HEM

Please renew or return items by the date
shown on your receipt

www.hertsdirect.org/libraries

Renewals and   0300 123 4049
enquiries:

Textphone for hearing   0300 123 4041
or speech impaired

D0363271

THE FALCON THRONE

THE TARNISHED CROWN
BOOK ONE

KAREN MILLER

www.orbitbooks.net

ORBIT

First published in Great Britain in 2014 by Orbit
This edition published in 2015 by Orbit

1 3 5 7 9 10 8 6 4 2

A CIP catalogue record for this book
is available from the British Library.

ISBN 978-1-84149-950-5

Typeset in Times by Palimpsest Book Production Limited, Falkirk, Stirlingshire
Printed and bound in Great Britain by CPI (UK) Ltd, Croydon CR0 4YY

Papers used by Orbit are from well-managed forests and other responsible sources.

MIX
Paper from
responsible sources
FSC® C104740

Orbit
An imprint of
Little, Brown Book Group
100 Victoria Embankment
London EC4Y 0DY

An Hachette UK Company
www.hachette.co.uk

www.orbitbooks.net

In memory of Fiona Churchward Whitehouse,
a bright light dimmed too soon

DRAMATIS PERSONAE
NOTABLE CHARACTERS

Old Kingdom of Zeidica

The King
Jelani of Osfahr, his dead queen
Salimbene, his heir
Barbazan, his physick

Duchy of Harcia

Aimery, Duke of Harcia
Balfre, his heir
Grefin, his youngest son
Jancis, Balfre's wife
Emeline, Balfre's daughter
Mazelina, Grefin's wife
Jorin, Grefin's heir
Ullia, Grefin's daughter
Kerric, Grefin's son
Joben, Balfre's cousin
Waymon, Balfre's friend
Paithan, Balfre's friend
Lowis, Balfre's friend
Terriel, a lord of the Green Isle
Alard, his heir
Robion, his nephew
Kierron, his nephew

Lord Herewart
Black Hughe, his youngest son
Curteis, Aimery's high steward
Ambrose, Aimery's Master Armsman

The Marches

Molly, mistress of The Pig Whistle
Diggin, her dead husband
Benedikt, her son
Iddo, The Pig Whistle's barman
Gwatkin, The Pig Whistle's stablemaster
Phemie, Molly's friend and a local healer
Denno Culpyn, a trader
Wido, a Clemen Marcher lord
Jacott, a Clemen Marcher lord
Bayard, a Harcian Marcher lord
Egbert, a Harcian Marcher lord

Duchy of Clemen

Harald, Duke of Clemen
Argante, his duchess
Liam, his heir
Roric, his bastard cousin
Ercole, Argante's half-brother
Lord Humbert, his chief councillor
Lindara, Humbert's daughter
Vidar, a disgraced baron
Godebert, his dead father
Lord Aistan, Harald's councillor
Kennise, Aistan's daughter
Ellyn, Liam's wetnurse
Master Blane, head of the Merchants' Guild
Arthgallo, a leech
Damikah, a witch

Principality of Cassinia

Gaël, Prince of Cassinia
Leofric, his chief regent
Berardine, Duchess of Ardenn
Baldwin, the late Duke of Ardenn
Catrain, his heir
Brielle, her sister
Derrice, her sister
Markela, her sister
Izusa, a witch

PROLOGUE

Trapped by the weight of a single cotton sheet, Salimbene listened to the bedchamber's sickness-tainted air rattle in and out of his chest. Something was about to happen, cataclysmic as an earthquake. His aching bones, his burning blood, the strange, knowing presence behind his eyes – they all told him. This night was an ending. His life, *this* life, was ending. Soon he'd be reborn. But as what, he didn't know. He couldn't see it. Not yet.

So he drooped his lacklustre eyelids low enough to deceive the physick . . . and waited.

Barbazan, done at last with his poking and prodding, his grunts and dire mutterings, retreated to the lamplit corridor beyond the chamber's open door. The king stood there, magnificent in a fine blue robe and priceless jewels. Four days since he'd dared cross the chamber's threshold. One more ominous sign.

'Is there hope?' the king whispered, too afraid to ask for the future out loud. His long, grey-striped beard was oiled and heavily perfumed, clouding him in a sweet stink. Even over the mingled stench of vomit and shit, suppurating flesh and useless incense, Salimbene could smell it: a blending of hyssop, sandalwood and jasmine. Royal scents, meant only for the great. 'Tell me, Barbazan. Is there hope, or must he die?'

Pitilessly revealed by the corridor's hanging lamps, the physick's face folded and stretched, malleable with grief. Or was it revulsion? Shit and vomit were commonplace in a sickroom, no reason for disgust. But this strange, disfiguring illness also brought boils and pustules and endlessly weeping lesions. Not a pretty suffering, only ugliness and filth. A gradual, stinking decay that not even the most obscure unguents could halt.

1

'My lord king,' Barbazan said, carefully. Lamplight shone on patches of sun-browned scalp, visible through his carefully crimped, brittle black hair. 'There is always hope.'

The king's face twisted. 'So you think he will die.'

'Whether your son lives or dies will be as Carsissus decrees, my lord king.' The physick's tone hinted at reproof. 'But I will fight to keep him.'

'And if that battle is won?' said the king. 'Do you tell me he is not near to ruined with this affliction?'

A moment, then the physick looked down. His hands fell to his sides, hiding in folds of moss-green lamb's wool almost as fine as that worn by the king. Barbazan made a rich living in service to Zeidica's ruler.

'Alas,' he admitted. 'But my lord king—' He looked up again. 'You should not despair. You are a vigorous man, and your new queen is lush. Surely another son will quickly follow, to sit your throne in his time.'

'I do not understand this calamity.' The king sounded stronger. Close to anger. 'Why am I punished, Barbazan? What sin is mine, to deserve this?'

Two frowning gazes slid into the chamber. Then the king shifted his resentful eyes to the physick's guarded face. What he saw there made him wince, and swallow.

'Speak your truth,' he commanded. 'Your words will not ruin you unless you repeat them elsewhere.'

'My lord king . . .' Barbazan shook his head. 'You know I am counted a great man of healing. In my sixty-five years I have seen all manner of sickness and death. No mysteries of the body remain for me.'

'I do know it. Why else would you be trusted as physick to my court? Seek not for praise, Barbazan. Answer me instead.' The king pointed into the chamber. 'What pestilence devours his flesh?'

'Great and gracious king, I cannot name it,' said the physick, full of sorrow and dread. 'I have never seen its like in my life.'

'Meaning what, Barbazan?'

'Meaning your son's affliction is not natural.'

'Not natural?' The king's head lifted, as though he braced for a blow. 'Do you tell me—'

'Alas, my lord king.' Barbazan's words were almost a groan. 'I fear your son's illness springs from some poisonous canker of the spirit.'

A terrible silence. Then the king and the physick pressed their palms to their eyes, swiftly, that they might be spared the sight of evil. They spat on the corridor's stone floor, expelling evil from their souls.

Watching them, feeling his heart labour in his wasted, painful chest, Salimbene felt a different, sharper pain. They were branding him unclean. They were calling him *cursed*.

The king wrapped his heavily ringed fingers about the diamond sunburst chain resting on his breast and squeezed until its golden links threatened to buckle. 'You are certain?'

'Yes, my lord king,' Barbazan whispered. 'Forgive me. I am.'

'And he cannot be saved?'

'I do not say that, my lord. But—'

'*Should not* be saved?'

Barbazan frowned. 'A question for a priest, I think.'

'I am asking you, Barbazan.'

'My lord king, I—' The physick placed his capable hands together, palm to palm. 'I am sworn to heal the body. Beyond that, my authority wavers.'

'Does it?' The king laughed, a harsh bark. 'Then I envy you. Because my authority cannot waver. As Zeidica's king I must be priest and physick both to my kingdom. And as its priest I must face every truth . . . no matter how painful.'

'What truth, my lord king?' Barbazan sounded fearful.

'That thanks to you I now understand my sin. My sin, Barbazan, was Salimbene's mother.'

'His – his mother?'

The king's lips pinched bloodless. 'Yes. For when I married that woman, I took to wife a witch.'

'My lord king . . .' Uncomfortable, Barbazan shuffled his feet. 'I know there were whispers. I dismissed them as the rotten fruits of jealousy. Instead of choosing a woman of Zeidica, your eye lit upon an outsider from Osfahr.'

'A *witch* from Osfahr,' said the king, his face dark. 'They breed them as a dog breeds fleas in that cursed place.'

'But my lord – she was examined. No flaw was found.'

'She was a *powerful* witch. As full of secrets as ever she was with child.'

'My lord king . . .' Barbazan risked his life to touch the king's arm. 'If you knew her for a witch . . .'

The king knocked the physick's hand aside. '*Know?* I did not *know*! She snared me in a web of wickedness, blinded me with her spells and evil conjures. It is only *now* that I see what has been hidden from me all these years. That rotting lump of flesh in there that you say is beyond all natural remedy? It is not my son.'

Barbazan's mouth dropped open. 'My lord?'

'She said he is my son, but she is dead and he is dying, unnatural, and *you*, Barbazan, can you swear to me that my seed gave him life?'

'If not your seed, my lord king, then whose?'

'No man's! Is it not plain? *She* gave him life, with foulest sorcery.'

'*Sorcery?* Oh, no, my lord king—'

'Can you swear she did not?' Sweat glistened on the king's brow. 'Before the god of healing, Barbazan, with a sacred stone in your hand, *would you swear it?*'

Now the physick was sweating, salt trickles running down his temples and into the grooves in his parched cheeks. He looked like he was weeping. 'My lord king, his face is yours when you were his age.'

'Are you deaf?' said the king, his eyes wild. '*She was a witch.* If her son wears my youthful face, it is her sorcery to blame. Her sorcery is to blame for *all* the ills of my life.'

'My lord king, what ills do you—'

'You are a fool,' the king spat, glaring. 'You call me vigorous but in nineteen years she birthed no other child. I call that ill!'

'Your son's birthing was bloody,' Barbazan protested. 'Your wife's body was ruined, after.'

'Another sign of sorcery! And it was sorcery kept me from discarding her when she was proved barren.'

Stepping back, Barbazan raised placating hands. 'My lord king, I do not think we can—'

'Is it not strange that her son sickened on the first blood moon since she died?' The king was breathing heavily, making the dangled

4

sapphires in his ears swing and flash in the mellow light. 'The blood moon, Barbazan! A witch's glory time, when all foul deeds are shrouded in murkiest night! If she did not conjure him to life with sorcery, why else would he fail when the moon rose bloody? Or do you say, physick, that his moral decay springs from *my* loins?'

Barbazan gasped. '*No*, my lord king.'

'No, my lord king,' the king said grimly. 'And well for you that you do not say it, for there is more than one physick in this world.'

'Yes, my lord king,' said Barbazan, his voice strangled. 'My lord king, these are weighty matters, far beyond my reach. I should return to your – to my patient.'

The king lifted a finger. 'Wait.'

Still as death on his pillows, from beneath his lowered eyelids Salimbene watched the king stare at him. Watched his lips thin, and the leap of muscle along the bearded jaw that had softened with the passing years. And as he watched, saw his fate decided.

'Go, Barbazan,' said the king. 'And never return. You are no longer needed here. See to my wife. I wish to know how many days must pass before my seed will fall on her fertile, natural ground.'

Barbazan's shocked stare leapt into the bedchamber, and out again. 'But – my lord king—'

'*You dare dispute me?*'

Shuddering, the physick bent almost double. 'No, my lord king.'

'Barbazan . . .' The king placed a fist beneath the physick's chin and forced the frightened man's head up. 'You said yourself, Carsissus will decide if he lives or dies. Is that not the truth?'

'Yes, my lord king,' Barbazan whispered. 'That is the truth.'

Lowering his fist, the king nodded. 'The solemn truth. For we are mortal, Barbazan, and flawed. The gods have no need of our interference.'

'No, my lord king.' Cautiously, the physick unbent himself. 'I – I will see to the queen, my lord. And in this matter—' A final, flickered glance into the chamber. 'I will trust the gods.'

'*Silently* trust,' said the king, his face full of dire warning. 'Barbazan, you are wise.'

Barbazan withdrew and for a long time after, the king stood silent in the bedchamber's open doorway. Salimbene waited, barely

5

breathing. There had been a mistake, surely. Surely he had misunderstood. For seventeen years he and this man had lived as king and prince. Father and son. Friend and friend. Friends did not leave each other to die, alone and in miserable agony.

Fathers did not condemn their sons to that.

Still unspeaking, the king reached for the chamber door's carved ivory handle. Tightened his jewelled fingers around it. Started to pull.

Salimbene sat up. The pain sank its talons deeper into his corrupted flesh, but he ignored it. With her dying breath his mother had warned him . . . but he'd refused to believe her. How could he believe her? He was the king's *son*. His pride. His joy. His heir.

'Please, my lord. Wait. Speak to me.'

The king said nothing. The door kept closing.

'*Father!* You'd abandon me? Leave me to die? *Why?*'

The door's closing paused. The king sighed. 'A true prince would not have to ask.'

A soft, final thud of wood against wood. The chamber sank into deeper shadow, its only light the small lamp on the table beside the bed.

Stunned, Salimbene screwed his crusted eyes tightly shut. Betrayal was a dagger twisting in his heart. Salt tears flooded his eyes, unstoppable, and spilled to sting the weeping lesions on his face. But not for long. Soon enough rage rose to burn away the grief. To burn away kind memories, leaving nothing but hate. And with the hate came fresh strength.

Beneath his wool-stuffed mattress was hidden a great secret. His mother's last and greatest gift.

Biting his scabbed lip, smothering the pain to a thin mewl, Salimbene kicked free of his sheet and half-rolled, half-fell, out of his princely bed. His linen sick-shirt tore free where seeping pus had glued it to his skin. Swift blots of blood spread across the older, yellower stains. He had to wait again, unevenly breathing on hands and knees, until he was strong enough to lift the mattress and grope beneath it. When at last his fingers touched the book of spells that had once belonged to his mother, Jelani of Osfahr, the true queen of Zeidica, it felt like a kind of coming home. Bound in gold-stitched calfskin, each stiff page covered with careful ink,

6

no Zeidican would know what the book said. Its words were written in Osfahri.

'*Keep this safe from prying eyes, my love*,' his mother had said in her native tongue, that they'd shared since first he learned to speak. '*No one can know you have it. Your life is forfeit if it's found.*'

Bidding farewell to him on her deathbed, she was so thin he was sure he could see the bones and slowing blood below her skin.

'*The key to my power, the same power that sleeps in you, is in this book, Salimbene*,' she'd whispered, despite her suffering. '*You feel the power waking, don't you? You've had the dreams.*'

Of course she'd known, without him telling her. Never in his life could he hide the truth from his mother. She was a witch. A sorceress of Osfahr. Since learning the truth of her as a child, just turned four, he'd held her life in his hands. But it had been safe there. She knew it.

'*When the time comes, use your magic freely*,' she'd told him, her sunken eyes brilliant even as the shadows closed in. '*Never fear it. Salimbene, my precious son, one day you will be a sorcerer king, the most magnificent the world has ever seen. This is your birthright. Do you believe me?*'

'*Yes*,' he'd said, weeping. Not sure if he did believe, only desperate to please her. '*But I know nothing of magic, of power. How will I—*'

Seventy-two empty days had passed since she died, and still he could feel her thin, cold fingertips on his wet cheek.

'*Everything you need is in the book, my son. Trust it. Trust yourself. But Salimbene . . . you must beware the king. After I'm gone he'll be a danger to you.*'

His father a danger? How could that be? Shocked, he'd tried to argue. But she wouldn't let him. And even as her gasping breath failed, and her brilliant eyes dimmed, she fought to save him.

'*Salimbene, I beg you. Do not trust the king! And know there is one more danger you must beware. The Oracle of Nicosia. It has the power to destroy you. Find it, my love, no matter the cost. Find it and destroy it. Only then will you be untouchable. Promise me, Salimbene. Promise!*'

So he'd promised her, not understanding, and then held her close as she died.

7

CHAPTER ONE

B rassy-sweet, a single wavering trumpet blast rent the cold air. The destriers reared, ears flattened, nostrils flaring, then charged each other with the ferocity of war.

'*Huzzah!*' the joust's excited onlookers shouted, throwing handfuls of barley and rye into the pale blue sky. The dry seeds fell to strike their heads and shoulders and the trampled, snow-burned grass beneath their feet. Blackbirds, bold as pirates, shrieked and squabbled over the feast as children released from the working day's drudgery shook rattles, clanged handbells, blew whistles and laughed.

Oblivious to all save sweat and fear and the thunder of hooves, the two battling nobles dropped their reins and lowered their blunted lances. A great double crash as both men found their marks. Armour buckled, bodies swayed, clods of turf flew. Their destriers charged on despite each brutal strike.

With a muffled cry, his undamaged lance falling, abandoned, Ennis of Larkwood lurched half out of his saddle, clawed for his dropped reins, lost his balance and fell. For three strides his horse dragged him, both arms and his untrapped leg flailing wildly, helmeted head bouncing on the tussocked dirt. Then the stirrup-leather broke and he was free. Squires burst from the sidelines like startled pheasants, two making for the snorting horse, three rushing to their fallen lord.

Heedless of the vanquished, the crowd cheered victorious Black Hughe, youngest son of old Lord Herewart. Hughe let slip his ruined lance, pushed up his helmet's visor and raised a clenched, triumphant fist as his roan stallion plunged and shied. The mid-afternoon sun shimmered on his black-painted breastplate, thickly chased with silver-inlaid etchings.

'Fuck,' Balfre muttered, wishing he could reach beneath his own armour and scratch his ribs. 'Did a more rampant coxcomb ever draw breath?'

Standing beside him, sadly plain in undecorated doublet and hose, his brother sighed. 'I wish you wouldn't do this.'

'Someone must,' he said. 'And since you refuse, Grefin, who else is there? Or are you saying our dear friend Hughe isn't ripe for a little plucking?'

Grefin frowned. 'I'm saying the duke will be ripe to toss you into the dankest dungeon he can find once he hears what you've done. You know he's got no love for—'

'Aimery clap his heir in irons?' Balfre laughed. 'Don't be an arse, Gref. His pride would never let him.'

'And your pride will get you broken to pieces, or worse!'

Hughe had pranced his destrier to the far end of the makeshift tourney ground, so his gaggle of squires could prepare him for the next joust. Ennis was on his feet at last, battered helmet unbuckled and tugged off to reveal a wash of blood coating the left side of his face. Much of his close-cropped flaxen hair was dyed scarlet with it. He needed a squire's help to limp off the field. As the shouting for Hughe died down there came a scattering of applause for Ennis, no more than polite recognition. Harcia's rustics had little patience for defeat.

Balfre shook his head. 'You know, if Hughe's a coxcomb then Ennis is a pickled dullard. Any donkey-riding peasant with a barley-stalk could push him off a horse.'

'My lord!'

Turning, he looked down at the eager young squire who'd run the short distance from their rough and ready tourney-stall and halted at his elbow.

'What?'

The squire flinched. 'Master Ambrose says it be time for your bout, and to come, my lord. If it please you.'

'Tell Ambrose to polish my stirrups. *Fuck*. Does he think the joust will start without me?'

'No, my lord,' said the squire, backing away. 'I'll tell him to wait, my lord.'

10

Balfre watched the youth scuttle to Master Armsman Ambrose. 'Speaking of pickled dullards . . .' He grimaced. 'I swear, Grefin, that turnip-head must've snuck into Harcia from Clemen. He's witless enough to be one of scabrous Harald's subjects. Don't you think?'

But his brother wasn't listening. Instead, Grefin was raking his troubled gaze across the nearby jostling villagers, and Ennis having his split scalp stitched by a tourney leech, and beyond him the small, untidy knot of lesser men who'd come to test their armoured mettle and now stood defeated, and the heavily hoof-scarred tilt-run with its battered wicker sheep-hurdle barrier, to at length settle on Hughe and his squires. The chuffer had climbed off his destrier and was exchanging his dented black-and-silver breastplate for one unmarked but just as gaudy. It would be a vaunted pleasure, surely, to dent that one for him too.

'Balfre—'

If this weren't such a public place, be cursed if he wouldn't hook his brother's legs out from under him and put his arse in the dirt where it belonged.

'Hold your tongue, Grefin. Or better yet, since you've no stomach for sport, trot back to the Croft and lift your lance there, instead. Plant another son in your precious wife. After all, you've only sired one so far. You must be good for at least one more.'

'Balfre, don't.'

'I mean it,' he said, keeping harsh. Refusing to see the shadow of hurt in Grefin's eyes. 'If all you can do is carp then you're no good to me. In truth, it havocs me why you came in the first place.'

'To keep you from breaking your neck, I hope,' said Grefin, still frowning. 'What havocs me is why *you* came! Look around, Balfre. We stand in an open field, far from any great house, and those who cheer and groan your efforts are villagers, herdsmen, peddlers and potboys.'

'So you'd deny the local churls an hour or two of entertainment? You're turning mean-spirited, little brother.'

Grefin hissed air between his teeth. 'It's a question of dignity. Aside from you, and Hughe, and Ennis, who of any note came today to break his lance? Not our cousin. Not even Waymon, and he's a man who'll wrestle two drunk wild boars in a mire.'

11

'Come on, Gref,' he said, grinning despite his temper. 'Even you have to admit that was funny.'

'Side-splitting, yes. And I'm sure the squires who broke themselves to save Waymon from being ripped wide from throat to cock laughed all the way to the bone-setter!'

'Grefin—'

'No, Balfre. You'll listen,' his brother said, and took his elbow. 'You're Harcia's heir. You owe its duke more than this joust against a gaggle of mudder knights fit only to ride the Marches.'

Wrenching his arm free, Balfre looked to where Ambrose and his squires stood waiting. His stallion was there, his unbroken lances and his helmet. Catching his eye, Ambrose raised a hand and beckoned, agitated.

He looked again at his niggling brother. 'Where and how I choose to romp is my concern. Not yours. Not Aimery's.'

'Of course it's Aimery's concern. He has enough to fret him without you risking yourself here. Those bastard lords of the Green Isle—'

Familiar resentment pricked, sharper than any spur. 'You can throw down that cudgel, Grefin. When it comes to the Green Isle, Aimery has his remedy.'

'Balfre . . .' Grefin sighed. 'He needs more time.'

'He's had nearly two years!'

'It's been that long since Malcolm died. But Mother died in autumn, and here we are scant in spring.'

'What's Mother to do with it? She wasn't his Steward!'

'No,' Grefin said gently. 'She was his beating heart. He still weeps for her, Balfre. And for Malcolm. Both griefs are still raw. And now you'd have him weeping for you, too?'

The chilly air stank of churned mud and horse shit. A troupe of acrobats was amusing the crowd as it waited for the last joust. Motley painted canvas balls and striped wooden clubs danced hand-to-hand and man-to-man through the air, the jonglers' skill so great they never dropped even one. From time to time they snatched a cap from a villager's head and juggled that too. The field echoed with delighted laughter.

Balfre glared at them, unamused. Aimery weep for him? That

would be the fucking day. 'I never knew you had such a poor opinion of my lance-skills.'

'This has nothing to do with jousting,' Grefin retorted. 'Please, Balfre. Just . . . let it go. Who cares what a sophead like Hughe mutters under his breath?'

'I care!' Blood leaping, he shoved his brother with both hands, hard enough to mar Grefin's dark green doublet. 'When what he mutters is heard by a dozen men? *I care*. And if you cared for me, *you'd* care.'

'I do! But Balfre, you *can't*—'

'Oh, fuck off, Grefin! Before I forget myself and give those gaping churls reason enough to gossip for a week!'

Grefin folded his arms, mule-stubborn. 'I don't want to.'

'And I don't care what you want.'

Holding his brother's resentful stare, unflinching, Balfre waited. Grefin would relent. He always did. There was a softness at the core of him that made sure of it. A good thing for Harcia he wasn't Aimery's heir. Such a softness would leave the duchy's throat bared to faithless men like Harald of Clemen.

At last Grefin huffed out a frustrated breath. 'Fine. But never say I didn't warn you,' he said, and retreated.

Still simmering, Balfre returned to Ambrose. The Master Armsman near cracked his skull in two, shoving his gold-chased helmet onto his head.

'For shame, my lord,' Ambrose said in his rasping voice, come from a sword-hilt to the neck in the desperate, long-ago battle that had made Aimery duke. 'Dallying like a maid. This might be a rumptiony shigshag we be at but still you should be setting of a timely example.'

Balfre bore with the reprimand. The armsman had served two dukes of Harcia already, thereby earning for himself a small measure of insolence. With a nod, he held out his hands so the turnip-head squire could gauntlet him. The burnished steel slid on cleanly, cold and heavy.

Ambrose started his final armour inspection. 'You been watching that rump Hughe?'

'I have,' he said, twisting his torso to be certain of no sticking points in his breastplate, which was gold-chased like his helmet and worth more than Hughe's horse. 'Nothing's changed since the last time we bouted. He still drops his lance a stride too soon, and sits harder on his right seatbone.'

'True enough.' Ambrose slapped his pupil's steel-clad shoulder. 'And shame be on his tiltmaster. But for all that, he be a brutey jouster. You'll be kissing dirt, my lord, if you don't have a care.'

'Then shame be on *my* tiltmaster,' Balfre said, flashing Ambrose a swift smirk. 'If I do kiss the dirt, I'll have to find myself a new one.'

Because this was no formal tourney they lacked judges to keep time or award points and penalties. There was the lone hornblower, though, for the sake of the ragged crowd. As Hughe remounted his restive stallion, one of his squires ran to the man and gave an order. Obedient, the appointed villager blew his horn to alert the crowd to the next joust.

Balfre nodded at Ambrose, then crossed to the wooden mounting block where his destrier was held fast by two squires. As he approached, one of them was doltish enough to shift too far sideways. The stallion lashed out its foreleg and caught the man on his thigh with an iron-shod hoof. Squealing, the squire crumpled.

'Maggot-brain!' said Ambrose, hurrying to drag him clear. Then he gestured at turnip-head. 'Don't stand there gawping, you peascod. Hold the cursed horse!'

The excited villagers set up another din of handbells and rattles and whistles. Stood at a distance in their second-rate armour, Ennis and the vanquished mudder knights cast envious looks at the stallion. Quivering with nerves, eager for the joust, the horse tossed its head and swished its thick black tail. As Balfre reached the mounting block it bared its teeth and snapped, strong enough to rip fingers from an unprotected hand.

'*Bah!*' he said, and punched the stallion's dish-round cheek. 'Stand still!'

Walking to and fro, the hornblower sounded another rallying blast, coaxing more raucous cheers from the crowd. On the far side of the tourney ground Hughe kicked his roan destrier forward, scattering his squires like beetles. One tottered behind him, awkwardly carrying his lance.

14

Rolling his eyes, Balfre picked up his reins, shoved his left foot into his stirrup and swung his right leg up and over his jousting saddle's high cantle. The moment he settled on his destrier's back he felt the animal tense beneath him, its breath coming in angry grunts. Not even his heaviest gauntlets muffled its throttled energy, tingling from the curbed bit to his fingers. Through the steel protecting his thighs and lower legs he could feel his mount's barrel ribs expand and contract, and the pent-up furious power in the muscular body beneath him. This was his best horse, and they were well-matched in both temper and skill. Only for Black Hughe would he risk the beast here. But Hughe was owed a mighty drubbing, and to be sure of it he'd chance even this animal.

With a decided tug he closed his helmet's visor then held out his hand. 'Lance!'

The weight of the carved, painted timber woke old bruises and strains. Stifling an oath, he couched the lance in its proper place, pricked spurs to his horse's flanks, then softened the bit's sharp bite.

The destrier leapt like a flycatcher, snorting. White foam flew from its mouth. Prisoned within his gold-chased helm, his vision narrowed to a slit and the crowd's roaring a hollow boom, Balfre laughed aloud. Aside from a writhing woman pinned on his cock, was there anything better in the world than a lance in his hand, a grand horse between his legs, and a man before him a handful of heartbeats from defeat?

No. There wasn't.

Snorting, ears pricked, the destrier settled into a stately, knee-snapping prance. He sat the dance with ease, guiding the stallion to the start of the tilt-run with nothing more than his shifting weight and the touch of his long-shanked, elaborate spurs. There he halted, and paid no heed to the crowd's wild cheering or the stallion's threatening half-rears.

'Black Hughe!' he called, loud enough to be heard through his helmet. 'You stand ready?'

'I indeed stand ready, Balfre!' Hughe shouted back. 'Do I have your pardon now, for the unseating of you later?'

'You'll have my pardon once you answer for your slur.'

'My lord,' said Hughe, defiant, then closed his own visor and demanded his lance.

As the hornblowing churl took his place midway along the rough tilt-run, horn ready at his lips, the watching villagers and mudder knights fell silent. Only the blackbirds kept up their squabbling, seeking the last grains of seed.

The horn sounded again, a single trembling note. Balfre threw his weight forward as he felt his stallion's quarters sink beneath him, felt its forehand lift, saw its noble head and great, crested neck rise towards his face. It bellowed, a roaring challenge, then stood on its strong hindlegs. Night-black forelegs raked the air. He loosened the reins, gripped the lance and spurred the stallion's flanks. The horse plunged groundwards, bellowing again . . . and charged.

Blurred, breathless speed. Pounding heart. Heaving lungs. Nothing before him but Black Hughe on his horse and the memory of his hateful taunt, dagger-sharp and unforgivable.

Seven thundering strides. Six. Five.

He tucked the lance tight to his side, closed his thighs, dropped the reins. Blinked his eyes free of sweat . . . and took aim . . . and struck.

A double shout of pain, as his lance-head impacted Hughe's armoured body and shattered, as Hughe's undamaged lance struck then glanced harmlessly aside. Pain thrummed through him like the ringing of a great bell, like the clashing of a hammer against the anvil of the world. His fingers opened, releasing the splintered remains of his lance. Then they closed again, on his dropped reins. He hauled on them, unkindly, and his destrier shuddered to a head-shaking halt. A tug and a spurring, and he was turned back to look for Hughe.

Herewart's youngest son was sprawled on the tilt-run's dirt like a starfish, his fancy breastplate dented, his helmet scratched, his brown eyes staring blindly at the sky.

'My lord! My lord!'

And that was Ambrose, the old, scarred man, running hoppy and hamstrung towards him. Turnip-head and another squire scurried at his heels. Hughe's squires were running too, the ones that weren't dashing after his ill-trained horse.

Ambrose, arriving, snatched at the destrier's reins. His pocked face, with its faded sword marks, stretched splitting-wide in a totty-tooth smile.

'A doughty strike, my lord, *doughty*! The best from you I've surely seen! Lord Grefin will bite his thumb, for certain, when he's told what he missed.'

Grefin. A curse on Grefin and his milksop mimbling. Balfre shoved up his visor, then kicked his feet free of the stirrups and twisted out of his saddle. The jar in his bones as he landed on the hoof-scarred ground made him wince. Ambrose saw it, but nobody else. He held out his hands for the squires to pull off his gauntlets, and when they were free unbuckled and tugged off his helmet for himself.

'Take the horse,' he commanded. 'I would speak to Black Hughe.'

'My lord,' said Ambrose, holding stallion and helmet now. 'We'll make ready to depart.'

The villagers and mudder knights were still cheering, the ragtag children shaking their rattles and handbells and blowing their whistles. He waved once, since it was expected, then turned from them to consider old Herewart's son. The lingering pains in his body were as nothing, drowned in the joy of seeing his enemy thrown down.

'Lord Balfre,' Hughe greeted him, his voice thin as watered wine. His squires had freed him from his helmet and thrust a folded tunic beneath his head. 'Your joust, I think.'

With a look, Balfre scattered the squires who hovered to render their lord aid. Then he dropped to one knee, with care, and braced an aching forearm across his thigh.

'Hughe.'

Black Hughe was sweating, his face pale beneath the blood seeping from a split across the bridge of his nose. More blood trickled from one nostril, and from the corner of his mouth. He looked like a knifed hog.

'I'm not dying, Balfre,' Hughe said, slowly. 'I bit my tongue. That's all.'

'And to think, Hughe, if you'd bitten it the sooner you'd not be lying here now in a welter of your gore, unhorsed and roundly defeated,' he said kindly, and smiled.

Hughe coughed, then gasped in pain. 'My lord—'

'Hughe, Hughe . . .' Leaning forward, Balfre patted Black Hughe's bruised cheek. Mingled sweat and blood stained his fingers. He didn't mind. They were his prize. 'I'm going now. Without your horse and armour. I didn't joust you for them.'

'My lord,' said Hughe, and swallowed painfully. 'Thank you.'

'Not at all. And Hughe, for your sake, heed me now. Remember this moment. Engrave it on your heart. So the next time you think to slight my prowess with my lance? You think again – and stay silent.'

Hughe stared at him, struck dumb. Balfre smiled again, not kindly. Pushed to his feet, spurning assistance, gave Hughe his armoured back and walked away.

Temper sour as pickled lemon after his fractious dealings on the Green Isle, Aimery of Harcia disembarked his light galley in no mood for delay. Not waiting to see if his high steward and the others were ready, he made his way down the timber gang-plank, booted heels sharply rapping, and leapt the last few steps with the ease of a man half his age. The surety of steady ground beneath his feet at once lifted his spirits. Ah! Blessed Harcia! Never mind it was little more than a stone's throw from the mainland to the Green Isle. He'd stick a sword through his own gizzards before confessing to a soul how much he hated sailing.

''Tis good to be home, Your Grace,' said his high steward, joining him.

Staring at the busy harbour village of Piper's Wade crowded before them, Aimery breathed in the mingled scents of fresh salt air, old fish guts, people and beasts. Some might call the air tainted, a stench, but never him. It was the smell of Harcia, his duchy, sweeter than any fresh bloom.

'We're not home yet, Curteis. Not quite.' He smiled. 'But this'll do. Now, let's be off. I can hear the Croft calling.'

His party's horses had been stabled against their return at nearby Piper's Inn. With their baggage to be off-loaded from the galley and transported by ox-cart, he led his people to the inn with purposeful haste, greeting the villagers who greeted him with a nod and a friendly word in passing, making sure they knew he was pleased to see them but alas, could not stop . . . only to be halted in the Piper's empty, sunlit forecourt by a wildly bearded man in embroidered rags.

'My lord! Duke Aimery!' Skinny arms waving, the man shuffled into his path. A soothsayer from the old religion, half his wits wandered off entirely. Lost, along with most of his teeth. Twig-tangled grey hair, lank past his shoulders, framed a seamed and sun-spoiled lean face. His pale grey eyes were yellowed with ill health, and sunken. 'A word, my lord! Your pardon! A word!'

It was held bad luck to spurn a soothsayer. Aimery raised a warning hand to his four men-at-arms. 'Keep yourselves. There's no harm here. See to the horses and you, Curteis, settle our account with the innkeeper.'

They knew better than to argue. As he was obeyed, and his scribe and body squire hastily took themselves out of the way, Aimery turned to the ragged man.

'You know me then, soothsayer?'

The soothsayer cackled on a gust of foul breath. 'Not I, my lord. The stars. The little frogs. The wind. The spirits in the deep woods know you, my lord. But they whisper to me.'

'And what do they whisper?'

Those sunken, yellow-tinged eyes narrowed. 'I could tell you. I should tell you. But will I be believed? Do you honour the spirits? Or . . .' The soothsayer spat. Blackish-green phlegm smeared his lips. 'Are you seduced by the grey men, my lord?'

The grey men. The Exarch's monks, harbingers of a new religion. It had barely scratched the surface of Harcia, though its roots grew deep in other lands. The soothsayer stared at him, hungrily, as though his reply must be a feast.

'I'm seduced by no one,' he said. 'Every philosophy has its truth. Speak to me, or don't speak. The choice is yours. But I'll not stand here till sunset, waiting.'

The soothsayer cocked his head, as though listening. Then another gusting cackle. 'Yes, yes. I hear him. A needle-wit, this Aimery. Prick, prick, prick and see the blood flow.' A gnarled finger pointed to the early morning sky, eggshell-blue wreathed in lazy cloud. 'Three nights past, my lord. As the moon set. A long-tailed comet. The sign of chaos. Were you witness? It made the black sky bleed.'

Three nights past at moonset he'd only just crawled into his borrowed bed on the Green Isle, head aching with arguments. 'No. I didn't see it. I was asleep.'

'Asleep then, asleep now.' Eyes stretching wide, the soothsayer shuffled close. 'Time to wake, my lord duke, and see the trouble festering under your roof.'

A clutch at his heart. 'What trouble?'

'There was a man who had three sons. Lost one. Kept one. Threw the third away. The fool.'

'What do you mean? What—'

'Be warned, my lord duke,' the old man wheezed. 'Unless you open your eyes you will sleep the cold sleep of death.' A rattle in the scrawny throat, a sound like the last breath of a dying wife. A dying son. 'And no right to say you were not told. You have to know it, Aimery. A long-tailed comet cannot lie.'

But a man could. A mad man, his wits scattered like chaff on the wind. Aimery stepped back. 'Be on your way, soothsayer. You've spoken and I've listened.'

'Yes, but have you heard?' The soothsayer shook his head, sorrowful. Or perhaps merely acting sorrow. Who could tell, with a mad man? 'Ah well. In time we'll know.'

It was nonsense, of course. He had little time for religion, old or new. But the soothsayer looked in a bad way, so he pulled a plain gold ring from his finger.

'Take this, old man. Buy yourself a warm bed and hot food. And when next the spirits whisper, whisper to them from me that a faithful servant should be better served.'

The soothsayer's eyes glittered as he stared at the ring. Then he snatched it, and with much muttering and arm-waving hobbled out of the forecourt.

'Your Grace,' Curteis murmured, arriving on soft feet that barely disturbed the raked gravel. 'Is aught amiss?'

Aimery frowned after the soothsayer, an indistinct bundle of rags vanishing into the high street's bustle. Mad old men and their ramblings. Throw a stone into any crowd and you'd likely strike at least three.

'No. Can we go?'

Curteis nodded. 'Yes, Your Grace. As it please you.'

They rode knee-to-knee out of the inn's stable yard in a clattering of hooves, with his body squire and his scribe and his men-at-arms close at heel.

'Be warned, Curteis,' he said, as they scattered pie-sellers and cobblers and fishwives before them along Piper's Wade high street, 'and share the warning with them that ride behind. I wish to sleep in my own bed under my own roof sooner rather than later. Therefore we shall travel swiftly, with few halts, and should I hear a tongue clapping complaint I swear I'll kick the culprit's arse seven shades of black and blue.'

'Yes, Your Grace,' said Curteis, smiling. He was well used to his duke.

With the past two weeks fresh in mind, Aimery scowled. 'I tell you plain, man, I've heard enough clapping tongues lately to last me till my funeral.'

'The lords of the Green Isle were indeed fretsome, Your Grace.'

'Fretsome?' He snorted. 'Snaggle-brained, you should call them. Vexatious. Full of wind. Especially that cross-grained fuck Terriel.'

'Your Grace,' agreed Curteis. 'Lord Terriel and his noble brothers farted many noisome words. But you set them well straight.'

Yes, he did. And woe betide a one of them who again dared defy his judgement. That man, be he ever so lordly, even the great and grasping Terriel, would find himself so handily chastised there'd be scars on his great-grandson's arse.

Bleakly satisfied, still impatient, Aimery urged his iron-dappled palfrey into a canter, then swung left off the high street onto Hook Way, which would lead them eventually to his ducal forest of Burnt Wood. If the rain held off and no mischance befell them, with the horses well rested they'd be in and out of the forest by day's end. Spend the night in Sparrowholt on its far side, leave at dawn on the morrow, ride hard with little dallying and with fortune they'd reach the Croft before sunset.

And so it proved. But when he did at last trot beneath the arching stone gateway of his favourite castle's inner bailey, feeling every one of his fifty-four years, he found himself ridden into yet another storm. For standing in the Croft's torchlit keep, clad head to toe in unrelieved black velvet, was old Herewart of nearby Bann Crossing. He trembled

21

in the dusk's chill, tears swiftly slicking his withered cheeks. Waiting with him, stood at a wary distance, Balfre and Grefin.

'What is this, Balfre?' Aimery demanded of his accidental heir, even as his gaze lingered on his youngest son. His favourite, now that Malcolm was dead. 'Why am I greeted with such confusion?'

He'd sent a man ahead, to warn of his arrival and stir the castle's servants to duty. As they hurried to take the horses and relieve Curteis and the scribe of their note-filled satchels, and the men-at-arms waited with their hands ready on their swords, he saw Balfre and Grefin exchange disquieting looks. But before his heir could answer, Herewart let out a cry cracked-full of grief and approached without leave or invitation.

'Your Grace, you must hear me! As a father, and my duke, only you can grant me the justice I seek!'

'Hold,' he said to the men-at-arms who were moving to protect him. Then he looked to his steward. 'Curteis, escort Lord Herewart within the castle. See him comforted, and kept company in the Rose chamber until I come.'

Very proper, though he was also weary, Curteis bowed. 'Yes, Your Grace.'

'Your Grace!' Herewart protested. 'Do not abandon me to an underling. My years of loyalty should purchase more consideration than that. I demand—'

'*Demand?*' Summoning a lifetime's worth of discipline, Aimery swung off his horse to land lightly on his feet. 'My lord, be mindful. Not even a lifetime of loyalty will purchase a demand.'

Herewart's colour was high, his wet eyes red-rimmed and lit with a burning fervour. 'A single *day* of loyalty should purchase the justice I am owed. And be warned, Aimery. Justice I'll have, as I see fit, and from your hand – or there will be a reckoning. This is not cursed Clemen, where *in*justice wears a crown!'

Silence, save for Herewart's ragged breathing and the scrape of shod hooves on the flagstones as the horses hinted at their stables. Aimery looked to his sons. Grefin stood pale, arms folded, lower lip caught between his teeth. There was grief for Herewart there, and fear for his brother. As for Balfre, he stood defiant. He knew no other way to stand.

22

Belly tight, Aimery looked again at Herewart. 'What has happened, my lord?'

'My son is dead, Your Grace,' said Herewart, his voice raw. 'My youngest. Hughe.'

The blunt words tore wide his own monstrous, unhealed wound. 'I'm sorry to hear it, Herewart. To lose a son untimely is—'

'You must know he was murdered,' Herewart said, bludgeoning. 'By your son and heir, Balfre.'

'*Liar!*' Balfre shouted, and would have leapt at the old man but for Grefin's restraining hand. 'It was ill chance, not murder, and he'd still be alive had you taught him how he should speak of Harcia's heir! The fault is yours, Herewart, not mine, that your son's bed tonight is a coffin!'

Aimery closed his eyes, briefly. Oil and water, they were, he and this son. Oil and flame. *Balfre, you shit. When will you cease burning me?* 'What ill chance?'

'None,' said Herewart, glowering. 'Hughe's death was purposed. Your son challenged mine to a duel and killed him.'

'*Duel?*' Balfre laughed, incredulous. 'It was a joust! I unhorsed him by the rules, and when I left him he was barely more than winded. How can you—'

'No, my lord, how can *you*!' said Herewart, a shaking fist raised at Balfre. 'My son made a ribald jest, harmless, and *you*, being so tender-skinned and pig-fat full of self love, you couldn't laugh and let it go by. You had to answer him with your lance, you had to goad him into unwise confrontation in the company of churls and mudder knights and take your revenge by taking his life! He breathed his last this morning; his body broken, your name upon his blood-stained lips.'

Pulling free of his brother's holding hand, Balfre took a step forward. 'Your Grace, Hughe's death isn't my—'

Aimery silenced him with a look, then turned. 'My lord Herewart, as a father I grieve with you. And as your duke I promise justice. But for now, go with Curteis. He'll see you to warmth and wine while I have words with my son.'

Herewart hesitated, then nodded. As Curteis ushered him within the castle, and the inner bailey emptied of servants, squires,

23

men-at-arms and horses, Grefin tried to counsel his brother but was roughly pushed aside.

'Balfre,' Aimery said, when they were alone. 'What was Hughe's jest?'

His face dark with temper, Balfre swung round. 'It was an insult, not a jest. And public, made with intent. I couldn't let it go by.'

'Grefin?'

Grefin glanced at his brother, then nodded. 'It's true. Hughe was offensive. But—'

'But *nothing*!' Balfre insisted. 'For Herewart's son to say my lance is riddled with wormwood, with no more strength to it than a pipe of soft cheese, and by lance mean my cock, never mind we talked of jousting, he questioned my ability to sire a son. He as good as said I wasn't fit to rule Harcia after Aimery. And that's treason, Grefin, whether you like it or not.'

Grefin was shaking his head. 'Hughe was wine-soaked when he spoke. So deep in his cup he couldn't see over its rim. He was a fool, not a traitor.'

'And now he's a dead fool,' said Balfre, brutally unregretful. 'And a lesson worth learning. My lord—' He took another step forward, so sure of his welcome. 'You can see I had no choice. I—'

'Balfre,' Aimery said heavily, 'what I see is a man possessed of no more wit and judgement at the age of three-and-twenty than were his when he was *five*.'

Balfre stared. 'My lord?'

'You killed a man for no better reason than he had less wit than you!'

'But Father – I was wronged. You can't take Herewart's part in this!'

Oh Malcolm, Malcolm. A curse on you for dying.

Aimery swallowed, rage and disappointment turning his blood to bile. 'Since last you saw me I have done nothing but ride the Green Isle, hearing complaints and chastising faithless lords who count their own petty needs higher than what is best for this duchy. And now *you*, Balfre, you encourage men to defy my decree against personal combat. What—'

'It was a *joust*!' Balfre shouted. 'You've not banned jousting. I was obedient to all your rules. I made sure of a tilt barrier, my lance was well-blunted, and I—'

'And you killed a man, regardless,' he said, fists clenched. 'Much good your obedience has done you, Balfre. Or me.'

Balfre's hands were fisted too. 'That's not fair. Father—'

'*Do not call me Father! On your knees, miscreant, and address me as Your Grace!*'

Sickly pale, Balfre dropped to the damp ground. 'Your Grace, it's plain you're weary. You shouldn't be plagued with the Green Isle. Appoint me its Steward and I'll—'

'Appoint *you*?' Aimery ached to slap his son's face. 'Balfre, if I let you loose on the Green Isle there'd be war within a week.'

'Your Grace, you misjudge me.'

'Do I?' He laughed, near to choking on bitterness. 'And if I were to break my neck hunting tomorrow and the day after I was buried you learned that Harald of Clemen had yet again interfered with Harcian justice in the Marches? Tell me, would you tread with care or would you challenge *him* to a joust?'

'Harald is a cur-dog who sits upon a stolen throne,' said Balfre, his lip curled. 'Thieves and cur-dogs should be beaten, not cosseted. If Harald feared us he'd not dare flout your authority, or entice Harcia's men-at-arms to break your decrees, or demand unlawful taxes from our merchants and—'

'So you'd challenge him with a naked sword, and slaughter two hundred years of peace.' Aimery shook his head, stung with despair. 'Never once doubting the wisdom of your choice.'

'Your Grace, there's no greater wisdom than overwhelming strength and the willingness to use it.'

And so the decision he'd been avoiding for so long, like a coward, was made for him. He sighed. 'I know you think so, Balfre. Grefin—'

Grefin looked up. 'Your Grace?'

'The Green Isle has been left to its own devices for too long. Therefore I appoint you its Steward and—'

Forgetting himself, Balfre leapt to his feet. '*No!*'

'Your Grace—' Alarmed, Grefin was staring. 'I'm honoured, truly, but—'

'Enough, Grefin. It's decided.'

'No, it isn't!' said Balfre. 'You can't do this. Like it or not I'm your heir. By right the Green Isle's stewardship is mine. You *can't*—'

Aimery seized his oldest son's shoulders and shook him. 'I must, Balfre. For your sake, for Harcia's sake, I have no other choice.'

'You're a duke,' said Balfre, coldly. 'You have nothing but choices.'

'Ah, Balfre . . .' Run through with pain, he tightened his fingers. 'The day you understand that isn't true is the day you will be ready for a crown.'

Balfre wrenched free. 'Fuck you, Your Grace,' he said, and walked away.

CHAPTER TWO

Some time later, alone with his father, Grefin blinked away weariness and cleared his throat. 'It wasn't murder, my lord. Balfre was angry. But he didn't murder Hughe.'

'Grefin, Grefin . . .' Staring into the Rose chamber's flame-leapt fireplace, Aimery shook his head. 'You always defend him.'

He felt his body tense. The spirits save him, not this brawl again. 'He's my brother.'

'And he's my son! But that doesn't—'

'The wrong son,' he muttered, then held his breath.

Slowly, Aimery turned. Seeing the naked pain in his father's face, Grefin shifted in his chair and looked down. 'I'm sorry.'

'You should be.'

There was a splash of dried mud on his woollen hose. He scratched at it, trapping dirt beneath his fingernail. 'My lord, I did try to stop him. But you know Balfre. And Hughe's slur was wicked. Drunk or sober, he meant to wound.'

Aimery turned back to the fire. 'Yet you still say it wasn't murder.'

His shoulders rose and fell. 'You'd have me brand Herewart a liar? Is that it?'

Hughe's father, scarcely comforted and spurning his duke's offer of a bed for the night, was on the road back to Bann's Crossing. Riding home to his dead son, laid out in his finery on a trestle surrounded by sweet candles and weeping women.

Remembering Malcolm, and their mother, Grefin watched his knuckles turn white.

'The old man claims you weren't there when Hughe fell,' said his father. 'He claims Hughe's squires told him you fought with Balfre, and stormed off.'

Curse it. If only he'd been permitted to meet with Herewart by his father's side. But no, he'd been kept out of the room as though he were still a child. As though he couldn't be trusted to speak the truth, dispassionate. As though speaking up for his brother was the same as telling lies.

'It's true Balfre and I fought,' he said, holding resentment at bay. 'And I left him. But I didn't go far. I saw the joust. I tell you, my lord, Balfre's not to blame. Hughe fell awkwardly. It was bad luck, that's all.'

Aimery swore under his breath. 'No, Grefin. It was bad judgement. There should never have been a joust. Can you admit that much, at least? Or is there *nothing* Balfre could do that you won't excuse?'

At the end, when the leeches had no more help for his mother and it came his turn to sit with her for the last time, she'd surprised him by rousing out of her stupor.

'You're the youngest,' she'd whispered. 'My wee babe. Even so, you're older than Balfre. I fear you always will be. Stand for him, Grefin. Take his part, no matter what. He's not like Malcolm was. Your father can't fathom him. But you do. You must. Always.'

He'd promised he would. Of course. But sometimes he wondered if his mother had known what she was asking.

'My lord . . .' Grefin braced his elbows on his knees and leaned forward. 'I'm not saying your anger is unjust. Balfre was wrong to call the joust. But must you make me the Green Isle's Steward in his place? He won't forgive it.'

27

Aimery swung round again. Though the chamber's candlelight threw shadows, they weren't deep enough to hide his rage. 'How can I make him Steward, Grefin? What will Herewart say, and the other lords, if I elevate Balfre the very day of Hughe's death?'

'Then wait,' he said, close to pleading. 'Let Hughe be buried with all sorrow and honour. Give Balfre time to express the regret I know he feels, even if his wounded pride won't let him show it, then—'

'I have no time for Balfre!' his father shouted. 'I've squandered too much time already! The Green Isle must be mastered now, not a month from now. A month from now will be too late. Since Malcolm's death it's grown monstrous unruly and I *won't* see us return to the battles and butcheries of my youth, with family pitted against family and no quarter shown. The day I lost my father, my uncle and both my brothers is burned into memory. How will *I* be remembered if I let such bloodshed happen again?' He struck his fist to the mantel over the fireplace. 'The fault here is mine. I kept holding back, waiting to name Balfre as Steward, hoping I'd see some judgement in your brother, the smallest glimpse of Malcolm in him, but all I've done is delude myself. Balfre's not fit to—'

'Now you are being unjust, my lord.'

'If that's your opinion, perhaps I'm mistaken in you too!'

Grefin leapt up, goaded beyond customary respect. 'Entirely mistaken, my lord, if you think I'll stay silent as you use me to punish Balfre!'

'I do *not* use—'

'Yes, you do! And I mislike it, very much. But because I see you have no choice, Father, I'll be your Steward. Only you must remember this. Balfre is still your heir. And if he's to be the duke you want him to be, in his time, you can't deny him the Green Isle's steward-ship for ever.'

Aimery struck the mantel again, so hard that in the hearth burning logs collapsed into charcoal. Sparks flew, hissing his fury. '*Whelp!* You presume to command *me*? Not even Malcolm dared—'

'Malcolm loved you too much not to speak his mind. And so do I.' Heart pounding, Grefin folded his arms. 'Balfre has every right to expect the stewardship. But I know he has to pay a price for Hughe.

And so does he. So I'll be your Steward of the Green Isle for one year. Balfre will accept that.'

Aimery's eyes glittered in the candlelight. 'He'll accept whatever I give him.'

'Father—'

'*Enough*, Grefin. Leave me. I need solitude, so I might think.'

Defeated, he sighed. 'Yes, my lord. But can I at least tell Balfre you'll speak with him before you retire?'

'No,' said Aimery. 'Keep him out of my sight.'

Torn, as he was so often torn between his father and the only brother he had left, he paused at the elegant Rose chamber's door. 'It's not his fault he isn't Malcolm. It's not his fault he lived, and Malcolm died.'

In the flame-crackled silence, Aimery's indrawn breath sounded loud. 'You think because you've made me a grandfather you're too old for a thrashing? You're not, Grefin, believe me.'

From his first squalling cry, Malcolm had been Aimery's favourite. And their mother had loved her sickly youngest son best. All his life Balfre had stood stranded between them, necessary, but not needed. Now, with Malcolm dead, he was needed . . . but not wanted.

'You should give Balfre a chance, Father. You never have. I think he'd—'

'*Enough, Grefin! Get out!*'

So much for building bridges. Grefin bowed. 'As you wish, Your Grace. Good night.'

Heartsick and still numbly disbelieving, Balfre prowled the confines of his lushly appointed privy chamber. *Grefin* was made Steward of the Green Isle. Grefin, best loved and faery-favoured. Grefin, who'd heard Black Hughe's black taunt and refused to lift a lance in his brother's defence.

'*Bastard!*'

Stomach roiling, rich red wine turned to vinegar in his mouth, he hurled his goblet at the wall. Heavy green Maletti glass shattered against Ardennese tapestry-work, the spilled wine staining its vivid hunting scene like fresh blood. He was hard put not to weep. Grefin's treachery buried dragon-talons in his bowels. No wonder he was bent in half. He crabbed sideways to a padded settle and dropped. The lamplit room stank of crushed, fermented grapes and betrayal.

A knocking at the door of the outer chamber turned his head. His useless wife was elsewhere and he'd dismissed the servants, so he was forced to answer the summons himself.

'Let me in.' Grefin, standing on the threshold. 'I've things to say.'

Balfre smiled. In his veins his blood bubbled, dangerous. 'Brother Steward. Come to gloat?'

'Don't be a noddle, Balfre,' Grefin said, impatient. 'Let me in.'

If he could change what had happened by beating his brother bloody, he would. But this war could only be won with words. He stepped back. 'Fine. Join me, and welcome.'

'You're alone?' said Grefin, leading the way into the privy chamber. 'Where's Jancis?'

'I don't know.' He made for the sideboard. 'My wife has taken to aping yours, and so does as she pleases. What do you want?'

'I told you. To talk.'

Picking up a bottle of brandy, he offered his brother a bright smile. 'Shouldn't you be celebrating your good fortune with Mazelina? Surely you've told her the happy news.'

'I wanted to see you first.' Grefin nodded at the brandy. 'Might I have some of that, if you've not emptied the bottle?'

'Of course, little brother. As if you need to ask. Isn't everything mine as good as yours?'

'Balfre—' Grefin stared, his brows pinched tight, then moved to the fireplace and thrust a fresh log into the lowering flames. 'This isn't my doing. I never asked Aimery to make me Steward.'

'Then refuse the appointment.'

'I tried. He won't let me.'

'Try harder.'

Grefin sighed. 'I can't.'

'Yes, you can. You just don't want to.'

Their gazes met, like the clashing of swords. Grefin was the first to look away. 'You can't blame Aimery for being angry. You did defy him, challenging Hughe. And he sees your defiance as a stain on his honour.'

'What of my stain? What of Hughe and his filthy tongue? Where's my honour if I don't dispute such rank and public slander? Or doesn't that matter?'

'Of course it matters,' Grefin muttered. 'But curse it, Balfre, you know what Herewart is. If he'd not seen you punished he'd stir trouble with the lords, say that Aimery tramples justice to protect his son.'

'So I'm trampled instead, my rights as Harcia's heir mangled like a hog's guts in the mud? Where's the justice in that?'

'Balfre, I understand you're disappointed. But try to see it through Aimery's eyes. He—'

'Fuck Aimery's eyes!' Shaking, he sloshed brandy into a fresh goblet. Drained it dry as those dragon-talons twisted deeper into his guts. 'We both know the old bastard won't keep this secret. Within the week all of Harcia will know I'm disinherited the stewardship, and by month's end Clemen will know it too. We'll hear Harald laughing all the way from Eaglerock.'

'Harald?' Grefin groaned. 'Why must everything come back to Harald?'

He stared. '*Why?* I swear, Grefin, you're as blind as Aimery. It's a fucking mercy you're not the one stepped into Malcolm's boots.' He refilled the goblet, hand still unsteady. 'At least not the whole way.'

'Not even part way,' said Grefin. 'I don't want to be duke.'

'Good, for you'd make a poor one!' he retorted. 'Don't you see, Grefin? Sooner or later Harcia will be mine. And if Harald still rules Clemen then? By the Exarch's balls, how will I keep us safe from that slavering mongrel if Aimery's already taught him I'm not to be feared! Has the old fool thought of that? Fuck if he has!'

Another sigh, then Grefin looked again to the brandy. 'Do I get a drink, or don't I?'

He walked away from the sideboard. 'Am I your fucking servant now? Pour it yourself.'

So Grefin tipped brandy into another goblet and drank, more deeply than was his habit. Balfre, looking over his shoulder, seeing the misery so close to his brother's plain surface, turned from the chamber's narrow, shuttered window. Fuck. Despite everything, and no matter how much he resented it, Grefin's honest pain could still pain him. They were brothers, tied hand and foot by blood and memories and death. Nothing could change that, though he often wished otherwise.

'How long have you had that doublet, Gref? A year? You should've turned it to dishcloths months ago.'

'When it's only been mended twice?' said Grefin, eyebrows raised. 'I don't think so. Besides, you keep the household tailor busy enough for both of us.'

He snorted. 'Spoke like a true nip-purse. Are you certain sure we're related?'

'Mother seemed to think so.'

'You do know she's dying again, from shame, seeing you put together like a third-rate Ardennese merchant with a hole in his money chest.'

Grefin tugged at his dark blue velvet doublet, unleavened by so much as a single pink pearl. 'Bite your tongue. I'm as well-dressed as a *second*-rate merchant, thank you.' Then he frowned. 'And don't speak of Mother like that.'

He raised a placating hand. 'Sorry.'

'It's just . . .' Grefin drank more brandy. 'I miss her.'

'I know.' A headache was brewing behind his eyes. He pressed a knuckle hard against his forehead, rubbing 'So. How was the duke when you left him?'

'Not sweet,' said Grefin, after an uncomfortable pause. 'Herewart's grief has left him raw.'

'Will he see me tonight?'

'No.'

'And if I want to see him?'

'Do you?'

He laughed, unamused. 'No.'

'Well, then.' Grefin nodded at the scattered shards of Maletti glass beneath the wine-spoiled tapestry. 'You broke a goblet.'

'And if I did?'

'It's a pity,' said Grefin, shrugging. 'They were Mother's favourites.'

And so they were. 'It was an accident.'

'Like Hughe?'

The sharp question stabbed him onto his feet. 'Meaning?'

Grefin's eyes had shaded to the cold blue of winter, and the grief in his face was turned to wariness . . . and doubt. 'You spoke to him, after the joust. Couldn't you tell he was mortal hurt?'

'I'm not a leech.'

'There was no hint, no sign, that he—'

'It was a joust,' he said, as temper stirred again. Tangled in all his adult feelings for the man Grefin had become, the childhood pride of a little brother tottering faithfully in his footsteps. Where was that little brother now? Where was the Grefin who thought Balfre could do no wrong? 'Sometimes men die when they joust. I never forced Hughe to ride against me. And I never hobbled his horse or sat a burr under his saddle or cut through his stirrup leather or weakened his lance. All I did was win. Is winning enough to make me a murderer?'

'I know you never meant Hughe to die,' Grefin snapped. 'But admit this much, Balfre. When you're angry you don't see straight. You don't even try. I think you saw Hughe was hurt and because he'd hurt you first, you just didn't *care*.'

He was sore tempted to smash another glass goblet. 'Why should I flinch for Black Hughe's spilled blood or weep because he's a corpse now, and rotting? He was an upstart, a brash-boy, he mocked his betters and never knew when to hold his nasty tongue. Did *he* care when he slandered me? Fuck if he did! So no, I didn't care he was hurt and I don't care he died of being the poorer man in a joust!'

Grefin's face twisted. 'You should.'

'And you should care I've had my birthright stolen. The Green Isle is mine, Grefin. Not yours.'

'The Isle belongs to Aimery. Whoever is named its Steward, that man holds it in trust for Harcia's duke.'

'And we both know I should be that man. *Please*, Gref.' Stepping close, he took hold of his brother's shoulder. 'Tell Aimery that for love of me you won't steal the Isle like a common thief.'

'I can't.' Shrugging free, Grefin put down his empty goblet. 'I've already said I'd be Steward for a year.'

Balfre moistened his lips. 'You've promised him that?'

'I have.' Grefin stared, defiant. 'For both of us.'

His hot blood had turned to ice, freezing heart and bone. 'I don't remember lending you my tongue. Tell me, brother, what else did I say?'

'Balfre—'

'*What else?*'

Grefin turned away, his own temper escaping. 'D'you think you can defy the duke and be winked at? Kill a man, and be winked at? So you'll wait one more year before you're Steward. That's *nothing*.'

'Says the man who's been made Steward in my place!'

'Oh, Balfre.' Turning back, Grefin shook his head. 'Can you think of no one but yourself? The duke held that old rump Herewart in his arms and *wept*. That old rump is broken with his grief. It was his *son* you killed. *Fuck*. I begged you not to hold that joust. Why, just once, didn't you listen to me?'

A good question, in hindsight.

Abruptly exhausted, Balfre dropped again to the settle. 'So that's that, is it? You're to be Steward and I'm to be made a laughing stock.'

Grefin dropped to the settle beside him. 'I'm sorry.'

As if that made any difference. As if that made what he'd done all right.

'Aimery does what he must for Harcia,' Grefin added. 'He might not be the easiest of fathers but he is a good duke.'

'Sometimes,' he admitted, grudging, then let out a slow breath. 'But mostly he scares me shitless. He loves peace so much he's afraid to think of war. He thinks Clemen is no danger. He thinks Harald—'

'Is a fool and a rascal who'll stumble into trouble without our help.' Grefin looked at him sidelong. 'And he's right.'

'I know you think so. But Gref, what if he's wrong?'

'What if he is? Are you saying the only remedy must be the spilling of Clemen blood?'

'Clemen's spilled our blood, in the Marches.'

'And we've spilled theirs,' said Grefin. 'We've both of us done our share of bleeding. But do you want Marcher squabbles spilled over the borders? Would you flood both duchies scarlet?'

'I'd never let it come to that. I don't want Clemen ruined. Just brought to heel.'

In the fireplace, flames flickered. Shadows danced on the

tapestry-hung stone walls. With a muttered curse Grefin braced his elbows on his knees and pressed his hands to his face.

'When we were boys,' he said, muffled, 'after Malcolm was squired to Deness of Heems and it was just the two of us, you always wanted to play King of Harcia. Remember? You brandished a wooden sword and wore a crown you wove from willow-wands, and when I wouldn't call you *Your Majesty* you'd get so angry . . .'

Balfre's heart thudded hard. 'Doesn't every boy dream of being a king?'

'Maybe.' Grefin let his hands fall. Shifted a little, to look at him squarely. 'But we're not boys any more.'

'More's the pity. Things were fucking simpler then.'

A startled moment, then Grefin laughed. 'Yes. They were.'

'And you have to admit, Gref, they'd be simpler now,' he pointed out, carefully careless, 'if the old kingdom returned and Harcia and Clemen were reconciled under one rule. Clemen's people would be happier were they rid of cursed Harald.'

Grefin thudded his shoulder blades against the wall. 'No doubt. Only the last king of Harcia died some two hundred years ago and those crowned days died soon after when the kingdom split. I know you still dream of the old Harcian kingdom reborn, Balfre, but you must know that's folly. It's far too late to turn the clock back.'

Said Aimery and his faithful echo Grefin. But they were mistaken. Ancient wrongs could be put right. Stolen thrones could be reclaimed. The Kingdom of Harcia had been mighty, once . . . and would be again, when he was done.

But that wasn't something he was ready to share with his brother.

'I know,' he said, heaving a deceptively rueful sigh.

'Do you?' Grefin frowned. 'Really?'

'Yes, really.' He punched a fist to Grefin's knee. 'It's late. You should go. Mazelina will be thinking I've shoved you down the garderobe.'

Grefin's answering smile was tinged with relief. 'Given into temptation, you mean.'

'Oh, go fuck yourself,' he suggested. 'Better yet, fuck your wife.' When his brother only stared, uncertain, he shoved. '*Go*, Grefin. I might sting over the Green Isle but if you think I'd throw myself from the top of the Croft for losing it, you're moonshot.'

'So . . .' Grefin stood. 'I'm forgiven?'

Balfre blinked. Forgiven? For capitulating to Aimery. For taking what wasn't his. For thinking he could speak on anyone's behalf but his own. *Forgiven?*

Grefin really was moonshot.

Maybe in a year, when – *if* – Grefin kept his word, and the Green Isle's stewardship passed from his brother's unlawful hands to his. Maybe then he could find it in him to forgive the day's betrayal. But not now, with Grefin's presumption of pardon so glibly thoughtless, so *arrogant*. So like Aimery he could spit.

'Yes,' he said, smiling, as the dragon-talons clutched anew. 'You're forgiven.'

The smile lasted until the outer chamber's door closed behind his little brother. Then he staggered to his feet, snatched up the bottle of brandy and poured what remained of it down his dry throat. Choked. Gasped for air.

'Fuck. *Fuck!*'

He was too angry to stand, had to rage about the luxurious chamber that served only to remind him of what he didn't possess. In every castle of Harcia it was the same, he and Jancis and her mewling daughter granted the apartments that had belonged to Malcom. He held no castle of his own, outright. A clutch of manor houses, yes, with villages and farmland yielding him wealth. After Aimery, before Grefin, he was the richest man in Harcia. But it didn't make up for his lack of moat and drawbridge and keep.

Grefin would have a castle, now he was Steward of the Green Isle.

The thought had him smashing the emptied brandy bottle onto the floor, sent him hunting for a fresh one. But then he stopped, panting. What was the point? There wasn't enough brandy in the duchy, in the *world*, to numb his rewoken, all-consuming pain. He needed a living distraction, something soft and warm. A woman.

'Jancis!' he roared. 'Jancis, where the fuck are you?'

He found his wife in the nursery, clad in unbecoming tawny wool, holding her swaddled brat of a daughter and talking with a servant. 'Get out,' he told the girl. She picked up her linen skirts and fled.

'My lord,' Jancis whispered, standing with the brat's crib between them. 'I heard. About Hughe, and the stewardship. I'm so sorry.'

Oh, but she was a colourless shadow, his wife, with her pale hair and pale skin and eyes like watered glass. So thin, so flat-chested, sunlight almost passed right through her. No wonder he struggled to sire a living son. Aimery was to blame for that. From misplaced loyalty to one of his nobles, Aimery had cradle-promised him to Jancis, and when Malcolm died forced the wedding upon him. After two sons miscarried he'd begged his father on both knees for release, but the old fulmet wouldn't let him put the barren bitch aside – even though her father was dead by then and couldn't be offended. So he was yoked to her until Aimery was bedded for good in his own coffin.

He could feel the brandy in his belly, burning like dragon-fire. 'How did you hear? Who told you?'

'I was with Mazelina in her apartments. We heard the servants gossiping.'

Fucking servants. He should rip out their tongues. 'And?'

'And what?' his wife said, tears rising. 'I don't understand.'

Held tight to her uninspiring breasts, the brat wriggled and cooed. Jancis started to look down, then stopped herself.

'And do you have a fucking opinion?' he demanded. 'Or is that too much to ask?'

His insipid wife's pale cheeks washed pink. 'I think it's wrong that Grefin's made Steward. Why did Aimery do such a thing?'

'Don't you mean *How am I to blame*, that Aimery would kick me in the balls before the watching world? Isn't that what you mean?'

Like his privy chamber, the nursery was generously lit with oil lamps and firelight. Jancis's plump tears glowed with a golden warmth.

'No,' she whispered. 'Of course not. However Hughe died, I know the fault's not yours.'

'Herewart says elsewise.'

Jancis gasped. 'Herewart calls murder on you? And Aimery *believes* it? That's why he's named Grefin his Steward? But – but that's wicked unjust!'

She was a barren bitch and he could never love her. So what did it say of him, that her swift defence of his honour was a balm, and welcome?

'What a needle-wit you are,' he said roughly, sneering. 'So sharp you must prick yourself twice a day, at least.' Her face paled again at the taunt. 'There'll be talk,' he added, needing to goad her. 'Will you stand it?'

Her resentful eyes met his. 'Will you?'

The tart reply was a surprise. Jancis hardly ever challenged him. Perhaps he'd like her better if she did. Perhaps if she had greater mettle she'd find the strength to give him sons.

And if mules were horses a peasant in the saddle could be mistook for a lord.

'Mind your shrewish tongue,' he said, skirting the crib to close on her. 'You're the cause of this, Jancis.'

The brat snuffled as her holding arms tightened. 'How is it my fault? I never—'

'Hughe's dead because he slandered me!' he shouted, backing her into the wall. 'And he slandered me because of *you*! What corruption is in you, Jancis, that your feeble body must spit out my sons before they're formed?'

'No corruption, Balfre! Indeed, you do me wrong!'

'*I* wrong *you*?' He almost laughed. '*Bitch!*'

'I'm sorry, Balfre,' she whispered. 'I'd give anything to give you sons. Perhaps if I could find a wise woman who knows of such things I might—'

'A *witch*? Woman, are you *mad*?'

She cried out. 'No, no. I won't look for one! I promise! Please, Balfre, don't—' She was weeping, half-turning to shield the brat, starting to slide down the wall. 'Don't hurt her!'

Like a man watching a mummery, he saw himself looming over his unwanted wife and girl-child. Saw his fist raised to strike. Saw her tears, and her terror. Heard the child's frightened wails. Sickened, shaken, he turned away. Never in his life had he struck a woman. *Any man who beats a woman makes of himself a beast*. A lesson learned at his formidable mother's knee. How ashamed she'd be, could she see him now.

Helping Jancis to stand, he felt her trembling fear of him beneath his hands and flinched. 'I'm sorry,' he said, as she settled the brat in its crib. 'Jancis . . .' Helpless, he stared at her. 'Fuck. I wish — I wish—'

She looked up. 'I know, Balfre. So do I.'

Without warning, his throat closed. 'It's not right that Grefin's made Steward. Ever since Malcom died, Aimery has looked for ways to—' He breathed hard, fighting the pain he resented so much. 'The honour of the Green Isle belongs to me.'

'Your father's made his decision,' Jancis said, shrugging. 'There's nothing you can do.'

Her defeated acceptance rekindled his anger. 'Fuck that. I don't accept it. You wait. I'll change the old bastard's mind.'

From atop the Croft's battlements, wind-tugged and shivering despite his padded doublet and heavy woollen surcoat, Aimery watched the summoned lords of his council clatter on horseback across the stone bridge leading to the castle's outer bailey. Though he stood high, and they were distant, he could tell they weren't happy. But then, neither was he.

Out of long custom, Harcia kept an itinerant court. As he travelled the duchy, showing his face, hearing disputes, he often met with his greatest barons. Together they nipped trouble in its rancorous bud, which meant a great council was held once, at most twice, in a year. Its holding was a disruption, an upheaval in many lives. That reckless Balfre was the cause this time would not endear him to the men cruel fate had decreed he'd one day rule.

Aimery sighed. If only Balfre understood that.

Horse by horse, Harcia's barons vanished from sight as they passed into the keep: Deness of Heems, Lord Keeton, Lord Ferran, Maunay of Knockrowan, Reimond of Parsle Fountain, Lord Orval. Last of all, Joben, Balfre's cousin on his mother's side. There was a younger cousin, eager for a place on the council. But history taught that dukes who favoured family over their duchy's loyal barons came to foul ends.

I must punish Balfre harshly in the eyes of every lord. Not just to save him, but to save myself too. And Harcia.

Footsteps behind him, and then a lightly cleared throat. Curteis.
'Your Grace, the council gathers in the Great Hall.'

'Let them wait. I'll come presently.'

'Your Grace.'

Alone again, Aimery feasted his gaze on the open countryside around the Croft. Once woodland had grown almost as far as the eye could see. But Harcia had cut down nearly all of its forests, hungry to turn tall trees into swift galleys. A mistake, that had proven. The men of Harcia weren't natural sailors. They failed to read the treacherous tides and currents of the northern sea. Those mistakes, and three seasons of vast storms, had wrecked Harcia's galleys to driftwood. One more reason for his duchy's struggle to find wealth in the world. Aside from the Green Isle's splendid horses, they had precious little. He was doing his best, sapling by sapling, to bring back those slain forests and with them the natural riches Harcia had squandered. He'd not see them reborn in his lifetime, but Balfre would. If he continued the work his father had started.

Balfre.

Aimery felt his breathing hitch. When would his son realise he must be a better man than the man who'd knocked Black Hughe from saddle to coffin? Than the man who blamed Jancis for their sorrows and looked with sour envy upon Grefin and his thriving son?

He must know he disappoints himself. He must know he breaks my heart.

Even so, there was courage in him, and the capacity for love. If he was spoiled a little, if he wasn't Malcolm, surely he wasn't yet rotten. Surely he could still be saved.

For Harcia's sake he must be.

Staring over his battlements, seeing in his mind's eye every village and creek and manor that by birthright he owned yet only held in trust, Aimery felt a sting of tears. As much as he'd loved Malcolm, did love Grefin, tried to love Balfre, did he love his harsh, rugged duchy.

Blinking away the sting, he turned from the battlements. He could hide up here no longer. Hard tasks did not soften with the passing of time.

* * *

Grefin was waiting in the Great Hall, in company with the council. In company with Herewart, returned to the Croft after Hughe's funeral, still dressed head to toe in mourning black. The old man's sharp grief was blunted, the pain instead settled deep in his bones and moulding his face into a portrait of permanent loss. Herewart had no place on the council, but he was owed this public apology.

'My lords,' Aimery said, raising a hand to acknowledge their sober greetings. 'Be seated. I'd not keep you longer than necessary. Grefin, stand with me.'

As they obeyed he took his own chair, the hugely carved ducal seat with its bearskin covering and bear-claw decorations. Let the bear's strength suffuse him, let its courage rouse his blood. Bears were mighty and ferocious. Bears did not weep.

He could feel Grefin at his right hand, high-strung beneath the outward calm. As always, dressed more like sober, self-effacing Curteis than a duke's son, in dark blue velvet lacking jewels and gold thread. That would have to change. Clothes proclaimed the man . . . or, in his case, the Steward. But Mazelina would see to that. His youngest son's wife was a lively woman of unbounded tact and common sense.

'My lords,' he said again, once his barons were settled, 'your summons to council arises from our dear brother Herewart's grievous loss. He knows my privy heart in this, but I'll share it now so none here might wonder. A son's untimely death is a sorrow no father should suffer. And I tell you *my* sorrow is doubled, for the part my heir played in Hughe's death.'

'Your Grace, we all grieve,' said Reimond of Parsle Fountain. Time-grizzled, with thinning hair and two fingers lost from his left hand. He turned to Herewart. 'Hughe was a fine man, boon friend to my own Geffrei. That he should die—'

'By mischance,' Joben said quickly, not caring if he gave offence. Only two years parted him and Balfre, and as boys they'd been peapod close. 'There was no malice.'

Reimond glowered, while the other barons tapped fingers and muttered. 'But there was temper, Joben. Temper and poor judgement. Your Grace—'

'Peace,' said Aimery sharply. 'This is not a debate upon the character of my eldest son. I know him, heart and soul, better than anyone. Balfre is—'

'Here,' said his son, unwelcome and gallingly disobedient, as he entered the Great Hall. 'Come to plead my case before Harcia's duke and his council.'

'Balfre, you *noddle*,' said Grefin under his breath, dismayed. 'What are you doing?'

The council, and Herewart, stared at Balfre as he approached. Not a popinjay this afternoon, but a sparrow, he wore an undyed linen shirt and mud-brown woollen hose. He came barefoot and bareheaded, not an ear- or finger-ring to be seen. Plain Grefin by comparison was turned gaudy bright.

Searching his barons' faces, Aimery fought to keep his own face still. Balfre's brazen defiance of established protocol was a barbed blade twisting in his guts. And he could see Reimond felt the same, his forehead knitted in disapproval. Indeed, only Joben showed any favour. Deness of Heems and the lords Keeton and Ferran echoed Reimond's unmasked disgust.

Heedless of their hostile stares, Balfre halted and folded into a bow. 'Your Grace,' he said, straightening, his steady gaze supremely confident. 'I come to you humbled, seeking forgiveness. When I blinked at your disapproval of rowdy sporting I acted out of youthful bravado, discarding your wise judgement for my own. Your Grace, you deserve much better. And before these great lords, whom I have also offended, I swear on my life I will never again fail you or Harcia – and I ask that you let me prove it by granting me all my rights as your heir.'

Breathing out softly, Balfre pressed a hand to his heart, making his words a solemn vow. Then, letting his gaze lower to the flagstoned floor, he folded first to his knees and then to utter prostration, arms outstretched before him in an extravagance of entreaty.

From a great, cold distance, Aimery heard the hall's air whistle in and out of his chest. There was rage . . . and there was, he now discovered, a place beyond rage. He stared at the stunned faces before him.

'Balfre is my heir,' he said, as though no time had passed, as though his other son had never entered the hall. 'And when I die he will be your duke. But the tragedy of Hughe's death makes plain that he yet has much to learn. Therefore I declare that for the span of a year and a day my younger son Grefin, here standing beside me, shall be hailed Steward of the Green Isle, my voice and my authority in that place.'

Reimond of Parsle Fountain cleared his throat. 'And if Balfre proves himself a slow learner?'

'For his sake, Reimond . . .' Aimery bared his teeth in a smile. 'I hope he proves otherwise.' He stood. 'My lords of the council, my lord Herewart, I invite you to withdraw with me and my well-loved son Grefin, that we might spill wine in memory of Black Hughe and then celebrate our new Steward!'

With every man watching, with Grefin breath-caught and torn, to his sorrow, he took a step forward . . . and stepped over his other son. Stepped again and kept walking, leaving Balfre prostrate and speechless in his wake. And as Grefin followed, and the other lords followed Grefin, he did not look back.

CHAPTER THREE

'Your Grace! Your Grace, please, another measure,' cried Lord Gerbod's wife, pouting. 'The hour is not so late and no man here prances a *roundelay* to rival you!'

Harald, Duke of Clemen, waved his hand in refusal then collapsed breathless into his high-backed, intricately carved wooden chair. Sweat trickled down his face, his spine, soaked the hair in his armpits and slithered over his ribs. But none here would notice, surely, and if they did – what matter? Though the night was cold he didn't sweat alone. Dancing was a sweaty business. No reason for any man here to glance at his sweating duke and wonder.

In his iron-banded chest, his heart beat hard and too fast.

'Wine!' he said, snapping his fingers, and wine came in a jewelled silver goblet. Scarwid playing servant this time, bowing and scraping. A tiresome tick, he was, his welcome worn out. The petty lordling would've been dismissed from this dull northern court long since, had his wife not been such a good fuck.

Harald drank deep, thinking of Gisla. He'd grown weary of her, too. There was nothing new there, he'd ridden all the tricks out of her. And of late he'd spied a possessive glint in her fine brown eyes. Her fingers, taking his arm, clutched him tight as though she owned him. Like all women she was a fool, thinking she held more worth than a pair of honey tits and the hot, wet hole between her legs.

But there was no need to worry. Roric would rid him of Gisla and cuckolded Scarwid when he returned from his errands. Neatly, discreetly, with a sweet smile and a gentle touch to belie the sting of dismissal. Good at that, was dependable cousin Roric. Harald smothered sly pleasure, thinking of it.

Perhaps I'll make him a baron, one of these days.

Or perhaps he wouldn't. Bastard-born, barred from ducal inheritance and lawful marriage, Roric relied on his duke for the clothes on his back – and everything else. As a baron he'd be granted property, have the means to provide for himself, and therein lay the key. Dangled prizes kept a man keen. A promise unfulfilled was a promise fat with power to guarantee loyalty.

Still sweating, Harald willed his thumping heart to ease. Tucked safely out of sight in his chamber was a cordial to aid him, and a thrice-incanted charm on a thin gold chain. But he could dare neither, not even in this lightly lorded court's glare. No stink of weakness could taint Harald of Clemen, with his two dead wives and five dead sons and the future of his bloodline yet in whispered doubt.

Tipping the goblet of wine to his lips once more, he stared over its beaten rim at his duchess, Argante. She claimed she was breeding again. She should be, the times he'd had her on her back since Liam's birth. Relief at the news of a second pregnancy hollowed him. For Liam was not enough. One ill breath and his infant heir was meat for maggots. Though this son was strong, not a sickly babe like the others, he wouldn't be at ease until the succession was made doubly safe. Fate was a fickle bitch. She'd toyed with him all his life.

She toyed with him now, her cruellest trick yet.

The leech he'd summoned in secret from distant Lepetto, trained in ordinary medicine – and certain arts more arcane – had left him the foul cordial and the charm and a stern-faced warning against every manner of gluttony.

'*Duke, not even you with your sharp sword can defeat death,*' he'd said, a thick foreign accent mangling his seldom-spoken Cassinian. '*It comes. You must accept it. But if it comes creeping or flying, that is your choice.*'

A fortune in furs and precious stones, the leech had cost him. That meant another tax. Clemen's lords would groan at it, but let them. He was Harald, their duke. Their lives belonged to him, and their treasure chests. That was the order of things. Dukes ruled. Lords asked what they could give and then gave it, smiling.

Well. If they knew what was good for them, they did.

Masking temper with a smile, he drained the goblet of wine and held it out, upside down. *Enough.* Obedient hands took it from him. He sat back, breathing more easily, the iron bands clamping his ribs loosened now to mere discomfort. Because he was always watched, he rested a benevolent gaze upon Lord Udo, taking his turn at dancing with Argante. Ah, but she was a hot little bitch. His cock stirred in his hose at the sight of her tits swelling above her low-cut velvet gown. He could fuck her now, before his court in this Great Hall, creeping death be cursed, and not a man would gainsay him. Even had one of the Exarch's sour grey celibates attended him here, he could fuck her. Rulers did that, if they wished to. Rulers were not ruled. The Potent of Khafur, he had as many concubines as shone stars in the night sky and he fucked them where and when he liked and any man who raised his right eyebrow lost his head before ever he could raise his left to comment more.

Harald and the Potent of Khafur, rulers and cock-brothers.

The thought made him laugh.

'Your Grace? Might I trouble you?'

And here was Lord Bartrem. Amusement fading, Harald looked at the man, an unimportant local noble recently widowed of a rich

Eaglerock merchant's only daughter. He knew already what Bartrem was after. Some four desperate letters had paved the man's road to Heartsong Castle. He'd been tempted to deny the nagging fool an audience, but prudence outweighed irritation. Bartrem's cause was lost when his wife drew her last breath, but there was no need to needlessly inflame the man, or his fellow northern lords. Not when the court must soon return to Eaglerock, at the other end of the duchy.

'Be brief, my lord,' he said, courteously enough. 'We dance and make merry tonight. Serious matters belong to the morning.'

'Yes, Your Grace,' said Bartrem, spindle-shanked and chinless, with watering eyes and bulbous nose. Lucky for him he had a proper bloodline. Without it he'd never have caught the merchant's daughter. 'Your Grace, I must speak on the question of Thania's wardship.'

'It's not yet decided into whose care your child will be placed.'

'Your Grace—' Bartrem took an impetuous step closer to the ducal dais, then stopped himself. He was trembling. 'She is too young for wardship. My child is not yet three.'

'Infant wardships are commonplace, Bartrem.'

'Your Grace, they are cruel!'

Harald stared until the man took a step back. 'Not as cruel as a household in want of a wife. Or do you tell me you've wed again? Strange. I don't recall granting you permission.'

'No, Your Grace,' said Bartrem, losing colour. 'Of course not. I know what's right and proper.'

'So you say.' He inspected the emerald ring on his thumb. 'And yet you'd leave your precious daughter without womanly guidance?'

'No, Your Grace. My late wife's mother dotes on the child. With my parents dead, she would gladly—'

'You expect I'd allow a child of noble birth to be raised by common hands?'

Bartrem swallowed. 'Your Grace, after me my goodmother is Thania's closest kin.'

'And common.' He let his voice chill. 'As Clemen's duke I have a duty to protect noble blood. I would no more hand your child to a trinket-trader for raising than I would gift a staghound puppy in my kennel to a passing peddler.'

'Perhaps Your Grace is misinformed,' said Bartrem, fingers clenched nearly to fists. 'My late wife's father, Master Blane, is a merchant of high standing. His purse could buy half the lords beneath your roof this night and scarce show its loss of coin.'

That was true. Harald looked again to his ring. The question to be answered was this: did Bartrem's goodfather Blane hanker after the girl because she was his dead daughter's child, or did he see her as a thing of value to be traded? It was possible. The man was a wealthy merchant, after all.

If his care is genuine and I gift the girl's wardship to a lord other than Bartrem, then I might well be strewing stones in my own path. But if I gift the girl to myself . . .

It was a tempting thought. Liam would need a wife one day. Or if not Liam, then the next son Argante gave him. Surely Master Blane wouldn't cry foul to see his daughter's daughter in the care of Clemen's duke. Such an alliance would sate any crude ambition – or deafen him to Bartrem's cries, if family matters were his only care.

And a rich merchant made family by advantageous marriage would surely be most convenient.

'Your Grace.' Bartrem's voice was dropped to a pleading whisper, almost lost in the minstrels' music and the dancers' merriment. 'Thania is all I have left of my dear Mathilde. I beg you, be merciful.'

The man was a fool. Harald flicked his fingers. 'Very good, Bartrem. I shall think on what you've said. For now you should forget your sorrows and join us in a dance.'

Defeated, Bartrem bowed. 'Alas, Your Grace, my heart is too heavy for dancing.'

'Then find a more smiling face in a cup of wine. We are merry here. Would you spoil that?'

'Never, Your Grace.'

As Bartrem withdrew, Harald looked for his wife. Tired of Udo, and who wouldn't be, Argante was dancing with Scarwid. Feeling his gaze upon her, she dropped Scarwid's hand. Smiled and trod the minstrels' spritely music towards her husband.

Harald felt his body stir anew. Young enough to be his daughter,

47

Argante, but what did that matter? It was her youth that gave him Liam, and would give him Liam's brothers. Youth gave her firm tits and silken skin and lust enough to ride him to a bull's roar. His heart, which yet beat too fast, beat faster still as her youth and her tits and her lust danced her to him, hands reaching, eyes dark with sweaty promise.

'Your Grace,' she said sweetly. 'You've not yet danced with me. For shame. What will the court say? That I am wilted, and you are tiring?'

He cursed his heart, unreliable, and the stern-faced Lepetto leech. He wouldn't fuck her now, but he would dance with her . . . and in the dancing every man and woman here would see the fucking to come later. They'd see their duke virile, the father of many living sons. The whispers would fall silent, the wondering gazes shift to someone else. Abandoning his chair, Harald caught Argante in his arms, held her in the proper way of the jaunty *craka*, away from his chest so she couldn't feel his cursed, stuttering heart.

She was laughing, her long honey-brown hair beneath the gold wire-and-pearl headdress bound tight to the fine bones of her skull, shimmering in the light of one hundred burning candles. Her almond eyes, tip-tilted and dappled hazel, shone brilliant in her fashionably pale face.

'Come!' she cried, dropped-pearl earrings swaying as her be-ringed fingers beckoned to the near-score unimportant northern lords and their ladies who ate his food and drank his wine, who owed him whatever he decided to take. 'We haven't yet danced our joy for the duke's son, and we must, else we anger whatever mischievous spirits yet dwell here. Those who've not been chased away!'

Their obedient laughter answered her, and soon after the soft sound of heels kissing the Great Hall's red-and-white tiled floor. Harald laughed too, because he was watched, because – despite the cordial and the dangerous charm – his chest pounded with a dull pain that never quite ceased. He danced for his heir and wished that Roric danced with them. He could pass Argante to his scrupulous, agreeable cousin and not a man in the hall would blink.

High above them in his nursery, in his charm-covered cradle, little Liam slept. Heart thudding with pain, with love as keen and sharp as a curved Sassanine dagger, Harald danced and dreamed days of glory for his son.

Night. Star-pricked, meagrely moonlit, and crackling with frost. Hiding in a copse of saplings and shadows, Roric pulled his rabbit-lined cloak closer about his ribs and listened to the distant, derisive barking of foxes. Winter might be on the turn but there was life still in the stubborn old man, one cold, miserly fist clutching fast to Harald's duchy. Waiting for the arranged signal from the castle, shivering, he breathed in ice and breathed out smoke.

It'll come. It must. Belden's with us. Save a handful, everyone in Clemen will stand with us. Love for Harald is dried up like a sun-scorched puddle.

Where he stood, at the copse's fringe, the deer-rutted, rain-pooled ground before him ran away in a long, lazy slope towards the castle's bright green lawns. Harald owned twelve such strongholds, scattered across Clemen like thrown knucklebones. This one, fancied Heartsong by some long-dead duke's lady, curtsied prettily to the surrounding countryside. No raised hackles here, no growling threats uttered in counterpoint to the singing of a naked sword. Heartsong was a fret-worked white stone jewel. A woman's castle, more manor house than fortress, lacking high, wide curtain walls and treacherous moat and impassable drawbridge. Argante's castle, where she held court over wellborn ladies twice her age and older, and in triumph wielded Harald's infant son as though the babe were a blade made of soft, swaddled flesh.

And so he was, in a way. Poor noble brat. Poor Liam.

Thinking himself safe here, safe everywhere, his monstrous arrogance a helm with its visor hammered shut, Harald debauched himself within Heartsong and without, never noticing, never *dreaming*, that—

The damp crack of a twig breaking underfoot heralded someone's approach. A familiar tread. A trusted friend, who'd taken a trembling, owl-eyed boy of seven as a page and guided his journey from childish tears to knighted manhood.

'My lord Humbert,' Roric said, not turning, his voice pitched low. 'You should remind Vidar that patience is an admirable virtue.'

For all Humbert possessed his own castle and a wealth of land,

and armour scratched and dented in scores of confrontations since the day he won his spurs, Harald's most leaned-upon councillor had of late become yawn by yawn more fond of a close ceiling than an open sky. Not weak, never weak, but attached to his comforts, there was no denying. Padded beneath his heavy mail with fat these days; more than a linen-stuffed jambon. Even so, despite his changes, he still boiled with courage. Offended, as most were, by Harald's greedy, vindictive ravagings, he was prepared to be called traitor, to risk his life that those ravagings might be ended for good and the duchy's happiness restored.

'Oh ho. So I'm Vidar's squire, am I?' Humbert retorted, his own voice conspirator soft and teasing. 'Come to bend my knee with querulous demand?'

Turning briefly from Harald's moonlit Heartsong, Roric clasped the older man's shoulder with leather-gloved fingers. 'No, my lord. If there's knee-bending wanted it will be me in the mud, not you.'

Humbert's untamed, black-and-grey beard trembled as his jaw worked against emotion. 'Don't be a fool, Roric. Knee-bending? You? Never. You're Berold's grandson.'

He couldn't long look away from the castle, for fear he'd miss the signal. 'So is Harald,' he said, turning back. 'More truly than I am.'

'Harald.' Humbert spat at their feet. '*That* for Harald. Your grand-sire would never know him. I could believe yon Harald was a cradle-snatched changeling, so far from the great Berold has your cousin run his course. Bastard or not, Roric, *you* are Berold's true heir. Not that bloat who wears the ducal coronet, breaking the heart of every man who should love him.'

'So you've said, many times. But—'

'Give me none of your buts!' Humbert said, fierce. 'It's the truth, boy, and so I'll remind you till the maggot doubt stops its gnawing of your guts.'

The barking foxes fell silent. Roric pressed the heel of his hand against the aching scar across his left thigh, where once a swinging blade had caught him. Not even his heavy cloak could keep out the cold and its torment of old, healed hurts. In the deeper gloom behind him, the muffled thump of horses' shifting hooves and a clinking of bits and stirrups.

'Roric . . .' Humbert stepped closer. 'You stand a stone's throw from your heart-rotten cousin, sword ready to defend Berold's duchy. At your back stand Clemen's best nobles and their men, pledged to fight in your name. Would you shame them? Shame me? Shame the lord Guimar?'

As ever, the mention of his dead father was salt rubbed in an open wound. 'Humbert, do not—'

'He was friend to me like none other, Roric. A count of such renown, the minstrels still write songs of him. And that brave man died full of fear, knowing his brother for a craven lumpet and his brother's child for much worse.'

'Even so.' Roric swallowed a sigh. 'It was my uncle Baderon born Berold's heir, not my father, and Harald born *his* heir with no taint of bastardry on him.'

Humbert growled his displeasure. '*Boy*—'

The fisted blow, when it came, rattled Roric's teeth and left a burning pain in his arm, even through the charcoal-hardened links of his mail. In the moon-silvered darkness Humbert's glare showed fear and fury.

'I see the maggot's in your brain, not your guts! You say this rumption *now*, as we stand ankled in mud with our sharpened swords thirsty for blood? You – you gormless bull-pizzle! You *tribbit*! What ill faery flapped its dust in your dreams that you'd spill—'

Roric raised a calming hand. 'First changelings, now faeries? I hope you don't speak of such things where an exarchite can hear you. Our pagan days are behind us, or so the Exarch holds.'

'I'll spit on the Exarch, and I'll spit on you after,' said Humbert, his barrel chest heaving. 'But first you tell me truly, Roric. Are you wishing you'd not started this?'

'Did I start it? Or did you? I scarce remember.'

Humbert snorted. 'What does it matter? The end is all. Harald's end, and his vileness with him. Are you feared, Roric? I'll not believe it. You've served your time in the Marches, your sword is blooded a dozen times over. Don't ask me to believe your courage fails you.'

'It doesn't. But Humbert, don't *you* feel the weight of this? No duke of Clemen has ever been deposed.' He shivered. 'Making history gives a man pause. So I've paused, my lord. I'm thinking.'

'*Thinking?*'

He loved Humbert almost as much as he'd loved Guimar, but love didn't kill less kindly feelings. 'You've known me seventeen years, my lord. Tell me when I didn't chew over my choices like a hound chews gristle.'

Another blow, fist to his back this time. 'Your chewing time is *done*, Roric! It's weeks you've had to chew this bone. What's changed? Are you telling me this whoreson Harald sings a sweet tune now, and you're the only man who hears it?'

If only he could say that. If only Harald had come to his senses. Instead, he looked at Humbert and shook his head. 'No. My cousin's voice is as ugly as ever.'

'And his deeds so foul they'd shame a soul-eater,' said Humbert, giving no ground. 'Let history tend itself. It's *right* we do here. Stiffen your sinews, boy. You swore to me, you swore to *them*—' His thumb jerked at the shadows behind them, at the men who'd pledged themselves to this night's dark task. '—and all those lords waiting down south in Eaglerock, that your heart was in this. Are you Guimar's son, Roric, or are *you* the cursed changeling?'

'Don't plague me with Guimar,' he said, teeth gritted. 'It's *because* I honour my father that I think on this task, even as I stand here prepared to shed his blood from Harald's body, if I must!'

When it came, Humbert's released breath was like a groan. 'It might not come to slaughter.'

'Might not, no. But Humbert, it might, and that will be a heavy thing to live with. And explaining it to Liam, when he's old enough to understand?'

Just the thought could make him heave.

'You want to turn tail, then?' Humbert demanded.

'I want to save Clemen!'

Humbert stepped so close that his sigh felt like a warm, ale-scented breeze. 'And if we could save it without riding roughshod over Harald, don't you think it would've been saved before tonight?'

Roric looked away, weary before he'd struck a single blow. 'Yes, my lord.'

'Yes, my lord,' Humbert echoed, close to pleading. 'And I'd call you my lord, Roric. I'd call you my duke.' His finger stabbed at

Heartsong, where Harald caroused unawares. 'But I can't call you either until that piece of offal is done with. And the only man who can see him done is you. The only head fit for Clemen's coronet is yours. No more of Berold's blood remains.'

'That's not true.'

'Infants die every day, boy! Who's to say Harald's brat will live to see another winter?'

A fair question. Humbert had buried his two sons untimely, and both of Guimar's true-born sons had died in their youth. Clemen's grass grew green over the bones of young men and dead babes.

But even so . . .

'Liam's not dead yet, Humbert. And by rights, Clemen is his.'

'This duchy has no need of a milk-suck,' said Humbert. 'Even if the brat does survive, what use is it to us? We need a man who knows how to wield a sword. I promise you this, Roric. Grant Harald's babe the coronet, trammel it with regents, as they've done in Cassinia, and the wolves of Harcia will be at our throats before summer's end.'

'Aimery has never—'

'It's not Aimery I fear! It's his curs't heir wants to spill our blood in the mire – and Balfre is mongrel enough to try!'

He wished he could deny it. But Balfre had long made it plain he saw Clemen as stolen land. With one whiff of weakness, Aimery's heir and his friends would ride the Marches flat in their haste to reclaim Clemen for Harcia. And whispers from Harcia cast doubt on Aimery's ability to stop him. Balfre was a hot-head, full of temper and bile. Fresh gossip held he now had innocent blood on his hands, an enemy killed under cover of rough play. That was the stamp of Aimery's heir.

'Roric,' said Humbert. There was iron in his voice. 'I want an answer. Do you honour your oath and wield your sword in defence of this plundered duchy, or do you forswear yourself and toss Clemen in the midden?'

His sword, belted close by his side. A knight-gift from Guimar, costly and much loved. Heavy with promises and oaths newly sworn, in secret. Harald's doom . . . or his own.

Doubt was pointless. In this, he had no choice. Closing his fingers around the sword's hilt, Roric drew breath to reply and end the untimely, unwelcome dispute.

'He'll fight, of course,' said Vidar, joining them. Cat-footed as ever, despite the halt in his stride. 'He loves Clemen as some men love their wives. And a pox on you for doubting it, my lord.'

Any other man speaking so to Humbert would find himself clubbed to his knees. Vidar, being Vidar, earned nothing more violent than a glare. 'We're not here to henhouse,' Humbert muttered. 'If you've a mind to be useful, keep an eye open for the signal.'

Vidar's scarred face twitched, the closest he mostly came to a smile. In the moonlight, the eye that hadn't been stitched shut glinted. 'My lord, I'll do my best.' Ignoring Humbert's angry chagrin, he jerked his chin at the castle. 'But since you mention it . . . the night wears thin, Roric, and there's still no sign we're welcome. Are you certain Harald's knave is to be trusted?

He frowned. 'Are you certain he's not?'

'How can I say?' Vidar's shrug was elegant. 'I must defer to your superior judgement, since I've little cause to cross paths with knaves.'

And that was Vidar in a nutshell. His insults, if they were insults, were always so agreeably couched in courtesy.

'I've no reason to doubt him, Vidar. I told you. Belden's uncle to a trusted squire, and vouched for.'

Another elegant shrug. 'If you say so, Roric. Though I must confess I save my trust for lords, not knaves.'

'Then you can breathe easy, Vidar,' Humbert said flatly. 'For it's Roric you're trusting.'

A brief bow, this time. 'Of course, my lord.' Then Vidar smiled. 'Good Roric, are we quarrelling? Let's not. We should save our temper for Harald.'

And that was Vidar, too, effortlessly shifting from veiled insult to open, easy accord. Sometimes it was hard to know the real reason he'd joined their cause. Did he truly believe it was just? Or was he simply seeking revenge for his father, and the chance to reclaim what Harald had stolen?

And in the end, did it matter? So long as Harald fell . . .

'Look!' said Humbert, pointing. 'There.'

A plunging star of light from the top of Heartsong's single tower keep. A flaming arrow. The signal.

Blood pounding, Roric turned. 'And that would be my knave, ready to unbar the castle's sally port to us. It's time. Vidar—'

Caught by the arm, Vidar swung about. His scarred face darkened with anger, swift as a wind-chased cloud crossing the sun. 'Roric?'

'Remember I want little Liam untouched,' he said, loosening his hold. 'Remind everyone, in my name. Harald's son is innocent of his father's sins, as all sons are innocent.'

Vidar, landless and tainted because of his own foolish father, bared his teeth in a grim smile. 'At least until they make their own choices,' he said, his single green eye unclouded with doubt or fear. 'And then they're men, Roric, who must answer as men.'

'Perhaps. But any man who spills a single drop of Liam's blood, be he noble or base, shall shed his own in a river. We haven't come to make war on infants. My lord—' He looked to Humbert. 'Go with Vidar to fetch the others, and our men-at-arms. We don't want to keep Belden waiting. He might lose heart and think we've mislaid our purpose.'

'A knave lose heart?' said Vidar. 'Shame on you for saying so, Roric. I've heard on the best authority that knaves are as noble as any lord in the land.'

'That's enough mischief from you, Vidar,' Humbert growled. 'Save your strife-making for Harald.'

Humbert and Vidar retreated into the copse's shadowed gloom. Grateful for the solitude, however brief, Roric stared at the castle and felt his gloved fingers cramp until his hands were made fists.

See reason, Harald. Find shame. For all our sakes, I beg you. Do not contest me, so all of us might live.

Liam was fussing.

'Oh, baby, baby, my wicked lamb! Waking so soon? Naughty!'

Swooping, Ellyn snatched up her beloved charge from his gilded cradle, hung with faery-charms no matter what the Exarch's mimbly priests said, and pressed him close to her milk-plump breast. Was he hungry? No, that wasn't his empty belly cry. She'd be leaking like a sieve if it was. No, he was just fussing, frit by a baby-dream and ripe for cuddling.

'There, my baby,' she crooned, as Liam grizzled and folded his fingers into her hair. His tiny nails scratched her neck. They needed paring again, growing as fast as he was. Nearly three full moons old now, and such a big boy. His wispy hair tickled her chin, chestnut-red like his handsome father's. And his slate-grey eyes would turn the duke's lovely amber-brown, she knew it. Such a beautiful boy, so fine she could scarce remember her own babe, strangled in its cord, blue and wrinkled and ugly. A mercy to lose the little bastard, her mother said, and it was true. That dead unwanted babe had brought her Liam.

Wriggle, wriggle, fuss. Would he never settle down?

'Hush-a-bye, hush,' she whispered, breathing him in, sweeter than summer roses. 'You'll wake the old cow, lamb. We don't want her mooing at us, do we?'

The old cow, Lady Morda, who only looked at Liam and made him cry. Nasty old woman had no business being in the nursery with her pinching, poking fingers, but what use a fifteen-year-old wet nurse saying so? The lady Argante would be deaf to that. At seventeen and shockingly fair, the duke's triumphant third wife knew everything already. Besides, the lady Morda was her kinswoman, so she could do no wrong.

'Come, baby,' Ellyn said, her cheek pressed to Liam's restless head. 'Shall we walk a bit? Take a little tit-tup? You'll sleep like a noddy one, won't you, once we've had ourselves a roundabout.'

Of course he would. She knew him front to back, knew his ten toes and his ten fingers and the reason for every tear on his rose petal cheeks. He was her baby, her Liam. What was Argante, Duchess of Clemen? Nothing but the vain, spoiled young woman who'd pushed him out between her legs.

'But you're my wee man, Liam, aren't you?' she whispered, walking him round and round the fine castle nursery, with its tapestries and velvets, stained-glass in the window, gilded shutters fastened tight against sly drafts, a brazier glowing with heat and candles enough to outshine the sun, as well as rushlights for the small hours. Nothing too fine for Duke Harald's heir. 'Liam is his Ellyn's wee man.'

Her wee man blew a sticky bubble, then started to wail.

'No, Liam,' she implored, jigging him. 'Don't you start that. You'll have me in such trouble. The old cow, she'll blame my milk.'

And then the lady Argante would hiss like a cat and tell the duke to find another wet nurse for Liam. If that happened, she'd die.

Walking as she jigged him, she crossed them to the narrow, gilded door opposite Liam's cradle. It was the lady Morda's chamber behind there, the privy closet she had claim to because the nursery was in her charge. No straw-stuffed pallet on the flagstones beside the cradle for that old cow. Holding her breath, Ellyn pressed one ear against the painted wood, but heard nothing save the lady's snores, rough as a hacksaw in a log.

'All mousey, lamb,' she whispered, backing away. 'So hush now, hush.'

Liam's wail stuttered into hiccups, but that was only the lull before the storm. There'd be more wails soon enough if she didn't keep him sweet. A longer walk, then. But it was night-time, the stone corridors chilly. Let Liam catch an ague and she'd kiss farewell to those kindly looks from the duke. He'd kill her with his bare hands, instead. His son was worth more to him than all the gold and jewels in Clemen.

Ellyn bundled her little lambkin into a fine scarlet-dyed blanket, the wool to make it brought over land and sea all the way from duchy Ardenn, in Cassinia. They grew the best wool there, everyone knew that. But even so, *ten gold marks* for three hanks of sheep's wool! Still, not even ten gold marks was o'erspending. Not for precious Liam. After he was safely snugged and gummy smiling, she wrapped them both in her coarse brown woollen cloak then slipped out of the nursery to wander Heartsong for a while.

The castle stood but three storeys high, not counting the kitchens and cellars below or the tower keep at one corner, and Liam's nursery was an eagle's eyrie on the uppermost floor. Expecting to find at least one of the duke's men-at-arms nearby, she was surprised to discover the corridor empty and echoing. She hesitated, uncertain. But then faint strains of music drew her towards the stone spiral staircase leading down to the four-sided minstrel gallery above the Great Hall, where Duke Harald and his duchess and the court amused themselves of a night.

Warm beneath the plain cloak as they took the tight-turning stone stairs one careful step at a time, Liam wriggled and cooed. Ellyn smiled, feeling the damp on her linen undershirt where her little man had drooled. Reaching the gallery at last, she stopped.

There was the missing man-at-arms, snatching a few moments of music to brighten a dull watch. Emun, his name. A bit rough, like all men-at-arms, and older than her by a tenyear, but not a bad sod. She'd known worse. Emun spun about, hearing her laced leather slippers on the flagstones, his knee-length mail coat rattling its own rough music. The fat candles set into the stone wall beside him betrayed his surprise and sudden, red-faced guilt.

Ellyn pressed a finger to her lips, giving him her best saucy dimples. Let the twinkle in her eye tell him she'd not tattle if he didn't, so he should stay and enjoy the music a bit longer. But Emun frowned, his thieved moment spoilt, his fear of the castle's serjeant too great. Because he had a ready, slapping hand, she stepped aside from the arching stone doorway so he could stomp past her and Liam and take the spiral staircase back to where he belonged.

She wasn't sorry to hear his footsteps fade away. She liked it best when she and Liam were alone.

'There, my lamb,' she murmured. 'Let's bide a while and listen, shall we? And watch your fine, handsome Dadda dance.'

'My lord Roric.'

'Serjeant Belden.' Roric, answering whisper with whisper, examined the man's rough-hewn face in the torchlight falling through Heartsong's narrowly opened sally port. Resignation there, a touch of fear, but no treachery. The man was standing firm. 'Is all ready?'

The castle's senior man-at-arms nodded. 'His Grace is at his pleasure, keeping company with his lords and ladies in the Great Hall. They're well-plied with wine, and mellow.'

'Your men? How many in all?'

'Fifteen.'

Still only a handful, then, even this close to the Marches. Harald's overconfident arrogance was serving them well.

'Where will we find them?'

'There are none in the hall itself, my lord. Two stand at its doors. Four have the roaming of the castle, roof to cellars. The rest I've posted where they'll do you least harm.'

'We crossed paths with no one outside.'

'No, my lord. I've kept every last man within doors. I didn't want to risk them seeing the arrow.'

Roric nodded. 'A clever thought.'

'My lord.' The serjeant chewed at his lip. 'My lord, about my men. I'd not—'

'I make no promises I'm not sure to keep, Belden. But I'll do my best to see they're not slaughtered.'

The serjeant sighed gustily. 'Yes, my lord.'

At his back, Humbert cursed. 'Roric! What's the hold?'

'No hold,' he said, turning. 'I'm making sure of our welcome.'

A burning torch was set in the stonework above the sally port. In its guttering light he saw Humbert's frown. Vidar's almost-concealed tension. Open tension in the shadowed faces of the lords who stood with him: Aistan, Farland, Hankin and Morholt. Disciplined behind them stood the two score of men-at-arms sworn to follow their lords. Not a one of them belonged to him, yet to a man he commanded them. If they died this night, their blood would wet his head.

'*Roric.*'

He looked again at Heartsong's guardian. 'Serjeant of the Guard, do you grant us entry?'

Belden's knuckles whitened on the edge of the sally port door, then he nodded. 'I do, my lord Roric. The castle is yours.'

CHAPTER FOUR

On the far side of Heartsong's gallery, across the lofty expanse of hall below with its tapestry-hung walls and wrought-iron candle wheels, Duke Harald's minstrels played their merry music so Clemen's lords and ladies might dance. Not dusty, out-of-tune travelling minstrels these, but clean, swift-fingered men paid to travel with the court and give the duke music whenever he wanted. Ellyn tugged her cloak aside so Liam could see and hear them, and smiled at his alertness.

'See, lamb?' she whispered, creeping closer to the wide oak railing. Not close enough for notice, though. Like Emun, she didn't look for trouble. 'That music, it's for you. And those rousty men with their tabors and little fiddles and pipes, they belong to you too. Or they will do, one day. Or if they don't, their sons will. Just like Clemen will be yours, when you're a man and your father is – is—'

She couldn't bring herself to say it, never mind Liam was too young for understanding. Looking down over the gallery's half-wall, where Clemen's northern lords and ladies caroused, she feasted her eyes on Duke Harald.

Tall and bold, he was, as Liam would be in his turn. The enormous beeswax candles and the golden firelight spilling from the wide hearth burnished his chestnut hair and his bronze silk tunic as he stood with two favoured noblemen, the lords Gaspar and Scarwid, clapping his hands and stamping his feet to the lively music. At nine-and-thirty years old, Duke Harald was past his prime, some would say. But those who said so, they didn't know him. They'd not seen the duke astride his coal-black destrier, with his favourite falcon hooded and fierce on his upraised wrist. They'd not heard him laugh or seen him dance or cross great-swords in the tilt yard with his bastard cousin, the lord Roric.

No one who'd seen any of that would dare call Harald *old*.

The duke's lady Argante was dancing, beautiful in her glittering headdress and pearl-sewn blue velvet gown, but she wasn't partnered with him. Not with the lord Roric, either, or poor Lord Vidar who did still dance a little, despite his troubles. They were gone from Heartsong, about great doings for the duke. Just now Harald's lady was dancing with Lord Ercole, her unwed half-brother. He was as plain as she was fair, which might well be why they danced. So she'd show to best advantage. It couldn't be for the joy of it, since there was no deep love between Lord Ercole and his half-sister. She'd heard Duke Harald's lady cursing him to her favourite damsel, Helsine. But that was because she'd caught the lord Ercole with his hand up

Helsine's skirt, fingers busy where they had no right to be and Helsine not protesting. Argante slapped Helsine's cheek as scarlet as Liam's blanket and raged until the girl's eyes near washed out of her silly head from weeping.

Not that the lady Argante cared so much what her half-brother did, or even Helsine. No, the tantrum at Helsine was because, like her brother, Duke Harald's fingers dabbled where the lady Argante thought they shouldn't and she couldn't shout at him or slap his handsome face scarlet.

'As if she had a right to,' Ellyn told Liam, safe in her arms. 'A duke does as he pleases. So hard as he labours for Clemen, what's a kiss and a fumble? All the fine jewels your father gives her, and the dresses, and the feasts, how can she grudge him? She flirts. I've seen her.'

And she'd seen the duke do more than flirt in shadowed corners and on many spiralling castle stairs, with fine ladies who sometimes sighed, sometimes sobbed. She hated them sharp as a knife, being touched like that, by him, so handsome with his curling chestnut hair and broad shoulders. It stirred her own hunger, that she'd fed just the once and a dead bastard to show for it. She dreamed of Duke Harald's fingers, sometimes, and woke wet and aching.

Her breathing half-hitched, Ellyn held Harald's son tight and trembled her longing.

Far below, in the Great Hall, the duke broke from his noblemen's company, snatched an armful of delighted lady and leapt into the dance. The falcon stitched into his bronze tunic dazzled its gold wings in the candlelight, talons out-thrust, sharply curved beak gaped wide. The other lords and their ladies, bound to obey the duke, joined in the dancing after him. Rubies flashed fire. Gold shone like the sun, and silver like sun-struck fresh snow. The nobles of Clemen at their play, no tears for them. No sorrows. Everything at their fingertips and nothing to regret.

Unseen above them, Ellyn danced with Liam in the minstrels' gallery, making him laugh. It was as close to joy as she would ever come, and she knew it. Too soon her wee man would be weaned off her. The lady Morda would take him and she'd be banished to the milch cows for her own milk to dry up.

'Liam, Liam,' she whispered, and wept as they danced. Then she had to stop dancing because, like an arrow from a blue sky, hunger struck hard in her belly. It took a lot of meat and bread to make all the milk Liam could drink. The duke knew that, so she had his leave to seek out the kitchen whenever she needed.

Down in the Great Hall, Duke Harald laughed. Wrapping Liam close again in his soft, scarlet blanket and her coarse cloak, feeling herself wrapped close in Duke Harald's carefree happiness, Ellyn left the music behind and went in search of hot, plentiful food.

As the iron-studded sally port's door groaned shut behind the last of his borrowed men-at-arms, Roric looked around the crowded guards' chamber at the grim faces of the lords who'd risked everything to follow him. In a few hours' time, either the sun would rise upon their victory or else on their hacked corpses. His guts tightened. If only this could be done without risking anyone else. If only it were as easy as killing his cousin. That would be no challenge. Harald trusted him. A simple matter, then, to slit his throat in the dark.

Simple . . . and dishonourable. The duchy deserved better, and so did Harald's infant son.

Silently, Humbert and Vidar and the other lords and their men-at-arms shed their cumbersome cloaks. Guttering torchlight played upon the blades of their swords, unsheathed for the stealthy crossing from copse to castle. Mouth dry, Roric fumbled one-handed at his own cloak pin.

'You barred the door, Serjeant?' he said, letting his cloak fall to the stone floor as Belden joined them.

'Yes, my lord.'

'Then find your trusted men outside the hall and tell them to be canny. Spread word to the rest after, quickly and quietly. Order them not to interfere. We've no wish to wade through blood spilled for misplaced loyalty.'

'But we will spill it,' Vidar added, 'if any man is fool enough to show us naked steel.'

Belden frowned, his eyes glassy with unease. Roric flicked Vidar a warning glance, then touched the man's arm. 'You've trained them to heed you, man?'

'Yes, my lord. Of course. But—'

'Good. Trust to that. And if any choose not to heed you what happens is their doing and no shame on you. They're not slaves, with their free will taken from them.'

'My lord,' said Belden, his voice strangled.

Hearing the fear, the doubt, Roric took the serjeant's shoulder in a firm grasp. 'What we do here is right, Belden. But right is rarely easy.'

Belden dragged a hand down his face, rasping stubble. 'It surely isn't, my lord.'

'Don't despair, my friend,' he said gently. 'When this is over Clemen will know you for its truest son. Now stand aside. Some of these lords and their men will go with you to secure Heartsong, but I'd have words with them first.'

'My lord,' said the serjeant, and withdrew to the mouth of the corridor leading into the castle proper.

When Belden was out of earshot, Roric shifted his gaze past Humbert and Vidar to Aistan, oldest and most experienced of the remaining lords. Next to Humbert, he'd worked hardest to bring Clemen's great nobles to this undertaking. But then Aistan had suffered more. With his wife and his daughter both debauched by Harald, his sister robbed of the lands owed to her from her dead husband and his own estates reduced to feed Harald's insatiable greed, he had every reason to want Clemen's rapacious duke thrown down.

'Be swift, Aistan, and stealthy,' he said. 'I prefer Harald completely surprised.'

Aistan nodded, content to be led by a younger, less experienced man because of his blood-tie to Berold. Roric felt his heart thud. If he let himself dwell on that, the burden might break him.

'I've no doubt the bastard will be surprised,' Aistan said gravely, amusing his brother nobles and their men-at-arms. 'Never fear, Roric. We'll clear the weeds from your path.'

'You heard what I told Belden,' he added. 'Honour it, as far as you're able. Temper just cause with mercy. There is one enemy here and his name is Harald.'

'Agreed,' said Aistan, as the other lords nodded. His lips curved in a small, grim smile. 'But when you face the real enemy . . .'

'Never fear, Aistan. My mercy is saved for those who deserve it.'

'Well said,' Humbert muttered, standing back to let Aistan and the others lead their purposeful men-at-arms out of the guards' chamber.

'And since we speak of Harald,' said Vidar, 'I'm wondering. Do we now bait the cornered bear? Or should we tarry some time longer, chatting?'

Ah, Vidar. But even as he opened his mouth to make a tart reply, Roric hesitated. 'Lord Aistan, hold,' he said, then slapped the stone wall to attract Belden's attention. 'Serjeant, to me.'

'Roric?' Humbert was frowning 'What's the—'

A touch to Humbert's arm hushed him. A moment later, Belden rejoined them. 'Serjeant, on any other night how many men would you set to prowling the castle grounds?'

'Three or four, my lord,' said the serjeant, puzzled. 'Depending.'

'Then find your four men closest to the hall and send them outside by any door but the sally port. You'll save them from harm and make our task the simpler. When that's done, and your other guards are subdued, leave the lords to their business and come back to me here.'

Relief and gratitude warmed Belden's sharp eyes. 'My lord.'

'That's a good thought, Roric,' said Vidar, as the guards' chamber began to empty. 'But I do question the wisdom of skulking here while Aistan and the others bring Heartsong to heel.'

'You're the one who called Harald a cornered bear,' Roric said, stifling anger. 'Would you face a bear without first sending in all the dogs?'

'*Enough*,' Humbert said, before Vidar could say more. 'Roric's made his choice. Now we wait.'

'And I suggest we wait at the other end of the corridor,' said Roric, gesturing with his sword. Shadows flickered along its gleaming, lethal length. 'After you, my lord Humbert. And you, Vidar.'

'More pottage, Ellyn?' said Nelda, keeping her voice hushed so the cook, her mother's crotchety sister and her only living kin, wouldn't rouse in her fireside chair and start beating anyone she could reach with a wooden spoon. 'Go on. There be plenty.'

The small night kitchen was drowsy warm with its flame-crowded hearth, and whispered full of music from the Great Hall above. Its long, wide bench was laden with dainty morsels waiting a summons from the duke. Leek and cheese tartlets, minced pork tartlets, tiny napwing eggs in aspic, pewter cups of frumenty and sturdy wheels of cheese. Fine food for fine nobles, floated down their elegant throats on the best wines in Clemen.

Squeezed at the bench's far end, Ellyn swallowed the last scraping of bean mush from her bowl and slumped a little on her stool. She envied the sleeping cook. Naughty Liam, keeping her awake so late and so long.

'More ale, I'd like,' she said, smothering a yawn. 'But I'm bellyful else, Nelda, and I thank you.'

'It be hard work, feeding a babe,' said Nelda, her shy smile come-and-gone. 'I'll fetch your ale.'

Hard work it surely was, feeding and holding. Ellyn wriggled a bit, trying to ease the ache in her arm from keeping Liam pressed close. She longed to lay him beside Nelda's bastard brat on its straw-stuffed pallet, just for a moment, but she couldn't. The cook might be snoring fit to rival Lady Morda but not even that old besom would snore through Liam, screaming. And scream he would, for certain, if his Ellyn set him down on the floor.

'Here,' said Nelda, pouring more ale. For all she was young and skinny, she hefted the pitcher as though it weighed light as air. 'Drink up.' With the tankard full again she stepped back, and sighed at sleeping Liam. 'Ah, he's a fine boy, Ellyn. It's strong milk you've got, him growing so fast.'

She swallowed half her fresh ale before answering. 'True, he's a bonny lamb. And yours, Nelda? Tygo? He seems fine, too.'

'Ais,' said Nelda, nodding. 'No sign of sickly on him, at least not so far. Not as brave as little Liam, though, for all he's a moon older.'

Ellyn hid her face in her tankard. And why would a kitchen drudge's brat be any like to her lamb, Tygo being planted in Nelda by a passing trinket-man, not a duke? But it seemed unkind to say as much, especially after that tasty pottage, so she drank more ale instead.

'If he stays small, he'll find work here on the turnspit, like little

Thom and his kind,' said Nelda, with a frowning glance at the three kitchen boys gnawing heels of bread along the wall beside the fireplace. 'My mam's told me I dursn't hope for more.'

With a ripe burp, Ellyn pushed the emptied tankard to one side. 'He'll be warm in winter, any road.'

'Ais, and soused in sweat othertimes,' said Nelda, sighing. Then she ruffled herself, like a hen. 'But tie my tongue for griping. There be fathers what drown their daughters' bastard brats, and mams as tell them to do it. Tygo's living and he's with me. I've no cause to gobble.' Stepping briskly, she returned the ale pitcher to its slab-sided stone jar in the corner furthest from the flame-warmed hearth. 'Not to you, leastways. You lost your own, I'm told. That's a sad thing and I'm sorry for it.'

Fussing with Liam's scarlet blanket, Ellyn made a grunting sound that could've meant anything. Let Nelda decide, it was easier.

'I'd ask you, Ellyn, if I could,' Nelda started, but then a coming-closer pattering of footsteps in the corridor beyond the night kitchen turned her. A moment later one of Heartsong's pages scuttled in, puffed up in his green velvet tunic and fine wool hose, a little Clemen lordling.

'An' it please His Grace the Duke,' the page piped, 'but he's wanting supper served.'

Because she had to, because this was a favoured lord's son and she was common as muck, Nelda spread her apron and bobbed a curtsy. 'An' it please His Grace the Duke,' she answered, 'fetch the other pages, sir, for you see the duke's supper is here ready and waiting.'

'I see it,' said the page, his eyes wide with greed. 'I shall return in a moment.'

'There now, Ellyn, you'd best go,' said Nelda, as the page scuttled out. 'For in a tricket I'll have him and his friends underfoot like mice. Aunt Cook, Aunt Cook—' An urgent hand shook the heedless woman's shoulder. 'Supper for the duke, Aunt Cook.' She turned to the kitchen brats. 'Come on, you little toads! On your feet!'

Wrapped once more in her coarse woollen cloak, Ellyn left the old woman snorting awake, the kitchen brats cramming the last of their bread and Nelda pushing her bastard brat to safety beneath the long kitchen bench, and made her own way with Liam back to their eyrie. One pause on the minstrels' gallery, to snatch a last glimpse of Duke Harald. For all his smiles he looked weary, packed about with pushing lords and ladies. After him for favours, always, they were. No matter what the duke gave them it was never enough. Never enough for the lady Argante, either. Greedy bitch. All the fine things he'd given her, and not once did she open her mouth to the duke if it wasn't to ask for more. She was in his lap down there, wriggling. What a cock-tease. The poor duke. He couldn't see her for what she was. Sick in love with his son, he was babe-blind. Why were men so stupid?

Holding Liam close, feeling the ache in her breasts that told her she was too full of milk, she hurried up the spiral staircase then along the stone corridor that led to the nursery. The man-at-arms, Emun, he was in his rightful place again. He saw her and rolled his eyes, finger pressed to his lips.

Slowing, she felt her heart thump. *Morda?* she mouthed, and he nodded. Sighing, she smiled her thanks. He smiled back, not such a bad man, Emun, even if he was rough. He'd not had to warn her. Could be he'd like a kiss sometime. He'd earned it. Sucking in a deep breath, she stepped into the nursery.

'*Slut!*' shouted Lady Morda, leaping forward with bony arms outstretched. 'Give the babe to me, you drabbish lightskirt!'

Even as Liam woke, Ellyn clutched him tighter and half-turned away. 'Please, my lady, you'll—'

Liam opened his gummy mouth and howled. It was his angry cry, his hungry cry, and her aching breasts spurted milk at the sound. Lady Morda stepped back. She knew that cry too. And she knew that whatever the duke's son wanted, that came first. Always.

The old cow pointed at the nursing chair. 'Sit,' she hissed. 'Feed him. I go downstairs to the duke. He will be told what you've done. Expect a whipping, at the least.'

Ellyn sat, unlaced her tunic, bared her breast and set Liam to suckling. Outside, in the corridor, Lady Morda was berating Emun. She'd see him whipped too, and perhaps a hand taken for good measure. Or an eye put out, his cock sliced off. He'd be sorry he let the sluttish wet nurse past him. Hating her, Ellyn stroked Liam's downy head. She'd speak up for Emun, she would. Tell the duke she'd waited till the man-at-arms had needed a piss, then slipped out of the nursery. She'd say she'd not meant to cause trouble, Liam was fussy, wanting a walk, and she was hungry. No harm was done. Duke Harald would listen. He gave her many kindly looks – and he had little care for Lady Morda. The old bitch wouldn't have the pleasure of maiming poor Emun.

Liam made happy little gurgling sounds when he sucked. Charmed by them, adoring him, Ellyn closed her eyes. Her lamb, her precious lamb. She'd keep him safe from Lady Morda, and every other harm.

Trapped in his chair, near-deafened by that old bitch Morda's shrieking rage, Harald felt his fingers itch for a sword. A cursed pity the court's niceties demanded a lack of naked blades and bloodshed. He couldn't even summon the serjeant to kill her for him, since Morda was cousined in some distant degree to Argante and so was thrust out of his reach. To his lords' and ladies' tittering amusement, and threatening to drown out his minstrels, the old sow was demanding the hide of Liam's wet nurse.

'But my lady,' he said, when the hag paused to draw breath, 'would you have me a tyrant? How can I chastise without cause?'

Morda's pebble-grey eyes bulged. 'Without *cause*?'

'Morda . . .' Standing beside him, slender fingers lightly rested on his arm, Argante favoured her kinswoman with a cool smile. 'His Grace is right. In your dismay you've not told us what the girl has done to earn this demanded whipping.'

'She took your son from his cradle!' Morda spat, her miserly dugs heaving beneath the green brocade bodice covering them. 'She wandered with him about the castle like a drab, heedless of the hour and chill, and if she did not show her privy parts to every man-at-arms in passing I am not a true servant to His Grace and that babe!'

More tittering. The court's pages, holding silver trays of cooling food, stared at the bitch and each other. Two smothered giggles. Harald felt his teeth grind. Morda was making a fool of him.

'You saw her drabbish? With your own eyes, this very night?'

'Saw her?' The high colour in Morda's sallow cheeks faded. 'No, I did not see her, not this time. Your Grace,' she added, warned by his glare. 'But I tell you truly, the wench is a—'

'Silence!' he said, thumping his fist to the arm of his chair. Of course the wet nurse was a slut, delivered of a bastard planted in her by some cowherd. But her milk was rich. Liam drank from her till he was bursting, and thrived. And she was a prime piece of flesh, young and eager to open her legs. He'd caught her looking at him more than once. Had Morda not haunted the nursery he'd have had the little wagtail pinned against a wall long since.

The bitch knows. She's jealous. If there's been even one man eager to thrust his cock between her skinny thighs I'll eat my best destrier. Raw.

'My lady Morda, your care for my son cannot be faulted,' he said sternly. The court must not think him chastened. 'But I fear you wrong his wet nurse. She dotes on the child, as all of Clemen dotes. If she walked him about the castle, then she did so with my leave. You well know Liam can be fretful of a night. Walking settles him.' Without looking at Argante, he eased his arm from beneath her fingers and closed his hand about hers. 'Is that not so, my dove?'

'Indeed, my lord,' she replied. 'But perhaps—'

Still smiling, he tightened his hold. 'There, lady Morda. You hear my son's mother. And now we are done. Return to the nursery and think no more of my son's wet nurse.'

No curtsy from Morda, only a stiff-necked nod. 'Your Grace.'

He would accept the implied insult, this last time. And in the morning he'd dismiss her. Let Argante pout. Did he not pour food, wine and coin into the open cesspit that was Ercole? For a half-brother, he'd do it. But not for the dried-up old bitch withdrawing in offended silence from his presence. The pages were still snickering, even as they continued serving their betters. Who did they belong to? Ah, yes. Meriet and Udo. He must devise a particular punishment, then. Sending to his court sons with no more breeding than a mucked hog.

Argante was yet to move, her hand still prisoned within his fingers. She knew better than to pull free, with so many eyes upon them. 'Harald . . .'

She might sound pleading, she might have gasped a little when his hand took hers, but in truth she didn't fear him. The first two women he'd made his duchess had feared him. He could break them

69

with a look. Water in their veins, not blood. Argante was full of blood. Full of temper and life. The kind of woman to breed strong sons.

'Harald,' she said, 'shall we enjoy another dance?'

He was weary. His chest hurt. But she was right, they should dance again. They should show the court that Clemen's duke and his duchess were as one in all things. There were no Harcian merchants here to send tales home to Duke Aimery and his ill-mannered heir, but Clemen tongues wagged too. And not even he could cut them all out.

He stood. 'A slow measure, yes. So I might savour your beauty.'

'And I your strength,' Argante replied, her smile brilliant. No other man in the room would know, as he knew, that behind the smile were surrender . . . and forged steel. She knew she'd lost Morda. And he knew she'd find a way to make him pay for that loss. It was the dance between them that did not end.

At his signal, the minstrels in their gallery shifted to playing a *chibinay*. And because he and Argante were dancing, everyone danced, and the pages were left to stand adrift and watch and not touch the uneaten morsels of food they held, on pain of losing their fingers.

Without warning, the music stopped.

As the patterns of the *chibinay* fell apart, Harald released Argante and stepped back. Tipping his face to the minstrels' gallery, he glared.

'I gave no command for you to cease your playing! Begin again or forfeit your coins! Forfeit your supper also, and the comfort you find beneath my roof!'

Still no music. A stifled gasp turned his head to the confusion of lords and ladies milling in the hall. Then a clatter, as one of the pages dropped his silver tray to the flagstones. Eggs in aspic burst wetly, scenting the air with expensive spices.

'Foolish, wasteful boy!' Argante snapped. 'Think you too highly bred for whipping? I'll choose the birch myself and—'

'Whip a child for a moment of fright?' someone demanded. 'For shame, Argante. Will you whip your son the same?'

The tangle of lords and ladies parted, hushed and staring.

'Roric?' Frowning, Harald watched his cousin's slow, steady approach. He was flanked by Humbert and crippled Vidar, some half-pace behind. In the stunned silence, Vidar's halting footsteps sounded loud. All three of them wore mail, held naked swords, looked warlike. 'Roric, what means this? Is it the Marches? Or does unprovoked Harcia bare its rotten teeth?'

Roric's unfashionably close-clipped dark hair was dirty. Smears of dried mud marred the high cheekbones gifted him by Guimar, and his deep-set brown eyes, the eyes every man could see in a painting of their grandsire, Duke Berold, were clear and cold. Unfriendly. He halted, mail coat chinking, the unsheathed sword a threat in his hand.

'No, Your Grace,' he said softly. 'Harcia doesn't threaten us, though we both know their duke is often sore provoked.'

Even as he felt a prickle of warning across the back of his neck, Harald lifted his chin. 'Cousin, you talk in riddles. Speak plainly. Is there trouble, or not?'

'Yes, Harald. There's trouble,' said Roric, his face so grim. 'And we've come to discuss it. No – no, don't bother to call the serjeant. Belden knows his duty and has done it. Your rule of Clemen is ended.'

Disbelief, then a surge of crushing pain. Half-blinded, Harald fought to hide it as Argante stepped forward.

'*Ended?*' she echoed, her beauty twisted into rage. 'It is not *ended*, you bastard, nor will it ever be. Harald was born your duke and will die so. This is treason! And before the sun rises Harald will see every one of you dead!'

'– have softened His Grace, girl, but be warned! My cousin Argante knows you for what you are, and *I* know you! We'll be rid of you soon enough!'

Ellyn waited for Lady Morda's closet door to bang shut behind her, then pulled a hideous face. 'Miserable old cow,' she muttered. 'His Grace will cast you out before he sends me away.'

In her arms, Liam heaved a huge sigh. Ellyn glanced down at him and breathed out her own sigh. Praise the spirits, he was sleeping at last. With all that milk in his belly, with luck he'd sleep until daylight so she could drowse a while herself. Stealthily she eased out of the nursing chair, then settled Liam in his cradle. He didn't stir, not even when she tucked his scarlet blanket around him. Looking into his innocent face she felt a love so fierce it was like a pain.

As she did every night when it was only the two of them, no

71

Morda to carp, she dropped to a crouch and whispered her way, one by one, around the charms strung onto her precious lamb's cradle.

'For health . . . for happiness . . . for keen eyes . . . for strong heart . . . for strength in battle . . . for wisdom . . . for love . . .'

With each whisper she kissed her fingertip and touched it to a gold disc, calling on its purpose and power for Liam. Trusting more to the old, half-forsaken ways than ever she would to what the Exarch's prosing priests said. It was Harald who put the charms on the cradle. Just one more reason to love the duke.

Last of all she touched the heavy gold ring, set with rarest tiger-eye from Agribia. Not a proper charm, not really. But it was the great Duke Berold's ring, his name written on the inside of the band. So that was a charm too, in its way.

When she was done, the spirits reminded of their duty to Liam, she fetched the nursery pot and pissed out the ale she'd drunk, grateful she didn't have to freeze her arse in the wintercold garderobe, like Emun. Then she curled up on her straw pallet, and closed her eyes to sleep.

Roric had to admire Argante's fluent fury. A torrent of abuse and she'd hardly paused to draw breath. Where had she learned such inventive curses? From Harald? Certainly he didn't seem surprised to hear the foul words tumbling from his youthful wife's tongue. Nor did he seem inclined to speak for himself. To the casual eye he was relaxed as he stood before them. A man who didn't know better might think him amused.

'Roric.'

And that was Humbert, his prompting spat from the corner of his mouth. He was right, of course. Argante's spittled tirade had lasted long enough.

'Have conduct, cousin! You sound like a bawd. Clemen's court is owed meeker manners than that.'

Stumbled to silence, Argante stared. 'I am not your cousin, I am the Duchess of Clemen,' she snarled, recovering. 'And I won't be schooled in manners by a snivelling, treacherous *bastard*.'

'No?' Roric shrugged. 'Then find someone acceptable to teach you, Argante, for you're as much a disgrace as your husband.'

She leapt at him. Fending off her clawed fingers with one raised arm, he captured her wrist and swung her about.

'Control your wife, Harald. She's spoiled and unlovely, but I'd not have her hurt.'

'Argante.' Harald held out his hand. 'To me.'

Writhing against restraint, Argante hissed like a cat. 'Harald! Why do you stand there like a bodkin? Summon the serjeant! I want this bastard knave chopped head from neck from knees! He dares *touch* me, he—'

'*Argante.*'

A flinch ran through her slight, velvet-clad body, then she stilled. Roric opened his fingers and watched her rejoin her husband, slowly, a falcon shamed to have lost its kill. He could feel Humbert and Vidar on either side of him, taut with purpose now that Argante was subdued. Around them, the heart-stopped court was a blur of shocked faces. Some stared at him, some at Harald, and the rest up at the minstrels' gallery where a double-handful of his borrowed men-at-arms stood to advantage, their drawn swords on show.

'So,' said Harald, stirring. 'Cousin Roric.' The hall's warm light revealed a sheen of sweat, broke sudden upon his forehead. Buried deep within his steady voice, a tremor. But was it fear or rage? There was no way to tell. 'I should've expected this. A wise man knows that sooner or later a cur dog will bite the feeding hand. But love closed my eyes. And now here you are, betraying what little noble blood you possess that's not tainted rotten by the whore who whelped you.'

Humbert muttered a curse. 'Roric, don't—'

'Peace, my lord,' he said mildly, though his heart pounded. 'My mother is dead a score of years. Harald's slighting words can't hurt her. Or me.'

Harald laughed. 'No? Roric, I have more ways to hurt you than there are spines on a hedgehog and I'll enjoy showing you each and every one.'

'Be quiet, Harald,' said Vidar, stepping forward. 'We're not here for a taunting, but to—'

'To disrupt the gaiety of my court!' Harald said, his voice sharply risen. 'And I promise you, I am *mightily* displeased!'

73

'Ho, are you?' Humbert retorted, scowling. 'Well, so are *we* displeased, Harald, with far more grievous cause than you. Now, marry your teeth together a time and hear what's to be done with Berold's duchy, that you held in trust and have treated worse than a poxed drab.'

Still holding Argante's slender hand, drawing her with him, Harald retreated to an ornate chair placed nearby upon a dais. With Argante haughty beside him, her fingers fiercely clasping his, he sat.

'Humbert . . .' A sorrow-filled sigh. 'What faithless Roric has promised you for this, I can't think. Nor you, Vidar. *Vidar*. So you lost your honour with your eye, did you? How sad. And now, like your unlovely sire, Godebert, you'll burn beneath a blue sky.' His gaze swept around the silent hall. 'Along with Humbert and Roric and every man standing with you. How your families will weep before I turn them out of their fine homes in rags, to wander friendless until they die starved to skin and bone in a rank, shit-filled ditch.'

'You would say so,' said Vidar. No sly humour in him now, only freezing disdain. 'And you'd do it, given the chance. If any part of you wonders what's brought us here, Harald, know *that* is why. Humbert's poxed drab would rule Clemen better than you.'

Releasing Argante, Harald stood. 'I am not *Harald* to dross, Vidar. Son of a dead traitor and now traitor in his own right. I am *Your Grace*. I am your *duke*.'

'You were, Harald,' said Humbert, his voice heavy with impatient regret. 'But no more. As your chief councillor, I—'

'You were!' Harald shouted. 'But no more. Your authority in this duchy is forfeit, *my lord*. Scarwid, step forth!'

'Scarwid?' Argante stared at her husband. 'You'd raise *Scarwid* to head of the council? A nothing lord from the north? Why? Scarwid's no more than a nodding arse in a chair. This honour belongs to Ercole.'

Harald's eyes were dangerous. 'Ercole?'

'Yes. You said you'd see my family gilded. You said you'd—'

He slapped her. 'Shut your mouth! You do not chew my private words before the court!'

'*Enough*, Harald!' Roric said, watching the white handprint on Argante's cheek swiftly blush red. 'Your bullying days are done with. Accept your fate, and set aside the ducal crown.'

'Or what?' Harald spat. 'You'll set it aside for me, still clasping my severed head?' Turning, he spread his arms wide in appeal to his silently watching court. 'My lords! Will you bear this? Will you not speak against such naked treachery? If *I* am so assaulted, who among you is safe? Scarwid! I have named you my chief councillor, have I not? Then come, my lord. Step forward, and be heard in defence of your duke!'

CHAPTER FIVE

S carwid, unmoving, cleared his throat. 'Alas, Your Grace, I must defer to Lord Humbert. He is head of Clemen's council.'

Clemen's council. Not Harald's. Roric felt his blood leap. The lines of loyalty were drawn, and not in his cousin's favour. Humbert had promised he'd deliver them, the lords of Clemen who'd not joined in this storming of Heartsong. Humbert with his rough charm and wide respect, the authority bred in him that had no need of threats or violence.

As the blurred hall resolved itself, as he considered Harald's other noble guests – Udo, Gaspar, Gerbod, Sagard and Vasey the most prominent – he saw in their faces the same resolution that hardened Scarwid. Only Ercole looked uncertain, and Ercole was of no account. Seated on the council to keep Argante quiet, he'd long since exhausted what meagre good will he owed to the blood he shared with his half-sister.

Harald saw it too, his lords' refusal to aid him as he might expect. Demand. A heartbeat's hesitation, then he sat again in his fine chair. Smiled, magnanimous.

'My lord Humbert, you've taken me unawares. You of all men know the proper way of things. We are far from Eaglerock, where it's custom for us to speak of weighty matters. 'Tis not meet that—'

'Yes, it is, Harald,' said Roric, swiftly. 'How many times have you told us that where you are, there is the rightful authority of Clemen? You *are* the court, and the law. Isn't that what you say?'

Harald's jaw tightened. Roric met him stare for stare, feeling his own muscles tense. Beneath the fury in his cousin's eyes there was hurt. But wasn't that to be expected? Harald had been generous in the past. Denied him the hope of marriage and children, yes, but made up for the loss with lavish gifts and favours.

Still. No gift, however grand, could excuse his crimes.

Seeing him resolute, Harald shifted his stare. Wiped him from his heart as a wave upon wet sand wiped away a seagull's tiny claw marks.

It shouldn't have stung . . . but it did.

'Lord Humbert,' said Harald, a sounding bell of rediscovered reason. 'You've served me twelve years, with your blood and your honour. In return I've shown you much favour. Yet now you come to me packed to the gills full of grievances?'

'Sore grievances, aye,' said Humbert, his eyes slitted. 'But they're not mine alone. The quarrels I have with you are shared.' He jerked his bearded chin. 'By them.'

Shifting, Harald lifted his gaze to the minstrels' gallery where Aistan, Hankin, Morholt and Farland had silently gathered and now stared down, their faces stony cold, their hands ominously resting on the hilts of their half-unsheathed swords. Four of Clemen's greatest lords, and only Hankin not been seen frequently at Eaglerock's court. Aistan and Farland had seats on the council. Harald's face, blotched with emotion, drained pale.

'You see?' Vidar's voice rang with contempt. 'This is a mighty chorus, Harald. Not a thin, forlorn piping.'

'A chorus that sounds throughout the duchy,' Humbert added. 'You'll find unhappy lords not only here, in your pretty castle, but throughout the length and breadth of Clemen.'

Instead of answering, Harald looked once more to Aistan and the other nobles. 'You perch high, my lords, like brooding carrion birds. Come down. Face me. Or do I ask too much?'

'Always, Harald,' Aistan retorted, his voice raised and carrying. 'But I'll face you. And whatever I say, you can trust I speak for us all.'

'Trust?' Harald's face spasmed. 'A turdish word, on your lips.' He snapped his fingers. 'Very well. Join us.'

As Aistan stepped back from the gallery's half-wall, Argante took hold of her husband's arm. 'Harald—'

'No,' he said, and seared her to silence with a look.

Aistan's tread on the stone stairs leading down to the hall sounded loud in the smothering hush. Waiting, no one spoke. It seemed they hardly breathed. One of the pages was weeping, the leg of his green hose stained with piss. And when Aistan finally appeared, tall and broad and dour, the bleakest enmity in his eyes, Roric heard more than one gasp.

'Aistan,' said Harald, fingers tight upon the arms of his chair, 'I can scarce believe your dagger's buried in my back.'

'No?' Aistan laughed. His sword was returned to its scabbard, but anyone who knew him knew how swiftly that could change. 'But why would you believe it, when you could believe a man would stand by and do nothing to avenge his ruined family. Truly, you're surprised?' He swept a gesturing arm up to the gallery, then around the hall. 'When the great men of Clemen you've not wronged can be counted on the fingers of a blind butcher's hand?'

Harald shook his head, sorrowful. 'Your accusations confound me, Aistan, though I see you think them true. Therefore, though we be leagues distant from Eaglerock, we shall call this a council, summoned in surprise – and do what we can to untangle this unfortunate misunderstanding.'

'Your Grace!' Trembling, Argante glared. She was as pale as her husband, but that came from the powdered chalk fashionably dusted from wide brow to pointed chin. Beneath that pretended pallor, her cheeks burned. 'You let unnatural kindness defeat natural rancour. These rough men are traitors, burst upon us with ill intent. Worse, they've turned the hearts of others against you. You *cannot*—'

'Cannot?' Harald said softly. 'Argante. Was such a word ever spoke in Berold's hearing?'

She was young and arrogant beyond bearing, but no man could accuse her of being snail-witted. Lips pressed tight, Argante folded her hands neatly, like an obedient wife, and lowered her gaze to the tips of her jewelled velvet slippers.

Roric let go his held breath, aware that Humbert and Vidar did the same. Aistan, his support declared, stood like a man carved from Harcian granite. The hall was so quiet the dull clinking of mail could be heard from the minstrels' gallery, where those borrowed men-at-arms kept watch beside their lords.

He took a measured step closer to his deceitfully courteous cousin. 'Harald, there is—'

'Hold your tongue, cur,' said Harald. 'I deny you my name, my blood, and any part of me. To think I treated you like a brother. Well might Humbert take me to task for that. Indeed, it shames me to—'

Enough. Give Harald the chance and he'd warp this encounter to his own benefit, make himself the man wronged and slither free of condemnation.

'Your Grace, you said you'd hear our grievances. Will you hear them, or did you lie?'

'I *said*,' Harald replied, his teeth bared, 'that I would listen to my barons.'

A light touch to his arm. Humbert. Throttling temper, Roric held his tongue. Beside him, Vidar shifted. Doubtless easing his bad hip, but also growing impatient. His grudge against Clemen's duke was even more personal than Aistan's. But though his rage was justified, it could never excuse blatant murder. No matter how cruelly Lord Godebert had died.

Feeling Vidar's temper tighten further, Roric frowned at him. Vidar's nostrils flared, but he let his sword lower until its point touched the tiled floor. Needing to ease the ache in his forearms, knowing the message it would send to Harald, Roric lowered his own sword-point likewise.

A small, triumphant smile curved the corners of Harald's ungenerous mouth. He had silenced his upstart cousin and doubtless believed he'd silence Humbert too, and Aistan, and all the other lords of his duchy. Even now he thought he'd prevail, blinded by the arrogance that had led him to this confrontation. So was Argante blinded, standing straight-spined beside him, her beeswax-dyed lips the colour of old blood.

Looking at them, Roric felt a sting of pity for his cousin's child, asleep in its cradle. Were Harald and Argante dog and bitch, a wise huntsman would never have bred them. What chance did the babe have, with such a bloodline? Poor Liam. Was there a way to save him?

We're kin. I'll have to try.

Smile fading, Harald smoothed a crease in the hem of his gold-embroidered bronze tunic. Candlelight set fire to the hearts of his ruby and emerald rings. Some of his colour was returned. He looked almost robust. Only the lingering sweat, and a pinch-mark between his eyebrows, hinted at anything amiss.

'And so, Humbert, council is in session,' he said. 'Speak now, or never. I am patient in this small time but even the deepest well must run dry.'

Humbert's turn to step forward. His large hand swallowed nearly all of his sword's hilt. He carried the heavy blade easily, a man full of martial memories, tempered like Rebbai steel. Harald would cut himself to ribbons on him, and bleed to death before ever he knew himself hurt.

'Your Grace,' said Humbert, with only the faintest hint of scorn, 'here are the grievances held by the lords and nobles of this duchy, by strength of which we claim the right of redress. First grievance: the gross and burdensome matter of untoward taxation . . .'

'Ellyn? Ellyn, wake up!'

Startled from her dropped-mouth drowse on her straw pallet, Ellyn dragged open her eyelids and blinked. 'Nelda? What do you—'

The kitchen girl's green eyes shone with fear, her arms clutching her bastard brat close. 'Ellyn, can I hide here? Please, say I can.'

'*Hide?*' With a grunt for her aching back, she sat upright. Looked first to Liam, sleeping mousey in his cradle, then to Lady Morda's closet – but its door remained slammed shut. 'Nelda, you can't be in here with your – with Tygo! He could start wailing any moment, and if you wake Morda she'll skin us both.' She stared past Nelda to the nursery door, left ajar. 'How did you get by Emun? He knows better than—'

'He be stretching his legs along the corridor,' said Nelda, unrepentant. 'I waited for his back to turn. Ellyn, there be trouble. Men-at-arms in the castle.'

Spirits save them, was the girl ale-giddy? 'Of course there are—'

'Not ours!' Nelda hissed. 'These be strangers, and lords I've never seen before. Ellyn, they be roaming the castle with bare swords. They came into the kitchen and set Aunt Cook in a tizzy! I couldn't help her. Tygo and me only just scribbled by them unseen.'

No . . . Nelda wasn't ale-giddy. She was a henwit. Ellyn scrambled to her feet. 'Then what are you doing here? Find the serjeant, tell him—'

'The serjeant be helping them!' Nelda sucked in a shuddering breath. 'He be telling Heartsong's men to keep their swords by their sides – and they are.'

She swallowed a surge of panic. *Liam.* 'I don't believe you. Not a word. You must've dreamed it.'

'Dreamed it when? As if I've slept since last dawn, working my fingers to blisters cooking for the duke!'

'But – Heartsong's serjeant? He wouldn't—'

'Ellyn, I *heard* him!' Nelda insisted. She was shivering with her fright. 'The castle's lost, I tell you!'

The banging open of the lady Morda's closet door spun them both about.

'Slut!' Muffled in a night-cloak, her grey-streaked hair bundled into a linen coif, the lady Morda stood furious in her narrow doorway. 'Is there no end to your wickedness?'

'My – my lady—' Ellyn replied, breathless. Stammering, because she did believe Nelda, even if the girl was a henwit. The kitchen drudge's terror was too real for fakery. Besides, why would she risk terrible punishment with a lie? 'Lady Morda, something's awry. Strange men-at-arms in—'

'What I see *awry*, girl, is—'

An iron jangling of mail, and Emun was in the nursery. 'What's the rout here?'

'The rout?' Hand raised to strike, Morda stormed at him. 'You worthless piece of dung! How did you let—'

'Emun! Emun, listen!' On a sobbing breath Ellyn leapt ahead of Morda. Knocking the woman sideways, ignoring her astonished gasp, she took hold of his arm. 'There's danger. We've got rough men in Heartsong.'

Suspicious, Emun stared. 'What men? I've not seen—'

'I have,' said Nelda, daring. She sounded close to tears. 'I—'

'This is nonsense,' said Lady Morda, her voice hoarse with temper. 'Bar these sluts in a cellar. That snot-nosed bastard, too. I want them—'

'*Emun!*' Ellyn shook him, making his mail rattle a promise of safety. 'Go and see. If I'm wrong I'll let them whip me. I'll let *her*—' she glanced at Morda '—do every terrible thing to me.'

'And me!' Nelda added. 'But it be true. With my own eyes, I saw those men.'

'Saw the bottom of an ale barrel more like!' the lady Morda retorted. 'As if any man in Clemen would endanger the duke!'

Emun opened his mouth then closed it again, uncertain. 'Ellyn—'

Oh, he was a *cock*. 'Please, Emun!' she nearly broke her hand slapping his mail-covered chest. 'What harm can come from looking?'

'Plenty,' said Lady Morda, grimly. 'For you and your sluttish friend.'

She only just kept herself from breaking a hand on the old cow. 'Good then! You go with him, my lady, and prove us wrong. Then you'll have your excuse to see me stripped and beaten, won't you?'

'My lady—' Emun stepped back. 'You should stay. Won't take me a moment to look about.'

'And leave you to lie for this slut?' Lady Morda demanded, uglier than ever in her hate. 'Make up some tarradiddle to soften the blow?'

Emun's beard-stubbled face coloured. 'My lady—'

'As if I'd not seen you sniffing after her. As if I didn't know you'd pin her against a wall were I not watching so close. You'll prove her a liar with me by your side. Out of here, churl. *Out!*'

He was a man-at-arms, and she was kin to Harald's wife, in charge of the nursery that held Harald's son.

'Go, Emun,' Ellyn said, struggling to smile. 'And have a care.'

He didn't want to leave them, but Morda gave him no choice. He bowed to the old cow, stiffly. 'My lady.'

Morda stabbed a finger at her. 'You stay here, Ellyn, you and this drab. Keep her and her bastard far from Harald's son. And never doubt the duke will be told of your wicked mischief.'

'Oh, *Ellyn*,' Nelda wailed, as the nursery door closed behind Emun and the old cow. 'I'm feared!'

'Yes, but hush,' she said, turning away. She and Nelda were of an age, but she felt years older. 'Or you'll wake Liam and then you'll know true strife.'

Ignoring Nelda's frightened snuffling, leaving her to cosset her bastard brat, she bent over the cradle. Bless the spirits, her precious lamb slept on despite the upset. Daring a fingertip to his soft cheek, she made herself breathe slowly until her heart left off its banging on her ribs.

'Ellyn . . .' Nelda whispered now. 'What do we do?'

'Do?' She stood straight and turned. 'Nelda, you heard what I—'

And then she bit her lip. *You stay here.* Yes, that was the sensible thing. Only there were lords in the castle, with their men-at-arms. Serjeant Belden was helping them. What did that mean?

Oh. Wild spirits save me. What if these lords are noblemen from Harcia? Not a soul of us thought Duke Harald would ever sire a son. Harcia must've doubted it too. What if Belden's sold his loyalty to Duke Aimery? He could have. And everyone knows what the Harcians are. What if – what if –

Nelda's bastard brat cried in protest as her hold on it tightened. 'Ellyn? You be frighting me. What thought's put that look on your face? What—'

Leaping to Heartsong's kitchen drudge, Ellyn pressed a finger to the girl's cold lips. 'Nelda. Listen. Do you love our duke?'

Mute, Nelda nodded.

'And his son? His beautiful Liam, who's to be duke after him? Do you love him too?'

Another nod, then Nelda pulled away. 'Ellyn—'

'No, no, just *listen*,' she said, fighting not to shout. 'These men in the castle, Nelda. They'll never hurt a babe. Noblemen aren't like that. But – but – we must make certain Liam's kept safe for the duke.'

'Safe?' said Nelda, bewildered. 'I don't—'

She took hold of Nelda's shoulders, thin beneath a kitchen-stained linen dress. 'Emun will be back soon. Him and Lady Morda, they'll be back,' she said quickly, as coaxing as she could. 'But one of those lords you saw, the ones we don't know, they could find us first. Nelda, they mustn't find Liam. You and me, we can't let any of them have the duke's son. Not when we can't be sure what they're about.'

Nelda's eyes were wide enough to nearly start from her head. 'But Ellyn, you said they'd not hurt a babe. You said—'

'I know what I said!' she snapped. 'And they won't. But don't you see? They could still take him and threaten to hurt him, so they can hurt the duke. So here's what we'll do. You and me. For Duke Harald. I'll take my Liam and go in there—' She pointed at Lady Morda's closet. '—and you'll stay out here with your – with Tygo. Look! You can sit in the nursing chair and – and Tygo, he can sleep in Liam's cradle. With all its charms dangling on it, see, so he won't go awry.'

Nelda's eyes filled with tears. 'You want to leave me here? Alone?'

Stupid henwit. 'No, no, Nelda, you won't be alone. I'm not leaving. I'm just going to sit with Liam in Morda's closet. So if one of those lords comes here, he'll not find us.'

'But he'll find me and Tygo,' said Nelda, tears spilling. 'What do I say then? What do I do?'

'*Nothing*,' she said, and tugged Nelda towards the nursing chair. 'You're only a kitchen drudge. They won't care about you or your little bastard. So you sit and wait for Emun. Or the duke! He'll come, for certain. And when he sees what you've done for Liam, he'll be so pleased, Nelda. He'll – he'll grant you a cottage, he will. And coins. A gold mark all your own, I'll bet. And the lady Argante, she'll give you some of her clothes, she'll be so grateful. Fancy! Silks and furs and could be a little ruby ring, too.'

'For sitting here?' said Nelda, letting herself be pushed into the chair. 'Ellyn, be you sure?'

Ellyn plucked sleeping Liam from his cradle. 'Yes! Certain sure. Don't I know them, Nelda? I'm wet nurse to their son. They *trust* me, you've seen that. So *you* can trust me. When I tell them how brave you are, how much you love Liam—'

'Ais, but—' Hope and doubt shook Nelda's voice. 'Lady Morda, she be—'

'Never you mind about that old cow,' she said, fighting not to look at the nursery door. Any moment it could burst open, any moment . . . 'The duke has no care for her, and what the duke decides is what happens. Nelda, you settle Tygo in Liam's cradle. He's never slept anywhere so fine, with all these lovely oil-lamps. They're scented. Don't the air smell sweet? Better than a kitchen full of cake! Your Tygo, he'll dream he's a duke! I'm taking Liam into the closet now. Once I close its door, not a peep. Not a hiccup. And whatever you do, if a lord does come, don't look our way. Best you forget we're in there. The duke will be here soon. All will be well. I promise.'

'Ais,' said Nelda, sniffing.

'And you promise to stay mousey?'

'I promise,' said Nelda.

Shaking, Ellyn closed the closet door on Nelda's trusting smile. The door had a latch and a wooden cross-bar to hold it fast. Struggling not to disturb Liam, she fumbled the bar into place. Hearing it thud home, she had to swallow tears.

Safe. Safe. We're safe.

Morda had left three beeswax candles burning beside her bed. *Three*, when she begrudged anyone else a single stinking tallow taper. Oh, she was a cow. And the bed, layered deep with softest wool blankets and a wolfskin coverlet on top. Luxury! And all she did was moan that Duke Harald did not esteem her.

'I'd like to esteem her,' she muttered, cradling Liam's head as she sank to the edge of the bed. 'Right off the top of Heartsong's keep, I would.'

The mattress gave way beneath her, a silence of wool and feathers. No crackling, prickly straw for Morda. Aching with nerves, she wanted to lie down, only that would be folly. Safe she and Liam might be, but safer still sitting up. She pressed her lips to his head, gently. He wriggled, the tiniest twitch, knowing who held him. Knowing who loved him more than anyone in the world. Even more than Duke Harald did, though she'd never say it out loud. But how could he? Duke Harald didn't suckle his son, Duke Harald hardly saw him but once or twice in a week. Duke Harald wanted more sons, in case Liam died. She could understand that. It was the way men were made.

But you'll not die, my baby. You'll live and be a duke.

No sound from Nelda in the nursery beyond the barred door. After so much fuss and upset, she'd half-expected to hear Tygo crying. Could be the brat was sickly. Best for Nelda if it was, and died. Bastard brats were a burden – unless they were born noble, like Duke Harald's bent-nosed cousin.

The beeswax candles burned bright. Staring at them, hating the thought of sitting in the dark, she dithered a moment then reached for the long-handled snuffer and put them out. Better darkness than discovery.

Time dragged its heels. Surely Emun would return soon. Surely—

A heart-cracking sound of timber striking stone as the nursery door crashed open. Nelda broke her mousey promise and screamed. Blind and trapped in Lady Morda's dark closet, Ellyn leapt to her feet. Bit her lip to blood when Nelda screamed again, and her sickly bastard screamed with her. A confusion of heavy boots on the stone floor, rough voices, a clashing of mail.

'*This is the child?*' A man's harsh demand. '*Harald's son?*'

Remembering this time, Nelda said nothing.

'*What is this? What do you do here?*'

A new voice. Familiar. Ellyn stuffed her fist between her teeth. *Emun*. At last.

'*Answer me!*' said Emun. '*You're bound to answer, for—*'

Metal scraping metal, a shocking sound. Metal plunging into flesh. A choked-off cry, full of pain. A woman's scream, not Nelda, and then a metal thud as something heavy struck the nursery floor.

'*Butchery!*' cried Lady Morda, shrill with fear. '*Murder! Foul murder! Where is the duke, send for the—*'

Another sickening sound of forged steel cleaving meat. Another thud, much lighter. No rattle of iron mail.

'*Hold!*' said a different voice, tight with anger and confusion. '*What are you doing?*'

A harsh laugh, another new voice. '*What I'm paid for.*'

Muffled shouts. A clash of sword blades. Breathless grunts and booted shuffling. A smash of wood. A desperate cry. A second iron thudding on the floor. A man's groaning curse, full of pain. Halting, dragging footsteps. And then a frightened baby's wail.

'*Please,*' said Nelda, weeping. '*Please, you be mistaken. Don't hurt us. I'm not – please, you mustn't – no – don't – don't—*'

Ellyn dropped to the soft bed and muffled Liam in wolfskin, so he couldn't hear that bastard brat and its babbling henwit mother die. When it was over she waited to be found, for the closet door to crash open, to feel the unforgiving kiss of steel, to hear Liam shriek like

Nelda's Tygo. To feel her lamb's blood wet her skin. Instead came another heavy, metal-rattling thud. Slow, this time, and with much laboured groaning.

Then the groaning stopped, and there was silence. Ellyn swallowed a sob. She and wriggling Liam were alone . . . and alive.

To Roric's surprise, Harald had said nothing throughout Humbert's remorseless onslaught of accusations. But, knowing his cousin, he knew the self-control wouldn't last. Behind the attentive mask Clemen's duke was seething. Humiliated. A muscle twitched in his cheek, chaotic, and a swollen vein throbbed an ominous warning at his temple.

Standing rigid beside her husband, Argante held his hand so tightly it seemed her bones must burst through the skin.

'Lastly,' said Humbert, shifting his wide-legged stance, 'we touch upon your ill-judged tauntings of Harcia. Against all sound advice you insist on provoking its duke! Like a boy with a stick you poke and you prod, flouting custom, flouting *law*. Inviting retaliation. They already resent us mightily for the wealth we possess and they lack. Do you think those wasps won't sting us, Harald? Do you think you can kick and kick at their nest and they'll say nothing? Do *nothing*?'

Harald laughed, sounding brittle. 'They've done nothing yet.'

'And that might easily change,' Humbert growled. 'I tell you, Harald, Aimery's list of grievances against you is growing. Before long it will match our own!'

'*Grievances?*' Trembling, Argante slitted her eyes. 'Better call them the petulant, self-serving whinings of an old fool. A fool who forgets himself, for you will surely address my husband as *Your Grace*, Lord Humbert, or I swear I'll see you—'

'Peace, Argante,' said Harald, still pretending compliance, and raised the hand she did not hold. 'Humbert has shed his blood for Clemen. He has earned the right to speak his mind.'

'Speak his mind?' Too angry to heed the warning in his face, she released her tight grasp of his hand and stepped down from the dais. Humbert stood his ground as she approached, bold as any man. 'What mind? The old fool's wits are scattered! He's forgotten where his sworn loyalties lie. Shed his blood for Clemen? He should bleed out every last drop. *That* will serve Clemen!'

Aistan cleared his throat. 'My lady, instead of berating Lord Humbert you should be on your knees thanking him. He has spared you in this, for you're young and poorly guided. But were he asked, he could list your misdeeds.'

'*My*—' Incredulous, Argante glared. 'You'd dare to besmirch *me*?'

'You besmirched yourself when you told lies about Lord Gerbod's cousin in Harald's name, so Gerbod's manor house in Bellham was made forfeit to your brother.'

'Liar!' Argante spat at Aistan, and whirled round. 'He's lying, Harald. Don't heed him!'

Looking away from his wife, Harald stared at Ercole. 'My lord?'

'Your Grace!' Ercole protested. He stood alone, abandoned by Scarwid and the rest. 'This is a foul slur, I swear it.'

Doubt and dislike clouded Harald's eyes as he considered Argante's brother. Then his expression smoothed. 'You hear my wife, Aistan. She knows none of it, and nor do I.'

Roric saw Aistan's face darken, saw his fingers unfurl and reach for his sword. They were poised on a blade's edge – and if they fell—

'I'm sorry, Harald,' he said quickly. 'It's true. Gerbod's family kept quiet out of fear you'd seek vengeance on them for speaking ill of your wife.'

Humbert snorted. 'Another failure. When no man, woman or child, be they of noble blood or common, can trust they're safe from the rapacious whims of their duke and his duchess, how terrible a day has dawned in Clemen. Which is why we stand before you now, Harald, and say: *No more.*'

All through Humbert's unflinching recitation, the other lords in the Great Hall had nodded and murmured as every terrible charge was laid down. Some of the complaints had touched on them personally, which prompted open agreement. Harald had never once acknowledged them, his gaze fastened to Humbert from beginning to end. But he paid them attention now, searching each face for even the smallest sign of comfort.

He found none.

'Harald?' said Argante, querulous. 'I'm tired of this. Send them away.'

Roric looked at Humbert, who scowled. *Your turn to speak*. He took a breath, but Harald nipped in before him.

'Ah. And now we come to the bitter truth. You think to sit *your* arse on my throne? *Cousin?*'

'I think almost any arse would sit there better than yours,' he said, shrugging. 'But I've been asked, and I've answered. If I can serve Clemen, I will.'

Harald smiled his scorn. 'If you serve it as you've served me, Roric, Humbert and his friends will be weeping soon enough.' The smile vanished. 'As will you. For if I'm to be the first deposed duke in Clemen, how long will it be until you're the second? Something difficult done once is never so difficult again.'

'Pay him no heed, Roric,' Humbert warned. 'He'll say anything to save his miserable hide.'

With a flourish of her heavy velvet skirts, Argante returned to Harald's side. 'This is naught but chittlechat. Send them *away*, Harald – and together we'll find a punishment to sweetly suit their foul crimes.'

'Are you *deaf*, you stupid bitch?' Vidar demanded, goaded past common sense. 'Harald is done, Argante, and you're done with him. Clemen has judged you, and Clemen spits you out like the rancid offal you are.'

With a shriek Argante leapt at him. This time it was Aistan who laid hands on her, swinging her off her dainty feet and shaking her like a ratting dog with its prey.

'Be silent, you spoiled slattern, or I'll snap your pretty, worthless neck!'

'Aistan, no!' Shoving his sword at Humbert, Roric stepped in. 'My lord, release her. This is the ducal court, not a shambles. Aistan! *Let her go!*'

Harald was on his feet, red-faced with fear and fury. 'Aistan, you're a dead man! I'll dagger you myself and feed your hacked corpse to my hounds! You cur – you—'

Roric shoved him back into his chair. 'Hold your tongue, Harald! *Aistan!*'

On a harsh, sobbing breath Aistan sprang his clutching hands wide. Argante slid to the tiled floor, weeping.

'Aistan?'

Aistan turned away, his face haggard. 'I'm done, Roric. Finish this.'

'Finish this?' Argante looked up. Tears runnelled the chalk dust caked on her face. 'Finish us, you mean. Why else are you here with swords?'

'To make sure you listen,' he said sharply. 'We've not come to spill blood. Harald—'

Ignoring him, Harald pushed out of his chair. This time Roric let him go to his wife. Watching his cousin gently help Argante to stand, he felt an unexpected pang of sorrow.

'I never wanted this, Harald. None of it. You should've been a better man. There was Berold to guide you. Why did you take the path to ruin?'

Harald's stare was vicious. 'I don't answer to you. *Bastard*.'

'He means to kill us, Harald,' Argante said, clinging. 'He means to kill our son.' Her hands flew to her mouth. 'Liam could be dead already, butchered in his cradle!'

'He's not!' Roric said, as Harald blanched. 'We have no quarrel with an infant.'

She shook her head, eyes glistening with tears. 'I don't believe you.'

'Then see for yourself. Humbert, go with her.'

'I will go,' said Harald. 'Liam is my heir.'

'Argante goes, or no one.' Roric held out his hand. 'Humbert?'

Stepping forward, Humbert gave back the sword he held in trust then offered Argante a brief bow. 'My lady? Lead the way.'

'Go,' said Harald, curtly. 'Bring Liam to me.'

Argante hesitated. 'But—'

'*Bring him!*'

With a last hate-filled glare, Argante fled the hall, leaving Humbert to lumber in her wake.

'Your son is safe, Harald,' Roric said, feeling the heavy stares of the silently watching lords. 'How could you think otherwise? That I'd harm him? Liam is family.'

Harald snorted, derisive. 'You seek to steal his birthright, Roric. My son is dreadfully harmed.'

'Its loss is your fault, not mine. I never told you to rule Clemen with your sword-point pressed to its throat.'

Harald looked at Aistan, then Vidar, up to Farland, Morholt and Hankin in the minstrels' gallery then back down to the other lords ranged against him.

'My lords!' he said, his voice raised. 'Is there not a one of you who'll stand with me against this upstart?'

A long and terrible silence. Not even Ercole answered. Instead, Argante's brother stared at the floor.

'I see,' Harald said at last. 'So it's to be exile?'

Roric nodded. 'With money enough, and comforts. Liam will want for nothing, Harald.'

'Nothing save his birthright! Tell me, Roric, where do you suggest that I—'

'*Murderer! Bastard murderer!*'

Startled, Roric turned to see the watching lords and their ladies cry alarm and scatter, the pages yelp and fling themselves to safety . . . and Argante, no sign of Humbert, running breathless towards him with a bloodied sword in her hands.

'*Murderer!*' she screamed again, her gold headdress discarded, her hair unpinned and flying, her blue velvet dress stained black and red. 'Liam's dead and burned in his cradle and Heartsong's set afire! Harald – Harald—'

Roaring in anguished rage, Harald threw himself forward. Roric dropped his sword and took the weight of his cousin, grunting as a clenched fist caught him in the eye. Half-blinded he swung them both about to see Argante still running, still screaming, her stolen sword raised to strike.

'Vidar – Vidar, no, *don't*—'

Vidar's blade ran her through, neatly, with barely a sound.

'*Argante!*' Abandoning Harald, Roric tried to catch his cousin's wife as slowly, so slowly, she slid off Vidar's sword. But dismay robbed him of strength. Blood flowed from the killing wound as Argante slipped from his grasp and struck the red-and-white tiled floor. The sword she'd foolishly brandished clattered beside her, useless.

He looked up, his vision blurred. 'Vidar . . .'

'You're welcome,' Vidar said, sounding sour. His one good eye glinted. 'Roric, she was no sweeter than a—'

Aistan's shout and the change in Vidar's scarred face spun him round. *Harald*. But whose sword was that he –

'Here!' said Vidar. 'Now end this!'

Roric snatched Vidar's offered, blood-wet blade and barely managed to clash it across the sword in frenzied Harald's grasp. His own sword, his knight-gift, tossed aside without thinking.

'Don't, Harald,' he panted, fighting to hold his ground. 'I'd not—'

With a practised flick of iron-strong wrists, his face bestial with grief, Harald deflected the blocking blade and slashed his stolen sword in a swift, lethal sweep. Roric twisted as he parried, felt sharp pain as the passing blade caught him, drove links of mail through padding and into tender flesh. Dimly he heard someone shout, heard women scream, saw lords and ladies scuttle to the far reaches of the hall. Dimly he saw Vidar and Aistan, helpless, able only to watch.

Blow after blow he blocked, feeling each heavy shock shudder through his forearms, into his shoulders, rattle his teeth. This was no tilt yard game, full of laughter and teasing. Harald was trying to kill him.

I never wanted this.

They ranged about the Great Hall, filling the air with furious sound. Turned the castle into a smithy, steel ringing against steel. Sweat dripped, chests heaved, shod feet slid and scrabbled on the smooth floor. A stinging hint of tainted smoke. Had Argante told the truth, then? Was the castle on fire? Someone had dragged her body away. White tiles were smeared red. Roric sobbed for air as Harald beat him across the place where his wife died, beat him onto the dais and off it, smashing the gilded chair to kindling, beat him nearly into the fire and howled in furious disappointment when a killing thrust failed.

'*Take him, Roric! Finish it! There's no saving him now!*'

Humbert.

He blocked another sword-thrust, grunting at the pain. His throat felt raw, his lungs shredded. His bones threatened to break. But Harald was the older man . . . and he was tiring too. Was tiring faster. His face was grey, and slicked with sweat. Slash. Parry. Block. Deflect. Slash—

Harald stumbled, going down hard on one knee. His head snapped up, eyes wide with pain, lips bloodied from a bitten tongue.

'*Roric*—'

'Forgive me, cousin,' he whispered, and pushed Vidar's bloodied sword through Harald's unprotected heart.

CHAPTER SIX

'*R*oric.'

For one dreadful moment, Roric thought it was his cousin speaking, enchanted back to life. But then a hand touched his slumped shoulder.

'Come, boy,' Humbert said, full of sombre grief. 'With me.'

He felt his breath hitch. *Liam*. 'No. Humbert, *no*. He was an infant, he was helpless. He *can't* be—'

Humbert shook his head. 'You must come.'

Of course. Vision blurred, he looked around the hall, at the court's silent lesser lords and ladies then at Aistan and the other great lords, and the men-at-arms staring down from the gallery. 'Remain here till I return. All of you. And don't be afraid. I'm not my cousin. You're safe with me.'

Leaving Vidar to retrieve his sword, and guard dead Harald, Roric climbed stair after winding stair until he reached Heartsong's nursery. It was still smouldering, oil lamps over-turned and broken, candles trampled, the smoke-thick air sickening with the stench of burned bedding, burned furs, burned tapestries and heavy curtains and brightly painted furniture.

Burned flesh.

Eyes streaming, forearm pressed to nose and mouth, he made himself step over the charred men on the floor, over the charred remains of the wet nurse and Lady Morda, and face what lay in the smoky ruins of the cradle.

'Liam.'

A dazzle of memories, sharp as shattered glass.

Harald cradling his newborn son, tears on his cheeks . . . Argante kissing her babe's forehead, her hard eyes softened with love . . . his own love, unexpected and fierce, as he held his cousin's child, so afraid of letting the little one fall . . . Liam, smiling up at him . . .

'Roric!'

Choking on bile, he flung away from the babe's burst, bubbled flesh and seared bones. Humbert followed him out of the nursery and into the torchlit corridor beyond, saying nothing as he bent double to heave and spit.

At length he straightened, wincing as his bruised, battered body groaned in protest. A sharp sting, as his bloodied linen undershirt pulled away from his skin. The side of his face and his eye ached fiercely, where Harald's fist had caught him. He wanted to weep, but couldn't in front of Humbert. On a shuddering breath, he looked at his foster-lord.

'I know, boy,' said Humbert, his own composure challenged. 'It's wicked.'

'Three dead men,' he said, his voice rasping. 'At least one of them must be Harald's. He never left Liam without a man-at-arms nearby.' He felt his breathing hitch. 'Spirits, Humbert. Could they *all* be his men? Did our men slay Harald's men-at-arms, slay Liam and Morda and the wet nurse, then set fire to the nursery to burn any trace of their crime before fleeing?'

'No,' Humbert said fiercely. 'Roric, why must this be murder? It's more likely to be mischance.'

'*Mischance?*' He nearly laughed. 'You can't believe that.'

'One man seduced to disobey you, I can believe. Just. One man, taking his companions unaware. But a clutch of traitors in our midst?' Humbert shook his head. 'That I won't believe.

'Harald claimed *he* had a clutch of traitors in his midst.'

'Don't,' Humbert commanded. 'Harald was the traitor here. Everything he touched, he tarnished.'

He could still feel his sword sliding through Harald's heart. See the light of life dying out of his cousin's shocked eyes. His belly heaved again, fresh bile rising. He didn't want to think about Harald.

'Once we've tallied our men, and Harald's, we'll know who lies dead,' said Humbert, breaking the heavy silence. 'But more than that? I'm sorry, boy. Best you make peace with the notion we might never know how this unfolded. Not for certain.'

'Make peace with it?' Roric stared, outrage overcoming sickness. 'Humbert, I said plainly Liam wasn't to be touched. And now he's *dead*. Harald's son. You'll never convince me this was mischance. Someone I brought here in good faith has betrayed me. How can I make peace with that?'

'How you do it is your affair. But if there is a villain here, and if we don't unmask him swiftly, then make peace with it you must. Aistan and the other lords won't stomach harsh suspicion. They had a bellyful of that with Harald.'

True. And if he even so much as *hinted* at ruling like his cousin . . .

'Make no mistake,' Humbert added. 'You need Aistan and the others to help you stamp your authority on Clemen. But to earn their trust you have to trust them. If ever they doubt you, this new house we're building will tumble to ruins at our feet.'

'And what of Liam?' Seeing again that ghastly cradle and its dreadful, stinking burden, Roric dragged a hand down his bruised face. Welcomed the clean physical pain that caused, better by far than the soul-sickness of a slaughtered infant. 'Doesn't an innocent babe deserve justice? Vengeance?'

'Not if justice and vengeance come at the expense of this duchy.'

'Clemen's people will expect me to avenge the murder of my own flesh and blood!'

'You can't say for sure it's murder.'

'*You* can't say for sure it isn't! And if—'

'*Roric*.' Heavy-handed, Humbert took hold of his shoulder. 'Think like a duke, not a man. No good can come of whipping up mopish sentiment for Harald's brat. Or in stirring Aistan and the rest with accusations of treachery. I know it sits sour, but in this mucky matter we'll best be served by never learning what happened.'

And to think he'd thought the night couldn't grow any worse. 'So you're saying I'm to wink at misdoing if it suits? Explain how that doesn't make me Harald!'

Humbert growled. 'Don't you go pushing words between my teeth.'

'My lord, there's a hall full of people downstairs who heard what Argante said, who *know*—'

'*Nothing*,' said Humbert, still glaring. 'Beyond what we choose they should know. They'll believe what we tell them, Roric.'

'How so sure, my lord?'

'Because they'll want to.'

Half-blind with nausea, Roric knocked his foster-lord's hand from his shoulder and turned aside. 'Humbert—'

'Tell me I'm wrong,' said Humbert, pitiless. 'Show me one lord who doesn't want this misery put behind us. Then tell me the peace of Clemen isn't worth such a trifle.'

He spun round. '*The truth is no trifle!*'

'Roric, you're a fool if you think a one of them will shed a tear for that dead babe.'

Staring at Humbert, he felt a different grief welling. *It wasn't supposed to be like this*. 'All the more reason for me to care.'

'You don't have the luxury of caring! Not like that. What kind of shepherd kills his whole flock for the pity of one sick sheep?'

'We're not talking about sheep!'

'I know what we're talking about, boy! Do you?'

His legs were shaking, worse than when he'd faced his first run at the ring in the tilt yard. His first blade unsheathed against him in anger. Humbert, his second father, was suddenly a stranger.

'You're glad Liam's dead.'

Humbert fisted his blunt hands on his hips. 'I'm glad he'll not grow to be a rallying point for traitors. And like it or not, boy, we both know that was always a danger.'

Perhaps, but it didn't make the nursery bloodshed any easier to stomach. Or his foster-lord's pragmatism any less brutal. Exhausted, all the pains in his body clamouring louder than ever, Roric took a deep breath and made himself stand straight.

'Fine. We'll do this your way. For now. But I still think someone betrayed me tonight, Humbert. And you know I can't rest till I know the man's name.'

'And I think you're mistaken. But I'll look into it. You have my word.' Softening, Humbert sighed. 'Roric . . . we knew from the outset this would be hard.'

Hard? He'd been ready for hard. Not for a moment had he thought Harald would let go of his duchy easily. But never in his deepest doubtings had he thought so much blood would be spilled. Loving Humbert, and in this stark moment thoroughly disliking him, he shook his head.

'What's happened tonight is an ill omen.'

'*No*,' said Humbert, and pointed a finger. 'Roric, I give you fair warning. Don't you start with any superstitious shite.'

'It is an ill omen,' he insisted. 'And its shadow will stain me for ever. Harald dead. Argante dead. And innocent Liam . . .'

Humbert thrust his bristled beard close. 'Vidar killed Argante, and with good reason. The bitch was mad with grief. As for Harald, it was his choice to pick up a sword. No one can blame you for defending yourself.'

For all he was a man grown, and blooded in the Marches, that look in Humbert's eye could make him quail as though he were seven years old again and caught in mischief. Was it the same for all men who yet had a father living? If so, then he should envy Vidar.

'And Liam?'

'I said it,' Humbert replied, his jaw tight. 'Babes die. Harald's brat could as easily have perished of plague. Now come, Your Grace. Steady yourself. There's much to be done before we can ride home to Eaglerock.'

Your Grace.

Feeling anything but graceful, feeling sore and sorrowful and soiled, Roric surrendered. 'Yes, my lord.'

'And first of our tasks,' said Humbert, in the voice that allowed no argument, 'is deciding what tale we tell those lords milled about downstairs . . .'

Waiting for Roric and Humbert to return, Vidar tried to ignore the cacophony of pains wracking his flesh and bones. Since his ruination in the Marches – and it would be four years gone come Summer

Rise, time running so fast, as he no longer could – not a day had passed without some kind of pain in it. At first he'd thought he must lose his wits. He'd not imagined any man could live with such constant, cruel suffering. But it turned out the leech treating him hadn't been an arrant liar after all. After a few months the scarlet screaming dimmed to a pale whisper, mostly, and mostly he'd learned how to ignore it. He took powdered willow bark on the whispery days, oil of lantrin when he had no choice, and was careful not to demand more from his scarred, half-butchered body than it could give. Well. Usually he was careful. But the hard ride to Heartsong couldn't be avoided. It had punished him, and thrusting a sword through Argante had only made the pain worse.

If he'd been alone he might've succumbed to the torment and groaned out loud. Swallowed more lantrin than was safe and endured the mad fever-dreams that followed. But he wasn't alone, and revealing the extent of his weakness before the men his foolish father had affronted was akin to cutting his own throat.

So, to distract himself, he watched Clemen's anxious northern lords and their quietly weeping wives without seeming to pay them any attention at all. One of his father's neat tricks, that. A pity Godebert had forgotten it, or else grown careless in its use. If he'd been sharper in his wits he might still be alive. The old fulmet.

He let his vaguely roaming gaze touch on the cooling corpse of Godebert's murderer. Harald had fought well, but Roric had fought better. For all his protestations of wanting to keep the bastard alive, he'd shoved a sword through the poxed mongrel neatly enough . . . which meant he could be ruthless if he had to. A point worth remembering. And likely it meant he'd not mourn Harald over-long. Or Argante. Or the babe.

Thought of Liam tripped his heart, set it beating a little faster. He was beginning to regret not dealing with Harald's son himself. The man he'd bribed to his service, sworn to Humbert but soured over an old slighting, had seemed safe enough. But with the deed done, niggling doubt was creeping in. Was the fear of a fearful death enough to keep the spiteful man-at-arms honestly suborned? Was the coin he'd paid the man, coin he couldn't easily part with, sufficiently purse-heavy that greed wouldn't tempt him to a little black dealing?

Because if he'd misjudged the bastard . . .

On the far side of the hall, Aistan stood deep in murmured conversation with the lords Hankin, Morholt and Farland. Clemen's mighty southern barons hadn't invited him to join their huddle. It seemed that till Roric said otherwise, Harald's tainting of him would hold true. His heart tripped again, thinking on it. Roric's promise he'd be restored to his inheritance was why he'd risked his life in this dangerous venture. Not even the chance to avenge his dead father had counted more than his hope of claiming the woman he lived for. Breathed for. *Lindara*. He had no chance of winning Humbert's daughter without first being washed clean of Godebert's enduring stain. And achieving his absolution had meant helping Roric rid Clemen of Harald. Yes, and ridding it of Harald's innocent son, too.

Now the thing was done, never to be undone. Clemen was saved from a tyrant and civil war, and Lindara was his. At last.

The thought almost had him smiling, despite the pain. He pinched his lips to kill it. He'd be thought most odd, smiling in the midst of blood and death. Then hidden joy gave way to surprise, as Aistan left his brother barons and crossed the hall towards him. A moment's hesitation as he passed by Ercole, sat on the tiled floor with his half-sister's body draped over his knees. Was the little shite's tear-stained grief genuine? Perhaps. Or perhaps Ercole wept for his purse, which would empty soon enough without Argante's influence to keep it filled.

'My lord,' Vidar said, as Aistan joined him.

Aistan nodded. 'Vidar.' Dispassionate, he looked at dead Harald, neatly composed at their feet. 'So,' he murmured. 'The whole rotten family cut down, root and stock. A good night's work, yes?'

'I doubt Roric thinks so.'

'Roric has a tender heart.'

'Not a fatal flaw, surely?'

'You think so?' Aistan's heavy brows lowered. 'A tender heart beats most usefully in a woman's breast, Vidar. Not a man's.'

'True,' he agreed. 'But you'll not fault our new duke for a little regret. Family is family, my lord. Even when it strays.'

A brief quirk of his lips showed Aistan understood, perhaps appreciated, the veiled reference to Godebert. 'Anyone who regrets Harald's death is a fool. Argante's too. She was a vain, greedy bitch.'

'They were indeed well-matched, my lord. But it's a shame about the babe.'

'The babe was trouble, delayed,' Aistan said sharply. 'Clemen's safer with it dead.'

Vidar nodded. 'Yes, my lord. It is.'

Which was why he'd risked his hope of Lindara to make sure the child died. For the sake of their sons yet unborn and the Clemen those sons would inherit, knowing Roric wouldn't do it, he'd taken it upon himself to stain his hands with innocent blood. Assuming, of course, that any child born of Harald and Argante could be innocent.

Still . . . he was guilt-pricked. And he hoped, in truth, that Liam had died without pain.

'Did you know,' said Aistan, watching him carefully, 'that Roric threatened to withdraw from claiming Clemen if Harald, Argante and the child were denied safe passage out of the duchy, and money to keep them in exile?'

'No, my lord, I didn't,' he said. 'But I can't say I'm surprised. It's because Roric's not Harald that we're content to make him our duke. Isn't it?'

Aistan grunted. 'Bastard or not, he's Berold's grandson. There could be no other choice.'

Not one that wouldn't lead to bitter conflict. Clemen's people set great store by bloodlines, its lords no less than any common man in a cow byre. Too many lived who remembered beloved Berold for any of Clemen's barons to step over Roric in pursuit of the ducal crown. That was why Roric's bastard birth would be winked at.

Aistan's mail chinked as he shifted his stance and glanced upwards. 'Roric and Humbert are taking their time.'

'Do you wonder?' Vidar said, shrugging. 'I might've been barred from court but my ears weren't stopped to gossip. I'm told Roric loved Liam. He'll be deep in grief.'

Aistan grunted again, unmoved. Then he turned a little, his gaze narrow. 'It was wrong that Godebert died as he did. I counselled Harald against execution. But even so, Vidar? Your father was guilty of stealing coin from Clemen's coffers.'

'I know that, my lord. And I'm guilty of being his son.' He stared at Aistan steadily. 'But not a single coin Godebert stole ever found its way into my purse.'

'Harald thought otherwise.'

'And you, my lord? What do you think?'

Rolling his shoulders, Aistan frowned at Harald's bloodstained corpse. 'I think that in a few hours the sun will rise upon a different Clemen. I understand Roric's sworn to reinstate you.'

'He has, my lord. Do you and your brother barons object?'

'I don't speak for them, Vidar. For myself, I'd call it justice. There was no proof you ever were part of Godebert's dishonourable scheme.'

'Fie, my lord,' Vidar said, temper rising. 'You'll turn my head with such heaping praise.'

'With your inheritance restored,' said Aistan, choosing to ignore the pricking words, 'you'll doubtless be seeking a wife to give you sons. Have you made a choice, or does your eye still wander?'

He'd served a difficult apprenticeship in the guarding of emotion, these last four years. Had emerged from it a master in hiding his heart. Hiding it now, Vidar favoured Aistan with his blandest of smiles.

'In truth, my lord, I've not dared to give that hope wings. Let Roric keep his word and then I'll dare to hope for sons.'

'You're prudent,' said Aistan, approving. 'And more than once before tonight you've proven yourself a man of courage. I have a daughter, Vidar, whom I love. Kennise. My youngest. Like you she's been hurt. I'd think that would mean you'd deal with her kindly.'

Kennise was the daughter Harald debauched. So what was this? A great lord seeking to dispose of an inconvenient nuisance? Did Aistan think that a physically ruined man, one shadow-tainted by a treasonous sire, might well struggle to find a father willing to bestow upon him a pristine child? That being in his own way as debauched as this Kennise, he'd fall to his knees in gratitude and humbly take Harald's leavings?

'You astonish me, Lord Aistan,' Vidar said, still smiling. The effort that took nearly shattered his spine. 'I lack the words to express how I feel. As I say, I can't hope to hope for anything just now. But when I can, I'll give your generous offer all the consideration it deserves.'

Aistan's dark, forbidding face lightened. For a moment he looked almost vulnerable, nothing like the man who'd confronted Harald.

'She's a sweet girl, Vidar. I don't offer her lightly. But she should have a chance at happiness, and—'

A stirring in the hall cut short his protestation. Roric and Humbert were coming down the stairs. Roric's face was a picture of resolute authority, but beneath the determined mask Vidar saw smothered shock, and grief. Treading the stone staircase behind him came Humbert, his expression impassive behind that grizzled beard.

'My lords,' said Roric, halting beside the Great Hall's dais. Not touching Harald's overturned and splintered ducal chair. Only standing near enough to it that no one present could miss the hint. 'It's with great sorrow I must tell you that my late cousin's child is indeed perished. Lord Humbert and I have close-inspected the scene of his unwanted and deeply regretted death and we are both satisfied that the babe died by a sorry mischance.'

Aistan stepped forward. 'Can you elaborate, my lord?'

'We can,' said Humbert firmly. 'For one of our men-at-arms had a few breaths of life left in him. Dying, he told us what happened. Hearing our men approach, the babe's wet nurse panicked. One of Harald's men, alerted by her shrieking, foolishly refused to surrender his sword when told. There was an affray – and in the mayhem all were cut down and a fire started. No one survived.'

Still huddled on the floor, Ercole lifted his tear-soaked face. 'Liar. *Murderer*.' Wild-eyed, he stared around the hall. 'Will none of you speak? Will none of you condemn this upstart bastard who killed my poor sister and her child?'

'Leave him be,' said Roric, as Humbert opened his mouth to chide. 'Lord Morholt? See the lord Ercole to his chamber and sit with him till he's more composed. My lords and ladies of the court—' His gaze swept around the hall. Lingered a moment on the childish pages, who'd collapsed by the cooling fireplace and drooped over each other like wilting daisies. 'My friends. This has been a tumultuous night . . .'

Letting Roric's soothing words wash over him, Vidar smoothed his face to blankness. So, did this mean he was safe? If the man he'd suborned was indeed dead then surely he was safe. Unless Ercole was right to call Roric a liar, and even now something sinister brewed for a private bubbling over. His heart was tripping again, the pulse in his throat throbbing like a wound. What a *fool* he'd been, to trust the brat's necessary killing to any hand but his own.

Now all he could do was trust that the dice had fallen in his favour.

His soothing speech ended, Roric bade Harald's guests to remain within Heartsong until the morning. As the stunned court began to withdraw from the hall, Vidar snatched Roric's attention.

'Let me be useful, my lord. I'll account for our men-at-arms while you attend to weightier matters.'

Roric shook his head. 'No need, Vidar. Humbert will do it.'

But Humbert was tangled with Morholt, both men trying to persuade a distraught Ercole to let go of Argante's body. He'd started keening. A terrible sound.

'Go, then,' said Roric, distracted. 'Tell Belden to hold his men in the guards' chamber and shackle any who might think to oppose us. Our men you can bring back here. And locate the castle's steward. Bid him secure himself and the servants in their quarters till they're sent for.'

'My lord,' he said, and left Roric to help deal with Ercole before he changed his mind.

Almost breathless with pain, he searched the castle. Heartsong's steward, a sweating wreck who babbled nonsense about a heart-spasmed old cook, was swiftly dealt with. The servants too. Belden, unharmed and near to tears, eagerly promised his men's obedience. That left only Roric's men . . . and his own particular problem.

But though he looked in every chamber, he couldn't find the man-at-arms he'd bribed to rid the world of Harald's brat. Which meant either the man was one of those foul, charred bodies in the nursery – or else fear had encouraged Liam's killer to flee under cover of confusion.

It made little difference. Either way, the deed could not touch him.

Light-headed with relief, almost able to forget the torment in his hip, he led what remained of Roric's makeshift, borrowed army back to the hall. Ercole was gone. So were Harald and Argante. Their blood remained though, dried and dark red on the tiles. While Humbert and Aistan and the other lords wrangled before the freshly fed fire, Roric stood apart and stared at the place where his cousin fell.

'Wait here,' Vidar told the men-at-arms, and crossed to him.

Arms folded, chin lowered, Roric didn't look up. 'You saved my life, Vidar. I'll not forget it.'

'Return what's mine, Roric, and I'll ask for nothing more.'

Roric's sideways glance was sharp. 'I said I would, and I will. You'd doubt my word? Now?'

'No, my lord. Of course not.'

'Good.' Sighing, turning, Roric lifted his head. 'You're weary, Vidar. You should seek a bed.'

'Before you?' He let his anger show. 'I don't think so.'

'Don't be a fool,' said Roric, kindly enough. 'You hide it well, but it's clear to me you're in pain. Go. There's nothing more you can do tonight. The rest of this is council business.'

'And no concern of mine.'

Roric nodded. 'As you say.'

'Very well, then. I'll withdraw.'

'I'll be starting back for Eaglerock tomorrow,' Roric added. 'I'd have you ride with me, if you think you can. We must discuss the details of your inheritance.'

Vidar swallowed the hot words crowding his tongue. He would be a fool if he let a thoughtless insult imperil his future. 'Thank you.'

'No, Vidar.' Faintly smiling, Roric touched his arm. 'Thank you. Now, good night. Sleep well and wake refreshed. For I give you fair warning, I'll not be dawdling home.'

'My lord.' Vidar bowed, not caring that courtesy stoked his body's pain to greater heights. Let Roric gallop from doorstep to doorstep, he'd keep pace with the bastard no matter the cost. 'Until morning.'

Limping from the hall, feeling the great lords' gazes follow him, he made sure to keep his expression suitably grave. But once he was alone, in a cramped chamber on Heartsong tower's third floor, he thought of Lindara and laughed, until pain and exhaustion felled him like an axe.

Gently imprisoned within her father's unfashionable Eaglerock townhouse, Lindara waited, and waited, and thought she might go mad. Two weeks gone, almost, since Harald died at Heartsong. Clemen was still in convulsions. Ten days since Vidar and her father and Roric had returned from the north. Three days since Harald, Argante and their babe were laid to rest without public ceremony in the grounds of Eaglerock castle. Two days since Clemen's new council was announced, with Humbert at its head. So far she'd seen her father five times, Roric once and Vidar not at all. Every morning she came downstairs, full of hope that this would be the day her beloved came to claim her. Every night, disappointed, she snuffed out her bedside candle and wept because he hadn't.

If only she knew why he was taking so long . . .

Biting her lip, she tied off a thread of green embroidery silk and held out her hand. 'Red, Eunise.'

Eunise, her nurse turned lady's maid, laid a length of red silk across her palm. She threaded her needle, fighting the urge to stab it in her eye. *Embroidery*. She was sick to death of it. Sick of dour old Eunise, this dayroom, her life. No wonder wild birds moped and died in a cage. Feeling savage, she jabbed the needle through the silk cushion cover she was stitching. What she'd not give for a gallop through Bingham Wood, following hounds in pursuit of a stag. But her father wouldn't hear of it. She must stay indoors, with Eunise, till agitated Eaglerock was millpond calm again.

'And when will that be?' she'd demanded, fretted to unwise confrontation.

'How should I know?' he'd replied, scarcely heeding her. Not caring, it seemed, that she was close to tears. 'Lindara, cease your carping. I've greater worries to task me than your fidgets.'

So here she sat, day after tedious day, stitching cushion covers. Going mad.

A knock on the dayroom door, then it opened. Gillie, the townhouse steward, crossed the threshold and bowed. 'My lady. Lord Vidar is come, seeking Lord Humbert.'

'You should send him away, my lady,' said Eunise, uninvited. 'Lord Humbert wouldn't like him bothering you.'

Perhaps she could stab her needle into Eunise's eye, instead. 'Show Lord Vidar in, Gillie.' And as her prunish maid hissed under her breath, added, 'Enough, Eunise. It would be impolite to send him away without a courteous explanation.'

Heart hammering, she waited. When the door opened again, admitting Vidar, it took all her strength not to leap into his arms. Not to drown in pity for him, take his tired face between her hands, kiss away the fresh lines of pain grooved deep around his eyes and his lips. Because she couldn't, must seem indifferent, she tucked the threaded needle into her embroidery and handed it to Eunise, then smoothed the folds of her violet skirts.

'My lord,' she said, offering Vidar a distantly polite smile. Eunise bristled close beside her, a guard dog ready to bite. 'I'm told you wish to see Lord Humbert. Alas, he's trapped in Eaglerock castle, and I can't tell you when next he'll be home. Roric keeps him monstrous busy. But if you'd care to leave him a message I'll be sure he receives it.'

Vidar's smile was as distantly polite as her own. 'A kind offer, my lady, but what I must say to your father is best said face to face.'

She nodded, the gracious hostess. 'Of course. Eunise—'

'My lady?' said Eunise, suspicious.

'Bring me a pitcher of Evrish wine, a plate of sugar wafers and two of the red glass goblets. I'd not send Lord Vidar away completely unsatisfied.'

Eunise tucked in her whiskered chin. 'My lady, Lord Humbert wouldn't approve of that.'

'And I don't approve of you disputing me! Will you go, or must I dismiss you?'

'My lady,' Eunise muttered.

'So, my lord Vidar,' she said, as soon as they were alone. 'Have you really come to see my father?'

Vidar grinned. 'Given I know full well where Humbert hides himself, what do you think?'

She nearly tripped in her haste to reach him. 'I think you're a cat-hearted knave! It's been *days* since you returned from Heartsong and this is the first I see of you? For shame!'

'Lindara, wait,' he said, catching her hands in his. 'We can't risk—'

'Peace,' she whispered, and swiftly kissed him. 'Eunise will be an age. The only Evrish in the house is buried deep in the cellar, still a-barrel. Vidar, Vidar, where have you *been*? I thought you'd forgotten me.'

'Forgotten you?' He grasped her hips and pulled her close. 'And will I forget to breathe, too?'

'Yes,' she said, kissing him again. Reckless, this time. Hungry. Laughed softly as his right hand left her hip to find a new home upon her breast. When they finally parted, too soon, she was flushed and aching. 'What news, my love? Has Roric kept his word?'

Vidar turned away. Limped to the dayroom's expensively glazed window, with its painted wooden shutters folded back, and looked into the budding Knot Garden below. 'Not yet.'

'I don't understand,' she said, staring. 'Why the delay? Without you he'd never have toppled Harald. Without you, Vidar, he'd likely be dead!'

'You know what happened at Heartsong?' he said, glancing over his shoulder.

'My father told me. You should know he praised your part in it.'

'Grudgingly, no doubt.'

'Praise is praise. And harder wrung from Humbert than blood from a stone.' She crossed to him and pressed her palm to his chest. His grey velvet doublet looked worn, the gilded pearls once stitched to it cut off for easy pawning. Not that she'd ever tell him she'd noticed. His pride mightn't survive it. The thought pricked her temper. 'Roric promised to reinstate you. You must demand he keep his word, Vidar. And if you won't, I will.'

'No, Lindara.' Vidar's hand covered hers, fingers folding, holding tight. 'Roric made it plain on the ride home that he can't restore my lands till he's formally proclaimed duke.'

'And when will that be?'

'No bastard has ever been made a duke. Your foster-brother's courting every baron and purse-heavy merchant and even some of the Exarch's priests, to be sure of his welcome.' Sighing, Vidar captured her face between his hands and rested his forehead against hers. 'My love, we must be patient. If I make a nuisance of myself I'll turn Roric from ally to enemy. Is that what you want?'

'I want what was taken from you restored, Vidar. I want you as my husband. By my side. In my bed.'

'Soon, Lindara. We'll have everything we want soon.'

She broke away from him. 'Why must it be *soon*? Why isn't it *now*?'

'Because of politics,' Vidar retorted. 'You know that. You're Humbert's daughter.'

She couldn't care less about politics. The politics of Clemen were ruining her life. 'Then will you at least make formal approach to my father?'

'Of course. As soon as the ink is dry on my inheritance papers.'

'Before then, Vidar! Tonight. Or tomorrow morning. But no later.' She lifted her chin. 'Else I'll think you've changed your mind.'

He gaped at her. 'Why would you think that?'

'With you so full of excuses, what else can I think?' She was tempted to slap him. 'Perhaps your conscience pricks you. You told me yourself how Godebert didn't want us matched, how he hated Humbert for not defending him to Harald. And when it comes to marriage you've never defied your father.'

'How could I?' Vidar said, incredulous. 'I was a boy of seven the first time he betrothed me. Eleven when the girl died and he chose another. But she's dead too and this time the choice is mine. Even if he still lived, Godebert would have nothing to say about it. Do you believe me? Lindara, say you believe me.'

She felt her eyes fill with tears. 'I want to.'

Like every lord in Clemen, Vidar wore a dagger on his hip. Not taking his hurt gaze from her, he pulled it free of its sheath. The sharp blade glittered in the sunlight shafting through the casement window.

'Shall I open a vein like the pagans of old and call upon Voss the Unforgiving to witness my honour?'

Suddenly she felt ashamed. The pain in him now had nothing to do with old wounds. 'Of course not.'

'Lindara.' Lowering the blade, he shook his head. 'That you could *doubt* me . . .'

'I don't,' she said, snatching the dagger. 'And I'll prove it. Here's my oath to you!'

Before he could stop her she plunged the dagger-point into the heel of her hand. Blood welled, daubing her fair skin scarlet and staining the lace on her sleeve.

'*My lady!*'

Startled, she turned. Eunise stood in the open doorway, whey-faced and shaking. The tray she held slipped from her unsteady grasp. Wine, sugar wafers and red glass goblets crashed to the floor.

'Oh, Eunise! Clumsy creature!'

In the ensuing confusion, as Gillie remonstrated with Eunise and another servant cleaned away the mess, Lindara slid Vidar's dagger back in its sheath then nudged him aside. The look on his scarred face pricked her eyes with guilt.

'Vidar—'

'Hush,' he said, tenderly scolding. 'Lindara, I love you. Naught matters beyond that.'

She swallowed a sob. 'I know. And I love you.'

'I wish I could kiss you,' he murmured. 'But I think I should go. If your Eunise was a faery I'd have turned to stone by now.'

'Stupid woman,' she said, with a glance at her glaring maid. 'I swear, I'll marry you for no better reason than to be rid of her!'

That made him smile. 'How touching. My lady, see to your wounded hand.'

After Vidar was gone, the townhouse felt twice as empty. Desolate, she let Eunise scold her for playing with daggers. Suffered the woman to smear ointment on her small hurt and bind it with a strip of linen.

Then she returned to her embroidery . . . because there was nothing else to do.

CHAPTER SEVEN

The Pig Whistle's battered oak door banged open, letting out the heat, letting in the night's bluster and a tall, shambling figure wrapped neck to knee in a leather travelling cloak. Standing just inside the public room, the figure shook itself like a roused bear and stamped its booted feet. Raindrops spattered. Clots of mud smeared the uneven flagstoned floor. Nat Bevver and his brother Tid, seated at their ease nearest him, looked up from their tankards and cursed the newcomer in the way that invited trouble.

But Iddo, ever mindful, rapped his cudgel on the inn's wide, scarred oak counter. 'Shutten the bloody door, ye feggit! Do it look like ye done wandered into a byre?'

'Iss, iss, see me shutten yer feggit door!' the bear shouted back, ignoring the offended brothers, and made his point by kicking the door so hard he came near to knocking it off its hardy iron hinges. 'And now I'll be having ale off ye, Iddo, since this be an alehouse and I got m'self a powerful thirst.' Gloved fingers unlaced the leather cloak, then with a flourish and a fresh raindrop spatter whirled it free of his broad shoulders. 'So where be m'sweet Mollykins? Mizn't I standing here pining for a buss?'

With a shake of her head at Iddo, Molly stepped out of the shadows beside her inn's heat-billowing fireplace. 'I'd buss a farmer's bristled hog afore the pressing of my lips to yon muggy cheekin, Trader Culpyn!'

Dropping the leather cloak, Culpyn let out a pleased roar and spread his arms wide. 'Mollykins! M'sweetie honey posset, m'tossy love! Come to Denno! Mizn't he been dreaming of ye since the last time he was here?'

Smiles and chuckles from her customers. Even the cross-grained Bevver brothers snickered. Molly pinched her lips tight to keep her own smile private. Denno Culpyn of Maletti was a rogue, but charming with it. Made him double dangerous. But money was money and no need to feckle a man with an appetite like his and a purse just as generous. To keep Culpyn amenable and herself undisputed mistress of the inn, she insinuated her broad hips between the public room's close-packed stools and benches to pinch his bearded chin before scooping up his rain-soaked cloak and hanging it on one of the stout wall pegs by the door.

'Welcome back, Denno,' she said, letting her smile show. 'Been a gormful long time since ye raised my roof with yer bellowing.'

Culpyn nodded, mournful, as he stripped off his battered gloves. 'And it's broke m'heart, Moll, not pressing my arse to a Pig Whistle bench these many moons.' He tucked the gloves into his wide leather belt. 'Haven't I missed yer good ale and yer good mutton pies?'

Could be he did. But she'd surely missed the way he carried letters into Harcia for her and her most trusted customers, asking no more for the favour than a free pie here and there. She'd found others to play messenger while he was gone, but not a one of them was reliable – or discreet – like Denno Culpyn.

Needing that certainty again, she widened her smile. 'I be right glad to hear it.'

There was an empty stool up by the far end of Iddo's counter. With a crook of her finger she led Culpyn to it as the rest of her customers, losing interest in the trader, returned to their tankards and pies, their dice and cards, lively conversations and guarded privy dealings. All kinds came to the Pig Whistle, from every corner of the Marches and far beyond, to do all manner of things. If they raised her no ruckus, and were careful not to bring any Marcher lords' men to her door with swords drawn, she made sure to mind her own business and not theirs.

'Press yer arse there, Denno,' she said, jerking her thumb at the stool. 'I'll fetch yer ale and pie.'

'What be he doing back in the Marches, after no hide or hair of him for months?' Iddo muttered as she tapped a fresh keg of ale to fill one of her large tankards.

She shrugged, used to his crotchets and jealousies, and loving him no less. 'Not to fret. I'll find out.'

Her famed mutton pies kept warm in the kitchen out back. Leaving Iddo to his guarding of the Pig Whistle's public room, she pushed aside the heavy leather curtain and went to fetch one. First, though, she looked to be sure her son was still sleeping righty-tight. And he was, tucked into his kitchen truckle by the ovens. Grown so big now, it surprised her every time she smiled down at him. Her Benedikt. Nigh six months old, and all she had left of the man she'd wedded and bedded. And poor dead Diggin was his father, she wouldn't think elsewise. The trouble that saw her raped and widowed in one foul night, she'd not have it touch her lovely son. His raven-dark hair and brown eyes came from Diggin, not that other man. The one Iddo had killed for her, and axed to pieces, and scattered for the wolves and ravens from one side of the Marches to the other.

'Molly!' Iddo's raised voice stirred her out of bleak memory. 'Another mutton and a chicken pie, hoppish!'

She tucked sleeping Benedikt's blanket a little closer, stirred the iron pot of beef and barley stew on the hob, then slid three pies out of the warmery oven and onto a wooden paddle and carried them out for eating.

With an eager chortle Denno Culpyn rubbed his wool-covered paunch as she put his pie and ale before him on the counter. 'Mollykins, yer a queen among women.'

'Then ye'll not refuse a royal demand for one shiny silver ducat, Trader Culpyn,' she said, holding out her hand.

'A ducat?' His astonishment wasn't all pretend. 'When y'asked me for copper nibs the last time I was here?'

'We had ourselves a hard winter, Denno.'

His fingers fumbled in the purse laced tight to his belt. 'That's what I be hearing, Moll.'

'And I heard whisper ye'd forsaken us poor folk of Clemen and Harcia to make yer fortune elsewhere.'

'So I did, Moll, so I did,' said Culpyn, with a heaving sigh. He dropped a silver ducat onto her palm then picked up his tankard. 'For as much as I love ye, there looked to be tidier profits elsewhere. All

111

set I was, to spend what's left of m'years trading m'wares around the west coast of Cassinia, the Quartered Isles and the old Kingdom of Zeidica, and even the Treble Kingdom too. Had m'self a doughty little cog, a gullish wave-skipper if ever I saw one.'

For all he was a bawdy tale-teller, she could feel the honest regret in him. 'Things turned foul on ye, did they?'

'Foul?' Culpyn tipped ale down his throat. 'Mollykins, m'love, y'can blame Baldassare for my arse on yer stool, so y'can. Young he might be, scarce more than a stripling, but never was a pirate more curs't to an honest trader than yon feggit barnacle.'

She'd heard of Baldassare. Most everyone had heard of Baldassare, no matter they lived landlocked and could go their whole lives not catching a glimpse of ocean or sails. A stripling, as Denno said. Rumour aged him at barely sixteen, but so fierce and fearless that men twice his age followed him eagerly into bloody plunder. A demon-sprite, he sounded. She was glad she'd never meet him. She had both hands full in the Marches.

'Sailed yer fine galley into the pirate king and here this night to talk of it, Denno?' she said, slipping his payment into the pocket stitched inside her blouse. 'Don't be telling me yer a man out of luck!'

Culpyn shoved a brimming spoonful of pie into his mouth. 'Luck?' he mumbled around pastry flakes and drips of gravy. 'It be luck to sail into that rampageous brine-thief three times, Queen Moll? To have every horn button and silver bracelet and garnet earbob and all m'pretty furs and laces plucked from m'fingers three times? *Luck?*'

He looked so aggrieved she had to pat his shoulder. 'Luck that yer head wasn't plucked from yer neck, Denno. Or yer clankit bones thrown into the Sea of Sorrows.'

'Oh, iss?' Indignant, he glared. 'So it be luck, y'call it, that y'were robbed of y'man but the Pig Whistle never burned?'

Iddo, wiping ale-spill and listening, put up his chin. Molly waggled a finger at him, not looking away from the trader. 'If yer minded to be hurtful, Denno Culpyn, I'll show ye my door. The Pig Whistle's done without yer ducats these past months. I'm tolerable sure we can muddle along again.'

Culpyn turned red behind his rough beard. 'Mollykins,

Mollykins . . .' He fished a copper nib from his purse and pressed it on her. 'That for m'feggit rude tongue, m'darling.'

'Hah,' she said, but she slipped the nib out of sight then cuffed him, lightly. 'Yer feggit tongue and yer dribbly manners. That be gravy on my counter!'

A guilty hunching of his shoulders, and he swiped the wood clean with one work-rough finger. 'Y'be a scold, m'darling Molly. Can I sweeten y'mood with news?'

News was always welcome. In her own quiet, careful way she traded in news as much as ale and mutton pie and beds for the weary. 'Fill yer belly, Trader Culpyn,' she said, pretending indifference. 'I've a mort of folk to wink at this night. Eat yon pie, slosh yer ale, and could be I'll sit and chumble-chop with ye after.'

Ignoring Iddo, who was rolling his eyes at Denno Culpyn's cheer, she busied herself with Pig Whistle business. Darkness might've fallen outside but it was early yet, and her inn sold its ale and pies and stew until midnight. There'd be plenty more bellies to fill before she closed the low-ceilinged, raw-beamed public room and sent her overnight guests to their beds in the travellers' dormer. Tankards to fill too, and refill with good ale. More cooked pies to pull from the warmery oven, new pies to push into the hot baking oven. Jokes to laugh at, questions to answer, gossip to marvel on, harmless, friendly fumbles to refuse without hurt feelings. She did it all with a smile, never forgetting her luck. Twice she dropped a hint to men prepared to pay her for news she told no other soul. In between serving ale and pies, counting coin and keeping order, Iddo hauled up two fresh ale kegs from the cellar and brought in huge armfuls of logs to keep the oven busy and the fireplace belching heat.

The inn's door banged open and shut another dozen times after Culpyn's blustery arrival. She was a queen of innkeepers, she knew all but four of the newcomers by name. Of those four, three she'd not laid eyes on before. Men far from their proper homes in Pruges, with oiled dark hair and inked skin the colour of acorns, they spoke Cassinian with little twists and odd mouthings that told her they spoke otherwise with greater ease. From their sober but well-made wool tunics and hose, she judged them traders, with goods for the selling in both Clemen and Harcia. But she didn't ask. She minded her

113

business. Their coin was plentiful, their manners polite enough, and that made them welcome no matter where they hailed from.

The fourth man she knew at once for a herald, even if it was his first time at the Pig. Though in truth, he was hardly a man. A youth, stringy with sinew and touched blue by the cold, dressed in mud-splashed leather leggings and battered leather riding boots reaching past his knees and a well-worn leather cloak to keep out the rain. She shoved him onto a stool in front of the fire, pinching him quiet when he tried to protest. Iddo fetched him a hot milk toddy, splashed generous with brandy. Beneath his discarded riding cloak the herald wore a dark red linen tabard over his green doublet, its stitched device of an arch-backed grey cat announcing to all and sundry that he served Harcia's Lord Reimond, of Parsle Fountain.

'Pie, young ser?' said Molly, once his teeth had stopped chattering.

The herald handed her his emptied toddy mug. 'Pie, yes. I've a cavern in my belly big enough for three bears.'

'It be a cold night for hard riding,' she said, flicking a look to Iddo so he'd fetch the pie. 'Come far, have ye?'

'Far enough,' he said, grimacing. 'I left my lord at first light, and come dawn I'm on the road again. You've a bed for me?'

Any duke or count's herald was found a proper place to sleep in the Whistle, no matter who else had to be pushed out to the inn's dormer. It was the common law, strictly upheld by the four quarrelsome Marcher lords.

'A soft bed, iss,' she said, nodding. 'And a hot breakfast to see ye on the road. A silver ducat's cost, young ser, as yer duke's agreed.'

'Your man in the stable swore my horse would be well kept,' said the herald. His lips had coloured from blue to pink, and the cramped, shivering hunch was gone from his slight body. 'Oats and hay and a blanket.'

'Gwatkin's a good man for horses,' she said. 'And his lad is the same. Don't ye fret on that. Now if ye be warmed enough, I'll set ye at the counter for yer pie and ale.'

Denno Culpyn, eating his steady way through a bowl of stew, gave the Harcian herald a friendly nod. 'Ser.'

Returning the nod, the herald eased himself onto a stool beside the trader. 'Good eve.'

'Might ye be travellin' all the way south to Eaglerock, and the duke of Clemen's castle?' Culpyn enquired, politely enough.

The herald hunched his shoulder. 'I don't speak of my lord's business.'

Molly caught Denno Culpyn's interested eye and frowned him to silence. Last thing she needed was word going back to the great men of Harcia that their heralds couldn't sup ale or eat a pie under her roof without some stranger sniffing and sidling where he had no right. The Pig Whistle stood handy at the biggest crossroads in the Marches, where all four of the Marcher lords' domains touched borders. Men of every stripe and allegiance passed her front door from sunup to sundown. It was the biggest and best inn for a dozen leagues around, but that didn't mean she could afford to cause offence.

'Young ser,' she said to the herald, 'I've mutton pie and chicken. Which would ye like?'

'I'll take one of each,' said the herald. 'And some hard cheese, and your largest tankard of ale.' He slipped off the stool, his gaze insolent and daring. 'For five nobles, mistress innkeep. Not a silver ducat.'

She swallowed, hard. 'Five nobles. On account of the botheration. Aye.'

'And I'll sup in my room.'

'Of course, young ser. Iddo?'

'Follow me,' said Iddo, displeased and nearly grunting. As the herald traipsed out in Iddo's wake, Molly rounded on Denno Culpyn and thrust her hand at him.

'Mollykins, m'sweet!' Culpyn protested. 'I was only being friendly!'

'Being nosy is what ye were,' she retorted. 'And it's half a silver ducat ye cost me.'

'Ye do know he'll likely pocket those five nobles he wrung from ye?'

If the herald did or didn't, that wasn't her trouble. She frowned at Culpyn, fiercely. Grumbling, the trader fished in his purse and counted out five small silver coins.

115

'It's mercy y'should have on me, Moll, all the troubles I've seen.'

'It's mercy I'm showing ye, Denno,' she said, plucking the nobles from his reluctant grasp. 'Have I sent ye to sleep in the stable with yer mules?'

'*One* mule I've got to m'name, Moll. That's how far yon curs't pirate sunk me, and him never to be found for hanging, they say, on account of foul, secret sorceries and dark conjurations that keep him and his sharkish men hidden from the world.'

She couldn't care less about such fanciful nonsense. 'Any more moaning off ye, Denno, and I'll have mercy on that mule of yers, and set ye to sleep in a ditch!'

Heaving a sigh, Culpyn poked his spoon into his stew. 'Y'be a hard woman, Molly.'

'And don't ye forget it.'

A raised hand from one of the Pruges traders at their table against the end wall turned her away. She fetched their empty tankards, brought them back to the counter and started filling them with fresh ale.

'See, Moll, y'do me wrong,' said Denno Culpyn, worse than any dog with a bone. 'I was only going to say to the young ser that if he do be heading Eaglerock way, he'll find it slow riding when he's still leagues from the city gates. The countryside down south be cragged bellyful with folk, on account of Clemen's upheavals.' He waggled his eyebrows. 'Y'know of that?'

Iddo's hands were big enough to carry three foam-topped tankards, but hers weren't. She loaded a wooden tray and hefted it. 'I've heard a thing or two.'

'Iss, m'sweetie Mollykins, but I'll noddle my pot if ye heard—'

Only a fool collected whispers in the open. 'Denno Culpyn, y'feggit, be I look to ye a woman on the snatch for a gossip?'

Leaving him to scrape his stew bowl clean and sputter heart-wounded protests, she served the Pruges traders their ale, gleaned a mite of useful tattle from them, then made sure to seeing her other customers were happy. She threw a few casts of dice at one table, laughing when she lost, offering one free ale to each man for her forfeit, and tarried at another to ask woodsman Rankin how fared his son, caught beneath a falling tree and hobbling yet. She settled an argument between the Bevver brothers, who brawled at the hint of a whisper of a slight, drank the good health of fur-trapper Lange for his wife's first babe-quickening, and let it be a brave and bonny boy, aye! Forester Lugo pulled out his whittled pipe and cheered the room with reedy music. Feet tapped, hands clapped, and for a time the world's many woes were drownded.

The door banged open and closed again, quickly. Molly saw who it was and rapped her knuckles on the counter. 'Iddo! Phemie's here. Keep these rascals tidy while her and me talk out back.'

'Moll,' said Phemie, sliding her heavy leather satchel from her shoulder to the kitchen's worn flagstones. 'I'm parched for tea, besom.'

'Besom yerself,' she said, grinning. 'T'aint me the wizened old healer woman.'

Phemie wrinkled her nose. 'Old is as old does. I be not fifty yet.'

'And ye'll see that a mort of years afore me, ye will.'

'Tush! And ye call yerself my friend!'

Making the tea, Molly chuckled. 'There be pie, if ye want one. Or stew. Help yerself.'

Comfortable in the Pig Whistle's warm, rich-smelling kitchen, Phemie cast her eye over sleeping Benedikt, gave a pleased nod, then ladled beef and barley stew into a bowl. Fragrant, meaty steam wafted from the cast-iron pot.

'Busy night.'

'Busy enough,' she agreed, feeling her belly gurgle. 'I'll sleep well, it be sure, once the door's bolted for the night.'

Phemie wasn't idly called the best healer in the Marches. 'Ye should be eating of yer own stew, Molly,' she said sternly, perched on the edge of a stool. 'Yer cheeks be wanting good colour, hen.'

'That's yer old eyes, playing tricks.'

Phemie's bowl was half-emptied already. 'Cheek me, besom, and that'll be my old hand playing tricks on yer arse. Ye said ye'd be finding another girl to help out. Where is she?'

'Dancing in the woods with the faeries,' Molly retorted, and dripped honey into Phemie's mug of tea. 'What be the use of finding another girl? She'll up and dance off with a passing peddler, like that Tossie did. Iddo and me manage, Phemie. Now, did ye bring the tooth posset for Benedikt?'

Phemie swallowed the last of her beef and barley. 'I brought ye the posset and a warning. There be spotted tongue in the eastern Marches. Best ye keep an eye on folk coming in from that direction.'

Spotted tongue? Curse it. 'Have ye told Lord Wido?'

'Word be sent,' said Phemie. With her stew bowl empty, she blew on the tea to cool it for drinking. 'To him and Lord Bayard, for Harcia. T'aint so dire yet. I've caught three men with it, none so bad the knife was needed. But ye do recall the last time the spot paid us a visit.'

She surely did. Nigh on thirty Marcher folk with their tongues sliced out of their mouths. Four had been children, ruined for life. *Traders*. They brought more than spices and ivory and fine fabrics from foreign lands, they did.

'I'll see Iddo looks at every new tongue till ye say the danger's passed.' She pulled a face. 'But folk won't be pleased.'

'Then I'll have old Gadifer drop his jaw and wag his stump at them who complain till they see reason,' said Phemie. 'Or do y'want the Pig Whistle burned to the ground like the lords burned the Jangling Bell for letting spotted tongue go by?'

'No!' Molly snatched up Phemie's used bowl and spoon and stowed them in the big oak tub for washing, later. 'Flap yer lips on that misery, would ye? When Bamfry hanged himself for seeing his doughty Bell a bonfire?'

'Bamfry were a weak-kneed gromble,' snapped Phemie. 'And that yer not. Ye've lost a sight more than Bamfry ever did and here ye be, proud and strong and thriving.'

Molly sniffed. Her friend's kind words touched her, but she was never one for being mawkish. 'So ye brought me a remedy for Benedikt's teething, and news I ain't pleased to hear. What else?'

Knowing when to leave well alone, Phemie hoisted her leather satchel onto the big kitchen bench and hauled out the pills and powders and possets a good inn kept to hand for the comfort and succour of its guests. Molly stowed them with care in her doctoring chest, locked it again, then handed over the six nobles good innkeeping cost her.

'Will ye stay the night?' she asked, as Phemie packed up her satchel. 'There always be room for ye.'

'Can't,' said Phemie, regretful. 'I be on my way to a first birthing at Deep Pond. The goatman's wife, with twins, poor soul. She's skinny as a lizard through the hips, so I'm like to be kept there nigh on a week. That's if the birthing don't kill her. Send word to me there if you see a spotted tongue.'

Two men came into the Pig Whistle as Phemie went on her way. Torbyn Groat, one of Lord Bayard's riding men, charged with keeping peace along the Marches' roads. The other was Lord Jacott's farm steward, Hamelen, come in as he'd said he would. Heart thumping a little harder, Molly caught Iddo's eye. Unhurried, he collected four empty tankards and joined her behind the counter.

'Trouble?' he said, his voice low.

Oh, she did love Iddo. He was her man of oak, her iron spine. 'Spotted tongue, Phemie says. Coming in from the east.'

No need to say more. Iddo put the tankards on the counter and made his way to the newcomers, genial and unbending. She couldn't hear what he said, but she saw the men startle, then let him look into their open mouths.

'Spotted tongue?' said Denno Culpyn, frowning. 'That be curs't news, Moll. I'm clean, I swear, but so y'don't have to ask . . .'

Coming close, she inspected his open mouth. 'Clean as a whistle. I be obliged, Denno.'

Iddo was coming back, Torbyn at his heels. Hamelen had settled near the door, in place of the Bevver brothers. They must have tumbled home while she was in the kitchen with Phemie.

'Ser,' she greeted Torbyn. 'Peace to ye, and welcome. Tell Iddo what ye be after and he'll see ye well supped. And can I make known to ye the good trader Denno Culpyn, come back to us after many adventures? Denno be full of a pirate tale, so he is, and eager to tell it.'

She'd raised her voice on that, loud enough to stir the interest of the tables nearest the counter. As men turned their way, in the mood for a rolic, she cocked a hinting eyebrow at the trader.

'A pirate tale, aye!' Culpyn said, leaping up from his stool. 'Tell me, friends! Have ever y'met a man what can swear t'ye true he's three times faced the pirate king Baldassare and lived to tell of it?'

And that was that. Not even Lugo's piping made for better

entertainment. Leaving Culpyn to his energetic mummery, and Iddo to tend Torbyn and the bar, she fetched a mutton pie from the kitchen, where Benedikt slept on, drew a fresh tankard of ale and carried both to the table by the door.

'Molly,' said Hamelen. He'd pulled a dice-pouch from his belt and was clacking the carved and painted horn squares between his scarred, nimble fingers.

She put down the ale and pie. 'Good eve, Hamelen. How goes Lord Jacott in these tumbled times?'

'His lordship goes well,' said Hamelen, tossing the dice aside. 'Though the times, they do be tumbled.'

'Have ye good news for me, Hamelen? It's sorrowed I'd be if I had to buy the Pig Whistle's mutton elsewhere.'

Lord Jacott's farm steward winked. 'Have a seat, Molly. We can natter mutton and geese and duck while I feast on yer pie.'

'– and there the curs't young barnacle stood, I tell ye, black as moonless night and thrice more the danger, even though he be scarce old enough to grow his beard! And if I dared ye to tell me what happened next, ye never could. So I'll tell ye free and easy, so I will. Friends, best y'pin back yer ears and believe every word . . .'

Hamelen snorted into his tankard. 'Now there be a rascal.'

'And a rogue,' she agreed. With a swift slip and slide of her fingers, she plucked a sealed letter from her apron-pocket and passed it to him, sleight-handed. 'But harmless.'

The letter vanished inside his workman's wool doublet. 'Another ten dressed chickens, yes?'

She smiled. 'And five more I'll pay for, Hamelen. And three geese and six duck. Yer last pigeons were scrawny. I'll hold till summer for the next. And I'll have three sides of mutton. Not too fatty, mind. Now, what news from Clemen? Be the naughty whispers true?'

'True enough,' said Hamelen, who traded Lord Jacott's farm produce . . . and other things on the side. 'Clemen's council tried to keep it secret but servants talk, and a lordling from Harcia rattled roundabout coin in the right places. B'aint a man-at-arms in Clemen be paid so much not a one would hold out his hand for more.'

Molly felt her belly tighten. So. Rumour had it right. Duke Harald was dead. And his duchess. And his son. All slain beneath their own roof where they'd thought to be safe. A terrible business, surely, whether the duke was loved or not.

'Be there a new duke?'

Digging into his pie, Hamelen shrugged. 'There be a man claiming so, by right of Berold's blood.'

Ah. That would be Duke Harald's bastard cousin. Roric. A sure recipe for mischief, him, not being pure of birth. If other claims were shouted, trouble would soon follow.

'Lord Jacott,' she said, her heart thudding. 'Does he sniff ructions in Clemen?'

'He do look a mite put out more than usual,' Hamelen admitted. 'He be called south to Eaglerock castle, and court. Lord Wido too. It's fast they'll be riding, no fanfare.' A swift, sharp look. 'But that b'aint Pig Whistle gossip, Molly.'

As if she needed telling. She knew which news to sell, and which to hold close. 'Do they look to stay here, passing through?'

Another shrug. 'Stay or fresh themselves. The lords and their high stewards will say which, not me.'

'*Have ye heard it told that yon beardless barnacle, Baldassare, would dance a man over a ship's side sooner than ask a ransom for his life? Well, friends, if y'heard it, I be here to tell ye, t'aint no lie! Didn't I see that young demon dance a good man to his death, with these eyes in m'own head?*'

Culpyn's wild tale had caught the imagination of every man in the room. Even the traders from Pruges, who must have pirate tales of their own, seemed amused. Molly leaned closer to Hamelen, not wanting to shout above the cries and urgings for the trader to go on, go on, what dread thing happened next?

'And what be the news from Harcia? Ructioned Clemen'll see them dancing, for sure.'

'Like a jester's dogs,' said Hamelen, leaning close from his side. 'But word is Aimery be holding off, for now. Still bruised from that killing business with his heir, he is, and not eager for more strife.'

And that was wise of Harcia's duke, to see how the winds in Clemen blew. 'So, Hamelen. Have you met him, this bastard Duke Roric?'

Hamelen swallowed ale. Belched. 'No.'

Neither had she, but she knew a little of him. Sharp with a sword but kindly, it was said. Phemie had stitched him once, after a skirmish with Harcia's Marcher men-at-arms out past Bollard's Marsh. Nasty business, that. Seven men and their horses lost. Harcia's Lord Egbert should've known better than to stand sword on that boggy ground. Them who escaped the skirmish said Harald's bastard cousin retreated soon after, so no more Harcians would perish for their feggit lord.

'Clemen wants this Roric, do they?'

'Eaglerock wants him.'

And in Clemen, the lords of Eaglerock were kings. Or nearly.

'– does he look like? Why, black as night, didn't I tell ye? And muscled like a hunting cat all the way from Agribia. Gold hoops in his ears, a ruby set in his nose, here, and emeralds braided into his hair. And his eyes, his eyes, green as the Sea of Sorrows where he plies his curs't trade. Friends, if y'asked me, I'd swear his mother was a soul-eater.'

'Lord Jacott,' Molly said, as her belly tightened again. 'Does he stomach this bastard?'

Tankard empty, pie eaten, Lord Jacott's farm steward picked up his dice then stood. 'I need to piss.'

It was his rough way of telling her he was done. Crude he might be, but she could live with it. Had to live with it, didn't she? The Pig Whistle made a good part of its living on the secrets Hamelen sold.

Hamelen, and a few others like him.

The farm steward went outside to the easery, and she joined Iddo at the bar to serve ale and bowls of stew and the last of her famous pies. Culpyn reached the end of his tale and laughed as he was cheered and clapped for a right one. He took himself off to bed in the dormer soon after, too tired, he said, for more jibberjab. But he'd happily chumble with her come the morning, and take any letters she wanted carried north into Harcia. Lugo started piping again and the night rolled on gently, customers going home or to their traveller beds in dribs and drabs till the oft turned-and-emptied hour glass behind the counter emptied for the last time, and had Iddo calling time.

She bolted the door behind the last man out and rested her forehead on the old oak, so tired. Sighed to feel Iddo's lips press against her mussy hair.

'I'll pass eye over the privy rooms and the dormer,' he said, rubbing her back. 'Then take Gwatkin and his lad their pies and ale, and see they got no stable strife.'

Her Iddo had a rough face and a broad nose. No woman would call him handsome. Diggin, he'd been handsome, but his good looks hadn't saved him. A living plain man was more use any day than a handsome one, buried.

'And I'll wipe down in here,' she said, smiling at him through her weariness. 'Then start on the kitchen.'

He pursed his lips. 'Hamelen?'

'Had news,' she said. 'We can talk on it later. Ye make sure that hoity-toity herald be sweet.'

The knock on the Pig Whistle's front door came as she mopped ale from the final bench in the public room. Curse it. Iddo hadn't quenched the bar's welcome torch yet. Dropping her damp wiping-cloth, she trudged back to the door, drew the bolt and pulled, ready to turn away the most parched of customers.

A girl stood before her, soaked to the skin, flame-flickered and shivering. In her arms, a bundled baby. It was mewling like a cat.

'Help us, mistress,' the girl whispered. 'Me and my brother, we're near to perished. Please, please, help. Don't turn us away.'

CHAPTER EIGHT

'– or where she come from! Keep her? Molly, ye've slopped yer common sense out with the swill!'

'I done no such thing, Iddo. Peg yer lips, man. Seems to me she be spirit-sent, for Tossie.'

'Oh, Moll . . .'

The voices softened, so Ellyn couldn't hear them any more through the heavy leather curtain behind the bar. Feeling sick, her belly a tangled ball of hope and dread, she held Liam in the crook of one arm and with her free hand plucked at her slowly drying linen skirt. The inn's fire burned boldly, not yet banked for the night. Its heat was like a faery-favour, reaching all the way to her bones. She was so *cold*. Aye, and hungry. They'd feed her soon, wouldn't they, the man and woman squabbling about her behind that leather curtain?

Liam squirmed a little, whimpering, grown so thin and feeble since she'd fled with him from Heartsong. Her milk was all but dried up, nightmares and not enough food or sleep to blame. The bastard Roric was to blame for it; that wicked, murdering man. That thief.

'Hush, lamb, hush,' she whispered, pressing the babe to her flattened chest. 'They'll feed you soon, lovey. They'll feed my little lamb, they will.'

They had to, surely. Whatever they feared of her, they couldn't fear an innocent child. Not when they didn't know who he was. Not when she'd never tell them, not ever. Not even if they beat her until her blood ran.

The leather curtain behind the bar creaked as it was pushed aside. Out came the big woman, Molly, and close behind her the even bigger man she'd called Iddo. He carried a serving paddle laden with a tankard, an earthenware cup, a thick slice of buttered rye bread and a bowl wafting aromatic steam. Ellyn swallowed the rush of juices into her mouth.

'Sit, girl, sit,' said Molly, slapping the bar's wide counter. 'Y'should be warm and dry by now.'

'Yes'm,' she murmured, approaching. 'Thank you.'

Molly held out her arms. 'And best ye give me that babe,' she added. 'Afore ye drop it.'

'Him,' she said, her hold tightening. 'Willem.' The name she'd decided for Liam the night she'd fled Heartsong. Not his true name, but near enough. 'He's Willem. He's my brother.'

'So he be Willem,' said Molly. Her lips were soft, but her eyes were watchful. 'And what name d'ye go by, lass?'

The woman's arms were still outstretched, and her man Iddo showed no sign of putting that food down on the counter. Since running from Heartsong she'd not let Liam go, not once. But she

124

was so hungry, and the man Iddo was staring. He reminded her of the heavy-shouldered black-and-brown guard dogs that prowled Eaglerock castle and its grounds at night.

'I'm Alys,' she said, her voice catching, and gave her precious lamb to Molly.

The big woman gathered Liam to her pillowy chest. He didn't protest, not even a whispery wail. 'Iddo.'

That was enough for the man to thump down the bread and bowl, the tankard sloshing with ale and the mug. There was a carved wooden spoon, too. Giddy with hunger, Ellyn nearly snatched it. Nearly wept at the first taste of warm beef and barley. She ate standing up, not needing a stool. Dipped the bread into the stew's gravy and swallowed, hardly chewing. Swallowed the ale after, rich with malt. She could feel Molly watching her, and Iddo. Judging her. Summing her up. She didn't care what they thought of her gobbling, no better than a pigherder and his pigs. All she wanted was somewhere safe for Liam.

'The lass could do with more stew, Iddo,' said Molly. 'And y'can bring me one of Benedikt's suck-tits.'

Iddo's sparse brows tightened into a frown, but he retreated behind the leather curtain again. Molly dipped a finger into the earthenware cup. When she pulled it out, it dripped white.

'Goat's milk,' she said as Liam wriggled in her firm grasp, scenting food. 'Nice and warm. Good for a baby. He'll take it from a suck-tit?'

Ellyn nodded. 'Yes. But—'

'My son sleeps in the kitchen, Alys. Benedikt. He be a few months older than Willem, here, by the look of it, but still on the milk. How long since yer brother supped?'

'A day and a bit,' she whispered. 'There was a village. A woman milked a drop from her cow. 'Twas all she could spare and I had no coin for more.'

Molly's gaze was sharp again. 'Y'took to the road with a sucking babe and not enough coin to keep him in milk?'

Tears rose, misty blinding. She'd never thought she could dry up so fast. And the copper nibs she'd run with, that were spent mostly on Liam, they'd trickled through her fingers like water.

'I never meant to harm him. I love Willem, I swear I do.'

Iddo came back with another bowl of stew and a suck-tit for Liam. There was such relief he'd be fed properly for the first time in days that her knees buckled. She dropped onto a stool.

'Hmm,' said Molly, then shook her head. 'Ah well. It be done. Best ye eat up, girl. Ye be almost as starved as yer brother.'

So she ate the second bowl of stew then wiped both bowls clean with the last of the rye bread, as Molly poured warm goat's milk into the kid leather suck-tit and filled Liam's belly. Not too fast, though. She knew not to make him sick. All the while, Iddo stood wide-legged by the leather curtain with his arms folded and his forehead creased. His head was good as bald, what little brownish grey hair he had scraped to stubble. There were old scars on his freckled scalp. From the size of him, and the promise of fierceness, she thought he could likely thump a drunken man senseless with one fist.

Molly's hair was long and rusty red, loosened by hard work from its braid which she'd pinned to her head. She was much younger than Lady Morda but looked just as stern, even though her deep-set brown eyes were gentle in her broad face as she fed Liam his warm goat's milk. She held him close, and easily. She knew about the care of babes, that much was no lie.

'Where d'ye hail from, Alys?' she asked, not shifting her gaze from eagerly sucking Liam. 'Be ye a Marcher lass?'

It was too dangerous to say yes. The Marches were a strange, mistrustful place where foreigners wandered freely. They were full of folk who obeyed lords from both Clemen and Harcia – or sometimes neither. No better than mules were Marcher folk, Duke Harald used to say. Not one thing or t'other and never to be trusted outright. Too often them as lived in the Marches liked to think they ruled themselves. Oh, how cross the duke would be if he knew she'd brought his son here.

Harald.

Ellyn felt her heart seize, remembering he was dead. Slain by the bastard Roric, who'd sent that cripple Lord Vidar to see Liam dead too.

'Alys,' said Iddo, his voice like gravel beneath a warhorse's iron-shod hooves. 'Ye give answer t'Mistress Molly.'

She flinched. 'Beg pardon,' she mumbled, shivering again even

126

though she was almost dry down to her skin. 'I'm from Clemen. A village. Berrydown.'

'T'aint known t'me,' said Molly, smiling at Liam and rocking him so the milk would settle. 'It be a goodly few leagues from the Pig Whistle?'

'A long way, yes. Days and days from the Marches.'

'Days and days,' said Molly. She looked up, her gaze sharp. 'And what brings ye to my door, lass, trudging days and days till ye near kill this child with hunger?'

She'd cobbled together a story after deciding on Liam's new name, knowing their only hope was to make the tale sad enough for pity. Over and over she'd told it, to carters and peddlers and milkmaids and alewives, with only the name of the village changing. She'd told it so many times she almost believed it, and didn't blink once as she stared into Molly's unsmiling face.

'If I'd stayed in Berrydown we'd be dead, we would,' she said, earnestly. 'My da, he's an ale-sop. He drinks and he drinks. He lost his temper with my ma, and he beat her head in. He beat me too. Lots of times. Broke my bones, once. See?' She thrust out her left forearm, snapped in a tumble from a farmer's bucking calf when she was six. Though it had healed well enough, there was a bump and a smudged mark like an old bruise. 'I was scared he'd beat Willem, I was. I had to run, to keep him safe.'

Molly raised eyebrows at Iddo, and Iddo pinched his lips. 'Her arm's been broke, man, y'can see that,' the woman said. 'And y'know better than most what an ale-sop be like.'

Iddo's folded arms tightened. 'The folk in Berrydown couldn't help ye, girl?'

'They never helped my ma.'

Still comfortably standing, Molly settled Liam's head against her shoulder. Full of milk and drowsy, he smacked his little rosebud lips and sighed. 'What age be ye, Alys?'

'I'm fifteen.'

'Poke out yer tongue.'

Bewildered, Ellyn looked at her. 'Mistress Molly?'

'Do as yer told!' said Iddo, stepping closer. 'Poke it out, or be off with ye.'

She poked out her tongue. Iddo peered at it.

'She be clean, Moll,' he said, and sounded sorry.

'There be a sickness, lass, comes and goes in these parts,' said Molly. 'The Marcher lords be mighty strict on it.'

Fear burned her. 'Willem.'

'He be fine,' said Molly. 'If he was sick, ye'd be sick with him. But to be sure, lass, answer this. Did ye come into the Marches from east Clemen? And best be warned, I can sniff a lie like a truffle hog.'

She didn't know what a truffle hog was, but she believed the woman. 'West,' she said, truthful. 'I swear it on Willem's life.'

Silent, Molly stared at her. She stared back, unblinking. She didn't need a fancy mirror from Ardenn to know she looked a fright, like the worst kind of wagtail strumpet who lifted her skirts behind one of Eaglerock township's misbegot slummish taverns. She'd not bathed herself head to toe since Heartsong. Her skirt was mud-stained, her hair brambled with knots. Her ragged fingernails were filthy and her breath stank. She knew it. If Iddo, misliking her, rode roughshod over Molly, if the woman let him . . .

'We had a lass here,' said Molly, her eyelids drooped half shut. 'Tossie. Yer age, she was. She served ale and pies, and cleaned the inn. She fed the hens and fetched their eggs. She milked the cow and the goat and minded my son Benedikt when I told her. Then last week she danced herself off with a peddler.'

Hope stirred. 'I never would.'

'She worked hard, did Tossie,' said Molly. Her rough, careworn palm pressed to Liam's cheek. 'Time to time, her fingers bled.'

'I don't fear hard work, Mistress Molly. I fear dying in a ditch with Willem.'

Molly shifted her hand to rest against Liam's gently breathing chest. His filthy blanket was in tatters. His linen nightshirt, the plain one she'd snatched up because a baby wearing it wouldn't look like a duke's son, it was filthy too. They shamed her, the blanket and nightshirt. But at least he looked like an ale-sop's brat and not the rightful duke of Clemen.

'I see shadows in yer eyes, Alys,' Molly said, looking up. 'I see shadows and gnarly dreams. D'ye bring trouble with ye under my roof?'

'Iss,' said Iddo. 'Keep the babe if ye must, Moll. But send this troublesome slut on her way.'

Ellyn leapt to her feet. Curse it. If only she hadn't sold poor Emun's dagger. 'You can't. Willem's mine. I don't bring any trouble. I'll work hard. I'll earn our keep. I'm not some Tossie, sniffing at peddlers, and I don't care if my fingers bleed. I'd do more than bleed for Willem. I'd die for him, I would.'

Molly lifted one thick, straight eyebrow. 'And would ye kill for him, lass?'

She already had. Nelda and Tygo. She'd do it again and never blink. '*Yes.*'

'Iddo,' said Molly. 'Can ye manage without me?'

Iddo dragged a broad hand across his chin. 'Moll . . .'

Molly's smile was crooked, and something of a comfort. 'Don't ye fret, man. I b'aint in danger. Be about yer business so I can tend to this babe, and Benedikt. Sun'll be up soon enough and we need our shuteye, we do.'

'Thank you,' Ellyn whispered, as Iddo stamped his way out. 'Mistress Molly, thank you.'

'No need for thanks, lass,' Molly said, briskly. 'Ye'll earn yer keep, never fear. Now come with me to the kitchen. We'll bathe yer brother there, then it'll be bed for both of ye. Ye'll have Tossie's room and the truckle Benedikt grew out of. I've his little clothes too. Ye can have them, and the skirts Tossie left behind her.'

Tears slid down her cheeks. 'I'm ever so grateful. You won't be sorry. I promise.'

'No?' Molly held the heavy leather curtain aside. 'I'd best not be. Now hush, and come along. I don't abide gabbiness, lass. Be warned.'

Peddler-sniffing Tossie had slept in the Pig Whistle's attic, tucked tight into a corner against the inn's steeply sloping thatched roof. There'd been more room in Lady Morda's closet. Liam's little truckle and a sleeping pallet took up most of the bumpy wooden floor. Three pegs on the wall were for holding her clothes. There was a pot to piss in, one tiny window behind an unpainted shutter, a single tallow candle for light and a narrow shelf to sit it on.

'This once ye can sleep till ye wake, lass,' said Molly, looming large in the doorway. 'Or till the babe wakes ye. Likely that'll come first. On the morrow ye'll use a tub, and when ye be presentable then we'll see what be what.'

She'd already settled Liam into her son's outgrown truckle, after bathing him in the kitchen and dressing him in a fresh nightshirt and a little woollen cap. He was fast asleep now beneath comforting sheepskin, his cheeks pink again, the horrible pinched look of him gone at last.

'Yes'm,' said Ellyn, bobbing. She forgave the woman her bossy ways because Liam was warm and fed and safe. 'Thank you.'

Molly's watchful gaze swept her up and down. 'Work hard, Alys. Mind yer manners. Mind Iddo. Give me no nincy-nonce and ye'll call the Pig Whistle home. That be my word, and my word be trustful.'

The door closed behind her. Ellyn let out a shuddery breath, bent low to put the smelly candle on its shelf then dropped to her pallet. It was straw-stuffed and lumpy, the coarse, roughspun blankets full of scratch. But after so many cold and hungry days on the road, now she felt like a duchess.

The thought woke memories of Argante, and she shivered.

Dead. They're all dead. Duke Harald and Duchess Argante and Lady Morda and Emun.

Nelda, too. And Nelda's bastard brat. The little baby Tygo.

Stifling a sob, she pulled her knees to her chest and buried her face. Would she never forget? Would the blood and spilled bowels haunt her till she drew her last breath? Would she wake every night for the rest of her life, seeing the flames devour the splashed oil, the silks and linens, the blood-soaked hair, the hacked flesh and split bone? Would she never stop smelling them as they blackened and burned?

Please, spirits. Please, please, let me forget.

She'd left Nelda and her brat to die because protecting Liam was her duty. She'd set the nursery ablaze because she had to confuse Harald's enemies, and she'd run because staying would have cost Liam his life. But she'd always meant to run back, as soon as she heard the danger was past. As soon as Harald put an end to his bastard cousin's wicked plot.

But that never happened. Instead a terrible truth had escaped

Heartsong and whispered fearful through the surrounding countryside. Duke Harald's cousin had slain him and taken the castle for himself. The duke's wife was dead too, and his infant son. Worse yet, Clemen's council and its great lords were with the bastard Roric. So Clemen had a new duke. And if he knew Liam was living . . .

She'd had no choice but the Marches. It was a rough place full of rough men, true, where duchy law bent to Marcher law and lawless men roamed and weren't always caught and punished. But the risk was well worth it. Not a soul knew her here. No one could question her story. She was Alys from Berrydown and little Willem was her brother. It meant she was dead to her parents, but she couldn't help that. Besides, they had another daughter and two strapping sons. She wouldn't be missed long. They might not miss her at all.

Warm in his truckle bed, Liam wriggled and sighed. Ellyn rolled it a little closer, and smiled down at his candle-shadowed face. Her precious lamb. Only . . . no. That wasn't right. Not any more. Liam was her precious falcon. Heir to his father's duchy and Clemen's Falcon Throne. Still smiling at him, she pulled up her travel-stained skirt and groped for the torn strip of linen she'd bound tight around her right thigh. There it was. And bound within it, Duke Berold's precious ring. Liam's inheritance and the proof that one day would see him topple that bastard Roric from his stolen throne and into his traitor's grave. On the morrow she'd find a place to hide it, and then she'd keep it safe there until Liam was old enough for revenge.

And if that meant she must be a Tossie in the Pig Whistle for the next fifteen or twenty years . . .

Then I'll do it. I'll be Tossie. And I won't let Liam forget.

Burning with fresh purpose, she pinched out the stinking tallow candle. Then she wrapped a blanket close to ward off the night's chill and bent low over Liam.

'Here's our secret, my loveykins,' she whispered, in the silence and the dark. 'Here's the truth, that you can't never tell a soul. Your father was brave Duke Harald of Clemen. Them wicked lords Humbert and Aistan and Vidar, they betrayed him, and the bastard Roric *murdered* him. The bastard stole your throne. But when you're grown, my little Liam, you're going to take it back.'

* * *

131

Curled up in bed beneath a goosedown quilt, in the shelter of Iddo's strong arms, Molly felt his heartbeat thud through her in the darkness and knew she was safe.

Iddo cleared his throat, restless and unhappy. 'I know ye be certain, but I won't lie to ye, Moll. I say the girl be trouble. Her and the brat.'

She dug her smooth fingernails into his broad, naked chest. 'He b'aint a brat, Iddo. Poor tiddy mite, with his miseries.'

'So ye believe the girl's tattle?'

'D'ye say ye don't? D'ye say no man never sotted himself sense-less and laid about his wife and babes with his fists, or whatever he could find?'

'No,' said Iddo, grudging. 'But Moll—'

'Y'know there be them as says I weren't never raped and widowed by them roguish men,' she said, sitting up. 'Y'know there be them as says Benedikt be yer bastard son on me, and we killed Diggin, Iddo, ye and me, to be clear of him. Ye know that?'

Iddo growled. 'I know any arse what says so where I can hear him, he'll be sorry.'

She lay down again, and took back his shoulder for her pillow. 'Men tattle, Iddo,' she said, as he pulled the comforter close. 'Can't cut out their lying tongues and say they had the spot. Ye got no proof the girl be a diddler. And the babe was half dead, Iddo. Ye'd turn him away?'

'No,' said Iddo, after a long silence. His cheek rested against her unbound hair, his slow breathing a lullaby. 'I be rough, but I b'aint cruel.'

She pressed her lips to his warm skin. 'Yon tiddy mite can grow up Benedikt's brother. I can't give him one else, Iddo. Them roguish men saw to that, didn't they?'

His arms tightened around her. It was her great sorrow, and he knew it, that she was barren since Benedikt's hard birth. Phemie, she'd done her best, but even she couldn't change what the raping and the hard birth had done. This babe, though, this little Willem, he could. He could be the second son she'd always wanted.

'And the girl?' said Iddo. 'If she be another Tossie, a slutty tramp and a wagtail, and never worth her keep?'

Then she'd be feckled and out on her arse, that Alys. But not Willem. Little Willem, he'd stay behind. She'd fed him, she'd bathed him, she'd seen his sweet smile.

Willem be mine.

'I say ye be wrong, Iddo,' she said, soothing. 'The lass'll earn her keep. How else d'ye think she'll live? She be orphaned, good as. The Pig Whistle be her home now. We'll have no trouble, ye'll see.'

Iddo grunted. 'Iss, Moll. If ye say so.'

'I do, Iddo. I do.'

And it seemed she was right. Young Alys minded her business and worked hard and showed no interest in men. Which was good for her, after Tossie. But three days later a different kind of trouble came to the inn.

'Mistress Moll, Mistress Moll! You're wanted, Mistress Moll!'

Molly put down her cleaver, wiped her mutton-mucky hands on a damp cloth, made sure Willem stayed sleeping in his truckle, then pushed aside the leather curtain out to the public room. It was late in the afternoon, the lull between nuncheon trade and night-time busyness. Only six passing-through men supping on ale and coddled eggs in the public room. A seventh man stood at the bar's oak counter, Alys dithery beside him. He was young and hard-muscled from much riding, and his blue-and-white tabard was stitched with a horned owl.

She nodded at him. 'Greetings. What's to be done for Lord Wido today?'

'Mistress Molly,' said the man. 'I am Berard, his lordship's herald. My lord rides a league or two behind me, on his way to Eaglerock castle. The day swiftly shortens, and he would sleep himself and his men beneath your roof this night.'

'Surely,' she said. After Hamelen's warning, she'd been expecting this. 'And what of Lord Jacott, d'ye know?'

'We meet with his lordship on the morrow.'

'So how many men do I feed tonight, young ser?'

'Counting Lord Wido and myself, Mistress, ten men,' said the herald. 'By Marcher law—'

'His lordship comes afore all men save a duke,' she said, a trifle sharpish, so he'd know next time not to muckle her. 'The law and me be well acquainted. Lord Wido and his men be most welcome at the Pig Whistle. Tell me, does his lordship take his lady with him to Eaglerock?'

The herald shook his head. 'Another time, Mistress Molly. There will be no court frivols that her ladyship might enjoy.'

No frivols, eh? So, it seemed Clemen's new duke was of a mind to be sure the Marches stayed settled afore he kicked up his heels. Not a fool, this Roric, the spirits be thanked.

'Ride back to his lordship, ser, and bid him come in good cheer,' she said, smiling. 'We'll have wine and meat aplenty for him, and a warm bed against the cold.'

'Mistress,' said the herald, and took himself away.

She turned to wide-eyed Alys. 'Run to Iddo, lass. He be in the vegetable garden. Tell him Lord Wido be on his way. And tell Kytte in the laundry I do want my bed stripped, and fresh linens for his lordship.'

Alys bobbed. 'Yes'm.'

With pies to finish and slide into the oven and stew to braise on the hob and jugged hare to bake, they'd be pinching time. Iddo came in with a basket of carrots and a pail of peas and Benedikt, covered in garden dirt from crawling. She scolded them both roundly then called Alys from her table-scrubbing to see her son washed and put in clean clothes. Iddo she sent out to warn Gwatkin of horses coming, then to chop wood, for the spirits knew they'd need a mort of it afore sunrise next. Little Willem woke fussing, so she warmed goat's milk for him and filled his belly. When Alys came back with a clean Benedikt she gave the girl her son and Willem to mind on the grassy stretch between the vegetable garden and the herb bed, with the carrots to scrape and the peas to pop from their pods.

After that it was cooking, as fast as she could. What a mercy she had the pastry rolled and ready. When the last pie was slid into the oven there was just enough time spare to pin on a clean apron before she and Iddo must needs stand themselves in the wide crossroad outside the Pig Whistle to greet Lord Wido.

'Molly?' Squinting, Iddo shaded his eyes and stared at the approaching horses. 'That be more than ten men. Looks like twice that, t'me.'

He was right. The horses trotted closer, and they had their answer. Blue and white pranced knee-to-knee with green and white, and a banner flag stitched with a badger kept company with Lord Wido's horned owl. A good thing they had the large dormer, and plenty of stables and chopped wood.

'Lord Wido's met early with Lord Jacott,' she said, sighing. 'The lords and their men-at-arms, they'll be sleeping cheek to toe.'

Iddo nodded, glumly. 'We'll be turning folk away.'

'Can't be helped,' she said. 'Ye know the law.'

Side by side, they stepped forward to greet Clemen's Marcher lords as the nobles drew their joined company of men-at-arms to a halt.

'Mistress Molly,' said Lord Wido, lean and fit and smiling astride a glossy chestnut stallion. 'As you see, I arrive on your doorstep with Lord Jacott.'

'I do see, my lord,' she said, nodding respectfully at Jacott on his fine acorn-brown horse.

'You have room for us?' said Lord Jacott, older than Lord Wido by a few years, and more portly. 'Say yes. My mouth has not stopped watering with the thought of your pies.'

She curtsied. 'Ye both be right welcome at the Pig Whistle, my lords. But I must tell ye, there be but one great bed. Ye can share that, or toss a coin for it and the loser take a privy room. Comfortable but less grand, my lords. I'll not feckle ye on that.'

Lord Jacott grinned. 'Mistress Molly, for an extra helping of your pie I will gladly take a privy room.'

Jacott was a good man, for a Marcher lord. She favoured him with her warmest wink. 'Seems to me, yer lordship, ye've earned the great bed and the pie, such tasty meat y'do sell me.'

'Hold on that!' Lord Wido protested. 'I think there's a coin toss in our future, Jacott.'

Stepping back, Molly raised her hands. 'My lords, I be a humble innkeeper, is all. I beg ye, don't—'

'Lord Wido! 'Ware Harcia!'

It was Wido's herald, seated on his horse behind the lords, who raised the shout. He was pointing down the left arm of the crossroad, to a second company of riders coming towards them at a canter. The lowering afternoon sunshine showed them liveries of black-and-gold, and black-and-scarlet. Two banners fluttered, one stitched with scarlet arrowheads, the other with three balls of gold.

Molly felt Iddo plucking at her sleeve. 'This be trouble, Moll,' he muttered. 'Best we step aside.'

Iddo had the right of it. Feelings between Clemen and Harcia's Marcher lords were lately sore bruised, what with Lord Bayard's men caught hunting a stag in Lord Wido's stretch of manor woodland. She let Iddo tug her off the road and into the Pig Whistle's beaten-earth forecourt.

Lord Wido spurred his snorting horse forward as the company from Harcia plunged and milled before him.

'Lord Bayard!' he called. 'I take it you and Lord Egbert are summoned to Eaglerock?'

Lord Bayard was a big man, strapped heavily with muscle. The scarlet arrowheads on his tunic and his black horse's trappings made promise of violence. So did his smile.

'*Summoned*, Wido? Does Clemen now *summon* the lords of Harcia?'

There was muttering behind Wido, as Clemen's men-at-arms took offence at Bayard's tone and sweeping look of contempt. Jacott turned to glare at them, then rode to join his brother lord.

'If the word was ill-chosen, Bayard, feel free to choose another.'

Bayard sneered. 'We are despatched south by our duke. More than that is no concern of yours.'

'As you say. Now, ride on. We stop here for the night.'

'At the Pig Whistle?' Lord Egbert laughed, deepening the pockmarks in his face and making the cloth-of-gold balls stitched to his black velvet doublet dance. 'A happy chiming. So do we.'

'I think not,' said Wido, still glaring at Bayard. 'There's no room for you, my lords, so I think you'll ride on. We are here first, we claim the right.'

Lord Bayard's face twisted. 'You claim so many rights, I do wonder how you keep them straight. If Clemen must be believed, you own every deer in the Marches and now every innkeeper's bed.'

'Hold, Wido!' Jacott snapped, as his brother lord's hand moved to his sword. 'The new duke will not thank us should we muddy his waters!'

'The new duke?' scoffed Bayard. 'Roric's not acclaimed yet, Jacott. But he should be, for he's fitting. A bastard lord for a bastard duchy, its castellans base venison-thieves and inn-scrapplers!'

The words were naked flame to spilled oil. Wido rode his warhorse at Bayard's proud beast. The stallions roared, half rearing, forelegs striking, trained to kill and willing. Lord Jacott kicked his horse into a leap, one hand reaching for Wido's reins.

'Hold, Wido! Enough! A dead stag isn't worth this! For pity's sake, think of Eaglerock! Egbert, you mumchance slipshod, speak up and keep the peace!'

But Lord Egbert paid him no heed, too busy fighting his own battle-eager stallion, and trying to keep himself out of the way. Jacott's desperate rein-snatch failed and he was almost unhorsed as his stallion tripped and stumbled. And all the men-at-arms, the hard, scarred fighting men of the Marches, they saw their noble masters argle-bargling and drew their own thirsty swords, eager to prove themselves loyal.

Molly held her breath. If these lords and their men slaughtered each other, what hope of hiding it? There'd be war in the Marches, rivers of blood where the roads used to be, and then how could she hope to keep the Pig Whistle's doors open? She felt herself shaking, felt Iddo shaking beside her.

'Feggit lords and their shammeries!' he cursed, as the lords' heralds, no fighting men, scurried themselves safe and the Pig Whistle's few guests spilled onto the forecourt to point and stare, boggle-eyed, at the men-at-arms jostling towards each other, shouting vile insults and slashing the air to ribbons with their threatening blades.

Lord Jacott was purple-faced with fury. Heedless of the danger, he spurred his gape-mouthed stallion between Bayard and Wido's horses.

'Come to your senses, Wido!' he bellowed. 'Or d'you want Roric to banish you out of your castle and lands?'

Before Lord Wido could answer, the sound of steel striking steel slewed them round in their saddles. Two men-at-arms, one Clemen, one Harcian, swinging their swords wildly . . . and blood spilled on both sides.

137

Scant heartbeats of silence, full of shock and anger and fear. The air trembled on the brink of calamity. Then Jacott wrenched his horse about.

'*Men of Clemen! Stand your ground!*'

For one terrible moment, Molly thought Clemen's men-at-arms would disobey. But then they heeded their furious lord, ramshackle, and Lord Egbert wheeled his warhorse on its haunches and rode it straight at Harcia's approaching men-at-arms. Seeing their own lord in danger of their drawn swords, the men-at-arms collapsed into confusion, trampling each other to get out of his way. Lord Wido, still red-faced, abandoned his quest to spill Lord Bayard's blood.

Dry-mouthed, Molly watched as a hasty truce was hammered between Jacott and Egbert, with Wido and Bayard glowering and all the tamed men-at-arms glaring their impotent threats. When it was done, Lord Jacott dismounted his stallion and stamped his way towards the Pig Whistle.

'Iddo,' she said, under her breath. 'Best ye get these lollygaggers inside. I'll see what the lord wants.'

He was her Iddo, he did as she asked without a brangle. As he bustled their guests into the public room, she met with Lord Jacott.

'A foolish misunderstanding,' he said, sweaty and jaw-jutted. 'I'd be obliged if you put it out of mind, Mistress Molly.'

'Yer lordship,' she murmured. 'There be two men wounded. Would ye have me see to them?'

A great wash of relief passed over his face. 'I would.'

He beckoned the two bloodied men-at-arms with a harsh gesture, not caring that one of them owed him no obedience, and as they limped forward she fetched her physicking chest. Then she did her best to bind their hurts, thinking all the while of Phemie peering over her shoulder. After that, the lords of Harcia rode on with their chastened men-at-arms behind them. Neither of them lowered their dignity to an apology.

She and Iddo ran themselves ragged after that, feeding Clemen's lords and their rowdy men-at-arms and emptying a dozen kegs of fine ale into endlessly out-thrust tankards. They crawled into their bed well past midnight and lay curled together, hand in hand, humming head to toe with weariness.

'Feggit lords,' said Iddo, around a huge yawn. 'If this be what a new duke in Clemen brings the Marches, we do be facing a mort of dark years.'

She wanted to argue, but he was right.

'A mort of dark years, Moll,' he said again, pulling her close. 'And best we prepare for it, afore we lose our way.'

CHAPTER NINE

Taking advantage of the most favourable winds, the light galley *Dancer* made a night crossing from the Cassinian duchy of Ardenn to the great harbour of Eaglerock township. Cloaked against the cold, and the sea spray whipping up and over the galley's side, Berardine of Ardenn brooded into moon-silvered darkness. As she stared, the *Dancer*'s hull sliced through the inky Moat, its parted waters slapping and hissing in protest. The galley's square-rigged sail creaked high overhead, bellied with eager air, and its prow dipped and heaved beneath her feet, but she rode each surge easily, as though she sat her swiftest horse.

A pity she couldn't simply ride the wide stretch of water between her royal duchy and Clemen. In nigh forty years of living, she'd never reconciled herself to boats.

The captain had promised her they'd reach Eaglerock harbour just after dawn. She didn't know how her sailing masters knew these things. She didn't need to. It was their business to know, and hers to be satisfied, and if they failed her they knew what they could expect.

Catching the sound of someone's approach, Berardine turned her head a little and waited.

'Beg pardon, Madam,' said the captain's mate, halting. 'Captain thought you'd fancy a toddy against the nip.'

She held out her hand. 'That is most thoughtful.'

'Madam,' said the mate, and put the warm tankard into her grasp. 'Were you wanting anything else?'

'Solitude.'

'Yes, Madam.'

Footsteps, retreating. She took a moment to enjoy the toddy's heat against her chilled fingers, then risked a taste. If it was goat's milk . . . but no. Wisely, the captain had seen fit to bring on board finest sweet cow's milk for her, and had liberally laced this tankardful with rum. She took a deeper swallow and smiled as the sailor's brew burned a smooth path all the way to her near-empty belly. Her appetite these past weeks had been shy, the news from Clemen too disquieting for comfort. Milk might be babe's pap, but it soothed her fretful stomach. She needed that, now more than ever. The days ahead were sure to be fraught with uncertainty, if not danger. To prevail she'd require all her strength and cunning.

Tucked within her jewelled bodice was a folded sheet of paper, the most recent report from her envoy to Eaglerock castle and its set-adrift court. She had no need to re-read it, though. After nineteen days of perusal she knew the letter's contents by heart.

My great and gracious duchess, greetings. In obedience to your wishes, I convey to you the current state of affairs in Clemen. Roric has yet to be formally acclaimed the duchy's duke, though his day-to-day dealings leave no doubt he is acting in that capacity. Alas, I cannot provide you with a reason for the delay. Also, though my original report holds true – Harald was not loved, so there is litle regret for this death – I must tell you Clemen's mood remains cautious. Prior to these events Harald's bastard cousin did not live large. Many do not know him, and lack of familiarity breeds unease. Despite this uncertainty, however, I see no reason to fear for your interests. Our traders here are confident. Ardenn is Ardenn, and will remain so.

And well it might, and must, for it was in trade with Clemen and, through it the duchy of Harcia, that she protected her own vulnerable duchy's sovereignty and her precarious rule. Lose Clemen and Harcia and she lost all. The dukes of Cassinia, emboldened, would fall upon wounded Ardenn in a frenzy . . . and she'd get no help from the men in charge of Cassinia's infant, orphaned prince. Those weak, selfish bastards were too busy feathering their own nests and appeasing the Principality's great lords.

'But they won't destroy me, or mine,' she declared to the wind-whipped water and the muffling night. 'On my beloved Baldwin's grave, I swear it.'

'Mama?'

She turned, frowning. 'Catrain. Why aren't you asleep?'

The galley was generously strung with oil lamps. In their leaping light Catrain's blue eyes gleamed mysterious. Tendrils of wavy, honey-gold hair escaped from her blue cloak's hood and flirted with the salty breeze. Though just fourteen, she seemed older. She was her dead father's daughter, Baldwin's image and delight.

'You're not, Mama.'

'Mind your tongue.'

Her three other daughters, hearing that tone, would have flung themselves at her in sobbing regret. Not just because they were younger, but because – well, because they weren't their sister.

Catrain laughed. 'If I bother you so much, Mama, you should've left me in Carillon.'

'The captain can always take you back there once we have reached Eaglerock.'

'Mama . . .' Joining her, Catrain slipped a confiding hand beneath the folds of her cloak and into the crook of her arm. 'He could, but he won't. You need my eyes and ears in Clemen's court. I'm the only one who can spy for you there unnoticed.'

Sometimes she feared her first-born daughter was too bright. 'Is that why I've brought you with me? To spy on our Clemen cousins?'

'Am I wrong?' Catrain sounded surprised. 'I couldn't think of another reason why you'd want me to come.'

Berardine stared into the night. Yes, she had another reason. But oh, how she dreaded shattering her daughter's innocence. There remained a little time, yet. Best divert her bright child with an answer that was the truth . . . but not the whole truth.

'Now that you're of age, Catrain,' she said with practised ease, hiding all doubts, 'I decided the experience of travel beyond our borders will stand you in good stead.'

Catrain nodded. 'Yes, Mama. I'm sure it will. But you do still intend for me to be your spy. Yes?'

'You are the heiress of Ardenn. I intend you should do your duty.'

'Exactly so,' Catrain said, pleased. 'I'll make a good spy, I think. What man ever looks past a pretty girl's tits?'

'Your father did.'

A careless shrug. 'Papa was different.'

Indeed he was. Different, and irreplaceable. Even now, after so long, there were days when the pain of missing Baldwin threatened to put her on her knees.

'He'd be so proud of you, Mama.'

Berardine kissed her daughter's cloaked head. 'And of you, Catrain. Though he'd despair at your impudence.'

Another laugh, this time a trifle wistful. Catrain had been nearly seven when Baldwin died. An impressionable age.

'I'll return to the cabin, Mama, if that's what you truly want.'

Even with the brisk winds, they faced at least four more hours of sailing. She couldn't stand on deck all that time. 'We'll both retire, in a moment.'

A stretch of silence as Catrain gazed up at the distant, glittering stars. Her face in profile was achingly pure. Looking at her, Berardine felt a pang of uncertainty.

Since his firstborn daughter's third birthday it had been Baldwin's determined desire for the child to marry into Clemen, and in doing so increase Ardenn's influence and fortunes. But such an intent, while laudable, failed to tell the whole story. At last she'd wormed the truth out of her husband. In defiance of the Exarch's strict teachings against soothsaying, Baldwin had claimed a knowing of it, and told her that if Catrain didn't marry Clemen then dire calamity would surely follow. He feared the greed of his brother dukes, and their arrogance. He was afraid they'd see Ardenn reduced to smoke and cinders before admitting Catrain was bloodborn to rule. Instead they'd seek to take it for themselves. Without a great duke as her husband, her champion, his heir and duchy both would be ruined. A soothsayer had told him so.

She'd found it hard to believe him, even though she wanted to. He was the father of her children and the king of her heart. Never once had he lied to her. But *soothsaying*? That was near as bad as sorcery. A great sin. Only he'd asked her to trust him . . . and of course she did.

Then, four years later, she lost her beloved Baldwin.

Within days of his death the dukes of Cassinia began dangling various sons before her in hopes of securing an advantageous betrothal to Catrain. Smiles turned to scowls when she refused. Compliments swiftly decayed into veiled threats. Besieged on all sides, she'd begun to weaken, even though she could see that Baldwin had been right to fear the dukes.

But just as despair threatened to overwhelm loyalty, a young woman came to her, slipping into Carillon's airy palace unchallenged. Like a shadow. Izusa, she called herself. Baldwin's muse, she claimed to be. Without preamble she'd sworn her fealty, promising her service in defence of Ardenn and in dear Baldwin's memory.

'Madam, three tokens will I give you by which my honesty can be judged,' she said. 'If even one of these tokens proves untrue you'll not hear from me again. But if I prove true, Madam, think of me . . . and I'll return.'

She'd stared at the young woman, trembling with hope and dread. 'What tokens?'

'Madam,' Izusa said. Her clear green eyes were fearless, her oddly matched features somehow attractive. 'Three days hence, in the midst of its pealing, the great bell in the great chapel of Carillon will crack. When the exarchites prepare the bell field to cast a new bell, there they'll discover the bones of a hunchback long since dead. Three hours after disturbing these mortal remains, a flock of night-crows will descend upon the chapel bell tower. Thrice will they circle it and then fall dead to the ground – save for one bird, which will sing more sweetly than the sweet-throated thrush. As the last note fades the bird will blush from black to gold and fly away into the blue sky, never more to be seen.'

'Ridiculous,' she said faintly. 'Night-crows don't sing.'

Izusa's full lips curved in a smile. 'One will sing, Madam. And all who hear it shall weep.'

Distraught with grief, more terrified of betraying Baldwin and his trust than imperilling her soul, she'd promised Izusa she'd wait to see if the strange predictions came to pass. Feeling foolish, missing Baldwin, on the third day after the soothsayer's visit she left her palace to pray in Carillon's great chapel.

And while she prayed, the great bronze bell in its tower cracked.

When word came to her of the crooked bones found in the bell field, she went to look. She watched the night-crows circle the chapel's bell tower, then watched them fall dead at her feet. And when the last songless crow sang like a sweet-throated thrush she wept . . . and barely saw it fly away golden through the veil of her tears.

The next night, like a shadow, Izusa returned.

'Madam,' she said, fearless, 'am I not a woman of my word?'

'How did you know those things would happen?' she'd whispered. 'What *are* you, Izusa?'

'Your servant,' Baldwin's soothsayer replied. 'Bound to you and yours for as long as there is need.'

'Bound how? Bound by whom? For what purpose? *I must know!*'

'Madam . . .' Izusa took both her hands. Held them, though she had no permission. There was something comforting in her touch. 'The more you know, the greater your danger. Shadows creep beyond these walls. Wicked men plot to wound you. Your daughter is not safe.'

She gasped. 'Catrain?'

'She must marry into Clemen,' Izusa declared. 'No matter who importunes you otherwise, Madam, you must stand firm.'

'Alone, Izusa?' She couldn't bear it. 'For how long?'

Izusa's smile was brilliant. 'You're not alone, Madam. You have me and the powers who sent me.' Then she scattered her ancient telling stones across the bedchamber floor. 'When your daughter is fourteen, and a woman, then will the wheel turn. Stand fast till then, Madam. For Ardenn and the love of the husband you lost.'

'Will I see you again?' she'd asked, watching Izusa return the telling stones to her rabbit-skin satchel one by one, with care. 'How can I reach you, if I need . . . guidance?'

'Fear not, Madam. I'll come if you need me.'

'And how will you know?'

'I'll know,' said Izusa, her eyes gentle, her smile strange. Then, like a shadow, she was gone.

So for the last seven years she'd stood fast. Though in the end the threats came to nothing, her rejection of those dukes' dangled sons had cost her much good will and roused unwelcome suspicions. Most valuable noble daughters were matched years before they reached the legal age to wed. While Baldwin lived there'd been no public complaint over Catrain remaining free, as there was still the chance of a son to inherit his duchy. But with that hope gone, since his death the critical whispers had grown louder. Baldwin's widow was the sole ruling duchess in Cassinia, and tolerated only by virtue of her widowhood. The thought of Catrain succeeding her and ruling outright, unwed, was unthinkable. The girl must marry and breed a son to inherit Ardenn. Though the prince's regents and the other dukes squabbled every other week, in this one matter they stood united.

As her daughter's fourteenth birthday approached, the regents' pressure increased. Berardine knew she was fast running out of time. Only the thought of giving her tender child to a man like Harald of Clemen stayed her hand. Then newly widowed Harald remarried, and the choice was denied her. When the news came ten months later that Harald had at last sired himself a healthy son, it seemed she must betray her beloved Baldwin and his dream. Harald would hardly betroth his infant heir to a girl of an age to have borne the child herself. She'd come to think she had no hope but to placate the prince's regents and marry Catrain within Cassinia . . . or else find another husband for herself and risk her life, and everything she held dear, on the slender chance she could birth a son to follow Baldwin.

Dreading that, she'd waited for Izusa to break her years of silence. And then, when the silence persisted, she wondered if all along she'd believed in a lie.

But now Harald and his son were dead . . . and the cousin who'd supplanted him was yet unmarried. It seemed Baldwin and his soothsayer had been right after all. Still, one doubt remained. Would the regents and the dukes accept his widow marrying his daughter and heir across the Moat?

She was almost sure they'd support her if she promised that Cassinia would receive a goodly portion of Clemen's trading wealth.

Gold was like oil, it calmed the most troubled waters. And the law was on her side. Nowhere in Cassinia's statutes was such a marriage forbidden. Why, foreign blood flowed through the veins of every Cassinian noble. As for Roric of Clemen being any kind of threat to the Principality, it went without saying that Catrain's husband would never take precedence over her in Ardenn. And he was unlikely to object to the role of consort when the marriage would be so advantageous to his duchy. Indeed, in offering Roric her eldest daughter she'd be honouring him, enriching him, beyond his wildest imaginings. Of course he'd agree to the match. He might be a bastard, but she'd never heard he was a fool.

'Mama?'

Berardine stirred out of frowning reverie. 'Yes?'

'Something troubles you.'

Yes, indeed. Her daughter was altogether too bright. 'Catrain—'

'Mama,' said Catrain. 'You fret over me, don't deny it. You should tell me why. I have the right to know.'

A fair point. Without Catrain's willing agreement to a match with Roric, Baldwin's wishes would be thwarted – and if her headstrong daughter felt bullied or tricked in this, she would surely baulk.

'Very well,' she said, casting a glance behind them to make sure they remained private. 'But you must keep your counsel on it.'

'I will.'

Catrain's hand was still tucked into her arm. Taking hold of it, lacing fingers, Berardine lowered her voice. 'While I did bring you with me to hear things I might not that will advantage or disadvantage Ardenn, it's not the only reason.'

A whispery giggle. 'I thought it wasn't.'

'You are Ardenn's future, Catrain, as surely as if you'd been born a boy. The choices you make will set our course for years to come.'

In the dancing lamplight, Catrain's expression was serious. '*My* choices, Mama?'

A shout from the captain's mate, bold but not alarmed. Then a thudding of feet and a flapping of canvas as the *Dancer*'s sail was trimmed to meet the shifting wind. The boat heeled and the deck beneath them tilted. Oil lamps swung, washing new shadow and light across Catrain's young, beautiful face as she easily kept her balance.

Berardine squeezed her daughter's hand. 'I know what's done in other noble families. But you have my word I'll never force you. Women are granted few enough freedoms in this world.'

'Mama . . .' Catrain wrinkled her nose. 'I think you're speaking of marriage.'

Pain and pride stabbed, sharply. For Baldwin to have his way she must lose this extraordinary child to a stranger. 'I am, Catrain.'

Her daughter seemed more intrigued than alarmed. 'And who would you have me marry?'

'You know our history, Catrain. How long ago it was nobles of Cassinia, many of the best of them from Ardenn, who tamed the wild men across the Moat and—'

'And birthed the Kingdom of Harcia,' Catrain finished, impatient. 'Yes, Mama. I do remember my lessons.'

'Minx,' she said, but without heat. 'Attend me. There has been some trouble in Clemen of late. Harald, who sadly was not a good duke, is no more. His cousin Roric will soon be acclaimed duke in his place.'

'How frightening for Clemen's people,' Catrain said softly. 'Not to have the comfort of a good ruler.'

Ah, but her daughter had a kind heart. She would make an excellent duchess. 'Yes, child. Most frightening.'

'So, it's this new duke Roric who's in want of a wife?'

'Indeed he is.'

A stretch of wind-whipped silence, as Catrain considered this. At last she released her breath in a long, slow sigh. Let her hood fall back, and turned her bold face to the water and the wind and to distant, night-shrouded Clemen. Her pretty lips curved in a knowing smile, so like her father's that the world almost stopped turning.

'Then, Mama, we shall give him one,' she said. 'The lucky, lucky man.'

'Lord Humbert! A word!'

Biting back an oath, for he had peculiar news to tell Roric and wanted no delay, Humbert turned and waited for Vidar to fight his way through the visitors passing to and fro beneath Eaglerock castle's portcullised outer gate. Heralds, town messengers, scholars, merchants, scribes, servants, a few minor nobles and even a brace of grey-clad exarchites, they jostled together in a noisy throng. With the changes thrust upon Clemen it seemed every man and his dog were eager to make themselves known to the officials of Roric's unofficial, fledgling court. The gatekeeper and his junior bailiff were hard put to sort wheat from chaff. As for Vidar, he elbowed his way past them without stopping, his frown a dare to challenge him.

The castle's red granite entry road, forbidden to horses, sloped steeply upwards from the outer gate. Halted halfway to the main forecourt, watching lame Vidar approach, seeing him gift the amblers in his path with a one-eyed glare fit to freeze the marrow, Humbert felt a grudging admiration. The man came on nimbly enough, though the odd hitch-and-twist in his gait lent him the look of a drunken sailor. That much could be said for him, he never once took to a litter and had himself carried about like a perfumed Sassanine. 'Twas a pity he wasn't as amenable in other ways. An even greater pity that Lindara held him in such esteem.

'Lord Humbert,' Vidar said with a scant nod, on reaching him. 'Do you go to meet with Roric?'

Humbert stared Vidar up and down, taking note of the shabby claret-coloured velvet and dimmed gold thread of his doublet. His undershirt was finest linen, but aged now, its lace trim about neck and cuffs looking tired. It was an open secret, how Vidar's circumstances daily grew more straitened. He must be perilously close to beggared, these days.

'I do, my lord.'

Vidar was glaring again. 'Then speak to him, sternly. He should've been acclaimed duke days ago. What's the matter with him? He threatens the duchy's calm with this dallying!'

Humbert waited for two messengers and a herald to hurry by. When they were safely past, with no one else close enough to eavesdrop, he raised a warning finger.

'Honest opinion or no, Vidar, you'll keep from offering it in public.'

Vidar's lips pinched. 'Yes, my lord. But do you deny I'm right?'

Instead of answering, he started again up the sloping roadway. Vidar hesitated, then followed until they reached the castle's wide, granite-paved forecourt. There, a little winded by the climb, Humbert puffed his way to the half-wall that bordered the sheer cliff side protecting Eaglerock's western flank. Looking over it, a man sweeping his gaze across the heart-stopping view could see busy Eaglerock township far below, and the boat-crowded harbour with docks and warehouses lining it both sides. Those long, high buildings were crammed floor to rafter with goods to be sent out into the world from Clemen, and goods brought in from as near as Ardenn and as far as Agribia and Ardebenia. Clemen's lifeblood, the flow of steady trade filling its coffers with gold from sales and taxes and tariffs and imposts. And all of it at risk now, thanks to Roric's dithering.

But he'd eat a month-dead weasel before admitting as much to Godebert's haughty heir.

Instead, he jutted his chin. 'When the last king of Harcia died, and when the foolish sons who survived him were done tearing his kingdom apart, who survived best? *Clemen*. We survived, and even thrived, despite famine and drought and the great pestilences of 1140, 1219 and 1392. We even survived Harald, the spirits be thanked. And now you say Roric would put the duchy in danger?'

Vidar pushed a strand of breeze-blown hair out of his face. 'Not on purpose. But it seems he's reluctant to claim the throne he took from Harald, and you can't deny that's making Clemen nervous.'

He snorted. 'I deny you've wit enough to fill a sucking babe's milk cup. Now come with me.'

The men-at-arms with their killing-sharp halberds, standing duty at the castle's entrance, knew him for Clemen's chief councillor and nodded without challenge. Humbert stamped his way across the entrance hall's tiled floor, leaving Vidar to toil in his wake as best he could, and took the first narrow staircase on the right past the enormous green marble sculpture of Paharan, Clemen's abandoned god of war. Eaglerock's exarchites were for ever on about having it hammered to dust but Harald, to his meagre credit, had always refused. He expected Roric would do the same, to remind the Exarch who was duke in Clemen and who wasn't.

Provided we can get his arse officially sat on the Falcon Throne.

He'd chosen this staircase because it was narrow and seldom travelled, meant for the use of men-at-arms defending the castle.

There was a cramped landing at its first bend, with an arrow-loop spilling a thin shaft of light. Humbert pushed his robed bulk onto it and waited. A few moments later Vidar caught up to him, his scarred face tight with anger and pain.

'My lord Humbert, I must—'

'Hold your tongue,' he said. 'For I'll have the rest of my say first.'

Vidar pinched his lips so tight they disappeared. 'My lord.'

'Good, then. Now, Vidar. Don't you take me for a fool. I know why you're so eager for Roric to formally claim his title – and I can't say I blame you. But if you think I'll bully him into rushing ahead for your sake, you're thrice the knothead I ever thought you might be.'

Vidar's scarred face flushed, then paled. 'He promised me restitution.'

'And you'll have it! Roric's word is good. You know that. But he's juggling more balls than a score of acrobats. Would you have him drop them all, and Clemen's future, for the sake of one man?'

'An easy question for you to ask, my lord,' Vidar retorted with heat. 'With a full purse in your doublet and no taint upon your name!'

Humbert sighed. He had no great love for this man, but the natural justice of his claim couldn't be denied. 'Roric values your friendship, and your patience, Vidar. If you think he'd slight you when you stood by him at the risk of your own life, and took a life in defence of him, you don't know him at all.'

'Forgive me, my lord,' Vidar said stiffly. 'But I judge men by what they do, not what they say. For weeks, all I've received from Roric is words. When it comes to deeds my purse is empty.'

'It won't remain so. You'll have your name and your lands returned to you.'

'When? He made it plain I'd have nothing till he was officially named duke. What stays his hand, Humbert? Why is he not yet acclaimed?'

Chewing his lip, Humbert scowled at the worn flagstones beneath their feet. It went against all instinct and honour to confide in Vidar . . . but keeping his counsel would only make matters worse. Feed the man's sense of grievance beyond any hope of placation.

'My lord . . .' He offered Vidar his most fatherly smile. 'You're feeling hard done by, and were I in your shoes I'd doubtless feel no different. I know few men who'd willingly swallow the same injustice twice.'

Vidar's expression darkened. 'More words.'

'Aye, more words, but with a purpose, I fancy. If you'd have the truth of it, Vidar, our friend Roric yet grieves the loss of Harald's babe. Putting it bluntly, his conscience pricks him.'

'His conscience?' Vidar stared. 'How so?'

Shrugging, Humbert hid his own growing irritation behind a mask of indulgent sorrow. 'If the child lived safe in exile I doubt he'd give it any thought. But it perished, and so he finds fault with himself.'

'The fault's not his. The brat died by mischance. Roric's a fool to shoulder the blame.'

He shook his head, making sure his features were well-schooled. Not by any slipshod hint could he tip Vidar to the notion that Roric remained convinced there was foul play behind the death of Harald's son.

'I know it, my lord, as well as you. And I've turned my face blue comforting Roric, trying to convince him he's innocent of any wrong.' Humbert spread his hands wide. 'But there it is. The babe was his own blood. Can you wonder at his dismay?'

'No,' Vidar said, grudging. 'But I can wonder at him dwelling so long and heavy on what won't be changed by a river's worth of tears. Harald is dead, and his line with him. Roric lives, and must live as Clemen's duke. And as this duchy's chief counsellor, and his foster-lord, it's your duty to see it done.'

Humbert swallowed a vexed sigh. It gave him wind, agreeing with Vidar. 'I know.'

'I don't say this for my sake,' Vidar added. 'But for Clemen's. I trust you know that too, my lord.'

'I do, I do. Yes.'

Glowering, he stared out of the arrow-loop beside him, down to Eaglerock's bailey. A host of riders was milling about, newly arrived it seemed. He squinted, trying to make out colours and badges. Eventually he recognised them.

'Ha,' he said, turning. 'The Marcher lords are here, all four, with twice more men-at-arms than they need.' He snorted. 'Foppets, to a man.'

Vidar raised his unscarred eyebrow. 'Roric summoned them?'

'He did. I told you, Vidar. He might not dance to the tune you'd play him, but make no mistake. He means to rule.'

Relief washed away the surprise in Vidar's face. Then came a familiar, cynical glint of amusement. 'So. The Marcher lords of Clemen and Harcia travelled here together without hacking each other to pieces? Perhaps there's something to the Exarch's doctrine of miracles after all.'

Humbert snorted, then tugged at his beard. After a night of contentious deliberations, during which very little was agreed upon, Roric had dismissed Clemen's council. Its lords remained in Eaglerock township, ready to reconvene when called. Prepared to grant Roric a trifle more leeway, as their unacclaimed duke came to grips with matters as they were and not how he wished them to be.

But only because I near twisted their arms off when his back was turned. Vidar is right, curse him. I've indulged the boy long enough.

'Do me a courtesy, Vidar.'

'Of course, my lord.'

'Hie yourself down to the bailey. Greet the Marcher lords with all courtesy, especially those bastards from Harcia, see they're halfway presentable then escort them to Heartsong's constable. In the meantime I'll tell Roric they've come.'

'My lord,' Vidar said, bowing. 'It will be my pleasure.'

Humbert banged a fist to his chest and belched, his swiftly souring temper no friend. 'I'm obliged.'

Halfway down the narrow staircase, Vidar halted and looked back. 'For Roric's sake I'm sorry that Harald's brat died. But it was for the best, my lord. What hope can Clemen have, without first the old book burned and the new book opened to an unwritten page?'

The distinctive drag-and-thud of his footsteps faded as he made his way down to Eaglerock's entrance hall. Staring after him, Humbert felt a prickle across his skin. Could *Vidar* be the one who . . . But then he shook his head. No. For all his faults, Godebert's son didn't lack honour. Why, hadn't he been prepared to consider the man as husband for his only daughter? He had, and were it not for Roric he'd say yes to the match. For his child's sake, he would. He could've learned to live with wind.

But Clemen came first. Though the boy didn't know it yet, Roric needed Lindara more than Vidar ever would.

I'm an old fool, is what I am. Vidar wouldn't pledge loyalty to us, then betray us at the first chance. Nor would Aistan or any other lord. It's as I held from the outset. Harald's brat died by mischance.

And there that terrible night must end. Roric had to accept it, and announce the day and time of his acclamation, and take a wife, and breed a son . . . and let his promise flower, to the good of all Clemen.

Eaglerock castle's largest and most splendid audience chamber was a lofty, intimidating room. Its floor was diamond-tiled in scarlet and black, its stone walls panelled in gleaming white ash inlaid with cherrywood, and its ceiling was a frescoed blue sky chased with white clouds and stooping falcons. One enormous stained-glass window behind the ducal throne admitted the chamber's only natural light. An unhooded falcon ruled the intricately designed glass, perched arrogant upon a steel-gauntleted fist. The cherrywood throne itself stood on a white ash dais, with talons for feet and outstretched falcon's pinions on either side.

Roric touched the throne's carved arm hesitantly, as though the polished, ancient timber might sear him for temerity.

'It won't bite,' said Humbert behind him, sounding impatient. 'Though I tell you, boy, I might if you don't soon sit your arse in the curs't thing.'

Resentment pricked. He let his hand fall to his side. 'Boy?'

'Well, it's a sham to call you *Your Grace*, isn't it, when you won't let the council acclaim you.'

'How many times must I say it, my lord? I still have unanswered questions about—'

'*Enough*, Roric! You're as answered as you'll ever be!'

Turning, he watched Humbert stamp his familiar, belligerent way toward him from the chamber's open doors. One of the guarding men-at-arms discreetly closed them, so they could bellow at each other in private. When they were face to face, his foster-lord thumped to a halt and fisted both hands on his soberly robed hips.

'D'you hear me?' Humbert demanded, flushed. 'Liam's dead. Let him lie. And for Clemen's sake let us here and now pick the time of your acclamation!'

'For Clemen's sake, Humbert, how can I?' he said, keeping reasonable with some effort. 'How can the duchy acclaim me, honour me, when—'

'Clemen honours *strength*, Roric! Not this womanish beating of your breast. It honours purpose and duty and men of their word!'

He stared. 'What does that mean?'

'It means my ears are still ringing from Vidar's angry complaints. And Roric, he's in the right of it. You made him a promise.'

'Which I will keep!'

'Before his arse starts hanging out of his threadbare hose, or after? I tell you plain, boy, he's so short of coin now he'll soon be eating his horse. And if you think Aistan and the others haven't noticed then you're tipped in the skull.'

'If Vidar's short of coin he can come to me. I'll—'

'Why should he? It's not charity he deserves, boy, it's a duke who keeps his word!'

Struggling to hold his temper in check, Roric began to pace the gaudy floor. 'I can't help Vidar till I'm legally acclaimed duke and I can't be acclaimed duke till Liam is avenged. For I know in my heart he was murdered and—'

'Are you truly such a lackwit?' Humbert roared. 'Is this how I raised you? How Guimar before me raised you? Does Berold's blood flow through your body or has there been a mistake?'

Brought up short, Roric swallowed. 'Humbert—'

'You know in your *heart*?' Humbert's fisted hands lifted, shaking. 'What cat's piss is *that*?'

'My lord, you taught me to trust my instincts. And my instincts—'

'I taught you to be a man your father would be proud of!' Humbert spat. 'At least, I thought I did. But it seems I was wrong. It seems you're more like Harald than I knew.'

'You're unfair!'

'What's *unfair* is that poor crippled bastard Vidar, limping to me one-eyed, with his hand out, begging for what he's rightfully owed!'

He made himself meet Humbert's furious glare. 'All I want is justice for Liam.'

'Well, you'll not have it!' Humbert retorted. 'A fart on your instincts, Roric. You've no proof of murder and no way of finding it now. All you're going to get is more bloodshed, because with every day you delay you give Harcia more reason to think Clemen's a lone lamb without its shepherd. Get it through your head, boy. *The brat's death is a blessing!*'

Humbert's words struck him like a hammer blow to his heart. 'What?'

'You were right about me, that night at Heartsong,' said Humbert, savage. 'I am glad Harald's son is dead. Clemen's best served with a clean page, unwritten. Heartsong's in the past. Accept it.'

'And if I can't?'

'Then Clemen will fall into chaos, making you more of a villain than curs't Harald ever was.'

Not a hammer blow, this time, but a long, thin blade neatly slid between his ribs. He could feel the blood flowing from his bruised and battered heart. His eyes were dry, though, all his tears wept out for Liam.

'I only started this for Clemen,' he said, voice low, throat aching. 'To save us from Harald.'

Humbert heaved his shoulders in a shrug. 'I know, boy. Now finish it. Or what was all that dying for?'

A terrible question, with but one answer. Humbert was right. No matter what he suspected, he had no proof. 'Fine, my lord. You win. I'll speak no more of Liam.'

'Good,' said Humbert, sounding equally shattered.

'Was there anything else?'

Humbert tugged at his beard. 'Yes, but it can wait. The Marcher lords are here.'

'I know. I saw them arrive.'

'They're likely on their way up now.' Humbert cleared his throat. 'Roric—'

Needing a moment, Roric pushed past him to the dais and took his place on the Falcon Throne. The cherrywood was cool beneath his hands as he grasped its carved arms. Never before had he sat it.

As he accustomed himself to the feeling, he released a slow breath and considered the man who meant so much to him.

'I've disappointed you.'

'Worried me,' said Humbert, the hectic colour fading from his face.

'And angered.'

'True,' Humbert agreed. He cleared his throat. 'I'm sorry if I was harsh, boy. You've a good heart.'

'But?'

'But sometimes I fear the goodness in you will over-rule the iron.'

Deliberately, Roric relaxed his tight fingers. 'And a duke should be iron first and foremost, with goodness trickled into the miserly nooks and crannies that remain?'

Humbert nodded. 'He should, Roric. And you know it.'

That thin blade, still rib-lodged, twisted. 'Alas, Humbert. I do.'

Humbert made to answer, then turned his head at a heavy rapping on the chamber doors. 'Enter!' he bellowed, then stepped back until he stood beside the dais. The doors opened, revealing one of the castle's stewards. Nathyn.

'Your Grace,' he said, bowing. 'I give you the Marcher lords, come to Eaglerock at your behest.'

CHAPTER TEN

*T*he Marcher lords.

Roric felt his heart thud. His first test, then. One he couldn't afford to fail. Not with Humbert's fiery words still heating the chamber's air.

'My lords,' he said coolly. 'You're welcome to court, and have leave to approach.'

Travel-stained and stubbled, their spurs muddied, their surcoats splashed, the Marcher lords came forward to bend their knees in respect.

'Be upright,' he said, gesturing. 'And receive my thanks, that you'd set aside all natural inclinations towards sport and come before me unbloodied.'

A swift exchange of glowering glances told him that if these lords were unbloodied, it had been a close-run thing.

Bayard of Harcia lifted his chin. 'Lord Roric—'

'*Your Grace*,' said Humbert, the watchdog.

Bayard's insolent gaze shifted. 'Oh? It's my understanding the lord Roric isn't yet acclaimed Clemen's duke.'

'A formality, soon to be dealt with,' said Humbert. 'Have a care, Bayard.'

'Your Grace,' said Lord Egbert, a swift glance blunting Bayard's dagger glare. 'Clearly we are clouded in confusion. Indeed, Duke Aimery confided his surprise that you'd send for us before first consulting with him.'

'I've no need to consult with Harcia on matters touching this duchy, or the treaties that bind your duke and me to the peace and protection of the Marches,' Roric retorted. 'Indeed, those treaties oblige me to be vigilant and impress upon the Marcher lords of Clemen *and* Harcia my dedication to their strictures. Besides, your duke was informed I wished to see his castellans. If that weren't so, would you be here? Lord Wido—'

Wido, who'd proven himself skirmishing in the Marches, inclined his head. 'Your Grace?'

'My late cousin Harald placed some great measure of trust in you. To my knowledge it was not *mis*placed. Should I now think elsewise, with Harald buried and myself duke in his place?'

'No, Your Grace.'

'And you, Lord Jacott. My cousin once told me you sometimes o'erstep your authority. He laughed, and called you *doughty*. But I wasn't amused.'

A muscle leapt along Jacott's tensed jaw. 'Your Grace.'

'Egbert!' he snapped. 'Why are you smirking? Do you think I'll wink at Harcian horseplay? Have you told Aimery that the bastard Roric isn't to be feared?'

Startled, Egbert of Harcia gaped. 'Your Grace—'

With a silencing look at Humbert, he leapt up from the throne, off the dais, and confronted the Marcher lords.

'For your sake, my lord, I hope you weren't so foolish. Or you, Bayard.' Prowling before them, remembering Guimar, and Berold, Roric slapped his once-wounded thigh. 'For there are scars on my body to prove that boast a lie – as well you know, for I was scarred in Clemen's service when Harcia forgot its honour and threatened the Marches' peace. Never doubt I'll risk more scars, and worse, should Harcia forget its honour again!'

'And what of Clemen's forgotten honour?' Bayard demanded. 'Do you say we've never been provoked?'

He let the silence lengthen, then shook his head. 'No. I say plainly, to your faces, that in dealing with your duchy Harald did forget himself from time to time. Tell Aimery I won't.'

'And we're to trust your word on that?' said Egbert. 'Not knowing you?'

'My lords.' His smile made Egbert blink. 'Doubt my honour and you'll know me soon enough.'

'Your Grace,' the Harcian Marcher lords muttered.

'And tell Aimery this, too, when he asks what was said here today,' he added, 'tell him Clemen is no lone lamb, wanting a shepherd. Our business is ours, and none of his, and there's no unrest here that should give him cause to hope.'

'Your Grace.'

With the Harcian lords cowed, at least for the moment, he halted before Wido and Jacott. 'As for you, my lords, don't think my sword will unsheath for Harcia alone. I wink at no man who flouts Marcher law or seeks to plump his purse at my expense – or Harcia's. Your manors and your men-at-arms are held from me, and it is to *me* you'll answer for any mischief.'

'Your Grace,' Wido and Jacott murmured, as one.

He smiled again, no less fierce. 'Then, my lords, you may withdraw. My steward will escort you to some food and comfort, after which you'll return to the Marches with all haste. And when you get there, be sure to spread the word. Clemen is well-defended. Peace will reign. Not war.'

'Ha,' said Humbert, once the chamber had emptied. 'That'll give Aimery something to chew on.'

'So, my lord. Was I iron enough for you?'

In Humbert's eyes, a glimmer of praise. 'It was a fair beginning.'

Typical Humbert, never satisfied. 'Then go and inform the council I'll meet with them tomorrow, at nine bells. It's time the date was set for my formal acclamation.'

Humbert bowed. 'Your Grace.'

Frowning as his foster-lord made for the doors, Roric felt memory tug. 'Wait, Humbert. Didn't you say you had more news?'

'I did,' said Humbert, swinging about. 'Vidar and the Marcher lords knocked it out of mind.'

'Well?'

'Berardine of Ardenn. Did you invite her to Clemen, Roric, then let slip telling me?'

What nonsense was this? 'Of course not. Why would I—'

'Because she galleyed into the harbour at first light,' said Humbert, fingering his beard. 'As far as I can make out, not a soul among our own people knows she's here. And for the life of me I can't imagine why she's come.'

Eaglerock township late at night was a place patchworked with silence and feverish goings-on. The bakers and the tanners and the seamstresses and the blacksmiths and the butchers, all the men and women who plied their honest daylight trades, at this creeping-towards-midnight hour, slept above or behind their premises and dreamed of purses filled with coin. In the township's grand houses Clemen's lords and ladies also slept, or else sported themselves behind their closed doors. But though eleven bells had rung, the torchlit waterfront taverns were still lively. The brothels, too, and the cockpits. Braziers burned on each street corner, little islands of heat in the night's chilly ocean.

Heat and light could also be found in the township's merchant district, where rows of warehouses and the plain dwellings of foreign trading factors huddled close to the waterfront, a fastidious stone's throw from the taverns and brothels. But it was no haven of ale-soaked levity, where carousing sailors and dock-men gambled and buxom wenches flaunted their breasts, promising more for a copper nib or two, and cutpurses taught the unwary a sharp lesson. No, the merchant district was sober and hardworking, where as many different tongues as there were trading nations could be heard, the speakers' voices raised in the pursuit of plump profits.

Though the harbour was closed from nightfall to dawn, Eaglerock's docks and wharves remained torchlit so the men who made their fortunes and risked their lives buying and selling goods in this busy part of the world could unload the wares from their late-arrived galleys, or fill their emptied ships with such treasures as Clemen had to offer: tinwork, and lavish leatherwork for fine lords and ladies and their horses. Jars of honey, dried fruits, smoked meats, a few looked-for medicinal herbs. Glazed earthenware, exquisite silversmithing and jewellery, delicate woodwork, and the finest illustrated manuscripts, for Clemen's artisans were renowned. Barrels of ale and cider, as good as any foreign wine. Horses, too, were shipped to Cassinia and beyond. The best of them were bred in Harcia, but Clemen rode not far behind.

Wrapped close in a leather cloak reaching past his knees, a waxed woollen hood covering his head and shadowing his face, Roric picked his way unchallenged along narrow, winding Hook Alley. Before stealing clandestine from his ducal apartments, he'd told his chamberman he had business abroad so the alarm wouldn't be raised if his bed was found empty. Aside from Theo, though, no one – not even Humbert – had an inkling of this jaunt.

What he'd share of it, in the end, would be decided by what he learned when he confronted Berardine of Ardenn.

One of Humbert's useful men, who by fortunate chance knew the duchess by sight, had noticed her unheralded arrival in the harbour then followed her to the home of Master Tihomir, Ardenn's trading factor in Clemen. It was clever of Berardine to stay with him. Ardenn's duchess amid the rough-and-tumble of the waterfront? It was unthinkable. So no one would think it, and she could pursue her business without the scrutiny of Eaglerock's many lords, its council and Clemen's unacclaimed duke.

At last reaching Harbour Street, making his way with care down the steeply sloping thoroughfare towards the richest of the merchant warehouses where Ardenn stored its bounty, Roric frowned. Whatever Berardine's business was, no matter how innocent, should Harcia get wind of it, or even her presence, unfriendly questions would be asked. If the sun shone too bright for too long, Harcia blamed its parched pastures on Clemen. And it had always resented Clemen's friendship and profitable trading with Ardenn. Given this provocation, what mischief might Aimery stir should it come out that Berardine had travelled to Clemen in stealth?

He didn't know, and had no desire to find out.

A lively breeze gusting up from the nearby harbour brought with it snatches of music playing in the taverns, whispers of laughter and teasing touches of spices carried from distant, mysterious lands. Roric took a deep breath, savouring the exotic hints. He'd always wanted to travel. As Clemen's duke he could find reason to sail abroad, visit all the duchies of Cassinia. Even venture so far as the famed City State of Lepetto in the Danetto Peninsula. Dreaming of it, a distraction from his worries over Berardine, he took another deep breath . . . and stopped.

He smelled *smoke*.

And then, as he breathed in again to make sure he'd not imagined it, he heard the waterfront alarm bell start to clang and saw an orange-red flicker of flames in the near distance. One of the merchant warehouses had caught fire.

Cursing, he loosened the tight lacings on his leather cloak, and ran.

Shouting. Screaming. A crush of shifting, staggering bodies. Mayhem and madness. Cold night turned to hot day, with leaping flames and billowing heat.

'*Help here, help here!*'

'*Aza g'ai rethuni, tibeno rethuni!*'

'*Rouse the harbour master! Rouse the town serjeant!*'

'*Milafasso! Tuk-tuk-tuk!*'

'*Water, I need water!*'

'*Out the way, y'crook-back lump!*'

Panting, coughing, Roric slipped and tripped to a halt. Nearly crashed to the stone-paved ground as a grim-faced Zeidican sailor burdened with a sloshing bucket in each hand barrelled into him and kept going towards the heart of the nearest burning warehouse. Six in all fronted this stretch of the harbour – and by the coats of arms nailed high and proud to their doors, four of the six belonged to Ardenn. Poor Berardine, to receive such a welcome. One of her warehouses was well alight, one smouldered ominously, with two others belonging to Ardenn's sister duchy Voldare in immediate danger.

Breathing hard, Roric stared around him. Had Berardine braved the night and the danger to witness Ardenn's losses? He couldn't tell. Chaos ruled.

Boots thudding on the dockside, cries of despair, of encourage-ment, howls of fury, shrieks of fear. The loud clanging of bells, the slap and splash of buckets being plunged into the harbour and hauled out again. A frantic sizzle and hiss as water met fire. Nightmare shadows. Choking smoke. The throat-closing, lung-bursting stench of charred wool, burning oil, melting metal, blazing wood.

The nursery at Heartsong. Liam's burned cradle. Liam's burned body. The silent, ringing echoes of Argante's fatal grief.

Roric shook his head sharply. He had no time for memories now.

'Here, y'gormless bollock!' a soot-streaked man shouted, thrusting an empty bucket into his hand. 'Don't just stand there!'

The bucket's handle had a rope tied to it. Desperate, he kneed-and-elbowed his way to the dock's edge, tossed the bucket into the churned harbour alongside all the other tossed buckets and hauled it out again full of water, muscles cracking. Kneed-and-elbowed his way back through the heaving crowd towards the fiercely burning buildings. A sudden wind whipped up, whipping sparks and embers with it. For a moment the world stopped and he stared at their savage scarlet and orange beauty as they danced and swirled and flirted with the night, hardly feeling his lungs sear and his eyes water from the heat and smoke. Not caring, not even frightened, only stunned because in the midst of destruction there could still be such *splendour* . . .

'It's no use!' someone close by bellowed. 'We won't save it! Let's do what we can for the rest!'

The bellower was right. The first warehouse to catch alight was swiftly burning itself into a timber skeleton. But the other five in the row, they still might be saved – and the rest of the merchant district with them.

Gasping in vain for clean air, he fought the warehouse fires like a knight of old battling a flame-breathing dragon. Fought alongside sailors from a half-score of nations, and Clemen dockmen, and Eaglerock taverners, and bare-breasted brothel wenches. Fought unrecognised and unremarked, just another soot-streaked face in the crowd. The heat was so fierce he could feel his exposed skin crisping, even as sweat soaked through linen and velvet. His leather cloak was a torment but he didn't dare throw it off in case someone recognised him. A stray, rueful thought occurred in the midst of the madness.

Humbert will skin me alive when he hears about this.

Above the shouting voices, crashing burned timberwork and roaring flames, a new and different sound. Skin-crawling, horrible: the screams of terrified horses. No man who'd heard it even once in battle could forget it, or mistake it for anything else.

Dropping his emptied bucket, Roric turned. Heard someone shout, 'Harcia's stables!' A handful of men abandoned the warehouse fires to run uphill and crosswise, heading towards that dreadful animal screaming and another ominous, scarlet-and-orange glow in the night.

He ran after them.

The fitful breeze swirling sparks and embers into a glorious dance had blown them high overhead, capricious, then dropped them onto the nearby roof of a barn housing Harcian horses meant for sale into Cassinia. Timber, hay and straw fed the swiftly growing flames . . . and in scant moments live horseflesh would feed them too.

Roric helped three other men unbar the barn's heavy doors and haul them wide. Almost deafened by the terrified horses as the animals neighed and kicked and squealed, they stared at each other in the growing glow of flame. Stared into the burning barn, swiftly filling with smoke. Where was the barn-man? Harcia would never leave its valuable horses unguarded, but there was no sign of him. Had he turned coward and fled?

'You there!' Roric shouted at the others who'd run from the waterfront, who hesitated now in the face of so much danger. 'Four

163

of you stand fast to take the horses we bring out. The rest of you find a way to block each end of this street! If the horses escape us we can't have them bolting free. They'll break their legs, and the necks of any man in their way.'

'You be going in there?' demanded one of the men who'd helped haul open the barn doors. Short and brawny, he had the olive-skinned look of southern Cassinia about him.

Roric glared. 'I am. And so are you – and you – and you! Or I swear by Clemen's falcon you'll be answering to the duke. Now, with me!'

He plunged into the madness. Through the smoke and leaping flame saw ten panic-struck animals still trapped in their stalls, wide eyes white-rimmed, flaring nostrils blood red, sleek coats foamed with the sweat of fear.

'Halters!' he shouted to the men who'd followed him, pointing at the hooks beside each stall's door. 'Let your animal free without one as a last resort only!'

Because he was Clemen's duke, and these strangers' leader, he had to go deepest into the barn. Leaving them to save those horses nearest to safety, he fumbled through the choking, flame-flickered darkness to the last stall on the right, hissing as his fingers blistered on hot timber and metal. The stall's door was already ajar. As he leapt to pull it open he nearly tripped face-first over the crumpled body at his feet. One swift touch found sticky-wet hair and crushed bone.

So much for Harcia's barn-man, poor bastard.

The horse that had killed him jinked and jittered in a corner. The thud of its iron-shod hoof against timber sounded as menacing as a sword-hilt pounding on a bossed Harcian shield. Muttering a plea for protection, Roric dragged the dead barn-man out of the way then scooped up the dropped halter. With his wary, smoke-smeared gaze fixed on the snorting stallion, he cleared his dry throat. It was like swallowing gorse.

'Steady, there, steady,' he crooned. 'I'm here to help, so stand steady.'

Many times in the Marches he'd gentled a warhorse driven wild by the stench of fresh blood and spilled entrails. He had the knack of calming fretful beasts. Dimly aware of raised voices at the front of the barn, of stall doors crashing timber to timber and shod hooves clattering on brick, he eased himself forward until his reaching fingertips met shivering, quivering muscle. The horse half-snorted, half-squealed at the touch on its arched neck, a heartbreaking cry for help, as above their heads the fire ate its ravenous way through the vulnerable barn roof and down its wooden walls.

'Steady, beast,' he said again, and in a single, deft move slipped the halter over the horse's head. Then he kicked the stall door wide, stepped back and tugged on the halter's lead rope. For one dreadful moment the horse resisted, torn between terrors. And then it leapt, like a great stag, through the open doorway and over the dead barnman, pulling Roric off his feet, tightening the rope around his hand almost to bone-breaking point. With his own great leap he lunged after it, grabbed hold of the halter's cheek piece, used his body weight to slow the horse's flight towards safety.

Outside the burning barn he threw the lead rope into waiting hands, then ran back inside. In those brief moments the fire's ferocity had increased. He twisted sharply sideways, nearly falling, as another man and horse escaped the inferno. Tried to hold his breath against the stink of burning hay, burning horseshit, burning horse. Whatever great prices the Harcians had hoped for these horses before tonight, they'd have no chance of fetching them after.

Another wild-eyed horse and its rescuer burst out of the smoke. No time to ask how many were left to save. There was at least one; he could hear the frenzied thudding of hooves against a timber stall. Thankful now for his leather cloak, for the woollen hood he pulled low to his forehead, Roric pressed his forearm to his mouth and nose and pushed through the blinding smoke. A sane man would say he'd taken leave of his senses, risking his life for a horse, but he couldn't leave a living thing to burn in this place, to burn as helpless Liam had burned.

Somewhere in the nightmarish smoke-and-fire gloom a voice cried out in anger. 'Stop it, you stupid creature! I'm trying to help!'

Shocked, Roric stumbled. That was a *woman*.

'Wait! Wait!' she shouted. 'I have to—'

And then a thump, and a muffled cry of pain.

'You, there!' he called, turning, half-blinded by smoke. 'Are you all right? Where are you?'

'Help me! Quickly! The stall door is stuck, I think the heat has warped it!'

She was in the second-last stall on the left, tugging at the stubborn door with one hand, fending off the panicked horse with the other.

Roric heaved the door open. 'You fool! What are you doing?'

'What do you think?' she snapped. 'I'm saving this horse!'

He stared down at her, dumbstruck. Not a woman. A *girl*. Her deep voice had fooled him into thinking her grown. Tall for her age, and slender, she was swathed in a dark woollen cloak, with a thick mass of honey-gold hair, now tangled and sweaty, escaping her hood's confinement. Her flawless skin was smudged charcoal black, and in the fireglow her eyes were eerily piercing. Crystal blue, the irises ringed a dark grey.

'Give that horse to me!' he said, finding his voice. 'Before it tramples you.'

It was taking all her girlish strength to keep hold of the lead rope. 'I can't. There's one more still trapped, and you must save it. Now move, ser, or *you'll* be trampled!'

Shocked anew, he stood aside. It was that or be kicked to the ground. Girl and horse pushed by him. A warning groan, and part of the roof at the barn's far end caved in, showering sparks and embers. Pitched high above the renewed roar of flame, a scream to freeze a man's blood and crack his bones to splinters.

The last trapped horse.

Men were shouting at him from the barn's burning doorway, waving their arms, urging him to flee. But he couldn't. Not yet. His debt to Liam was far from paid . . . and he could still see the challenge in that reckless girl's blue stare.

Staggering, barely able to breathe, refusing to see the ravenous flames, feel their heat, admit the rest of the barn could collapse on him any moment, he searched for the horse. Found it, and felt the tears leap to his eyes. The poor beast was truly trapped, its quarters pinned beneath a burning roof beam. The anguish in its almost human eyes nearly stopped his heart. Sobbing, he kicked his way into the smoke-filled stall. Fumbled beneath the folds of his leather cloak for the dagger on his hip, pulled the blade free . . . and plunged it deep into the horse's throat. A twist, a wrenching downward pull, and it was done. Blood gushed, mercifully swift. Sizzled and smoked on the burning wood, the hot ground. One whispery groan and the horse collapsed, released from torment.

Three unsteady strides beyond the confines of the burning barn and the ruined building fell in on itself. Shuddering, his lungs heaving, Roric whirled about. Fountains of sparks flew skywards, caught in a swirling updraft, despite everything still beautiful. A crowd had gathered in the road to shout and point and keep hold of the rescued horses.

He seized the nearest man's arm. Shook it. 'The girl! The girl! Where is she?'

'Girl?' The man boggled at him, confused. 'What girl? I never saw no girl. B'aint no girls in this muckery, scunner! You done got yourself knocked on the head!'

No use arguing. She must have abandoned the horse and run, afraid of getting into trouble. So he'd never see her again. Ah, well. She was only a girl . . . and the world was full of them.

Turning at the sound of freshly raised voices, he saw that the Harcian horse-copers had finally arrived to claim their stock and bewail their losses. This was no place for the unacclaimed duke of Clemen.

Sliding into the shadows, Roric made himself scarce.

'Your Grace?'

Weary to the marrow of her aching bones, heartsick at the losses Ardenn had sustained, Berardine continued to stare through the unshuttered window of the dayroom in her trading factor's house. It had provided an excellent view of the harbour, the docks . . . and the chaos of the fire. All the coin her duchy poured into Clemen's greedy hands, the harbour fees and galley tolls, the warehouse rental, the import taxes, the haulage imposts, the foreign trading levies and poll taxes, and still it could not muster sufficient men and buckets of water to save Ardenn's warehouses from burning.

Shame on them. Oh, shame. It was enough to make a grown

woman weep. But she couldn't. She was Baldwin's wife. How could she disgrace him, betray him, by showing such weakness?

'I'm sorry. Madam?'

Turning slowly, because she must not appear eager to look away from the carnage, Berardine raised an eyebrow at dishevelled Master Tihomir. 'Yes?'

'Madam—'

'Yes, Tihomir. What do you want?'

Short and portly, he shifted uneasy feet. 'Madam, there is a man.'

She waited for a moment, then raised both eyebrows. 'And?'

Her factor had yet to clean all the soot from his round, fleshy face. Beneath the fire's lingering evidence his stubbled cheeks were pale. Lines of strain tugged the corners of his mouth into decline.

'Oh, Madam!' he wailed. 'I told *no one* you were coming, or that you would be my most honoured guest. I swear it on my life. I serve you honestly, diligently, my loyalty is beyond reproach.'

'That's for me to decide, Tihomir, not you,' she said, her reply sharp, unhesitating, even as her thoughts raced. Someone had betrayed her presence in Eaglerock. If not the trading factor, then who? 'This man. He asks for me by name?'

Tihomir nodded, miserable. 'Madam, he does.'

'Who is he?'

'He won't tell me.'

'A rude rascal, then.'

'I tried to send him away,' said Tihomir, his voice rising, cracking. 'I told him he was wrong, that you weren't here. He refused to heed me and – and—' He swallowed, convulsively. 'Madam, he is very tall and strong.'

'Has he a sword?'

Tihomir shook his head. 'No, Your Grace. But he looks no stranger to bloodshed with a blade.'

She stiffened her spine. Straightened her shoulders. 'Admit him.'

'Madam!' Jaw dropped, the factor stared. 'Is that wise?'

'Look out of the window, Tihomir. Dawn fast approaches and the entire merchant district is still frantic after the fire. Would you have this tall, strong man on your doorstep at sunrise, for all and sundry to see and wonder on?'

'Madam,' he said, wilting. 'But I'd not have you meet this stranger unshielded. Shall I send for our warehouse men, for protection?'

'The men who failed to notice until it was too late that the warehouses they're paid to safeguard were on fire? Those men, Tihomir?'

He looked close to tears. 'Madam,' he whispered, and withdrew.

Waiting for him to return, Berardine repinned her heavy, coiled hair and smoothed the folds of her deep-pink damask dress. Beneath its pearl-sewn bodice, and her chemise, she could feel her skin damp, feel the too-swift thudding of her heart against her ribs. This man . . . this unknown, inconvenient man . . . what mischief had he come to make? To whom did he owe loyalty? And how would she foil him? Her belly churned, sickly. But it was too late now for regret, that she'd brought Catrain with her to Eaglerock.

A hesitant tapping on the dayroom door, which her trading factor had closed behind him. She folded her hands before her and lifted her chin. 'Come.'

The door swung wide, revealing Tihomir and the stranger who'd refused to give his name. Indeed he was tall, and lean, and strapped with militant muscle. Young yet, but clearly mature. He wore a soot-stained, spottily burned leather travelling cloak, thrown back over his broad shoulders. Beneath it his plain doublet and hose showed greatly the worse for wear. His coppery hair, kinked with the hint of a curl, was close-cropped and filthy, stuck to his well-shaped skull with dried sweat. His bronze-brown eyes were red-rimmed, watchful, set a trifle too widely over a crooked, once-broken nose. His mouth was generous, his chin determined. Not a handsome man, but neatly made. There was something teasingly familiar in his looks.

He met her steady stare calmly. 'Madam. Please, be easy. I've not come to do you harm.'

'No?' She nodded at his hip. 'Then surrender your dagger.'

The merest hesitation, then he tugged the weapon from its plain sheath. The dayroom was lit brightly enough to reveal the blade stained with dried blood, imperfectly removed. She heard her breathing hitch before she could stop herself. Furious, she glared at her trading factor, who was staring at the staining blood in unabashed horror.

169

'Take that dagger, Master Tihomir, and bring it to me.'

Fingers trembling, Tihomir plucked the dagger from its owner's loose grasp and proffered it to her.

'The blood isn't human,' the man said, his gaze never leaving her face. 'One of the Harcian's horses was trapped in its burning barn. I couldn't save it.'

'So you killed it?'

He shrugged. The gesture was indifferent. The look in his eyes was not. 'They'll be compensated.'

'I see. So I'm to believe you're free to dabble your fingers in the duke of Clemen's purse?'

His lips twitched. There wasn't a hint of fear or deference in him. 'You are.'

Tihomir was still holding the bloodstained blade between trembling thumb and forefinger, as though he expected it to cut his throat at any moment. Taking pity on him, she took it from him. A beautiful weapon, despite the marring blood. Certainly no poor man-at-arms' possession. Her fingers sat comfortably about its leather-bound hilt and her forearm, taking its beautifully balanced weight, gave no protest at the burden. Its edge was sharp. She could easily imagine it cutting a horse's throat. Or a man's.

Careless, she tossed the dagger onto the seat of the high-backed chair beside her. 'And what of my compensation? Ardenn lost a small fortune tonight.'

'Those losses will be addressed, Madam.'

'You say,' she retorted, finding herself aggravated by his arrogant certainty. 'And who are you to say it?'

He looked at Tihomir. 'Leave us.'

Though her factor was no fighting man, and the night's woes had deeply shaken him, he'd not been named Ardenn's trading representative on a drunken whim.

'I'll do no such thing, you sly rogue!' Tihomir said, vigorously indignant. 'This is my house and we are in the presence of my great and gracious duchess. I'll not abandon her to the likes of—'

'Tihomir,' she said, forestalling him. 'You may go.'

'But, Madam, I cannot—'

'*Tihomir.*'

With a last resentful look at her uninvited visitor, Tihomir obeyed. He left the dayroom door ajar this time.

To show the man she was unafraid, and in command of herself, Berardine crossed to another chair and sat. Fixed her arrogant visitor with the cold, impersonal look she'd cultivated in the weeks following Baldwin's death, when every lord in Cassinia assumed she would meekly answer to him.

'Who are you? And be warned, I shan't ask you again.'

'I'm Roric, Duke of Clemen,' the man said promptly. 'Though I confess the formalities aren't yet observed.'

She blinked. Was he a lunatic, to saunter into this house and make such an outrageous claim? He must be, surely. She wished now she'd sat herself on top of his dagger. Better yet, thought to tuck one of her own down the front of her bodice.

Clemen's self-styled duke smiled. 'I'm not lying, Madam. Or mad. I promise.'

It was the smile that eased her suspicion. Easy, unselfconscious, touched with a hint of self-mockery. As though he knew better than anyone how ludicrous he sounded and wasn't afraid to admit it. Relaxing, just a little, she considered him more closely from beneath circumspectly lowered eyelids.

This was Roric? The man she wanted for Catrain? This bold, almost insolent, horse-killing, peace-breaking noble bastard who'd spilled family blood for the sake of ambition. Or honour. Or whatever reason had provoked Harald's bloodthirsty dethroning. This was Roric, the late and widely lamented Berold's illegitimate grandson?

Well . . . they shared the same hair colour. And knowing Berold's likeness, since a portrait of him gifted to Baldwin's mother still hung in Carillon's palace, she could see now that his bastard grandson had the ghostly look of him in the eyes, and the way he stood his ground, unafraid. He wasn't dressed like a duke, unacclaimed or otherwise. But then, what did a duke wear when fighting fires and killing horses?

She straightened an emerald ring upon her finger. 'An outrageous declaration, ser. You can prove it, I suppose?'

'Only a fool with a death-wish would pronounce himself Roric, surely,' he said, still amused, 'when the lowest man-at-arms in Eaglerock could with one glance say it was untrue.'

Curving her lips, she kept her eyes cool. 'In other words, you can't.'

'Berardine . . .' There was a stout wooden settle pressed against the wall. Roric crossed to it and sat, leaning back, his arms loosely folded. 'In my time at Harald's court—' Some raw memory killed his lingering amusement. Shadowed his gaze, pinched his lips. 'My cousin trusted me with letters you wrote to his council. Half-blinded I'd still know your handwriting. And while I'm a stranger to Master Tihomir, I was friendly with Master Locksill, the man he replaced. Your former factor can marry my face to my name. That is, if the word of an Eaglerock man-at-arms isn't good enough.'

Berardine looked at her neatly clasped hands. The change in him, mentioning Harald, was too raw for deception. It set her suspicions at ease. This was indeed the man she'd come to secure for her daughter.

'Tell me, Roric,' she said, intending cruelty, needing honesty. 'Did you mean to kill the babe, or were you simply careless?'

Tears sprang to his eyes. 'I didn't kill Liam.'

'Someone else, then? On your orders.'

'*No*,' he said harshly. 'The babe's death—' Biting his lip, he pressed folded arms to his ribs so hard it was a wonder he could breathe. 'It was an accident. One I deeply regret.'

'Do you?'

'Liam was my flesh and blood! More than that, he was innocent. I would *never* harm him, or order him harmed!'

She knew a score of men who could speak those words with that same wounded passion, summon the same touching tears to their eyes, and she'd never believe them. Roric, she believed. The knot of fearful anxiety lodged beneath her breastbone eased. Perhaps she could give Catrain to this man and not feel like a whoremaster selling a bawd.

'I'd be interested to know how you found me,' she said, letting go the matter of Harald's slaughtered son. 'Don't say I have a Clemen spy in my court.'

Roric smiled, briefly. 'Blame sharp Clemen eyes rather than shadowy deceit. You were recognised, Madam.'

'By whom?'

'Does it matter?'

She frowned. 'You know it does.'

'By one of Humbert's men.'

Sharp relief. She wasn't betrayed, then. It was a comfort, after a night of much discomfort. 'Who else knows I'm here?'

'To my knowledge? No one.'

Again, she believed him. There was an honesty in Roric that she found both refreshing and alarming. Whatever seedlings of duplicity he'd managed to find in himself that had let him cozen Harald, best he nurture them swiftly. No great ruler could afford the luxury of an untarnished conscience.

'I meant what I said, you know,' he added, watching her. 'About compensating Ardenn for what was lost in those warehouses. Fire is always a danger, but I saw chaos tonight. I'll make sure we do better next time.'

'Make sure of it,' she said. 'For while I'll take Clemen's coin, gladly, some things can't be bought twice. Tihomir tells me there were priceless manuscripts that burned.'

Roric winced. 'I'm sorry.' Then, unfolding his arms, he leaned forward, his eyes intent. 'Why are you here, Berardine? What do you want, that you must ask for it in secret?'

This time she straightened all five of her rings, rubbing a smudge from her favourite ruby, noting a small pink diamond loosened in its gold clasp. Shoddy work by the goldsmith. She'd not buy from him again.

'Berardine?'

Never had she imagined brokering Catrain's marriage in such a fashion, filled with smoky sorrow and lacking sleep. She felt gauche and ill-prepared. Like a supplicant, not a duchess. Taking a deep breath, she lifted her gaze to meet his.

'It's a delicate matter, Roric. One close to my late husband's heart, and mine, that concerns Ardenn's future, and Clemen's . . . and most importantly yours. Will you hear me out? Or would you rather play the grand duke, and leave here as ignorant as you were before you came?'

CHAPTER ELEVEN

Before Roric could answer, the dayroom's door pushed open.

'Mama?' said Catrain, entering. 'Why are you—' But instead of finishing her question she stopped, staring at Roric. '*You!* What are you doing here? Did you save the horse? Please, please, tell me you did!'

Startled, Berardine watched Roric leap to his feet. 'The horse? No. I'm sorry,' he said, as surprised as her daughter. 'But I didn't let it suffer. It was the best I could do.'

Catrain, who loved horses more than gold, was blinking back tears. 'At least you tried. Those other men wouldn't even do that much. Cowards. I hate them. I hope *they* burn one day!'

'Fierce maid,' said Roric. He sounded approving. 'I'm quaking in my boots all over again.'

Catrain smiled at that. Though she wore an unremarkable green woollen dress, girdled about the hips with a plain leather belt, and her riotous hair was bundled haphazard into an unjewelled caul, her youthful beauty remained undimmed. Her expressive eyes revealed unfeigned admiration and interest. Roric's gaze, sharply attentive, showed rapt attention.

Both had forgotten they weren't alone.

'Catrain.' With an effort, Berardine relaxed her clenched fingers. 'Am I to understand you left this house during the night? Without permission? Or an escort?'

Recalled to dutiful obedience, Catrain turned. Saw how much strife she was in, and looked down. 'I'm sorry, Mama.'

'Why did you do it?'

'I wanted to see for myself what was happening.'

174

'And you escaped the premises how?'

'After you came to see I was unfrightened, I crept downstairs and hid in the pantry,' Catrain muttered, belatedly shamefaced. 'And when the uproar over the fire was loudest, I slipped out the back.'

Of course she did. Curious, resourceful and undaunted: Catrain was Baldwin's daughter in every way. 'And how did *seeing things for yourself* lead to a burning barn full of horses?'

Blushing, Catrain fidgeted her feet. 'I heard some men shouting about stables on fire, and then I heard the horses in distress. I thought I could help.' She looked up, beseeching. 'Mama, I *had* to. I couldn't just leave the poor things. That would've been cruel.'

She felt sick. And furious. All the while she'd stood in this dayroom, watching from a safe distance as Ardenn's warehouses burned, thinking her precious daughter was out of harm's way upstairs, the wicked child had been running loose in the riotous streets, no better than a tavern brat, caring only for *horses*.

'You risked your life for Harcian nags?'

Roric cleared his throat. 'I can't deny she was foolish, Madam. But your daughter was monstrous brave, too. You can be proud of that.'

'Can I?' she said coldly, berating him with her stare. 'And the next time she's monstrous brave, and it kills her, will pride smother my grief? Or undo the damage her disobedience will have wrought?'

'Life is uncertain, Madam,' he said, unflinching. 'Some of us die old, and some die young, and few of us have a say in it. What matters is how we live. And if we live without courage, then better we never lived at all.'

Unimpressed, Berardine snorted. 'Fine words, my lord. Most noble, I'm sure. But I wonder if you'd speak so swiftly in her defence if Catrain were your wife tonight, instead of my daughter.'

'Wife?' Catrain's eyes widened. 'Mama – is this *Roric*?'

'Wife?' Roric echoed, looking sharply between them. Then a disconcerted understanding dawned in his eyes. 'Berardine—'

With all her careful plans in smoking ruins now, she took a moment to settle her breathing and ease her spine. 'One moment, my lord. Catrain, leave us.'

Wisely, her daughter made no argument. 'Mama,' she murmured, bobbing a dutiful curtsy. Then she smiled at Roric. 'Your Grace.'

The door closed firmly behind her. Shaking his head, Roric returned to the settle. 'So this is why you've come to Eaglerock? To broker a marriage between Clemen and Ardenn?'

She showed him nothing but cool self-control. 'You find the notion abhorrent?'

'I find the notion astonishing,' he said, and laughed. Not a mocking sound, so that was something. 'Marriage. With your daughter. With that – that *child*.'

'Catrain is fourteen. By law she is a woman, and of marriageable age.'

Roric raised a hand. 'Laws are ink on paper. To my eyes, she's a child.'

'But a brave one. You said it yourself. And not . . . unattractive.'

A gleam in Roric's eyes as he silently acknowledged her daughter's beauty. 'You're serious, Berardine? You're offering me Catrain?'

'I am.'

'Even though I'm a bastard, and killed my cousin for his throne?'

'Bastard or not, you're Berold's grandson,' she replied. 'Duke Berold was much respected in Ardenn. He even courted Baldwin's grandmother, briefly. So you see, there is precedence. As for the manner of your cousin's demise . . .' She discounted Harald with a shrug. 'History is littered with untidy successions.'

A muscle leapt in Roric's cheek. 'If I made Catrain my duchess, her home would be here in Eaglerock. Or do you suggest I rule Clemen from your late husband's palace?'

She should be pleased, really, that he was a man who didn't let beauty blind him to awkward truths.

'Are Clemen and Ardenn so far apart?' she retorted. 'I think my presence proves they're not. The dukes of Clemen are in the habit of travelling. If you travelled a trifle further than usual, what harm is there in that?'

He drummed dirty fingers on his knee. 'And what does the Prince of Cassinia think?'

'The Prince of Cassinia is a milksuck.'

'Who has a council of regents.'

She shrugged. 'There is no law in Cassinia barring a marriage between you and Catrain.'

'The prince's regents could write one.'

'They could,' she agreed. 'At their peril. Cassinia's dukes are coming to treasure their growing independence from the crown. And what constrains Ardenn today might constrain one of them tomorrow. The dukes of Cassinia aren't fond of constraint.'

'Neither was Harald,' said Roric, very quietly. 'It didn't end well for him.'

Troubled, he pushed off the settle and began roaming the dayroom as though it were his own to wander. Sunrise flooded brightly through the window, making the paler light of lamp and candle almost disappear. Shifting in her chair, Berardine saw that the long night was catching up with him. Weariness slowed his movements, bruised shadows beneath his eyes.

'Believe me, Roric, I'd not intended to raise this matter with you in such a tumultuous fashion,' she said, softening her voice with sympathy. 'But events, it seems, have trampled me. And since the ice is broken . . .'

Halted before the window, Roric rested his fingertips against the uneven glass. As though he would reach out and touch the blackened warehouses. Give comfort to those the fire had burned most deeply, and lend strength to the men who still toiled amidst the hot ashes.

'You've taken me unawares, Beradine,' he said at last. 'I'd never thought to marry.'

'No? But surely every man dreams of a son.'

'Every man, yes,' he said, wry. 'But not every bastard.'

'You're no longer a bastard, Roric. You're Clemen's duke.'

'Almost.' Letting his hand fall, he glanced over his shoulder. 'Can I trust you with a confidence?'

'Of course.'

'It was never my ambition to create my own lordly house. I meant to caretake Clemen for Liam. Keep it safe for him till he was grown, and able to rule in his own right.'

She blinked. 'A noble thought, Roric, but impractical. You have to know Harald would have raised his son to hate you.'

'Perhaps. But I was prepared to bear the burden of Liam's hatred.' He grimaced. 'Believe me, the burden of his death is far worse.'

'I'm sure it is,' she said, smothering irritation. Roric might have time for maudlin sentiment, but she didn't. 'And I'm sorry for your grief. But now Clemen needs its future secured. And for that, you must marry and have sons.'

'With Catrain?'

'I think so.'

Roric turned, his expression sardonic. 'Cassinia has no eligible men?'

'None good enough for my daughter.'

'But I am. When you know nothing about me.'

'Roric.' She stood, meeting him stare for stare. 'Am I a fool? What I need to know of you, I know.'

'You need to know I'd never surrender Clemen to Cassinian rule.'

'Nor would I ask you to. I seek an alliance that would enrich both our duchies. Is that really so unthinkable? Clemen and Ardenn already share a rich history. Indeed, you sprang from us. The blood of my distant forbears flows through your veins. Together, Roric, I know we can achieve great things.'

He took a moment to examine his grimy fingernails. 'And if I married your daughter, would I be named Duke of Ardenn?'

'No,' she said, fighting the urge to fiddle with her rings. 'But your son would be. Could you content yourself with that?'

Roric smoothed a hand over his close-cropped hair. Frowned at the fresh soot smears on his palm. 'I could. But that's not the same as saying I will. You must know, Berardine, I can't answer you now. I'll have to discuss your offer with Clemen's council.'

'You can answer me this. Do you truly not mislike Catrain for her hoydenish antics with the horses?'

The corner of his wide mouth quirked in a fleeting half-smile. 'No. I don't mislike her. For that, or anything else.'

Well, then. Perhaps the Exarch was right, and there was a god after all. 'That's a start.'

'You and Catrain should go home to Carillon,' he said. 'Tonight. I'll have no swift decision for you, and you can't stay here for days on end. Word of your presence will spread, and that could cause trouble for both of us. Make sure Tihomir sends me a reckoning of your losses and I'll see you're promptly recompensed.'

She nodded. 'That's generous. I'm pleased to see it. I'd not wed my daughter to a miserly man.'

He held out his hand, and she returned his bloodstained dagger to him. Sheathing it, he favoured her with another half-smile. 'The generosity is yours, Berardine. Catrain is a rare maid.' He bowed. 'Have a safe journey home, Madam. I'll show myself out.'

Much, much later, long after Tihomir had been despatched to warn the *Dancer*'s captain that he should be ready to sail his galley home to Ardenn that night, Catrain crept back into the dayroom. For once in her mischievous life she was properly subdued, as befitted the properly brought-up daughter of a duke.

'Mama?' she said, demurely standing before her. 'Duke Roric. Will he have me?'

Remaining seated, Berardine looked at her. A needle-sharp pain pricked remorseless behind her dry, tired eyes. 'I don't know.'

Catrain swallowed. 'Because of the horses?'

'No. He admires you for the horses. I think he's the only man breathing in the world who would.'

'Oh.' Catrain tried, and failed, to smother a smile. 'I see.'

Abruptly furious, she fought the desire to slap her oldest daughter – and lost.

'*Mama!*' Shocked, one hand pressed to her blotched cheek, Catrain gulped for air. 'I'm sorry, I—'

'I'm not interested in *sorry*, Catrain! What use to me is *sorry*, with Roric returned to his castle and us dismissed home to Ardenn, and all my careful plans for our meeting gone up in flames and smoke like that horse!'

Tears spilled from Catrain's beautiful eyes. 'But you said he didn't mislike me. You said—'

'I know what I said! But this is a delicate business, child. And what must *you* do but blunder through it like a farmhand in muddy, hobnailed boots!'

Still weeping, Catrain crumpled onto the settle. 'I'm sorry,' she whispered. 'Must we really go home? Aren't we invited to Roric's court? I'd have done well there, Mama. I'd have learned lots of useful secrets for Ardenn. And – and I think I'd have made Roric like me.'

Remembering his small half-smile, Berardine sighed. 'Liking you isn't the rub. Roric likes you already.'

'Then there's still hope? He and I might yet be married?'

Perhaps . . . but she was far from sure. All her plans for Catrain, and Ardenn, had rested on her meeting with Roric. A meeting the time and place of which she had planned to control, where she'd intended to charm and cajole and persuade until Harald's bastard cousin gave her the answer she wanted. But thanks to Lord Humbert's man, who'd seen her, and the warehouse fire, which had ruined the night, she controlled nothing.

But that wasn't Catrain's fault.

'Mama?'

Temper cooled, she regretted losing it. The only spark of brightness in this muddy mess was that Roric had found something in Catrain to admire. She opened her arms. Catrain rushed to her, and they embraced.

'Don't fret, child,' she said, stroking her daughter's neatly contained hair. 'This is a setback, nothing more. We might leave Eaglerock on tonight's tide . . . but we'll be back again soon enough. I know it.'

For Izusa had promised the marriage would happen. And Izusa was never wrong.

'*Marriage?*' Humbert stared, incredulous. 'With *Ardenn*? What, is the widow gone mad?'

Seated in their half-circle of chairs in Eaglerock's council chamber, the rest of Clemen's councillors muttered agreement with Humbert's shocked demand. Seated separately, his chair raised upon a modest dais, Roric examined their faces as he waited for the fuss to die down. Did any man here think the notion of Clemen's duke wedding Catrain was worth serious consideration?

Humbert didn't, clearly. And from his look of derision, neither did Aistan. Scarwid huffed and puffed as though trying to recover from some mortal insult. As for Farland and the lords Hyett and Egann, they seemed just as unenthused. Only Ercole, banished to the council's outskirts, slumped in his chair with apparent disinterest. Perhaps it was lingering grief for Argante. With Ercole it was hard to tell. Pouting disdain was all he'd ever shown his fellow councillors. This morning, though he was dressed head-to-toe in velvet and jewels, with his gilded hair newly shorn and slicked with Rebbai pomade, he looked like a petulant child.

'My lord . . .' Farland glanced at his fellow councillors. 'Are we to assume you declined the duchess of Ardenn's kind offer?'

'Preposterous offer, you mean,' said Humbert. 'I can't believe she'd make it.'

Scarwid raised his eyebrows. 'You weren't present, Humbert?'

Every gaze shifted to Humbert. 'He was about other business on my behalf,' Roric said, as his foster-lord's face flushed. 'As for Berardine, I told her I needed time to ponder her proposal before answering. And I have thought on it, ever since I left her.'

'That long?' Humbert growled. 'Why? You can say *no* in half a heartbeat.'

Their eyes met. In Humbert's stare, hurt disbelief. Roric looked away. He'd deal with his foster-lord later.

'It troubles me,' said Aistan, fingers tapping his knee, 'that Berardine would enter Eaglerock under cover of darkness. If the offer is genuine, why be clandestine? Cassinia breeds perfidious men as a dog hatches fleas, but even so this seems out of the ordinary sly.'

'What does it matter if the offer's genuine?' Humbert demanded. 'It's a nonsense. Unthinkable. No duke of Clemen has ever married outside the duchy!'

Ercole stirred out of his sulking slump. 'There's a first time for everything. Isn't Roric proof of that?'

'Mind your manners,' said Humbert. 'Within this chamber you'll address him as *Your Grace*.'

'But I'm addressing you,' Ercole said, sneering. 'My lord. And I'm wondering why you're so hot to dismiss the widow's daughter.'

'Ercole, if you need an explanation then—'

'Do you mean to make it law, Humbert, that no duke of Clemen can wed beyond our borders? That seems presumptuous, even for the man who arranged my sister's slaughter.'

Spurred to his feet, Humbert rounded on Ercole. 'Bite your tongue, you mewling little cockshite! You're here on sufferance and—'

'*Enough!*' Roric shouted over the angry protests of his council. '*My lords, hold your peace!*'

Glowering silence. Humbert thumped back into his seat, face florid, beard jutting. Ercole, arms defiantly crossed, glared at the chamber's woodbeamed ceiling.

'My lords . . .' One by one, Roric frowned at them. 'I won't have this. Clemen must be guided by sober, self-disciplined men. If you can't control yourselves, how will you help me control this duchy? Ercole. Ercole, look at me.'

Unwilling, Ercole lowered his gaze.

'For the last time, Argante's death was never intended. Your sorrow is my sorrow. But I won't let it weaken this council or our duchy. For Clemen's sake, can you set your grief aside? If you can't, you're no good to me.'

Still, glowering silence. He could see in Humbert's face that his foster-lord was willing Ercole to quit the council. And Humbert wasn't alone. Not a man present wanted Argante's half-brother to remain. The decision to keep him had been politically prudent, not popular.

And because Ercole knew it too, knew how deeply his presence irked, he shook his head. 'I would stay a councillor. Your Grace.'

'Then be warned, Ercole. I'll tolerate no more of your outbursts.' He turned to Aistan. 'To answer your question, my lord, I don't doubt Berardine's offer was genuine. As for why she made it clandestine, I didn't ask.'

Aistan was scarcely containing his contempt. 'Because you knew she'd lie?'

Spirits save him. Aistan loathed Cassinians as though they'd done him some mortal harm. 'I assumed it had something to do with the vipers' pit of Cassinian politics.' Masking irritation behind a smile, he added, 'Or else at the last moment she regretted her choice of gown, and preferred not to display her poor taste in public.'

A ripple of uneasy amusement from the council, defusing the tension.

Lord Egann, elderly and most often timid, chosen councillor by

Harald for his accommodating ways, cleared his throat. 'My lord, how did you know Berardine was in Eaglerock?'

He made sure not to look at Humbert again. 'I was told.'

'Why didn't you tell us?' said Ercole. 'Why did you meet in secret with the widow?'

This time Ercole's comment sparked no furious outcry. Instead, Farland nodded. 'Yes, Your Grace. Why?'

And here it was. The first real challenge to his authority. If he didn't meet it, his rule would be over before it truly began.

'My lords, as Clemen's duke there will be times when I keep my own counsel,' he said. Addressing all of them, but looking at Humbert. 'Best you become accustomed to that.'

'But now the matter's in the open,' Humbert said, his right hand tight on the arm of his chair. 'And we can talk of it. We must talk of it. Roric, you can't marry the widow's brat.'

'Humbert's right,' Aistan agreed. 'Marrying Ardenn would yoke Clemen to every duchy in Cassinia, mire us in their festering feuds. We'd never know peace again. Nor can we wink at the hornet's nest such a marriage would stir with Harcia. You can be sure Aimery would view it as a grave threat.'

'He might even declare war!' said Scarwid.

Hyett was frowning. 'Indeed. Balfre would urge him to it. Given half a chance.'

Fervent exclamations as the council imagined the worst. Remembering the damage Harald had caused in the past by trying to mute them, Roric waited for their consternation to die a natural death. Instead let his mind wander, to contemplate Catrain. An unusual girl. Beautiful, yes, but beauty had limited uses. A duke was better served by a wife of wit and intelligence and courage, who could pass those attributes onto his sons. Catrain was in abundant possession of all three. And she was compassionate. He wanted that in a wife, too. The thought of marrying an Argante broke him into a cold sweat. So it was a pity he couldn't risk Berardine's daughter. But even though Catrain had caught his interest, stirred him, he could never put personal desires above Clemen's welfare.

Do that, and he'd be no better than Harald.

'My lords,' he said, judging they'd had enough time to express themselves. 'Rest easy. I've no intention of wedding Catrain. The advantages such a match would bring us – and there are many, you can't deny it, in trade and influence – still don't balance the scales. Cassinia's arrogance is well known. The prince's regents would soon be citing history as precedent, and seek to dabble their fingers in our business. Berardine has no power to stop them.'

'Perhaps she doesn't mean to,' said Farland. 'Perhaps she's come at their behest.'

'I don't think so,' Roric said, after a moment. 'Else there'd have been much public display. I suspect she hoped to settle things before ever the regents' council sniffed her intention.'

Aistan grunted. 'All the more reason to refuse her. If she thinks to hoodwink her own liege lord's advisors she proves herself the most poisonous viper of all.'

'And then where would we be?' said Hyett. 'We mustn't forget – like mother, like daughter.'

'So it's settled,' said Humbert. 'You're refusing the widow's offer.'
Roric raised an eyebrow. 'Haven't I said so?'

'But you will marry,' said old Lord Egann. 'That's not in doubt?'

Their eagerness to settle Clemen's future he could well understand, but he was starting to feel like a prize stallion. '*Yes*, Egann. In due course, I'll marry. In the meantime, leave me to deal with Berardine. To you, my lords, I leave what we've already agreed upon: the preparations for my acclamation and the restoration of the merchant district. And now we're done.'

To his complete lack of surprise, Humbert lingered in the council chamber until they were alone. Being private, his foster-lord let slip his deferential mask.

'So what's all this, boy?' he demanded. 'I thought we'd decided to confront the widow together and afterwards, once we'd learned her intentions, agree on what the council should be told.'

'I changed my mind.'

Humbert stared. 'Without consulting me?'

'My lord—' His fists were clenched so tight behind his back he could feel his fingernails biting his palms. 'The spirits know I never hungered to be Clemen's duke. But now I am, and so I will be. *Must* be.'

'You'd be a duke in secret?' Humbert retorted, red-faced. 'Treating your councillors with contempt? Roric—'

'No, Humbert,' he said fiercely. 'Not here. And not now.'

Humbert's jaw worked as he throttled his temper. 'Fine. At Arthgallo's, then. Three bells. Don't be late.'

Watching his foster-lord stamp out of the chamber, Roric released an unsteady breath. Defying Humbert was difficult. Painful.

'I'm sorry, my lord,' he murmured. 'But I must be my own man.'

The leechery's treatment chamber stank worse than a slave-infested Zeidican galley. Stripped to his linen drawers, snuffling through his stench-stuffed nose, Humbert glared around the caverny room crowded small and cramped with its laden shelves and roof-beams, its stacked boxes and burlap sacks and reeking barrels. What a collection of foul, pestilent concoctions. Filthy foreign powders! Galling, misbegot twisteries of nature! There, that bottle. Full of some animal's eyeballs. And that one? Birds' claws, shrivelled and knobby. He'd cut his own throat before swallowing one of *them*. And those knotted ropes of herbs, dangling from above. Looked like dried-up, sun-bleached lengths of horse intestines.

Faugh.

Every time he came here he swore he'd never come back. But then his head would start aching, or the twenty-years-gone sword thrust through his left thigh would wake again, complaining. The swollen joints in his right hand. His right knee, cracked in a joust the same year he won his spurs.

I'm getting old. That's my misery. All my years and youthful follies are finding me out.

The trouble was, as everyone knew, there couldn't be found anywhere in Eaglerock township a better leech than Arthgallo. Not in all of Clemen. No, nor the Marches and Harcia, either. So it was suffer in silence, suffer loudly at the hands of some inferior fool . . . or put up with whatever remedies Arthgallo decreed were required.

His movements as neat and precise as a chicken pecking wheat, the leech pinched up yellow powder from a stained wooden box on his bench and dropped it into his stone mortar. Pinched blue powder, and black powder, then a rustling snatch of dried leaves from a green

185

silk bag. The bag was scrawled over in odd-looking runes. Foreign writing. Maybe pagan.

Humbert sniffed. An exarchite would raise a fuss and confiscate the bag and its contents, most likely. As a councillor of Clemen he should express his own dismay. But he wasn't going to. No exarchite he'd ever met could ungripe him like Arthgallo. Not even Badouim with his incense and mumbled prayers. Show him an exarchite who had the healing touch and maybe he'd raise a complaint about pagan runes and so forth. But until then . . .

The leech looked up from his cluttered bench, smiling cheerfully. He was always smiling cheerfully. Most likely because he never swallowed his own potions.

'Not much longer, my lord. Nearly done. Not cold, are you?'

Four coal-burning braziers breathed heat into the leechery. It saved a nearly naked man from freezing, with the disadvantage of warming every stinking thing in the place to eye-watering strength.

Humbert sneezed. 'No.'

'Good, good,' Arthgallo said, beaming. Stringy strands of his grey hair had escaped his canvas leech's cap to straggle about his cadaverous face. Their tips were swiftly staining blue, black and brown. Similar stains marred the front and sleeves of his worn roughspun robe. 'Not to fret, my lord. I'll have you hoopish in a tricket.'

Feeling more and more apprehensive, even as his taut guts griped, Humbert watched Arthgallo pour a thin stream of dark green oil out of its glass flask and into the mortar. Frowned as something grey and chalkish was crumbled in after.

'What's that?' he said, suspicious.

Arthgallo waved a dusty hand. 'All part of the cure, my lord.'

Well, yes, but that wasn't an answer, was it? However, there was no use pressing the curs't man. When it came to his cures Arthgallo was as close-mouthed as a cold oyster.

A short time pounding the slop of ingredients with his pestle, and the leech was done at last. Trying not to breathe too deeply – the stench from the mortar paled every other stink in the room – Humbert blinked.

'You don't expect me to swallow that muck, do you?'

'Swallow it?' Arthgallo's spare frame shook with laughter. 'And kill my favourite patient? No, my lord, no. This is a liniment, of sorts.'

'Oh.' Liniments he understood. It was the 'of sorts' that had him fretsome. 'And that's all? You'll not bleed me?'

'Lightly, my lord,' Arthgallo said, pulling on a pair of supple calfskin gloves. 'A little leech-kissing, I think. You're not fevered, so a proper gushing would do more harm than good. Now, if you'd be kind enough to lift your arms?'

Stoically, Humbert endured the slathering of his armpits, his belly and the soles of his feet with the putrid slop in the mortar. Then he grimaced and winced his way through the attachment of ten thread-like, wriggling bloodsuckers to his shrinking flesh.

'Very good, my lord,' said Arthgallo, standing back to admire his handiwork. 'I doubt you'll need more letting than that, but we'll see.'

Eyes stinging from the fumes, Humbert nodded. 'Good.'

'Now, my lord, if you'd care to—'

The bright jingle of a bell, as the outer door to the leechery was opened. Frowning, Arthgallo turned. 'How peculiar. I set the door sign to "Closed". I'm sorry, my lord, I'll just—'

Humbert cleared his throat. 'I think you'll find your visitor's come to see me. Pass him through, Arthgallo, then wait outside till we're done. And should someone else turn up wanting you, see to them best as you can out there, with no mention of me or him. Understood?'

'My lord,' said Arthgallo, comfortably incurious, and did as he was told.

Soon after, the thick leather curtains dividing outer leechery from inner treatment room parted, and Roric entered. Nose wrinkling, he pushed back his concealing hood then flung aside the folds of his long woollen cloak.

'My lord,' he said, with a sharp nod. 'You couldn't think of a sweeter place to talk?'

Considering him, Humbert swallowed a sigh. Beneath the dark grey cloak Roric wore a plain brown doublet and brown hose. Good enough clothing when a man wished to draw no attention. But since he'd worn the same clothes in that morning's council meeting, it seemed the boy needed reminding yet again that he must peacock or else be thought a common lob.

'I can think of half a dozen easily, but we'll not be noticed here.'

Roric grinned, briefly. 'True.' Then he frowned. 'You're all right, Humbert? What's amiss?'

A week hence and this man would be formally acclaimed Clemen's duke. Already, anticipating it, there was a change in him. The hesitant, conscience-wrung Roric of Heartsong had vanished. In his place stood this man who, despite his feeble attire, was grown bold and decisive, the man he'd urged this former foster-son, the son of his heart, to become.

How disconcerting to find himself . . . disconcerted.

'Amiss?' he said, striving to sound as cheerful as his leech. 'Nothing turbulent. Gripe. The old trouble. Not to fret. Arthgallo will see me hale and hearty.'

Still frowning, Roric cast a doubtful look about the shadowy chamber and then at the dangling, gorging leeches. 'I know you set great store by his cures. But you're a braver man than I am, Humbert, to throw yourself on this mercy.'

'Wait till you're my age,' he grunted. 'You'll find then it's less courage and more desperation. Roric, when do you mean to refuse the widow?'

A hint of temper in Roric's eyes. 'It's not even a full day yet since she made her offer. Don't mankle on it, Humbert. I said I'd deal with her, and I will.'

'But you ordered her home to Ardenn, at least?'

'Of course. She leaves tonight.'

Well, that was something. 'Then you've time to tell her the answer's no before she sails.'

'What?' Roric laughed, disbelieving. 'You want me to go back to her? In broad daylight? Humbert, have those leeches drained the sense from you, along with your blood?'

'I don't say meet her again! Spirits forfend, boy. One mistake of that stripe is enough. Send her a note!'

'And make it look like I'm falling over myself to reject her daughter?' Roric shook his head. 'I don't think so, Humbert. She'll be wounded as it is. You think it's clever politics to add insult to the injury?'

Humbert scowled. It would be easier to argue if he weren't standing in his drawers, painted with foul-smelling slop and hosting a feast of leeches.

'Clever politics is making sure that if word of the offer is ever breathed about Clemen, or reaches Harcia's ears, your refusal is long since writ in stone! For if it's not you can be certain someone will make mischief!'

A pinching of Roric's brows acknowledged the truth of his observation.

'And I'll say this, Roric, since we're blunt speaking,' he added, feeling his own wounded feelings prick. 'It hurt that you broke this business to the council with me not a whisper the wiser beforehand.'

Eyes hooded, Roric made a great show of poking about Arthgallo's crowded bench, as though the muckery of leechcraft was of deadly importance.

'I'm sorry,' he said at last. 'That wasn't my intent.'

What did intent matter? It was deeds that counted. But even worse than being hurt, he'd felt his fellow councillors' surprise as they realised he'd not known of Berardine's offer. It was galling. And it weakened him . . . which made him angry. After all he'd risked for Roric, the boy owed him more loyalty.

'Why did you meet the widow alone the moment my back was turned?'

'I told you. I'd have Aistan and the others know I'm my own man.'

'Fine. But why not at least tell me first thing this morning, what you'd done? Why leave me looking a fettled fool in front of the council?' A nasty thought jabbed. 'Did you keep clap-tongue because you're tempted?'

'By Catrain?' Roric picked up a dried bassa root. Stared at it closely, as though he were interested. 'No.'

But his denial was too slow. Humbert felt his belly churn. 'You've seen the girl? Berardine risked bringing her to Eaglerock?'

'And if she did? If I saw Catrain? What does it matter? I've said it plain. I'll not wed with her.'

'What *matters* is you never told me! Roric—'

Roric looked up sharply. 'I'm not blind, Humbert. Or deaf, or

189

wanting wit. People wonder if I'm not too beholden to you. They wonder if I can't make a decision without first I seek your opinion. Or your permission.'

'What people?' He laughed, disbelieving. 'You don't mean that little cockshite Ercole?'

'Not just Ercole,' Roric insisted, mule-stubborn. 'Aistan and the rest stood with me against Harald because they had no other choice. But if they come to doubt me—' He banged his fist on the bench, making cups rattle and boxes jump. 'Harald was right. I'm vulnerable.'

Breathing deeply, Humbert waited until he could trust himself not to shout. 'All the more reason to refuse Berardine sooner rather than later. Then marry a fine Clemen girl who'll give you fine Clemen sons.'

Another silence, as this time Roric inspected the contents of the nearest slumped burlap sack. He was frowning again. At length he turned, wiping his ochred fingers down the side of his cloak.

'I was angry at first, when Harald told me I'd never marry,' he murmured, his eyes blurring as he gazed at the past. 'But in time I came to see he was right. Look at the strife noble bastards have caused in the Danetto Peninsula.'

'That's Danetto,' he said. 'And Harald is dead. Now marriage and siring sons is your duty.'

'I know,' said Roric, his voice edged. 'It's just . . . I'm not in love.'

Caught unawares, Humbert banged his chest, coughing. '*Not in love?*'

Roric's cool gaze narrowed. 'You've dropped a leech, Humbert.'

'I'll drop you, boy!' he said, still wheezing. Refusing to look at the gorged and bloated bloodsucker plopped from his cheek to the floor at his stinking feet. '*Not in love?* What mumfoolery is this?'

'It's not unheard of, that a man should love his wife,' said Roric, defensive.

'It's unheard of he should think of love first instead of last! Especially when that man is a duke!'

Still defensive, and resentful with it, Roric took to pacing. Kicked a box of bones in passing, and cursed.

'Mind your temper,' Humbert growled. 'Arthgallo sets great store by his leechcraft.'

Roric's withering glare scorched him head to toe. 'I can tell.'

Another blood-fattened leech lost its hold and plummeted. He wrestled with the urge to pulp it under heel. 'Roric . . .' Wheedling now, because the boy was curdled and needed a light touch. 'Is it you've got some misgivings about the notion of matrimony?'

'Of course I do!' Roric snapped, goaded. 'When I take a wife it'll be to sire sons upon her, no better reason. The least woman in Clemen deserves more kindness than that.'

'You think you won't be kind? Don't be a fool, Roric. You're no Harald. Guimar and I between us raised you more knightly than that.'

'Yes, you did.' Sighing, Roric fetched up at the leech's work bench and leaned his hip against it. 'But . . .' He pressed thumb-and-fingertip against his closed eyes. 'For all the pitfalls in wedding with Ardenn, I think there are as many to dance around when choosing a homegrown wife. Past plagues have winnowed Clemen of its daughters.'

Yes, and its sons. As if he needed reminding, with both his boys lost to the last ravaging foul pestilence. Ailred and Collyn. The lack of them was a never-healed ache in his heart.

Roric blinked at him, belatedly remembering. 'I'm sorry, my lord. I didn't mean to – all I meant was that it's meagre pickings among our best houses.' Disconsolate, he slumped. 'I might do better casting a wider net.'

'Ha!' Humbert flicked a third sluggishly wriggling leech from his flesh. 'Like Harald did, in catching Argante? No, Roric. Be taught by your bastard of a cousin in this. What man in his right mind puts his best warhorse to a common carting mare, even if her hide is glossy? You can't do it. One Ercole at court is enough.'

Roric grimaced. 'True.'

And now they'd come to it. Mouth suddenly dry, and not because of the heat and stink, Humbert scratched under his armpit, where Arthgallo's congealing slop prickled his skin. But there was no use beating about the bush. Best simply to say it, in the voice of authority that Roric had obeyed since he was seven years old.

'There's only one answer to this puzzle, boy. You'll marry Lindara.'

CHAPTER TWELVE

'*Lindara?*' Roric slid his hip off the bench. 'Humbert, are you touched? Should I summon the leech?'

Chin jutting, beard bristled, Humbert slitted his eyes. 'D'you tell me there's a girl better bred anywhere in Clemen? You can't, for you'll not find one. And she's comely enough, if I say it myself. Takes after her mother, spirits be thanked. Why not wed with Lindara, when your heart's not given elsewhere?'

'*Why not?* I've just told you! I must be careful to put some distance between us or turn the other lords sour!' Roric dragged a hand down his face. 'You should find another leech, Humbert. Arthgallo's cures are addling your wits.'

'Fine,' he said, hands fisted. 'Marry Lindara and I'll step down from the council. Will that answer? Make my daughter your duchess and I'll not set foot in Eaglerock again.'

All the temper in Roric's eyes cooled. 'What?'

'You heard aright. Name Aistan your chief counsellor and pasture me like an old nag. Or if Aistan chafes, name someone else. Anyone save Ercole. I'll go lambish, Roric, my vow on it. Only wed with Lindara.'

'Humbert, I don't want you to go lambish, or naglike, or in any animal fashion! What use to me will you be cooped up in Larkspur castle? I need you in Eaglerock.'

Touched by Roric's heartfelt dismay, Humbert pretended interest in the sole of his foot. Arthgallo's muck had dried hard, and was itching.

'Didn't you just say I'm a cause of trouble to you, boy? Surely you'll be better off if I'm not here for you to stumble over.'

'That wasn't my meaning! I can't have Clemen's nobles think you lead me round by the nose, but of course I need your counsel. How else can I be duke?'

'You can be duke however you choose,' he said. 'And wherever I am, boy, you'll still be duke. This time tomorrow, or by the end of next week, I could be dead from my weight of years. One day I will be. D'you tell me you mean to stop being Clemen's duke when I die?'

'Don't talk rumption, Humbert,' Roric snapped.

He salted his foster-son with a glare. 'There's no rumption in plain truth. And I'd die a happy man if my Lindara was your wife.'

Groaning, Roric again slumped his hip to Arthgallo's bench. 'Does Lindara know you're offering her to me?'

'She knows it's her duty to marry. And she knows the obedience owed her father.'

'Ha! You mean she doesn't.'

'Never you fret about Lindara.' He raised a warning finger. 'Listen well, Roric. You must wed. Soon. Before those lords who do have eligible daughters start dangling them in front of you. If you're promised before ever they raise their hopes you'll save all of us much grief.'

'Perhaps,' Roric said after a moment, reluctant.

'For certain! Tell me, what happens if Aistan thinks to thrust his youngest girl into your path?'

'Kennise? The daughter Harald—'

'The same. What if Aistan decides he's owed recompense for Harald's debauching of her? What if he says marriage with his ruined daughter is the price of his support?'

'Aistan wouldn't,' Roric said, disconcerted. 'He's an honourable man.'

'An honourable man whose pride was deeply wounded by your cousin. Would you wound him afresh by spurning his child?'

Roric was shaking his head. 'What Harald did to Kennise was wicked. She bears no blame. But even so, Aistan *knows* I could never wed with—'

'Never?' Humbert rolled his eyes. 'Before we took down Harald, boy, all of Clemen knew a bastard could never be made duke. Yet there you stand. The girl was a virgin. She's not pregnant, and she's been kept in seclusion since Harald had her. As for her bloodlines, they're near as good as Lindara's. What grounds would you have to refuse Aistan's offer?'

'Why can't I simply say no?'

'He'd want a reason, Roric. And whatever reason you gave him, no matter how crafty, he'd take offence at it. Aistan's a good man, but pricklesome when it comes to his family.'

'Most men are.'

'And there you make my point!' he said, itching to shake Roric until the boy saw sense. 'Every lord of Clemen whose daughter you reject will want a reason. And every reason you give is bound to raise hackles. You'll be surrounded by offended nobles. Is that how you want to start your rule?'

'Humbert, even if you're right . . .' Roric rubbed a hand over his face, then started pacing afresh. 'You can't deny Aistan and the rest of the council are watching how close you and I stand.'

'Keep them sweet with honours and prestigious tasks and watching is all they'll do.'

'So you say,' Roric muttered, stepping round a toppled pile of dried batwings. 'But depend on it – they'll say I seek to enrich your house at the expense of every other great noble's family.'

'I have no house,' he said roughly. 'It died with my boys. You know that, Roric. You stood beside me as it fell. The day these ageing bones of mine are buried, my name will be buried with them. In giving you Lindara I look to secure her future. What dutiful father leaves his only child undefended? As for Aistan, I—'

'Don't tell me again to send you from Eaglerock, Humbert, for I won't!'

'Then stand your ground. Show Clemen's lords your teeth. Aistan and the rest, they might not want another Harald but they do want a man who'll snarl at Harcia when he needs to. Snarl at them first and prove you can.' He shrugged, shaking the leeches still bloating themselves on his blood. 'And if you must, claim you're lovelorn for Lindara.'

Roric threw him a look. 'But I'm not.'

'Then lie,' he said, brutal. 'Clemen's future is worth a lie. Besides, you like her well enough. Or did my eyes deceive me as you grew to manhood under my roof?'

Another glowering look. 'Liking isn't loving, Humbert. You don't think she deserves love?'

Humbert thought of Vidar. There was love there, and it would lead to nowhere but disaster. 'Love isn't everything, Roric. Most times it isn't anything at all.'

'You're harsh,' Roric whispered, halting, his back turned. 'Humbert, she's your *daughter*.'

'All the more reason for you to have her.'

'My lord . . .' Slowly, Roric turned. 'What if I can't make her happy? I don't want to hurt her. I don't want her to hate me.'

'Hate you?' Humbert scoffed. 'My fortunate daughter will kiss your feet.'

'And if she doesn't?'

'D'you think I've not lost nights of sleep over this?' His arms spread wide in appeal. 'Ever since Harald's first son died in its cradle our duchy has danced on daggerpoint. Now you must settle Clemen's nerves by giving it your undoubted heir. And the woman who'll cause the least roilery in that is Lindara. She's impeccably bred, she's not foreign, and there'll be no question you're the sire of the sons she'll bear you.'

'Even so . . .' Fists on his hips, Roric breathed out sharply. 'I'd speak with her first.'

He could easily have plucked the leeches from his chest and thrown them at the boy. 'To what end? Clemen's noble daughters wed their father's choice, and that's that.'

'And if Lindara's heart is given elsewhere?'

Vidar. Curse the inconvenient bastard. With an effort Humbert kept his face blank, because Roric knew him too well. 'Lindara's heart is in *my* keeping. She trusts I'll give it to a worthy man. And you are worthy, Roric. How else could I love you like my own flesh and blood?'

Roric's obdurate expression softened. 'And I you, my lord.'

'Then we're agreed? You'll wed her?'

Still, Roric hesitated. 'Humbert . . .'

'Then name me another girl, *any* girl, you'd make your duchess in Lindara's place!'

Silence, as Roric stared at the leechery floor. From the outer chamber, the faint sound of voices as Arthgallo tormented other suffering souls.

'You can't, can you?' Humbert demanded, when he'd waited long enough. 'You know I'm right.'

On a sigh, Roric lifted his head. 'It seems you are.'

'Then it's done,' he said, scalded with relief. 'But you'll let me tell Lindara. As her father, that's my task. Now, Your Grace, you'd best be on your way. Arthgallo's not finished with me and I've some shreds of dignity left.'

Half-smiling, Roric looked him up and down. 'You do?'

Humbert threw a leech at him.

After some time spent poking and prodding his patient, followed by much pulling of his pendulous lower lip, Arthgallo at last decreed there should be another round of bleeding.

'For caution is a comely thing, my lord Humbert, and leeches are not hard to find!'

With the second bleeding endured, then there was the swallowing of a foul concoction, upon insistence.

'I know, my lord,' said Arthgallo, leavening cheer with a smidgin of sympathy. 'It seems the gods of healing are blessed with a poor sense of humour, when that which succours us would make us heave our guts upon our boots.'

Belly protesting and tongue shrivelled, Humbert glowered at the leech. 'Enough of that pagan shammery, man. Now, are we done? Or have you more misery in mind for me?'

No, they were done. Plucked free of bloodsuckers, sponged clean and dressed again, Humbert paid Arthgallo four silver ducats then took his leave. Ah, the relief of breathing fresh air again! Well. Fresh after the stink of the leechery. Much cheered by it, and by the easing of gripe in his guts, he made his way out of the alley and onto wider Leech Street, which was thronged with townsfolk on foot and on horseback.

Few of Clemen's nobles troubled to walk about the duchy's towns and villages. What they needed was fetched for them, given into their hands by merchants and traders and servants. Most of Clemen's great lords and their ladies kept to themselves, disdaining the dust and mud of the streets. When forced to stir, they went on horseback. For himself, he never found it demeaning to rub shoulders with the ordinary people. No, he deemed it important. Like a hunting hound he scented the air, seeking the smallest hint of danger, of blood on the brink of being spilled. In the days following Harald's violent passing, he'd smelled that kind of trouble. Then he'd hourly expected the clarion-call of disaster. Had held his breath and pinched his thumbs and prayed the peace would hold. A dark time, that in his darkest moments he feared might not pass.

But it did. He could smell no danger now. Only the everyday stinks to be found in any busy township – horse dung, ox dung, puddled piss, wood smoke, baking bread, roasting meats, the distant sear of the tannery and the iron tang of the forge. Blowing through all of it, fresh salt from the harbour laced with the wetness of fish. And still, lightly lingering, an exotic memory of burned spice.

Walking crosswise from Leech Street down to the merchant district, because he wanted to quietly see for himself how the repairs to Ardenn's ruined warehouses progressed, Humbert nodded at the few who recognised him without the help of his house badge, the antlered stag, stitched to his russet brocade doublet. At the top of Bakers Way he paused, to see who the gathered crowd was jeering. Ah. Some fool of a baker who'd been caught adding chalk or gravel or even wadded cobwebs to his loaves. Pegged into a pillory, the dishonest man was weeping as his furious victims hurled dead rats and rotten eggs and sloppy stinking cow shit into his face.

Humbert snorted, and moved on. Serve the jackanapes rogue baker right. Shit in his eyes and perhaps a broken nose for good measure would teach him not to fartle with Eaglerock's bakers' beadle, with his heavy stick and dour opinion of those who'd flout the baking laws.

After Bakers Way came Salt Street, and after Salt Street the rabbit warren known as Chandlers Square. That tipped him into steeply sloping Anchor Road, running all the way to the harbour, cutting the merchant district in half.

With every step he took he could feel Eaglerock castle looming behind him. Feel the weight of knowing how much he'd asked of

Roric, and still asked, and would yet ask, pressing down on him like a great hand, threatening his breath and his bones.

But he'll not fail me. And he'll not fail Clemen. If I thought he would, or could, I'd never have started this.

Upon reaching the site of the warehouse fires, Humbert found an unobtrusive shadow to stand in. Work on the gutted buildings had started just after sunrise. Now, with the sun sliding towards the horizon, that work was well underway. The din of hammers and wood saws, of stonemasons and blade-grinders, rang raucous in his ears and drowned the wider noise of harbour and township, as nearly a score of men laboured to rebuild what had been lost to the flames. He caught sight of Ardenn's trading factor, Tihomir, red-faced and dishevelled, trying to bully two Eaglerock clerks sent by Roric to keep an account of the damages. Whatever Berardine's man was demanding, the clerks appeared disinclined to agree. Not so much as a flinch, as the widow's lickspittle brandished a fist beneath their intransigent noses. Good. Offer Ardenn a pared fingernail and it would take a man's arm all the way to his shoulder.

Imagining Clemen married into Cassinia, Humbert felt his guts grind and gripe anew. But then he mastered himself. Only a fool wasted time dwelling on what might have been . . . and he was no fool. That danger was knocked aside like an inexpert sword thrust. Clumsy Berardine was ordered home, and she'd not be coming back. All that remained of the sorry business was the need for him to tell Lindara she'd soon be wed, and so made Clemen's duchess.

Lindara.

'A pox on it,' he muttered uneasily, rubbing his brocade-covered belly. 'And spirits save me. For she'll see herself ill-used, I know it, though I'm giving her the moon.'

Because preserving lemons was a way to keep her dead mother close, Lindara never let her father's cook near the task. Working in the townhouse's citrus-scented small kitchen, her hair wrapped in a coif, her plain linen dress swathed in an apron and her needle-pricked fingers stinging from spilled juice, she smiled through misty tears as she remembered how she and her mother had preserved winter's end lemons together. Salt in the bottom of a pottery jar. Sharp knife slicing through each plump fruit, exposing the firm, pale yellow flesh. A hearty salt rub, inside and out. Then squash the salted lemon into the jar. When the jar was full, add more juice then seal it with a cork stopper and a generous slather of warm wax.

She could still feel the press of her mother's lips to her childish cheek in reward for a task well done. Hear her mother saying *'Never stint on the salt, Lindara. It's the key to a good preserve.'* That was why she insisted on purchasing Evran salt from Cassinia. That had been her mother's first choice. Let Humbert grumble at the cost, so long as he paid it.

Oh, it made her heart ache, how much she missed her mother.

'My lady,' said Eunise, from the kitchen doorway. 'Lord Humbert has returned from the town, and sends me to fetch you.'

Not looking up, she eased her paring knife through a new lemon's thick rind. 'You may tell my father I'm occupied, and will come to him by and by.'

'My lady,' said Eunise, disapproving. 'He bids you come at once.'

She put down knife and lemon with care. It was important, then. *Vidar. Vidar. Please let it be Vidar.* 'At once? What's amiss?'

'Amiss? I know naught of amiss, my lady. Lord Humbert's not in the habit of confiding in me.'

Eunise's snappish reply turned her towards the doorway. Since Vidar's visit, and that business with his dagger, her former nurse's manner had been tender as a gorse bush.

'Very well,' she said. 'But you'll stay here and make certain the cook keeps his fingers off my preserves. Lord Humbert's in his closet?'

'Yes, my lady,' said sour Eunise.

Breathing tight, Lindara made her way from the kitchen to her father's privy chamber, where he often worked on council matters not concluded at the castle. At its closed door she hesitated. He'd not like to see her garbed like a servant. She should take a moment to remove the coif and apron, find a jewelled caul for her hair. But then she remembered she was cross with him for keeping her caged in the townhouse. She opened the door without knocking, dressed how she liked.

'You wanted me, my lord?'

Seated in a wood and leather chair, one hand nursing a goblet of wine, the generous candlelight showed the great Lord Humbert weary. His grizzled beard was finger-tangled, a sure sign of perturbation. Seeing her, he frowned.

'Why do I pay silver ducats by the handful for ells of velvet when you'd as lief dress like a kitchen drab?'

'I'm preserving lemons, my lord. Salt and juice will ruin velvet.'

'Ah,' he said, his voice softening. 'Your mother's recipe?'

'Of course. And I've not finished yet, so—'

'Never mind your lemons, girl. I've something to tell you.' He jerked his chin at the closet's empty chair. 'Sit.'

Breathing tight again, she obeyed. 'How went it with Arthgallo?'

'The man's obsessed with leeches,' her father said, scowling. 'I've lost less blood skirmishing in the Marches.'

'But you feel better?'

'I'm not dying. But enough of that. Lindara, I've news. You're to wed with Roric. You'll be Clemen's new duchess, and mother to its next duke.'

'What?' she said faintly. She could hear her heartbeat, pounding in her ears. 'Wed with Roric? But – I thought—'

'Thought what?' he said, staring.

She was going to be sick, surely. Vidar had failed her. He'd promised to speak with Humbert, secure her father's blessing, and broken his word. Or his courage had failed. He'd never admit it but Godebert's folly had scarred him. Now he cared what others thought, when he'd never cared before. But she didn't. She never would, no matter what happened. So she must be brave for both of them.

She gave her father stare for stare. 'My lord, I can't wed with Roric.'

Humbert thudded his goblet to the small table by his side. 'You can and you will. It's been arranged.'

Just like that. No thought for her. She had to blink hard, to banish the sight-smearing anger. 'By you?'

'Yes, by me. Roric and I agreed on it this afternoon, in the leechery.'

'The *leechery*?' Somehow, she found the strength to stand. Her legs were trembling, and her hands. 'You bartered me to Roric while you were being fed on by *leeches*?'

Humbert's face darkened. 'Don't you take that tone with me, girl. I—'

'Did he ask for me? Roric? Or am I to be thrust upon him against his will?'

'And don't talk trumpery! Roric knows your value, Lindara, he—'

'Roric thinks of me as a *sister*!' she shouted. 'I've no desire to marry him, my lord. You *know* who I would wed!'

Still seated, Humbert glared up at her. 'Even before the Marches ruined him Vidar was never good enough for you. He's the son of a traitor. And blood proves itself. You know it.'

'I know a man isn't a staghound,' she retorted. 'Or a stallion, or any beast. You can't judge his worth with a studbook, or by what his father did. Vidar is a good and valiant man and he loves me. Roric doesn't. I won't wed him. I love Vidar.'

With a grunt, Humbert stood. His beard was jutting, an ominous sign. 'Weren't you listening? I've made you a duchess. That you'd argue such good fortune only proves you're too childish to choose for yourself.'

She put up her own chin, fresh rage smothering fear. 'Childish, my lord? I'm eighteen. Four years a legal woman.'

'Legal to wed,' her father said, his eyes cold. 'But until that day you're in my care and you'll do as you're told. Vidar's denied you, Lindara. Best make your peace with that.'

Make her peace with it? How could she? Oh, why wouldn't he understand? 'Please, my lord. If you love me, don't do this.'

'*If* I love you?' Humbert roared. 'It's *because* I love you that I do it! I was ready to abandon my duty to Roric for this marriage. To resign from the council so the likes of Aistan wouldn't carp!'

'And what of your duty to me? Don't you care that I don't want this? I've pledged my heart and soul to Vidar. The thought of wedding Roric makes me feel like a whore!'

Humbert seized her arms, his calloused fingers cruelly biting. 'Has Vidar touched you? Has he *breached* you? If he has, girl, I swear I'll—'

'No,' she said, her voice breaking. 'How could you think it? Vidar has his honour, and I have mine. My lord – Father – *please*—'

Releasing her, Humbert stepped back. 'You prate to me of honour.

Of *duty*. What of your duty to me, Lindara? What of the honour owed to our name? Your brothers are dead. Our house will die with me. The only hope for our bloodline lies with the sons born of your body. And you'd waste our nobility on *Vidar*? You'd choose Vidar over *Roric*, the great Berold's grandson?'

'I'd choose love! Without it life is a desert!'

'You know nothing of life, girl! You're a foolish, featherbrained chit.'

'I know my mother loved me,' she said, a tempest of tears rising. 'I know she'd never forgive you for forcing me like this!'

Humbert slapped her. 'Your mother would never forgive me for letting you marry the crippled, one-eyed son of a traitor! A man who only stood against Harald so he could fill his empty purse!'

'That's unfair! You're unfair!' she said, as the spilled tears flowed down her stinging cheek. 'You said it yourself, Harald's judgement was unjust. Whatever Godebert did, Vidar *never—*'

'It was never proven,' said Humbert. 'There's a difference.'

'Not to me! And if he was good enough to risk in your deposing of Harald, how can he *not* be good enough to sire my sons?'

'When it comes to wedding and bedding you, girl, Vidar isn't good enough to wipe my shitty arse! *Love* him? One day as Clemen's duchess and you'll barely remember his name.'

'That's not true.' Half-blinded, she dropped to her knees before her father. Reached out with trembling fingers and touched them to his hand. 'Please, my lord. I'm begging you. Don't make me do this.'

He snatched his hand away as though her touch were poison. 'So I'm cursed, am I? Ailred dead, Collyn dead, and a daughter who cares more for her own childish, passing fancies than she does for the duty and honour owed her sire and her house!'

'And so am I cursed!' she cried. 'With no mother to defend me, and a father who'd sacrifice my happiness in pursuit of his own lust for power!'

He slapped her again, so hard he felled her. 'You're an ungrateful bitch, Lindara! Defend you? Were your sweet mother here, girl, she'd *disown* you! Your rank disobedience would break her heart!'

Her head was ringing from the force of his blow. Sobbing, because she was hurt in body now as well as in heart, she hid her face in her folded arms so her father wouldn't see what he'd achieved. She heard his breathing harshen as he bent close.

'Listen well, Lindara, for I'll not say this again. You'll wed with Roric, or with no man. The choice is yours. Life in Eaglerock, as Clemen's duchess, cared for by Clemen's duke, who'll deny you no luxury your heart could desire – or a barred, barren chamber in Larkspur until you die of old age, withered and alone.'

Stunned, she kept her face hidden. He didn't mean it, surely. Humbert was a hard man, toughened by years of conflict in the Marches, by his great griefs, by the burden of trying to constrain Harald at his worst, but . . . he couldn't mean it. He couldn't do that to his own flesh and blood, his only daughter, the sole child of his body yet living.

'Don't test me, girl,' said Humbert. 'Don't think to play my sympathies, like a harp. In the matter of this marriage I'm no more yielding than stone.'

So. He did mean it. And what was she to do? Short of murder, she had no defence against him. He was the great Lord Humbert. She was his daughter. Every law, every opinion, sat firmly on his side. And clearly Roric was willing to abet him in his bullying. There was no hope for help there.

'*Lindara*. I'll have your answer.'

She couldn't defeat him, at least not face to face. Her father might deserve a dagger plunged and twisted in his belly but the mother who'd loved her, who'd taught her how to preserve lemons, would never want her to do it. She'd have to find another way to win. A sly way, a cunning way. A woman's way, in this world where men's wants mattered most.

Slowly, she sat up. Used her juice-stained apron to dry her tears. The sharp citrus scent gave her strength. She breathed in deeply, and felt hatred like acid etch itself into her soul.

'My lord,' she said, lifting her dry eyes. 'All my life I've been your obedient daughter. If you decree Roric is a better match for me than Vidar then I'll bow to your wishes, and wed him.'

Humbert frowned. 'And no more caterwauling for Godebert's second-rate heir?'

Caterwauling, he called it. Her desperate cry from the heart. He was a monster, her father. 'His name shall never again pass my lips.'

'Good then!' said Humbert, and held out his hand. He was still stern, but his eyes were warmer. 'I knew you'd be sensible. You'll thank me one day, Lindara. When you're holding your son, the next duke of Clemen, you'll thank me.'

She let him help her stand. 'Yes, my lord,' she murmured, her gaze downcast. 'And I'm sorry I was vexatious. You took me by surprise with this news. I never thought I'd be Clemen's duchess.'

'Nor me,' he said, and laughed. 'Fate's wheel turns strangely.'

Looking up, she pretended anxiety. 'I fear to fail you, my lord.'

Another laugh. 'Fail me? For shame, girl. You only fail me when you're undaughterly. Promise me you'll mind your manners and we'll be honey-sweet.'

As if she were one of his hunting bitches caught sniffing after the wrong dog. She smiled at him, deceitful, and showed him only what he wished to see: a biddable daughter, brought meekly to heel. 'I promise. Now, if you please, I'd return to my lemons.'

'Yes, yes,' he said, briskly jovial. 'And as for dinner, you may suit yourself. I dine with Aistan tonight. We've council business to chew on.'

'Then I shall join you for breakfast.'

'In the morning I must break bread with some exarchites.' He rolled his eyes. 'I'll return for you in the afternoon. We'll see Roric then, together, and you'll tell him how he's made you the happiest maid in Clemen.'

'Yes, my lord,' she said, and curtsied. 'Thank you, my lord.'

She closed his closet door very softly behind her. Hurried back to the small kitchen and snatched up her sharp knife. And as she stabbed and stabbed more lemons, imagined the juice they spilled was his blood.

That night her sleep was fitful, haunted by dreams of betrayal and despair. At last, any hope of rest abandoned, she watched the false dawn give way to the rising sun, then daylight, and while the sky lightened she plotted her revenge.

'Eunise,' she said, as her old nurse laced her silk-and-velvet striped sleeves to her bodice, 'there's a herbary woman I've heard tell of in the township. She has a little shop in Comfrey Lane. I'd have words with her this morning. D'you see that sealed letter on the chest, there? Tell the runner-boy to deliver it, so she might be warned I'm coming.'

Eunise's busy fingers ceased their lacing. 'A herbary woman, my lady? Are you unwell?'

'No. But I am to be married, Eunise. And since my first duty will be to give Clemen a healthy heir, I must—'

'My lady!' Eunise was near to squealing. 'Do you marry the lord Roric?'

Of course the old wretch would be delighted. 'You're not to breathe a word of it beyond these chambers, Eunise. If you do I'll see you beaten and locked in a cupboard, I swear!'

Fingers trembling now, Eunise began lacing the other sleeve. 'No – I mean yes – oh, *my lady*! This is wondrous good news! You must be so happy!'

Yes, indeed. Happy as a man being dragged to the gallows. 'I'm the most fortunate of maids, Eunise.'

'But my lady, what need is there for some untried herbary woman recommended by idle chatter? Master Arthgallo—'

'Is a man. I've no desire to unburden my womanly heart to him.'

'But—'

'Eunise, don't *scribble*! Would you spoil my morning with your carping? Surely I may be allowed to choose my own physick without you pecking at me like a crotchety hen!'

Eunise's sallow cheeks flushed. 'Lord Humbert relies on me to—'

'Lord Humbert scarcely remembers you exist,' she snapped. 'And he knows better than to meddle in womanish affairs. Now do as you're bid. Give my letter to the runner-boy then bring me my breakfast.'

Defeated, for the moment, Eunise withdrew. Glaring at the closed chamber door, Lindara resisted the urge to stamp her foot like a child. One thing was certain: she'd not take the old baggage with her when she began her new life in Eaglerock castle. As Clemen's duchess she'd have her pick of ladies to serve her. And when she chose her privy companion she'd be sure to honour a young maid who'd know her place and understand where her loyalties must lie.

No more Eunise! For that mercy alone it might be worth wedding with Roric.

Her breakfast arrived as she was pinning her hair into a jewelled caul. Humbert's brutality had robbed her of appetite but she ate her coddled eggs and warm bread roll with feigned enthusiasm. Afterwards, to kill time, she made lists of what clothing she'd take with her to the castle. Eunise argued with her choices. Of course.

And then it was mid-morning, and she could leave to visit the herbary woman . . . who was more than a herbary woman if the whispered gossip were true.

Comfrey Lane was narrow and shadowed, its shabby shops weatherworn and looking unprosperous. Silently cursing the need for Eunise's prune-lipped company, Lindara frowned her old nurse into holding her tongue then picked her way along the rain-softened ground till she found the door she sought. The stout timber was splintered in several places, its ironwork pitted with rust.

'Wait here,' she told Eunise. 'Let no one enter till my business is done.'

Eunise stared at her, owlish. 'My lady, I don't care for this. Lord Humbert wouldn't like to see you in such a riffraff place.'

No, he surely wouldn't. And if she didn't cozen Eunise the carping misery would tell tales. 'Take heart,' she said, pressing her old nurse's hand. 'Perhaps I have been misled, but we've come all this way. I'll know in a few moments if this woman can help me or not.'

With a reassuring smile, she pushed the herbary door open and stepped inside.

It took a moment to see in the gloom. Like Arthgallo's leechery the air was thick with mysterious scents. Some sweet. Some sour. Some almost putrid. She felt her mouth dry as she breathed them in. Her head swam. Her vision blurred. Something hissed from the pooled shadows beyond the few fat, wax-dribbled candles lighting the room. A cat? No. A lizard. Green-scaled and spiny, it blinked orange eyes and scrabbled sharply curved claws on a jar-crowded bench.

'My lady Lindara,' said a soft, oddly accented voice. 'You are welcome.'

Lindara strained to see who'd spoken, but all she could make out was a slight figure standing in an archway, draped and swathed in a colourful, clinging fabric. 'How did you know—'

'I have your letter, my lady. You wrote it, yes? Signed it, yes?'

'Yes,' she whispered. Her heart pounded so hard it hurt. 'But—'

'Then I know you, my lady.'

'Come out of the shadows. Let me see you.'

The herbary woman laughed, low and husky. 'You are your father's daughter.'

'Yes. I am. So don't—'

'Peace, my lady,' said the herbary woman. 'We have a long road to travel. We should travel it as friends.'

'Friends don't hide from each other. Friends share their names.'

The lizard hissed again. Thrashed its tail. One of the jars on the bench fell to the floor and broke, releasing such a sour odour that Lindara felt herself gag.

'Silly *disdis*,' the herbary woman chided, stepping out of the gloom. The fabric swathing her made a slithery sound. 'Be unafraid, my lady. Little Shoupa is a pet.'

She didn't care about the lizard. Astonished, she stared at the herbary woman. 'Where are you from? I've never seen anyone like you before.'

The woman smiled, revealing crimson-stained teeth in a delicate face pale as finest Khafuri alabaster. Her dark hair was cropped so short it seemed painted on her skull and her moss-green eyes, large beneath highly arched dark brows, stared as though she could see into another's soul.

'I come from Osfahr, my lady.'

'The people of Osfahr are dusky-skinned.'

'Most are, my lady. But some are not.'

Lindara swallowed. 'And why is that?'

'I cannot say, my lady. Why are some dogs spotted and others plain?'

She lifted her chin. 'Tell me your name.'

'Tell me your purpose.'

'I thought you said you knew me. If that's true then you know why I'm here.'

'Do I?' Another husky laugh. The herbary woman wore green-enamelled copper bracelets. They jangled on her thin white wrists. 'And if I do? My lady?'

'*Tell me your name.*'

This time the woman's smile kept her crimson teeth hidden. 'You may call me Damikah.'

'Does that mean Damikah isn't your real name?'

'Yes. Yes. Your father's daughter.' With long, slender fingers Damikah plucked a sheet of folded paper from the folds of her dress. Eyes half-closed she caressed it, her head tipping to one side. 'So sorrowful, my lady. For all your freedoms, still a prisoner. Bound at every turn by the wanton whims of men. Greatness thrust upon you, whether you'd have it or not.'

Her letter. Handwritten and signed. A few terse words. No explanations. And yet Damikah knew. Blinking back a sting of tears, because the herbary woman sounded truly sad for her, Lindara took a deep breath. Let it out with a shudder.

'I need help. Can you help me?'

Damikah held up the letter. It caught fire. The flame consuming the paper burned green. 'Yes, Lindara. I can help you. If you're willing to pay the price.'

Humbert had to be punished. Roric too, for meekly, weakly, agreeing to the marriage without thinking of her first. 'I'll pay anything. I'll do anything. Tell me what to do.'

The letter had burned to nothingness. Not even ash remained. Damikah crossed to the bench and picked up her lizard. The creature settled on her shoulder, blinking.

'Bring in Eunise, my lady. The old woman looks odd, standing outside my door.'

Eunise? 'But—'

'I shall serve her tea,' said Damikah, softly. 'And what she sees and hears, she will forget. I promise.'

'Damikah . . .'

A gentle smile. A hint of rage. 'Do not worry, little Lindara. Here is where power lies. I shall share it with you . . . and you shall have your revenge.'

CHAPTER THIRTEEN

'Your Grace. Here is Lindara, come to give thanks for the great honour you'd bestow upon her and our house.'

Roric waited until he could be sure his face was schooled, then turned. Wheezing from his climb up Kite Tower keep's many spiralling stairs, Humbert offered a breathless, perfunctory nod.

'We couldn't meet in the Knot Garden, Roric?' he added, blotting sweat from his forehead with his embroidered linen sleeve. 'You've turned my shanks to beef jelly, asking to meet in the clouds.'

Roric shrugged. 'I'm fond of the view. And I'm too easily found in the Knot Garden. This is a moment for privy discussion, not meat for idle gossip.'

'Hmmph,' said Humbert, unmollified. With an impatient tut-tut and a finger snap, he beckoned Lindara forward. 'Greet His Grace, daughter.'

Lindara obeyed. Gowned in brocaded blue silk, exquisite as Borokand amethyst, her rippled dark gold hair meshed in a richly jewelled caul, she dipped into a curtsy. 'Your Grace.'

And that was wrong, for so many reasons. This was *Lindara*. Embarrassed, he held out his hands. 'Don't. To you, always, I'm Roric.'

A hesitant moment, and then she placed her cool palms atop his. 'Roric.'

Struck dumb, he stared at her. They'd studied lessons together as children. Chased hound puppies and each other when no sour grown-ups were there to stop them. She was terrified of spiders. Her favourite colour was green, her favourite instrument the lute. Above all things she loved hunting. She rarely wept. She never cheated. She always bested him in games of chess.

'I'd be alone with your daughter, Humbert,' he said, not taking his eyes from Lindara's pale, composed face. 'Make yourself comfortable in my apartment solar. We'll join you there presently.'

Of all Eaglerock's tower keeps, the Kite stood tallest. As its stout oak door thudded closed behind Humbert, Roric took Lindara's hand and led her to the red granite battlement overlooking Eaglerock township and its harbour. The afternoon was cool and clear, no clouds marring the bright sky. In the watery distance, smudging the horizon, a dreamy hint of Cassinia. Of departed Berardine's Ardenn. A brisk breeze tugged at his hair, his doublet, coaxed rustling whispers from Lindara's gown.

'I love Clemen,' he said softly. 'I never knew how much until I knew how far I'd go, what I'd do, to keep it safe.'

Her sigh was lost in the breeze. 'You went far indeed, Roric.'

'Unforgivably far?'

'That's not for me to say.'

'I say it is.'

'To chide you would be to chide my father,' Lindara said, faintly reproachful. 'You'd have me disloyal?'

She was playing word games. It wasn't like her. 'Telling the truth is never disloyal. In the end it's the only loyalty that matters.'

Her fingers tightened around his. 'You count truth the greatest virtue, Roric? Being true to one's honour. To one's heart and one's word.'

'Yes,' he said, looking down at her. 'Without that, what else matters?'

For the first time, she smiled. Brilliantly. 'Nothing.'

'Well, then?'

Her smile faded. 'Well, then, I think Harald was a bad man and a worse duke. Clemen was suffering. Something had to be done.'

'Do you wish I hadn't done it?'

'How should I answer you? When it's been arranged that I'll benefit so richly from what you did?'

It was market day in Eaglerock. The town square was thronged, and the streets, and the two main roads leading to the city gates. He counted nine galleys tethered at the docks, another six sailing the lively harbour. A thriving township. His township, now.

Their township.

He still had hold of her hand. Heart thudding, he turned her towards him. 'I have to know, Lindara. Are you content to be my duchess?'

Her eyes widened, as though the question surprised her. 'Of course.'

'Lindara . . .' He shook his head. 'I love your father as dearly as ever I loved Guimar but I'm not blind to his faults. I know how he is when he thinks he knows best. Has he browbeaten you into this match?'

A fleeting touch of sorrow in her wide, guileless eyes. 'When Humbert looks in a mirror, Roric, he sees an old man. He wants no fears for my future. And he wants strong sons for you, and for Clemen.'

'Yes, but what do *you* want?'

'Roric . . .' Slipping her hand free of him, she laid her palm against his chest. 'You sound uncertain. Did Humbert browbeat you?'

How could he tell her? The truth would only wound. And Humbert was right. Clemen's duke had to marry, and Lindara was better than any other choice. 'No. But I'd have you happy.'

'Being chosen by a duke, what woman could be anything but happy?'

'And love?' he said, troubled. 'What of love?'

Her fingers tapped against his doublet. 'But I do love you, Roric. Just as you love me.'

'We love each other as friends, Lindara. Is that enough for you?'

She laughed, as though he were being foolish. 'It's a start. Many nobles wed with far less.'

'So there's no other man you'd rather have? You swear?'

This time she pressed her palm to his cheek. Her gaze was fearless. 'I'm yours, and blessed for it. We'll give Clemen fine sons.'

He'd kissed Lindara many times, on her cheek, on her forehead, but never on her mouth. She tasted cool and sweet. Chaste. She remained utterly still. Felt . . . indifferent. Her palm on his chest would feel his heartbeat, undisturbed. Behind his closed eyes he saw

Catrain of Ardenn, alive with passion and fury, a firebrand of a girl. His heart leapt. He stumbled backwards.

'Roric?' Now Lindara's gaze hinted at distress. 'Am I displeasing?' Her breath caught. 'Or is there someone else for you?'

'There's no one. I'm sorry, Lindara, I—' He tried to laugh. 'Don't you find this strange? I find it strange. As though, of a sudden, I never knew you. Never saw you before this moment.'

Her pale cheeks coloured. 'I do feel a little uncertain. But I'm sure that must be natural, for a maid.'

Did she know about Catrain? About Berardine's offer? Surely Humbert wouldn't have told her. He didn't dare ask. 'You'll make Clemen a fine duchess, Lindara. You'll make me a fine wife. I promise I won't disappoint you.' Hearing himself, he grimaced. 'Well . . . I promise I'll try.'

Turning, Lindara looked again at Eaglerock township. Then, taking his hand, tugging him with her, she walked all four sides of the tower's square, blustery platform.

'Does it make you quail, Roric?' she said at last, sweeping her pensive gaze over the green fields, the neat hedgerows, the deep shadows of Bingham Forest and the higgledy-piggledy rooftops of cottages and farms and a half dozen distant, noble estates. 'Knowing that all this rests in the palm of your hand? That every life, great and small, must be lived, or lost, obedient to you?'

Again, he tried to laugh. Felt sick. 'It does.'

'You mustn't worry,' she said, her fingers squeezing. 'I'll not let you bear the burden alone.'

A warm rush of tenderness. He lifted her knuckles to his lips. 'Thank you, my lady.'

'Roric . . .' A shy look from beneath lowered lashes. 'I'd have a favour of you.'

'Name it.'

'Once we're wed my first duty must be to give you an heir. And I'll do it willingly. You shouldn't doubt that. It's just . . .' She smiled, coaxing. 'It means I must forgo my hunting. So couldn't the court ride out tomorrow? I know the deer and boar won't be summer fat, but still I think we'll find good sport. Would you grant me one last frolic? One last mad, horseback romp?'

How could he refuse her? She was right, her life was about to change. Irrevocably. Only . . .

'You're afraid I'll take a fall?' she said, and sighed. 'Roric. When did I ever fall a-hunting?'

'Never,' he admitted. 'But—'

She laid a cool finger across his lips. '*Never* is the right answer.' Her pressing finger caressed him. 'We needn't take the whole day. Think of it as a wedding gift. I'll ask no more of you, I promise.'

A morning's hunting. It was a tempting thought. Fresh air, a good horse, and a few hours free of fretting care. 'I'll get no peace till I surrender, will I?'

Dimples winked in her cheeks. 'None.'

He heaved a sigh. 'Very well, then.'

'Fraud!' she said, and tweaked his nose. 'As if you're not as eager to chase after hounds as I am! Now come, Your Grace. We should rejoin my father before he gripes himself into another visit to Arthgallo.'

They found Humbert pacing the solar like a mare fretting for its weaned foal. On seeing their faces he let out a pleased roar then embraced them both, heartily.

'By the spirits!' he declared. 'I knew you'd suit. Matching you is the best thing I ever did. Duke Roric and his duchess, Lindara. The minstrels will compose such songs . . .' He cleared his throat. 'Daughter, our carriage sits in the castle forecourt. Wait for me within it.'

'My lord,' Lindara murmured. 'Roric.' She gave them both a dutiful curtsy, and withdrew demurely from the solar.

'I've given this much thought, boy,' said Humbert, still gruff with emotion. 'You'll wed privily, the morning of your acclamation. A thimbleful of witnesses only, no public pomp. For all the duchy's glad to be quit of Harald, there's yet some sympathy for Argante and the child. I'll not have it said you danced haper-scaper on their graves. Let some time pass and we'll have a wedding feast or some such thing belike it. But not yet. It's too soon.'

It surely was. He'd kept his word and not mentioned Liam again, but grief still gouged. 'Agreed. But I'll have Lindara acclaimed duchess by my side. I won't give Harcia any excuse to raise quibbles.'

'That's wise,' said Humbert. Then he snorted. 'But I still think it ramshackle you've sent for those Marcher pules Bayard and Egbert.'

'Harcia must witness me made duke, Humbert. Would you rather I called on Balfre instead?'

'Yes, yes,' Humbert muttered, because he'd long lost the argument and knew that, too. Then he cleared his throat again, sounding suddenly ill at ease. 'Now. Roric. There's a last thing I'd tell you, for it's something you should know. Vidar looks kindly upon Lindara.'

'Looks kindly?' Roric stared. 'You mean he *loves* her?'

'He's never asked me for her,' Humbert said swiftly. 'But his feelings are somewhat . . . tender.'

Tender. 'Why didn't you tell me this before?'

'I'm telling you now. Besides, it makes no difference. I've never favoured Vidar. Not for Lindara.'

'Humbert . . .' He had to unclench his fingers. 'Lindara told me her heart is untouched. Is that true?'

'My daughter's as fair a maid as you'll find in Clemen,' said Humbert, glowering. 'And if you think I'd foist a soiled kerchief upon you, boy, then—'

'That's not what I'm asking! *Does she love him?* Will she break her heart wedding me?'

'No!' said Humbert, nearly shouting. 'What d'you take me for? A man who'd ruin his only child's happiness?'

'So you're telling me Lindara comes to this marriage willing.'

Humbert's stare was belligerent. 'Did she say so?'

'She did.'

'Then you're answered, aren't you?'

He was. And to call both Humbert and Lindara liars would be the height of folly and cruel, besides. They were family. They loved him. And he loved them.

'What of Vidar?'

'You'd mope for his feelings?' Humbert tucked in his chin. 'I never knew you and Vidar were grown so close.'

'We aren't. But—'

'Well, then,' said Humbert, and rocked on his heels. 'What's the missmuss? Vidar's a worldly man. He knows how things are done. If Lindara meant so much to him he'd have spoken up long ago.'

'How could he, after Godebert?'

'Roric,' said Humbert, shaking his head, 'Vidar knows full well that stain will soon be washed away. He could've come to me. He didn't. That's all you need to know.'

'Then if his passion is so shallow, and Lindara never shared it, why would you—'

'Because a duke must know the heart and mind of every man who kneels to serve him. And I've no doubt Vidar will sting over this. He's shiteful of pride, that one.'

'What if it's more than pride? What if you've misjudged the depth of his feelings?'

'I haven't.'

He made it sound so simple. It wasn't. 'Vidar saved my life, Humbert.'

'And you'll reward him, boy. But not with my daughter.'

Suddenly weary, Roric rubbed his eyes. 'All right. But I'll ask you not to say anything to him about me and Lindara. I'll break the news to him tomorrow. While we're hunting, or soon after.'

And there was a conversation he could easily live without. But that was his life, now. Difficult conversations. Uneasy choices. Hurting people's feelings so he could serve the greater good.

Humbert was scowling. 'Hunting? What's this?'

'Lindara begged a favour. It's a small thing, when she must stay safe once we're wed so she can bear me healthy sons. Don't puff about it, my lord.'

Humbert raised his hand, capitulating. 'Your Grace, I am your humble servant. When and where do we assemble for this hunt?'

A humble servant? Humbert wouldn't know *humble* if it bit him in his bath. 'Bingham Forest. I'll send a messenger with details by tonight. Now take your daughter home and cherish her, for I know you'll miss her when she's gone.'

After sending for the steward Nathyn, and arranging the hunt invitations and messengers to deliver them, Roric returned to the welcome solitude of the Kite Tower. There he paced, ignoring the dancing air and splendid views and the fact that Badouim, Eaglerock's most senior exarchite, had long been waiting to meet with him. He couldn't care less for spiritual matters. Not after hearing what Humbert had to say.

Vidar cares for Lindara.

Curse the man. Curse him. And every sprite in Bingham Wood curse him too.

The wounded boar plunged out of a thicket, all hot, dripping blood and razor tusks and deep-set eyes on fire with rage. Plunging after it, baying and slavering, the heavy-shouldered hounds Roric inherited from Harald.

''*Ware His Grace!*' someone shouted.

Cursing, Vidar wrenched his horse aside as a mud-splattered Roric spurred past him, reins in one hand, heavy spear in the other, chasing the boar. His face was alight with fierce, joyful determination and he urged the hounds forward with stirring cries.

Another mud-and-leaf-muffled thundering of hooves, then someone else shouted. '*Give way! Give way! Mind yourself, Vidar!*'

And that was Aistan, hard on Roric's heels. Thundering with him were Humbert, Scarwid, Farland and that pisscock Ercole. Cursing again, Vidar held back his blowing, agitated horse until the knot of nobles was safely ahead, then gave chase. Off to his right, keeping rough pace with him, he could hear more riders crashing through the forest, and the baying of different hounds in pursuit of their own prey. The hunting pack had split. Did Lindara ride with them? He'd glimpsed her once so far that morning, when he arrived late at the rustic hunting lodge Harald had built at the forest's edge. But Humbert kept her close. He'd had no chance to speak with her or even catch her eye.

A fresh thunder of hooves. A distant flash of sunlit colour between Bingham's mighty oaks. Scarlet velvet, indigo leather, a shadowed gleam of dappled grey hide and chestnut. Then tawny velvet, and bright blue, and brown leather. A golden bay horse, two brown horses, and a black with white legs. Even with his half-ruined sight he knew none of them was Lindara. And then he saw her, brilliant in hunter green, riding her favourite pied gelding. She turned her head. Saw him. Such a look on her face! Startled, he glanced beyond his horse's ears. Roric and the others were losing him. If he didn't kick on he might well miss the kill.

Turning back to find Lindara, vanishing and reappearing and vanishing again as she threaded the narrow forest trail with customary, reckless skill, he saw her still stricken, as though she were newly bereaved.

Fuck the kill. Let Roric have it.

Heedless of his horse's hocks he wrenched the animal sideways a second time, forcing it so close between two burled oak trunks he came perilous near to crushing both of his knees. And then he rode dangerously hard, though his ruined hip burned with pain, determined not to lose the other pack, and his beloved.

A score of pounding strides and he'd caught them.

'Lindara!'

She'd slowed her pace, was riding conspicuously last. And since she *never* let herself fall behind she must want him to join her. As he reached her side she nodded, but there was no smile, no laughter. The Lindara he loved always laughed during a hunt.

Feeling sick, churned with fright, he matched his horse's pace to hers.

Ahead of them the hounds' baying changed pitch, yelped higher and more lustily. Woodcocks and silver pigeons burst from their leafy hiding, escaping into the forest-fretted sky. Vidar stood awkwardly in his stirrups, stared over the heads of the riders in front of him at the creature being hunted. Another boar in panicked flight, Harald's hounds snarling and snapping at its bristled rump. It swerved leftwards, desperate, and the hounds swerved after it. A fallen tree, slanting, crushed spring-green undergrowth, blocking their path. The boar blundered under it but the hounds leapt it freely, as though they had wings, and the following horses leapt it too. Side by side with Lindara, Vidar felt his horse gather itself beneath him, felt its quarters drop, its shoulders lift. Her horse was a mirror. They cleared the fallen tree as one.

And still she didn't laugh.

A cry of triumph from the leading riders as they burst into a clearing. The hounds yelped their excitement. The boar let out a grunting squeal.

'We have it! We have it!' And that was Gerbod, who never let a man or woman ride by him. 'Go to, dogs, go to!'

More yelping, snapping, snarling. A hound shrieked, then was silent. Milling confusion, steaming sweat, stamping hooves, excited voices, as the hunting pack of nobles surrounded the stricken boar.

'Vidar, with me! Quickly!'

Startled again, Vidar spurred his horse after Lindara. At a swift trot, neatly ducking under branches and skirting Bingham's great oaks, she guided him away from the sounds of slaughter in the clearing. When the shouting and barking were dulled to a whisper, she stopped. Took a moment to be certain they were alone, then swung her horse around to face him.

'I was told not to tell you this, but I don't care,' she said, reckless. 'Vidar, I'm to wed Roric.'

The breath left his body as though he were a boar, run through his pounding heart with a spear.

'Wed Roric?' he croaked. 'You can't.'

She spurred her horse forward until they were close enough to touch. But his beloved didn't touch him. Her gloved fingers were tight on the reins, and her eyes glittered in her bloodless face. 'I must. Humbert has given me to him, and there's no taking me back. Make your peace with it, Vidar, as I have.'

The jangle of steel bridle work, as his horse rubbed a sweaty cheek on its knee. In his head, a dreadful roaring. In his body, so much pain.

'*Peace?*' He choked down the rising bile. 'You wanton bitch! You bawdy strumpet! You never loved me, did you? All along you've wanted Roric. You want the power he can give you. I was only ever—'

'You know me better!' she cried, her voice catching as tears spilled. 'On my knees, on my *belly*, I begged Humbert to spare me. I told him I had one love in this life, *you*, and that if he loved me he'd not force me into Roric's bed. He wouldn't listen. With my brothers dead he wants immortality through my children. He said my first duty as his daughter was to him and to Clemen and that in marrying Roric I'd serve both, and do him honour.'

'*Honour.*' Sweating, freezing, Vidar pressed the back of his hand to his mouth, praying he'd not vomit. Breathed hard for a moment, then let his hand fall. 'What would Humbert know of *honour*, when he whores out his daughter for the sake of a ducal crown?'

'I'm no whore,' she said, chin lifting. 'I'm no bitch or bawdy strumpet. If you love me, guard your tongue.'

'*If I love you?* Lindara—'

'You know I can't refuse my father,' she said, as though he hadn't spoken. 'I wed Roric or die a prisoner in Larkspur castle. Please—' Her lips twisted in a bitter smile. 'Don't say you'd rather I died.'

As if he would! 'Does Roric know you love me?'

'I'd be a fool to tell him, wouldn't I? He might send you away – and Humbert would beat me till my bones break.'

'And what of Roric? Does he love you?'

'No.'

'Does he know *I* love you?'

'I don't know. But even if Humbert told him, it's made no difference.'

He lost sight of her then, his eye blurred with stinging tears. 'I'll kill him,' he said thickly, feeling his hand move to his dagger. 'I'll kill them both.'

'And kill yourself? Don't you be a fool.'

'You'd have me do nothing?' he demanded, smearing his face dry. 'Stand by as Roric fucks you without love, and do *nothing*?'

'No,' she said, her voice like ice. 'I'd have you fuck me and put your son on his precious Falcon Throne.'

Stunned to silence, he stared at her. 'You're mad,' he said at last.

Now she was smiling, not with joy, but wintry hate. 'I'm not.'

'Lindara, it isn't possible. You *can't*—'

'But I can,' she said, still smiling. 'And believe me, I will. I can turn Roric's seed to salt and he'll never know, or even suspect.'

He breathed out, slowly. 'How?'

'Babies and birthing are women's business. There are potions, and certain charms.'

'*Sorcery?*'

Her cold smile widened, baring her teeth. 'That's what men call it. Women call it something else.'

'Whatever you call it, if you're discovered it means death!'

She shrugged. 'I won't be discovered.'

'You don't know that! Lindara—'

'Poor Vidar. Are you frightened?'

He'd never heard her so cruelly mocking. 'My love—'

'Don't call me that!' she spat. 'If I was *your love* you'd have claimed me from Humbert weeks ago and this wouldn't be happening!'

She blamed *him*? 'Lindara—'

'What's it to be, Vidar? You mean nothing to Roric and Humbert. *I* mean nothing. Will you fight them with me? For I must fight. If I do nothing to avenge myself then I deserve—'

Raised voices, approaching. Laughter. A rhythmic drumming of hooves.

Lindara spurred her horse back a pace. 'We mustn't be seen. *Go*. I'll find you later, for your answer.'

As she urged her horse into a canter, abandoning him, Vidar kicked his feet free of his stirrups and slid to the damp, leafy ground. Scooped a handful of sticky mud and dirtied his face, his russet doublet, the side of his hunting leathers and his horse's knees. A moment later Roric appeared between the trees, flanked by Humbert and Aistan. Seeing him, they slowed their horses to a halt.

'Vidar!' said Roric. 'We wondered where you were. Never say you were unseated!'

What was his pride, next to Lindara's safety? He winced, not needing to pretend any physical discomfort. Hunting was a torment. 'Alas.' A slap on his horse's neck. 'The beast stumbled.'

'Are you much hurt?'

Oh, so now the bastard would feel his pain? 'Not to speak of.'

'You missed two fine kills,' said Humbert, jubilant. Dried blood smeared his sleeve, flecked his beard. 'The court will eat well tonight.'

Aistan, also blood-flecked, frowned. 'Vidar, can you ride?'

To answer, and to hide the sudden burn of fury, Vidar re-mounted. Never mind that he was clumsy, that because of his hip he had to hop and clutch and haul. Settled into his saddle, with a blank stare he dared them to say a word.

'My lords,' said Roric, 'I'd speak privately with Vidar. Ride ahead to the hunting lodge and make sure those boar are dealt with as they should be.'

Humbert cleared his throat. 'If it's all the same to you, Roric, I'd like to find my daughter. Aistan knows what he's about when it comes to boar. Don't you, Aistan?'

'Fine,' said Roric. 'I'll see you both at the lodge.'

'Is something wrong, my lord?' Vidar asked, all friendly deference, once they were alone. It was vital that Roric never suspect his seething hatred. 'That shite Ercole's not raising a riot, is he?'

Roric shook his head. 'He knows better. Vidar, I've news for you. I doubt you'll like it.'

'Tell me,' he said, as the late morning's filtering sunlight turned to snow on his skin. 'Is it Harcia? Do Aimery's Marcher lords cause trouble on the eve of your acclamation?'

'I could almost wish they did,' Roric murmured. 'Vidar, I'm wedding Lindara.'

Even though he knew already, even though he'd braced himself to hear the familiar words, it was like being spear-skewered a second time.

'I'm sorry,' Roric added. 'Humbert tells me you're fond of her.'

'*Fond?*' He laughed, feeling sick. 'My lord – Roric – I *love* her.'

A stricken look in Roric's eyes. 'Oh.'

'Can you say the same?'

'Lindara is dear to me.'

'So you can't,' he said, hearing his voice crack. 'Roric—'

Roric nudged his horse closer. 'It's a matter of state, Vidar. Of what's best for our duchy.'

He could easily smash Roric's earnest face to blood and bony splinters. 'Why Lindara? Clemen is full of women. Fuck, the *world* is full of women.' Another strangled laugh. 'For you, at least. For a duke. For me there's only one. Choose someone else.'

'Vidar . . .' Roric rubbed a gloved hand across his face. The gesture left a smear of boar's blood in its wake. 'I would, if I could. But my choices are more limited than you want to believe and I *must* put Clemen's welfare first. So for our duchy's sake you'll let Lindara go . . . and I'll wed her.'

He wanted to shout *You arrogant shit, she doesn't love you! She loves me!* But he couldn't. The truth would put Lindara in danger. His only choice was deceit. To play the obedient courtier and let Roric think he'd won. But he didn't dare surrender without any fight.

'Is this why you haven't restored what's mine?' he said, hearing his voice grate. 'Have you kept me noble in name only so Humbert would never take my suit seriously?'

Roric flinched. 'No! Vidar, I promised you'd have all you're owed, and you will. You'll have more. I'll grant you your choice of a ducal estate, and a seat on the council. Your name will be a byword for courage and honour far beyond Clemen's borders.'

In other words the bastard thought he was a whore, to be bought. 'I risked my *life* to sit your arse on Harald's throne.'

'And I'm in your debt for that,' said Roric. 'But would you truly ask me to put you before all of Clemen?'

Silence, save for the natural sounds of Bingham forest and the quiet clinking of their horses' bits. His breathing unsteady, Vidar let Roric see the depth of his pain. 'You know how I must answer.'

'Then what else is there to say?'

'You can tell me one thing. When you asked Lindara to marry you . . . did you know my feelings?'

'No.'

'And if you had known?'

'I truly am sorry, Vidar.' Roric smiled, sadly. As though his sorrow mattered. Then he held out his hand. 'I hope one day you can forgive me. And I hope you'll take that seat on the council. I need all the good men around me I can find.'

Vidar stared at the drying bloodstains on Roric's gold-embroidered leather glove. More than anything he wanted to slap the offered hand aside, reject Roric's insulting bribe. But a seat on the council would keep him in Eaglerock, near Lindara. Which was imperative if he was to fall in with her mad plan.

A plan that now tempted him like a sweet sugar plum.

Slowly he let himself be clasped wrist-to-wrist. 'All right. I'll take that council seat, Your Grace. As for a ducal estate . . . Coldspring leaps to mind.'

'Coldspring,' said Roric, not quite hiding the wince. 'You have excellent taste, Vidar.'

'In all things.'

Roric's grasp tightened. 'And what of forgiveness?'

'Treat Lindara well. Make her happy. I'll not forgive her tears.'

'Thank you, Vidar,' said Roric, releasing him. 'I won't forget this.'

Shaking, he watched Harald's bastard cousin ride away.

'And nor will I forget it,' he whispered. 'For you're all the same, you great men of power. You see the rest of us as puppets and play with us as you will.'

Harald had called him a traitor. And in Harald's eyes, he was. But nothing he'd done had been a betrayal of Clemen. Ridding the duchy of Harald had been an act of loyal love. But to cuckold Roric, trick him into naming another man's son as his heir . . .

Then he would be a traitor.

But how could he forsake Lindara? So wounded. So used. Her father's pawn. Roric's convenience. No one to think of her, protect her, *love* her, but him. And what was he? A disinherited, landless fool who'd put off making his declaration until it was too late, leaving the woman he loved vulnerable. A fool who'd risked everything for Roric, who'd arranged the murder of an infant, only to be kicked aside like a cur dog, his feelings counting for naught. For that he was owed his own revenge.

If I am traitor, what of it? He betrayed me first.

Eaglerock castle contained the finest library in the duchy. Late that night, Vidar ran Aistan to ground there, amidst the leather-bound books and hand-painted manuscripts and industrious silence. Aistan looked deeply weary, his lean face pale in the library's generous lamplight. Scattered books lay open before him, and on a sheet of ink-smudged paper much untidy writing.

'Vidar,' he said, looking up, 'did you want something?'

'A little of your time, if you can spare it.'

'I can.' Aistan set down his quill. 'Join me.'

Vidar pulled out one of the heavy oak chairs on his side of the long, broad library table and sat. 'Thank you, my lord.'

A glimmer in Aistan's dark, deepset eyes. 'As a rule such formality isn't held between fellow councillors.'

'Ah. So you know.'

'Roric announced your appointment this afternoon.'

And here was a chance to nip speculation in the bud. 'He made me the offer this morning, after the hunt. That's why he sent you and Humbert ahead. Do you mislike it?'

'You've earned the honour.' Aistan tapped his calloused fingertips to the table. 'He also announced his plan to wed with Humbert's daughter.'

He feigned surprise. 'Lindara?'

'The same.'

'And do you mislike that?'

Aistan shrugged. ''Tis a better notion than he marry with Berardine of Ardenn's heir.'

No need for feigning this time. '*What?* Whose brain-rotted idea was that?'

'It was the widow's doing. She came here in secret and threw her brat at Roric's feet. Fortunately, he rejected them both.'

Fortunate for Clemen but not for him. Lindara would still be his, had Roric agreed. Curse the bastard for loyalty.

'Mind you,' said Aistan, after a moment. 'If you'd have the truth I suspect he was tempted. Tell me, Vidar. D'you like our new duke?'

An odd question, without warning. Vidar felt instinct stir. 'I like him well enough,' he said, meeting Aistan's hooded stare. 'We're too different to be close, but there's much to admire in him.'

'There is. Though he's young and still unseasoned when it comes to murky political waters.'

'He has Humbert to guide him.'

A muscle twitched in Aistan's cheek. 'Humbert's not infallible.'

Something was brewing here. Not regret, nothing so dire. But a seasoned caution that might well be useful, in time. With Roric now his enemy he needed Aistan's good will . . . and more.

'Does something concern you?' he prompted. 'I'm not a babble-monger, Aistan. We speak in confidence.'

Silence, as Aistan weighed him. Then the deepest lines carved into his careworn face eased. 'Berardine of Ardenn is a proud woman, and stubborn. If she has ambitions in Clemen one rebuff won't kill them. She'll seek another way to pluck the plums from our pie.'

'And you fear Roric won't see her for what she is till it's too late?'

'I fear he looks for the good in people and is swift to give them the benefit of the doubt,' said Aistan, heavily. 'Long after such benefits should be exhausted. You remember how much persuasion he needed to stand against Harald.'

Indeed he did. 'I agree he's unseasoned and sometimes too trusting. But what can we do, my lord? Roric is our duke.'

'And we are his councillors. Whose first duty must lie with Clemen. It's why we threw down Harald.' Aistan's fingers tapped again, restless. 'I'm doing what I can to keep Berardine constrained, but should the widow prove wily, Vidar, will I have your support to stand more fiercely against her?'

'Against her or anyone who threatens Clemen's peace,' he said promptly. 'I'll risk Roric's anger before our duchy's future.'

Aistan smiled. 'It heartens me to know I wasn't mistaken in you, Vidar.'

And here was the opening he'd sought, the chance to pursue his reason for seeking Aistan out so late.

'You weren't. My lord, if I might touch upon a personal matter? You'll recall the offer you made me in Heartsong. Your daughter's hand? I've kept silent till now because my position remained uncertain. But with all doubt removed, I wanted to—'

'I'm sorry,' said Aistan. 'But it seems I spoke too soon. Kennise . . . ' His eyes glittered. 'She's not well.'

'She rejects marriage?'

'She fears it.' Aistan sighed. 'And after Harald's cruelty, how can I rage? You know there's talk of the Exarch wishing to establish one of those women's contemplative houses in Clemen?'

'I'd heard mention.'

'What do you think?'

He thought he was spirit-cursed. First Lindara lost to him, and now Kennise? Marriage with Aistan's daughter would've done him much good – and helped disguise what he and Lindara planned to do.

'Aistan,' he said slowly, 'I think it would be a mistake. I'm wary of the Exarch, just as I'm wary of Berardine and Harcia. Of all those who'd seek to undermine Clemen's sovereign authority. And anyone who denies the Exarch's love of power is a fool.'

'True,' said Aistan. 'But Kennise has her heart set on it. She finds the world burdensome.' Another sigh. 'And my heart breaks, knowing that for Clemen's sake I must deny her.'

'So there's no hope she might soften?'

'Vidar, I'm sure she will. Be patient. Every girl desires marriage. In time Kennise will find her courage.'

'I don't doubt it,' he said, accepting his temporary defeat. 'For she's your daughter, my lord. And you are a great man.'

Aistan grimaced. 'That's not for me to say. What I can say is that I'm a busy man.' He picked up his discarded quill. 'So if you'll forgive me . . .'

Swallowing a grunt of pain, Vidar pushed his heavy chair back from the table. 'Of course, Aistan. My thanks for your time.'

Making his uneven, circuitous way out of the castle, Vidar fought the urge to curse out loud. It was likely that now, with his new position and new estate of Coldspring glossing over his physical deficiencies, the maidens that might've been shown to Roric would be shown to him instead. And not a father among them would be as useful an ally as Aistan. Perhaps he should ask Lindara to procure him a love charm to sway Kennise.

Because while he could put off his own marriage a little while . . . it wasn't something he could put off for ever.

CHAPTER FOURTEEN

Berardine sailed into Carillon harbour on a rising tide and a swelling of hope. It was late. The night sky was dimmed with cloud, the city's joyful bells silent. Once her galley was docked in the Royal Pool she bundled herself and a drowsy Catrain into the closed litter she'd left handy for her purposes, and chewed at her lower lip as four panting sailors hurried them home to the palace.

Come to me, Izusa. I need to know what I must do now.

Perhaps there was some gentle sorcery, a kindly love charm, to nudge Roric of Clemen where Ardenn needed him to go. Nothing malicious. Nothing harmful. She'd not endanger his soul . . . or her own. And especially not Catrain's. But there had to be *something* Izusa could do. Or why else was the woman a witch?

She'd confided in Howkin, Baldwin's trusted majordomo, her purposed journey to Clemen, and left him to divert attention from her absence. But since she was returned so soon it was doubtful he'd needed to exercise his imagination.

'Madam!' he said, startled, answering her swift summons once she and Catrain were neatly and secretly slipped back into the palace. 'I did not expect to see you again before next Chapel Day.'

Seated on a velvet-covered chair in her official dayroom, deliberately unattended by her ladies, Berardine smoothed a fold in her pearl-grey damask skirts. 'My purpose was somewhat diverted, Howkin.'

More than once Baldwin had declared that the majordomo would tear his own heart from his breast with his teeth before ever he'd betray their house. Watching him closely, she saw a fierce disappointment leap behind his well-schooled servant's face, and was comforted.

'It pains me to hear you say so, Madam,' he said. 'I know you had high hopes for your gracious daughter's settlement.'

'I still have them, Howkin. Diverted is not the same as defeated.'

He brightened. 'No, Madam. That's surely true.'

'It's possible I was o'erhasty in my eagerness to settle Catrain. Clemen yet remains in turmoil following Harald's hasty despatch.'

'If true, 'tis a pity,' said Howkin, downcast again. 'You at least met with its new duke? This bastard, Roric?'

He was bordering on insolence, but she was prepared to disregard it. Lacking Baldwin, missing him so hurtfully, Howkin's solid loyalty was an echo of her beloved's steadfast support.

'Roric and I did meet, Howkin,' she said, toying with her favourite ruby ring. 'And it went well. Catrain impressed him. But now that I've assuaged your curiosity you'll promptly forget you ever heard me mention his name.'

'Madam,' Howkin murmured, pricked into remembering his rightful place. Candlelight gleamed on his grey hair and doubled itself in his blue tunic's bright brass buttons. 'Not a whisper of him shall pass my lips.'

'Very good.' Bone-weary, she fought the urge to slump. 'Was I missed, Howkin?'

'Exarchite Lamesh requested an audience, Madam, but did not press the matter once I explained you were slightly indisposed.'

Lamesh. The Exarch's most trusted priest in Ardenn. A good enough man, but persistent. 'What did he want?'

'Madam, he declined to enlighten me.'

She smothered brief amusement. 'Best you send to him come morning. Invite him to attend me here.'

'Yes, Madam.'

'There's nothing else I should know?'

'I don't believe so, Madam.'

'Then you're dismissed, Howkin. And thank you.'

He bowed with infinite correctness, then left her. For some time she sat in her extravagant chair, relieved to be neither aboard a wave-lurched galley nor trapped within a swaying litter. Through the closed door that led to her inner apartments she could hear the whisperings of her ladies, those twittery hens, roused to excitement by her return. They thought she and Catrain had travelled into the countryside for a mother-and-daughter retreat. They'd been told to sew their lips on it, and she had no reason to think them disobedient. It was the height of accomplishment to be named one of Berardine's ladies. There wasn't a hen among them who'd risk her place or her family's wrath by speaking out of turn.

Because she'd stir alarm if she kept them waiting any longer, she abandoned the rare pleasure of solitude and suffered herself to be curtsied and smiled at, exclaimed over, disrobed and bathed and scented and lotioned and encased in demure embroidered linen. Not a man's hand upon her anywhere. No more a wife but a widow, a living doll, excised of passion. Her ladies' possession. Ardenn's bride.

When she could bear no more of their fussing she sent them away, pleading a megrim. At least that wasn't a lie.

Alone in her dark chamber, in the desolate bed she'd shared with Baldwin, she sought in vain for sleep. All her treacherous fears, unbridled, stampeded inside her painful skull. What if Roric failed to understand the great honour she'd offered to bestow on him?

What if he rejected Catrain or – worse – allowed his personal desires to be over-ruled by his council? For all he was a man comfortable at court and blooded in the Marches he was still a child when it came to his authority. Did the maggoty worm of his bastardy gnaw at the heart of him? It was a greater taint in Clemen than in many other realms. Why that should be, she had no idea. Noble bastards abounded elsewhere, to little ill-effect. Well, save the Danetto Peninsula of course. But they were mostly mad in Danetto. Everyone knew that.

He spoke of Catrain kindly. I did not mistake the look in his eye, the hunger. He'd happily play the bold ram to her sweet ewe. And for all his protestations I saw that other hunger. Ambition. Isn't he Harald's cousin? Berold's grandson? He springs from a lusty blood-line, never mind he's not bred true.

And then there was Izusa. How could she doubt Baldwin's choice? Doubt the proofs the witch had given? She might as well doubt the sun . . . or the memory of her husband.

Izusa said Catrain and Roric would marry. I must hold on to that, no matter who'd dissuade me. Izusa, Izusa. You promised to be my guide. Come to me, I beg you, and set my mind at ease.

Exhausted, her head pounding, at last she slid into sleep. She dreamed of Baldwin's kisses . . . and when she woke, her cheeks were wet.

Though the waiting was worse than frostbite, Catrain showed nothing of her growing impatience to those in Carillon who liked to watch her. If she'd learned one thing from her mother it was the importance of patience. Cats who splashed too soon in a fishpond caught nothing but duckweed in their claws.

As Baldwin's heir she had her own small court, confined within the larger orbit of Ardenn's duchess. She was far from independent, sadly, but at least her position was recognised. She no longer had to share the palace nursery with her annoying little sisters. That was important. For if Ardenn couldn't take her seriously, how could she expect the prince's regents and Cassinia's dukes to see her as anything but a wayward girl-child in need of supervision and male guidance? How could she hope to keep Roric in his place as her consort? Because no matter how much she liked Clemen's new duke, that was all he could ever be. The notion that Baldwin's heir would allow the man she married to rule her or her duchy was nonsense.

Since no ruler could afford to be ignorant, much of her time was taken up with learning. Each day a procession of tutors put their prize pupil through her paces, like an expensive minstrel's palfrey. Resigning herself to the familiar humdrum after the excitement of Eaglerock, she danced for them, and pranced for them, sang sweet songs in four different tongues and calloused her fingers on lute-strings for them. She embroidered exquisite tapestries and cushion covers, recited the lineages of every royal house in Cassinia unto the fifteenth generation, tried to care about the wool trade, shamed the palace horsemaster with her knowledge of colic, stumbled somehow through the complications of Ardabenian mathematics . . . and through it all daydreamed of that surprising man, Roric. Her husband-to-be.

But then, to her dismay, she realised she was beginning to forget his face.

On the morning of the sixth day since she'd sailed home from Clemen unbetrothed, she dismissed her language tutor, ordered her matronly attendants to lose themselves in a convenient garden maze, and went in search of her mother. They'd scarcely laid eyes upon each other since returning to the palace. First it was the Exarchite Lamesh, then a delegation from Maletti, then the monthly royal Court of Assizes, followed soon after by another delegation, this time from the Duchy of Grayne, and on its heels a trading envoy from Harcia. The demands upon Duchess Berardine never ended. And she understood that, of course she did. Wasn't she Baldwin's daughter? The heir to Ardenn?

But surely the least Mama can do is tell me when Roric and I are to wed. I hardly think that's too much to ask.

The southern tower of the palace was devoted to the cogs and wheels of governance, both seen and unseen. The grand throne room and its succession of antechambers occupied the entire top floor, loftily floating above Carillon's general population. The rest of the tower was a rabbit warren of closets and offices and storerooms and libraries, where the sweaty machinations of the minions whose task it was to transform Berardine's decrees into deeds were performed, day in and day out, without respite.

Knowing that one day those decrees would be hers, the minions answerable to her, Catrain had for some time made sure her face was familiar there, and that she knew who did what for Ardenn, and why, and how. When she did become duchess she'd not be taken by surprise.

But that was the future. Until the day she claimed her birthright she was as constrained by proper protocols as any subject in the duchy.

'My lady Catrain,' said Howkin, bowing. 'How may I serve you?'

If her mother were a house then Majordomo Howkin would be its door. Neatly painted, hinges well-oiled, and most usually locked. Knowing better than to try charming him, Catrain offered him a regal nod.

'Howkin. Please tell my mother I'd beg a few moments of her time.'

'Certainly, my lady. If you'd care to wait here?'

As Howkin withdrew from his antechamber into her mother's – formerly her father's – official ducal study, she swept a deceptively disinterested gaze across his parchment-covered desk. But the majordomo's spiky handwriting was hard enough to read right side up. Upside down it was impossible. She could make out a few names she recognised: nobles from other duchies, Exarchite Lamesh, the duke of Pruges, even the fearsome Baldassare. She felt her skin prickle. What was that wicked pirate up to now? And did anyone expect her mother to stop him?

Surely not. Surely nobody could think Ardenn could or should—

'My lady,' said Howkin, reappearing. 'Duchess Berardine invites you to sit with her.'

The last time she and her mother had spoken at length, in Eaglerock, things hadn't gone at all well. She could still feel that dreadful stinging slap across her face. How completely the blow had killed her lingering excitement over Roric, and the fire, and the way she'd helped save most of Harcia's trapped and burning horses. Berardine's apology, afterwards, had done little to soothe the pain. Words. Just words. They couldn't undo what was done.

Remembering that moment, Catrain hesitated. Howkin closed the study door behind her, but she remained a few steps over the threshold. As always her gaze went first to Baldwin's portrait, hung on the wall behind his elaborately carved mahogany desk. For all her turmoil, she smiled to see him. Dark gold hair, deep-blue eyes, a determined chin rescued from stubborness by that thumbprint of a dimple. His lips too thin for beauty, but for ever hiding some amusement. Lingering on his dear face she felt the ever-present ache deep in her heart and didn't resent it, because he was her father and she loved him. She missed him every day.

Of course she loved her mother too . . . but it was different for mothers and daughters. Everyone knew that.

Berardine stood at the window with her back to the room. Stood very still, staring out over her glorious, sunlit city of Carillon. Waiting for her mother to acknowledge her presence, Catrain gave herself over to thought.

As always, these days, Berardine looked magnificent. While Baldwin lived of course she'd dressed as the wife of a great duke ought, in softly flowing fine wools and velvets, and wore glistening ropes of pearls and gold beads around her neck. But she never appeared more grand than her husband, never garbed herself so richly that next to her he'd seem poor. Baldwin had been the brilliant sun, she the moon content to shine less brightly by his side.

But with his death that, along with everything else, had changed. Lusciously plump Berardine lost her spare flesh to grief. Lean as a Lepetto hunting dog now, she encased herself in heavy, whalebone-stiffened silk brocades sewn all over with seed pearls and gold nuggets and jet beads and jewels. This morning she wore a midnight-blue gown, stitched intricate with gold thread flowers whose every heart was a glossy, faceted sapphire.

Before Eaglerock, her first adventure into the wider world, Catrain had never paid her mother's attire much attention. Berardine was Ardenn's duchess, of course her clothing was the most opulent of any woman in the duchy. Since returning from Clemen, though, she'd realised there was more to her mother's astonishing dresses than mere show. In Eaglerock, for the first time, she'd seen her mother uncertain. Seen her at the mercy of someone else. A man.

And seeing that she understood a profound and sobering truth. Like a knight, Berardine daily dressed for battle, and within her costly carapace did all that she could to rule her inherited duchy invulnerable, like a man.

It was a stern lesson for a daughter to learn. That even her mother, the most powerful woman in Ardenn, in Cassinia, could be afraid. Could find herself in danger, like every other woman.

She never told me. Why didn't she tell me? How am I old enough to marry but too young to know that?

Staring at her silent mother, who stood statue-like before the chamber's window, Catrain felt a fresh stirring of unease. It was improper for anyone, even a daughter, to speak to Ardenn's duchess before being spoken to by her first, but . . .

'Mama?' She took a step closer. Her mother's unnatural stillness was making her pulse leap. 'What's amiss?'

Sunlight sparked on sapphire as her mother took a deep breath. Shifted, just a little, and held out her left hand. Her ringed fingers clasped an unrolled letter. They were shaking. Her many rings were sparking, just like her dress.

'Read this, Catrain.'

Mouth suddenly dry, she crossed the beautiful hand-woven Rebbai carpet like a doe venturing onto thin ice. And with every cautious step thought she could hear her life splintering.

'Who is it from, Mama?'

'*Read it*, I said.'

Catrain stopped. Swallowed tears. First the slap in Eaglerock, and now a voice so sharp and hard it could chip flint. Berardine was turning into a stranger. Her own fingers unsteady, she took the letter. Blinked until her vision cleared then waited for the attractively scrawled words to make sense.

'*Berardine, what I must tell you isn't yet common knowledge, but to keep you waiting longer for my answer would be discourteous – and unkind. Three days from now I will wed the daughter of my chief councillor, the lord Humbert. I've known Lindara since I was a boy. We deal well together, she and I, and in choosing her I choose the path of least upheaval for my council and my duchy. Please believe I was honoured by the offer of your daughter's maiden hand.*

Believe too that in refusing Catrain I make no criticism of her. In truth I found her delightful, and were matters here different then I might well follow my heart instead of my head. Please tell her I wish her every happiness in life. As for myself, I hope in time you will forgive me, so Clemen and Ardenn can remain the best of friends.'

The letter was signed simply, without flourish, *Roric*.

Catrain felt her breathing hitch. Felt her fingers twitch with a fierce impulse to rip the letter to shreds. She mastered it, but only just.

'Well. And there I thought Clemen's duke was clever enough to know he'd never find a better wife than me.' Hearing her brittle voice waver, she braced her shoulders and lifted her chin. She was Baldwin's daughter. Roric would *not* make her cry. 'Never mind, Mama. We won't lose sleep over a fool. We'll put our heads together and find someone else, someone far better than Harald's bastard cousin to be my consort in Ardenn.'

Berardine's indrawn breath sounded harsh. Painful. 'There is more, Catrain. And worse.'

She looked at the second letter her mother held out. Worse? Roric had rejected her. What could be worse than that?

'Mama—'

'Be silent and read it,' her mother said coldly. 'You cannot learn too soon about the perfidy of men.'

Roric's rejection hurt and offended her. But she'd much rather that than the fear now curdling in her throat. Her mother had become a pagan goddess, icy and remote. Fright-sweat damped her temples, her armpits, the palms of her unsteady hands. She tossed Roric's rejection onto the seat of a nearby chair and took the second letter.

'To Berardine, Duchess of Ardenn, from the Regents' Council of His Most Sovereign and Serene Highness Prince Gaël,' it read, the heavy parchment gilded, each cursive character exquisitely formed with expensive ink by a master scribe. *'Madam: we understand you have sought for your husband's eldest daughter and heir, Catrain, a match with the bastard murderer and traitor Roric, self-styled Duke of Clemen. Be apprised of His Highness's grave*

displeasure at this news and know you are summoned before this council, in the company of Baldwin's heir, to explain your grievous actions.'

Catrain stared at her mother's sword-straight back. 'Could it be a forgery?'

'No. That is the prince's seal.' Berardine snorted. '*His Highness's grave displeasure.* As if a milk-sucking babe feels grave displeasure over anything but the emptiness of its wet nurse's tit. Oh, Catrain! These men who want to rule me. Curse their blood, curse their bones, and their tiny little cocks.'

Startled by her mother's crudity, she dropped the regent's letter. Hid her confusion by hastily retrieving it from the carpet. 'What are you going to do, Mama?'

'Do?' Berardine turned away from the window. As befitted an icy pagan goddess, her cheeks were pale as snow. 'What can I do, Catrain, but obey this arrogant demand? A duchess is not a prince, nor even a prince's regent.'

Hidden by her long wool skirts, her knees were shamefully trembling. 'Will they punish you for offering me to Roric?'

'No. They'll bluster and they'll threaten, but they've no power to do more.'

She wanted to believe that. She wanted to believe her mother believed it. But behind Berardine's cold self-control there was a fear that matched her own. She could feel it.

'Mama . . .' She had to wet her dry lips. 'What if they decree I'm to marry a man of their choosing?'

Berardine's eyes glittered like frozen glass. 'They won't.'

'They might! What if—'

'There is no *what if*, Catrain. Do you think I'd allow the regents to wed you *anywhere* without my consent? Do you imagine Ardenn would allow it?'

A surge of relief. Her mother was right. She was Baldwin's daughter, adored by his people. Let the regents try to force a marriage and the whole duchy would rise in protest. That was Baldwin's power, seven years after his death. And the regents knew it. She was safe.

Or was she?

Chilled, she looked again at the regents' unfriendly letter. 'If that's true, Mama, then why am I summoned?'

'Because the prince's keepers seek to beat two mares with one stick,' Berardine said, derisive. 'You're to be duchess after me, remember? They want you subdued, while you're still young.'

It seemed the most likely explanation. And yet . . . 'What aren't you telling me, Mama? I thought we agreed I'm no longer a child.'

Instead of answering, her mother crossed the chamber to Baldwin's imposing desk and sat behind it. Her restless fingers tapped his fabulously expensive silver-filigreed onyx inkwell, the one gifted to him by his second cousin's youngest daughter, who'd married the heir to Duchy Trehnt. Still cold, her eyes watched the play of light on her pearl and ruby rings.

Catrain followed her to the desk. 'Mama? *Please*. If yesterday I was old enough to marry, then today I'm old enough to know the truth.'

With a shuddering sigh, her mother looked up. 'Prove it. Read the regents' letter again.'

And what did that mean? Had she misread it the first time? Missed some hidden message or meaning? One uncertain glance at her mother, then she scanned the letter a second time.

. . . *we understand you have sought for your husband's eldest daughter and heir, Catrain, a match with the bastard murderer and traitor Roric* . . .

Oh! Of course! Like a ninny she'd let herself be blinded by the pain of Roric's rejection. The regents understood there'd been a match sought? How? Unless – unless—

'So,' said her mother, darkly pleased. 'It seems you have the makings of a duchess after all. Yes, Catrain. We were betrayed.'

'Not by Roric,' she said quickly. 'He's not that kind of man.'

'You don't know that. You don't know him.'

'Yes, I do. When we saved those horses, I—'

'*Not another word about those wretched horses, Catrain!*'

No fool, she fell silent. But she knew she was right. At court a man could hide his true face, wear a hundred different masks, disguise the stench of evil with a soaking of sweet perfume. But fire burned away all pretence. Surrounded by smoke and flame she'd seen Roric for who he really was. And for her sins, between heartbeats, she'd fallen in love with the man he'd shown her . . .

. . . but she wasn't going to think about that. Not yet. Not until she could think of him without wanting to weep. But that didn't mean she could leave him undefended.

'It wasn't Roric, Mama.'

'You'd accuse our sailing captain? Or Master Tihomir? Or perhaps this betrayal is Howkin's doing!'

She felt her face flush. 'I'd say rather the lord Humbert's behind it! His daughter's to marry Roric, isn't she? What if he wanted to make certain, and so sent word to the regents of our meeting in Eaglerock to stir trouble for us.'

'Humbert?' Berardine murmured. Her gaze softened as she considered. 'That's a clever thought, Catrain.'

Judging it safe enough, Catrain sat in a tapestried chair without asking permission. 'And if not Humbert, then it was another of Roric's councillors.'

'You seem very sure.'

She was. Her history tutor didn't leave every lesson smiling for no reason. 'Clemen's noblemen deposed Harald for their own purposes as much as for the duchy. I'd wager every pendant in my jewel-case they think Roric the bastard owes them his fealty more than they owe any to him.'

Now her mother's gaze was intent. 'Meaning they'd never permit him to marry you. Or indeed any maid safely beyond their control.' A strange look passed over her face. 'I should have seen that. And I would have seen it, only—'

'Only what, Mama?' she said, uneasy. Her mother's stricken expression was disturbing. 'I don't—'

Berardine stood. 'It's nothing, child,' she said, her face snowfall-smooth again. 'A passing thought, of no import.'

She didn't believe that, but there'd be a better time to pursue further truths. 'So, Mama.' She tossed the regents' letter onto her father's desk. 'When do we leave for the Prince's Isle?'

'We don't,' her mother said, frowning. 'I'll be confronting the regents alone.'

'But Mama—'

'Don't argue! Their quarrel is with me, Catrain. I'll not have you dragged into it!' Berardine turned to the portrait on the wall behind the desk. 'Your father would never forgive me for that.'

'The regents won't forgive you for leaving me behind!'

'I've made my decision.' Her mother nodded at the door. 'Now, be a good girl and go. I've much to arrange and little time at my disposal.'

And that was that. Defeated, Catrain dropped into a curtsy. 'Madam,' she said, the dutiful daughter, and did as she was told.

Berardine departed Carillon at dawn the following morning. Catrain watched her mother's carriage out of sight, her throat tight, her eyes stinging. Then she set about killing fear with duty. Thirteen days later a troop of royal men-at-arms trotted menacingly into the ducal palace's forecourt.

'I'm sorry, my lady,' Howkin said, his voice choked. 'But they're sent by the prince's regents and they have a warrant. Look.'

Outwardly stony-faced, inwardly panicked, Catrain took the parchment he thrust at her. Read it quickly, willing her heart not to beat right through her chest. The warrant gave no hint of what had been done with her mother, just tersely commanded that she present herself before the regents' council without delay. Like the first letter it was signed by Lord Leofric, maternal uncle to the prince.

Howkin's fingers were clenching and unclenching, betraying his agitation. 'Captain Markus awaits your answer, my lady.'

Captain Markus could go piss himself. But since that wasn't the kind of thing Baldwin's daughter could say out loud, she nodded at her father's majordomo.

'Tell the good captain that as Prince Gaël's loyal subject I shall of course obey. I suppose I'm to be given enough time to pack suitable clothing?'

'Captain Markus indicated his desire to depart Carillon within the hour.'

'Carrying me piggy-back behind his saddle?' she asked. 'Or am I permitted the extravagance of a coach?'

'Neither,' said Howkin, smiling despite his dismay. 'The captain understands my lady is an intrepid horsewoman and hopes she is fit enough to ride with him and his men.'

That made her stare. 'He wants me to travel for nearly a week without a suitable female companion?'

'I did object, my lady,' said Howkin. 'You have the regents' word your honour won't be touched.'

'Do I?' she said sourly. Ordinarily there was nothing she'd love more than several days of cross-country riding on her favourite horse, without the burden of a complaining female companion. But the thought of agreeing to anything this captain wanted made her teeth ache. 'And if it turns out I'm not as intrepid as he's heard?'

'My lady . . .' Howkin hesitated, then heaved a mournful sigh. 'I think it prudent to accommodate him. I fear Captain Markus is a man lacking both patience and humour.'

She glanced out of her dayroom's window. 'And common sense, apparently. Or else he's blind. It's raining, Howkin.'

'The captain seems indifferent to rain, hail or shine.'

Well, didn't he sound charming? 'Very well. Inform Captain Markus I'll meet him downstairs in an hour. Then tell the stables I want Otebon groomed and saddled. Oh – and have the kitchens send me up a meal to eat while I'm packing. Nothing too heavy.' She smiled, unamused. 'Or likely to excite the bowels. I don't suppose this dour captain wants to be stopping every half-league or so.'

'Very well, my lady,' said Howkin, his eyes bright. 'And if you'll excuse me saying so, could Duke Baldwin see you now he'd be ever so proud.'

The comment caught her off-guard. Hiding emotion behind a frown, she nodded. 'Thank you, Howkin. Now, best not keep the captain waiting.'

'My lady.'

'Howkin—'

Pausing, he turned. 'My lady?'

'I don't suppose – I mean—' She lifted her chin. 'Did Captain Markus bring any word from the duchess?'

Howkin seemed to shrink a little. 'No, my lady. I'm sorry.'

Yes. And so was she. Sorry . . . and afraid.

*   *   *

It was tempting to be late downstairs purely on principle. But she didn't delay, because she was her father's daughter and Baldwin always said only a fool made an enemy without good reason.

Captain Markus, grey-haired and wiry, was polite enough, but aloof. His men, ten of them, were likewise fit and unapproachable and, echoing their captain, indifferent to the soft, soaking rain. They surrounded her in the palace forecourt like wolves circling a lone lamb, and at Markus's barked order hustled her away in his wake.

Snatching a last look behind her she saw Howkin and her bevy of matronly attendants and her sisters, Brielle, Derrice and Markela, standing on the palace steps. Every one of them was weeping.

She wanted to weep too, but she'd die before she let the regents' wolves see how much she feared the future she was riding towards.

For five gruelling days, from before dawn until deepest dusk, they rode hard on their tough horses and she rode harder still to keep up. They left Ardenn behind, crossed first into Trehnt and then into Rebbai. Captain Markus made no allowance for her. Each night, as they bedded down in this plain inn, or that one, all he asked was whether she could continue. And though her body shrieked in protest, all she ever answered was yes. Beyond that, she thought, to him and his men she might've been a block of wood.

They reached the Prince's Isle late on the fifth day after leaving Carillon. But when dusk fell, instead of stopping for the night Captain Markus kept riding. Then dusk gave way to darkness and still he kept riding, willing to risk the horses beneath a sliver of miserly moon.

By the time they stumbled through the imposing gates of the prince's palace, Catrain was so bone-shatteringly weary she could hardly remember her own name. Impersonally rough hands pulled her out of the saddle, stripped off her riding cloak, hustled her indoors. Too tired and hungry to care about the whispers and stares that followed her, she let herself be chivvied through the palace until she reached a large, gilded chamber warm and bright as noon with burning candles. Blinking at the three men and one woman who stood before her, Catrain cleared her throat.

'Where is my mother? I demand that you take me to the Duchess of Ardenn.'

The oldest of the three men was dressed head-to-toe in black. His black hair was oiled and close-cropped, his beard badger-striped grey. He looked at her with brown eyes containing no warmth at all.

'Little girls don't make demands. They hold their tongues and do as they're told.'

'I am not a little girl. I am Baldwin's daughter.'

The man smiled, a snarl of teeth. 'You are one of Baldwin's daughters. As for your mother, she's returned home.'

Knives of fear, stabbing. 'Without me? I don't believe you!'

'Believe what you like,' he said, shrugging. 'I am Lord Leofric. This is Lord Auberon.' He gestured to the red-haired man to his right. 'And this is Lord Beyden.' A gesture to his left, at a bald man with a paunch. 'We are the prince's regents.'

'Yes, I know,' she said. 'My lords, why am I brought here?'

Leofric nodded to the elegant woman standing off to one side. 'This is my wife, Lady Leofric. She will have the governance of you, while you're in our care.'

Terrible waves of heat and cold were washing over her like storm-surge. 'What do you mean, in your care?' she said faintly. 'Where is my mother? I want to see my mother! I want – I want—'

The bright room dimmed as her vision blurred, as her bones turned to water and she crumpled to the floor. The last thing she heard, before darkness claimed her, was a woman's voice whispering into her ear.

'*Hold your tongue, my husband said. The prince and his regents don't care what you want.*'

'What?' Berardine said blankly, staring at Howkin. 'How can Catrain be gone? Gone where? With whom? Man, what—'

Howkin was wringing his hands. 'Madam, madam, the regents sent for her. Days ago. With a warrant. I was sure you knew. And when word came to me your carriage was sighted I assumed you were bringing her home!'

The regents. Those duplicitous, treacherous bastards. 'What warrant? Show me.'

Howkin sent for the warrant and, surrounded by tearful servants, she read it. Crushed it in her fist when she was done. 'Get out. All of you. And if you value your freedom, don't come back till I send for you.'

Wisely, not a one of them protested. As Howkin and her ladies trickled out of her dayroom, she retreated to her privy chamber and slammed the door shut.

'Madam,' said a soft voice. 'You are troubled. Let me lift your cares.'

Berardine felt her heart near stop with fright. Then she saw it. A slender shadow standing against the night-drawn curtains. Memory woke. *Izusa*. She moistened her lips. '*You*. How did you get in here?'

'Does it matter? You're in no danger.'

'I promise you, one of us is. You said you'd give me counsel, but it's been *years*, Izusa. Where were you?'

'Madam . . .' Izusa sighed, chiding. 'I said I'd come if you needed me. You've not needed me till now. And now I'm here. Let me help.'

'*Help?*' Sick with rage, Berardine snatched a cushion from a nearby chair and threw it. 'Liar! Deceiver! Slither from my presence the way you came and *never* show your face again!'

Unperturbed, Izusa stepped forward into warm candle-light. 'Do not fret, Berardine. Your daughter is safe.'

'She's been taken by Leofric and his lapdogs! How is she *safe*?'

Fox-red hair curled in twists and tangles around Izusa's narrow face. 'The regents will not harm her. You have my word.'

'Why should I believe you? Everything you've ever told me was a lie!'

'Everything?' Izusa's lips curved, briefly. 'Berardine.'

She wanted to slap and scratch the witch's hollow cheeks until the blood ran. 'You told me she'd marry Roric!'

'True,' said Izusa. 'But did I say when?'

'*What?*'

'Catrain will marry Roric, Madam. When the time is right.'

Still smiling, cat-confident, Izusa settled herself on the edge of the large four-poster bed. Patted the marten-pelt coverlet beside her. Dazed, Berardine started towards the bed then caught herself, just in time, and instead chose an unpadded wooden settle. She was duchess here, not Baldwin's soothsayer.

'Explain yourself,' she said coldly. 'Or things will go ill for you.'

If Izusa was frightened, she didn't show it. 'You are angry.'

'Indeed! How amazing. You must be a witch.'

'Madam . . .' Another chiding sigh. 'The regents have taken your daughter so they might keep you constrained.'

'I don't need you to tell me that!'

'Then what can I tell you?'

If she asked the witch a question, she'd be admitting she trusted the answer. But who else could she confide in? With Baldwin dead, Catrain stolen, she had nowhere else to turn.

'Is this Roric's doing, Izusa? Did he betray me to the regents?'

'No, Madam. It was Aistan. One of Roric's closest lords.'

'Then Roric—'

'*No*, Madam. Aistan acted alone. In this, Roric's hands are clean.'

So. Catrain was proven right. A small comfort. 'Hear me, Izusa. I won't leave my daughter to the regents' tender care. Nor will Cassinia's dukes tolerate their conduct. When they learn—'

'Cassinia's dukes find your rule unnatural, Madam. They will do nothing to help you so long as Catrain remains unharmed. And even then . . .' Izusa shrugged one shoulder. 'But never fear. Your daughter *will* remain unharmed, provided you do nothing rash.'

The words struck her like lead and sank to the bottom of her soul. 'What are you saying? That I must accept this – this *theft*? Abandon my child to the craven cowards who stole her?'

Izusa nodded. 'For now.'

'I can't do that.'

'*You must!*'

Shocked, Berardine waited for the wildly leaping candle-light to calm. Then she looked again at the woman she'd trusted for Baldwin's sake. The witch who promised miracles. Who knew things no one could know.

'I'm frightened, Izusa,' she whispered. 'I don't know what to do.'

Izusa's smile was kind, and confiding. 'I know, Beradine. But if you trust me, all will be well.'

She kept the severed baby's head in a box carved out of ash.

'*Izusa,*' it said, its grey lips fondling her name.

The thrill of him sizzled through her, as though his fingers had touched her nape. 'Salimbene.'

'*Have you seen the duchess?*'

Izusa nodded, eager. 'Yes. I've just come from the palace.'

'*Were you noticed?*'

The thought of his anger sickened her. 'No. I swear it.'

Silence. The head's lips drooped, like an old man's, showing a hint of rotting gum. Wood smoked and crackled in the crumbling fireplace, throwing shadows against the sagging, cracked wattle-and-daub wall. She lived poor here, in this slummish Carillon cottage. Just as he wanted. Everything, as he wanted.

'*Izusa.*' The head's closed, sunken eyelids twitched. '*How much did you tell her?*'

'Only that Catrain is safe. Nothing more.'

The lips smiled. '*Good. And now you're done with Berardine. Make your way to the Marches between Clemen and Harcia. Kill the herb-woman Phemie, and take her place as a travelling leech.*'

He wasn't calling her home? She wanted to weep, but that would displease him. 'Yes, Salimbene.'

'*Make haste, Izusa. I will find you there.*'

The drooping infant lips stilled. He was gone. Soon after, the severed head collapsed into dust. Letting her tears fall, she unbound what remained of the binding rite and burned the box. Then she set fire to the hovel . . . and disappeared into the night.

CHAPTER FIFTEEN

Eagle-eyed Joben was first to see the trader and his two burdened mules, plodding along the dusty road leading to Pikebank township, where twice a year the Great Southern Horse Fair was held.

'Ho, Balfre! What's this?' he said, pointing ahead.

Balfre grinned at his cousin. 'Sport.'

There was nobody else on the narrow, rutted road. The fair had opened two days earlier, and every village for leagues around had emptied itself into the town, to rowdy and trade and bawd with the horses as an excuse. Easing his destrier from canter to trot, Balfre raised a clenched fist. It was the only command he needed to give. Joben, riding on his left flank, Paithan on his right, with Lowis and Waymon behind them, eased their horses too. Once they were all prancing, he encouraged his stallion forward until he was clearly in the lead.

'Now,' he said, still grinning, 'let's see what this tardy merchant has to say for himself.'

The trader rode a spavin-shanked, goose-rumped, flea-bitten nag, and the mules were no better. Their sway backs sagged beneath the weight of the laden panniers they carried. The man's lowered face was shaded from the sun by a wide-brimmed leather hat, his linen shirt-sleeves rolled up to reveal hairy, muscular forearms burned a deep summer brown, where they weren't scarred. His leather leggings were scratched and he wore a long dagger belted at his side.

'You there!' Balfre shouted, approaching. 'Stand and account for yourself, in the name of Duke Aimery!'

The trader looked up slowly, as though roused out of sleep. Pushing his hat back, revealing the acorn-brown skin and wide, flat cheekbones of one Maletti-born, he gaped as though he'd never seen well-bred horses before.

'M'lord?' he called, not halting his nag and mules. 'What be the trouble? Mizn't I a proper man, minding his own tidy doings? What be the cause to stop me in my tracks?'

'Hark to him,' said Paithan loudly, spitting contempt. 'Fucking Maletti churl. Someone should raze their precious city state to the ground. Everyone knows they shit the plague in that place. Maybe we should strip him naked and burn his clothes, for fear he carries it.'

'What?' the trader yelped. 'Strip me? When I b'aint offering no soul a wigget of harm?'

As his companions laughed, Balfre laid a hand on his sword-hilt.

'I'll decide if you're harmful or not, man. Stand, I say, or I'll cut the legs off you so you can sit on your arse for the rest of your short life.'

The trader wrangled his horse and mules to a standstill. 'Iss, iss, m'lord. I be stopped, see? No cause for ye to go waving a sword at innocent I, who never had a single plague boil a day in his life.'

Balfre halted his own horse in front of the man, then waited until his companions had formed a menacing half-circle at his back. 'What's your name?'

'Denno Culpyn, m'lord,' said the trader, sweeping his hat from his head, revealing close-cropped and grey-threaded dark hair. 'Bonded merchant trader, as I am, and riding peaceful to Pikebank fair with fine, fancy wares for the lords and ladies of Harcia.'

Waymon laughed, sneering. 'Cheap and nasty trinkets, more like.'

'No, m'lord, no trumpery, or call me a feggit!' Culpyn protested. 'Mizn't I be an honest man?'

'How should I tell?' said Balfre. 'I've never laid eyes on you before.' He took his time raking a cold stare over the trader, his nag and his burdened mules. 'The fair began day before yesterday. You can't be much of a trader if you don't know that, and come so late to Pikebank.'

'I do know it, m'lord,' said the trader, grimacing. 'But I got m'self felled in the Marches, y'see. Lost four days shitting and heaving till the sickness passed. But t'weren't plague!' he added hastily. ''Twas belly gripe. A nasty thing, but no more fearsome, m'lord. I swear.'

A plausible excuse. But even so . . . 'You claim you're bonded to travel and trade in Harcia? Prove it.'

'Trading passes in my saddle bag, m'lord,' said the trader, self-righteous. 'All proper signed and sealed, they be. And the leech's nod, m'lord, showing I b'aint diddled with plague. Denno Culpyn knows better than to cross out of the Marches without his papers, he does.'

He held out his hand, eyebrows raised. Hid amusement as his companions added the weight of their gazes to his.

Fumbling, the indignant insolence leaking out of him like water through a dented sieve, the trader dismounted, perched his hat on his saddle, unbuckled a saddle bag and pulled out a folded, much travel-stained sheet of parchment and a sheet of rush-paper.

'See, m'lord?' he said, brandishing it. 'Denno Culpyn mizn't no truth-twister.'

With a wave of his hand Balfre summoned the man closer. Took the parchment and unfolded it. The inked permissions were faded, the attached seals of Harcia and Clemen old and cracked, but the bond was in order. So was the leechery clearance, signed the day before.

'You were trading in Clemen before crossing into Harcia?'

'Iss, my lord, that be so. I traded in Clemen, and in the Marches.'

'And where else in Harcia do you think to peddle your goods?'

'That be hard to say, m'lord.' The trader plucked at his whiskery chin. 'Depends on how swift I sell in Pikebank. Could be I won't get a stride further. A great many of yer lords and ladies come to Pikebank for the horses, m'lord, and in my experience they've a powerful liking for fine wares.'

'Fine wares, yes,' he said, and was pleased to see blood rise beneath the trader's skin.

Uneasy, Culpyn shuffled his feet. 'Forgive me if I be a feggit slow worm, m'lord, but be there trouble in Harcia, that ye'd ribble me for no reason? Yer good duke's not fallen amiss again, has he?'

'Mind your tongue. My father is none of your concern.'

That had the churl's jaw dropping. 'Yer father, my lord? Then ye be—'

'Count Balfre,' he said, not bothering any more to hide his amusement. 'Aimery's heir, and the next duke of Harcia.'

Culpyn looked near to shitting himself. 'C- Count Balfre.' He managed an awkwardly dashing bow. 'M'lord. Heard of ye, of course. Famed through all the Marches, ye be. And a feggit for it if ye b'aint.'

Scowling, Balfre threw the battered travelling bonds at Culpyn's feet. The paltry Marches? Before he was done he'd be famed far wider than that. 'Empty your saddle bags and panniers.'

The trader's deep-set eyes widened. 'M'lord?'

'You heard Count Balfre, churl!' Waymon said roughly. 'We'll see your wares on the ground, or your blood. Choose which!'

It was odd, really, how the big, blustery men always shrank when they were put to it. Indeed, the trader's fingers never once touched his dagger. Instead, pinch-lipped and pale beneath his Maletti skin, Culpyn reluctantly obeyed. As short bolts of figured silk and muslin bags of jingling jewellery, bundles of embroidered doeskin gloves, stitched oilskin packets of rare herbs and spices and various other foreign treasures fell one by one to the dusty ground, Balfre idly considered his four companions.

Three useful nobles and a cousin. All in all, he'd chosen his closest confidants well. Cousin Joben first, of course. Family was important. Then Lowis of Parsle Fountain, and Ferran's wayward, reckless son Waymon. Paithan had joined him last, after much careful wooing. A particular triumph, weaning Black Hughe's brother from that troublesome old rump Herewart. Their father's heirs, every one. He was pleased to see, watching them watch the trader, there wasn't a squeamish glance between them, not a soft heart to be found. He had no use for soft hearts. What he needed was ambition, hungry for being unfed. And in these men he had it. His companions were eager to inherit, as he was. Stifled by their sires, as he was. Ripe to pluck the fruit they wanted, heedless of tradition . . . as he was.

Six years now, I've bided my time. Danced to Aimery's never-silent pipe. Played my part as the contrite and dutiful son. Smiled and smiled and smiled at the great Steward Grefin, every time he sets foot off the Green Isle.

Only thinking of his brother made his teeth ache, like biting ice. He'd have to practise his smiling on the ride back to Cater's Tamwell. Doubtless Grefin had reached the castle by now, with Mazelina and their happy brood. Two more brats Grefin had sired since leaving the mainland for his little island fiefdom. But only one was another son. That was some consolation. And now they were all returning to Harcia's capital to celebrate Aimery's sixtieth birthday.

The old man should have another palsy and be done with life. He's past his prime. Worn out. And Harcia's weeping to be reborn.

'Balfre,' said Paithan, beside him. 'Culpyn's done.'

On a sharp breath, Balfre frowned at the haphazard piles of tumbled goods on the road. Then he stared at the trader, whose hand rested on one supposedly-empty saddle bag. There was something possessive, even furtive, in the gesture. Suspicion prickled.

'Done? I don't think so.' He raised his voice, giving it a sharper edge. 'Culpyn. What is it you don't want me to see?'

A small flicker of resentful defiance lit the trader's eyes. 'M'lord? Here be all my trinkets and wares, ruined for yer pleasure. B'aint another mossle to show ye, my word on it.'

'Your word?' He leaned forward. 'Man, I'd take poison before I'd take your word. *What's in the saddle bag?*'

'Nothing, m'lord! Nothing!' But Culpyn's snatched hand told a different story. Caught in a lie, his face reddened with frightened guilt. 'M'lord, they be letters, is all. Little letters, a few chicken scratches. No harm in 'em. I mizn't a man as would hurt yer fine duchy.'

'Letters for whom? Written by whom?'

'Writ by all manner of Marcher folk, m'lord, as need me to ride with 'em into Harcia. When they can't, y'see, on account of not being travel bonded.'

Balfre laughed. 'Fuck, Culpyn, do you expect me to believe you scamper about the Marches on that nag, with those sorry mules, collecting letters like a royal messenger?'

'No, m'lord,' the trader whispered.

'Well, then?'

'M'lord—'

'Answer me!'

'M'lord . . .' The trader stared at his battered boots. 'It be true I mizn't no fancy, scampering messenger. A fine woman I know, trusted by all the Marcher lords, she is, she holds the letters from folk then passes 'em to me, and I pass 'em on after.'

'And does this paragon have a name?'

Culpyn didn't want to tell him that, either. His fingers clenched and unclenched, his jaw tightened, his throat convulsed as he swallowed. Then his gaze lifted to the Harcian knights ranged before him.

'Molly,' he muttered.

'And who is she? This *Molly*?'

'I told ye, m'lord. She be a fine woman. Taps a sweet keg and bakes a greely mutton pie in the Pig Whistle Inn, at the big Marches crossroads. Her place, it be. Run tight as a drum.'

249

The Pig Whistle? He'd heard of it. 'And does she write letters too? This fine, trustworthy innkeeper?'

The trader shrugged, helpless. 'Iss, m'lord. Sometimes. No harm there either. No harm in any of 'em. Just little bits of gossip, they be. Just as I told ye, m'lord, no danger to Harcia.'

'How would you know? Do you read them? These letters?'

Culpyn stepped back, shocked. 'Read 'em? No! I mizn't no sticky-beaker. I *told* ye, m'lord. I be an honest trader doing a kindness for a friend.'

Nothing so innocent would break a man into a rolling sweat . . . and the trader was sweating. And that meant a lie. Denno Culpyn might well be a man who sold goods for coin but it was clear as the sun overhead he was something else too. A messenger for spies, or perhaps a spy himself. Traders were widely travelled – and they weren't all as they seemed.

'The letters, Culpyn. I'll have them.'

Culpyn blinked. 'M'lord?'

'*I'll have them.*'

'But – m'lord – Count Balfre—' The trader raised an imploring hand. 'Molly, she do trust me to see 'em safe delivered. She promised others, trusting me.'

'And if you speak another word, Culpyn, you can trust I'll see you safe delivered to a fucking dungeon. *The letters.*'

On the brink of tears, Culpyn took a bulky, twine-bound packet from the saddle bag and surrendered it. Not bothering to even undo the twine, Balfre slid the letters into his doublet.

'Waymon. Lowis.'

Like well-trained boarhounds, they knew what he wanted. Unmoved, he watched as they beat the trader into a bruised and bloodied heap. The nag and the mules shuffled uneasily, heads tossing, but the beasts were too weary to bolt. Culpyn grunted and moaned and tried to protect his face and balls, but Waymon and Lowis were jousters, men who wore steel armour like silk. Brash Denno Culpyn was no match for them.

When he was sure the lesson had been learned, he snapped his fingers. Waymon and Lowis stepped back.

'Give me the travelling bond.'

Lowis retrieved the torn parchment from under the flea-bitten nag's cracked, poorly shod hoof and handed it over, then he and Waymon remounted their horses.

'Culpyn,' Balfre said, nudging his stallion closer to the shuddering man curled on the ground amidst his trampled wares. 'Look at me.'

Culpyn forced open his swiftly swelling eyes. 'Iss, m'lord?'

'What you do in Clemen is your business – and that cursed bastard Roric's. But my business is Harcia. You're no longer welcome here.' He pulled Aimery's seal off the parchment and snapped the worn, faded wax disc in half. Tossed the pieces away. Tossed the parchment and leech pass after them. 'If you're found in my duchy again you'll swing from a gibbet. Understood?'

Culpyn nodded, wincing. 'Iss, m'lord.'

'And don't linger in the Marches, either. Harcia's Marcher lords will be told of you, Trader Culpyn. Best you limp back to Clemen with your tail between your legs and find yourself a bed in one of Eaglerock's middens. Better yet, swim back to Maletti. For there'll come a time soon when the likes of you won't be safe anywhere within my reach.'

Breathing harshly, dribbling scarlet from his broken nose and the splits in his eyebrow and cheek, Culpyn staggered to his feet.

'This b'aint right,' he said thickly. 'I be an honest man. I mizn't done a thing wrong to ye.'

Balfre looked down at the trader's ruined wares. 'Your taste in trinkets offends me. And that's offence enough.'

'M'lord,' said the trader, and bent to start retrieving his goods.

'Those are forfeit, Culpyn. Now go, you ignorant shit, before I run my sword through those mangy beasts of yours *and* through you for good measure.

Wisely, Culpyn held his tongue. Collected his useless travel bond, then the mules' tether reins, clambered grunting into his saddle and rode away slump-shouldered from Pikebank, back the way he'd come, in the direction of the Marches.

Waymon nodded at the jumble on the grass. 'You don't want any of that?'

'The jewellery,' he said, shrugging. 'If it's still any good. And the spices. You can ride the rest to rags.'

'Balfre,' Joben said quietly, holding back while the others continued their sport. 'Those letters. What are you thinking?'

Yes. The letters. He could feel them tucked between his velvet doublet and linen shirt. 'I'm thinking they're my concern, cousin. Not yours.'

Joben rubbed a gloved finger over his lips. 'I beg to differ. You might be Aimery's heir, but I sit on the council.'

'As do I. Your meaning, Joben?'

'If those letters somehow pose a threat to Harcia—'

'What threat?' he said lightly, smiling as Waymon leaned half out of his saddle to piss on a tangled twist of green and blue silk. 'You heard the trader. They're full of Marcher peasants' gossip.'

'If you believed that, he'd still have them. And since he doesn't . . .'

Balfre looked sideways, one eyebrow lifted. 'It means nothing. I'm a malicious fuck, Joben. Didn't you know?'

'You're a suspicious fuck,' Joben retorted. 'Balfre, if there's danger to Harcia in those letters then—'

'Then I'll tell Aimery. But it's more likely I'll be wiping my arse on them in the garderobe.' He lifted his reins, frowning. 'And speaking of the good duke . . . we should be on our way, cousin. Doubtless my father is roaming Tamwell castle in a temper because I've not returned to make a hue and cry over Grefin's return.'

'Grefin.' Joben pulled a face. 'And how long does our celebrated Steward of the Green Isle plan to stay in Cater's Tamwell this time?'

Too long, most likely. Grefin was loved best when loved from afar. 'Who can say?' he said, shrugging. 'It's Aimery's castle. He'll decide. Paithan! Waymon! Lowis! Enough of that. I want to ride.'

Obedient, his companions abandoned their destruction of the trader's wares, handed over the rescued jewellery and spices then fell behind him, in their accustomed place.

Wheeling about, the packet of letters heavy against his ribs, Balfre spurred his stallion towards home.

It seemed as though every man, woman and child in Cater's Tamwell and its surrounding villages had turned out to cheer the Green Isle's Steward and his family. Riding up from the river, where their galley was docked, with Mazelina laughing and smiling and waving by his side, and the excited children in the flower-decked pony cart trundling behind, Grefin smiled and waved too, hiding his hurt. Knowing his father had grown frail, he'd not expected to see Aimery waiting to greet him at Tamwell Landing. But he'd hoped, half-expected, that Balfre would be there.

Which only goes to show I'm a fool.

The river Tam formed a large, lazy loop around Cater's Tamwell, the duchy's largest and most prosperous township. In older days, Balfre's dead and dreaming time, the king's seat in his kingdom of Harcia. Usually a visitor come by galley to Tamwell castle would moor at Castle Landing and enter its high-walled grounds through the river gate. But since this was no usual occasion, instead the start of a three-day celebration for Aimery's landmark birthday, the Steward of the Green Isle, his family and his attendants were making a grand entrance. The township's high street was lined four deep with excited Harcian folk on both sides, everyone whistling and shaking rattles and throwing barley-seeds dyed yellow and red. Though he was worried for his father, Grefin couldn't help feeling touched.

But on second thought, it's probably best Balfre's not here to see the fuss. He'd only ferment the barley into more bitter ale.

Nothing had been the same between them since that dreadful council meeting six years ago, when Balfre had abased himself and their father stepped over him as though he were driftwood . . . or a dead dog. For himself, he'd given up saying he was sorry. Perhaps Balfre's forgivness would come, one day. But the more he asked for it, the more he showed how much it mattered, the longer Balfre would deny him. Like it or not – and he didn't – that was his brother.

'My love, you've stopped waving,' said Mazelina, riding so close that their knees touched. 'Have you broken your arm?'

He looked at her, startled. Splendid in green velvet and cloth-of-gold and pearls the size of walnuts, her brow clasped by a gold circlet studded with emeralds that matched her leaf-green eyes, she was everything he could ever desire. Nearly eight years married, and her beauty still stopped his heart.

'What?' he said. 'No. I was just thinking.'

'About Balfre.' She wrinkled her nose. 'You really shouldn't, Grefin. You'll get heartburn.'

That made him laugh. 'Hush. Wait until we're behind castle walls before you disparage Aimery's heir.'

Mazelina shrugged, indifferent. 'Wave, my lord Steward,' she suggested. 'Or you'll leave hurt feelings in your wake.'

She was right, of course. But that was nothing new. So he waved at the cheering, delighted people of Cater's Tamwell and its surrounding villages as he rode beside Mazelina along the length of the high street and up the winding approach to Tamwell castle, which stood atop a weathered granite outcrop commanding a sweeping view of the township and the river.

Aimery was waiting for them in the castle bailey, smothered in a fur-lined robe though the day was summer warm, and relying on a gold-fretted ebony cane to keep him steady.

'He's grown so thin,' Mazelina murmured, as they halted their horses. 'And his hair is all turned white. Oh, Grefin. I never thought to see Aimery of Harcia look *old*.'

'Hush,' he said again, glancing behind them at the pony cart. 'The children might hear you.'

More than a year had passed since he'd last seen his father, soon after the palsy felled him. Before they left the Green Isle this time Curteis had written to warn of Aimery's changes, so there'd be no shock at their first sight of the duke. A kind, clever gesture. But even so, he was shocked. Oblivious to the bustling as servants rushed to take charge of the horses, the children, the Steward's attendants, Grefin slid out of his saddle and threaded his way through the crowd. Halting before his father, he dropped to one knee and bowed his head.

'Your Grace.'

'My lord Steward,' said his father. His voice had grown reedy, like the rest of him. 'Welcome home.'

Grefin felt Aimery's hand come to rest lightly on his head. Blinking back the sting of tears, he looked up. 'I'm most happy to be here.'

'Prove it and embrace me,' said Aimery, his own eyes wet. 'Or I'll think you naught but a flattering knave.'

They embraced, laughing, even though it was awkward thanks to Aimery's cane. Holding his father tight, Grefin felt through the bulky robe just how much flesh Harcia's duke had lost, how much muscle and strength. The discovery killed laughter. Made it hard for him to breathe.

'Peace, Grefin,' his father whispered into his ear. 'I'm not dead yet.' Then, letting go, he stepped sideways and held out his arm. 'Behold the fair Mazelina, who grows more radiant with every passing year. Come, daughter, and kiss me. You've been too long from my sight! And you children too! Let me see how much you've grown!'

Feeling someone approach behind him, Grefin turned as Mazelina and their excited sons and daughter greeted the duke. Curteis. His father's faithful steward was more careworn than when they'd last met, but his smile was as wryly self-contained as ever.

'My lord Grefin.'

'Curteis. You're well?'

A respectful half-bow. 'Well enough, my lord.'

'And Duke Aimery? The truth, mind. I'm not a babe seeking sugar suckets.'

'His Grace . . . is His Grace,' said Curteis, after a moment. 'A lord of infinite dedication.'

'In other words he's working too hard, and won't listen to you or his physicks or any sensible man.'

'Indeed, my lord.' The steward's lips quirked, hinting a smile. 'Though you did not hear me say so.'

'Of course I didn't,' he agreed. 'And Balfre? Tell me, is my brother even here?'

Curteis's confiding expression cooled. 'No, my lord. Your noble brother is elsewhere about the duchy. But His Grace anticipates his heir's imminent return.'

'Ah. And what of our travel chests?'

'Safely arrived from the dock, my lord, and taken up to your apartments.'

Grefin clapped him on the shoulder. 'Truly, Curteis, you're a marvel of efficiency. I—'

'Curteis!'

'Your Grace?' said Curteis, smoothly stepping forward, an illuminated illustration of the perfect courtier.

Aimery's sickly pallor was suffused now with faint colour, his faded eyes alight with pleasure. 'Curteis, see my gooddaughter and her brood within the castle, to their apartments. Have the kitchens bring them food. I'd steal some privy time with my Steward.'

'Your Grace.'

Leaving Mazelina and their chattering gaggle of offspring in Curteis's capable care, Grefin followed his father out of the emptying bailey.

'My lord? Where are we going?'

'To the wine cellar,' said Aimery. 'I can't so much as look at an empty goblet indoors these days, without Curteis near frowning me into a spasm.'

'And you think *I* won't frown? When the goblet's full?'

Aimery's fleeting smile was full of well-remembered mischief. 'I think you'll grin like a giddycrake if it means I'll share my last bottle of Lambardi sunwine.'

Grefin laughed, delighted, feeling his gathered tensions abruptly ease. 'Your Grace, I have missed you.'

'Not as much as I've missed you, Grefin.'

The castle's wine cellar sat next to the buttery, where muscular milkmaids skimmed cream, churned butter, and made cheeses both soft and hard. Their energetic voices carried through the high, open window and into the bailey. Comforted by their simple cheer, Grefin unbarred the cellar's heavy oak door, lit the oil lantern that hung on the hook beside it, then stood back so his father could make his way down the steep stone stairs before them. To go first himself would be to offer insult.

He didn't breathe easily until they both safely reached the last stair.

'Here,' said his father, handing over the lantern. 'Make yourself useful.'

The cellar was cool and caverny, its stone walls limewashed stark white, its floor unevenly flagstoned with Harcian granite. Lantern shadows leapt floor to ceiling like pagan dancers as they made their way past neat rows of oak barrels, bloated with drunken promise. At the rear of the cellar, just beyond the last barrel, they came to a rickety cupboard and an old three-legged stool.

Aimery rested his cane against the wall. 'Wine's in there. There's just the one chair, so you'll need to set your arse on the floor. Won't do your young bones any harm.'

'Yes, Your Grace.' Grefin rested the lantern on top of the cupboard, then pulled its doors open to reveal a dusty, cork-sealed bottle and a dull pewter goblet. 'If you'll take the throne, I'll do the honours.'

Snorting with amusement, his father lowered himself stiffly onto the stool. 'The goblet's yours. I'll keep hold of the bottle.'

After Aimery had poured him a generous splash of rare, expensive sunwine, Grefin arranged himself cross-legged on the cold floor. Met his father's gaze with a hinting smile.

'A toast. To you, Your Grace.'

Aimery tapped bottle to goblet. 'To your mother. And Malcolm.'

'The spirits keep them,' he said, and drank. The wine was exceptional. He wondered if Balfre knew it was here, and decided not to ask his father. Or ever mention it. Not even to Mazelina.

'Grefin.'

He looked up. 'My lord?'

'You continue doing fine work on the Green Isle.' Aimery's eyes were warm with approval. 'I hear nothing but good of you from every lord. Even that rogue Terriel thinks you shit rainbows – and if that's not a miracle, I don't know what is. You've made me proud. You make Harcia proud.'

Praise from his father came rarely. 'Thank you, Father. I've enjoyed myself a great deal on the Isle and count many of its lords as friends. But . . .' He rubbed at a stain on the goblet. 'Perhaps it's time you brought me home. Balfre must be ready to—'

'No.' Lowering his raised hand, Aimery frowned. Daring argument. 'You'll stay the Steward. I need your brother here, under my eye, where I can watch him.'

'You still don't trust him? After all this time?'

His father took another swallow of wine. Coughed a little, and wiped his mouth on his blue woollen sleeve. 'Balfre's behaving himself well enough, it's true. Does what I ask, what the council asks, without complaint or shirking.'

'Then what more do you want?'

'He needs more seasoning.'

Swallowing a sigh, Grefin pulled his knees close to his chest.

This was why his brother refused to forgive him. If their father would soften, even a little, for even a moment, then Balfre would be able to let go of his grudge. But until that happened . . .

'Is he still whisper-close with Joben?'

'He is,' said Aimery, fingers drumming his knee. 'And of late, not only with your cousin. He's boon companions with Reimond's heir, Lowis, these days. And Ferran's loutish oldest son.'

Waymon. Grefin felt a tug of unease. Since leaving the mainland he'd heard some startling stories. If even half of them were true, it seemed Waymon had learned nothing since that nonsense with the wild boars. What was Balfre thinking, keeping a man like that close? No wonder Aimery hesitated to loose him on the Isle.

'You knew already?' said Aimery, closely watching.

'Jancis wrote as much to Mazelina, and Mazelina told me.'

Aimery pursed his lips at the mention of Balfre's unproductive wife. 'And did Balfre's little rabbit tell Mazelina he's also riding with old Herewart's heir?'

'With *Paithan*? But Paithan hates Balfre.'

'Not any more,' said Aimery, eyebrows lowered.

'And this worries you? I'd think you'd be pleased. For when Balfre is . . .' He stared at the floor, unable to continue. 'What I meant was—'

'Untie your tongue, Grefin,' his father said dryly. 'You're no Osfahr witch, to hasten my death by speaking of it. And you're right. When Balfre is Duke of Harcia he'll need the friendship of his lords.'

'Then—'

'But no lord can take the place of a brother,' Aimery continued, implacable. 'And until I see Balfre turn towards you, not away, you'll be my Steward of the Green Isle. Not him. Now pass me your goblet.'

Grefin sighed as his father poured him more wine. 'You're angry because he's not here. It doesn't matter.'

'It matters to me.'

Another silence. They both drank, moodily. Then Aimery cleared his throat. 'And that's enough talk of Balfre. Where do we stand with Clemen?'

Another contentious subject. 'Nowhere yet,' he said, guarded. 'I've sent Roric word, as you wanted, and now I wait for his reply.'

'Sent word how?'

'Carefully. I have a man who knows a man who knows another man who—' Grefin made a rolling gesture. 'You know how it goes. Whispers in alehouses. Not-so-chance meetings in this alley, and that one. Coin dropped in the pocket of the right trader at the right time.'

Aimery didn't look pleased. 'Sounds havey-cavey to me.'

'Perhaps, my lord, but this is a havey-cavey business.' With an effort he soothed his stirring temper. 'I'm told I might receive answer through someone at Pikebank fair, but I shouldn't wager more than a copper nib on it. What can I say?' he added, as his father glared, unimpressed. 'When we can't speak in the open, when we must sneak like thieves through little holes in the wall, then—'

'If I could approach Roric openly I would,' his father retorted, still glowering. 'But Harcia and Clemen are so belligerently bound by generations of old scars and half-healed wounds, there's no easy way of starting afresh. Look at the Marches. Every other month, a new squabble to quash. No, Grefin. First let Roric prove himself the man I hope he is. Then will I speak up. But until I can trust him I must trust *you* to break new ground in my name. Another reason to keep you as my Steward. On the Green Isle you're free to act in this unobserved. Here, in the court's glare, you've no chance of that.'

'I know,' he sighed.

'But?' his father said, challenging.

'But I think you're wrong to keep this from Balfre. As your heir, he's the one who should be reaching out to—'

'Don't be a fool! Balfre can know *none* of this until a binding treaty between Harcia and Clemen is signed!'

'And if you think he'll not take monstrous offence at that, then—'

'I don't care what he takes, Grefin! Don't you understand?' Aimery was near to shouting, his brow suddenly stippled with unhealthy sweat. The lantern's glow reflected fire in his bloodshot eyes. 'Roric is mired. He can't see past his own troubles. His every waking thought is consumed by Clemen's woes. I've waited six years for him to look up and see your dangerous brother. I can't wait any longer! I might not be at death's door yet but my candle is burning low. I should've approached Clemen's duke long since, but like a fool I thought I had all the time in the world. I don't. And I'll not die leaving Harcia prey to Balfre's misplaced ambitions.'

'Really, Father?' He swallowed a groan. 'You still believe Balfre dreams of uniting the two duchies beneath his rule?'

Aimery stared. 'You don't?'

'I believe he has the right to answer the accusation! Instead you've convicted him as a man for the things he said when he was a boy!'

'He wasn't a boy when he killed Black Hughe,' Aimery said, with an emphatic jab of the wine bottle. 'And what he believed then, Grefin, about crushing Clemen and restoring the old kingdom of Harcia? He still believes it. Depend on that.'

'Has he said so? In your hearing?'

'He doesn't have to. I know him. He's my son.'

'And you're his father. *Talk* to him. Bring him into your confidence. He'll listen, I know he will. He—'

'Don't, Grefin,' said Aimery, his face twisting. 'False hope is the poison that kills good men. The cause of peace is too important to risk entrusting to your brother. If Harcia and Clemen can find a way to break with the past, chart a new and more prosperous future together, then it must be found while I am living, and still Harcia's duke.'

'And if you succeed, my lord? Without Balfre? If you're right about his ambitions, what will stop him from burning the treaty the moment a physick pronounces you dead?'

Aimery smiled. 'You'll stop him, Grefin.'

'*I* will?' He wanted to flee the cool wine cellar and forget he'd ever agreed to this madness. 'My lord, your confidence is flattering but likely misplaced. I doubt Balfre will—'

'Fuck your doubts!' Aimery bellowed, dashing the bottle of sunwine to the flagstoned floor. Smashing it to glass shards, splashing the grey granite red. 'And fuck you. Can I now trust that walking cane there more than my own son? Do you abandon me, Grefin? When I am at my weakest, feeling death's icy breath on the back of my neck, desperate to give this duchy the greatest gift it's ever known, do you turn your back? *Do you?*'

Grefin scrambled to his feet. 'No! And fuck *you* for even asking! Whatever storms the future holds, I know we're best served if Harcia and Clemen weather them as friends. And more than that, I know the thought of what Balfre might do once you're dead and he's duke freezes your heart. For fuck's sake, if I thought for a moment he'd not outgrown his childish dreams my heart would freeze too! But I don't think that, Father! For six years Balfre's served you, been your eyes and ears and strong right arm in this duchy. He's earned your trust, my lord. Please. You must *trust* him.'

Breathing heavily, Aimery got to his feet. There were tears in his eyes. On his cheeks. 'Don't you think I want to? Can't you see it *wounds* me, to speak of my heir like this? But better I be wounded than I slay Harcia – and Clemen – for love. You and I alone must forge an alliance with Roric, and soon. So that when I die, and Balfre is made duke, we'll have travelled Harcia too far down the path of friendship with Clemen for your brother to turn us back.'

Staring at his father, seeing the tremors running through him, the chalky pallor of his face, Grefin knew he was beaten. 'All right.'

'All right,' Aimery echoed, once he'd mastered himself. 'If you hear nothing out of Pikebank fair, it could be that Roric mistrusts your first letter, thinks it some kind of trap. So if you must, send to him again. Will you do that, Grefin?'

Heartsick, he nodded. 'Yes, my lord. I will.'

CHAPTER SIXTEEN

Standing with Mazelina in his old Tamwell castle bedchamber, watching their candlelit children sleep like peas-in-a-pod in his old bed, Grefin felt such a wave of love crash over him that for a moment, he couldn't breathe.

'They grow so fast,' he murmured, his arm tight about his wife's slender waist. 'It was only yesterday that I saw Kerric born. Last week, when Ullia cut her first tooth. And Jorin. How can Jorin be nigh on *seven*?'

Mazelina kissed his cheek. 'Are you feeling your age, my lord Steward?'

'Before we left the Isle, Terriel asked me if I'd given thought to where Jorin will be fostered.'

'I hope you slapped him for his insolence. Jorin's too young to be a page.'

'You know he's not. Malcolm was but a few months older.'

'Malcolm was Aimery's heir!' she said hotly. 'Grefin, I won't have it. What Jorin should know, you can teach him. We don't need to send him away.'

In the bed, their children stirred. Ullia, though she was a girl and younger than Jorin, threw a protective arm over her brother. Little Kerric cuddled close.

Grefin smiled. 'She's like you. A tigress.'

'And if you don't wish to feel my claws you'll abandon any thought of fostering Jorin with Terriel.'

'Mazelina . . .' Sighing, he stroked her unbound hair. 'I'm tired. Let's not fight. We can decide Jorin's future later.'

'All right,' she agreed. 'What did Aimery want?'

He released her. 'I said let's not fight.'

'*Balfre*.'

He knew much of her disdain rose out of pity for Jancis. And that she resented his brother bitterly for refusing to forgive him the Green Isle. It was useless asking her not to take sides. Her love was fierce, her loyalty unyielding. So long as Balfre hurt him she would never give his brother the benefit of any doubt.

'Come,' he said, taking her hand. 'I'd not say more in front of the children.'

Safely private in their own tapestried chamber, seated before the fire the castle needed, even in summer, they stared into the leaping flames and wondered who would speak first.

'I think it's time you told me what egg you and Aimery are hatching,' Mazelina said at last. She never could abide uncomfortable silence. 'And if you love me, Grefin, don't tell me there's no egg.'

'You *won't* like it.'

'I don't like being kept in the dark.'

'I know.' He sighed. 'I'm sorry.'

'Aimery doesn't mean to name you his heir instead of Balfre, does he?'

'No! Of course not! Why would you—'

'Because he doesn't trust your brother. And why would he? Balfre's sly.'

First his father, now his wife. Why did they keep forcing him to pick up a cudgel in Balfre's defence?

'That's unfair, Mazelina. He's angry, not sly. And who can blame him? I looked him in the eye and swore I'd serve on the Green Isle for a year. No more. But six years later I'm *still* its Steward and—'

'That's Aimery's doing. Balfre shouldn't blame you for it!'

'Except he does,' he muttered. 'And there we are.'

She slapped his arm. 'Oh, *Grefin*. Don't you see? His festering resentment is dangerous! What will happen when he's made duke?'

'Well, he's not going to slaughter us, if that's what you fear. He may be angry but he's still my brother.'

'So you say.'

He could feel his temper fraying. 'D'you want to know Aimery's purpose, or not?'

Her turn to sigh. 'Fine.'

She kept silent as he unburdened himself of his burdensome secret. And when he was done, laced his fingers with hers and kissed them.

'I've disobeyed him, telling you,' he said. 'You can't so much as hint that you know.'

She kissed him again. 'I won't.'

The relief of sharing the truth with her made him feel light-headed. 'And now that you know, what do you think?'

'I agree with Aimery,' she said at last, frowning into the fire. 'Clemen must be dealt with before he dies. But Grefin . . . I fear you and your father haven't properly thought this through.'

'We have!' he protested. 'How can you—'

'No, *listen*. All this time, and Roric has yet to sire a son. Or even a daughter. After Harald's trouble begetting an heir, how much longer will Clemen wait? Its lords have already deposed one duke for another.

It could happen again. They must be thinking by now they could've found a better man.'

'There was no better man. Berold's bloodline ends with Roric.'

She scoffed. 'D'you tell me there's not a lord in Clemen who fancies his own house a match for Berold's?'

Spirits save him. 'I wish I could.'

'And that means any treaty signed between Harcia and Clemen might well come to nothing, should Roric be pulled down for lacking an heir.' She rested her head against his shoulder. 'Of course, it's more likely Balfre will spoil things before ever that comes to pass.'

'Enough, Mazelina!' He shoved her off him. 'Must we spend the whole night talking about my brother?'

Tousled, she smiled, slowly. 'I hope not.'

Beyond the castle's stone walls, dusk had fallen. With Aimery fatigued and early in his bed, like the children, and Balfre not yet returned, there was no feasting or dancing. And he'd had more than his fill of intrigue and argument for one day. So what was a man with a beautiful wife to do?

'Wench,' he growled, and reached for her. 'Let's see that hope come true!'

Because there was no getting rid of the man – at least, not yet – Balfre greeted his father's steward with a friendly nod.

'Curteis. You're up early. First light's not yet broken. I hope all's well with His Grace?'

The steward bowed. 'Quite well, my lord. But he was concerned you hadn't returned yet, so posted runners along the road. I had good warning of your approach.' He bowed again, to Joben and the others, standing at a discreet distance in the castle's magnificently appointed entrance hall. 'My lords. Welcome again to Tamwell.'

'My brother and his family, Curteis,' he said. 'They're safely arrived?'

'Indeed, my lord. Two days ago.'

And there was a criticism, wrapped in a smile. Insolent bastard. 'Good. But I'd not disturb them, or my father, till I'm more present-able. We've ridden hard for many leagues, and we're tired and famished. Find my cousin and dear friends a chamber each, and be certain the kitchens send us food. Oh, and plentiful hot water for bathing. In case you hadn't noticed, we stink.'

'Guest chambers are already prepared, my lord,' said Curteis. 'But as I say, His Grace has been worried. I think you should—'

'No,' he said flatly. 'When you see my father, you may say I'll join him later today. My brother, too.'

The steward bowed again. 'As you wish, my lord.'

Idiot. Turning, Balfre smiled at his weary, travel-stained companions. 'Go with Curteis. He'll see you settled.'

'My lords,' said Curteis, one arm sweeping towards the impressive oak staircase that led, eventually, to the South Tower's fifth floor. 'If you'll follow me?'

Listening to the fading footsteps as Curteis led Joben and the others to their rest, Balfre looked around the hall, with its rich tapestries and old swords, the mounted stag antlers, the costly glazed pots from Agribia, and in the iron-shuttered windows panes of stained-glass, awaiting sunrise. By the spirits, he loved this castle. So much history. The home of Harcia's kings. The day couldn't come soon enough that it would be his.

Though he was a tough man, muscles and sinews hardened by years of training in the tilt yard, of more jousts and hunts than he could remember, still his legs protested as he climbed the stairs to his own apartments.

Safe behind his closed bedchamber door, he sat with a groan on the edge of his bearskin-covered bed and pulled from inside his leather doublet the only one of Culpyn's letters he'd not burned on the way home.

He'd read the fucking thing so many times now, the cheap, flimsy rush-paper was close to falling apart. He unfolded it yet again and looked at it, even though blindfolded he could recite every carefully crafted, treacherous word.

Cousin – for so I'd call you, though we have never met. It's my father's belief that our two great families, so long estranged, should seek to leave the past in the past and join hands in present friendship. I know, and he knows, that this is easier said than done. But I ask you to think on what such a friendship might mean to both of us. And I beseech you, cousin, on bended knee, that you do take this

265

proffering of friendship as honest coin, for so it is. There is no deceit here, and nothing but the truth. And to prove myself I do enclose this ring. I think you will know it.

Balfre touched his grimy fingertips to the single name, flourishingly added. *Grefin*. Not that he needed it. He knew his brother's quaint penmanship as well as his own. As for the ring, Grefin's cryptic hint suggested their father had sacrificed his favourite cabachon emerald. How touching.

He turned the fragile rush-paper over.

Cousin, Roric had replied. *I return this letter to you not in rejection, but so you'd know I did receive it, and the ring, and believe your offer to be no more or less than what it seems. Tell your father I take his words to heart. I have no answer for him yet, save to say I will consider well what you've said – and that I too believe there is much to be gained from friendship.*

A more cautious man, Roric had chosen not to sign his name. But of course the letter came from him. It could've come from no one else.

The urge to rip the rush-paper to tatters, piss it to sludge, was so strong he had to toss it aside and walk to the window. Not caring that he'd squander the heat granted him by the braziers left to burn in his room, he unbarred the shutters and pulled them wide.

Spread below him was the river, and the sleepy township of Cater's Tamwell. Far beyond them lay the Marches and beyond the Marches . . . Clemen. A duchy of thieves. A maggotry of bandits. Living fat and prosperous on the spoils stolen from Harcia.

And my father would be friends with them. My brother would, with his own hands, plunge Roric's dagger into our hearts.

Revolted, his belly roiled. Bending over, he vomited bile onto the oak-beamed floor. And then, as he waited for the sickness to pass, he blinked back tears of fury and weakness.

The Exarch claims there is one god in the world, one power. Perhaps he's right. By what chance did I discover Grefin's letter to Clemen? No chance, surely. That finding was meant. There are powers in the world that will aid the right man.

But even if it was mere chance, did it matter? The letter was his.

The advantage his. Aimery and Grefin had tried to hide their treachery from him, and they'd failed.

And before I'm finished they will rue their fucking betrayal.

On the letter's outer wrapping, which had been sealed with cheap green wax, someone had scrawled a name he'd not recognised. Some nobody, a Master Belchet, to be found at an alehouse in Glasson, three days' onward ride from Pikebank. He'd burned the wrapping with the other letters, but would remember the name – for all the good it would do him. Master Belchet, even if the name wasn't a cockstory, would likely not be found within twenty leagues of Glasson.

A knock on the chamber's door returned him to the bed. There he slipped the letter beneath the bearskin, commanded the servant to enter and bade the man to leave his tray of food on the sideboard.

Alone again he ate, ravenous, like a starved wolf. Then he closed and barred the shutters, stripped off his stained and stinking clothes and crawled into bed . . . to dream of vengeance, and spite.

The sun was pulling down shadows as Molly slid the last of the night's first-batch pies into the oven. With a pleased nod she thudded its heavy iron door shut, then pressed her hands into the small of her back. The aching eased, she set about lighting more kitchen lamps to fight the dark. Through the unshuttered window she could see Iddo, puffing as he rolled a fresh barrel of ale out of the cellar. On the grass nearby, too close for her comfort, Benedikt and Willem squealed and chased each other like puppies.

'Iddo!' she shouted. 'Mind them boys! Drat it, where be Alys?'

'Penning the hens!' Iddo shouted back. 'Breathe easy, Moll. I b'aint fool enough to roll a barrel over yer precious tadpoles.'

She snorted. *Breathe easy*, he said. What a man. He'd never say it if he were the one to push Benedikt out of his pain-wracked body. Ah, Benedikt. A prince of mischief, her son, and that Alys's hot-footed brother no better. For all the girl's chestnut-haired Willem was the younger boy, it seemed to make no difference. Not a day went by that he and Benedikt didn't dare each other into trouble. Climbing trees on the crossroad at the Pig Whistle's front door. Plucking long feathers from the cockerel's tail. Teasing the guard dog on its iron chain, the brute Iddo bullied her to get on account of the latest troubles between the Marcher lords.

Turn her back, it seemed, and before she could hiccup one of those boys was leaping both of them into strife.

Seeing Alys trudging up from the hen coop, she braced her hand on the window frame and leaned out. 'Look lively, girl! I want them scamps damp-clothed clean and fed before we fill to the rafters, d'ye hear? Or ye'll be the one sent to yer bed with no supper!'

'Yes, Molly!' the girl replied, and stirred herself to a stumbling run.

Benedikt and Willem rushed towards her, clamouring for play. Molly watched, approving, as the girl swept them along with her, saying no, but keeping them sweet. Not a bad lass, that Alys. A good worker, and doting on both boys. Not a strumpet like that Tossie. Came to a bad end, her, and no surprise there. The man she'd danced off with wrung her neck soon after, and didn't that serve the little lightskirt right.

Alys bustled the boys into the warm, pie-scented kitchen, and set about smearing them cleanish with a soapy rag. Hiding a smile at their moaning, as though shifting dirt was kin to killing them, Molly ladled steaming mutton stew into earthenware bowls, buttered bread, fetched two apples and two spoons, and set the food on the old wooden table.

'Eat up, ye forest imps. And then it's to bed.'

Beneath its tousled crown of black hair, Benedikt's small, handsome face collapsed in dismay. 'Bed, Ma?' he wailed. 'But—'

He looked so much like his father, it was a pain to deny him a thing. But spoiled boys grew into spoiled men, and then she'd be ashamed. Or heartbroke, if he strifed himself into the kind of mischief that ended with a noose.

'One more word, I'll break a wooden spoon agin yer arse,' she said, rapping her knuckles on the top of his head. 'There be men riding to the Whistle this night as don't care for rompish boys.'

Benedikt scrunched his shoulders round his ears, knowing she meant it. But Willem stared at her with dark-flecked amber eyes that sometimes surprised her, they were so grown-up.

'What men be they, Molly? And why dursn't they care for boys?'

'They be Marcher men, about their lords' great business. And I won't have ye or my Benedikt spitted on a sword for pestering underfoot. Now eat or go up hungry. It be all the same to me.'

Her son and Alys's brother exchanged conspiratorial looks, then plunged their spoons into the fragrant, carrot-plumped stew. They could chatter like magpies, these two, and then say as much to each other without sharing a word. Uncanny, it was. When she wasn't laughing, it made her wonder. She'd wanted a brother for Benedikt, and was glad chance had given him one. But she never thought a stranger's child could be as like to her own as flesh and blood . . . which Willem was, though in looks the boys were chalk and cheese.

The kitchen's leather curtain slapped heavily as Iddo stamped in from the public room. 'That ale barrel's unbunged so ye can get to counting the ale pots, Alys,' he said, with a jerk of his chin. 'And see the benches wiped. There be thirsty folk coming along the road a ways.'

Wary, for in all these years Iddo still hadn't softened to her, the girl bobbed a curtsy. 'Yes, Iddo.'

'Moll . . .' Taking hold of her elbow, he tugged her back to the window, out of the boys' earshot. 'What's this about Marcher lords' men coming? And why do them boys get told of it before me?'

She didn't snap his nose off, for he'd had a long hard day. Instead she pulled the window's shutters closed and dropped their iron bar in place. 'I was going to tell ye,' she said, soothing. 'In a quiet moment. While ye were walking yer rabbit snares in the wood, Izusa stopped back in, on her way to runcing Nonny's new babe. There be fresh trouble brewing between Wido and Bayard.'

Iddo scowled. 'How bad?'

'Bad enough, Izusa says. The lords' men came to blows over some mischief with a woman. Blood be spilled and threats made. There be not so much as a copper nib's worth of good will to be found in the matter. She says there be talk of a Crown Court to settle it. And in the meantime, we're like to see scores of Marcher men riding at all hours to keep the peace.'

'Or break it to kindling.' Iddo dragged a hand down his stubbled face, rasping. 'A Crown Court, Molly? With all that muck and upset?

Curse the feggit bastards. Why don't them lords teach their men to keep cock in britches?'

She patted his arm. 'I know.'

'And us barely sorted after them ructions over Bayard's loose horses.'

Which Bayard had blamed on Wido's men. And before that, the clash between Egbert and Jacott over rights of way through the stretch of Stoke Woods as was called common ground. Every time they blinked, it seemed, the Marcher lords were finding reasons to brandish their swords. No wonder Marcher folk had started pinning charms to their undershirts and rousing the old blood ways from sleep.

Iddo huffed out a breath. 'So these Marcher men as are coming. Which lord do they belong to?'

'Wido, Izusa says.' She pulled a face. 'Best we cross fingers Lord Bayard b'aint of the same mind, for with tempers sore and blood running steamy . . .'

'*Bastards*,' said Iddo, thumping a fist to the wall. 'I'll see m'cudgel be good to hand.'

'And bring the dog in,' she suggested. 'Could be they'll mind their manners with that brute chained to the bar.'

'I will. But Moll—' Iddo touched his finger to her forehead. 'What other sour news did that young herb-witch bring ye? For she did, I can see it. There be shadows in yer eyes.'

She slid her gaze past him to Benedikt and Willem, who were busy spitting apple seeds at each other. As a rule she'd cuff the pair of them for roistering at table, but this once she was grateful they were distracted. Even so . . .

'Later,' she muttered. 'In bed. I'll not speak of it now.' Then she poked him. 'And don't ye be calling Izusa a herb-witch. She b'aint no Phemie, but for all she's foreign and peculiar she knows her leechcraft. And we do be right fortunate to have her, all in all.'

Eyes wide, Iddo fastened his fingers on her wrist. 'It b'aint spotted tongue again, Moll?'

The last outbreak had reached their stretch of the Marches two months after the night Alys and her brother fetched up on the Whistle's doorstep. Close to four months, it scourged them, more virulent than the oldest Marcher man or woman could remember. The filthy pestilence took eleven of their regular customers, including both Bevver brothers and forester Lugo and Hamelen, Lord Jacott's farm steward. Worst of all, it took Phemie. Sad, sad days. Iddo, her man of iron, had been plague-skittish ever since.

'No,' she said, softening. 'Something else, Izusa says, and far away yet. She only told me what to look for 'cause we get traders from all parts passing through. And there be an end to it, Iddo. Now see to that dog and—'

They both turned at the sound of the leather curtain, slapping. 'Molly,' said Alys, flustered. 'Lord Wido's Marcher men are come. There be a dozen of them claiming a bed each, hungry and thirsty and banging fist to bench.'

A bed each? She'd be putting folk to sleep in the hen coop. But the lords' men had to be kept happy. So while Iddo and Alys plied them with food and ale, she hustled Benedikt and Willem upstairs, promising both boys a cracky whipping if they dared set foot downstairs again. And then it was rush, rush, rush, for alongside Lord Wido's rowdy men there were her half-score of regulars, a clutch of wool traders from Clemen, three quarrelsome Zeidican merchants – no sign of plague on them, thank the spirits – two Harcian messengers and six travelling exarchites. The Pig Whistle's public room fell silent when they walked in, long grey wool robes swishing round their ankles. Even Wido's men stared, ale pots and pie spoons stuck halfway to their mouths. But the exarchites were fasting and only wanted somewhere to lay their heads. So she settled them in the dormer, because not even the Marcher lords dared offend the Exarch, no matter how far away he was. Then she rushed back to her kitchen to rescue mutton pies from burning and slop fresh stew on the hob to heat.

She was so fretted she almost didn't hear the banging on her kitchen's back door. Cursing, she wiped her hands on her apron.

'*What?*' she demanded, wrenching the door open. 'D'ye think I b'aint so busy I can—'

'Mollykins. M'sweet Molly,' said the battered man swaying before her. 'Be a honey posset, would ye, and let me come in?'

It was the trader, Denno Culpyn, beaten black and blue.

He moaned as she shouldered him to Benedikt's seat at the table.

Coughed in pain as she pushed him down, and snatched hold of her apron as she turned away.

'Moll – Moll – don't leave me!'

'I got t'leave, ye half-plucked goose! B'aint that a full roaring public room ye can hear, demanding of its pies and stew? Just sit there and rest yer aches and dribbles till I can find a moment to slap a poultice or three where they might do ye some good.'

He stared at her woefully. 'I be in a right muck, Moll.'

'Never ye mind,' she said, patting his shoulder. 'I'll see ye set to rights in a trickle.'

But it was a good while longer than that before she could heave a deep breath and haul out her physicking box to tend him. With Iddo and Alys warned to stay on the other side of the leather curtain, she put fresh water to boil, fetched some soft cotton rags, and lined up her bottles and jars.

Denno didn't want to strip to his linen drawers so she could inspect every inch of marked skin, but weren't most men no more than overgrown boys? And didn't she know how to handle their fussing? Shivering, though the kitchen was warm enough, the trader suffered her poking and prodding, the stinging poultices and burning ointments that, thanks to poor Phemie's teaching of her, would put him on the slow road to healing.

'Ye be a fortunate feggit, Denno Culpyn,' she said at last, holding up his shirt to him so he could re-dress. 'Though a blind man on a dark night could see all them bruises, ye've suffered no brokit bones, no split flesh what b'aint on yer face, and even if ye do be pissing blood there don't be a bit of ye so squashed inside it won't mend.'

'How can y'be certain?' he said, doubtful. 'Y'be a fine woman, Moll, but no fulsome leech. Where be Izusa? I tell ye, I weren't in no way sure of that odd wench, but she sorted the boil on my arse a treat the other day, iss, and made the difference when that bloody flux came on.'

'Denno Culpyn, may ye hang for an ungrateful wretch,' she snapped. 'I ought to black yer other eye!'

He sniffed. 'But m'nose, Moll. It feels brokit.'

'It be flattened a bit,' she admitted. 'But since ye can snuffle wind, I say ye'll mend that too. Now—' She tugged his shirt over his head, helped him slide his green-and-purple mottled arms into the sleeves, then started lacing it up. 'For payment, ye'll tell me who put ye in this muck state. Don't tell me ye've fallen foul of a Marcher lord?'

'No, Moll,' he said, and shuddered. 'It were Count Balfre did this.'

'*Balfre?*' she said, staring. 'Aimery's eldest? Harcia's heir? Denno Culpyn, *what* did ye—'

'Don't ye scold me deaf, Moll,' he entreated. 'I did nothing, I swear it. He took agin me, is all, for coming in on m'lonesome, late to Pikebank. One look and ye'd think I rode a mule over his mother. He ruined m'travelling papers. Banished me. Can't never cross into Harcia agin, or trade the Harcian Marches. His men trampled m'pretty wares and beat me, all on his say-so.'

Stunned, feeling sick, she bent to pick up his leather trews. 'And the letters?'

'I be sorry, Moll,' he said, sounding more humble than ever she'd heard him. 'He took them.'

Her heart clutched tight. 'Every one?'

'Iss,' he whispered. 'I tried to hide 'em, but yon Balfre . . .' Another shudder. 'Mollykins, I be a man as have stood toe-to-toe with the curs't pirate Baldassare. And hand on m'heart, I'd face that barnacle agin, gladly, before ever I looked a second time in Count Balfre's eyes. That feggit man's got ice where his heart ought to be.'

Because Denno was helpless, she helped him pull on the leather trews. Kept herself fussing, so he'd not notice her face. All the letters taken . . . even the one she was paid two silver ducats to see safely to Pikebank horse fair. That she'd slipped to Denno along with some harmless tittle-tattle, and the trader no wiser. So, a calamity. She'd already spent the ducats and there was no getting them back. Should she confess all to Tybost, the farm steward who took dead Hamelen's place? No. How could she? Tybost might tell Clemen's Lord Jacott she'd played him false . . . and that would put the Pig Whistle at risk. Put *Benedikt* at risk.

Just the thought of that made her dizzy.

So she'd say not a word. Let Jacott think what he liked, he'd never think to accuse her. And besides, what happened wasn't her fault. She'd done what she was paid for. After that? Faery business.

'Moll?' said Denno, plucking at her sleeve. 'Can I have a bed? I'll ride on come the morning. Won't stay underfoot.'

He was a rogue and a rascal, but she did like him. And he was useful. 'Dormer be full to the rafters, Denno. Ye can sleep in the stables, and I'll not ask for a copper nib.'

'Ah, Moll.' His smile was sad. 'Y'be in m'heart like a queen. What a sorrow that when I ride out, I won't never ride back.'

'Never? But—'

'Risk trading the Clemen Marches, and Harcia's men-at-arms riding me down?' Wincing, he shook his head. 'Can't do that, Mollykins. B'aint I a canny man, as knows when he be knocked to his knees?'

She believed him. He was broken. Which meant one less useful man in her life, curse it. But she'd make good despite his leaving. In the end, she always did.

'I be sorry to hear it, Denno,' she said. 'Maybe one day ye'll change yer mind. Now be off to the stables with ye. I got customers as want m'pies.'

The outer bailey of Tamwell castle flew so many bright pennants it was a wonder the walls and battlements didn't fly away altogether. The colourful emblems of every noble Harcian house flapped and snapped in the brisk breeze; badger and ram and boar and kestrel, hound and horse, cup and sword. A vivid, martial display. A reminder of Harcia's long heritage, stretching back in time to the dimmest past . . . when the emblems of Clemen's nobles proudly flew with them side by side, in friendship. The dim past. The dead past. A past that might yet come back to life.

Seated on a great dais, honoured by the day's flowery joust, Aimery stifled a frown. *I only hope I live to see it.* For here he was, a duke turned sixty. *Sixty.* Most of his life behind him and nothing but uncertainty ahead. He could count on one hand's fingers, the dukes of Harcia who'd seen sixty. Thumbs would tally the dukes who'd lived longer than that. He could pray to the Exarch's god, or to a passing sprite or faery, that he might become a big toe. A duke famed for dying bald and old. But he doubted prayer would save him. Ruling a duchy aged a man. And a duke with a troublesome heir aged faster again.

There was a man who had three sons. Lost one. Kept one. Threw the third away. The fool.

Six years on, and even though he tried hard to dismiss them, the old soothsayer's cryptic words still had the power to chill. But so did he have power. He was nobody's fool. With Grefin beside him, he would defy even a long-tailed comet. Balfre would not have his way.

A raucous bellowing of applause and acclaim rose from the attending noblemen and their families as the jousting knights came to the end of their third pass, untouched. Their fabulously decorated armour, made for show, not proper killing, flashed silver and gold and painted colours in the afternoon sun. Their stallions sidled, heads tossing, as though disappointed to be held back in the joust. For on pain of dire consequence, they had been. This was his birthday celebration, for everyone else a happy occasion.

Aimery of Harcia would have no Black Hughes today.

Their horses standing flank-to-flank, facing the dais, each mounted knight uplifted his visor. Revealed, his unsmiling nephew Joben and young Lord Brandt, lately stepped into his inherited estates at Gosfyth. Given a choice, proud Joben would never tilt against such a minor lord. But saving one, the day's jousts were drawn at random. And it would do Joben good to climb down off his pride – if only for an hour.

Aimery stood, masking unsteadiness, and accepted his knights' fist-on-heart homage with a raised hand. More cheering and applause from the nobles ranked on their bench seats below and to either side of him. It followed the knights out of the bailey.

As he resumed his gilded ducal throne, and Master Ambrose's squires rushed in to set the tilt-run aright before the highly anticipated final joust, Mazelina touched her hand to his arm, laughing. Down in the bailey, Tamwell's minstrels re-started their cheerful piping to entertain the crowd.

'And now it's Grefin's turn! Oh, Your Grace, I can't envy you. Your heir and your Steward to joust each other. Perhaps they could

275

both fall off, and satisfy honour without causing you to take sides!' She leaned forward, looking across him. 'What d'you think, Jancis?'

Aimery shifted his gaze. Balfre's colourless wife sat at his right hand, and though she was coloured head-to-toe in crimson damask, and gold, and rubies, still she looked as pale as a moon maiden from pagan lore. Her face, so unexpressive, seemed a chalk mask.

Stirred to pity, as every day she stirred him, though he couldn't much like her, he forced a cheerful smile. 'Indeed, Mazelina. You might have hit upon the answer. But I dare say our dear Jancis would prefer to see her husband the victor. Jancis?'

She might choose not to answer Grefin's wife, but to ignore Harcia's duke was unthinkable. 'Your Grace, I confess to having no opinion,' Jancis murmured. 'I've no fondness for the joust. It's very loud, and I worry the horses will be hurt.'

By the Exarch's balls, even her voice was colourless. No surprise she was only delivered of one daughter. She was a mimbly woman, the wrong choice for Balfre entirely. That was his mistake. But for good or ill the two of them were bound and only death could part them. Were Jancis to be released, and marry again, and bear a son, the damage done to Balfre would be impossible to mend.

But if he remains without a son, at least Harcia won't be ruined. It has Grefin and his sons. The future is secure.

And that was the only reason he could sleep at night. Especially these days, with his health so much a trial.

Bright and beautiful Mazelina, his beloved Grefin's beloved, was trying to dance over Jancis's blunder.

'—is a worry a horse will be hurt, yes, but I think they love jousting as much as the men do, Jancis, truly. You know they're dreadfully stubborn creatures. Almost as bad as a husband. I doubt you could make a one of them run the tilt if it didn't want to. Isn't that so, Your Grace?'

He patted her knee. Her gown was cloth-of-silver, embroidered blue, but she dimmed even that radiance. 'My dear Mazelina,' he said, his smile entirely unforced, 'I cannot fault you.'

'Here they come,' said Jancis, as the crowd of nobles stirred to excitement. 'I pray no one is hurt.'

And so did he pray it, to whoever was listening. If he could have, he'd have kept his sons from this joust. Though Balfre had been volubly contrite for his lateness in returning to Cater's Tamwell, had begged his father's forgiveness so meekly, and in public – but mercifully not dressed in homespun and cast face-down on the floor – still a maggot of doubt was in him. From the time Balfre had burst into the world, furiously squalling, he'd never once forgiven a slight. And though he tried to hide it, there remained rancour over the Green Isle's Stewardship.

But he'll not hurt Grefin for that. Not here. Not like this. He might be a hot-head. The wrong stamp of man to make a duke. But worse? I'll not accept it. For all his faults, he is my son.

He watched Balfre and Grefin ride their glorious stallions into the bailey on a storm of acclaim. Balfre's gilded armour was part-painted crimson, Grefin's steel polished eye-searing silver and flourished in sky blue. They each wore their ladies' colours in scarves tied to their breast-plates. The silk fluttered gaily, danced by the same breeze dancing the house pennants over their heads. Visors raised, they halted before the dais. Balfre said something. Grefin looked at him, and laughed. Balfre said something else, his grin so wicked it must have been ribald. Both laughing, they lifted their gazes, crashed gauntleted fists to their hearts. Aimery stood, his own heart pounding, and raised his hand in salute. The lance-squires ran forward, armed the combatants, then withdrew.

'Hold my hand, Your Grace,' Mazelina murmured, as he sat. 'I'm so nervous I might faint.'

He did as she asked. Her palm was damp. So was his. He'd have held Jancis too, but her hands were kept from him, clasped tight in her lap.

The pipers ceased their trilling. Three horns blew a loud fanfare. The noble crowd fell slowly silent, until the only sounds were the snapping of pennants and the stately thud-thud-thud of the destriers' hooves on the close-cut bailey grass as Balfre and Grefin, their visors lowered, rode to opposite ends of the tilt-run.

A single trumpet note, high and sweet. The horses fought against bridle and bit, eager to joust. Their riders steadied lances . . . dropped reins . . . pricked sharp spurs to glossy flanks. Aimery held his breath, and sank his teeth into his lip. With great, grunting whinnies, ears pinned back and eyes gleaming, his sons' stallions charged.

And with one punishing blow of Grefin's lance, Balfre crashed to the ground.

CHAPTER SEVENTEEN

There was a feast in the castle's Great Hall after the joust, with enormous platters of venison and boar from the Marches, swan and goose, pike and sturgeon and delectable eel. There were dainty minced chicken pies and cartwheels of cheese, honeyed damsons and apricots, endless flagons of wine, and cherry juice for those who disdained the effects of fermented grape. There was music and dancing and no grey-faced, grey-robed exarchites to frown the birthday revellers into sober behaviour.

Aimery and his sons and their wives enjoyed the highest of high tables, proudly displayed for Harcia's nobles to see. Nearest to them, duly honoured, Harcia's councillors, their wives and their heirs. Almost as honoured, Balfre's closest companions. Even Joben, as yet unmarried, had forsworn his fellow councillors to carouse with Paithan, Waymon and Lowis, the young men loudly basking in the ducal heir's esteem. Seated at the hall's other damask-covered trestles, distantly overlooked by the antlered skulls of stags long since killed and consumed, many lesser nobles of Harcia, with sons and daughters attending. It was good to see them here. Marriages might come of the day's celebrations. Another reason to celebrate. And long as fine Harcian sons wed with lissom Harcian daughters, and were fruitful, his duchy would live on long after his death.

Lastly, of course, there were his beloved grandchildren, seated at their own small trestle, ruled over by their nurses. Grefin's three mischief-makers, and poor, wan little Emeline. Balfre's sickly daughter. Old enough now to know how deeply she disappointed. And how could she not, when she was the image of her mimbly mother?

At the far end of their table, flushed with wine and astonishment, Grefin flung an unsteady arm around his brother's neck. 'To the moment I draw my last breath, Balfre, I'll remember this day. Never before have I jousted *you* out of the saddle!'

Balfre, just as wineish, clumsily kissed Grefin on the side of his head. 'But you did, brother, and I have the bruises on my arse to prove it. And let me tell you how it happened, since you seem so amazed.'

'Yes, yes, do tell us,' Mazelina implored. 'For I promise you, Balfre, we're as amazed as my husband!'

Everyone within hearing laughed at that. Aimery knew he could easily weep, so great was his relief. Neither son harmed in their bout, and both so joyful, so comradely. After years of strain and sourness, he'd never thought to see them in such smiling accord. And that was Balfre's doing as much as Grefin's. He'd taken his defeat lightly, been swift to laud his victorious brother. No churlish frowning, only admiring delight.

So . . . had he misjudged his heir, then? Perhaps Grefin was right. Perhaps he'd never been fair to Balfre, who wasn't Malcolm and never could be. Perhaps the time had come to take a leap of faith. Trust that Balfre wouldn't dishonour him by plunging the duchy into a maelstrom of strife.

'My Lord Steward,' said Balfre, comically serious, as the laughter died down around them. 'It's clear to me that while serving our gracious duke in the Green Isle, you have become a doughty knight. Mighty of virtue, strong in sinew, inviolate of purpose. Indeed, the very paragon of jousters!'

Grefin clapped hand to heart. 'Why, thank you, my lord Count. Such praise leaves me speechless.'

'Not so very speechless, since that's your tongue I hear flapping.'

More raucous laughter, drowning the court minstrels. Mazelina

279

was wiping her eyes. Even subdued Jancis smiled, her be-ringed fingers clasped round the stem of a goblet full of cherry juice.

Eyes wide with mock-hurt, Grefin offered a seated bow. 'Forgive me. It's just I—'

'Be quiet, fool!' roared Balfre. 'Can't you see I'm still talking?'

'Do hush, Grefin,' said Mazelina, unsteady with mirth. 'Or he's like to tip that jug of wine right over your head!'

Thrusting aside discomforting thoughts, at least for the moment, Aimery banged a fist to the trestle. 'At fifty silver ducats a barrel? Not if he wants to sit his horse inside a week! I might be officially declared an old man, but there's yet strength enough in my arm to give a wayward son a good thrashing!'

'Fear not, Your Grace,' said Balfre, shaking his head. 'I've long since grown out of the wasteful gesture. But if I might be allowed to finish?'

'By all means,' said Grefin, hiccuping. 'Never let us distract you from your purpose.'

Balfre smiled. 'I won't, Grefin. On that you have my word. Now – as I was saying – you've impressed me, little brother. I am mightily impressed.'

'Go on, go on,' Grefin encouraged. 'I've waited years to hear you say this.'

'And if you don't cease interrupting, I swear you'll never hear it again!'

More laughter, as Mazelina pressed a hand over her husband's mouth.

'Speak swiftly, Balfre, I beg you. I fear your defeat has gone straight to his head!'

'Swiftly then,' said Balfre, grinning. 'As my lady commands. Swiftly, Grefin, while I admire you, as an honest man I must add this to my praise. That while your jousting skills are proved impressive, most impressive is the fact that at the ripe old age of twenty-eight you've at last learned how not to fall off your fucking horse!' Standing, he raised his wine-filled goblet. 'Your Grace! My lords and ladies! I give you the Steward of the Green Isle, jouster without peer, Aimery's beloved youngest son and my little brother. *Grefin!*'

'*Grefin!*' Harcia's nobles echoed, and drank, and drummed their feet on the rush-strewn stone floor.

As servants carried in fresh platters of meat and refilled wine jugs from the kitchens, and the gathered nobles turned to each other for more eager talk, Balfre put down his goblet and dropped to a crouch between Grefin and Mazelina. Grin fading, he pressed his palm to his brother's cheek.

'Grefin,' he said, his voice lowered to keep his words at their table. 'I think you know I've been angry with you. For a long time, monstrous angry. I've blamed you and resented you for things that weren't your fault. I'm sorry. Will you forgive me?'

Grefin grasped his brother's shoulder. 'Of course I will. As if you need to ask.'

'I think our father would disagree with that,' said Balfre, and turned. 'Am I right, Your Grace?'

Feeling his eyes sting with tears, Aimery nodded. 'You are. But there's no shame in a man admitting a fault. Indeed, there's honour in it. Your mother would be proud. As I am.'

'Then I have your forgiveness too?'

'Yes, Balfre,' he said, his voice breaking. 'You most assuredly do.'

'Your Grace. Your Grace, I'm sorry . . .'

Curteis.

Looking at his faithful steward Aimery saw the trouble that creased the man's forehead. 'What is it?'

Curteis bent low. 'Your Grace, word's come from Lord Bayard. There has been – an incident – in the Marches.'

The Marches. His precarious hope. Flooded with dismay, Aimery fought the urge to look at Grefin. 'How bad?'

'Alas, Your Grace. There are deaths on both sides.'

Fuck. His heart was hammering too hard, his treacherous body rebelling at unwanted news. 'Who's to blame? Do we know?'

'The waters seem fearful muddied. Our Marcher lords are blaming Clemen, while their lords blame us.'

'Curteis, you surprise me.'

'Indeed,' Curteis murmured. 'Your Grace, can I assume you'll meet with the council on this?'

Curse the council. Men who'd leap at once to belligerence, in whom he could not confide. 'After the feast, Curteis. Make arrangements.'

'Father?' Grefin said softly, as Curteis discreetly withdrew from the hall.

With an almost painful effort, Aimery relaxed his fisted fingers and rested them in his lap. 'Not now. The acrobats are come.'

'But—'

'*Not now, Grefin.*'

An awkward silence. Then Balfre gestured at an untouched wine jug set down by a passing servant.

'Is that Grayneish red at your elbow, Gref? If it is I'll take some, before you and the fair Mazelina drink it all.'

'Balfre!' protested Mazelina, as chastened Grefin struggled to reply. 'How could you say so, when 'tis well known by all who know you that a full barrel of Grayneish red is not safe in your sight!'

And so to more laughter, and playful bickering, as the hall filled with leaping acrobats and the spritely music of tambourines.

'This is a nonsense, Aimery,' grunted Reimond of Parsle Fountain, his craggy face carved even sharper by candlelight. 'What happens in the Marches is Marcher lord business. Let Bayard and Egbert settle it.'

Muttered agreement from his fellow lords, gathered in the North Tower's council chamber.

Frowning, Aimery tapped the scrawled parchment brought in haste by one of Bayard's men-at-arms. 'We've seven dead, all told, a score more wounded, and Wido of Clemen making grave threats. I fear this is already spilled beyond the Marches.'

'It's unacceptable!' Ferran said, banging his fist to the chamber's robust oak table. 'Who is this Wido, to demand Harcia take all blame? To bluster he'll have that bastard Roric force us to a Crown Court if we don't show our belly? And what's Bayard about, letting himself be bullied by this shite?'

'It sounds to me Bayard's grown too feeble for the Marches,' said Joben. 'Clearly he can't even control his men. Perhaps it's time another lord was sent to govern in his place.'

Aimery spared his nephew a frowning glance. Here was ambition, scenting the air. 'I won't deny Bayard has questions to answer. Yes, and Egbert too. But I'll be the one asking them, Joben. And I'll decide what's to be done if the answers aren't to my liking.'

'I say we call Wido's bluff,' said Reimond. 'Let him run to Roric bleating for a Crown Court. Let Roric demand one.' He smiled, grimly. 'Let him demand the sun rise in the north, too, and rain fall when he farts. Since when does Harcia do as Clemen demands?'

Grefin cleared his throat. 'My lords, I understand your reluctance to seem weak in the face of Wido's threats. But let's not forget that at the heart of this strife there lies a woman, dead.'

'A Clemen bawd,' Deness of Heems said curtly, seated across from him. 'A strumpet, who lifted her skirts without care and got no more than she deserved.'

'And because the bawd was careless, Harcian men-at-arms have died!' Ferran added, glowering. 'Weep for them, Grefin. Not for a wanton jade.'

'I do weep for them, Ferran,' Grefin retorted. 'But you can't dismiss this death so lightly. Murder must be answered.'

Joben scoffed. 'You don't know it's murder! Wido calls it murder, but Bayard—'

'Bayard's report is garbled, to say the least,' Grefin retorted. 'We don't even know yet who killed this woman, or why. What if she was innocent of any provocation? What if one of our Marcher men is guilty of the crime? Do we shield him because he's Harcian? Do we wink at unlawful killing because the slain woman was from Clemen and kept no clean sheets?' He swept his hot gaze around the table. 'My lords, if you're seeking trouble with Roric, *I* say that's a good way of finding it!'

More than muttering this time, as the council pounced on provocation. Letting their shouts wash over him, Aimery slid his half-lidded gaze sideways to Balfre, at his right hand, who was yet to speak. There was no telling from his bland expression what he thought. But surely he agreed with Reimond and the others, who thought any concession to Clemen an even greater crime than murder.

Grefin and the rest of the council were still arguing. If it weren't so late he'd let the bickering run its course, for the pleasure of watching his son argue cantankerous Ferran into silence. But he was sixty years old, and weary, and these days ill-health rode him meanly wherever he walked.

'*Enough!*' he said, and slapped his palm to the table with a crack like a hunting whip. 'The answer's simple. If Wido asks his duke to call a Crown Court and Roric refuses, there the matter will end. Bayard and his men will answer for the spilled blood to us, privily. But if Roric says yea, then there *will* be a Crown Court, for I promise you, my lords: to refuse him will cause more bloody strife between our duchies.'

Lord Keeton, a mild man whose talents lay more in the realm of coin-counting than swordplay, smoothed back his lank hair. 'And if it does come to a Crown Court, Your Grace, will you speak for Harcia?'

'What?' said Joben, appalled. 'Duke Aimery defend a bawd?'

'He'd not be defending a bawd,' said Grefin. 'He'd be standing for Bayard's accused men.'

Deness of Heems was ferociously scowling. 'And if it's proven they killed her, it amounts to the same thing. Would you see your father tarnished by this, Grefin?'

As every stare turned to him, Grefin sighed. 'Of course not. *If* there's a Crown Court, with His Grace's leave I'll speak for Harcia.'

Reimond of Parsle Fountain shoved his chair back, just a little. Caring nothing for the fate of a dead bawd, and impatient to be on his way. 'So, then. It's settled?'

Every stare shifted. Feeling the weight of them, Aimery looked at his folded hands. An old man's hands. Three knuckles were swollen, and pained him in the cold. Once-smooth skin was turned wrinkled, blotched brown, wormed with veins. It made him angry, to see them.

'No,' he said, and looked at Grefin. 'I'll not keep you kicking your heels in Cater's Tamwell while we wait to see how this plays out. There's a chance the Marcher lords might yet settle this themselves. And if they don't, it could be days, or even weeks, before Roric decides for or against a court. You're Steward of the Green Isle. Your duties lie there.'

Shocked, his son struggled to remain respectful. 'But, Your Grace—'

'*Grefin.*'

Grefin swallowed. 'I'm sorry.'

And so he should be, letting his passion for justice trample good sense. Given the delicacy of their barely fledged negotiations with Clemen, it would be madness for Grefin to thrust himself into the harsh glare of this tawdry affair. He could be seen nowhere near important men of Clemen, could take no part in legal proceedings from which Clemen might emerge bruised . . . or where Harcia might be proven the troublemaker. However would Roric trust him, did he mire himself in murder?

Deness of Heems heaved a sigh that was mostly a groan. 'Even so, Aimery, if worse comes to worst someone must speak for Harcia and we're all agreed it can't be you. Send Reimond. Or me. But—'

'I'll do it,' Balfre said quietly. 'I might lack Grefin's broad experience as Steward, but in the last few years I've settled my share of disputes around the duchy.'

'That's true,' said Ferran. 'And settled them well, what's more.'

'Your Grace.' Balfre turned. 'Crown Court or no, peace must be restored in the Marches. If you send me to oil the waters, Wido can't claim we're treating Clemen with contempt. And whatever the truth of this woman's death, Ferran's right. Bayard and Egbert have failed you. Who's better placed to punish? Deness, or Reimond . . . or Harcia's next duke?' His breath caught. 'Meaning nothing by that, Your Grace.'

May the spirits give him strength. Both of his sons grown men, yet so afraid of what must come. 'I take your meaning, Balfre, and take no harm from it. Indeed, you speak good sense.'

He let his gaze drop again, signalling his need for thought. Send Balfre to the Marches? The suggestion had merit.

If he shows himself wise in his dealings with Clemen's Marcher lords then perhaps I can bring myself to believe Grefin's right, and my fears for the future are unfounded.

Something he would never have considered possible, before Balfre's heartfelt reconciliation with his brother scant hours before.

Looking up, he nodded. 'Very well, Balfre. I'll leave this sorry business in your hands. And Curteis will go to the Marches with you, for you may trust his advice as you'd trust mine.'

'Of course, Your Grace,' said Balfre, properly sober. 'And thank you. I'll do my best not to disappoint.'

'Balfre! Balfre, wait!'

Smothering impatience, Balfre slowed until Grefin caught up with him on the North Tower's torchlit staircase, leading down to the castle's entrance hall.

'Such a surfeit of vigour,' he complained, and clapped a hand to his brother's shoulder. 'No wonder you and Mazelina have so many children.'

Startled, Grefin blinked. 'What?'

'Nothing,' he said, shaking his head. ''Twas a jest. And a poor one at that.'

'On you, yes,' said Grefin, discomfited. 'It must be hard, after so long, to only—' He cleared his throat. 'You and Jancis, have you tried – I mean to say, is there no hope you might yet—'

'What is it the exarchites preach? "In the divine there is always hope." So there you have it. Jancis prays. And I pray someone or something is listening.'

'I'm sorry.' Then Grefin smiled, a little tentative. 'So. How's your arse?'

'Still bruised,' he said, starting down the stairs again. Although deliberately losing the joust was worth a hundred bruises, to see his brother and father so eager to believe the lie. 'Like my pride. But don't apologise.'

'I wasn't going to,' Grefin said, his smile widening to a grin. 'The memory of you on the ground today will keep me warm on cold winter nights.'

Because it was necessary for Grefin to think they were friends again, true brothers, he started a mock-scuffle, as they'd scuffled in childhood with Malcolm. They took the last dozen shadow-flickered stairs down to the hall laughing and grappling, hips bumping, shoulders thumping, and laughed all the harder to see the affronted expressions on Reimond and Deness's austere, lordly faces as the councillors made their way to the staircase leading up to the East Tower, where they were being housed during Aimery's birthday celebrations.

Panting, Balfre tousled Grefin's hair. 'Did you want something? Or did you waylay me only to gloat?'

'Isn't gloating enough?'

'Fuck you.'

Grefin mimed himself arrow-shot, grinning. 'Muck-tongue.'

'Mankworm.'

'Mouldywarp.'

'Arselick!'

Two servants, a cord of firewood slung between them, startled as they came into the extravagantly candelit hall from the bailey.

'Now look what you've done,' said Grefin, nudging. 'Next they'll run weeping to Curteis and he'll scold you all the way to the Marches.'

Balfre felt his lip curl. 'I'm not in the habit of being scolded by servants.'

'Curteis is more than that, and you know it.'

Curteis was a fucking inconvenience. But no matter. Soon enough, like Grefin, he'd be swept aside.

'And Aimery's right,' Grefin added. 'He'll serve you well, should it come to a Crown Court.' Surrendering to a yawn, he scrubbed crooked fingers through his hair. 'But if I can be of any help before you ride out – if you ride out – if I'm still here? You've only to ask.'

With the wood-burdened servants huffing their way up the stairs to the East Tower, and everyone else safe behind chamber doors, they were alone again. Balfre felt his eyes narrow.

'I see. You think the task's beyond me.'

'Of course I don't! But—'

'But you're Steward of the Green Isle . . . and I'm not.'

Grefin looked at him. 'I thought we were past that.'

Fuck. Could he be more doltish, letting the rancour show? Lovingly, he rested a hand on his brother's shoulder. 'We are, Gref. Long past. I meant every word I said today. I'm proud of you, and I'm sorry. If you'd not found it in your heart to forgive me . . .'

Grefin's expression shifted from wary to embarrassed. 'I told you, there's nothing to forgive. The Green Isle is rightfully yours. I never should've said I'd take it, not even for a year. And once that year was up I shouldn't have let Aimery talk me into staying. I should've argued harder. I owed you that much.'

'And if you had, would he have listened?'

'Most likely not,' Grefin muttered. 'But I should've tried.'

Once, that admission would've counted for something, perhaps even healed the unhealed wound in his heart. Instead, the wound tore wider. Because he knew now how false his brother was. What a traitor he'd become, in league with Aimery against Harcia. Wooing Clemen. Offering the hand of friendship to that usurping bastard Roric.

Life is most strange. If Grefin had stood firm, if the Green Isle had come to me as I wanted, I might never have learned what he and Aimery are planning. And being ignorant, I'd have been too late to save us.

Seething, he pulled his brother close, held him tight. Conjured tears, because tears were important when selling a lie, even to the gullible. 'It means *everything*, Gref, that you forgive me. And I want to tell you something, that I need you to believe. I'm well-pleased not to be Steward. You're where you should be, on the Green Isle. And I'm where I must be, here, learning how best I can keep Harcia safe. If you never trust another word I say, trust that.'

'I do,' said Grefin, tightening his grasp.

He wanted to laugh at that. Instead, he forced a kind of choked sob. 'Good. But don't think you won't be the one hitting the ground arse-first next time we joust.'

'There's a fine boast!'

Stepping out of his brother's embrace, he grinned. 'Not a boast. A promise. Tell me, Gref, would you really school me so I'll not make a fool of myself in the Marches?'

'Of course.'

'Then school me now. Tell me what you've learned on the Green Isle that I should know. It's too early for bed. And besides . . .' He grimaced. 'I'm in no mood for Jancis. If you love me, keep me from her. We're happiest apart.'

Grefin's lingering smile faded. 'Balfre—'

'Don't,' he said sharply. 'You'll be wasting your breath. Now come, my lord Steward. Let's walk Tamwell's wall together and talk of happier things. Like murder.'

* * *

Emeline had taken poorly, soon after the feast.

'She's like me,' said Jancis, bathing her feverish daughter's brow with lavender water. 'The smallest morsel of rich food and her belly revolts. I did warn her not to indulge, but . . .'

Mazelina dipped a fresh linen cloth into the half-full pewter basin on the bedchamber floor. 'But like any child, she doesn't care to seem different.' She frowned. 'I hope her cousins didn't incite her.'

'Even if they did, Emeline knows better. This will be a lesson for her. Disobedience is always punished.'

And there was Jancis in a nutshell.

'Still. You can't really blame her, not wanting to miss out on a pleasure. Especially when my brood gobbles everything in sight without so much as a hiccup.'

'Indeed.' With an effort Jancis smiled, half-hearted. 'They're fine, healthy children, Mazelina. Life on the Green Isle suits them.'

'It might suit Emeline, too. I wish you'd bring her for a visit, Jancis. I'm sure you'd do well away from court for a little time.'

Jancis looked down at her sadly plain, afflicted daughter. 'Away from Balfre, you mean.'

'No, that's not what I—' Only it was, and they both knew it. Biting her lip, Mazelina twisted moisture from the lavender-scented cloth. 'It hurts to know you're so unhappy. You deserve better. Perhaps were Balfre deprived of your company for a month or more he'd learn to appreciate—'

'It would make no difference,' Jancis said calmly, exchanging her used cloth for the fresh one. 'Even when he's here, he scarcely notices me. Save for fucking, when the need arises. When he's not scratched that itch elsewhere.'

'*Jancis!*' She looked quickly at Emeline, but the child was restlessly fretful, her eyes barely open. 'That's a dreadful thing to say. Especially in front of—'

'The truth is often dreadful. As for my daughter, you may believe she's heard worse.'

The trouble was she did believe it. Every time she and Grefin came back to court she was vividly reminded of what a misery her goodsister's marriage had become. The unfairness of Jancis's predicament cut her, knife-like. Made her feel guilty for her own unclouded happiness.

'Don't reproach yourself, Mazelina,' Jancis said, reaching out. 'Or fear that I begrudge you the joy I'm denied. Do you think I'd see the world weeping because I can't laugh?'

Or bear a son. And here she sat, with two. Her vision blurred. 'The Green Isle is an old land, Jancis. I've met herb-women there with healing powers so strong they put Tamwell's leech to shame. If you'd come, if you'd let them—'

'Do what? Feed me foul potions? Gabble pagan chants over my shrivelled, barren womb?' Jancis withdrew her hand. 'I won't do that. Not even for a son.'

'But if they *worked*, Jancis. If it meant you could give Aimery's heir an heir, then surely—'

Jancis turned away. 'At the cost of my soul? I thought you cared for me, Mazelina.'

'You sound like an exarchite,' she said, staring.

'So what if I do? The Exarch's priests have been a great comfort. When I falter, they keep me strong.'

'So you've considered it?'

'Of course! Even though Balfre forbade me. But the exarchites showed me I was wrong.'

'Oh, *Jancis*. What do those grey men know of how a woman suffers?'

'And you?' Jancis bent again over her daughter, smoothing dull, mousey hair back from her damp cheek. 'What do you know of it?'

She leapt up. 'I thought you said you don't begrudge me?'

'I'm sorry,' Jancis said, flushing. 'I know you mean well. But you can't help me, Mazelina. No one can. Aimery refuses to sunder my marriage. And so long as the duke is obdurate, Balfre and I must endure.'

'So you've asked him? Aimery?'

Jancis sighed. 'I've begged him. Many times. The last time, he forbade me to mention it again.'

'And Balfre?'

Instead of answering, Jancis again cooled Emeline's over-heated skin. She was as pale as her daughter was flushed, and her thin, near-translucent hand trembled.

Frightened, Mazelina crouched at her side, by Emeline's low bed. 'Jancis? What's Balfre done?'

Another pallid smile. 'Tell me. You and Grefin. You confide in each other?'

'Of course,' she said, cautious. 'But if you're worried I'll tattle your confidences then—'

'Balfre tells me nothing.' Jancis looked up, her gaze unseeing. 'Days go by, and we hardly speak.'

'But?' she said gently, so full of sorrow her throat hurt.

Jancis shrugged. 'He's my husband, and I know him. Better than he thinks. People call him a hot-head. And I'll not deny his temper.' Her hand crept to her cheek, as though remembering a blow. 'But he's changed, Mazelina. He used to blurt things out in anger, or when he was in his cups. Not any more. He holds his tongue, these days. He knows raging isn't the only way to get what he wants.'

'And what's that?'

'Freedom,' Jancis whispered. 'When Aimery dies he'll be free. Of me. Of Emeline.' She released a shuddering breath. 'It won't be long now, surely. Aimery's an old, sick man. Balfre knows all he has to do is wait. And if he can wait, so can I. He's not the only one chafing for freedom.'

Jancis sounded so bleak she wanted to weep. Started to say something, then turned as she heard the outer chamber's door open.

'That's Balfre,' said Jancis, tightly. 'You should go.'

There was no use protesting the fear in her. The resignation. Jancis was right. Until Aimery died she was trapped here. Until Aimery died, she had to endure.

'Fair Mazelina,' Balfre greeted her, as she met him in the outer chamber. 'Did you come seeking Grefin?'

'No, to gossip with Jancis. I miss her, on the Green Isle.'

He raised an eyebrow. 'Really?'

For Grefin's sake she tried to like him, but he made it almost impossible. 'You should go to her, Balfre. Emeline is ill.'

'Again?' he said, indifferent.

Not knowing how to answer that, she searched his handsome face instead. The man who'd opened his heart to Grefin, who'd admitted his faults with grieving eyes. Was he real? Was he this man? Could she trust him with her husband, who needed so badly to trust?

Balfre tilted his head. 'I've made you angry.'

'A little,' she admitted. 'But then few men are born to be great fathers.'

'Like Grefin.' His jaw tightened. 'And Aimery.'

'Aimery?' She hesitated. Then, striving to be just, remembering that if Jancis was trapped in misery so was he, she sighed. 'I'd not call Aimery perfect.'

A flicker of surprise. 'No? Best you don't repeat that where Gref can hear you.'

'Where Grefin loves, he oft loves blindly. He'll forgive any hurt done him, no matter how cruel. Which means those who love him must be less forgiving.'

'Why, Mazelina,' he said, amused. 'Is that a warning?'

She tilted her chin. 'If you like.'

Laughing, Balfre kissed her forehead. 'Good night, dove. You'll find Grefin in your chambers.'

He was right. She did. And, standing unnoticed in the doorway watching the lordly Steward of the Green Isle blunder about the room on hands and knees, their three crowing children crowded on his back, didn't realise she was weeping until he at last saw her there.

'Mazelina! What's amiss?'

'Amiss?' Feeling the dampness on her cheeks, she hurriedly smeared them dry. 'Oh, nothing. Nothing. Everything's fine.'

Ullia, dark curls bouncing, waved her plump little arms. 'Mama! Mama! Come play! You can be my warhorse. We'll joust Jorin and Kerric and make them fall off!'

'Ninnypants!' Jorin scoffed, and poked her with his elbow. 'Girls don't joust!'

Ullia's lower lip quivered. 'I can joust if I want. Can't I joust, Papa?'

'Well, Mama?' said Grefin, catching wriggly Kerric's ankle with one hand to stop him sliding onto the floor. 'Can she?'

Turning, Mazelina closed the chamber door. Took that moment to breathe deep, until she knew she could trust herself to speak. There was nothing she could do for Jancis, or poor unwanted Emeline. All she could do was love her own family . . . and pray that one day her happiness might become theirs.

She turned back again, showing them nothing but delight. 'Of course she can, my lord Steward! Come along, Ullia. I'll be your fearless warhorse – and we'll make ninnypants of them!'

Leaving Jancis to nurse her useless, sickly daughter, Balfre spent the night in their apartment's outer chamber, slumped in a chair by the fire. He was too het up for sleep. For the first time since he'd stumbled across that fucking letter from Roric, he could see a chance to thwart Aimery's puling plan for peace with Clemen. And all thanks to a Clemen whore, who'd got herself murdered in the Marches.

There was justice in that. A glorious retribution.

Though some of the council doubted, he considered it almost certain a Crown Court would be convened. Far less certain, and most surprising, Aimery's decision to let his unwanted heir speak for Harcia. He'd offered himself to show willing, not because he thought his father would agree. Yet more retribution. The unseen powers were on his side. So he didn't dare waste the opening they'd given him. Had to turn uproar to his advantage, use every weapon he could find in the pursuit of his grand dream.

The rightful conquering of Clemen.

As night trudged towards dawn he kept the fire in the hearth burning and let his imagination run riot. Considered this thought, discarded that one until, like a puzzle, a plan began to take shape. It was made up of many pieces: the bits of advice Grefin had offered him as they tramped Tamwell's wall . . . the letter he'd taken from the trader, Culpyn, in Roric's handwriting . . . his own skill with pen and ink, the gaining of which he'd once resented . . . and the friends he'd made, and how best he could use them.

Hours later, the sun rose slovenly beyond the castle's thick stone walls. Fingers of daylight pushed between the outer chamber's barred shutters to lie idle on the floor. His empty belly rumbled. His full bladder complained. He heard the drift of voices from the bailey far below. Caught the scent of baking bread wafting up from the ovens.

Tamwell was awake.

Hastily breakfasted, and changed into a gold-embroidered russet doublet and sober black hose, Balfre took himself downstairs to the bailey's stables.

'My lord,' said Waymon, surprised to see him, and let go his stallion's hind hoof. 'Do you need something?'

The stables were bustling. Too many pricked ears. 'I do, Waymon,' he said. 'Walk with me.'

They left behind the restless horses, the scurrying stable boys, and the farrier roaring his forge to hot life. Waymon, blindly trusting, let himself be led over the causeway and onto the narrow path that threaded dangerously along the edge of the cliff overlooking the river.

Reaching the one place along the cliff path that kept them hidden from curious eyes, Balfre halted and turned. 'Forgive the mystery, Waymon. But we mustn't be overheard.'

'My lord,' Waymon said, his pockmarked face tightening, 'I know there's trouble. My father keeps council discretion, but I can tell he's worried.'

Balfre nodded. 'There's been a murder in the Marches. The bastard Roric intends to throw it at Harcia's feet. Worse, he's made our Marcher lords uncertain of their loyalty.'

'Bayard and Egbert?' Waymon gaped. 'Suborned to treachery?'

'I fear so.'

Shaken, Waymon looked down at the distant river, and the flat-hulled barges floating their ponderous way towards Cater's Tamwell. On the fresh morning breeze, the skirling shriek of a hunting eagle.

'*Fuck*, Balfre,' he said at last, 'this is terrible news.'

'And with Clemen ruled by that murdering bastard Roric, I fear there's worse to come. But you can't whisper a word of this, my friend. The stakes are too high.'

'Of course, my lord. My lips are stitched.' Waymon dragged the back of his hand across his mouth. 'What's to be done with them? Bayard, and Egbert.'

'Nothing kind. Waymon . . .' He folded his arms, like a man struggling against some great pain. 'Do you love me?'

Waymon's eyes widened. 'My lord, you know I do.'

'And if I commanded a task of you? Something difficult. Something . . . dark.'

'Then I'd do it. Without question.'

He hid a smile. 'Even though your hands may be stained with blood? Harcian, as well as Clemen?'

'*Anything*,' Waymon said, vehement, his mud-brown stare intense. 'Name it.'

'Ah, Waymon.' Balfre embraced him. 'I knew I could count on you.'

Waymon hesitated, then returned the embrace. As though they were brothers. 'Always. Never doubt it. I'm your man till the day I die.'

To his surprise, the declaration touched him. If only Grefin possessed even a thimbleful of Waymon's loyalty. Taking a deep breath, he stepped back. Shook off unwelcome melancholy. 'And I'm yours.'

'What is it you need me to do, my lord?'

'Nothing. Not yet,' he said. 'Matters are still unsettled. All I know for certain is I'll be riding to the Marches, soon. And when I go, Waymon, I want you by my side.'

'Me?' Waymon frowned. 'Not Joben? Or Paithan?'

Never. His cousin and Black Hughe's brother were useful, but neither man was what he needed. Waymon might dress like a popinjay but on the inside, where it counted, Ferran's son was a rabid wolf.

He smiled, gently. 'Not this time. To prevail in the Marches, I'll need you.' He thumped a fist to Waymon's gaudy saffron-and-crimson striped chest. 'Now come. We should return to Tamwell before we're missed. And remember – not a word to anyone. Harcia's future depends on your silence.'

295

CHAPTER EIGHTEEN

Harsh grunts. Rank sweat. The desperate, degrading thrust of flesh into flesh. There'd been pleasure in it, once. Desire and revenge entangled, feeding upon each other, swelling into a furious, endless burst of joy. Once there was laughter. A long time ago, delight.

Wearily, Vidar felt his straining body empty. Felt Lindara's weak shudder in response. She winced when he pulled himself out of her. Sighed as she fumbled her heavy green velvet skirts over her hips. Then she reached for her sleeves, set carefully aside with her elaborate emerald chain on the spiralled stone steps beside them. Her face was pale in the mean rushlight, no lingering flush of fulfilment.

'Help me lace them up.'

Once, three years ago – a moment ago, a lifetime – they'd torn her gown's bodice in their haste to disrobe. She'd had to lie to her lady's maid after, then find plausible reason to dismiss the woman to make certain she'd never cause strife. They'd taken more care since. Even now, with passion perfunctory, they made certain not to repeat that dangerous mistake.

Black hose rucked down to his knees, cock limp and deflated below the edge of his black velvet doublet, he laced her blue-and-gold striped sleeves to her bodice. Three years ago she'd stripped almost naked, and maiding her had made him smile. Gave him reason to fondle her breasts one last time beneath soft, rose-scented linen, and whisper scandalous things in her ear.

Three years later they removed only her sleeves. And met to fuck quickly, in empty stairwells and chance closets, no more lingering in moonlight, entwined in gold-embroidered sheets, fucking at their leisure while Roric was absent from Eaglerock.

Lindara flicked him a cursory look as she made sure of her pinned hair. 'You look ridiculous. Dress yourself, for pity's sake.'

There'd been a time when she'd laughed to see him so foolish. A time when she'd coax his limp, naked cock back to rampant life. When a single caress would make him iron again, and invincible. He dreamed those times now. Dreams were all he had left.

Pulling up his hose, lacing the points, tidying his shirt and doublet, he gritted his teeth against the grinding ache in his ruined hip. It hurt like shite to fuck standing, in a stairwell. But since Lindara decided where they'd meet, and even Humbert's pet leech Arthgallo couldn't undo his body's damage, he had to live with it. At least the leech's draught of poppy and yasfar dulled the worst of his pain.

'By Damikah's reckoning I've one more day fertile,' she said, fastening the emerald chain about her neck. 'So we should fuck again tomorrow. But not here. Perhaps in the wine cellar. Or the tapestry storeroom. I'll leave a note in the usual place by nine bells, once I decide.'

Abruptly exhausted, he looked at her. 'Fuck again to what end?'

'What do you mean?' she said, staring.

She was brittle, and so was he. Both of them thinned to breaking point. But he was tired of holding his tongue. Tired of pretending all was well when they both knew it wasn't.

'You set great store by your witch.'

'And why wouldn't I? She keeps Roric a gelding.'

'So you say.'

'And what do *you* say? That she's lying?'

'Or nowhere near the witch she claims to be. All this time fucking, Lindara, and you've still not borne my son. Or even my daughter.' He felt his breath hitch. 'You've never even miscarried.'

Trembling, Lindara folded her arms. The fine lines time had etched round her eyes deepened as she frowned. 'Then you do blame me.'

Perhaps he did. But how would it help to say so? 'Your witch promised us a healthy son.'

'She also warned it might take time.'

'How much time? What we dreamed of six years ago, that we've schemed and lied and fucked for ever since? It hasn't happened. Would you have us fucking in secret for *another* six years?'

'And what if I would, Vidar?' she demanded. 'I'm not leaving Eaglerock. Are you?'

He hesitated. He'd intended to talk of it, but not like this. Not in a stairwell.

'Vidar?' she said slowly. '*Are you leaving?*'

Trapped, reluctant, he looked into her accusing face. 'No. But I stand at a crossroad. There is a choice I have to make.'

'What crossroad? What *choice*?'

She sounded genuinely baffled. 'Lindara,' he said, feeling lost. How could she know him, love him, yet fail to understand? 'My title and estates were restored to me years ago, and still I haven't married. Surely you've heard the whispers?'

He watched her consider his question. Saw her eyes narrow as she realised what he was trying to say.

'Really?' Her cold stare raked him. 'You think people wonder why you're unwed?'

And that hurt, as she'd intended. 'Don't,' he said roughly. 'And don't pretend you can't see the danger we're in. Every week that passes, every time we meet like this, we—'

'Danger?' She laughed, scornful. 'Trust me, Vidar, we're in no danger. Roric suspects nothing. All he can think of is Clemen and its woes.'

'Your childless state being one of them!'

Her eyes glittered in the meagre candlelight. 'Roric forgives me that. So who are you to chide?'

'If he knew the reason for it he'd not forgive you.'

'Do you want to stop?' she said, stepping closer, hands fisted by her sides. 'Is that it? Because this is proving more difficult than we thought, do you want to abandon our revenge? Does it no longer matter to you, *offend* you, that every time he fucks me it feels like a rape? Do you no longer love me? Is that what you're trying to say?'

'*No*,' he protested. 'But—'

'Or perhaps you think it isn't rape,' she said, as though he'd not spoken. 'Because he doesn't use me violently. Because I'm not some peasant woman plundered on the battlefield as a reward for bloody slaughter.'

She was twisting his words, twisting *him*. 'I don't think that. You're unfair.'

'*Unfair?*' she spat. 'What do you know of unfair? You, a man, who'll never be treated as property or a witless doll. You think yourself hard done by because Humbert married me to someone else? You arrogant shite. Until you know what it feels like to be the one who's bartered, who must play the compliant whore and smile and smile and smile with every fucking, don't you *dare* stand there and moan to me about *unfair*.'

Did she know she was weeping? He thought she didn't. Her rage was too hot. Risking further fury, he pulled her close to his chest.

'I'm sorry. I'm sorry. I should've killed him in Bingham forest.'

'And claimed what, after?' she retorted, her tear-stained voice muffled against him. 'That he tripped over a tree-root and fell on his own sword?'

'Stranger things have happened. In Cassinia. Or so I'm told.'

'Fool.' On a shaky, indrawn breath she elbowed out of his arms. 'There was no hope ever of killing Roric. And I never wanted you to try.'

'Not then. But now?'

Even in despair, she was beautiful. 'Not even now. For nothing's changed. Clemen must have a duke . . . and despite his failings, Roric has the people's love.'

'They could learn to love another.'

Her eyes hardened. 'They will love our son.'

'If we have one.'

'*We will!*' Breathing harshly, she glared at him. Repinned her loosened hair. 'So. You want to marry. Have you a woman in mind?'

'Aistan's youngest daughter.'

'Kennise?' Surprised, Lindara raised an eyebrow. 'Didn't she bury herself alive in that exarchite women's house you failed to talk Roric out of permitting?'

A failure that still rankled, and Lindara knew it. She sought to punish him. 'Aistan has coaxed her back into the world.'

'So you can wed her? Why her?'

There was no point now in the keeping of secrets. 'He offered her to me at Heartsong, the night Harald died,' he said, weary. 'I made excuses. I thought I'd be marrying you. And then – it was too late.'

'Kennise,' she said, tasting the name as though it were something sour. 'You can do better.'

'I doubt it. She's impeccably bred. And marrying into Aistan's influence can do me no harm.'

'Kennise,' she said again, with such disdain. Then she smirked. 'I wonder what Godebert would say to you wedding and bedding Harald's soiled leavings?'

She could be the cruellest woman. More cruel even than Argante. 'So I'm to feel pity only if the raped woman is you?'

'Kennise is old,' she said, refusing to admit her fault.

'She was barely fourteen when Harald had her. She's younger than you.'

Lindara flinched. It pleased him to see it. 'I don't understand, Vidar,' she whispered, turning away. 'Not once have you ever talked of wanting to marry. After so long . . . why now?'

'Oh, *Lindara*!' He wanted to shake her. 'Did you truly think any son I sired on you would be the only son I'd ever want? I have a duty to my dead father. I'm thirty-five next month! If I should die without a legitimate heir then Godebert's line ends. The thought of that fills me with shame, and fear.' He felt a stab of bitter pride. 'And though I may be scarred, lame and half-blind, Aistan says Kennise will have me. But she won't wait for ever . . . and neither can I.'

Silence. Then the faintest of sighs. 'Do you love her?'

'I've never met her.'

Lindara glanced over her shoulder. 'And yet you'd wed her.'

'If not her, then someone else.'

'And us, Vidar? What of us?'

'What do you mean?'

'You know what I mean!' she said, spinning to face him. There was fear in her eyes. 'Wife or no wife, nothing can change. You swore you'd help me revenge myself on Roric, and on Humbert. I won't let you break your word.'

Fuck. He was so tired. And his hip was on fire. If he didn't sit down soon, he'd fall. 'I wasn't going to.'

'Damikah insists I'm not mismade,' she said, as though he'd not

300

spoken. 'We will have a son, Vidar, and he *will* be Roric's heir. I can give him stronger potions. I can take them myself. There are charms and incantations, too. Damikah knows.'

He reached for her again. 'Sorcery? No. I forbid it.'

'The choice is mine,' she said, trying to twist her shoulders free. 'You can't stop me.'

This time he did shake her. 'You know I can. You know I will. No revenge is worth your *life*.'

Lips trembling, she stared up at him. 'Then you do still love me.'

'*Lindara*.' He framed her face with his hands. 'Sweet fool. I never stopped.'

Her beautiful eyes were full of tears. 'Prove it.'

'I'll see your witch,' he said, after a moment. 'There must be a potion I can take.'

'You don't need one.'

'You don't know that.'

'Yes, I do,' she said, her smile wry. 'Or did you think I'd not find out about the bastard on your estate?'

Shocked, he watched her retreat to the arrow loop in the stairwell wall and breathe in cold, fresh night air.

'That's why I must risk Damikah's strongest elixirs,' she said, her back to him. 'And dabble in questionable magics. Because despite what she tells me, I fear the fault here is mine.'

And now his heart was burning. 'It's true, I've one bastard born at Coldspring. But I've fucked more than one woman there. It could be I'm to blame. Arrange for me to see your witch. I'll swallow whatever foul concoctions she thinks will help.'

'All right,' she said, reluctant. 'But even swallowing them . . . you'll still wed?'

'Lindara—'

She pressed her hands to her face. 'I know. I know. You must.'

'But not tomorrow,' he said, closing the terrible distance between them. Taking her in his arms again, and gentling her cheek to his chest. 'We still have time.'

'How much?'

'Enough,' he said, and kissed her. 'Don't you know, Lindara? I'd steal time from the spirits for you.'

301

'Vidar . . .' Her clever fingers reached for him. 'I was hateful. Forgive me.'

Pleasure drowned his fiery pain. As his ruined vision blurred, he gasped. 'But won't Roric—'

'Roric's busy,' she murmured, unlacing him. Sliding down him to her knees. 'Talking politics with Humbert. Don't think of him. Think of me, and the son we'll make.'

It was madness to stay. To risk all for another hasty fuck. But her fingers were a torment, and so was her tongue. Panting, he surrendered. Groaned, and moaned her name. So what if she was sometimes hateful?

She was Lindara. She was his life.

'. . . sorry, Your Grace. It pains me to say so, but I lack a simple answer where Cassinia's concerned.'

Glowering, because it was late and his joints were aching, Humbert rapped his knuckles to the arm of his chair. 'Come, come, Master Blane. No need to be a mimbly waddler. Speak plainly to His Grace. He's not Harald. You won't suffer for it.'

'Humbert.' Roric flicked him a warning glance, then smiled at the merchant. 'Don't take his lordship's scold to heart, Blane. With you so recently returned from nearly four months of merchant trading he's anxious, as I am, to hear what you have to say about our cousins across the Moat.' He gestured at the goblet on the small table beside the merchant's chair. 'But before we talk in earnest, would you care for more wine?'

'More – well, indeed, that's very kind, Your Grace,' Blane said, then stared, bemused, as Clemen's duke rose from his own chair and played servant to pour it.

Humbert rolled his eyes. Spirits save him. He'd lost count of the times he'd told the boy not to lower his dignity in such a fashion, but did Roric listen? He did not. Neither did he pay heed to sound advice regarding the proper way to conduct this kind of meeting. They should be formal, in one of Eaglerock's grandly appointed audience chambers, where no man was allowed to forget the weight of ducal might. Instead here they were, in Roric's shabbily comfortable privy closet, with a cheerful fire burning and the boy playing host as though they were three cosy friends. It was ridiculous. Especially when the treasury owed wealthy Master Blane, head of Clemen's Merchants' Guild, a great deal of coin.

'More wine, Humbert?' said Roric, after refilling the merchant's goblet.

He covered his own with the flat of his hand. Lowered his brows. 'No.'

'So, Blane,' said Roric, ignoring his pique, and sitting again. 'Paint me a picture of Cassinia as it stood when you left. And then tell me honestly how it seems to you *we* stand there – and don't think to spare my feelings.'

Hastily swallowing, Blane set his goblet aside. The rich wine had stained his neatly barbered flaxen beard dark red about the chin. 'Then I won't. Alas, Your Grace, when it comes to Cassinia I fear we're kneeling, not standing. That curs't principality's naught more than a cauldron of simmering strife. It bubbles up, spills over, and blights everything it touches. Like poison.'

Which was precisely what Aistan and Vidar had told the council earlier that week. The same sobering report from two different, reliable sources. And now here was a third.

Unhappily thoughtful, Roric picked at a loose thread in his fine grey wool sleeve. 'And?' he said at last. 'I'd know the worst.'

'The worst, Your Grace?' Blane shook his head. 'I doubt we've seen the worst, though what I've seen is bad enough.' He snatched up his goblet again and drank like a man in need of courage. 'Though we're still barred from Ardenn, with the restoration of our trading rights in Cassinia's other duchies I did for a time think we were looking at better days. But I fear I hoped too soon.'

From the careful corner of his eye, Humbert saw Roric's face tighten at the mention of Berardine's duchy. *Berardine*. Curse the meddling bitch. In offering her daughter to Roric she'd given Cassinia's regents a blade that had been pressed to Clemen's throat ever since. The duchy's slow decay had started the moment she set foot in Eaglerock.

And still the boy felt pity for her. As though she weren't the scribe of her own miserable fate.

'Ardenn's duchess,' Roric said, abruptly. 'How does she fare? Do you know?'

'Berardine?' Blane blinked. 'Why, she's still prisoned in her own duchy, Your Grace, but no worse than that. At least I heard no ill rumour to suggest otherwise.'

'And her daughter? Catrain?'

'Ah.' Blane swallowed more wine. 'She's dead, Your Grace.'

'*Dead?*'

'That's the general opinion. For certain she's not been seen alive in Ardenn – or anywhere else – for some years.' The trader grimaced. 'Which only worsens our predicament. Without a son to inherit Baldwin's duchy, when Berardine dies the other dukes will fight over it like dogs with a bone.'

Roric cleared his throat. 'But the duchess has other daughters.'

'All married off, Your Grace. And even if they weren't, after the disastrous widow there'll be no more women permitted sole rule in Cassinia.'

'No,' said Roric, his gaze dangerously unfocused. 'I dare say you're right.'

Shifting in his chair, needing to ease his aching bones, Humbert knocked his booted foot against Roric's ankle. A timely hint. Let the boy be distracted by Berardine and her dead daughter and they'd not escape the merchant's company before sunrise.

'What news else, Blane?' he said briskly. 'No need to dwell on Ardenn. His Grace knows already where Clemen can and cannot trade.'

'But he doesn't, my lord,' Blane said, banging his emptied goblet on the side table. 'And nor does any man who thinks to do business in Cassinia these days. That's what I've been trying to tell you! For in Cassinia these days up is down and down is up and the rules change from moment to moment, on a whim!'

Roric turned. 'Patience, Humbert. We need to hear him out.'

And that was true, though he wished it wasn't. He didn't care for Master Blane. Rich men who opened their coin chests to dukes oft had a nasty habit of thinking they'd made a purchase, not a loan. Resting his chin on his chest he gestured at the merchant.

'Very well, Blane. We're listening.'

Blane smoothed his wine-stained beard, the costly rings on his fingers catching the firelight. 'Your Grace, allow me to illustrate my point. This last venture, we travelled particularly to Duchy Hardane – being given reliably before we sailed that the noblemen there favour tawny silk above all. Now as everyone knows, the best silk-dyers you'll find anywhere live in Clemen. So at great expense I shipped in highest-quality silk from the Quartered Isles and had it dyed here. But when we arrived in Hardane, we were told tawny silk is forbidden in the duchy, by order of the Regents' Council!'

Despite himself, Humbert was intrigued. 'For what reason?'

'Because, my lord—' Blane hissed a breath between clenched teeth. '—the duke of Hardane's nephew insulted one of the regents while wearing a tawny silk doublet.'

From the look on Roric's face, it seemed he didn't know whether to laugh or howl. 'I'd not heard that, Blane.'

'Nor I, Your Grace,' Blane said glumly. 'Or I wouldn't have carted twenty bales of tawny silk all the way to Hardane.'

'*Twenty* bales?' Humbert snorted. 'A foolish risk.'

'No, my lord,' Blane said, not quite hiding his resentment. 'The duke of Hardane's nephew is passionate fond of tawny silk. And whatever he esteems becomes wildly popular with the nobility. If he'd not ruined himself with the regents I'd have turned a pretty profit. As it was . . .'

'You had to bring it back again?' said Roric, all sympathy.

Blane heaved a morose sigh. 'No, Your Grace. I was able to sell the stuff eventually. To a passing Hentish merchant. At a steep loss.'

'What?' Humbert stared. How was it this man headed the Merchants' Guild? 'You couldn't get a better price for it elsewhere in Cassinia?'

'I tried, my lord,' Blane said stiffly. 'But the duke of Lambard's third cousin is wed to that same insulted regent's wife's brother, so the duke refused me an audience. Next, I approached Duchy Voldare, but the duchess of Voldare is feuding with the duchess of Rebbai, whose second son is betrothed to the youngest daughter of another regent's—'

'Clap tongue, for pity's sake!' Humbert snapped. 'D'you think His Grace has time for this nonsense?'

Blane pinched his lips. 'My lord, you asked.' Pointedly shifting his gaze to Roric, he adjusted the guild medallion resting on his breast. 'Your Grace, the unhappy truth is that Cassinia writhes like a viper's nest with dispute. Its dukes see a slight in a smile, a deadly insult in a sneeze. And while it shouldn't be our business, they make it so. You'd need a soothsayer to tell you which duke was trading insults with which, and whether our travelling papers will be honoured – or torn to shreds for the offence of trading with a neighbour who one day is seen as friendly and the next declared a bitter foe! I tell you plainly, these quarrelsome dukes are as constant as a – as a – *frog*. And when they aren't fighting each other they're fighting the prince's regents! Which gives our merchants no respite, for the end result is the same. Much knavery on Cassinia's roads. And that means fistfuls of coin in hired protection for the avoiding of it, to our great detriment.'

Roric picked up his goblet, but didn't drink. 'You say all our merchants face these dilemmas?'

'Every one, Your Grace,' said Blane. 'But alas, there's more. Even when the dukes stop their feuding long enough to catch breath, from one day to the next Clemen's merchants can't be sure how much we'll be taxed from duchy to duchy, or if we can use the donkeys we hire at port-fall or must hire more afresh every time we enter a different duke's lands, or whether what might be lawfully – and profitably – sold yesterday can still be sold today. Or tomorrow!'

'But what of the regents? Don't they see the rule of law enforced? What you're describing sounds monstrous unfair.'

'Ha! Your Grace, the regents know better than to stir the dukes against them. Indeed, I think they think it useful to keep the dukes busy with their squabblings. So they wink and nod at floutish behaviours, interfering only when they must. And then, to keep the dukes sweet after, they let pass certain imposts their duchies owe the crown and instead wring them from us!'

Humbert exchanged a troubled glance with Roric. This was worse even than Aistan had reported.

'I'll be blunt, Your Grace,' Blane added. 'Matters can't continue in this fashion.'

'No,' Roric murmured, and sipped his wine. 'I see that.'

'And there's something else.'

'What?' Humbert prompted, as the merchant worried at the emerald dangling from one heavy lobed ear. 'Don't hold back now, Blane.'

'It's Prince Gäel,' Blane said heavily. 'Rumour has it he's quite mad.'

'Mad?' Roric set down his goblet. 'How can a child be mad?'

Blane shrugged. 'Some say he foams at the mouth. Others say he holds tongue for weeks at a time and walks about his grand palace quite naked, but for one shoe. This whisper claims he sees a mirror and runs screaming, that whisper swears he thinks himself a dog. Every tale is different, but at the heart they're all the same.'

'That Cassinia's prince is mad.' Roric pushed to his feet and crossed to the closet's hearth, where cheerful flames still leapt. Head lowered, he rested his forearm on the carved oak mantel. 'Poor boy. To lose father and mother, and then his wits.'

Humbert scowled at the scant swallow of wine left in his goblet. A pity he'd not let Roric refill it. He could use a good dose of strong grape. This news was ill indeed, and came as a surprise. Not even Aistan had managed to nose it . . . and the implications for Clemen were dire.

'It's also whispered the regents will do anything to conceal their prince's madness,' Blane added. 'They've spies in every mouse hole, and every butt of ale. But though they've killed some who've spoken, and locked others away, the truth slithers free.'

'And serves to embolden Cassinia's dukes,' Humbert growled. 'If the whispers prove true, they'll not accept the rule of a mad prince. I'll wager every one of those cockshites goes to bed at night dreaming of a crown.'

Blane's earring swung vigorously as he nodded. 'Aye, my lord, aye! 'Tis only a matter of time before they do more than dream. And they won't care when their ambitions tear Cassinia apart . . . and us with it.'

'*If* the whispers are true,' said Roric, turning back to them. 'There's a chance they're false, Blane. Spread by one of the dukes to bolster a claim to the crown.'

'That's possible,' Blane said slowly. 'But what's certain is that between the growing ructions in Cassinia, and the difficulties we face when we try to trade further afield – pirates, and dangerous, ill-natured waters, and skullduggery from nations who don't care to share their spoils – *and* a new plague come down from Agribia, touching the Treble Kingdom and Zeidica and even the Danetto Peninsula, or so that Hentish merchant told me, well . . . Clemen's in for yet more hardship and heartache. How are we expected to survive?'

The shadows in Roric's eyes deepened. Seeing his distress, Humbert fought the urge to sink a fist into the merchant's expensively clad paunch. *Cockshite.* Did Blane think Roric blind to the duchy's growing burdens? Or was he offering a veiled warning? *You owe me money, boy. Don't forget it.* As if Roric would, or could, forget the debt when every day he faced the many troubles that had forced him to borrow so much coin, and tormented himself over his imagined failings like an exarchite who beat his own back with a knotted rope.

'You needn't worry on that score, Blane,' he said, standing. 'Everything possible is being done to see Clemen's set to rights.'

'Of course, my lord,' Blane said. 'But I thought it should be said.'

'And I'm – *we're* – grateful for your insights,' said Roric. 'Isn't that so, Humbert?'

He sniffed. 'I'll be grateful for an assurance that Master Blane won't repeat what's been discussed here.'

'My lord.' Blane unfolded from his chair and offered a frosty bow. 'You have it.' Turning to Roric he bowed again, more warmly. 'Your Grace. If there's nothing else you need . . . ?'

Roric's smile was faint, and strained. 'Only your promise you'll not refuse me further counsel.'

'I'd refuse you nothing, Your Grace. You've only to ask. Good night.'

'Good night, Master Blane. Beyond the door you'll find a squire waiting to see you safely out of the castle.'

'Thank you.' A sharp nod. 'Good night, Lord Humbert.'

He grunted something suitable. Tried to catch Roric's eye as the merchant shrugged into his warm outdoors cloak, fastened his crimson-enamelled cloak pin then pulled on his gloves. But Roric was staring into the fire, heedless.

Hand on the chamber's door-latch, Blane turned. 'One last thing, Your Grace. If I might be so bold.'

Humbert gritted his teeth. Spirits curse the garrulous shite. What now?

Encouraged by Roric's nod, Blane settled on his heels. 'If Clemen's merchants are to weather these harsh times, Your Grace, we need Ardenn's coin. So whatever must be done to reclaim our trading rights there, I urge you to do it.'

'Again I'll advise you to clap tongue, Master Blane,' Humbert snapped. 'Clemen's not subject to arrogant Cassinian demands – and any man thinking the duke's council would travel the duchy down that road is a fool.'

Blane's eyes narrowed. 'That's as may be, my lord. But better the council swallows its pride than the rest of us in Clemen swallow gruel, and hear our children wail with hunger, because we can no longer afford to put meat and bread on our tables.'

'He's right, Humbert, and you know it,' Roric said, once the merchant was gone.

'I know nothing of the sort! Who's Master Blane, to be ordering Clemen's council? Or its duke?'

'He's a good man who fears what lies ahead for our duchy.' Sighing, Roric retrieved a length of wood from beside the hearth and fed it to the lowering flames. 'As I do.'

'Roric, if you're about to start blaming yourself again I swear I'll—'

'*Don't*, Humbert.' Bone-white weary, Roric rubbed the back of his hand across his eyes. 'You say I can't blame myself, but who else is there to blame? Have I convinced Cassinia's regents to stop punishing us for Berardine and Catrain? No. Did I prevent even one fresh outbreak of plague in the duchy? Or blistermouth? Or fish rot? No, no, and no. Have I been forced to borrow coin from wealthy men like Master Blane? More than once. And have I sired a son to sit the Falcon Throne after me? No, Humbert. I haven't. So tell me, my lord. Is this how you'd measure *success*?'

Humbert jutted his beard. 'And I suppose you're to blame for three poor harvests in a row, too. For the flooding in eastern Clemen and the parched soil everywhere else.'

'Perhaps not, but I haven't been able to ease the pain those natural miseries have caused and for that I *should* be blamed. I'm Clemen's duke.'

Ah, the spirits save him. First Harald, who cared so little . . . and now Roric, who cared too much. He felt like a pendulum, swung between two impossible extremes. And resented it, for his bones ached. He was getting old.

But who could look into Roric's face and not feel a mote of pity?

'I know what's brought on this mopish mood. For the last time, boy, the widow's fate is *not* your fault.'

'And what of Catrain?' Roric's jaw tightened. 'She might be alive had I wed her instead of Lindara. And your daughter would doubtless be a mother by now.'

'Suckling brats sired by that shite Vidar! Is that what you'd wish on me? Would you wish it on *her*?'

'I wish Lindara nothing but happiness.' Taking up the fireplace poker, Roric stabbed at the flickering flames. 'Which, it seems, she can't find with me.'

A chill of fright. 'What d'you mean by that?'

'Nothing,' Roric muttered. 'Never mind me, Humbert. I'm tired.'

'Roric.' Anger and frustration drained away, leaving him shaken. 'If there's strain between you and Lindara, it can't be wondered at. But you're young enough still, both of you. There'll be children. And then all will be well. Isn't that what Arthgallo says? To be patient, for you're not mismade. You or Lindara.'

The stirred firelight played over Roric's face, grown thinner with the weight of Clemen's trouble. 'He does.'

'Well, then.'

'Well, then . . .' Taking a deep breath, Roric glanced over his shoulder. 'Humbert, I think I must go to Cassinia.'

Fists on hips, he stared. 'Go to – Roric, are your wits faery-snatched? Go to *Cassinia*? For what purpose?'

'To meet face to face with the prince's regents.'

'And do what? Beg for scraps from their table? Promise them what they want till we're no better than their subjects? Over my dead body!'

'Humbert—'

'*No*, Roric!' Seizing the boy's shoulder, he wrenched him around. 'You are duke of Clemen, not a pustuled, penniless scapegrace forced to seek charity from your betters. *Go to Cassinia?* You can't!'

Sighing, Roric shrugged himself free. 'You heard Master Blane. Matters there are dire for us, and growing worse. But it's not simply that we still can't trade in Ardenn. Or that Cassinia's unruly dukes cost our merchants coin they can't spare. It's the prices they charge us for their mutton and beef and wool, now that our herds are so thinned by blistermouth and footrot. It's their tardiness in paying the tolls and taxes their merchants owe here, knowing we can't afford to sanction them as they've sanctioned us.'

'Then send a delegation, Roric! But—'

Roric laughed, bitterly. '*Another* one? Surely the last four I sent prove how easily the regents disregard letters and envoys. But they'll have a harder time disregarding a duke. Besides, Humbert.' A faint, sardonic smile. 'While I might not be pustuled, I'm most certainly penniless. Or almost.'

He could easily tug his beard out by its roots. 'You cannot go to Cassinia! The council won't abide it!'

'I don't require the council's leave, Humbert,' Roric retorted, his face hardening. 'Nor can it be told my business till I'm safely arrived at the prince's court. Not when we could never uncover who it was betrayed Berardine to the regents. That same man could well betray me.'

Yes, tug out his beard and throw every hair into the fire. 'Not that nonsense again. It was a Cassinian betrayed the widow. Her judgement's so poor I'll wager she had a score of trusted courtiers lined up to do it. Roric—'

Roric banged his fist to the fireplace mantel. '*Enough!* I must go. For what do I have left to me but personal persuasion? Short of declaring war on the regents. Is that what you want? For Clemen to take up arms against the Prince's Isle?'

'Say the word, boy, and I'll lead an army there myself!' he shouted. 'On foot, and the faeries curse my bunions.'

'Oh, *Humbert*.' Discarding the poker, Roric dropped into his chair. 'I know you would. But that's no answer.'

'Neither is you bending your knee to the prince's regents.'

Roric looked up. 'You don't think Clemen is worth a little bruising of my pride?'

'And if foul play should befall you?'

'That's a risk I'll have to take.'

His heart was shrivelling in his chest. 'There must be another way.'

'There might be,' Roric said, after a moment. 'But you'll like it even less than the thought of me bending my knee to Cassinia's regents.'

There was something worse than that? He couldn't imagine it. Certainly didn't want to hear it. But it seemed he was to have no peace this night.

'Tell me.'

Instead of answering, Roric stood again. 'We'll need more wine.'

So he waited, while Roric uncorked a fresh bottle of rich Dolchetti red and filled both their goblets to the brim. Half emptied his own in one swallow, refilled it, then wandered the small chamber looking at the tapestried nobles hunting their hounds around the walls, seemingly oblivious to the falcons flying over their heads. The colourful panels were years old, but still exquisite.

'Come, boy,' Humbert said at last. 'There's no sharp sword that loses its edge for the staring at it. Tell me, and have done.'

Roric halted by the closet's shuttered window. Touching one of the cast-iron studs buried in the seasoned oak, for a moment he looked as green and uncertain as the youth who'd so long ago left his home for fostering.

'Aimery seeks to broker a formal peace between our duchies.'

He put down his goblet, untouched. 'What?'

'If such a peace were brokered, we could ask Harcia for help. Then I'd not need to bruise my pride with the regents.'

He shook his head, unsure of his hearing. 'How do you know Aimery wants peace?'

'He sent me a letter. At least Grefin did, at his father's behest.'

'When?'

'Recently.'

'And how d'you know it comes from Aimery?'

'There was a signet ring sent with it, once worn by the last Harcian king's son, Bannor. Or as we prefer to know him, Clemen's first duke.'

He blinked. 'A *ring*.'

'It's genuine, Humbert,' Roric said, his voice edged. 'I recognise the seal.'

'This letter. Have you replied to it?'

'I have. With caution.'

'Oh, you *have*. I see.' Now his shrivelled heart was pounding fit to burst through his ribs. 'And you never thought to tell me?'

'I'm telling you now.'

'*Roric!*' He snatched up his goblet and threw it. 'You – you – maggot-brained *shite*!'

Looking down at his red-splattered grey doublet, Roric grimaced. 'And that's a sad waste of good wine. No, Humbert, be quiet.' He lowered his hand. 'I waited to tell you because I needed time to think. And I replied swiftly to Aimery because I'd not have Harcia's duke stir this publicly before I'm ready.'

'You're mad to think we can trust Aimery or his sons. *Twice* mad to hope they can row Clemen out of the weeds. This is a ruse, boy. They know we're struggling and—'

'And it could be you're right,' Roric said flatly. 'Or it could be Aimery's genuine. But even if he is genuine, Humbert, and even if I could persuade Aistan and the rest to hear him out fairly, and *even if* we could broker a peace . . . that will take months. So what choice do I have but to beg an audience with Cassinia's regents?'

He felt so old, he could weep. 'When would you go?'

'Soon.'

'And how—'

'Blane will help me.'

'And the council?'

'You'll keep order until I return.'

'What of Lindara?'

'I'll tell her. But not a soul else. Humbert—'

'I know, boy,' he said, and heaved a gut-wrenching sigh. 'I know. You don't have a choice.'

CHAPTER NINETEEN

For all that Lindara's chambers were in a thick-walled stone castle, still she'd made them elegant. Pale and delicate, like the inside of an empty egg. Pushing the door wide, Roric steeled himself to enter. He never failed to feel clumsy here, a brute man in a woman's soft, scented world. Or perhaps it was Lindara who made him feel that. Six years of marriage and yet she so often seemed distant. Unreachable. A mystery he was destined never to comprehend. As children they'd been friends. But as husband and wife . . .

'It's nearly midnight, Lindara,' he said, closing the door behind him. 'The servants are abed, sleeping. Why aren't you?'

Seated by the fire, her unbound hair flame-gilded, she set aside her embroidery frame. 'I could ask you the same.'

'Humbert and I had much to discuss. We met with Blane, of the Merchants' Guild.'

'And had a rowdy time, it seems,' she said, looking him up and down.

He touched fingers to the wine-stains on his doublet. 'You mean this? An accident.'

Her chamber robe was luxuriously modest, the blue-dyed, pearl-sewn linen covering all her body, save her beautiful face and her swan neck and her pale, slender hands. He loved her hands. Loved the length and straightness of her fingers, the gentle shine of their narrow, neatly shaped nails.

He couldn't remember the last time her nails had scratched his back in passion. When coupling was more than a desperate duty. An open wound beyond healing, or so it seemed.

'An accident, Roric?' In her glass-grey eyes, a cynical gleam.

'Are you sure? Or did Humbert lose his temper and throw a goblet at you?'

He was so tired. So sad. Without asking, he sat on the edge of her bed. Their bed, when he joined her in it . . . but still. It always felt like hers. Because he'd not infect her with his mood, he dredged up a smile.

'Don't tell me. You were hiding behind one of the tapestries.'

She picked up her embroidery frame again. Frowned over a loose stitch. 'You shouldn't let him bully you. He's a great one for that, my father.'

'I don't. He wasn't. I did something that distressed him.'

'Then isn't it fortunate he had no sword to hand?'

Roric let himself fall backwards onto the bed's squirrel-skin coverlet. 'You're too sharp with him.'

'And you're not sharp enough.'

'Oh, Lindara . . .' He rested his forearm over his closed eyes. 'Must we quarrel?'

The sound of her steady breathing. The faint pop-hiss-pop of needle and silk thread passing in and out of her embroidery. Greedy crackling, as flames devoured dry wood.

'What did you do?' she asked, at last. 'To distress him.'

She was his wife, and he trusted her, but not with every secret. He couldn't tell her of Grefin's letter. Or his reply. Not yet. 'Lindara . . . I must go to Cassinia.'

'To see the regents? To make them relent in their slow strangling of Clemen?'

She was also her father's daughter. She never needed him to explain.

'Humbert mislikes the notion greatly.'

'Humbert is wrong,' she said. 'But of course he won't see it.'

'Oh, he sees it. And he mislikes that even more.'

A soft chuckle. 'I've no doubt.'

Ribboned through her amusement, the echo of a thin, sour bitterness. Knowing her so well, he thought he was the only one who ever heard it. Perhaps Humbert did. But if he did, he never said so. For himself, he often wondered if their marriage was to blame for Lindara's wariness of her father. Wondered but didn't ask out loud. What was the point of hearing the answer? Even if his wife chose to tell the truth, nothing would change. They were bound together, duke and duchess. And for his life he could see no safe way to break that bond.

'Who will you tell, that you're going to Cassinia?'

He sat up. 'No one else now, save Master Blane. I'll use him to get me there, secret and safe.'

'You're keeping it from the council?' Lindara wrinkled her nose. 'That's probably wise.'

'You think so?'

'Let me guess.' Setting aside her embroidery again, she joined him on the bed. 'Humbert doesn't.'

'He still disbelieves Berardine was betrayed by one of us.'

'Might've been betrayed,' she said. 'You've no proof. And I agree with Humbert. No Clemen lord would willingly plunge us into the turmoil we're suffering, thanks to the widow.'

Reluctantly, once they were married, because he feared she'd hear whispers regarding the reason for the regents' sanctions, he'd told her about Berardine's offer. Dismissed it as moondust and never mentioned the fire, or the stables, or Catrain's heartstopping courage. He was sometimes foolish, even thoughtless, but never entirely dull of wit.

Catrain. Grief, stabbing like a dagger out of the shadows. *Catrain is dead*.

Lindara touched his shoulder, lightly. 'Roric. You can't let my father's bearish moods distress you.'

'I don't. It's Blane who's distressed me. I knew matters were difficult for us in Cassinia, but . . .' He rubbed at the needling pain in his temple. 'Of late they've gone from difficult to dire. And if I fail with the regents, if I can't convince them to forgive a crime we didn't even commit, then—'

'You won't fail,' she said, slipping from the bed. 'You defeated Harald. You'll defeat the regents.'

'I wish I could be so sure. Lindara—' Reaching out, he caught her by the wrist. Her pulse leapt beneath his fingers. 'I'd stay tonight.'

Golden eyelashes lowered, she sighed. 'Roric—'

'Can't I stay?' he said, and pulled her to him. 'I'm your husband, Lindara. Let me stay.'

He knew he was begging, and hated it. Hated knowing she'd never warmed to him in her bed. In her body. She tried to hide it, but he knew. And so, because he wasn't Harald, could never be Harald, he tried hard not to demand more of her than Clemen required. He'd not be begging now, only after Blane, and Humbert, he wanted to be touched. Needed badly to be touched. He was tired of grief and loneliness. He was tired of aching with fear. Why couldn't he ache with passion, instead? What was so terrible about making love to his wife? And they might even make a son. But as his lips met hers, tasted hers, he felt her shrink. Felt her shudder . . . and not with pleasure.

He let go of her, anguished.

'Roric!' she said, as he fumbled blindly for the door. 'Roric. Please. *Wait.*'

'For what, Lindara?' Pain hammered through his skull. 'What would you have me do? Beg pardon, like a servant, for overstepping my bounds?'

'Of course not!' Pale as milk, her eyes tear-glimmered, she retreated to the bed. Tugged aside coverlet and blankets, revealing linen sheets and the long bolster pillow beneath. 'I'd have you stay. I'll feel better in the morning. I – I have a touch of quease now. But your company will be sweet.'

'Will it?'

'*Yes!* Come.' She patted the pillow. 'Sleep. It's so late, and you're weary. Sunrise will see us both mended. We can sport then.'

He let her persuade him. Stood docile, like a child, as she fussed him out of his stained doublet, linen shirt and wool hose. Naked, he crawled into her bed and hardly felt her draw blankets and coverlet over his skin. He heard the damp sizzle, smelled the beeswax smoke, as she pinched out the chamber's candles. In the fire-glowed darkness she slid beside him, rustling in a cotton shift. She wore her night clothes like armour, and he lacked the skill to strip her bare.

'When do you leave for Cassinia?' she whispered.

'As soon as I've arranged matters with Blane.'

'You and Humbert have a story to give out, for while you're gone?'

'We will have.'

'Good,' she said, and kissed his uncovered shoulder.

Scant minutes earlier, the gesture would have excited him. Now, unstirred, he rolled onto his side.

She kissed him again, on the nape of his neck. 'Sleep well, Roric. And don't worry. All will be well.'

He wished he could believe that. He wished he couldn't taste bile and bitterness at the back of his dry throat. But as he listened to her breathing slow, and deepen into slumber, and closed his eyes praying for the pain in his head to cease, he thought it more likely nothing would ever be well again.

'Quickly! Quickly! Down to the lake! Aistan's dwarves are water jousting!'

Like a flock of screeching, multi-coloured Ardabenian parrots, Eaglerock's exquisitely dressed courtiers abandoned their quoits and their skittle-bowling and the pouting challenge of the archery butts to flee across his lordship's immaculately green lawn in search of rowdier entertainment.

Scowling after them, Humbert drained his tankard of foamy beer. *Water jousting dwarves?* What next? Zeidican monkeys on sheepback? Or perhaps a quartet of dancing mules. If this was a proper way for Aistan to celebrate his youngest daughter's unexpected betrothal he'd row himself to Zeidica, find a monkey, and eat it.

Of course, the girl was about to marry Vidar. Perhaps dancing mules and drowning dwarves weren't so far wide of the mark.

'More beer, my lord?'

Yes, indeed. More beer. How else to survive this nonsense until he could politely escape? 'Don't stint!' he ordered the helpful servant manning the impressive row of kegged beer barrels that marched along the edge of Aistan's trampled lawn. 'Not too much foam.'

Refortified, and beginning to wonder where Lindara had got to, he followed in the wake of the parroty courtiers and wound his way through Aistan's bee-swarmed formal gardens, heading for the lake. Encouraged by the fine weather, marigolds and daisies and pansies and fetch-me-fancies bloomed colourfully riotous in their neatly tended beds. Elsewhere in Clemen the lack of rain had left fields and gardens alike parched. But Aistan had coin enough to spare for servants who were tasked to keep his gardens hand-watered. Scenting the warm air, the succulence of salt-packed beef roasting in the coalpits dug for the occasion on the gardens' far side, near the clipped yew-hedge maze.

Breathing deep of a good feast's promise, Humbert patted his blue velvet belly, and smiled.

Cloud-reflected and limpid, the estate's small, ornamental lake sat like a mirror on the far side of the rambling country manor house Aistan called home – when he wasn't resident in Eaglerock, attending council meetings and overseeing duchy matters. Usually there were black swans floating on the lake's unruffled surface, looking down their red beaks like haughty Danetto courtesans.

But the water jousting dwarves had driven them away.

'Fuck,' Humbert muttered, heedless of the beer dribbling out of his tilted tankard. 'Should ever a man live so long to see such trumpery goings-on?'

With the cultivated lawn sloping towards the lake's muddy edge, he could see comfortably well over the heads of Aistan's pointing, laughing guests. He thought Lindara must be among them, but instead of searching her out, as he'd meant, he stared with horrified fascination at the mumpery Aistan had decreed must entertain the day. Or perhaps his youngest daughter had decreed it, in which case Vidar, by marrying her, was about to be punished in a most satisfying way.

Since warhorses rarely swam, or came equipped with oars, the jousting dwarves – in two short teams of four – rode each in a long, narrow skiff barely more water-worthy than a hollowed out log. Sunlight dazzled on the jingling silver bells sewn to their silly, pointed felt caps, their puffed, striped sleeves, the striped hose covering their short, bandy legs and into their long, plaited beards. One team affronted the eye in saffron yellow and hunter green, the other sported garments of wincing puce and peacock blue. Three dwarves from each side frothed the lake with churning oars. The fourth dwarf stood in his skiff's prow, a padded, beribboned wicker lance clutched hamfisted and defiant in hands no larger than a child's. Urged on by the eager courtiers lining the lake's shore, the skiffs wallowed towards each other with all the grace of drunken sows.

Shaking his head, Humbert noticed he'd spilled nearly half his beer onto the grass at his feet. With a ripe curse he tipped what he hadn't wasted neatly down his throat.

'Huzzah! Huzzah!' Eaglerock's courtiers cried. 'Huzzah! An unseating!'

Startled, he looked again at the lake. Now there was an empty skiff rocking upon it, and four bedraggled dwarves in the water, waving green and yellow arms in the air. Floating forlorn beside them, four green and yellow felt caps stitched with silver bells too waterlogged now to make a joyous noise. The other team of dwarves, victorious, leant overboard in their dismay.

Humbert raised an eyebrow. So there was one question answered. It seemed dwarves couldn't swim.

A rallying cry from Roric's courtiers. Then five bold young men plunged out of the crowd and into the lake, splashing their way to the waving, spluttering dwarves. Cheers and laughter and hilarious advice accompanied the gallant rescue. Four of the courtiers thrashed back to shore towing a dwarf each behind him, safely anchored by his soggy, plaited beard. The fifth courtier pushed the other skiff in, loudly urged on by the dwarves who'd won the joust and in doing so appeared to have lost the wherewithal to row.

Jubilation as the rescued dwarves were carried unharmed to dry ground, as their triumphant, diminutive brothers joined them, as all eight little men were passed from hand to grasping hand and tossed overhead, to shouts of delight. And then the deep sounding of a gong from the ivy-covered manor house.

Time to feast the betrothed couple with salt-roasted beef and rich wine and every mouth-watering delicacy Aistan's kitchens could devise.

Humbert at last found his elusive daughter as he took a seat at Aistan's elaborately decorated high trestle, placed upon a makeshift dais in the manor house's large rear courtyard. They'd travelled to Aistan's estate together, in the ducal coach, but no sooner had a servant handed her down its steps than Lindara had flitted off to mingle with the lords and ladies of the court.

'My lord,' she said, as he wrangled his way onto the low bench beside her. 'Do you enjoy yourself?'

He grunted. 'I suppose 'tis better than riding a hobbled horse through the Marches.'

'As excellent as that?' She laughed. 'I'm sure Aistan would be glad to hear it.'

Aistan, flanked by his mousey daughter and lame Vidar, was playing his part as host, moving from trestle to trestle. Even though the groom-to-be was Godebert's sour, crippled son, he seemed pleased enough the girl was about to wed. More pleased than she, if her sallow face were any guide. Those years spent in the company of pious women behind high exarchite walls had done her no favours. She looked thin inside her costly gown, as though the jewel-crusted violet velvet was a burden. The twined gold-and-silver circlet about her brow seemed too heavy for her to bear. And Vidar? He looked weary. Oddly sad behind his smile. Just as Roric looked, these days.

Reminded, Humbert frowned at his daughter. Lowered his voice and leaned close. 'What are you doing, girl, that Roric is miserable in your marriage?'

Startled as though dagger-pricked, Lindara let slip the manchet she'd plucked from a passing servant's tray. The soft white bread fell to her trencher, turning swiftly dark red with beef juices.

'My lord,' she said, teeth gritted, 'this isn't the time or place.'

Their long trestle was crowded with Aistan's most important guests: his wife, his two older daughters and their lords, Roric's other councillors and their wives. And of course that cockshite Ercole, still clinging leechlike to the small portion of power he'd inherited from Argante. Still not married, but rumoured to be wooing somewhere. Before them, crowding the courtyard, Aistan's less favoured guests raised their voices in vigorous conversation and loud, bawdy amusement. There were no strangers here, no foreigners, no exarchites and therefore no restraint. After the tense and moody atmosphere at court, here was a chance to abandon dignity and push cares to one side. Added to their chorus, the polite murmurings of well-trained manor staff, the cheerful pipings of three boy squires, and the gaudy minstrelling of musicians hired to brighten the festivities.

'We'll not be overheard in this raucous,' Humbert said, frowning. 'So give me answer. Why is Roric unhappy?'

With a brittle smile his daughter thrust her spoiled bread at another passing servant. 'My lord, he lacks a son.'

'So I've noticed.'

Colour high, she pretended interest in her wine. 'Roric complains of me?'

'Has he cause to?'

'My lord, I—'

'Your Grace! My lord Humbert!' Aistan, approaching, still in the company of the betrothed couple. 'How do you enjoy the day?'

'Aistan.' Humbert raised his goblet, brimming with wine. 'The day is most fine, as is your hospitality. My lady Kennise, 'tis a warming thing to see you so happy. Vidar—'

Rich in pearls and brown velvet, Vidar sketched a twisted bow. The scars dug into his face were silvery pale in the sunlight. 'Humbert.' Another bow. 'Your Grace.'

As Lindara murmured something indifferently appropriate, looking past Vidar instead of at him, Humbert crooked a confiding finger. Vidar took a cautious half-step closer to the trestle.

'Humbert?'

'Many of us thought you'd abandoned any hope of marriage, my lord,' he said, expansively genial. 'But it seems we were wrong, and I'm right glad of it.' Smiling in his beard, he felt a rare burst of good will towards the man who'd once foolishly thought himself good enough for Lindara. 'The lady Kennise will grace your table and be a fine mother to many sons, I've no doubt. Sons that will serve Clemen as their father serves it. With honour.'

Vidar's lips twisted into a familiar, sardonic smile. 'You're too kind, my lord.'

'I'm as kind as I need to be, Vidar. No more and no less.'

'Don't be alarmed, Kennise,' said Lindara, breaking the taut silence. 'My lord father's blunt manner is famed throughout the duchy. After six years skirmishing together on council, you can be sure Lord Vidar knows he only jests.'

Vidar bowed again, his unscarred eye glittering. 'Indeed, Your Grace.'

'As do I,' said Aistan's daughter, blushing. 'For you'll hear nothing but praise for the great lord Humbert beneath our roof. Your Grace—'

Lindara reached a hand to the girl across the food-laden trestle. 'Now, Kennise. Didn't I tell you already that I'm Lindara to my friends?'

'Yes, you did. I'm sorry, Your – *Lindara*.'

'Excellent,' Lindara said, squeezing the girl's hand then letting go. 'Vidar—'

'Your Grace?'

'You must take special care of your betrothed. She's a dear, sweet lady deserving of every kindness.'

Aistan, his neat beard turned mostly grey, rested a heavily ringed hand on Vidar's shoulder. 'Vidar treats her like a hothouse bloom, Your Grace, so gentle and considerate. My beloved daughter couldn't have found a more perfect knight – and no loving father could find a better man to claim his child.'

Lindara's reply was lost in a fresh gale of laughter from the feasting courtiers as the water jousting dwarves came tumbling into the courtyard, chased by a pack of tiny, yapping dogs. The miserable little curs were dressed in spangled green felt harnesses sewed over with yet more silver bells.

With one of his rare smiles, Aistan stepped back then nudged his daughter and Vidar closer together. 'Take your seats, my dears. Eat and drink your fill. The feast is being held in your honour, after all.'

'My lord,' said Vidar, taking Kennise by the hand. 'You don't join us?'

Aistan nodded. 'In a moment. I'd take Humbert aside first. Humbert?'

'Of course.' Hastily spearing a slice of beef on the point of his knife, Humbert levered himself off the trestle's bench and shifted with Aistan to stand against a nearby ivy-covered brick wall. As he chewed his meat he eyed the ridiculous antics of the dwarves and their rattish dogs, unimpressed.

'Don't blame me,' said Aistan, raising his hands. 'They're my wife's doing. All the way from Maletti, they've travelled. Favourites at the Exarch's Palace, I'm told.'

'And still the Exarch could part with them,' he said, scowling. 'Hard to believe.'

Aistan sighed. 'Ah well. They make Kennise laugh, and that's something. There was a time I feared she'd never laugh again.'

Well, if that was the case best she laugh her fill while she could. For surely marriage to crippled Vidar would be no laughing matter. If Harald's rough handling hadn't soured the girl on bedsport, doubtless Vidar's maimed body would. But that wasn't anything he could say to her father. Doubtless Aistan was simply relieved to finally get Kennise off his hands.

'You wanted a word?' he said, around another mouthful of beef. 'Not more trouble brewing, I hope.'

The yappy dogs were turning somersaults and leaping through the dwarves' looped arms. Laughter filled the three-sided courtyard, the clapping of hands, the stamping of feet.

'Have you heard from Roric?' said Aistan, turning a robed shoulder to the mayhem. 'When will he return?'

Humbert wiped his knife on his forearm. 'Not from Roric, but Arthgallo. The leech says our duke's megrims still plague him and Roric's to stay solitary in his country leechery a few more days yet.'

'I don't like it, Humbert,' said Aistan, fingering his beard. 'Is Roric sickly? Is this why—' He pulled a face. 'Forgive me. But is this why your daughter's womb has yielded no fruit?'

It was the first time anyone had dared ask the question to his face. There were whispers, of course. Eaglerock's corridors and passageways and chambers echoed with anxious, circumspect speculation about why Clemen's duke still lacked an heir. He ignored it. Did his best to shield Roric from it – though the boy, no fool, knew as well as he did that tongues wagged more and more.

But if Aistan, of all men, was prepared to openly confront the question . . .

'Are you challenging the validity of Roric's marriage, my lord?'

'No!' Aistan said quickly. 'I supported it at the time and I still support it, Humbert. Roric had to wed, without delay, to help quash Berardine's intentions and calm Clemen after the turmoil of Harald's death.'

'He did,' Humbert agreed, frowning. The dwarves were dancing on the trestles now, their bright red booted heels hammering so hard the platters of beef and pies and braised lettuce were leaping. The yappy dogs danced with them. Any moment one of those hairy runts was going to piss in the wine, he knew it. How many of the little shites could he spit on a sword with a single thrust? Surely Aistan had a spare blade laying around here somewhere.

'And I thought,' Aistan added, 'that your daughter, a well-bred virgin, was eminently suitable to be Roric's wife.'

Which meant what? That if Harald hadn't debauched his youngest girl, Kennise would this day be duchess of Clemen and Lindara would be the one struggling to fuck with a half-blind cripple?

'My daughter is still eminently suitable,' he said mildly, since this was no good time to offer Aistan offence. He shifted his gaze to her, beautiful and self-contained and talking amiably with Aistan's wife. 'As for her womb, Arthgallo assures me 'tis fertile. And so is Roric's seed. Our duke is a trifle worn down by Clemen's burdens. That's the nub of his trouble. Arthgallo will soon put him to rights, Aistan. You'll see.'

Frowning, Aistan brushed crumbs from his doublet. 'I know you place great faith in this leech of yours,' he said at last. 'But I must tell you, I fear – and I'm not alone in this – the matter might be beyond his skill. We can't forget that Roric is – was – Harald's cousin. And Harald's seed proved unreliable.'

How discomfiting to hear his own dark doubts given tongue. Especially by a man as sober as Aistan. But he wasn't about to concede anything. Not until his back was pressed hard to the wall.

'Harald's seed, I grant you. But Berold's never was. And his son, Roric's sire, my dear friend Guimar, bred true. As will Roric. You may depend on it.'

'I hope you're right,' Aistan said. 'For it's not just me depending on it. Clemen's people are desperate for an heir. For a reason to celebrate! Especially now, in the midst of so much hardship.'

'Which we both know can be pressed home to Cassinia.' Humbert turned a stern gaze back to his host. 'We'd be suffering far less did they not keep a poisonous dagger-point pricked against Clemen's heart.'

A stricken look passed over Aistan's face, wiping away any lingering joy for his daughter. 'Indeed,' he murmured. 'The regents have proven most vindictive. Far more so than—'

'Than you'd heard?' He snorted. 'Does your memory fail you, Aistan? You're the one who warned us of them when Berardine offered Clemen her daughter.'

'Look,' said Aistan, jerking his chin. 'The dwarves are done with their madcappery. Excuse me, Humbert. I must thank them, and encourage my guests to generosity.'

Under cover of Aistan's speechmaking, Humbert took his seat again and filled his belly with partridge pie. There was beef remaining, but he didn't trust it. Not after those yappy dogs. The dwarves handed round their felt caps not drowned in the lake, and Aistan's guests filled them with silver coins and golden hair pins and the cheapest rings from their fingers. For himself, he wasn't about to part with so much as a grey hair plucked from his beard. Only one of the dogs fixed him with its beady eyes and growled until he surrendered, and tossed in a copper nib.

After that came the malmsy-soaked damsons, the sugared figs and the apricots swimming in syrup. He ate his fill of those, gladly, and washed them down with ice-chilled sweet wine.

With that the feast ended, but there were more festivities planned. Aistan and his wife and his unwed daughter and Vidar led the revellers out of the courtyard and onto the grand lawn, where the minstrels struck up a dancing tune. Excusing himself on account of a bad knee, Humbert folded himself grateful onto a stout stool set near the yew-hedge maze entrance, accepted a foaming tankard from a servant, and settled to watch.

It was a pretty sight, he'd not argue. The ladies in their jewel-sparkled, colourful gowns. The lords in their colourful doublets, with jewels in the garters they wore to keep their hose from slipping down. Light-stepping and full of mirth and wine, ringed fingers clapping, heads tossing, elbows akimbo and knees snapping high, like palfreys. Even Vidar wasn't disgracing himself entirely. A miracle. Though his stiffly correct holding of Aistan's daughter, and the girl's shrinking response, didn't promise much in the way of a passionate marriage.

Lulled almost to drowsing by syruped apricots and beer, Humbert watched his daughter dance a *timmory* with Aistan and felt a pinch of regret, that Roric wasn't here. Let the court see the boy dance with Lindara and for certain many whispering tongues would be stilled.

The music changed. Time to take a new partner. Aistan handed Lindara to Vidar. Circling the trampled lawn, Eaglerock's courtiers continued merry, with laughter and teasing and not a little horseplay. Now they danced a whirling *feranti*, the kind of dance to make an exarchite wag a chiding finger. Arms circling lissom waists. Hands clasping hands. Faces scandalously close.

Humbert sat up abruptly, like a man doused in winter pond water. Step for step with Lindara, Vidar was dancing like a whole man. Dancing and smiling. Not dutiful, but tender. And Lindara – Lindara –

Throat scalded with bile, he watched his daughter betraying Roric. Every inviting step, every leap, every laughing curtsy and hot glance a treachery. And when the music changed again, when it was time for his daughter and her crippled lover to part, he watched their pressed palms linger in a slow, sliding kiss. Praise the faeries or the spirits or even the Exarch's god that the court was too breathless and giddy from dancing to notice them.

But he'd noticed.

Blinder even than Vidar, Humbert stumbled into the seclusion of the yew-hedge maze, bent over, and vomited up every mouthful he'd swallowed of Aistan's food and drink.

The strumpeting whore. I'll kill her for this.

He wasted no time in learning the whole truth of his daughter's wanton misbehaviour. The matter had to be discreetly uncovered in all its ugliness, then disposed of before Roric's return from Cassinia. In case he'd not been the only one whose eyes were opened during that dance. He set his best man to the filthy task. Egann. Stubborn, reliable and patient, his loyalty not to be doubted, his skill as a clan-destine without compare.

Four nights later, seeing him lurking in a shadowed corner beyond the council chamber, Humbert crooked a finger in passing. Egann fell into step beside him, his felt-soled boots whisper quiet on the worn stone floor.

'Well?'

'I fear 'tis worse than you suspected, m'lord,' Egann said, his voice conspirator soft. 'I did find foul doings, blacker by far than a naughty wife. I'm right sad for it.'

327

And that was an impertinence, but he was too heartsore to make a meal of it. 'Were you seen?'

'Not by any soul what counts.'

Chilled despite his furred robe, and washed through by a sudden wave of weakness, Humbert stopped short of the torchlit staircase before him and fumbled at the cold wall to keep himself steady.

'Foul doings, you say.' Clammy sweat damped his skin. 'How foul, man? What kind?'

Egann advanced three steps down the spiral stairs and cocked an ear, listening for approaching footsteps. Satisfied they remained alone, he looked up.

'The witching kind, m'lord.'

'*Sorcery?*' He pressed a fist to his roiling belly. Though he'd hardly eaten since the feast at Aistan's, still he wanted to be sick. 'Are you certain?'

'Your daughter's maid led me straight to the witch's haunt, m'lord. Down in the township, where she pretends to deal in harmless herbs and suchlike.'

'And Lindara's embroiled? You're sure of it? Couldn't the maid be—'

'No, m'lord. There be no mistake.'

He wanted to weep like a woman. Howl like a gored hound. 'The maid. Where is she now?'

'Out of the way, m'lord. She won't be squealing of this to the duchess.'

'And the witch?'

'Chained and waiting.'

'Take me to her,' he said, standing straight again. 'I'd hear what this sorcerous bitch has to say.'

Eaglerock's dungeons honeycombed the rock on which the castle was built. Disobedient servants were held there, kept cold, fed stale bread and water, punishment for petty crimes. Lawless men of the township, sometimes, when their guild masters sought harsher revenge than a day in pillory, were pelted with dead rats and rotten eggs. Men were whipped in the dungeons, suffered their pilfering fingers to be broken, their lying tongues pierced through, or cut out in the worst cases. Rapists lost their cock and balls to a heated knife then were hung in chains, dripping hot tar, till their joints popped. Other men, caught plotting, were made to long for such minor pains.

As Egann barred the cell's heavy door, Humbert stared at the woman secured by wrist and ankle to the wall. Smoky torchlight showed her passably beautiful, though she was sickly pale and her hair was shorn closer than a sheep after fleecing. Her face was bruised, one cheek swollen. A cut on her lower lip, scabbed with dry blood. Her embroidered linen chemise was torn, revealing generous, blue-veined breasts marred with more bruises. But her tits didn't stir him. He was years too old for lust.

'I know you,' she said, her voice oddly accented. 'Lord Humbert.'

He nodded. 'And I know you. *Witch*.'

'I'm no witch. I'm a herbary woman. The only magic in me is what lies atwixt my legs.' She thrust her hips, obscenely suggestive. 'Shall I magic you, my lord?'

'I'd fuck a dead goat first. What is your business with the duchess of Clemen?'

The witch's green eyes widened as she feigned mystified surprise. 'We have no business.'

'You were taken with her maid. The girl gave you coin. What was it for?'

When she didn't answer, he raised his hand. 'Egann?'

'Her shop in the township were rank with sorcerous filth, m'lord. Men's parts sealed in jars, I found. Dried dog tongues. Unnatural creatures. Stinking pills and potions. And a baby's head in a box.'

He turned, revolted. '*What?*'

'It fell to dust when I touched it.' Egann shuddered. 'But m'lord, I know what I saw.'

'This other foul muck. You have it safe?'

'Yes, m'lord. And the creatures are dead.'

'Good.' He turned back. 'Look at me, witch.'

The heavy iron chains holding her clanked as she rolled her head against the cell's stone wall, then slowly opened her eyes.

'Tell me what I wish to know and Egann will snap your neck clean.'

She spat at him, sneering.

'Egann,' he said, and stepped back.

Not even a witch could hold out against a tarred, knotted rope wielded by a man of experienced purpose. Flogged naked, flogged bloody, in the end she broke.

Sickened, Humbert listened to the witch's foul babblings. Learned what she and Lindara had done to Roric, and wept. When the witch was done, reduced to pulped flesh and pain and keening like a madwoman, he left her to Egann and went to find his daughter.

'My lord,' said Lindara, rising from her settle as he shoved her chamber door wide. ''Tis very late. Is something amiss?'

'Leave us,' Humbert commanded her gaggle of shocked attendants.

Cheeks flushed, Lindara nodded. 'You may go, ladies. And be sure to close the door.'

Alone with his daughter, he looked around the richly appointed room. 'Amiss, Lindara? Yes. You could say that.'

'Is it Roric?' she said, breathless. 'Have Cassinia's regents harmed him?'

'Don't pretend you care about Roric,' he said, his face stiff, his voice chilled. 'I saw you with that cockshite Vidar, all but fucking him on Aistan's lawn as you danced.'

'My lord, you're monstrous unfair! Whatever you think you saw, you're mistaken.'

No, no. He wasn't about to let her outface him. 'I'm not,' he said grimly. 'I know you're cuckolding Roric.'

'My lord!' Her eyes glittered with feigned indignation. 'How can you slander me so? I *never—*'

'*Hold your lying tongue, harlot!* There's no point denying it. Your maid's taken and the witch has confessed all!'

For a moment she stood there, frozen. Then she sank again to the settle. Clasped her slender, elegant hands in her lap. 'I see.'

'You say you're not spreading your legs for Vidar? Then who d'you spread them for, girl? Whose bastard would you have Roric raise as Clemen's next duke?'

'Oh,' she said, lifting an eyebrow. 'So now you object to bastards?'

If he slapped her once he'd keep on slapping, till she was as raw and bloody as her dead witch. To be safe, he moved aside.

'Hold your tongue, then. It doesn't matter. Whoever the cockshite is, your trullish legs are closed to him now.'

'My maid,' she said, after a furious silence. 'Merget. You say you have her?'

'I do.'

'Did she—'

'Betray you? No. More's the pity for her. I had the little bitch followed, after I saw you and Vidar dancing.'

A marble statue, Lindara sat there. Not a hint of remorse. 'How resourceful.'

'You don't ask how she is.'

'Does it matter?'

And this was his daughter. Revolted, Humbert folded his arms. 'Fetch me the witch's potions, girl. Keep none back, for these apartments will be searched. And in the morning you'll see Arthgallo. He'll leech you clean of the filth you've swallowed.' And he'd see Roric purged too, though convincing Arthgallo to lie about the reason would be no mean feat. 'Then you'll fuck with your husband till you give him an heir.'

Her chin lifted. 'And if I won't?'

'*You will*. Or so help me . . .'

A tear trailed down her bloodless cheek. 'Do you mean to tell Roric?'

'And break his heart?' Despairing, he shook his head. 'I don't understand you, girl. For six years that boy has loved you and defended you and forgiven you his lack of a son. And all the while – *all the while* . . .' He breathed out, hard. 'But you'd best be warned, Lindara. I'm not so forgiving. Cross me again – or breathe a word of this to Roric – *to any soul* – and I'll see you're put down like the bitch you are. Better by far that he mourn your corpse than learn the truth.'

The tear had dried. She stared up at him, saying nothing. Her eyes were cold, and defiant.

'Fetch those potions,' he said hoarsely. 'The sight of you makes me sick.'

She obeyed, filling a small, tooled leather chest with the witch's wickedness. Then in silence she handed the chest to him, and in silence he took it.

'Humbert,' she said, as he reached the chamber door, the chest hidden beneath his robe. 'You call me a harlot – but if I am, it's what you made me. I never wanted Roric, but you forced me to take him. When you should've been a loving father, you played the brothel-keeper instead. So if you're looking for someone to blame, look in the mirror. My conscience is clear.'

Halted, he turned his head until he could see her from the corner of his tear-blurred eye.

'Give Clemen's duke a son, Lindara. Or die in chains like the witch. Those are your only choices. And don't think to run. You'd never escape the castle.'

He banged the chamber door shut on her wordless rage.

CHAPTER TWENTY

Through the long, dragging night, as she restlessly paced her bedchamber, Lindara held fast to one small consolation – that no matter what Merget might confess, she could never point an accusing finger at Vidar. The silly girl had no idea of her mistress's trysts with a lover. All she'd ever done was collect Damikah's pills and potions and bring them back to the castle. As for the witch . . . yes, her confession was calamity. But though she'd known there was a lover, she'd never been told his name. So Vidar must be safe, surely. Not even Humbert would dare persecute a man whose crime he might suspect, but couldn't prove.

Unless he finds a way to snatch Vidar into secret keeping and there torments him till he breaks, and tells the truth.

Outrageous, yes, but she wouldn't put anything past her father.

With his sons dead, all Humbert cared about was becoming grandsire of a duke. He'd not flinch at committing more underhanded brutality. Not if it meant revenging himself on the man who'd nearly cost him his dream. And Vidar had no family to speak of. No one with power to stand for him against the second-most powerful man in Clemen. Aistan wasn't family yet. Let one whiff of scandal touch him – let Humbert so much as *hint* at matters unsavoury – and Vidar would never wed with pathetic, dowdy Kennise. Aistan would discard him faster than a cook throwing rotten meat into the midden. Which meant Vidar's only hope was that he'd be protected by Humbert's need to protect himself.

At least, that's what she believed. Had to believe. For if she couldn't believe it she'd break to pieces.

Eventually, exhausted, she stumbled against a carved bedpost and clung to it, a shipwrecked survivor in the stormiest of seas. Merget taken. Damikah dead. And with her last moontime proof of an empty womb, not even the hope of Vidar's child to sustain her. Six years of secret striving laid to waste in a matter of hours.

Humbert saw us dancing. We betrayed ourselves dancing. One lingering look, one private smile, and we're undone?

Oh, she could weep. And so was she punished for encouraging Roric to discourage sour exarchite prohibitions against harmless frolicking.

Dawn came at last. Slumped on the floor at the foot of the bed, wrapped in fox-fur, she heard the stirring of her ladies beyond the chamber door. Someone knocked, tentatively, and called her by name. When she didn't answer there was another knock, more determined. She wanted to scream at the ever-present, chattering magpies.

Go away. Leave me be. Don't you know my life is ruined?

But if she didn't let them in to help with her chamber pot, to bathe her face and breasts and arms with rosewater, brush her hair and braid it with pearl-sewn ribbons, lace her into linen and fine wool, garter silk hose upon her legs, fit her feet with velvet slippers, drape her bodice with gold chains and prick pearls through her ears, they'd shriek an uproar to bring Eaglerock castle crashing down upon their heads.

Humbert returned just as a kitchen steward was setting out her morning meal of manchet, curd cheese, apricot paste and cider.

'Be gone,' he said to the steward, and her ladies, jerking his thumb at the outer chamber's carved and gilded doors. 'Her Grace will call when she needs you.'

She might be Clemen's duchess, but Humbert was master of any room he chose to enter. Her people obeyed without comment. Only two would meet her gaze. They might be magpies, but they weren't dullards. They knew something was amiss.

It galled her to sit, but her legs were shaking. All her self-control was in her face, so he might not see her afraid. Had she loved him once? Possibly. As a little girl. In those long-ago days when she could amuse him. Before he saw her as his pawn, to be moved about the chessboard of his life on a whim.

Spine sword-straight, breathing ordered, she carefully arranged her dark blue skirts. Watched him from beneath lowered lashes as he helped himself to her bread and cheese, and her cider. Often he dressed in bright, lavishly jewelled doublet and robes, but this morning his clothing was sober. Dark brown. Dull green. Only a hint of flashing bronze. He wore a flat black velvet cap with the smallest curling white feather, and only one heavy gold ring. His signet ring, used to seal the fate of anyone he chose to mislike. Eyes narrowed, considering her, he licked a smear of soft cheese from his thumb.

'Your maid's dead.'

Though she tried, she couldn't hide her shudder. 'Did you kill her?'

'No. The bitch hanged herself. Sometime in the night.'

A buzzing in her ears as the chamber whirled drunkenly around her. A horrible looseness in her bowels. Would she need a change of dress?

'Poor Merget,' she said, hearing her voice alarmingly distant. 'I'll give coin to one of the exarchs, so he can sing for her soul.'

Her father's calloused thumb and finger caught her chin, forced up her head. 'Not that it makes any difference,' he growled. 'Not with your witch having told me all I never wanted to know.'

If she pulled away from him he'd strike her. She could see it in his angry, resentful eyes. So she lowered her gaze, submissive, the perfect picture of a chastened child.

'Egann is here,' he said, releasing her. 'He'll escort you to Arthgallo. After you return—'

She risked an upwards glance. 'You don't escort me yourself?'

'There's a council meeting,' he said. 'With Roric gone, I must preside. Egann has my confidence. I warn you, girl. Don't test him. After you return from the leech, you'll not set foot beyond these chambers till I give you leave.' He raised a finger. 'Which won't be before Roric's home again, so you'd best have plenty of embroidery to pass the time.'

Was she duchess of Clemen, or no more than a servant? Staring at her father's broad, robed chest, not daring to risk him seeing her contempt, she wondered if he ever thought of that. If he ever, if only once, stopped to think of how he spoke to her.

She thought not. The great lord Humbert knew as much of courtesy as a gadfly did of swordplay.

'And what do you suggest I tell my ladies?'

He glared, beard trembling as he worked his broad jaw. 'That your maid was found dead this morning in the township. That you're sore dismayed by this news and seek a remedy for your grief. And that you'd bear the grief alone, so they should quit Eaglerock for the day. I want them gone. I'd not have them squawking while these chambers are searched.'

Or spreading inconvenient gossip, either. 'Is that all? My lord?'

'For now. Eat your breakfast. Arthgallo's expecting you.'

She remained seated after he left, and stirred only when her ladies fluttered in . . . and it was time to tell more lies.

'My lords, I must protest!' Scarwid, red-faced and bolder than once he'd used to be, slapped the arm of his chair to underscore his unhappiness. ''Tis all very well for you, with your estates lying safely south of the Muckle River. But for those of us north of the Muckle, where blistermouth took two out of every three sheep, if it weren't for the exarchite houses there'd be even more fear and hunger to contend with! And you'd have this council thank them with another tax? For shame!'

His fellow councillors launched into heated protest at being so berated. Seated in Roric's chair, facing them, Humbert took a deep breath and willed himself calm. Nigh on two hours he'd been trapped in the council chamber with his contentious colleagues, who of late could scarce bid each other good morning without coming to blows. It seemed Clemen's mounting woes were become some kind of pestilence, infecting Eaglerock's court with fear and division. A pity he couldn't call upon Arthgallo to give every man here a purge.

Arthgallo. Reminded, he quelled his own fears. Last night he'd despatched Egann to the leech with the witch's foul pills and potions and a brief note explaining Lindara's use of them and how she must be safely purged. Once he was done with this mumpery he'd hie himself to the leechery so he might learn the worst outcome of his daughter's treacherous conduct. He could only pray she'd not poisoned herself past any normal use. And as for Roric . . .

Arthgallo will see him right. He's more than a match for a dead Osfahr witch.

Heart painfully thudding, he wiped suddenly damp palms down the front of his doublet. Then he stood, commanding the attention of Clemen's squabbling councillors.

'*Clap tongue, my lords!* You sound like a rabble of Khafuri bazaar vendors!' Having gained their affronted attention he sat again, heavily frowning. 'State your objections one at a time, if you please.'

A moment of silence, as they stared at each other. Then Aistan steepled his fingers. 'A question for you, Scarwid. The blistermouth outbreak. Can you tell us how it started?'

'How should I know?' said Scarwid, harassed and offended. 'Am I a shepherd? And what has it to do with—'

'Everything,' Vidar said curtly. 'Since the Exarch's priests are to blame for Clemen's loss of more than half its flocks.'

Vidar. Curdled by a surge of hatred so overpowering, so visceral, that for a moment he couldn't breathe, Humbert stared at the floor. Never would he believe Lindara's denials. It was this fuck, this cockshite, she'd turned traitor for against Roric. All that remained to do was find a way to punish him – without revealing his crime.

And he would, no doubt of it. He'd not lived to a ripe age without cunning and sly wit.

Scarwid was spluttering. '—to prove such a rank accusation, Vidar! I promise you the exarchites in my district are good, decent men!'

Vidar was staring at Scarwid with his one cynical eye. 'You defend them most passionately, Scarwid. Are you a convert to their mopish cause?'

'And if I am?' Scarwid's face reddened. 'What's my spiritual life to you, I'd like to know?'

'Nothing,' Humbert said loudly, before the cockshite could reply. 'In Clemen a man's soul is his own business.'

'His soul, perhaps, but not his sheep,' Vidar said. 'The exarchite houses north of the Muckle River brought in animals from Danetto already sick with blistermouth. The pestilence spread from their holdings.'

Faugh. Knowing now what he knew, if Vidar told him it was raining he'd send a squire to make sure. 'What folderol d'you talk now? Beasts entering Clemen from other lands are inspected in Eaglerock harbour by an animal leech. Blistermouth has ready signs, even before the pustules form. Do you tell me our harbour leeches are blind, not to see them?'

'Blind or bought,' said Ercole the indolent, sprawled in his chair. 'And my coin is on bought. The harbour's a hotbed of corruption. Any fool knows that.'

'Not this fool,' Humbert growled. 'Watch your step, Ercole.'

Dead Argante's half-brother hesitated, then waved a compliant hand. Obedient still, but these days inclined towards brief outbursts of rebellion. Humbert curled his lip. Rumour had it Ercole was eyeing Master Blane's orphaned granddaughter for a wife. The Bartrem girl, like Scarwid, hailed from north of the Muckle, but with her father's death she'd shifted south to bide with Blane and his wife. The thought of the merchant wedding her to Ercole churned his belly. The last thing Roric needed was that little shite marrying into rich pastures.

But he couldn't fret on it now. Let Ercole's ambitions be a problem for another day.

Shifting attention to this day's problem, he levelled a look at Vidar. 'Talk is cheap, my lord. What proof prompts you to make these accusations?'

337

Vidar reached into his doublet and withdrew a folded, sealed sheet of heavy paper. 'This proof, my lord. Though I doubt corruption in the harbour's so bad – yet – as Ercole fears, still for some time I've had misgivings. So I looked into it, discreetly, and found this.'

'You looked into it?' Humbert said, taking the proffered document. 'Without bothering to inform His Grace?'

'Vidar raised his concerns with me,' said Aistan, mildly enough – though his eyes were sharp. 'And upon sober reflection, I advised him to do as he thought best.'

'You didn't advise him to raise these concerns with Clemen's duke?'

Aistan smoothed the edge of his beard. 'As demonstrated by his continued absence, Humbert, Clemen's duke has enough proven troubles to deal with. I'd not care to burden him further without cause. Would you?'

They were seated side by side, Aistan and the cockshite who'd soon be made his goodson. Now they stared at him as one man, and as one man dared him to stir the matter more. And because he couldn't – not here, at least, and not now – he was forced to let them believe they'd bested him.

'Even so,' he said, feeling every muscle in his body harden with resentment. 'You set a poor example, my lords. *I'd* advise you not make it a habit.'

'And I'd know what gave you cause to look meanly upon the exarchites in my district,' said Scarwid. 'Unless you want to deny persecution, and claim you but stumbled by accident upon—'

'I did learn the truth by accident, yes,' Vidar said, shifting to look at Scarwid. 'But that doesn't make it any less true. And if you must know, Scarwid, I have for some time worried over the exarchites' encroaching ways in Clemen. They—'

'Oh, yes,' said Scarwid, scornful. 'Such wanton wickedness, the exarchites' charity! We should be hiding ourselves under our beds in terror at their generosity!'

'It's not their charity I fear,' Vidar snapped, 'but their deceit.' He gestured at the paper he'd handed over. 'In his hand Humbert holds signed confessions by two of the harbour's animal leeches, who were paid to wink at the proper inspections for the exarchites' sheep.'

Scarwid was near to leaping from his chair. 'And who paid them, Vidar? Can you prove it was Clemen's exarchites? For that makes *no* sense. In case it 'scaped your notice, my lord, this epidemic of blistermouth has hurt the exarchites along with the rest of us!'

Vidar shrugged. 'Perhaps. And perhaps not. If their intent was to ingratiate themselves with the north's lords and its ordinary people, I'd say they're doing right well. For here you are, Scarwid, a respected northern baron and one of the duke's councillors, defending their honour as though it were your own!'

Leaving Roric's lords to bicker, Humbert broke the wax seal on the document and swiftly scanned it. What he read left him sickened. He'd never believe Ercole's careless accusation of rampant harbour corruption, but it seemed Vidar's assertion was true. Or true enough that the council would need to probe the matter further, and officially. At the very best there'd been mistakes made. And at worst . . .

But Scarwid was right. Why would the exarchites bring ruin upon themselves? Unless *Vidar* was right – which meant someone was playing a deeper game. But was Clemen the purpose? Or only a pawn?

He looked up. 'Vidar. Where are they now, these self-confessed rancid leeches?'

'I have them,' said Aistan. 'They were taken into custody upon my authority and are being held under guard till they can be more strictly questioned. Here, of course. In Eaglerock's dungeons.'

Silence, as the rest of the council stared. Feeling a slow prickle of sweat beneath his sober doublet and robe, Humbert deliberately relaxed his hold on Vidar's proof before his fingers crushed it.

'Taken into your custody when?'

'Last night.' Aistan spread his hands. 'I did try to advise you, Humbert, but you were nowhere to be found.'

'Under the circumstances,' Vidar added, 'we thought a little presumption preferable to these sorry miscreants leaping aboard some outward-bound ship and making their escape before we could bring them to account. Though perhaps . . .' He raised his unscarred eyebrow. 'You disagree?'

'I don't,' Ercole muttered, close to a snigger.

'And I do,' Scarwid said. 'In His Grace's absence Lord Humbert is the council's highest authority. We cannot—'

Aistan frowned at him. 'We can and we must, Scarwid, if Humbert is also absent and the matter is urgent. Or do you recommend that as Clemen's councillors we sit on our hands and do nothing, though we see the duchy in danger?'

'In danger? From two animal leeches? My lord, you—'

'Clap tongue, Scarwid!' Tossing the leeches' confessions onto the floor, Humbert stood. 'I don't care for Aistan's high-handed approach – nor Vidar's – but it's Clemen that matters most. We'd do better to solve this knotty problem than waste our breath in more bickering.'

'I don't call it bickering to challenge this challenge to your authority,' Scarwid retorted. 'When Harald offered me the chance to undermine you, Humbert, I refused him. I'd made you a promise and I honour that promise yet.' He spared Aistan and Vidar an angry glance. 'We northern lords are constant. We don't blow in the breeze.'

'But do you fart in it?' Ercole wondered. 'For that would be expedient, Scarwid, to hide a noisome act within another act not of your making. Isn't that how you've climbed so high? As I recall you stood back and let Harald be—'

Humbert turned on him. 'Not another word, Ercole. There's been enough mischief out of you for one day.' He looked sideways. 'See what you've wrought, Aistan? Is this what you wanted?'

'What I want,' said Aistan, 'is for Roric to take his rightful place in this chamber. Clemen has no need of an absent duke.' Defiant, he swept his gaze around his fellow councillors. 'Is that not so, my lords?'

All of them, even Scarwid, nodded and muttered their assent.

'You see?' Aistan was glaring. 'And you can be sure, Humbert, that if Farland were here he'd say he felt the same. We are *none* of us content with this inconstant state of affairs!'

'There's no *state of affairs*, Aistan,' Humbert retorted, feeling fresh sweat prickle and slide down his spine. 'Inconstant or otherwise. How many times d'you need to hear it? Roric's unwell, and when he's mended he'll return. And who are you to question that? Since when does a subject lord demand explanation of his duke?'

340

'Since that subject lord and his friends gave him his crown,' said Vidar. 'Something it seems you've forgotten, Humbert.'

Another stark silence. Glaring at Lindara's lover, the treacherous cockshite, Humbert found it hard to breathe. Rage was in him, burning his vision red with blood. A good thing there was no sword to hand, else Vidar would be spitted as once he'd spitted a woman crazed with grief.

Scarwid was on his feet. 'My lords, let us collect ourselves, I implore you! We do Clemen a grave disservice to let temper sway us from proper—'

A fisted thudding on the council-chamber door. They all turned at the sound. Then the door swung open to reveal Roric's most trusted steward, Naythn, neat in Eaglerock livery and out of breath from running. Crowding behind him, a travelstained, grim-faced man-at-arms.

Humbert felt his heart sink. 'What's amiss, man?'

'My lord, forgive the intrusion,' Nathyn said, offering a curt bow. 'But I've a man here sent by Lord Wido, in the Marches. Inskip.' He urged the man-at-arms forward. 'Tell Lord Humbert and the council your news.'

Stubble-cheeked Inskip, his build wiry, his skin seasoned like old leather beneath his chain mail and padded doublet, touched dirty fingers to his widow's-peaked forehead in salute.

'My lords. There's been a murder, and more blood spilled on account of it. Lord Wido sends me for to tell you the duke must convene a Crown Court, no delay.'

'A Crown Court?' Humbert echoed. 'That's a drastic request, man. Why can't Wido and Jacott settle this themselves? They have the authority. Indeed, 'tis their purpose.'

The man-at-arms shook his head. 'My lord, ever since that black day Lord Wido's tried reasoning with Harcia, but he has no joy in it. Their Marcher lords cry innocent, they claim they're the ones wronged, and Aimery drags his heels. In truth, I think he waits for Clemen's response.'

'Who's murdered?' said Aistan, rancour forgotten in the face of fresh disaster.

'The wife to one of Clemen's Marcher woodsmen, my lord. Bayard of Harcia's men did come across her lonesome, and thought to make sport of her, against her will. Me and a handful more of Lord Wido's men, we heard her screaming.' Inskip looked down, his face dark with memory. 'But we were too late, my lords. And caught bloody-handed with their britches down and their cocks waving, Bayard's men did their best to keep themselves from justice.'

'And succeeded?' Vidar said sharply. 'For shame.'

Inskip's head jerked up. 'Two of us were killed trying to take them, my lord. Three of them died, resisting. The other three, wounded, did flee. Me and Lord Wido's other man left breathing, we dursn't go after them. By law Clemen can't set foot in the Harcian Marches without leave, as your lordships must know.'

'Yet these Harcian ruffians did not fear to accost a Clemen woman on our soil?'

'My lord, they accosted the woodsman's wife along Marches Way, as is counted no-man's-land and open to all.'

'Open to all brazen butchery!' Scarwid said, visibly moved. 'And rape! Lord Humbert, these are pernicious tidings! Surely we must—'

Humbert jabbed a pointed finger. 'Clap tongue, Scarwid. Nathyn—'

Nathyn stepped forward. 'My lord?'

'Show Wido's man-at-arms to food and comfort. As for you, Inskip—'

The man touched fingers to forehead again. 'Iss, my lord?'

'Go with His Grace's steward and hold yourself ready. You'll be wanted again soon enough.'

'Iss, my lord.'

As the two men withdrew, Humbert stamped across the flagstoned floor to the chamber's narrow, iron-barred window. He needed his back to Aistan and the others. Couldn't afford to show them his face, else they see every murderous thought rioting in his skull.

Peace with Harcia, Roric? Go begging to Aimery for help? Trust those bastards because they sent you sweet, wooing words and an old ring? Not till I've taken my last breath, I swear.

'Humbert . . .' Heavy footsteps behind him, as Aistan approached. 'Megrimed or not, and no matter your leech's advice, Roric must come back to Eaglerock. He must formally convene a Crown Court so this bloody business can be dealt with.'

He looked down at his clenched fists. Felt his heart clench in his chest. 'Aistan—'

'*No*, Humbert!' Aistan took his shoulder. Pulled him about. 'These murders demand justice, and there can be no delay. You heard what Inskip said. Aimery is watching. If we show timid, Harcia will grow bold.'

'I know that,' he said, staring past Aistan's angry face to look at the faces of their fellow councillors. Every man was alarmed. Even Ercole had stirred out of habitual peevishness and spite. 'But a Crown Court is no trifling matter. Before distressing Roric with this news we should learn more of these murders, then ponder the pitfalls of any action and—'

'Humbert, are you gone mad?' Vidar demanded. 'You're not this duchy's regent, to play at being duke. Roric must be told of this, so he can act swiftly and decisively to put Harcia in its place. You've no authority to pronounce yea or nay on that, or decide what Roric should or shouldn't know.'

'I have every authority!' he said, chin jutting. 'Given me by Roric himself. And I say—'

'You've *no* authority to usurp him! Did he lie senseless somewhere, or dead, perhaps you might—' A sharply indrawn breath, as Vidar's one good eye widened. '*Fuck*. Humbert – where is Roric?'

'What?' said Scarwid, the word a strangled yelp. 'Vidar? What are you saying?'

With his twisting limp, Vidar came closer. 'Humbert knows what I'm saying. Don't you, Humbert.'

'Answer Vidar, my lord,' said Aistan, the lines in his face carved deeper now with cold suspicion. 'Where is our duke?'

Like a cornered stag, he had nowhere to run. He and the boy had agreed that, should it be needful, he'd tell the council the truth of their duke's whereabouts. But not in his wildest dreaming had he thought it would come to this.

Curse Aimery. Curse Bayard. Curse every Harcian born.

'Where's Roric?' he roared. 'Not deposed by foul means, by *me*, if that's what you're thinking!'

Hands on hips, meanly triumphant, Ercole swaggered forward. 'But he's not unwell, either. Is he?'

'He is not,' Humbert admitted, knowing to his chagrin that he'd flushed red. 'Roric's gone to Cassinia. He pleads Clemen's plight with the prince's regents, in hopes to secure better terms for the duchy's merchants and the right to trade again in Ardenn.'

'*Cassinia*?' Incredulous, Aistan looked to Vidar, then the others. 'He's in *Cassinia*?'

'That's what I said, Aistan. It's good to know you're not deaf.'

'But – *Cassinia*?'

'Well, I suppose he could've gone to Danetto, but since the regents aren't to be found in Danetto, I—'

'Who travels with him? Surely he doesn't risk himself *alone*?'

Humbert tugged at his beard. That was another argument he'd had with stubborn Roric. One he'd as good as lost. But he wasn't about to confess as much to Aistan.

'No,' he said, repressive. 'His Grace is not alone. And more than that I'm not permitted to say.'

Vidar's face was tight with temper. 'Whose idea was this, Humbert? Yours?'

'No, it was *not*. Believe what you want of me, all of you, only believe *this* while you're about it. I did *not* favour Roric bending his knee to Cassinia's regents. I think it a fool's errand and so I told him. But he would go and he is the duke and I am his loyal councillor, not his father to deny him permission!'

Shaking his head, Aistan turned aside. 'You're right. I don't like it, but you're right. Roric is Clemen's duke. He may speak for his duchy however he sees fit.'

'Without so much as a passing thought for our advice?' said Ercole, bristling. 'I find that offensive.'

'And I find you offensive, Ercole, but there you have it,' Aistan snapped. 'We're both of us limed fast in what can't be changed. Besides. The spirits know we're in desperate need of a remedy in Cassinia. If Roric can soften the regents' hearts to us . . .' He pinched the bridge of his nose. 'I pray he can, for all our sakes. But – Humbert, when do you expect him to return?'

'I can't say, Aistan,' he sighed. 'But I'd hazard he'll be gone another two weeks. At least.'

Despite the tension sprung up between them, their eyes met in alarmed understanding. Matters involving Harcia could swiftly tumble into calamity. They both bore the scars of desperate skirmishes in the Marches, where together they'd served Berold as younger, wilder men.

'That's no good,' Aistan said softly. 'This business with the woodsman's wife can't wait.'

No, it surely couldn't. Unchecked trouble in the Marches might easily, swiftly, spill over into Clemen. They had no choice. On Roric's behalf the council must declare a Crown Court.

And if Roric doesn't like it, if he fears it might risk the chance of friendship with Aimery? Well. Won't that teach the boy not to jaunt off on a whim.

'Very well,' he said briskly. 'We'll send Inskip back to Wido with instructions to inform Harcia's Marcher lords they're to prepare for a Crown Court, and that he and Jacott should do likewise.'

'And who'll preside there for Clemen?' said Ercole. 'You, Humbert?'

'Of course,' said Scarwid, for once not hiding his mislike of the little shite. 'Lacking His Grace, who else? Certainly not you, Ercole.'

As they fell into fresh squabbling, Humbert was struck with a notion almost blinding in its clarity. Letting his gaze shift surreptitious to Vidar, he came near to laughing out loud. For in her sad misfortune, the woodsman's wife had done him a grand good turn. Had given him the perfect chance to rid Roric of his secret enemy and remove Lindara from temptation without any man at court being privy to his purpose.

'My lords!' he said, and clapped his hands. 'Must I send you to bed without your supper?'

Scarwid and Ercole turned away from each other like chastened brats. Paying them no heed, Aistan fingered his chin. 'You can't preside at a Crown Court alone, Humbert. For Clemen's dignity, if no other reason. I can—'

He punched a light fist to Aistan's shoulder. 'My thanks, but no, old friend. I'd have you learn the truth of those corrupted animal leeches you saw fit to arrest.'

'But you must have—'

'I'll take Vidar with me,' he said. 'For, like us, he's experienced in the Marches, and knows too well the taste of Harcia's treachery. Isn't that so, Vidar?'

Vidar bowed, the scars on his face hiding whatever he was thinking . . . or feeling. 'Indeed, my lord.'

'Then we're agreed?' Humbert spread his arms wide. 'Vidar and I will seek justice for Clemen in a Crown Court. In my absence, Aistan will oversee whatever daily matters that arise. And this council shall continue its good shepherding of the duchy till Roric returns from Cassinia . . . with good news, spirits willing.'

Exchanged glances. Then a murmuring of agreement.

'*Excellent*,' he said, nodding. 'Then I declare our business here done.' He offered Vidar the blandest of smiles. 'Come, my lord. There is much to do and discuss ere we leave for the Marches.'

Cassinia's duchy of Rebbai grew green and prosperous and sweetly scented beneath a gentle sun. As he rode a succession of carefully purchased horses hard across its rolling countryside, lavishly patch-worked with barley and oats and rye, and past vineyards drunk with ripening grapes, Roric thought of bewildered Clemen – here parched, there sodden – and was dismayed. When his horse's drumming hooves stirred fat brindled cattle and black-faced sheep in their lush pastures to eye-rolling alarm, he remembered the bonfires his people made of Clemen's butchered, blistermouthed ewes and rams. How for days at a time his duchy's air stank of charred meat and bones and burned fleece. How the stench had woken nightmares of Heartsong, leaving him sweaty and reluctant to sleep. And he remembered what the man Bellows, who Master Blane insisted must ride with him on this mad venture, had told him as they sailed from Eaglerock harbour to Gevez, Rebbai's main seafaring port. Most folk he knew, Bellows glumly confided, were feeding their families pigs' feet and ox tail and little more nourishing than that, besides eggs. And the eggs only two or three, no more than thrice a week.

The fear in Bellows' eyes – and worse, the hope – had left him clumsily speechless. But it also hardened his resolve to wring conces-sions from Cassinia's regents. The principality was so rich. It could afford mercy, and generosity. And since it seemed the regents had forgotten that, it was his task to remind them.

It rained twice and stormed once on the long ride from the coast to the Prince's Isle. Undeterred, Roric pushed on. Coming to Cassinia in this fashion was a fearful risk. He couldn't afford to shrink from a little rain or lightning. Bellows, a good man, didn't complain. Only pulled his oiled-leather cloak's hood lower, and joked that at least the foul weather would keep the brigands indoors.

But in a good sign, they were never held to ransom by trouble-makers. That was thanks to Bellows, who knew Rebbai's byways and bridle tracks better than a native, and made sure to keep them well off the traders' routes. Their horses stayed sound. The inns they slept in didn't rob them. And they were accosted by the duke of Rebbai's men-at-arms just once – as they skirted the duchy's sprawling capital to rejoin the main road leading to the Prince's Isle. Even then, their luck held. Master Blane was known and respected. His travel papers and his personal letter of authority for his men were accepted without dispute.

Roric made sure to express his appreciation with a generous gift of coin.

They passed out of Rebbai and into the Prince's Isle with no trouble. Long ago, the Isle's royal territories had encompassed vast tracts of Cassinia. In those dead days the dukes had been under-thumb, no more than timid, obedient vassals to the crown. But as the fortunes of the royal house ebbed, like a slow tide, so did Cassinia's dukes grow bold and crafty. One by one, little by little, they challenged the weakening royal authority. Castle by castle, year by year, and prince after hapless prince, they amassed their own power. And what they took they held, and never gave back. The Prince's Isle shrank steadily, till what had been a great realm became a mere memory of greatness.

'Remember this, Your Grace,' Blane had warned, standing with him on the dock before he boarded the merchant's swift cog. 'Cassinia's regents are determined to protect their prince's dwindled influence. And I'm sure in their secret hearts they dream of curbing the ambitious dukes, even of restoring the Isle's majesty and might to its former glory. So while I admire you, and wish you every good fortune and hope for success, don't think for a *moment* they'll look at you twice, should what you're asking for conflict with their desires.'

Each night, after bedding down, Roric heard Blane's warning echoing in his ears. He did his best to disregard it, or at least not let it daunt him. In this mad venture it would be so easy to be daunted. And what would happen to Clemen then? What would happen to Bellows and all the men like him, whose families were going hungry for want of an *egg*.

So no. He'd not be daunted. He'd reach the regents . . . or die trying.

Seventeen relentless days after leaving Eaglerock, he and Bellows halted their exhausted horses before the grand, golden gates of the prince's palace. Behind them, spread like a rich damsel's skirts at the bottom of the steep hill they'd just climbed, Varence, Cassinia's royal city.

Coughing, Bellows dragged a dirty forearm across his face. 'There now, my lord,' he croaked. 'Did you ever see the like?'

No, never. Awestruck, Roric stared across the palace's vast, immaculately gravelled forecourt at the slender limestone towers capped each with a crimson witch's hat spire, the four-storeyed wings joining them with their steeply gabled roofs tiled crimson and gold, the countless glass windows glittering with sunlight, the exquisitely proportioned formal gardens laid out on each side. By comparison, Eaglerock castle was little more than a glowering pile of red stone. A clenched fist belligerently raised at the harbour.

He shook himself. *Enough of this*. Let Clemen's duke quail before limestone and glass, and he was defeated before uttering a single word on his duchy's behalf.

'Bellows,' he said, shifting in his saddle. 'We'll part company here. Go back and wait for me in the Crown and Garland.'

Bellows hunched his shoulders. 'But, my lord—'

'I've no need of you,' he said, fishing within his leather doublet for his coin purse. 'Here.' He held out a silver ducat. 'This will purchase prompt service.'

Bellows was staring at the coin as though it was poison. 'My lord, I'm sworn to your side till we see Eaglerock again. Master Blane won't like that I—'

'You needn't fear Master Blane. I am his duke, just as I'm yours.' He smiled, to soften the reprimand. 'You're a good man, Bellows. But what I do now, I must do alone.'

Heaving a great sigh, Bellows took the silver ducat. 'As you wish, my lord. Though I'll be honest, I don't see why.'

The reason was simple. Another warning from Blane. 'Your Grace,' the merchant had said, frowning with worry. 'Bellows will see you safe and swift to the prince's palace. But after that, you'd do me a kindness if you left him safely to one side. If you must know, I don't trust the regents. I'd not have him used against you, or against me because I helped you.'

Roric clapped a hand to Bellows's arm. 'You don't need to understand. Just obey.'

For a few moments he watched Bellows ride reluctant down the sloping road. His horse flicked an ear, its only protest at being abandoned. Then he turned back, to stare again at the palace.

Cassinia's royal emblem was a lion, rampant. Now here he stood, Clemen's falcon, at the mouth of the lion's den. And if he wasn't careful . . .

'Up, nag,' he said, pricking spurs to his horse's flanks. His heart was beating hard, as though he'd just run a race. 'Time to spread my wings.'

CHAPTER TWENTY-ONE

The prince's palace was as elegant inside as outside. Bronze statues of frolicking wood faeries, displayed on green marble pedestals, graced its glossy, cream, marble-floored entrance hall. The floor-to-ceiling windows were framed by crimson silk brocade drapes, captured and fastened with tasselled gold silk cords. The walls were covered in cream silk, hung with paintings of past princes commanding on horseback, or surrounded by an adoring wife and richly clad children. Standing guard, one in each corner, most fabulously etched and inlaid suits of armour. The helms were magnificent: a snarling lion, a fanged wolf, a shrieking eagle and a roaring bear. Sunlight streaming through the undraped glass dazzled on polished steel. Roric found himself breathless at the exquisite craftsmanship. There wasn't an armourer in Clemen whose work could match it. And it was doubtful Eaglerock's treasury contained enough coin to purchase even one fantastical helm – or so much as a gauntlet.

Mouth suddenly dry, he tugged at his scuffed leather doublet. From the corner of his eye caught sight of himself in a mirror, and winced. So much for his bath and barbering at the Crown and Garland. Travelling as a simple merchant's man, he'd not been able to carry court finery with him into Cassinia. So he'd donned his one remaining clean linen shirt, done his best to polish his boots, and trusted his ducal bearing would carry him the rest of the way.

Looking around him, he wondered if that wasn't a mistake. Perhaps he should've risked a little velvet and a pearl earring.

The click of a door latch. Turning, he saw a cunningly concealed panel in one silk-covered wall swing wide. The gate guard who'd confiscated the daggers sheathed on his hip, strapped to his left forearm and tucked into his right boot had escorted him into the palace, then remained to guard him while the regents' steward was fetched. Now the man straightened smartly out of his slouch.

A thin, middle-aged courtier with sleekly pomaded brown hair stepped into the entrance hall and closed the panelled door behind him. Elegantly supercilious in cloth-of-silver livery, wearing a blue-enamelled silver chain of office, he dismissed the gate guard with a flick of his fingers, then approached. In his flat grey eyes, almost hidden, a gleam of derision.

'You claim to be Roric, duke of Clemen. Is that correct?'

Roric looked at him steadily. 'It's no claim. If you've seen the letter I gave to the gate guard, and the signet ring, you'll—'

'Yes. I've seen them.'

'I've seen them *Your Grace*. And you are?'

'Docien.' The courtier hesitated, then inclined his head in the merest hint of a nod. 'Your Grace. Steward to the prince's regents.'

'The letter and my ring. Where are they, Docien?'

The steward smiled, his eyes still flat. 'Being authenticated, Your

Grace. A precaution your own steward would take, I've no doubt. If he knew his business.'

'I'd be a fool to present myself as Clemen's duke if that were a lie, don't you think?'

'Certainly, Your Grace. But the world is full of fools. As I'm sure you've noticed.'

He'd not sailed for days and ridden scores of leagues to bandy words with a palace servant. 'Docien, shall we dispense with the pleasantries? I've come to see the prince's regents.'

'So I'm given to understand, Your Grace.' The steward frowned. 'But if you'll forgive my plain speaking? The odd manner of your arrival, your lack of warning to their lordships – or an invitation – and your—' His flat gaze travelled up and down. '—colourfully rustic attire . . . it's all somewhat alarming. The regents are, to put it bluntly, taken aback. This visit could hardly be described as *formal*.'

'Agreed,' he said. 'But it is urgent.'

A raised eyebrow. 'To you. Your Grace.'

So. The regents were determined to twist his tail. A good thing he'd not brought Humbert with him. By now his foster-lord would be bellowing fit to shake those glorious suits of armour to pieces.

'It was never my intention to alarm or dismay, Docien,' he said, mild as milk. 'Or to rudely impose. I only desire to speak with the prince's regents on a matter of mutual concern. If my arrival is inconvenient, I'll express my regret and offer to wait somewhere less conspicuous until their lordships are comfortable that I am who I say I am. At which time, we can talk.'

The steward's eyes narrowed, considering him. Then he bowed. 'Allow me to show you into the gardens, Your Grace.'

Hiding an impolitic smile, Roric followed the steward out of the palace into warm, late morning sunshine and the sleepy droning of bees. There Docien left him, with a veiled warning that while there were guards in the palace grounds, he'd not be disturbed.

The gardens, viewed closely, proved as elegant as everything else in the Prince's Isle. Densely green hedges were immacutely trimmed to knee height, or carved with pruning shears into dragons and griffins and unicorns and nymphs. Water splashed into marble basins through the mouths of sculptured, snarling lions. Marble benches in deep blues and blood-reds and pale greens and purest white, their feet styled like lion claws, offered the weary visitor somewhere to sit. Narrow paths gravelled in blue and white river pebbles meandered between flower beds bursting with fragrant blooms. Jewel-winged butterflies danced above them, flirting with the bees. Breathing deep, feeling his head swim with so many mingled scents, Roric recognised daisies and snapdragons and roses and violets, but there were a half-dozen vibrant blossoms he'd never seen in Clemen. Dotted haphazardly, delicate trees with trailing branches that dripped creamy petals like falls of Harcian lace.

And most curious of all, tall wooden poles striped white and red, white and blue, white and green, each supporting a carved wooden creature painted vivid, unlikely colours and lavishly tipped with gold. Here a black panther spotted crimson and white, and over there a crimson bull sporting a wreath of blue roses. A purple hare with silver whiskers. A coiled green snake with yellow eyes and bronze fangs. Extraordinary. They seemed almost alive. He shivered, half-believing they *were* alive and watching him with their glossy glass eyes.

Achingly aware of the toll the many days' hard travelling had taken, Roric abandoned his garden wandering and sank gratefully onto a marble bench. At first he sat upright, alert for the first sign of the steward Docien's return. Turning his thoughts resolutely from Clemen, so far away, determined not to imagine the worst happening as soon as his back was turned, he rehearsed what he intended to say to the prince's regents. Thought of how he'd persuade them to leave the past in the past and let his duchy's merchants back into Ardenn. But before long, his eyelids started to droop . . . his head lolled sideways . . . and the droning bees droned him to drowsy sleep.

A soft, childish giggle rowsed him. Blinking, pushing out of his sideways slump, he looked around. He was alone. Another giggle. No, not alone. But where—

Ah. There. A short stone's throw distant, a boy-child crouched within a trailing, lacy latticework of slender branches. Staring at him, Roric saw an impish face, shadow-mottled and pale as moonlight, crowned with curling silver-gilt hair. Greenish-hazel eyes fringed with long, oddly dark lashes. A slight frame lacking any pudginess of youth. Aside from his scarlet wool mittens, he seemed to be naked.

The boy met his startled stare boldly. Revealed pearly teeth in a mischievous smile. 'Shhh,' he confided. 'I's hiding.'

Charmed, Roric propped his elbows on his knees and nodded, gravely. 'Yes. I can see that.'

'But you can't see me,' the boy added, imperious. 'I's a faery sprite. I's magical. I's—'

'Gaël! *Gaël!* You little wretch, where are you? Oh, please, do come out. You *know* they'll whip me for losing you!'

And that was a young woman's voice, anxious and coming closer. Mouth open – *Gaël? Was this Cassinia's prince?* – Roric spared the boy a last look, then stood and turned to face the unlucky servant sent to seek her truant sovereign.

Tall for a woman, and reed slender, she was dressed in a severely plain dark blue linen dress. It covered her from throat to wrists to ankles, leaving only her face and hands bare. Her hair was hidden in a white linen coif, save for an escaping tendril that clung to her cheek. It was a beautiful honey-gold, and shone in the sunlight. Her eyes were crystal blue, like the waters separating Clemen from Cassinia. Her nose was fine and straight, her lips full, her gently flushed skin flawless. Even flustered, she was graceful.

She saw him, and stopped. Her eyes widened, her lips parted, and she caught her breath in surprise. '*Roric?*'

And then he knew her. Six years had wrought changes, but he knew who she was. '*Catrain.*' Stunned, he felt his heart crashing against his ribs. 'I thought – I was told – you were dead.'

Tremulously smiling, she came closer. 'To the world, I am dead. And for my mother's sake the world mustn't know any different. Roric – I'm sorry, Your Grace – why are you here?'

He scarcely heard the question. Relief had almost stopped his ears. This was Catrain, *alive*. In sending her from Eaglerock he hadn't caused her death. He wanted to touch her, just to make certain, but kept his fingers fisted by his sides.

She was waiting for him to say something, her expression a mingling of pleasure and alarm. What had she asked him? Oh. Yes. 'I'm waiting to see the regents. Clemen suffers badly from their sanctions, and the squabbling of Cassinia's dukes. I've come to better arrange matters.'

She grimaced. 'Your Grace, you mustn't—'

'Not Your Grace. Roric.'

'Roric.' A small headshake. As though she, like he, found this meeting hard to believe. 'Truly, you're wasting your time if you think Leofric and his brother regents will show you or Clemen mercy.' A shadow darkened her lovely face. 'They don't know the meaning of the word.'

'The regents mistreat you?' Anger surged. 'What you said before, about a whipping, was that—'

'It doesn't matter,' she said, with a wary glance around them. 'And speak gently. In this place I think they can eavesdrop on your dreams.'

He had to take a deep breath, to calm himself. 'But it does matter. You're kept a prisoner.'

'I'm less trammelled than I used to be,' she said, shrugging. 'I've learned how to behave. Please, don't imagine me locked in a dungeon with naught but rats for company and rancid gruel to eat.'

She was as courageous at twenty as she'd been at fourteen. But even though captivity had failed to break her spirit, still it was bruised. He could see it in her eyes, and the way she held herself – for ever braced against a blow.

'Catrain.' He had to breathe deep again. 'I'm so sorry. I wish . . .'

She shook her head. 'Don't. What's done is done, and that was done long ago. I know you married elsewhere. Lindara? Isn't that her name? Are you happy, Roric? I want you happy. How many children do you have?'

He could lie. He should lie, to spare her. But this was Catrain. Dishonesty would insult her.

'I have no children, my lady. And no. I'm not happy.'

'Oh,' she whispered.

They stared at each other, choked to silence by their separate and mutual griefs. A single tear, welling, spilled down Catrain's cheek.

A wild scuffling to one side, then, as Cassinia's little prince burst out of hiding. 'Bad man, bad!' he shouted, his impish, moon-pale face flushed bright red. 'You's making Cattie cry!'

Putting his head down, the boy charged. Roric tried to avoid him, feared hurting him, but he lost his footing on the loosely pebbled pathway and slipped to one knee. With a shout of angry triumph the boy snatched up his ungloved left hand and bit him.

'*No*, Gaël!' Catrain gasped. Wrapping her arms around the child's slight, naked body, she snatched him aside. 'Oh, you wretch! You'll have the guards on us!'

Glowering, his mouth sulky, the boy stamped his bare foot. 'I's not a wretch, Cattie! I's a magical sprite!'

'No, my lord, you are a prince,' Roric said, shaking his smarting hand. He should've left his gloves on. 'And no prince worth his royal blood sinks his teeth into another man's flesh.'

'I do,' the boy retorted. Spinning about, he waggled his naked rump in defiance, and blew a loud raspberry like a fart.

Roric smacked him.

'For shame!' he said sternly, as the boy stared at him in wide-eyed shock. 'To behave so in front of a lady. Beg her pardon, at once.'

The prince of Cassinia burst into tears.

'Oh, no, don't cry, lambkin,' Catrain begged him, and lifted him into an embrace. As he wrapped his arms and legs around her, and hid his face against her shoulder, she frowned over his silver-gilt hair. 'That was unwise, Roric. I might be the only one in this forsaken place who truly cares for Gaël, but he's still the prince. If the regents find out you chastised him . . .'

His curs't hand was still smarting. The boy had come close to drawing blood. 'Will you tell them?' he muttered. 'Will the boy?'

'No,' she sighed. 'He'll keep it secret, if I ask him. Gaël and I keep many secrets.' She kissed the snuffling, hiccuping boy's temple. 'Don't we, sweeting?'

'Catrain . . .' The way she held the child, so tenderly, touched him out of temper. 'It's whispered beyond the palace gates that Cassinia's prince is—' he mouthed the word '—*mad*.'

Her chin came up, and in that gesture he saw again the young girl who'd dared him into those burning Harcian stables.

'And if he is?' she said fiercely. 'Do you say it's his fault?'

'No. But—'

'I should think not. Yes, it's true he's . . . troubled. But he's

355

orphaned, Roric, and in his way he's as much a prisoner as I am. Never expect me to abandon him.'

'I don't. I wouldn't. But Catrain . . .' He felt a dreadful fear for her, rising. 'In befriending him, and sharing secrets, you're playing a dangerous game.'

'As if I need you to tell me that, Your Grace,' she retorted, with a wry smile. 'But I've been playing it since I was fourteen, remember. And as you can see, I'm still standing.'

She was astonishing. And, may the spirits save him, he wanted to kiss her. It shocked him, how much he wanted to taste her lips. A heat he'd not felt in years burned in his blood. It wasn't love. It was more than lust. And it was more honest, more demanding, than anything he'd felt for Lindara in months. Afraid that Catrain would see the desire in his face and be alarmed, or disgusted, he turned away. Pretended to be making sure they were still unobserved.

'Yes,' she said, her voice softened with regret. 'I must go. The palace guards were loitering by the garden entrance when I came in, but they could start to prowl at any moment. Roric . . .'

Praying he could trust himself, he turned back. Cassinia's prince had fallen asleep in her arms. He'd lost one of his scarlet mittens, and a bare thumb was stuck in his rosebud mouth. He was the age Liam would be now, if Harald's son had survived Heartsong. The old pain stirred, mingling with this fresh grief. Poor, pitiful little Gaël. Orphaned and moonstruck, at the mercy of the regents. What would become of him? What would become of Catrain?

'You mustn't be frightened for me,' she said, watching him. 'I'll be fine, Roric. I promise.'

'You can't promise that,' he protested. 'You can't promise anything. Catrain, for pity's sake—'

Shaking her head, she started to back away, slowly. 'No, Your Grace. You can't save me. I have to save myself. But there is one thing you could do for me.' Her face started to crumple, but with an effort she stayed strong. 'Or – you could try.'

He wanted to follow her. He knew he couldn't. 'Name it,' he said, his voice breaking. 'Anything.'

'Get word to my mother. She knows I live, but little more. Tell Berardine you saw me, and I'm happy – and—'

'I will, Catrain. I swear it.'

'Thank you,' she said, and turned, and fled back to the palace with Cassinia's mad prince.

Alone again, more shaken than he cared – or dared – to admit, Roric returned to the marble bench. But he was too stirred up to drowse again. That Berardine's daughter, Baldwin's heir, should be kept prisoner here, a political pawn, no better than a glorified nursery maid? It was offensive. How could Cassinia's dukes abide it? Surely they could see the danger, that what the regents would do to one they might eagerly do to them all? But no. It seemed they were too busy with their squabbles and he was helpless, his hands tied. Catrain was right. Somehow, she would have to save herself.

Fretting, he remained on the marble bench and waited for the regents' steward to return. Time passed. Then it dragged. The day dragged behind it. Shadows lengthened. The garden cooled. His empty belly began to rumble. When a palace guard at last came to fetch him, the afternoon had sunk almost into dusk.

'Your Grace,' Docien greeted him, as he returned to the palace's entrance hall. 'I do apologise for keeping you so long.'

The steward stood beside a blood-red marble table, set against one wall. Looking at it, Roric saw laid there the note he'd written, his signet ring, and his three useful daggers.

'Alas,' Docien added, so smooth, so courteously vicious. 'The regents are not able to meet with you, Your Grace. But they have asked me to convey this message. With regards to Clemen, Cassinia is satisfied with matters as they stand. If you have concerns, you'd be wise to look closer to home for the remedy. Perhaps you're not aware, but you brought a fourth dagger with you. You'll find it stuck between your shoulder blades.' The steward bowed. 'Have a safe, swift journey back to Eaglerock, Your Grace.'

As the cunning door in the wall slid shut behind the steward, Roric retrieved his belongings from the marble table. There was rage in him, cold and vast, but it would have to wait. Silent, he slipped on his ring, sheathed the daggers, stowed the note inside his doublet, then followed the guard out of the palace and back to the gilded gates where his horse was waiting. Silent, swung into the saddle and rode back to the Crown and Garland.

'My lord!' Bellows greeted him eagerly, rising from his chair in the parlour. 'How did you fare? Did you—' And then, seeing him close, his face fell. 'Oh.'

Feeling like a traitor, rage giving way to grief, Roric briefly clasped the man's arm. 'I'm sorry, Bellows. The regents were . . . disinclined to help.'

'I'm sure you did your best, my lord,' Bellows murmured, shoulders slumping.

His best? *Fuck*. He could hardly have done any worse. But hadn't Catrain warned him? And she was proven right. Humbert and Blane, too. He'd wasted his time coming to Cassinia. Wasted coin. Risked a good man. And for what? For nothing. He could imagine what Humbert would say. And as for the rest of the council . . .

You brought a fourth dagger with you. You'll find it stuck between your shoulder blades.

The steward Docien's barbed comment could mean only one thing. He'd been right, and Humbert wrong. Someone they both knew, another councillor, had told the regents about Berardine's marriage offer. And now Catrain was the regents' prisoner, because of that man.

'My lord?' said Bellows, alarmed. 'Are you all right? Them curs't regents didn't offer Clemen violence, did they?'

'What?' He stared. 'No. They offered us nothing. And keep your voice down, you fool, before you talk us into trouble.'

Bellows looked at the pinewood floor, abashed. 'Beg pardon, my lord.'

Splendid. Now he sounded like Harald, snapping the nose off an underling because he was piqued. Taking a deep breath, he thrust aside anger, and humiliation, and his fear for Catrain. 'Never mind, Bellows. I'm disappointed, and jogged out of sorts.'

'Yes, my lord. And no wonder.' Cautiously, Bellows lifted his gaze. 'My lord, what do we do now?'

There was only one thing to do. Learn the name of the man who'd betrayed Clemen – imprisoned Catrain – and see that he paid full price for his treacherous disloyalty.

'We eat,' Roric said, pretending a better mood. 'I'm famished. Then we sleep. And at sunrise, we start for home.'

* * *

The Marches had been buzzing like a kicked-over beehive for weeks. First it was the dreadful murder of Woodsman Gannen's wife, and the mad slaughter between the Marcher lords' men-at-arms that followed. Then, what with all four Marcher lords swords-drawn over the bloodshed, and pointing fingers every which way except at their own men, and the roads ridden to ruts by more men-at-arms meant to be keeping the peace but really looking for trouble, it seemed the Marches were like to catch fire. Gossip became the favoured coin. Some folk claimed to have seen goblins in the woods, others swore there'd been balefire on their rooftops. Jesslyn from Bluebell Hollow said he'd found a nest of two-headed worms, and the evil creatures had burst into blood when his gaze touched them. Every palm was damp with nervous sweat and every tongue was wagging. Charms and sprite-frights were nailed above doors and windows and dangled openly around folks' necks. Not a soul could hazard what might happen next. When the answer came, at last, a bolt of lightning couldn't have struck any harder.

'A Crown Court *here*?' Glad of stout Iddo at her back, Molly stood among her empty public room's tables and smoothed the front of her bloodstained apron. Chicken's blood, of course. The faeries knew when she'd be red with mutton blood again. 'In my Pig Whistle?'

Pero, Duke Aimery's herald, tall and skinny with faded pock scars marring his cheeks, looked down his bony nose. 'Woman, you'd be mort unwise to raise ruckus over this. Say yes to Count Balfre, and be done with it.'

Recalling Denno Culpyn's blood and bruises on him from that beating, she tucked in her chin. Then she looked at the herald who'd come all the way from Eaglerock.

'And this Lord Humbert of yers, Ser Dunsten. *He* pushes for the court to be held under my roof?'

As lean as his brother herald, but more comely, even though he was older and bald as an egg, Dunsten nodded. 'Mistress Molly, he does. For where else in the Marches can our unhappy lords meet to settle this contention? Your inn is one of the largest, and the best known, and sits convenient at the Crossroads. In belonging to no one lord, you could say the Pig Whistle belongs to all.'

'A feggit for that, ser!' she retorted. 'The Pig Whistle belongs to me. I've the signed and sealed charter to prove it and if you'd like I'll doddle upstairs this moment and fetch it.'

'There's no need to trouble yourself, Mistress,' Dunsten said hastily. 'I'm afraid you mistook my meaning. Your freehold here's not in dispute.'

She sniffed. 'Good, then. Just so we be clear. Now. How long would this Crown Court go on for?'

Dunsten spread his leathery hands. 'As many days as it takes to reach a verdict.'

'As many days as Harcia and Clemen decide,' said Pero, his crooked teeth bared. 'It's not for you to quibble, woman. Your permission to hold the court here isn't required. If you can read, you know what's in your precious signed and sealed charter.'

Iddo's warm hand on her shoulder. His warm breath against her cheek as he whispered. 'They be in the right, Moll. Ye can't refuse a lord's lawful request.'

As if she didn't know that. But because she could read, she knew everything that was lawful. 'Unruffle yer feathers, sers. I'll give the Pig Whistle to yer lords for their court – at a price. Ye'll give me coin for the food I cook ye, the ale and cider ye drink, and any bed as gets slept in. Coin for yer horses what muck m'straw and eat m'fodder. Coin for the coin lost to me, since I'll have no customers while yer lords argue this out. And coin to pay for what they break while they be arguing.'

Pero's face darkened. 'That's a saucy tongue you keep, mistress.'

'A saucy tongue what can tell tales to the lord as puts them fancy clothes on yer back,' she said, and shrugged off Iddo's tightening fingers. 'I won't be browbeat under m'own roof, Ser Pero. Ye be a Harcian man, iss? Come to us all the way from Cater's Tamwell, I'll allow, for ye first time in the Marches. Well, here be a little lesson for ye. Us all as lives here be Marcher folk, see? Clemen-bred or Harcian or born to a different land and come to live here by accident, we be Marcher folk first. And we don't take kindly to a raised voice – or fist.'

'But I think you might run from a raised sword, yes?'

'Come, Pero,' Dunsten said, stepping forward. 'Mistress Molly asks for what's lawful, nothing more. Mistress Molly—' He gave her a swift smile, shaded with pleading. 'You'll tender our lords a fair and honest reckoning at the court's end, and receive your lawful coin in return. Agreed?'

'I be a fair and honest woman, ser. Not a copper nib more than I be owed will I ask for. And I'll reckon to feed yer lords and their men pies and stew as'll have 'em weeping to leave the Marches.' She folded her arms, daring him to argue. 'Though I confess they won't be mutton, on account of the troubles.'

With a great show of disdain, Pero distanced himself from Dunsten. 'The Crown Court is set to start in two days' time, Mistress Molly. You have that long to tell your regular customers they won't be welcome till it's done. Do what you must to warn away travelling merchants and the like, and make this inn of yours presentable before our lords arrive. My duke's heir is a fastidious man, used to cleanliness and comfort. If either is lacking, you'll regret it.'

As Pero stamped out, Molly raised an eyebrow at Dunsten. 'And now ye'll tell me this Lord Humbert of yers be a man of the same stripe?'

'Lord Humbert is a great man,' said Dunsten, with quiet pride. 'I'm proud to serve him – and His Grace, Duke Roric.' He looked around the public room. 'My lord will find no fault here, I'm sure. And I'm sure he's sorry that the Court must put you to some trouble.'

'Ser Dunsten, I'll tell ye what puts me to trouble,' she snapped. 'Marcher men as can't keep their cocks laced in their breeches. For if they could there'd be no woman dead, no blood spilled, and no lords come to clutter under m'feet!'

Dunsten grinned. 'Pero's right about one thing. You, Mistress Molly, have a saucy tongue indeed!'

'And it'll talk ye into strife, woman, surely it will!' said Iddo, aghast, as the Pig Whistle's door closed behind Clemen's herald. 'Moll, ye can't scold a lord's man like he were Benedikt, or the other one!'

'Iss, I can,' she said, truculent. 'I just did. And *don't* call Willem *the other one*! Ye do know how that frets me.'

As cross as she was, Iddo waved a finger under her nose. 'Never ye mind scolding me, neither, ye besom! Wido and Bayard and them others, they be one hat of eggs. But here we do have Aimery's heir and a great lord of Clemen blowing to our doorstep. Take it into yer head to offend *them*, Molly, and with one puff they'll blow us all into the woods.'

He was right, but she was in no mood to admit it. 'Let 'em puff. I meant what I said, Iddo. Them fancy counts and lords and their heralds, they can clankit in gold armour from head to toe, they can, but the Pig Whistle's my inn and I'm the queen of it, y'hear?' She looked past him. '*Alys!*'

The leather curtains behind the bar parted, creaking, and the girl came out of the kitchen, her apron all over flour, her floury linen sleeves pushed back to her elbows and fingers shiny with butter. 'Yes, Molly?'

'There be lords and counts and the faeries-know-what coming to us from Harcia and Clemen for a feggit Crown Court, on account of that poor murdered Thea and how not a one of 'em's man enough to own the foul deed. Finish the pastry for tonight's pie crusts, like I showed ye, then do me a tally of what is and ain't in the dry cellar. It be a mort load of pies we'll be baking, by and by.'

The girl stared, speechless, no more wit in her than a hammered sheep.

She clapped her hands. '*Alys!* Did ye fall deaf when m'back was turned?'

'No, Molly,' the girl said, her voice a strangled whisper.

'Then do as yer told!'

'Yes, Molly.'

Shaking her head as Alys scuttled back into the kitchen, Molly caught Iddo's look. It made her scowl. No matter what she said, or how many times, he wouldn't warm to the girl. Worse, lately he'd started the habit of beetling his brow at little Willem, too. Though why he'd do that she couldn't guess, or make him tell.

'Not a peep out of ye, man,' she snapped. 'Or it be a cold bed ye'll find me keeping. The girl's snockled with the news, and who could blame her?'

'Iss, Moll,' said Iddo, rolling his eyes. Then he grimaced. 'Two days. T'aint much time to be fetching the ale we'll need for all them lords and men, and the firewood, and every other curs't thing they'll want – or think they want.'

'Not much time at all,' she agreed grimly. 'So do tell why ye be standing in front of me, flapping yer lips 'stead of getting to work!'

They were alone, so he kissed her. 'That feggit saucy tongue, woman. It'll be the death of ye one day!'

'And I'll be the death of ye, Master Iddo,' she retorted, and because they were alone gave his cock a quick squeeze. 'Now be off with ye, so I can see what that Alys be up to. Like as not she's let them boys up-end a sack of flour all over my kitchen floor!'

Lost in wild thought, and churned so sick with fear that the aches of her hard day felt no worse than a tickle, Ellyn hardly noticed when Liam started tugging at her long, skimpy plait. It wasn't till he pinched her, and used her proper name, that she paid attention. They were safe in their tiny attic bedroom with the door closed, the inn being shut for the night and Molly and Iddo tucked up safe where they couldn't hear. But that made no difference. He was old enough to know better.

'*No*, Liam,' she said, and poked him. 'I'm Alys. You *mustn't* call me Ellyn.'

Amber eyes clouded with crossness, he bounced on his knees beside her on the narrow bed. 'You call me Liam when I'm s'posed to be Willem.'

'It's not the same. I'm not a little boy. I won't forget and call you Liam when we're not alone up here.'

His lower lip poked. 'You might.'

'I won't.

'You might,' he said, scowl scrunching. 'And I b'aint a little boy.'

She sighed. 'Not *b'aint*. Speak proper, Liam. And anyway, you are a little boy, and you'll be one till I say you're not. Now, it's late. I'm blowing out the candle. Best you hop into your truckle.'

His mouth dropped with dismay. 'Without my story? But why? I can't go to sleep without my story!'

Pain was pounding through her forehead, and her throat felt drier than dirt. 'Can't you, Liam? Just this once? For me?'

Those wide eyes, so like his father's, filled with ready tears. 'Please, please, I want to hear my story. I'm sorry I called you Ellyn. I won't do it again.'

'Oh, *Liam*.' She snatched him close and crushed her cheek against his hair. 'Don't fret, lamb. It doesn't matter. I'm not gnarly with you really.'

How could she be? When he called her Ellyn she could forget Alys, the girl she'd had to become. Instead she could remember who she'd been. Who she still was, in her secret heart. The girl gifted with Duke Harald's baby son. The only soul in all the world who knew the truth of him, and kept it safe.

'Promise?' he said, his chin wobbling.

She kissed the tip of his nose. 'Promise.'

'And you'll tell me my story?'

'Of course I will.'

So she told him his story, the tale of Liam the rightful, dispossessed duke of Clemen, great-grandson of famed duke Berold, and he recited it with her, under his breath. And as she told it, speaking her lines without thinking like a player who'd played just one part over and over, for years, her mind poked and prodded at Molly's dreadful news.

Clemen coming to the Pig Whistle? What cruel faery trick was this? If only she knew which lords that bastard Roric was sending. If only she dared ask. But of course she couldn't. Not with Molly already prickled about the ructions of a Crown Court, and Iddo still watching her with eyes that never warmed.

She tried to think cheerful, convince herself there was no danger. After all, no more than a handful of Harald's nobles had ever laid eyes on her. Chances were they'd never recall a wet nurse. What great lord, aside from Harald, would ever notice a girl like her?

Only . . . only . . . she couldn't be sure of it. One of those lords *might* remember her. And if even one of them came to the Pig Whistle and glimpsed Liam . . .

He's the image of his father. Anyone who knew Duke Harald will see it.

She wanted to rock and whimper, but she'd only fright her little lamb. He was snuggled in her lap, grown too big for cuddling really, he was such a big, strong boy. But cuddling comforted both of them. She was mother and sister to him. He was her lambkin, her treasure, the reason she drew breath.

Should she run with him? She could run. Only he loved living here in the Marches. In the busy Pig Whistle Inn. He loved Benedikt, as good as his brother. Running from Benedikt would break his little heart. Besides, where could she take him that wouldn't plunge them both into peril? Not Harcia. Not back to Clemen. There was the Marches. Nowhere else. Besides. Here in the Pig Whistle, she wasn't a lowly, hardly noticed wet nurse. So many people knew her now. Knew her face, knew her false name. And they knew Liam.

And most everyone hereabouts knows Molly, one way or another. If I run, I'll make her angry. She loves Liam too. Far and wide she'll tell folk, don't trust a hair on that Alys girl's head. She mistreated that boy and stole him and I want him back. And they'll listen, 'cause she's Molly. They'll hunt us down, and catch us.

And what would happen to Liam then?

Safe in her arms, he wriggled. 'Ow, Ellyn! Ow!'

'Sorry, lamb,' she said, loosening her hold. 'Didn't mean to squash.'

He looked at her, puzzled. 'Ellyn? Has one of them rough'uns hurt ye? I'll fix him. You tell me who he is.'

Oh, the faeries protect him. Six years old he was, a little boy . . . with the courage of a man. Of a duke.

She kissed his forehead. 'Nothing's the matter, lamb. Come, let's finish your story. And then, cos you're a good boy, I'll tell you about the feast the duke held when you were born.'

Later, when her sweet Liam was asleep in his truckle bed under the attic chamber's shuttered window, she lay in the dark and tried to calm her pounding heart. Nowhere to run. Nowhere to hide. And the lords of Clemen coming . . .

Oh, spirits, help me. We have to keep Liam safe.

CHAPTER TWENTY-TWO

R iding at a slow jog-trot to the first day of the Crown Court, in company with Humbert and Clemen's herald and its ruinously inept Marcher lords and the two Marcher men who'd failed to save the Clemen woman and instead spilled Harcian blood, Vidar counted himself most harshly used. For surely it was a sour jest on Humbert's part to bring him to this misbegotten wasteland now, of all times: fourteen years almost to the day since last he'd set foot in the Marches. Fourteen years since he lost his eye and the good use of his leg, battling Harcia. When every bright dream he'd had for himself had floundered and foundered in a gushing of blood.

It had to be deliberate. Humbert had *been* there the day he was so grievously wounded, along with the lords Grevill and Mostyn and six men-at-arms. Harcian's men had come upon them in the shadowy depths of Barrows Wood, a part of the Marches counted as Clemen's domain. Chastened Wido ruled there now, but then the task had fallen to Grevill. He'd died defending his territory, along with two of his men. And of those who survived, not a one escaped blooding. Not even Humbert, and in his day he'd been fearsome with a sword. Of them all, his own wounds were the worst. He'd come perilously close to joining Grevill in death.

Everything blighted in his life could be traced back to that maiming.

And yet, remembering it all, as he must, Humbert would still drag him back here. Why him? Why not Aistan? His soon-to-be goodfather was a greater lord than disgraced Godebert's son and had fought in the Marches with distinction more times than the man on the brink of marrying his daughter. That business with the bribed leeches was a feeble excuse for Humbert to use.

For all his bluster, he's a patient shite. This is his chance to punish me for taking a seat on the council. Not a day in his life has he wanted to share anything with me. Not a laugh, not Lindara . . . and for certain, not power.

A fist thumped to his knee jolted him back to his surroundings.

'Pay attention, Vidar!' Humbert growled, riding beside him. 'Precious little use you'll be here if you can't keep your wits from wandering!'

With some effort he bit back an acid reply. For Clemen's sake its great lords must be seen in accord. The bloody aftermath of murder had left Clemen's men-at-arms on the jitter. Knowing their own lords had failed them, they looked to the duke's councillors for the justice they deserved. And with rumours of evil omens flying thick as snow in winter, he and Humbert couldn't be seen at each other's throats. So he swallowed fresh resentment and showed Lindara's father a meek face.

'I'm sorry, my lord. You said something?'

Humbert heaved an impatient sigh. 'I *said* are you certain you've a grasp of the facts in this matter? For we'll reach the Pig Whistle shortly, and for Roric's sake I'll not have you ill-prepared.'

The question was as good as an insult. Over the past five days he and Humbert had kept close in Wido's manor house, doing little more than strip this matter's carcase to its bones. They'd mercilessly interrogated Wido and Jacott – the lazy fools, grown fat and complacent in their little fiefdoms. When all was said and done they'd be answering to Roric for their costly mistakes. Inskip and his fellow survivor Sorren were closely examined too. No fault there, they'd done what they could. The murdered woman's husband told them of the other times his dead wife had been rudely accosted by Harcian men-at-arms not kept in check by any lord. A whole day, they'd spent, talking to Clemen's Marcher folk, and many a similar tale were they told. So yes, he was comfortably acquainted with the facts. But if he answered the insult, not the question, he might start something he couldn't finish. At least not without risking his place at court.

And without court, there was no Lindara.

'I'm tolerably sure I'll not disgrace you, my lord,' he replied, perfectly courteous. 'But feel free to examine me, if you like.'

That earned him a glower. 'Am I your bloody tutor, then?'

'No, my lord. I'd just have you confident I won't take a false step.'

Humbert grunted, then lapsed into silence.

The road taking them to the Pig Whistle meandered through sparse, straggling woodland. The morning was cool, the air damp, echoing with the muffled clop-clop of hooves striking hard-baked earth softened by a recent storm.

Feeling the ache building deep in his hip, because time in the saddle and damp weather always woke his lightly sleeping pain, Vidar denied the urge to press fingers into his scarred flesh. Weakness revealed would be his undoing – and not only because Humbert looked for it. Harcia's wolves would be seeking it too. Especially Aimery's heir. Of late Balfre had earned a reputation for dispensing harsh justice . . . and his lack of love for Clemen was hardly a secret. What might have been swiftly dealt with had a different Harcian lord been sent to the Marches – Balfre's gentler brother, Grefin, say – now promised to be a protracted, hard-fought affair.

Curse it.

Someone riding behind him exploded into a volley of ripe sneezes. It sounded like Wido, also feeling the damp. He and Jacott, kept company by Herald Dunsten, trotted in front of the two witnessing men-at-arms, Inskip and Sorren, and another score of men besides. The men-at-arms rode their tough Marches horses, but Clemen's lords and its herald sat astride conspicuously unwarlike palfreys. And though every man making his way to the Crown Court wore a dagger sheathed at his hip, swords had been left behind at the manor house or the barracks. Likewise they rode without benefit of mail, or even boiled leather armour. A strict rule of the Crown Court. Bloodshed lay in the past. This was a time for peace and brotherly reconciliation. Any man, even a lord, who broke the law by being martial would receive an uncompromising rebuke from the Court, and face far worse than that on his return home.

As the road began curving lazily leftwards, Dunsten urged his lean, caparisoned horse forward.

'Lord Humbert, Lord Vidar,' he said, joining them. 'The Pig Whistle inn lies just around this bend.'

And so it did, and there it was, sunlit in the distance. Remembering, Vidar frowned. 'I hope their ale's improved, Dunsten. It was sorely flat, the last time I was here.'

'Clap tongue, Vidar,' said Humbert. 'Dunsten, ride on. Warn the innkeeper we're coming.'

So warned, there were eager boys ready to take their horses once they'd dismounted in the Pig Whistle's tidy forecourt. Dunsten, looking relieved, told Humbert that Balfre and his people were yet to arrive. The innkeeper, a tall, broad woman, curtsied indiscriminately and bade them welcome.

'And if ye be hungered or thirsty, m'lords, there be ale and cider and pies we'll serve ye. Ye need only to ask.' She gestured at the trestle boards and benches set up along the low wall furthest from the inn's open front doors. 'All be made ready in the public room for the court, so I thought to serve ye out here.'

'Cider,' said Humbert. 'For we want clear heads.'

The woman curtsied again. 'Iss, m'lord.'

As Humbert gathered with Wido and Jacott, beard bristling as he reminded them, yet again, of how to conduct themselves in the court, Vidar idly followed the woman inside and took his time wandering around the room. Nodding approval at the arrangement of tables and benches for the legal proceedings, he was startled by the splash and clatter of tankards dropping to the floor. He turned awkwardly, pain hissing air between clenched teeth, to see a serving girl standing before him, her apron cider-soaked, her face stricken as she stared.

'*Alys!* Ye clumsy wench!' the innkeeper shouted, carrying her own tray laden with foam-topped tankards.

The maid crouched, face hidden as she scrabbled for the tankards she'd carelessly dropped. 'Sorry, Molly. Sorry.'

'Do that again and I'll show ye sorry on yer skinny arse. Just ye—'

'Lord Vidar?'

He turned back, to see Dunsten in the public room's doorway. 'What?'

'Lord Humbert asks that you join him. Count Balfre and his Marcher lords have come.'

Leaving the innkeeper to her scolding of the stupid wench, he followed Dunsten out to the crowded forecourt, which was heaving like an anthill with the arrival of Harcian lords and men and horses . . . and its next duke.

Though he'd never before laid eyes on Balfre, there was no mistaking Aimery's arrogant heir. And not because he wore gold-stitched leather, and pearl-sewn velvet, and rings worth as much as Roric's three best horses. No. Authority was stamped into him like a master swordmaker's mark on his finest blade. And like an unsheathed sword, he stood before grizzled, aged Humbert, glittering in the cool sunlight and honed to a killing edge.

'Lord Humbert,' he said, his dark head briefly dipped. 'I give you Duke Aimery's cordial greetings.'

'And I Duke Roric's greetings to him,' Humbert replied. Though his attire was rich in its own right, compared to Balfre he looked dull. 'And you. Count Balfre, here is Lord Vidar, a trusted member of my duke's council.'

Watching Balfre watch his limping approach through the noisy mill and roil, Vidar saw in the man's eyes an indifferent curiosity . . . and a kind of impatient contempt. As though crippling wounds sustained in battle were somehow an affront. As though no man worth his mettle would choose to live a cripple rather than die.

'Count Balfre,' he said, halting. ''Tis a pity to meet like this.'

Balfre smiled, a swift sneer. 'My lord, 'tis a pity to meet.'

'Count Balfre! Count Balfre! Lord Waymon rides for us as though a soul-eater were after him! 'Ware riot, my lord!'

And that was Pero, Harcia's herald, shouting from the middle of the crossroad outside the inn. The note of alarm in his voice alarmed all four Marcher lords and their men. Hands slapped to daggers. Heads lifted like scenting hounds, eyes narrowing, shoulders bracing. Enticed by trouble, men-at-arms spilled out of the forecourt to meet riot with bared teeth.

'Wido! Jacott!' Humbert bellowed. 'Tell your men to hold fast! Balfre—' He raised a warning fist. 'Tell your lords to do the same! This is a Crown Court, there can be no—'

'The Court's not convened yet,' Balfre retorted. 'And Waymon is my man.'

Spitting curses like broken teeth, Humbert shoved after Balfre as he forged a path through their menacing men and into the road. Painfully aware of his one eye and aching hip, Vidar limped in their wake.

Balfre's leather-clad man Waymon, fair-haired, his lean face knife-scarred and full of danger, hauled his sweat-foamed horse to a rearing halt. The bloodstained body slung over its neck slid free to thud onto the muddy ground.

'My lord Balfre! My lord—' Panting, Waymon leapt from his saddle. 'Ride for Harcia! We are betrayed!'

'How betrayed?' Balfre demanded. 'Waymon—'

With a shuddering groan Waymon pressed a hand to his side then held it out, blood-soaked, for everyone to see. 'My lord,' he said, choking with pain. 'As I rode to join you I came across this scoundrel. Something about him raised my hackles. And when I challenged him, he attempted my life! I had to kill him, or let him kill me. Count Balfre, he is Clemen's man.'

'*What?*' Astonished, Humbert looked at Balfre. 'This is not Clemen's man. All my men are here with me!'

'Are they?' With a fierce look, Balfre bent over the body and rolled it face up. Then he stepped back, pale with fury, and pointed to the emblem stitched on its dirty tunic. 'That is a falcon badge, Humbert. Only a man of Clemen might wear it. And those colours, bronze and black? Duke Roric's colours, I believe!'

Humbert was staring at the dead man. 'I don't know him,' he insisted. 'I've never once in my life laid eyes on him. Have you, Vidar?'

He limped closer. Frowned down at the dead man's blood-and-mud smeared face. 'No, my lord. Never.'

'So you deny him,' said Balfre, as Harcia's Marcher lords and men muttered, an ugly sound. 'And will you also deny the bleeding wound he opened in my good friend's side? Perhaps you'll claim Waymon plunged a dagger into himself!'

'No,' said Humbert. 'But—'

'But what, *my lord*?'

Humbert raised his fist again, shook it at Balfre. Turned his glare on Harcia's Marcher lords, then on Clemen's. 'This is not my doing!

371

Nor can any man lay it at the feet of my duke! Wido! Jacott! Is this your mischief?'

'No, Lord Humbert,' said Wido, his own glare aimed at the Harcians. 'I say this is Bayard and Egbert's foul mashery, so they might escape blame for an innocent woman's death!'

'That's a lie, you poxed mule!' Bayard of Harcia retorted. 'This is none of our doing. And it was your men maimed and killed mine after they murdered their own cunting whore!'

'Clap tongue, every one of you!' Humbert shouted above the rising discord. 'Or I'll—'

'Have a care, Humbert,' said Balfre, his face wolfish. 'Lay your hand on a man of Harcia and I'll take it from you with a single blow. And if you think I can't, my lord, ask your friend Vidar. He knows a Harcian blade cuts cleanly. Don't you, Vidar?'

Hatred rose in him, so thick and hot he almost spat it out. 'I know Harcians are cowards who attempt the lives of women and children.'

'And which one are you?' With a derisive laugh, Aimery's dangerous son bent again to the dead man and began to unlace the corpse's blood-soaked clothing. Humbert stepped forward in protest.

'What are you doing, Balfre? Leave the man be!'

'But he's not a Clemen man, Humbert,' said Balfre, with a scathing glance. 'So why should you care if – ah. And what is this?'

Triumphant, he withdrew a letter from inside the dead man's tunic. The folded, sealed rush-paper was partly soaked in blood. Balfre peered at it.

'A missive,' he said, frowning. 'For Lord Humbert.'

Humbert held out a shaking hand. 'Then give it to me!'

'No,' said Balfre, and ripped the letter open, scattering shards of cracked wax. '"*Humbert*",' he read aloud. '"*Upon reflection, I cannot believe we'll find either justice or Harcian friendship in the Marches. Aimery is duplicitous, like every Harcian duke before him. I've no doubt this Crown Court will be a sham. Therefore you'll show the Harcian murderers no mercy and obtain their swift deaths. Roric.*"'

A brief, shocked hush, and then a furious outcry as the four Marcher lords and their men began hurling curses and threats and spittle at each other. The wounded man Waymon turned from Balfre's side and started berating Wido and Jacott.

'Give that letter to me, I said!' Humbert shouted over the uproar, and lunged to snatch it out of Balfre's grasp. 'I'll decide for myself if the curs't thing's genuine, my lord!'

With Balfre not arguing, or attempting to retrieve his prize, Humbert retreated a little distance and turned his back on Aimery's son. Vidar joined him. Seeing the familiar pen strokes on the blood-stained rush-paper, he felt his guts cramp.

'I don't understand,' Humbert muttered, as he closely examined the letter. 'Surely Roric's still in Cassinia. If he'd returned we would know. So how could he have written – and yet—' He thrust the letter sideways. 'The signature's ruined with blood but it is his penmanship. Wouldn't you say?'

Warily, Vidar nodded. 'I would. And though it's bloodstained, that looks like his signature. Perhaps Master Blane sent him word of the Crown Court. It is common knowledge in the duchy now.'

'Warned him by pigeon? That could be,' Humbert admitted, reluctant. 'I suppose.'

'But this.' He tapped the rush-paper. '*Harcian friendship*. Humbert, what does that mean?'

'I don't know,' Humbert said, scowling. 'Ask Roric, when next you see him.'

He didn't know? Acutely aware of the shouting and threats and curses flying behind them, Vidar stared at the letter. His guts were cramping again. Because he thought Humbert did know. He thought Humbert was lying. But why? What was Lindara's father trying to hide?

Then, before he could challenge the old bastard, Balfre approached, wounded Waymon a half-pace behind. 'My lord Humbert! I'll have your answer. Did your duke pen the letter, or no?'

Swallowing an oath, Humbert turned. 'It seems he did. But—'

'So you admit your duke's treachery!' said Balfre, spreading his arms wide. 'And his intent to murder innocent men!'

'I admit no such slander,' said Humbert, seething. 'Roric of Clemen is no more a murderer than I am. There's a mystery here, Balfre, and I'd delve it to the dregs before—'

'And give you time to catch your breath, to further muddy the waters? Even send some sly man of Clemen into the shadows with a sword?'

'Clap tongue, boy,' Humbert growled. 'I warn you.'

'Or what?' Balfre taunted. 'What would you think to do to me, old man, you and that broken limpjack by your side?'

'For one thing beat your insolent arse bloody, as your fucking father never did, to his shame!'

Wincing with the movement, Waymon unsheathed his dagger. Its blade showed dull in the sunlight, sticky with the dead man's blood. '*Hold*, you Clemen cur! One step towards my duke's son and I'll—'

'Murder!' a Clemen man-at-arms shouted. 'Murder! The bastard Harcians would kill Lord Humbert!'

Mayhem.

Seeing the vicious glee in Waymon's face, Vidar grabbed Humbert's arm and yanked him backwards. As the letter slipped from his fingers Humbert roared in protest and pulled free, groping for his dagger. Vidar tried to hold him.

'No, Humbert, don't—'

And then three men-at-arms, swearing and slashing, thumped into his treacherously weak side and knocked him off his feet. One trod on his hand, another kicked him in the belly. The third one, stumbling, dropped both knees on his injured hip then pressed him face-first into the road. His good eye was full of dirt. He couldn't see a fucking thing. Somewhere close by he heard Humbert bellow again, half in anger, half in pain. He tried to regain his footing, but the blow to his hip had ruined him. On fire with agony, all he could do was wallow in the mud like a pig waiting for slaughter. Dagger clashed against dagger as the fighting rose fast to fever pitch. Men screamed. Shouted. Fell. He could smell piss and shit, fresh blood: the mingled stench of desperate battle.

At last he managed to flail himself upright. Smear the dirt out of his eye. Everywhere he turned men were fighting, some with daggers, some with fists and feet, slashing and stabbing and punching and kicking. At least a half-score were down already, wounded or dead. One of them was Wido. He looked for Humbert. Couldn't see him. With a grunting, sweating effort he stood. Looked again, heart pounding. Four grappling men – two from Clemen, two Harcian – tumbled apart panting, and there was Lindara's father, one hand fisted in a Harcian Marcher man's torn tunic, the other slapping the fool silly, snapping his head from side to side. The old bastard had lost his dagger, his doublet's left sleeve was ripped and soaked with blood.

On his blind side, sudden movement. He heard it, felt it, the old instincts bludgeoned awake. Slewing round, he saw Waymon. Face bloody, hand bloody on a blood-stained dagger, the Harcian was pushing through knots of furiously fighting men, making for Humbert. He shouted but his voice was lost among the chaotic sounds of battle. Then a scream louder than the rest and almost in his ear swung him rightwards in time to see Balfre, his back turned, almost close enough to touch, drop a Clemen man with one wild slash of his blade across the face. The count's foot slid in the bloody mud and he went down on one knee.

Wrenching his dagger from its sheath, Vidar leapt for Aimery's son. Pain shot through his body, brilliant and scarlet. Stinking air rasped in his throat. His empty hand reached, caught hold of Balfre's hair. Pulled the Harcian bastard backwards, off-balance, and braced himself to take the weight. His damaged hip screamed a protest.

'*Waymon!*' he shouted, dagger-point pricked to Balfre's straining throat. '*Hold, Waymon, and drop your blade – or see me kill your duke's heir!*'

The bastard heard him. Even as his scarlet-streaked fingers closed on Humbert's upraised arm, he turned. Saw his precious Balfre a heartbeat from having his throat cut. The look on his bloodied face blinked from rage to terror.

He dropped his blade.

The bloody skirmish's aftermath saw the Pig Whistle's public room fill near to the rafters with wounded, moaning men from both duchies. Its forecourt was crowded with dead bodies, three of them Marcher lords. And the fourth, Lord Jacott, was like to die of his injuries. Too stunned for scolding, Molly did what she could to save those men most grievously hurt.

'Now, my lords,' she said sternly, once the first desperate rush was done, and pointed a sharp finger at Balfre, then Humbert. 'I'll do what I can to bind up the rest. But ye'll need to leave yer dispute outside. Seems t'me there's been enough blood spilled for one day. Iss?'

The lords stared at each other, simmering with resentful rage. Around them their broken men whimpered and groaned. She held her breath, waiting. From the corner of her eye glimpsed stealthy Iddo behind the bar, reaching for his cudgel. Then Lord Humbert nodded.

'No more trouble,' he grunted, his grizzled, blood-flecked beard not hiding his pain.

Count Balfre said nothing. He just stalked outside.

Mindful that once the muck settled she'd have to deal with Clemen's great men, Molly offered Humbert a curtsy. 'Thank ye, m'lord. Now best ye take a seat while I see t'yer arm. Ye look fit to fall over.'

Humbert grunted again. 'I'm blade-tickled, Mistress Molly, not dying.' He jerked his beard at the wounded men laid head to toe on the floor. 'See to them first.'

And that surprised her. 'Iss, m'lord. If ye say so.'

Leaving Humbert to suit himself, she picked her way to the bar, and Iddo.

'Moll . . .' He pulled a face. 'We can't be leeching all these men. If one dies, d'ye think his lord won't blame us for it?'

'That Humbert won't,' she said firmly. 'Besides, Iddo. What d'ye think they'll do if we *don't* lift a feggit finger and one of 'em dies?'

She had him there, and he knew it. They got to work.

Gaping dagger slashes were poulticed then bound with strips of torn sheets, and finger-stumps dipped into the stinking tar Iddo heated in the kitchen. Broken bones Molly splinted, as best she could. At first the pitiful cries of pain scraped at her nerves but after the first hour she hardly heard them. Even so, the task was a bloodsoaked, waking nightmare. No matter how many wounds she bandaged, the number of men needing her never seemed to shrink.

When Izusa rode by the inn, saw the shambles and stopped to offer help, she near collapsed weeping on the woman's neck.

Izusa cast one long, steady look around the ghastly public room, then patted her shoulder. 'Not to be cackled, Moll,' she said in her oddly accented deep voice. 'I'm on my way to leech a goatman at Crookleg farm, but he can bide a while. I've a fulsome herbary bag with me. You and me and Iddo, we'll see these messy men put right.'

Molly closed her eyes, drowning in relief. To think she'd resented Izusa, for taking poor dead Phemie's place.

Another three hours it needed, to properly clean and stitch and poultice and splint every wounded lord and man-at-arms. Two men died while they waited, but it couldn't be helped. When at last they were finished, Molly walked Izusa out to the forecourt. It had been emptied of corpses. The dead from each duchy were piled into carts. The wounded who could ride sat subdued in their saddles. Those who couldn't ride waited in their own carts. An exhausted melancholy muffled the dusking air.

'I can't thank ye enough, besom,' she said, pressing a hand to Izusa's arm. 'Me and Iddo, we'd have been pickled for certain if ye'd not stayed to aid us.'

Izusa smiled her crooked smile, gaze resting on stormy-faced Count Balfre. He stood in the skirmish-scarred, bloodstained road, beside the cart loaded with the Harcian dead, listening to Lord Waymon's urgent whispering. Not a nice man, that Waymon. He'd cursed foully while his wounded side was being poulticed.

'Of course I helped, Molly,' the healer said. 'Leechwork is my calling. It's only a pity I couldn't have done more.'

Molly snorted. 'The pity is these lords can't keep their feggit daggers sheathed. Can ye believe it? Wido, Bayard *and* Egbert perished! After this muckle I'd not pay ye a copper nib for a Crown Court. Not in the Pig Whistle or anyplace else. Poor woodsman Gannen won't see justice in this life.'

Shrugging, Izusa looked away from Balfre. 'Isn't that the way of it, when nobles come to blows?'

'Surely, and there be a right disgrace. I tell ye, Izusa, we'll have no peace in the Marches for—'

'Mistress Molly.'

She turned. Humbert, his arm stitched and bandaged and bound to his barrel of a chest, stepped into the forecourt. Behind him limped crippled, half-blind Lord Vidar – and what a surprise *he'd* 'scaped with no worse than kicks and bruises. A just reward for bringing the bloodshed to an end, even if he was one of the reasons it started.

'Iss, m'lord?'

Weary and grim-faced, Humbert gave her a nod. 'We'll leave now. My thanks for your good services. And yours, Izusa. Duke Roric will hear of them. I'll send men in the morning to fetch our other horses. You'll be paid for their keep.'

'Iss, m'lord,' she said, standing back so they could pass.

She and Izusa watched Humbert exchange some last, cold words with Count Balfre, then swing himself stiffly onto his waiting horse. Lord Vidar, who'd been handsome before his face was ruined, struggled onto his own fine palfrey, then the two lords rode away. The men-at-arms who could ride, and the carts filled with Clemen's dead and wounded, followed. A sad procession.

'I must go too,' said Izusa, as one of the stable boys appeared leading her plain nag. 'Or the goatman won't pay me.'

Count Balfre didn't bother to offer his thanks. He was too busy staring after Izusa as she jogged her horse into the dusk. Not to be wondered at, really. She had a look about her, did Izusa, though she were thin and foreign, with that wildly curling, foxy hair.

'And I b'aint sorrowed to see the back of *him*, Moll,' said Iddo, coming out to join her as the Harcians departed. 'A right cruel one, Count Balfre. He fair makes my skin crawl.'

Denno Culpyn had said the same, and she had to agree. Would've told Iddo so, too, but before she could say a word all thought of Balfre fled. Because it was then her boys came home.

When the fighting started it was Alys's notion to run with them into the woods. She'd said yes, not wanting Benedikt and Willem in harm's way, or frighted by the screams and the hot, spilling blood. But now here they were at last, grubby with playing and not a scratch between them, clamouring to know what happened while they were gone.

'Never ye mind on that, ye ructious imps,' she said, tweaking their ears. 'Ye'll eat yer supper now, and then go to bed.'

'Why the frowning, Moll?' said Iddo, as she watched Alys chivvy her protesting scamps indoors. 'The girl b'aint what I much like, but she took good care of them boys. First thing she thought of, keeping them safe.'

Was that true? Or was Alys's first thought for herself? It was hard to forget the look on the girl's face when she saw Lord Vidar. Faery-struck, she'd seemed. Heartshot and trembling with fear. It made no sense. Why would the girl be frighted by a man she'd never met? Her fear woke memories of the night she and baby Willem turned up on the Pig Whistle's doorstep, a shadow of that same fear darkening her eyes.

But there'd be no mentioning that to Iddo. He was prickly enough about Alys already. Instead, she kissed her man's bristled cheek. 'What a feggit day. Go fetch them lads from the stables, Iddo, so ye can scrub the blood out of the floorboards and put the room to rights. I'll feed them impish boys, then we'll feast ourselves on chicken pie. The spirits know I baked enough!'

Later, as Iddo and the stable boys drank cider and drowsed and played leap-button in front of the fire, she left them to their laughing, took a lit lamp and climbed the stairs to speak to Alys, who'd taken herself to bed. For until she had the truth out of the girl, the reason why she'd so feared the sight of Lord Vidar, she knew she wouldn't rest.

The attic chamber's door was on the latch, candlelight showing under it and down its slivered edge. And murmuring through the crack, Alys. Telling Willem a story when he should be fast asleep. Molly drew her breath to scold, raised her fist to rap the door. Keeping the boy jiggety when he needed his rest? What was the girl thinking?

And then she heard what Alys was saying . . . and the blood in her turned to ice.

'So that's who you are, Liam. Great-grandson of Berold, son of poor slain Harald, and the rightful duke of Clemen. And once you're a man grown, my lamb, what will you do?'

'I'll find that bastard Roric,' said Willem, so bold. 'And I'll cut off his feggit head.'

'Exactly right, my lamb. That's what you'll do. But can you tell anyone about it?'

'No,' said Willem. 'Not even Benedikt. It be a secret. Yours and mine.'

For a long time Molly stood there with the raised lamp, hardly daring to breathe, biting her knuckles till her tongue tasted blood. Little Willem? That imp? Son of Clemen's duke that was killed? How could that be?

But then she remembered again the look on that wicked girl's face when she saw crippled Vidar . . . and knew, sick with terror, that it was the dreadful truth.

Willem's the proper duke of Clemen. Not that bastard Roric. And if Clemen finds him here, they'll take him. If he's found here, they'll kill us all.

Kill Benedikt. Kill Iddo. Burn the Pig Whistle to the ground.

Shivering, she watched her bitten knuckles tap lightly on Alys's door. Heard herself say, kindly, 'I need ye a moment, Alys. Can ye come back downstairs?'

She waited. The door opened and Alys slipped out, her nightdress half-covered in a woollen shawl. The girl was cross, but trying to hide it. 'Is something wrong, Molly?'

She shook her head. In her veins, the ice crackled. 'No. Go on, now. I promise it won't take long.'

She let the girl go first. And as Alys's bare foot touched the third worn wooden tread from the top, shoved hard between her shoulders and sent the girl tumbling down the rest.

Thud, thud, bang, crack. Alys sprawled at the foot of the stairs, twisted on her side. Ice-cold, Molly followed until she was halfway down. Then she clutched at the banister and drew in a sobbing breath.

'Iddo! Iddo! Come quick! That Alys, she's fallen down the stairs!'

A gasp from above her. Turning, she saw Willem – Liam – Harald's son, the spirits save them – standing at the top of the stairs with his chestnut hair tousled and his amber eyes wide enough to pop. His nightshirt was patched and darned, and barely came to his knees. He was growing so fast. He'd be a tall man, one day.

'Back to bed, imp!' she told him, and tried to shield him from seeing Alys.

But Willem – Liam – ignored her. 'Ellyn!' he cried. 'Ellyn!'

She caught him with one arm, held him kicking and struggling. 'Ellyn? Who's Ellyn?'

For a heartbeat he slumped limply against her. Then he started struggling again. 'Nobody. She's Alys. She's hurt. Let me go!'

So. Even the wretched girl's name was a lie. Everything about the little bitch had been a lie. And if Iddo ever found out—

Thudding on the lower stairs, and then there he was. Seeing Alys crumpled on the shadowy landing, he hesitated.

'Be she dead, Iddo?'

He held his calloused palm in front of the girl's face. 'No, Moll. She be breathing. But I fear she's mortal hurt.'

Not dead? She swallowed a curse. 'Best ye get her into bed. I'll sit with her. Ye can take Willem afore the fire.'

He frowned. 'I don't like to move her, Moll. Could be she's got bones broke.'

'Ye have to move her, man. She can't stay—'

A low, faint moan. The girl's hand twitched. And then, in the lamplight, Alys – Ellyn – slowly opened her eyes.

'*Willem.*'

The boy was struggling so hard she was going to drop the lamp. No need for Clemen to burn down the Pig Whistle. She'd do it herself.

'Here, Iddo! Take him!'

She stumbled down the rest of the stairs, poor distressed little Willem slipping from her grasp. Iddo snatched him free, whirled him away.

'Wait, Iddo. Keep him by a moment.'

Putting the lamp down, Molly knelt by Alys's side. Even in the rosy light the girl's skin was sickly pale. Her eyes had drifted shut. A thread of blood trickled from her nose and over her parted lips. Another thread dribbled from her ear, staining the neck of her night-dress. Such a bloody day, they'd had.

She leaned close. 'Alys. Can ye hear me?'

Another faint moan. A flutter of lashes. 'Molly? Where's Willem?'

'He's here, girl. I've got him.'

Alys breathed in, a raw, shivering sound. Her fingers twitched again. 'Molly . . .'

The girl's voice was failing. Molly touched her cheek. She was cold. Another shivering breath, then she opened her eyes. They were already starting to cloud.

'Willem,' she whispered. 'I risked my life for him, I did. I killed for him, Molly. I'd do it again. Keep him safe. Don't let . . . don't let . . .'

The girl died.

'Here, Iddo,' Molly said, and held out her arms. 'Let Willem come. Let the poor mite say goodbye.'

It cracked her heart wide, to hear Willem sobbing over Alys. Or Ellyn. Or whoever she'd been.

Killed for him, did she? Well. And so did I.

'No, no,' Willem hiccuped, clutching the girl's lifeless hand, his face hidden against her breast. 'Don't be dead. Ye can't be dead.'

Remembering how she'd grieved for Diggin, Molly pressed trembling fingers to her lips. She wanted to weep too, though Iddo was dry-eyed. But she'd not whip herself. She'd done what she'd done and she couldn't undo it. Wouldn't if she could. Willem was her family, just like Benedikt and Iddo. She'd never beg pardon for keeping her family safe.

But kneeling there, in the lamplight, battered by Willem's stormy grief . . . she was sorry to have hurt him. Still, he was just a little boy. Time would pass, and he'd forget this night and its cruel pain.

Forget Ellyn. Forget Liam. And forget he was a duke.

CHAPTER TWENTY-THREE

Standing before the window in Wido's oak-panelled library, feeling the sharp ache in his daggered arm, Humbert stared across the mole-pocked lawn to the straggling woodland that fringed the manor's unkempt grounds. Summer in the Marches started late and lived a short life. Wood burned in the fireplace, flames crackling loud and smoky. The chimney wouldn't draw cleanly. Poor household management. But that was Wido, wasn't it? Half-arsed. No proper judgement. Scant wonder the man was dead and order in the Marches lying in ruins around his corpse.

Almost he could wish Wido's crime had been enriching himself at Roric's expense. But no. The shite had spent his trusted time in the Marches squabbling with Harcia's Bayard and Egbert, pursuing petty vendettas against them and their Marcher men while turning a blind eye to his own men's misconduct. Within a day of his arrival here, he'd sniffed out Wido's failings. Yes, and Jacott's too. A pair of rotten peas in the same fucking pod.

And we in Eaglerock were fool enough, complacent enough, to take Wido and Jacott's reports at face value and dismiss Harcian complaints as shite-stirring. But no more.

Brooding, he wondered if he was doing the right thing. It sat ill to reward Vidar when the bastard deserved beheading. But try as he might he could think of no better remedy. Clemen was already precarious. Its brittle nerve could never withstand Lindara's wicked plot coming to light. No. He'd brought Vidar with him intending to leave the cockshite behind in exile, as punishment for daring to touch Roric's wife. He must stay his course. So long as he kept a close watch on Godebert's son – and he'd already sent for Egann to be his eyes and ears here – all would be well.

The library door opened. He heard the limping cockshite and his walking cane tap-and-drag into the room. Heard the door shut, then Vidar clear his throat.

'You wanted to see me?'

He turned. Vidar was leaning heavily on his cane, his one-eyed gaze wary. Not a knife-mark did he carry from the bloody debacle at the Pig Whistle, but the herb-woman who'd done her best for Clemen's wounded, and then come to the manor house that morning to see how they were faring, claimed Vidar was badly knocked about, his damaged hip hurt again. And true enough, he did look to be walking worse than ever. But looks could be deceiving. Vidar's looks most of all.

Six years on the council, nodding and smiling. Six years pretending he had Roric's interests at heart. And all that time . . .

Humbert clenched his jaw. Every time he believed his rage

conquered it woke again, and he wanted to knock Vidar to the floor and beat the shite to death with his bare fists.

'Humbert?'

'Tell me, Vidar,' he said, jutting his chin, 'how long have you been fucking my daughter?'

The look on Vidar's face was an admission of guilt. Not that there was any doubt.

'Answer me. You're crippled, not deaf.'

Too late, Vidar tried to pretend. 'If that's a jest, it's a poor one.'

'*Jest?* Vidar, you cockshite, it's treason. *How long?*'

'I admit nothing!' Vidar said hotly. 'Who accuses me, my lord?'

'No man. You accused yourself. When you danced with Lindara at your betrothal feast. So many people betrayed in one afternoon. Like father, like son. Godebert would be proud.'

The amethysts gold-stitched to Vidar's dark blue doublet shivered light as his breathing changed. A muscle leapt along his tight jaw. Under his spoiled eye, a nervous tic.

Glowering, Humbert raised a warning finger. 'Don't waste your breath denying this. *I know*. I have confessions. Lindara. Her maid. And the witch.'

Instead of protesting he knew nothing of any witch, Vidar swallowed. 'You'd see your daughter ruined by the taint of sorcery?'

'Ah.' He breathed out, slowly. 'So you knew the woman she used to ruin Roric was foul.'

His one eye glittering, Vidar eased his bad hip. Seemed prepared to go on blustering . . . then abruptly surrendered. 'Not till recently. I thought she was—' He sighed. 'But I doubt you care what I thought. Or believe that I'd have kept Lindara from her, had I known.'

'You're right. I don't.'

'You think me a traitor.'

'*Think?*' The urge to beat and batter rose again, blinding. 'You pissing whoreson! She's the wife of your duke!'

'An unwilling wife!' Vidar's voice was shaking. 'Wed to a man who never deserved her. Who never cared for her, not truly. Not like I do.'

Humbert stared, disbelieving. 'What womanish drivel is this? Have you never heard of *honour*?'

384

'You think Roric has honour? He married Lindara knowing I loved her. Thinking I held my love so cheap that I could be bought with dirt and grass and a seat on his council.'

'And you *were* bought!' Sweating, Humbert clutched at a nearby straight-backed chair. 'Like a two-copper whore you took what Roric offered – then you turned traitor and spat in his face. You planned to put your bastard son on the Falcon Throne!'

Vidar straightened, the effort blanching his unscarred cheek. 'Fine. I'm a traitor. But we both know I'm not the only one.'

'*What?*'

'You think I don't know how you threatened Lindara, to make her wed with Roric against her will?' Vidar's face twisted with contempt. 'What man who loves his daughter would treat her like that?'

'And what man with a daughter would see her wed with the likes of you?'

'Aistan.'

Humbert snorted. 'To his everlasting shame.'

They glared at each other, the air between them thick with loathing. A faint splattering sound, as rain began to spit against the window.

'So?' Vidar said harshly. 'What now? For as much as we both know you want to kick my corpse, you can't afford to call my life forfeit. Not when you're desperate to keep this matter close.'

Jaw tightened to breaking point, he scowled. 'Don't be too sure.'

'But I am sure,' Vidar retorted. 'You love Roric too much to let it come to light. You love yourself even more. What a shame you didn't think to kill me yesterday. You could've blamed my death on a Harcian and no one would ever know.'

'Believe me, I was tempted.'

But with Vidar dead he'd never trust Lindara to keep her mouth shut. Godebert's son breathing was his only way to keep her tame.

'Come, Humbert,' Vidar said, near to taunting. His old self again. 'Don't play coy. I'd know my fate.'

Humbert released his hold on the chair. 'As soon as Jacott can travel, if he doesn't die, I'll be leaving for Eaglerock with him, and Wido's body, and their families. You'll stay behind. I'm giving you

Clemen's Marches, Vidar. And your life will depend on you keeping the peace.'

'You're mad,' Vidar said, after a choked silence. 'You expect me to rot in this forsaken place? For how long?'

'You'll not limp back into Eaglerock before Lindara's given Roric two healthy sons. At least. Clemen will have its future, and you're no part of that. You failed, Vidar, you and my daughter and that whore of a witch you found.'

Despite the fire, the room was chilly . . . but a bead of sweat rolled down the side of Vidar's face. It almost looked like a tear.

'You have no right,' he whispered. 'Roric is duke in Clemen. Not you. If he—'

'Roric's been guided by me since he was seven. If I tell him you're best suited here, then here is where you'll stay.'

A short, bitter laugh. 'And you call me a cockshite. Humbert—' Vidar's fingers were white on his walking cane. 'I saved your life yesterday. Is this how you'd thank me?'

'You're not owed thanks. You've been fucking your duke's wife.'

Vidar took a lurching step forward. '*My* wife, Humbert. In my heart, she's my wife.'

More sentimental slop. Some faery had addled the bastard's wits. 'In your heart and nowhere else, Vidar. Stop thinking you can sway me. Lindara is lost to you. And I swear, if you fight me on this I'll see that she suffers for the rest of her life. Then I'll have your head for a paperweight and take my chances after.'

Vidar knew him well enough to know that was no idle threat. He seemed to shrink, his confidence shrivelling. In his face a stark and genuine grief. Seeing it, Humbert felt an unwanted pang of sympathy.

'Godebert was ever a weak and profligate lord,' he said roughly. 'Watching you grow from boy to man, Vidar, I had hopes you'd redeem him. And you did, somewhat. In your early years. For certain you've never lacked physical courage. I can admire you for that much.'

'High praise,' Vidar said, savagely sarcastic.

'No. A brute beast has physical courage. More is asked of a man.'

Silence, as Vidar contemplated his fate. 'And so I'm disposed of,' he murmured, at last. 'Out of sight . . . and out of mind.'

'And it's more than you deserve. Though I'll say this. Despite what you've done, I know you love Clemen. Your treachery is personal. Born of weak, slighted feeling.'

'Does that mean I keep Coldspring? And my other estates?'

He had to leave the man with some hope, else risk him doing something worse. 'If you behave yourself. If you make it plain to Roric that serving him here is your heart's desire and serve him well, then yes, you'll keep your property. And because I'm not a cruel man, I'll let you have Aistan's spoiled daughter to wife.' He shook his head, wearied with disgust. 'Get a son of your own on her, Vidar. You owe that to Clemen, if not Godebert. Our duchy needs all the strong sons it can breed. Keep peace in the Marches. As close as my eye will be on you, keep yours close on Harcia. What Aimery does next will decide if it's to be peace between us, or war.'

Vidar hesitated, then cleared his throat. 'And yesterday's bloodshed? The letter, and the man who brought it? His murder by Balfre's man?'

'Never you mind on that,' said Humbert. 'You can leave that to me.'

Crushed with disappointment, Aimery fingered the torn letter Balfre had given him. There was dried mud on it. Dried blood. But though some of the words were obscured, he could read enough to know they spelled the death of any hope he'd had for peace with Clemen.

'I'm sorry, my lord,' Balfre said, subdued. 'I wish I came with better news.'

'There's no doubt Roric wrote this?'

'None. Humbert confirmed it is his hand.'

'And he killed Bayard?'

'Yes.'

'And Vidar slaughtered Egbert?'

'I saw it.'

He frowned. 'Vidar's a cripple.'

'That didn't stop him from trying to slit my throat.' Balfre retorted, and pulled down his shirt.

Aimery stared at the scabbed dagger-cut in his son's flesh. 'You never said you were wounded.'

'I bled a little. That's all.'

'All?' said Grefin, standing with his back to the privy chamber's unshuttered window. 'You nearly died.'

His face was disciplined, but Aimery knew his younger son. Grefin was anguished by Roric's duplicity.

As I am. I offered him peace and friendship. He answered me with slaughter.

Both his Marcher lords murdered, and all of their men. His lax hand trembled on the arm of his chair.

'Your Grace—' Balfre dropped to one knee. 'May I speak plainly?'

In the face of dire provocation, this reckless son had conducted himself with remarkable restraint. There was hope for him after all . . . and cause for pride.

He nodded. 'You may.'

'I know you dream of a lasting peace with Clemen. Harald made it impossible, but I think you felt there could be a fresh start with Roric.'

'I did, Balfre,' he said, fighting the urge to look at Grefin. 'A wise ruler seeks peace.'

'Yes. But he must be careful where he places his trust. Roric has proven that base blood will out. He's a festering thorn and must be plucked from Harcia's flesh before he poisons us all.'

Aimery watched the muddied, bloodied letter slip out of his grasp. Flutter like an autumn leaf to the floor. 'You want war.'

'*Want?*' Balfre clenched his fists. 'Never. But Clemen has butchered two of our lords. Would you have Roric think he can kill us without consequence? Have Harcia's lords think you'll see them buried unavenged?'

'You hope to insult me into warfare?'

Balfre stood. 'No, my lord. But you—'

'I share your anger, Balfre,' Grefin said quietly. 'But there's blame here on both sides. Bayard and Egbert were often contentious with Wido and Jacott. And our Marcher men followed their lords' poor example.'

Balfre snatched up the fallen letter and brandished it at both of them. 'So you'd discard proof in Roric's own hand that he'd deal falsely with Harcia? *Father*—' Tumultuous, Balfre dropped to his knee again. 'Must the proof be written in *your* blood before I have leave to act?'

Moved by his angry fear, Aimery rested a hand on his son's head. 'Before we make countless Harcian widows? Yes, Balfre. It must. But keeping my sword sheathed is not the same as trusting Roric. I will never trust Clemen's duke again.'

'Nor should you, my lord. The bastard played you false.' Balfre sighed. 'Father . . . I'd make a suggestion. For on the ride home from the Marches I gave our dilemma much thought.'

Aimery sat back. 'What would you have me do?'

'Thanks to Grefin, we have order in the Green Isle. Let me bring that same order to the Marches. Grant me the authority to uphold the law in your name. Make me your Marcher lord.'

Aimery tapped a finger to his chin. 'A moment ago you were urging me to war. Yet a Marcher lord's first duty is keeping the peace.'

'That's true,' Balfre admitted. 'But a weak peace is no strength. A weak peace leads to bloodshed. I can uphold Marcher law *and* give Clemen reason to think twice before spilling any more Harcian blood.'

'It's not a bad idea, Father,' said Grefin. 'As your heir, Balfre's authority is unassailable. I doubt Roric would dare test him.'

What treacherous Roric would do, he could no longer imagine. 'Perhaps,' he said, frowning. 'But Balfre – a Marcher lord must be concerned with every man's welfare. Could you deal fairly with Clemen if a man of Harcia was found in the wrong?'

'Yes, my lord,' Balfre said, still kneeling. Not humble, for he could never be that, but with his natural arrogance tempered, at last. 'Which I think you know, or you wouldn't have sent me to speak for you at the Crown Court.'

No, he'd sent Balfre to the Crown Court to prove himself trustworthy.

And when he could've slaughtered Humbert, slaughtered Vidar, wreaked his vengeance upon Clemen, he stayed his hand and came home to seek my guidance.

What else should Balfre do to prove himself worthy of trust?

'You'd need another lord to aid you. The Marches are too big for one man.'

'I'd take Waymon, Your Grace.'

'Not Joben? Or Lowis? Or even Paithan?'

'No,' Balfre said, regretful. 'Harcia needs Joben's voice on the council. Lowis's health is uncertain. And with Herewart growing feeble, Paithan should be close at hand. His father will need him far more than I.'

'Waymon,' said Grefin, uneasy. 'I know he's your friend, Balfre, and I'd not smear him, but . . .'

'He can be wild,' Balfre said, looking at his brother. 'But he saved my life in the Marches. In time he'll season. If he's given the chance.' He almost smiled. 'As I have.'

Aimery pinched the bridge of his nose. Waymon wouldn't be his choice, either. But Balfre had earned the right to decide. Just as he'd earned the right to rule the Marches.

'Very well, Balfre. You are my Marcher lord.'

Balfre leapt up, brilliantly smiling. 'Thank you, Your Grace. I swear on my honour, I'll not disappoint.'

'I know.' He released an unsteady breath. 'Now, you've come to me straight from the road, weary and travel-stained after much hard riding, and though you keep close counsel I know you're heartsore over Bayard and Egbert and our slaughtered men. Eat, sleep, and put aside sorrow for a time.'

'Your Grace,' said Balfre, and turned. 'Grefin.'

Grefin crossed to his brother, folded him into an embrace. 'I'm proud of you, Balfre. I doubt I'd have kept my head, if I'd been there.'

As Balfre departed, Aimery let himself slump. His weakened body was trembling, and grief threatened to break free.

Grefin reached for him. 'Father—'

'Don't, Grefin,' he said harshly. 'There's nothing you can say. Balfre is right. Clemen has ever been greedy and deceitful. Shame on me for thinking that could change.'

'Not shame,' said Grefin, his voice thick. 'Never shame. There can't be shame in an honest seeking after peace.'

He shuddered. 'Say as much to Bayard and Egbert. See if they agree.'

'*Father*—'

'No, Grefin.' He raised a defensive hand. 'You mean well, and I'm glad you badgered me into letting you stay in Cater's Tamwell till Balfre returned. But I'd be alone. Go and play with your children. They'll be grown and you'll be an old man, soon enough.'

'Your Grace,' Grefin murmured, and did as he was told.

Aimery waited until the chamber door shut before he let the tears fall.

'Well, leech? Will Lord Waymon be spared?'

'Count Balfre!' The startled castle leech dropped his bone needle and length of boiled horsehair. 'His lordship's life is not in peril. The wound is more a long gash than deeply penetrating. Most fortunate.'

No, not really. Waymon had taken great care not to kill himself by accident. Inspecting the unstitched and freshly bloodied dagger-wound in Waymon's side, Balfre raised an eyebrow.

'Were you not satisfied with the herb-woman's stitchery?'

The leech sniffed. 'There were gaps, my lord. Ill humours were gathering.'

'She had worse wounds than mine to mend,' said Waymon, grinning despite the pain. Bloodied linen cloths were scattered at his feet. 'Count Balfre used his dagger on those Clemen filth with lordly skill.'

He frowned Waymon to silence. 'A few proper stitches is all Waymon requires, leech?'

'Yes, my lord,' the leech said, cautious. 'With a good daubing of speedwell ointment after, and a linen bandage to finish. I've one here, soaking in a tincture of cockleburr, comfrey and goldenseal.'

'Then go seek a patient elsewhere,' he said. 'I know my way around a needle.'

Not pleased, but no fool either, Tamwell's leech withdrew from the stone-walled infirmary. Balfre latched the door behind him.

'My lord?' Waymon was eyeing him like a skittish horse. 'Are you sure you—'

'You wound me, Waymon,' he said, crossing to a bench where the leech's tools were neatly displayed. 'I could slit your throat and stitch it shut again well enough.'

Waymon laughed, uneasily. 'I'm encouraged to hear it. I think. Have you seen the duke?'

Ah, Waymon. A little murder and mayhem and he thought they were almost equals. But this wasn't the time to put the upstart in his place. Waymon was yet useful . . . and knew more than enough to be dangerous. He must be kept close.

'I've just come from him.'

'How went it?'

With his back turned he didn't have to school his face. But he made sure to keep the aggravation out of his voice. 'Sadly,' he said, choosing a fresh bone needle. 'Aimery's grieved by the loss of good Harcian men, and his grief grieves me. I did what had to be done but it gives me scant pleasure.'

'Better a little pain now than a great pain later. Clemen is a festering sore.'

Indeed. He fished a horsehair from its jar of spirits, and threaded the needle. 'Though one good thing has come of this shambles. I'm named Harcia's new Marcher lord.'

'Truly? 'Tis excellent news, Balfre!'

Waymon sounded astonished, but pleased. Just what he wanted to hear. 'It's a solemn duty.'

'You'll perform it well. When do you leave?'

'Soon.' He crossed back to Waymon, who immediately looked skittish again. 'Clemen must remain cowed. Now, my friend, hold your arm out of the way and grit your teeth. This will pinch.'

Womanish, Waymon yelped at each popping bite of the needle and closing tug of horsehair. Yelped louder as ointment was slathered across the wound, then groaned as the herb-soaked bandage was wound around his ribs.

'Thank you,' he said, when the task was done. 'But don't take it amiss if I say you were born to be a duke, not a leech.'

'I won't. Waymon . . .' He settled his hand on the man's shoulder. Showed him nothing but the duke's loving son, a good friend. 'You must think me monstrous ungrateful, that I've not yet spoken of what you did for me in the Marches.'

Waymon flushed. 'My lord, I failed you in the Marches. I didn't stop Humbert from claiming the trader's body.'

True. But while the mistake still rankled, he was prepared, this once, to forgive. Humbert might have the body, but bodies rotted. He, on the other hand, had retrieved the forged letter. And it was the letter that gave him the leverage he needed over Aimery and Grefin. Which meant he had the power. All Humbert had was putrid flesh.

He gave Waymon's shoulder a light squeeze. 'No, my friend. Everything I asked, you did, even when what I asked was difficult. And I know it was difficult. Not killing that lone trader and dressing him in Roric's livery, but wounding yourself. Killing Bayard. And maiming our own Marcher men so they'd not survive.'

'You killed Egbert, and some of our men,' Waymon said, shrugging. 'How could I flinch, when you didn't? Besides, they failed Harcia. They failed you. What could any of them expect for that but death?'

He sighed, as though impossibly burdened. 'I'm glad you feel that way. There are many who'd think my judgement too harsh.'

'Not I,' said Waymon, fiercely. 'Can a meek lamb rule Harcia?'

The man's unswerving loyalty was a balm to his scorched spirit, which hadn't healed from Aimery and Grefin's betrayal. Might never heal. Some wounds were too deep. Some betrayals beyond forgiveness.

'Many would say yes.'

'Then they're fools, my lord. I'd rather be dead in a ditch than suffer the lordship of a lamb.'

Well. That was one thing they had in common, at least. Balfre wandered idly back to the bench, where he'd left the jar of speedwell ointment unsealed. Pushing the cork plug into its neck, he glanced over.

'The letter from Roric I gave you to put with the Clemen man's body. I know you must have questions.'

'Well—' Waymon hesitated. 'Balfre, I don't need—'

'No, but I'll explain,' he said, smiling. 'I owe you that much. How the letter came to me, it's best you don't know. I'd keep you safe whenever I can. But how I came by it meant I couldn't easily reveal its existence to Aimery. And so . . . a small deception. Dishonesty in service of a greater truth. If that disturbs you, then—'

'I told you, Balfre,' Waymon said, sombre. 'Whatever you need. Ask me, and it's done.'

Returning to him, Balfre slid his hand to the back of Waymon's neck, pulled him close so he could press their foreheads together. 'Such loyalty is a rare gift. Worth more to me than a lake of molten gold. I'd reward it. Come to the Marches, Waymon. Be my strong right arm.'

Waymon jerked back. 'Balfre! Me? But what—'

'My cousins are our friends and are good men, and I love them,' he said. 'And I'll have need of them, in time. But they lack your heart, Waymon. They would've stayed their hands in the Marches. Doubted what they were asked to do. Doubted me.'

'Then they're fools too,' said Waymon. 'Because what you did saved Harcia from Clemen's treachery.'

'No, Waymon. *We* saved it.'

Struck dumb, Waymon swallowed.

'Now, my friend, you should eat a hearty meal, then rest,' he said. 'As I intend to do. For the task before us is daunting and we shall need all our strength.'

The next morning, after a poor night's sleep, disheartened by Roric's duplicity and fretting for Aimery, Grefin found that not even Mazelina's gentle company or his children's laughter could soothe him. So he took refuge in childhood memory, and sought out the place where he used to hide as a boy: the crooked branches of an old apple tree, in a far corner of the bailey. There he sat, knees pulled close to his chest, and brooded.

Balfre found him there an hour later.

'We should talk,' his brother said, fisted hands on his hips. 'Just the two of us.'

He pulled a face. 'I'm not in the mood, Balfre.'

'Too bad. I am.'

There was no point protesting, so he climbed out of the tree and walked across Tamwell castle's outer bridge with his brother, thinking they'd wander along the cliff or maybe through the township. Find a quiet tavern and hide themselves in a corner. But no. Instead, Balfre led him down to the river and threw coins at a wherryman for the use of his sturdy little boat.

With a comfortable sigh, Balfre settled himself on a bench seat, his back to the stern. 'You're the youngest. You can row.'

Bastard. Grefin hunched onto the wherryman's seat, took hold of the oars and wrangled the wherry away from the dock and into the lazily flowing river. The wherryman stared after them, shading his bemused face with his hand.

'Mind, now,' said Balfre. 'The river's well-travelled and this doublet's not for swimming.'

He was right. The river Tam was Harcia's highway, thronged daily with wherries and barges unless it was a hard winter and the water froze. Then horse-and-carts used it like a regular road, and children tied shingles to their shoes and slid about in riots of laughter, and older boys held archery contests under the sparkling, ice-blue sky. Two hundred and sixty-odd years ago the Tam's waters had flowed through the Marches and into Clemen. But Harcia's duke in that time, Gorvenal, he'd put an end to that. Summoned every able-bodied man and boy in the duchy to the slow, narrow river bend beyond Cater's Tamwell and turned them into an army of spadesmen. Upon his command they'd diverted the river back into Harcia. And though Clemen had howled and pleaded and threatened, Gorvenal stood firm . . . and Clemen didn't fight. That was something to remember, in these uncertain times.

Glancing over his shoulder, then left and right at the wherries gliding beside them, making sure he was in no danger of a collision, Grefin heaved a sigh. 'Balfre, where are we going?'

Balfre waved a vague hand. 'Does it matter? Surely even you can't get lost on a fucking river. Now put your back into it. It's past time you worked up an honest sweat.'

If he'd not needed both oars, he'd have smacked his brother with one.

Feeling his muscles loosen as he worked into the rhythm of the task, feeling the impersonal tug of the flowing water and the strength it cost him to keep the wherry driving straight, he deepened his breathing. The air smelled of the midden, and open fields, and damp ploughed soil, and cattle.

'I'm wondering,' he said, watching Balfre watch the cottages and countryside glide by. 'When you leave, will you take Jancis with you?'

Balfre grimaced. 'No.'

'So you'd not object if she spent a little time on the Green Isle with me and Mazelina?'

'I would. Aimery needs her to tend him.'

'Balfre, she's nursed Aimery since he fell ill. She's tired. A respite will restore her spirits.'

'What the fuck do you care for my wife and her spirits?' said Balfre, staring. 'Besides, surely Mazelina is trouble enough on her own.'

Grefin thought a moment before replying. If only Balfre weren't so prickly when it came to talk of marriage. It touched too near the question of children, of sons. His disappointment, and how he blamed that on his wife.

'It's Mazelina who's asked me to ask you. She's fond of Jancis. She says the wives of men like us must love each other like sisters.'

'Men like us? I suppose that's an insult, is it? *Men like us*.'

'Balfre . . .' He shook his head, amused by his brother's outrage. 'Can you call us easy? Were you a woman, would you wish to be married to you?'

'Instead of you? Fuck! What do you think?'

'I think that when it comes to my wife, I know which battles to fight and when I shouldn't even bother unsheathing my sword.'

'Fuck.' Disgruntled, Balfre worried at the ruby ring on his thumb. Then he shrugged, an irritable twitch of one shoulder. 'Fine. Take Jancis back with you. Keep her for all I care.'

A double-sailed flat barge wallowed by them, laden with slabs of blood granite quarried in Danstun, three days' ride to the north. Breathing hard, Grefin struggled to hold the wherry against the barge's heavy wash. He could hear shouts and curses as the river's wherryman fought to keep their own boats steady.

Balfre was laughing as he swayed in time with their boat's plunging. 'What did I say, Grefin? An honest sweat. But I warn you – tip me into the Tam and I'll wring your fucking neck!'

A great deal of honest sweat saved him. Danger past, and the river settling, Grefin blotted his face on his sleeve. 'You lazy shite, Balfre. You could've lent me a hand. I swear, one of these days I'll kill you.'

Balfre grinned. 'Not if I kill you first.'

That deserved an eye roll, and got one. Rowing again, he considered his brother. Wondered if he should risk speaking further about Jancis. Probably not. But when would he have another chance? They mightn't see each other for a year. Perhaps longer. And Balfre was hurting, though he did his best never to show it.

'You shouldn't fret over Jancis. When Aimery—' No, he still couldn't say it aloud. 'When you're duke, you can put her aside. Choose a wife more to your liking and breed a son on her instead.'

'You astonish me,' Balfre said, after a staring silence. 'Truly.'

'Why? I'm not Mazelina. A duke's wife – the heir's wife – owes him a son. Jancis is no bad woman, but she's failed you.'

'Our father's made it plain, Grefin. I must keep Jancis to wife.'

A mistake on Aimery's part, but no amount of argument would change his mind. 'And so you will. While he's duke.'

Frowning, Balfre slid the ruby ring from his right thumb and fiddled it over the scarred joint on his left. 'But if I keep her to wife after his death, as Aimery wants, and as Harcia's duke die without a son, you'd follow me.' He inspected the ring again, then pulled it off his left thumb. As though the fate of the world rested upon which thumb wore a ruby. 'Fuck, Grefin. If Clemen kills me in the Marches you'll be Aimery's heir. I'll wager that thought gives you a thrill.'

His turn to stare. 'D'you think that's my ambition? That having tasted power in the Green Isle I now covet all of Harcia?'

The ruby ring was back on his brother's right thumb. One arm resting along the wherry's side, Balfre shrugged. 'Don't you?'

'No! Is this what you wanted to talk about? Because if it is—'

'Keep your voice down, Grefin. We've got wherrymen on either side of us and sound carries across water.'

Maybe so, but it was still hard not to shout. 'I've no desire to be duke of Harcia. And fuck you for thinking I'd rejoice at your death.'

Balfre smoothed his breeze-blown hair. 'It seems I've offended you.'

'And hurt me. When did I *ever* give you cause to doubt?'

'Never,' said Balfre. 'I'm sorry, Grefin. My mind's wandering to dark places. Blame Roric for that.'

For that, and so much more. 'Then what did you want to talk about?'

'Aimery. I must go to the Marches and you must return to the Green Isle – with my wife, or without her. But losing both of us will weigh on him. You know it.'

Shifting on the bench, Grefin eased his rowing and looked back to see how far they'd come. A goodly distance. Tamwell castle appeared not quite so forbidding. Looking again to Balfre, he set the oars to holding them steady.

'What are you saying? Has the leech confided more in you than he'll tell me?'

'The fucking leech hardly gives me the time of day. But I'm not so green I can't hear what isn't said. Aimery will never again be the man he was. And the next fit might—'

'Must there be another one?' he said, his mouth dry. 'Does the leech suggest there will be?'

'Grefin . . .' Now Balfre was impatiently pitying. 'You're not so green either.'

No, he wasn't. But the thought of his father's death was as cruel a hurt as thinking of Mazelina taken from him, or one of his children.

'Then if you must go, and I must, what's to be done?'

'I think . . .' Falling silent, Balfre searched the distant riverbank, as though he might find there the answer to a problem that was already answered. 'Grefin, if we can keep him from worrying,' he said eventually, his voice low and unsteady, 'then there's hope we'll keep him with us the longer. So while I pick up the pieces in the Marches, you need to bind the lords of the Green Isle ever closer. They heed you now for Aimery's sake. Make them heed you for your own. If I can tame the Marches, keep Clemen penned safe behind them, and you can keep the Green Isle sweet, what will there be in Harcia to fret him? And without fret . . .' He sighed. 'There's hope.'

'Perhaps that is the best we can do for him. Only . . .'

'It seems too little,' Balfre said. 'I know.'

They fell silent. Another barge blundered past, this one carrying sheep. Penned on the flat deck, their anxious bleating floated over the water.

'Life is strange,' Grefin murmured, turning to watch the barge. Mutton-sheep, he guessed, bound for slaughter. Even at this distance he could see their fleeces were good only for mattress stuffing and the stripping of lanolin. 'Who'd believe we'd be brought close again by Aimery's faltering health, and Clemen's treachery.'

'Who said we're close?' said Balfre, then laughed. 'Grefin, Grefin . . . you're as gullible as those fucking sheep, I swear.'

And here was the Balfre of his childhood: wicked, mischievous, absent for too long.

'Cockshite. You're the only man I know who'd see a trusting nature as something to disparage.'

'Then you know the wrong men,' said Balfre. 'Which explains why you're such a fucking soap with those oars. Shift over, brother, and let me take one. Or it'll be the middle of next week before we're home.'

Aimery hosted a feast to honour Harcía's new Marcher lord. A quiet affair, no acrobats or jonglers. Minstrels, of course, but they were instructed to keep the recent deaths of Bayard and Egbert in mind.

Just before the sweetmeats were brought into the hall, Balfre joined Waymon, Joben, Paithan and Lowis at the trestle he'd set aside for their privy use. He didn't have to look back to know his father was watching.

'My friends,' he said, signalling a servant to bring them a fresh flagon of wine. 'I know you wish you were all coming with me, but I'd ask you to be patient. I have important plans for each and every one of you. Wait to hear from me and know that you're as much a part of Harcía's future as I am.'

An exchange of looks up and down the trestle's bench. There'd been loud dismay when he'd told Joben and the rest that it was Waymon who'd be at his right hand in the Marches.

Joben had dragged him aside, flushed with temper. 'I'm your cousin, Balfre. How could you count him over your own blood?'

He'd kissed Joben's cheek. 'Because you're blood. Who else can I trust to speak my mind while I'm gone?'

'Are you sure, Balfre? Waymon's wild,' Paithan protested.

'A wild man for a wild place,' he'd replied. 'Have no fear, my friend. I'll handle him.'

Only Lowis had been indifferent. Lowis, whose cruel streak was less reliable than Waymon's, but who'd make a useful messenger . . . and a blunt instrument, now and then.

He'd expected their disappointment. But it would count for nothing, in the end. One day he'd be their duke. Their riches – their lives – dependent upon his largess. Let them pout. It didn't hurt him. All he had to do was snap his fingers and they'd come to heel.

After carousing a while with his lords, he left them to their belching and made his way around the hall, speaking to every noble guest and every merchant summoned by Aimery to bid him farewell. He spoke last of all with feeble Herewart.

'My lord,' he said, kneeling beside the wit-wandered old rump. 'Once I did you a grave wrong, and I never begged your pardon. So I beg it now, and thank you for the gift of friendship with your heir. Paithan does you proud, Herewart, as I hope to do my father proud while I serve him in the Marches.'

Herewart's rheumy gaze roamed his face. 'I do pardon you, Balfre,' he said, his voice cracked and seamed beyond its years. Grief for Hughe had broken him, and he'd never mended after. 'You're to be my Paithan's duke, so I'd not have us cross-purposed. He tells me you're a changed man and if he says so, I'll believe it.'

All around them, nods and murmurs of approval. Balfre bowed his head in a show of grateful humility, then shifted his gaze just far enough to look at the high table. His father was smiling. Grefin was smiling. Even his useless, barren bitch of a wife was smiling. As pleased to see him go as he was to leave, most like. Only Mazelina's eyes were cool and guarded, watching him. But then, for all her pretending at friendship, she'd ever been his enemy. It didn't matter. His brother's wife would be dealt with in time.

When I'm king and she's no one. Her fucking time will come then.

CHAPTER TWENTY-FOUR

Molly was in the kitchen, stirring a fragrantly simmering pot of rabbit stew, when Iddo pushed his way past the leather curtain. 'Moll.'

One look at his face told the tale. More trouble. Biting her lip, she glanced at the boys, sat quiet at the table eating their noon meal of bread and cheese and pickled onions. Willem was woebegone, missing Alys, and Benedikt was woebegone for him. She had them sleeping in her chamber now, because of Willem's bad dreams over the girl's death.

She still regretted it, causing Willem pain. And lying to Iddo, who could never know the truth. But what did it matter that she was pricked with miscomfort? Her lies, and what she'd done, kept them safe from the peril that dreadful, deceitful Alys had plunged them into. And with a tad more time gone by Willem would surely stop dreaming — and screaming.

Iddo slapped the wall. 'Moll. Ye've got to come. It be them feggit lords again.'

'Which lords?' she muttered. 'To my mind they be all of 'em feggits.'

'Balfre and Vidar.'

Vidar. Her heart pounded. Of all the lords to be put in charge of Clemen's Marcher lands, why did it have to be *him*, a man who'd spent time at dead Harald's court? Afraid Iddo would see her fear, which would only stir him up, she plunged her wooden spoon back into the rabbit stew.

'What d'they want?'

'I didn't ask!' Iddo said, astonished. 'Think I want a dagger 'twixt my ribs, woman, asking them two lords their business?'

Frowning, she jerked her chin at the boys. *Mind yer tongue, man.* 'Don't be foolish. 'Tis a reasonable question.'

'Iss,' Iddo retorted. 'But ye know as well as I do, Moll, they b'aint reasonable men!'

Swallowing a curse, Molly clapped the lid back on the cast-iron stew pot. Teased to leaping at shadows, Iddo was, these past few days – and the faeries knew he wasn't alone. Three days before, word had reached the Whistle that Aimery's son Balfre was returned as Harcia's new Marcher lord. Nobody she spoke to since was frolicsome at the news. Bad enough that familiar Jacott was on his slow way back to Eaglerock, too hurt ever to sit another horse, Izusa said, with crippled Vidar left behind in his place. There were whispers already from Clemen's men-at-arms, on how stern and unforgiving he was. Him and his man Egann. Wicked hard, both of them. Now here was Balfre, the son of Harcia's duke, and the Crown Court slaughter had shown them the kind of man *he* was. So what hope for peace and quiet did the poor Marches have, with those two brawling lords holding all the power and no one to caution them?

She'd told Izusa there'd be trouble. For once she wished she was wrong.

'*Molly*,' Iddo said, nervously impatient. 'What be amiss with ye? Them lords—'

'I know, I know,' she said, wiping her damp palms on her apron. 'Where are they?'

'In the forecourt. I did bid 'em to hold there, so they could speak private if needed.'

Clever thinking. But if she didn't play the welcoming innkeep they'd be under her feet soon enough. And above all things she had to keep Vidar away from Willem. 'I'll see to 'em. Best ye get back to the bar. Boys, ye bide here.'

Making her way through the public room, she frowned her dozen or so busybody guests to prudent silence. Then, as she stepped over her own threshold and into the forecourt, she felt her heart sink, because them feggit lords were facing each other like tomcats and Aimery's handsome son Balfre, he had *such* a smile on his face.

'—reward for your courage you're exiled to the Marches,' he was

402

saying. 'Perhaps next time you'll think twice before thinking to slit my throat.'

'My lords!' she said loudly. 'Be ye both welcome again to the Pig Whistle. Was it ale ye wanted? Some tasty beef pottage, perhaps?'

Both lords shining in velvet and glittering with jewels, looked at her. Refusing to wilt under their scrutiny, she lifted her chin. No curtsy this time. They owed her for all the spilled blood no amount of scrubbing could get out of her floor.

'Count Balfre and I would discuss Marcher affairs,' said Lord Vidar, his voice cool. 'You must have a room set aside for privy matters.'

'Iss, my lord,' she said. 'I do.'

'Take us to it and make sure we're not—'

As his one-eyed stare moved past her, she heard the patter-patter shuffle of small footsteps and two smothered voices. She turned. Benedikt and Willem, agoggle in the public room's open doorway. And what was Iddo doing, to let them slip by? *Useless* man.

Dry-mouthed, she raised her hand to them. 'Into the kitchen, ye rompish goblins, or I'll be breaking a wooden spoon across yer skinny arses!'

Her boys retreated, unwilling, eyes wide as they took in the splendidly dressed Marcher lords.

'My sons,' she said, turning back. Feeling sick. She didn't dare look at Vidar's face. 'Naughty but no harm in 'em. My lords, if ye'd follow me?'

She led them into the Whistle and up to the small, pleasantly furnished chamber kept aside for important guests. Hurried downstairs to dish pottage into her best bowls. Thrust the steaming bowls on their serving tray at Iddo, told him to draw two tankards of their best ale and take it all up to their lordships, fended off questions from the public room and escaped back into the kitchen. It took every bit of strength she had not to heave her guts into the sink.

Now she knew how Alys had felt. Heartshot. Beyond terror. She could feel the nervous boys behind her, waiting for a scold. In front of her the rabbit stew simmered on the hob. Upstairs, over her head, Lord Vidar of Clemen was eating her pottage and drinking her ale.

Vidar, who'd known Duke Harald. And here was Harald's son under his feet.

Vidar saw him. He saw Willem. And no matter how I try to stop it, he'll likely see the boy again. Or one of his fancy friends from Eaglerock will see him. They'll see him, and see Harald in him. It only be a matter of time. And then – and then—

They'd take Willem. They'd take the Pig Whistle. To keep, or to burn. They'd take her and they'd take Iddo and like as not hang them both. And Benedikt, her precious Benedikt, he'd be orphaned and alone. Or they could hang him too. Clemen's lords in Eaglerock pretended to care for the Marches but that was mostly for show. Mostly they cared because the Marches kept Harcia at arm's length. Marcher folk didn't matter. What was one hanged boy to them?

Lord Wido cared for us, but he's dead. Lord Jacott cared, but he's gone. And I'd hang myself afore believing Lord Vidar would lift a finger to save Benedikt's life.

So the burden was hers. Again. Protecting her boys, the Pig Whistle, Iddo? It was for her to do. Again. And having killed to protect them, what wouldn't she do?

As though she watched another woman, she watched her hands reach for the bubbling pot of stew.

Ye can't. He's a little boy. He meant no harm. Ye could kill him.

But even as the words wailed inside her head she was picking up the cast-iron pot and swinging round, swinging hard, knowing exactly where innocent Willem stood.

They sat opposite each other in the Pig Whistle's small upstairs chamber, both pretending they were alone. Pretending they'd come for a meal, nothing more. But even though the pottage was tasty, the ale rich and deep, Vidar thought he might as well be eating dirt and drinking swill.

He'd been a fool to demand this meeting. Balfre couldn't help himself; the shite offered insults the way marshland belched noxious fumes. Why had Aimery's heir even bothered to come? Not to admit any faults on Harcia's part, that much was plain. The bastard—

From below stairs, muffled, a woman's cry. A child's high-pitched shrieking. Thudding feet. Men's raised voices.

Balfre lifted his head like a boarhound scenting game. Pushed his chair back from the table and stood, fingers touching his dagger's hilt.

'Don't stir yourself, Vidar,' he said, viciously polite. 'I'll see what's amiss.'

And what could he do but nod agreement as he swallowed his mouthful of barley and beef? Balfre had seen how painfully he moved. His bad hip burned yet from the Crown Court skirmish and the relentless physicality that had followed, forced upon him by Lindara's father in the crowded days before his departure. Hours of drilling Clemen's men-at-arms and riding through its Marches territory, making himself familiar with every copse, every stream, every pond, every holding and the men and women who dwelled there. The healer-woman Izusa had given him pills more potent than he'd ever taken, but nothing could kill the pain outright.

Listening to the light thud-thud-thud of Balfre's boots as the shite ran downstairs to make sure the inn wasn't under attack, Vidar drained his tankard of ale and wished, for the thousandth time, that he'd kept his mouth shut and let Waymon butcher Humbert. But a lifetime of loyalty to his duchy wouldn't let him. A lifetime of loyalty – and his love for Lindara. Who hated her father yet loved him too. Or loved some small part of him, deny it though she might. He knew how that felt. To love and hate a father. For all his grave sins, didn't Godebert haunt him still?

So for Clemen and my beloved I saved Humbert's life. And now I'm prisoned in the Marches, at Humbert's mercy, his man Egann my keeper. Soon to be prisoned in marriage to Kennise . . . and no Lindara to unlock the cage.

His bones ached for her. His heart ached. Every night he dreamed of her, and woke every morning soaked in his own seed. Humbert said she was lost to him. He refused to believe it.

The old bastard won't live for ever. And then she'll be free. She'll run from Roric and I'll run from the Marches and together we'll run till we find our peace.

A foolish yearning? Perhaps. But what else did he have to sustain him? Yes, of late he and Lindara had been unhappy. But that could change. It would change. As soon as Humbert died.

But until that happy day he had only one choice: serve Clemen, and endure.

Thud-thud-thud. Balfre was returning. Vidar swallowed his last mouthful of beef, napkinned his lips clean, and sat back in his chair like a man without a care.

''Twas nothing,' Balfre said, pushing the door closed behind him. 'One of the innkeeper's brats burned itself.' Sitting again, he grinned. 'She's got a spare, so no harm done if it dies.'

He couldn't care less about the innkeeper's brats. 'Balfre, we must find common ground if we're to keep peace in the Marches.'

Still grinning, Balfre raised an eyebrow at him over the top of his tankard. 'Must we?'

With an effort he kept his fingers relaxed. He would not, *would not*, let himself be provoked. 'It's no secret Harald winked at misdoings here that soured you on Clemen. We don't blame you for hard feelings. Harald was not a good duke.'

'Well, you're bound to say so,' said Balfre, shrugging. 'Since he executed your father. For treason, yes? I see it runs in the family.'

For one dreadful moment, he thought Balfre meant Lindara. Then he realised the bastard was referring to Harald's killing.

'We never sought Harald's death,' he said, his jaw tight. 'We offered him honourable exile. It was his choice to fight.'

'Then perhaps he wasn't such a bad duke after all.' Impatient, Balfre banged his tankard to the table. 'Vidar, I didn't come here to rake over Clemen's tedious history. What you do with your dukes is your affair. What matters is the present. Harcia's duke, my father, though sorely grieved by recent calamity, seeks to leave the past in the past. If Clemen agrees not to pursue the murder of the woodsman's wife, Harcia will turn a blind eye – this once – to Roric's double dealing. We'll call it an error of youth and let the matter lie.'

Vidar dropped his gaze. So. Harcia wanted peace. It was the outcome he wanted, that Humbert demanded he obtain, but Balfre's dismissive contempt was beyond bearing. He'd never survive being trapped in the Marches with the bastard if he let him ride roughshod from the start.

'You have no proof of double dealing,' he said, looking up. 'One letter isn't proof. But there's no doubt the woodsman's wife was murdered, or that Harcia's men-at-arms were—'

Balfre stood. Not amused now, but angry. 'So it's just words with you, Vidar? You mumble for peace and prepare to spill more blood? Fine. If it's bloodshed you want then Harcia will oblige.'

So much for survival. Aimery's heir was even more volatile than rumour had whispered. Without kid-glove careful handling he'd rush them all to ruin.

'*Wait*,' he said tersely. 'Did I say I wanted blood?'

'Then what do you want? Tell me. That is, if you know.'

I want Eaglerock. I want Lindara. I want to dance on Humbert's grave.

He met Balfre's hot, derisive stare. 'I want peace. And so does Roric. Clemen agrees to your terms. We'll leave the past in the past and call this a fresh start. But you'll keep your men on a tight leash, Balfre. I'll do the same, and with luck our paths won't need to cross more than once a month. If that.'

'Done,' said Balfre. 'Just be sure you keep your word.'

He let Balfre leave first, so the arrogant bastard could think he'd won. And so Aimery's son couldn't bear witness to his pain. Sitting so long had tightened his sinews. His body groaned when he stood. Groaned as he limped his slow way downstairs. Groaned as he hauled himself into his saddle. And wept as he rode back to the manor house, that had belonged to Wido and which now he must call home.

Izusa was picking hedgerow herbs on the edge of her cottage wood-land when one of the Pig Whistle's panting stable lads found her.

'Can ye come to Mistress Molly?' he gasped, leaning out of his ragged pony's old, patched saddle. 'Her boy, he's been hurt.'

She felt a sickening lurch in the pit of her belly. *Not Liam. Please, not Liam.* 'Which boy? How is he hurt?'

''Tis Willem,' the lad said. 'I din't know what be amiss, but I heard him howling. Can ye come?'

Howling. She felt the earth tilt. 'Of course. I just need to fetch my satchel. Tell Molly.'

As the boy drummed his heels against the pony, urging it to a canter, she snatched up the sack of herbs and ran like a hunted doe to her cottage. If Liam perished, Salimbene would have her heart. Oh, how had she not *known*? Had she grown complacent? Or worse, were her powers failing?

Even if Liam lived, Salimbene would surely discard her if they were.

The thought of being tossed aside by him had her sobbing for breath, fumbled her fingers as she made sure of enough poppy and fevermoss and knitbone in her satchel. When she was satisfied, she hefted it outside, fetched her nag from its tethered grazing, banged on its saddle and bridle, strapped on the satchel, and set off for the Pig Whistle.

At least she had one consolation. Molly had straight away sent to her for help. That was welcome proof she'd grown indispensable to this stretch of the Marches. It was what she'd been working towards. What Salimbene had planned. Perhaps, hearing that, he'd forgive her for Liam.

It had been a simple task, killing the old herb-woman Phemie. Long ago Salimbene had given her the power to walk silent through the world, being seen by men only when it suited her. Or him. No curse had killed the old woman, just a drop of poison. A lingering death that mimicked the capricious cruelty of nature and let her death be called plague-kill without question. After that it was simply a matter of making people sick, as she'd made that trader Denno Culpyn sick, then waiting until fear stalked the Marches like a ravenous beast. Only then did she reveal herself. Izusa, the healer, with no plan to stay in these parts . . . except that she was needed. And being needed, would remain.

But only for so long as Salimbene desired.

Clemen's Lord Wido, unaware he was galloping towards his death, had granted her the use of dead Phemie's cottage. It lay in one of his woodlands so he imagined it was his. She'd taken it, gladly, and placed around the modest daub-and-shingled dwelling so many runes and curses that not a living soul would ever remember she'd lived there or what she looked like. Unless, of course, she wanted them to. Soon after that she arranged a dead baby, for its head. Then Salimbene found her and she was whole again.

But if she failed him . . . if she failed him . . .

When she reached the Pig Whistle, the stable lad who'd come to fetch her took the nag and told her she'd find Molly indoors. Iddo, tending the public room, nodded when he saw her and told the serving wench they'd taken on to show her upstairs.

'Izusa!' cried Molly, wringing her hands. 'At last. I tell ye, there be an ill faery under my roof. First that ruckus on the doorstep, then Alys goes tumbling to her death, and now this. The imp stood behind me while I was at the hob and when I turned round with the stew pot I—'

'Yes, Molly, I see,' she said, moving to crouch beside Liam in his truckle bed, pressed against the wall in Molly's bedchamber. 'You broke his nose and burned him.'

The woman's true son, little Benedikt, stood high-strung beside his foster-brother. 'But ye can heal him, iss?' His piping voice shook. 'He won't die?'

Stripped out of his roughspun shirt and propped up on pillows, Harald's son was a wounded, sorry sight. Nose bent and bloody. Forehead, cheek and shoulder blistered scarlet and weeping. His eyelid was swollen. Had the stupid woman made of him another Vidar? The child was shivering, pain taking its toll.

Molly made a growling sound. 'What did I say, ye wretch? Be hushed!'

Her son wilted. Reaching out, Izusa stroked his wild, dark hair. 'Not to fret, Benedikt. I won't let him die.'

Harald's son, misnamed Willem, bore her interfering fingers with surprising strength. He whimpered but once when she mostly straightened his nose, and shed only a few tears at the bite of the poultice she slathered on his burned flesh. When she gave him a poppy posset he gagged, but drank. All the while, Benedikt stood close and encouraged him. Patted his good shoulder. Promised all kinds of rompish fun just as soon as he was healed.

As for Molly, she stared. Stuffed with guilt, and silent. Stupid, careless woman. Should Salimbene want her punished it would be no hardship to obey.

Finished with her leeching, Izusa helped Liam ease properly into his bed. Benedikt helped too. He was a sweet boy.

'The poultice will stop any festering,' she said, turning to Molly.

'Change it morning, noon and night for three days. I'll leave you the herbs. But he's going to scar. And that nose of his, it'll stay crooked.'

'His eye?'

'Not blistered. I'll know for sure when the swelling's gone, but I think he'll keep his sight.'

Molly pressed her work-rough hands to her face. 'The spirits be thanked.'

'Let him sleep,' she said, touching the back of her hand to Liam's unburned cheek. He was already drowsy, the poppy doing its work. 'When he stirs he'll likely fever up. Steep him in a yarrow bath. That should do the trick. Poor mite. He'll feel worse before he's better.'

'Ye'll come again on the morrow?' Molly said, anxious.

Izusa smiled. She'd never seen the innkeeper so turmoiled. And serve her right, for Liam's sake. 'First thing.'

'I want to stay,' said Benedikt, tugging Liam's blanket smooth. 'Can I stay? I won't fret him.'

Molly frowned. 'Ye have chores, Benedikt.'

'He'll do no harm, Molly,' she said softly. 'Let him stay. It'll ease Willem if he's not alone when he wakes.'

'On yer bed, then,' Molly told her son, pointing to the other truckle tucked in behind the door. 'And if I hear a mouse peep from ye, it'll be the wooden spoon.'

Downstairs in the kitchen, Izusa portioned out the herbs and ointments and powdered poppy that Liam would need overnight. When she was finished, her satchel repacked and fastened, Molly pressed a silver coin into her palm.

'Thank ye, besom. I don't know what I'd do without ye.'

She slipped the coin into the leather purse belted at her waist. 'Don't fret, Molly. I'm not going anywhere. As for your Willem, he'll come right. I'll make sure of it. For you'd best believe I'll die before I let that boy come to harm. Now, take care of your customers. I'll see you again in the morning.'

Her plain nag was weary, she'd ridden it so hard to the Pig Whistle. So she let it amble its way back to the cottage. Though summer was fading some warmth remained in the sun. She tipped her head back to bathe her face in it, let it melt the lingering fear.

Harald's son may be healed . . . but there was still Salimbene. She couldn't keep this from him. That would surely mean her death.

Returned to her small dwelling, she unsaddled the nag then penned it beside the cottage with water from the well, an armful of hay and a scoop of oats. That done, she went inside. Before she left the Pig Whistle, Molly had gifted her a skinful of rich rabbit stew. She warmed it in a kettle over her hearthfire, and washed it down with a mug of strong ale. Then, her heart thudding, she lit more candles, fed the fire to leaping, and fetched her wooden box. She never knew how long it might take for Salimbene to answer her call. Sometimes he came to her swiftly. Sometimes he took hours.

All she could do was wait for him . . . and trust that he'd come.

With a snarling shout, Balfre ducked under Waymon's swinging arm, hooked one bare foot around his ankle, pulled hard while he thrust sideways once with his hip. Waymon went down. Balfre followed him. Plucked Waymon's dagger from his numbed, wide-spread fingers and thrust its point under his chin. Sprawled on his back, gasping for air, Waymon turned himself to stone.

Laughing, Balfre slapped Waymon lightly on the cheek. Then he bounced to his feet and turned to his watching men-at-arms, gathered raggedly around the barracks tilt yard of Bayard's manor that he'd taken for his own. 'A little trick I learned from my father's Master Armsman, Ambrose.'

Uneasy mutters. Sideways glances and some shuffling feet. Harcia's men-at-arms didn't know what to make of their new lord. Sagged into soft-bellied indiscipline by Bayard and Egbert's neglect, their taunting squabbles with Clemen's men spilling a little blood here and there but provoking more rancorous word play, these men thought themselves much deadlier than they were. Between them, at the Pig Whistle, he and Waymon had put down their sword-brothers with no more difficulty than if they'd been ladies' lapdogs. What he needed was wolves.

And when he was done with them, wolves he would have.

'I was two years of age when Ambrose first put a sword in my hand,' he said, sweeping his gaze across their blankly wary faces. He held up Waymon's dagger. 'It was made of wood, not much bigger than this. When I was three, I rode my first pass in a joust. I sat a pony. Ambrose faced me on foot. He sent me tumbling. When I snivelled, he beat me with the flat of his blade. *For shame, my lord Balfre*, he said. *You are a duke's son.* I learned my lesson. I took many more tumbles but I never snivelled again. *You—*' He sharpened his gaze. 'Are all snivellers. You think you're fine, fighting men but you only play at war. You take the duke my father's coin and you piss it against a tree. You jeer at Clemen, and catcall, when you should stand fast for Harcia. *Make no mistake.* Your snivelling days are done. I'm about to beat you with the flat of *my* blade until you beg for mercy. *Waymon.*'

'My lord,' said Waymon, joining him.

'Let's begin.'

In all, Harcia boasted some fifty men-at-arms to protect its Marches territory from Clemen's incursions. He'd ordered half to the tilt yard to train with him and Waymon this afternoon. The other half he'd confront in the morning. Waiting for the uneasy men to strip themselves to britches and bare feet, he smiled. Single out one or two for particular humiliation, batter the rest to their unsuspecting knees, and word would swiftly spread that Aimery's son Balfre was no soft, pampered lord.

'So, my friend,' he said, glancing at Waymon. 'Are you ready to teach these fucking shites a sharp lesson?'

Sweaty and dirt-streaked, his cheekbone bruised, Waymon grinned. 'Not ready, my lord. Eager.'

As was he. Putting crippled Vidar in his place at the Pig Whistle had only whetted his appetite for sport. He slapped Waymon's arm. 'Good. But no maimings. I don't mind blood and bruises but I'd leave them with all their limbs.'

For more than three hours he and Waymon put Harcia's men-at-arms through their paces. Kicked their legs out from under them, tossed them onto their backs, cut them and bruised them and rubbed their lapdog noses in how much they didn't know. When at last the light was fading, and he was satisfied they'd learned their lesson, he called a halt to the drubbing.

'You could be worse,' he told his Marcher men, strewn panting and bloody around the foot-churned tilt yard. 'Those of you who were worse got themselves gutted at the Pig Whistle. Me, I say they died of shame. That old cockshite Humbert took the most living men home. What's shame, if not that?'

Mynton, the barracks captain, hawked and spat blood. 'My lord, what d'ye tell us? Do we prepare for war?'

'With Clemen?' He laughed. 'Every day is war with Clemen. Roric the bastard would kill us all, had he the chance. But Aimery loves you. He'd keep your blood in your veins – as would I. For now. So until Roric breaks the peace we'll wage a war without blood. We'll keep the Marches bloodless and every day we'll train. Because one day Roric will put his sword to our throat. And when he does I'd have us ready to plunge our sword through his heart.'

More muttering, this time tinged with cautious pleasure. This time Balfre hid his smile. These men were beaten but not broken, which was precisely his intent. Mynton and two others, men he'd made sure to wound enough for leeching, he told to remain. Dismissing the rest to the barracks bath house, he sent Waymon to fetch him needle, thread and hot water. When they came he neatly cleaned and stitched the wounds he'd inflicted.

Mynton stared as he cautiously flexed his slashed forearm. A stringy man of middle years, he spoke with a faded hint of the Green Isle in his voice. In his pale blue eyes, a grudging gleam of respect.

'Thank ye, m'lord.'

Balfre nodded. 'You did well. You'll do better. See the men settled for the night.'

'M'lord,' Mynton said, with a jerky half-bow. 'Brindle. Poley. With me.'

As the men-at-arms snatched up their boots and tunics and limped through the falling dusk towards their barracks, Waymon cleared his throat. 'Balfre, a good lord should know his men. I'd bathe and sup with ours.'

A surprising request. Making sure to seem indifferent, he shrugged. 'If you like. If my company's grown so dull.'

Waymon flushed. 'My lord—'

'Fuck, Waymon. You're as easily gulled as a virgin. Go. Somehow I'll survive a solitary meal for one night.'

After pulling on his shirt, doublet and boots he returned to the manor. Its soft-footed steward Fulcher met him in the modest entrance hall and handed him a wax-sealed parchment. 'My lord, this came while you were at the tilt yard.'

'I'll be in the library,' he said, taking it. 'Bring me food and wine there.'

Comfortably cradled in his chair before the fireplace, he opened the letter. It was from Grefin, hastily penned the morning of his departure from Cater's Tamwell.

I'm off home to the Green Isle, Balfre, with Mazelina and the children. You should know Jancis decided not to come. Again, I wish you well in the Marches. I know you'll keep Aimery's peace, no matter how provoking Clemen might be. Speaking of the duke, I've sent for a leech who I'm told has worked wonders with other men afflicted like our father. I'm hopeful, as I know you'll be, that with his help we can keep Aimery with us for many years yet. Stay safe, brother, till next we meet.

Balfre tossed the letter onto a nearby side table, darkly amused, then stretched out his legs and let the leaping flames dazzle him. Ah, Grefin. So earnest. So transparent. So useful, from time to time. By all means let a new leech eke a few more years out of Aimery. He could wait. He had time. He had a great deal to do before he was ready to become the new king of Harcia.

His belly rumbled, complaining. Fulcher arrived with his evening meal and, laughing softly, he started to eat.

She was drowsing, drifting, when at last the severed baby's head in its wooden box stirred, then answered.

'*Izusa. You called me.*'

Heart beating wildly, she slid from her chair to the cottage's rush-mat covered earth floor. Forced herself to look into the severed head's grey, prunish face.

'Yes, Salimbene.'

'*You stink of fear, Izusa. What has happened?*'

Near to weeping, she told him.

'Forgive me. I saw no sign of danger or—'

'*You say the boy will live?*'

'Liam will live. I swear it.'

'*Then you have not failed me. You are forgiven, Izusa.*'

Believing him, she let her tears fall. And when the head's dead lips quivered, then stretched into a brief smile, she laughed. Her blood bubbled with joy.

'What other tasks have you for me, Salimbene?'

For a little while he didn't answer. She sat on her heels, content with silence. Content with knowing she'd kept his trust even though Liam was hurt. Candlelight flickered. From the night-dark woods outside came the screech of a hunting owl. Then the head's dead lips quivered again, and the sunken eyes behind their cobweb eyelids shifted.

'*Balfre of Harcia is settled in the Marches?*'

'He is. But I've not seen him.'

'*You will, in time. In time you will do more. But do not go to him, Izusa. Wait for him to come to you. When he comes – and he will come – you will give yourself to him. In giving you will take him. And then he will be mine.*'

Balfre to be her lover? No hardship, that. She'd fucked other men for Salimbene. Some had been old. Some gross. None were as handsome as Aimery's heir.

'Yes, Salimbene.'

'*We come to a fallow time, Izusa. Liam must grow out of childhood, and Aimery grow more feeble. Clemen must weaken further while Roric sinks into despair. Serve me in the Marches. Be a friend to every lord and humble woodsman. Listen to every whisper, and whisper them to me.*'

He wanted her close by while Liam grew out of childhood? That meant she'd be living in the Marches for years, be kept from him for years. Bubbling joy curdled to misery. But she couldn't protest, or defy him. He was Salimbene.

'I will,' she said, trembling. 'I'm your eyes, your ears, your beating heart. Command me and I'll obey.'

She received no answer. Salimbene was gone.

'*Now remember, Liam, you're no ordinary boy. You're brave Harald's true-born son, Berold's great-grandson, and the rightful duke of*

Clemen. Keep the ring hidden and don't tell a soul till you're old enough to take back the Falcon Throne from that bastard Roric who stole it from you.'

Twisting beneath his blanket, Liam whimpered out loud. It hurt to dream of Ellyn. He missed her so much. But he couldn't stop dreaming of her. If he stopped he'd never see her again. Never hear her tell him his story, and other stories of his father the duke, or feel her holding him safe and tight. In his dreams she wasn't dead. She wasn't broken on the attic landing. In his dreams she was smiling and he wasn't alone.

'Ellyn,' he moaned. 'Ellyn.'

A small finger poked his shoulder. 'Willem? Are ye awake?'

Oh, there was a terrible pain in his face and his shoulder. It wasn't the deep, dull ache of missing Ellyn. This was bright and hot, like fire. He could hear himself snuffling. He could only open one eye.

Poke, poke, poke. '*Willem.* D'ye want Ma?'

Benedikt was kneeling beside the candlelit bed. His peering face was blurry, and screwed up with fright.

'Wha' happened?' he said, and frighted himself. He sounded mushy, like Iddo that time a drunk trader punched him in the mouth.

'Ye got hurt,' said Benedikt. 'This morning. Don't ye remember?'

It was hard to think past the pain. He wanted to cry with it, only Ellyn said dukes didn't cry. His father, Harald, never cried. He had to make his father proud.

'In the kitchen?' he said, uncertain. 'Molly – she hit me with the pot.'

'Not on purpose,' Benedikt said quickly. 'Willem, who's Ellyn?'

A stabbing in his chest, worse than the fire in his face. He'd said her name out loud? But he'd promised he'd never tell. Every night he promised, even though she was dead. And even though this was Benedikt, a duke always kept his word.

'What?' he mumbled. 'No. I said Alys. I was dreaming. Benedikt, I feel sick.'

Benedikt scrambled to his feet. 'I'll fetch Ma.'

But before he reached the chamber door it opened. Iddo loomed in the doorway, his face scrunched in a scowl.

'Molly wants ye for supper,' he said, crooking his finger at Benedikt. 'Get downstairs, imp, quick.'

'Iss, Iddo,' said Benedikt. 'Look. Willem's awake.'

Iddo let Benedikt squeeze by him, then came into the room. Arms folded across his barrel chest, he kept on scowling. He had a good face for bad temper, all suspicion and scars.

Blurry-eyed, silent, Liam stared up at Molly's man. Iddo didn't like him. But that was fine, because he didn't like Iddo. Iddo had been mean and hard to Ellyn. More than once he'd made her cry.

One day, when I'm Duke Liam on the Falcon Throne, I'll make him pay for that.

'Ye be a careless brat, Willem,' Iddo said, his eyes cold. 'Diddling about under Moll's feet. A mort of coin to Izusa, this'll cost us. Coin we can't spare.'

It hurt to speak, but he had to. He had to make sure Iddo knew that *he* knew what was in his black heart. 'You wish I'd died.'

Iddo caught his breath, then quirked a ragged eyebrow. 'I wish ye'd never come here. Cut yer finger and ye'll bleed trouble. I knew it the moment that slattern Alys brought ye under this roof.'

'Don't call her names!'

Iddo took a step forward, arms unfolded, one fist raised. 'Keep a civil tongue, brat, or—'

'Iddo! Iddo!' Molly scolded, bustling in. 'Must ye fret the boy now? Go fill the tin tub with warm water. He'll need a yarrow bath, Izusa says. Then see to that crowd in the public room. We be in for a busy night.'

Iddo always did what Molly told him, even when he didn't want to. He left, and Molly bent low over the truckle bed to fuss. She wasn't Ellyn but she loved him. And he was fond of her.

'There now, imp, don't mind Iddo,' she said, her smile trembly. 'Ye gave him a fright, is all. Ye gave me a fright too. But never fret. Izusa says ye'll mend just fine.'

Of course he would. He was brave Harald's true-born son. And though he was just a boy now, one day he'd be a man. Then he'd take back the Falcon Throne the bastard Roric had stolen from him . . . and after that, he'd make the bastard pay.

CHAPTER TWENTY-FIVE

R oric travelled home to Eaglerock from Cassinia with gloomily silent Bellows, all the while thinking of little more than Catrain. The precocious child had become a startling woman. A woman who stirred him, challenged him, in every way his wife didn't. Couldn't. Such a mistake he'd made, marrying Lindara. Had he made another, leaving Catrain unprotected and at the regents' mercy? Perhaps. Though he'd had no other choice. At least now he knew she was alive, he'd not killed her. There was comfort in that. And while she lived, there was hope . . . even though knowing how she lived, knowing her every breath depended on the regents and their whims, was almost as crushing a burden as the belief that she'd died.

But while the thought of Catrain kept him sleepless, twisted a dagger of loss in his side, it was far easier to dwell on Berardine's unattainable daughter than contemplate his contemptuous dismissal by the men who held her prisoner. Or what Humbert would say of it. Or how his council would react.

Most of all, he didn't want to face the almost certain truth that he nursed a traitor in his midst . . . or that discovering the man's identity was likely impossible. Not when every lord on his council, even Humbert, had at one time or another expressed a keen dislike of Cassinia. And when all of them, united, had opposed any notion of him wedding with Catrain.

He had no proof of treachery. Only suspicion and the snide taunting of the regents' steward. It wasn't enough. Without a confession – which he knew he'd never get – he was powerless. Without a confession he was condemned to live uncertain of his certainty. To spend his days looking into the faces of men who'd sworn him their loyalty and wondering: *Did you lie?*

From the start he'd sworn to do nothing that wasn't in service of the duchy his revered grandfather Berold had served till the day he died. But little Liam had perished, and every endeavour since had crumbled to ash. He'd been right, that night in Heartsong. The babe's death was an ill omen. Folk who still followed the old ways would call him faery-cursed. And though he, like many men, had let his tenuous belief in the old ways lapse, when grief and doubt plagued him, when every good intention soured to bitter failure, it was easy to believe he had angered the unseen powers.

His task now was to learn how he might appease them.

Foul weather dogged every cantering stride from the Prince's Isle to the Rebbai coast. The sea crossing from Gevez to Eaglerock was a misery of wind and rain and battering waves; the elements so harsh they even kept pirates at bay. He and Bellows between them heaved up most of every meagre meal they ate. Blane's sailing master wanted to turn back to Gevez. Only the harsh truth that they'd come more than halfway stopped him.

After four heartstopping days and nights, the weatherbeaten cog sailed into Eaglerock harbour at dusk, just before the evening curfew. Roric's salt-stung eyes blurred at the sight of Eaglerock castle looming over the township. He'd take its rough-hewn strength over Cassinia's elegantly refined prince's palace any day. Alerted by pigeon-message of their departure from Cassinia, Master Blane waited to greet him on the almost deserted, torchlit dock. Cautiously swathed in a woollen robe and hood, the merchant took one look at his duke and winced.

'Your Grace. 'Tis good to see you safely home. If you don't mind me saying, I think you'd be wise to wait for darkness before you return to the castle. You're welcome to come and sit with me a spell. Take in some good strong wine, eat a hot pie.'

Roric dragged a hand down his weary, heavily stubbled face. Desperate as he was to reach Eaglerock, the merchant was right to advise caution. 'I'll do that, Blane. Thank you.'

''Tis no trouble, Your Grace. Besides, I've news to share.'

Blane's grimace sent his spirits plummetting. 'Not good news, I take it.'

The harbour curfew bell sounded; deep-throated bronze strokes bouncing off warehouse walls and echoing over the rippled water. Work might continue throughout the salt-scented night on board the tethered cogs and galleys, in the warehouses and their offices, but not until daylight would more boats be welcome at the docks.

'It could be worse, Your Grace,' the merchant said, once the bell fell silent. 'Though it's true I—' Recalling they weren't alone he frowned at Bellows, silently waiting a few steps distant. 'Be off home with you, man. We'll talk by and by.'

'Bellows.' Roric turned to his erstwhile companion. 'You have my thanks. And my help, if ever you should need it.'

Bellows bowed. ''Twas my honour to serve you, Your Grace.' Another bow. 'Master Blane.'

'This way, Your Grace,' Blane said, gesturing. 'Let's have you away from prying eyes.'

Settled beside a glowing brazier in the merchant's cluttered, lamplit trading office, with the promised wine and pie to fill his raw, empty belly, Roric listened with growing despondency to the man's brisk tale of Clemen's most recent woes.

'So as I said, Your Grace,' Blane finished, rising from his chair to refill his duke's goblet, 'matters could be worse. True, we've lost Lord Wido, and still might lose Lord Jacott, so rumour has it. But by the skin of his teeth, Humbert's kept peace in the Marches and dealt the curs't Harcians a bloody fright.' He sat again. 'Which is better than the Harcians being able to crow a victory over us.'

Roric hid his dismay with a deep swallow of wine. Fresh trouble in the Marches? So much for brokering a peace with Harcia. Had Humbert been right, then? Was Aimery's overture of friendship no more than a feint, a deception, meant to cozen him into complacency? He'd believed Harcia's duke was sincere. Had intended to meet secretly with his younger son, Grefin, so they could talk face to face about the future of their duchies. Now it would seem he'd been played for a fool. Just as Cassinia's regents had played him. So who was he? Roric the bastard, a man with more hair than wit.

Feeling Blane's stare, he looked up. 'You keep yourself well informed.'

'I must, Your Grace. My livelihood depends on it.'

And what was that? A subtle reminder that dukes weren't the only men with power? As if he needed one when he was still smarting from his harsh schooling at the regents' arrogant hands.

The brazier's heat was starting to wane. As he fed it more rough-hewn lengths of wood, Blane glanced sideways. 'And you, Your Grace? How did you fare in Cassinia?'

Roric swallowed more wine. He couldn't afford a bald lie. Not when the merchant would surely winnow all he could from Bellows.

'Not as well as I'd hoped. But neither am I bereft of hope. Clemen and Cassinia are too strongly tied for any permanent estrangement.'

A man well-used to masking himself, Blane kept his composure. But not even he could hide all his disappointment. 'So you did make progress, Your Grace? Clemen's merchants can expect more fairness and less uncertainty from Cassinia's regents?'

'Blane . . .' He smiled, apologetic. 'My lords of the council would take it most amiss did I discuss matters of state with you before them.'

Sitting again, the merchant raised his hands. 'Indeed they would, Your Grace. Forgive me.'

'Of course.' Time to shift the subject. 'You didn't say if Lord Humbert was returned from the Marches.'

Blane slapped his knee. 'No more I didn't. Yes, Your Grace, he's back. And a grand welcome Eaglerock gave him. 'Twas a warming sight, to see so many smiling faces. There being so little to smile at of late.'

Another sly dig. What else did it say of him, that a mere merchant felt safe in his prodding? Was this proof of another mistake? In trying so hard not to be Harald, did he give the impression to men like Blane, to his council lords, yes, and Aimery of Harcia, that Roric the bastard needn't be feared? Or even respected? Well, if he did, then more fool him. And shame on him for not following Berold's example.

After the Marches and Cassinia, that must change. *He* must change . . . or lead Clemen to its destruction.

Glancing at the sliver of uncovered window, Roric saw that night had well and truly fallen. He stood. 'Thank you, Master Blane. Your service and your discretion won't be forgotten. But I'd beg one last boon. Have you a horse I can borrow? I'd rather not walk to the castle.'

Yes, there was a horse. Obscured by his leather riding cloak, keeping its hood pulled low, Roric returned to Eaglerock. The stable staff knew better than to fuss at the sight of him but there were raised eyebrows and wide eyes. After warning the stable master against idly tattling tongues, he slipped into the castle by way of a double locked, tree-hidden postern gate to which only he and Humbert held the keys.

Humbert.

After hearing Blane's news, finding his foster-lord swiftly was paramount. Never mind he was exhausted, filthy, desperate for a bath and a bed that kept still. Never mind he was aching to the marrow of his bones.

'Your Grace!' Mouth open, his favoured steward Nathyn gaped. Looked up and down the stone corridor outside his chamber, one hand groping for the wall. 'When did you – *how* did you – I wasn't told—'

Roric slapped the man's arm. 'Never mind that, Nathyn. I'd know Lord Humbert's whereabouts. Is he in Eaglerock, or at his town house?'

'Oh.' Nathyn's amazement melted into consternation. 'Your Grace, Lord Humbert sits with the duchess. I am sorry. Her Grace is unwell.'

'Unwell,' he said blankly. 'What do you mean?'

'Her Grace has been bedbound for some days, my lord.'

Days? Lindara had been suffering for days. While he dreamed of Catrain, pining for what might have been. Turmoiled with guilty confusion, he cleared his throat.

'Bedbound why, Nathyn? What ails her?'

'I don't know the cause of it, Your Grace. There is a purging of her bowels and – and—' Nathyn swallowed. 'Her womanly parts.'

He felt the world tilt. 'Is my wife in danger?'

'Your leech, Arthgallo, says no, Your Grace, but—'

Not waiting for the rest, he abandoned the steward and ran. By the time he reached Lindara's apartments he was breathing hard and close to staggering. When he nearly fell into her candle-bright dayroom, her flock of attendants gasped and dropped their tapestries. Nodding at them, far beyond vapid pleasantries and protocol, he threaded his way across the room, scattering Lindara's ladies like a fox amongst a flock of hens.

Humbert, drowsing in a chair by the bedchamber's shuttered window, jerked awake as its door closed. Straightening slowly, he stared.

'Roric!'

A maid he didn't recognise was on a stool beside the bed. She stood, and dropped a curtsy. 'Your Grace.'

Another nod, but his gaze was fixed on Lindara. Chalky pale, she lay like a wax doll beneath the squirrel-skin coverlet drawn up to her chin.

'What happened, Humbert?'

Humbert creaked to his feet. Snapped his fingers at the maid. 'Wait outside.'

'My lord,' she said, and quietly withdrew.

'*Humbert.*'

'Don't fret, boy,' Humbert growled. 'Arthgallo swears she'll come right.'

'So Nathyn said. *What happened?* Is it a pestilence?'

Humbert tugged at his beard. 'No. No. Not a pestilence.'

He knew that uneasy tone, and the way Humbert tugged his beard when he was perturbed. Or defensive. 'My lord, I'm in no mood for shibbling.'

'Fine. The girl and I had words, after you left,' Humbert snapped. 'I lost my temper, accused her of not doing enough to bear your son. Which is only the truth, boy, like it or not. So when my back was turned she swallowed some fool herbary she thought would ripen her womb. Instead it made her sick.'

His legs watery, all of a sudden, Roric took hold of the bed's carved corner post. 'You had no right.'

Humbert jerked up his chin. 'I have every right. She's my daughter.'

'And I'm her husband!'

'Roric—'

'*No.* Humbert, I don't care if you meant well or not. You overstepped. My marriage is a private matter.'

'And your lack of an heir is a public concern! Do you deny it?'

How could he, when he'd added his own voice to Humbert's and the rest of the council's every time they broached the same fears to childless Harald? Besides. He lacked the stomach for an argument now.

'No, my lord. But I'll thank you to clap tongue the next time you feel an urge to meddle. This is painful, Humbert. Please, leave us to find our own way.'

Arms folded, Humbert glowered. 'All right – *if* you swear to me you'll give yourself over wholly to Arthgallo. No more mimbling prevarications. Let him leech you without reserve.'

'I do now!'

'You do not and we both know it. Roric, the day you took the Falcon Throne you surrendered your body to Clemen. As one of Clemen's keepers, I tell you I'll not be denied on this. I've looked the other way for too long. The duchy must have its heir. You'll give Arthgallo free rein.'

Roric stared at the floor. It did no good to resent Humbert's high-handed manner. This was his life. Lindara, his wife. Catrain was a dream and wanting her a childish yearning. For his sake, and for the duchy, he had to accept the harsh truth.

'There's something else,' Humbert said. 'After you left for Cassinia—'

'I know,' he said, looking up. 'The Marches. Blane told me.'

'*Blane?* That poxed, dribble-tongued—'

'Never mind cursing him! What does it matter how I found out? Humbert, how did that business with Harcia turn so bloody so fast? And why did you come back to Eaglerock so swiftly? If Wido's dead and Jacott's crippled, who is—'

'Vidar,' said Humbert, challenging. 'I left him behind as Clemen's Marcher lord.'

'*Vidar?*' He stared, astonished. 'Humbert, have you gone mad?'

'I have not. Roric—'

'No, truly, are you moonstruck? Explain yourself!'

'Not here,' Humbert said quickly, his gaze shifting from Lindara to the closed chamber door. 'Arthgallo's leechery. There's something you must see.'

'*Now?*'

Humbert snorted. 'No, boy. Next full moon.'

He wanted to argue. He wanted to fall face-first into sleep. But if he knew what Humbert's beard-tugging meant, he also knew that look in his foster-lord's eye. It was the same look he'd seen the night Humbert had taken his arm and whispered, '*Come with me, Roric. We must talk about Harald.*'

Releasing the bed post, he moved to Lindara's side and bent to kiss her pale, cool cheek. So frail, she didn't stir. Illness had smeared shadows beneath her closed eyes. But the tight dissatisfaction in her face, caused by his failure to make her happy was smoothed away. Beneath the marks of suffering he could see again the woman he'd married. The girl he'd grown up with under Humbert's fostering roof.

This is my fault. If I hadn't failed Liam, let him perish in fire, she'd be happily married elsewhere. And I'd be what I was meant to be: a caretaker duke.

'Humbert, are you certain she'll recover?'

'Arthgallo is. But she'll be weak for a time. She'll need careful handling.'

'She needs more than that,' he murmured, stroking her hair. 'And I'll see that she gets it. I've been a poor husband. I must put that right.'

Impatient, Humbert gestured at the closed door. 'Roric—'

'I know,' he said. 'Arthgallo's leechery. Let's go, then. And I'll tell you what I learned from Blane on the way.'

'Your Grace! Lord Humbert!' Arthgallo straightened his canvas skull cap, askew on his head, then smoothed the front of his singed, stained smock. 'This is a—' His expression sharpened. 'Her Grace? Is there some change? Do you need me to—'

'No. My daughter sleeps still,' Humbert said, casting a frowning look up and down the leechery's laneway. Its other doorways remained dark, windows shuttered, no lamplight behind them. 'We're here on – that other matter.'

'Ah!' Stepping back from his leechery door, Arthgallo beckoned. 'Come in. Come in. We're quite alone.'

With a nod at Arthgallo, Roric entered the leech's arcane world. The candle-yellow air within was thick with fresh, peculiar stinks and the throat-tickle of lingering, greasy smoke. He coughed. Coughed again. Startled as Arthgallo took hold of him, without permission, and pushed him towards the nearest puddle of light.

'The door, if you please, my lord Humbert,' the leech said. 'Drop the bar across it. We don't want to be disturbed. Now, Your Grace – let us have a closer look.'

No use protesting. Arthgallo rarely heeded protocols and Humbert would only tell him to clap tongue. So in silence he bore the leech's poking fingers and muttered comments.

At last Arthgallo finished. Puffed out his sunken cheeks. 'For shame, Your Grace. This will not do. You are underfed and underslept and—' His gaze slid towards Humbert. '—and as the leech charged with your good health, I tell you *it will not do*.'

'The duke knows that, Arthgallo,' said Humbert. 'And he's agreed to a proper leeching. Isn't that so, Your Grace?'

'A proper leeching?' Arthgallo was staring at Humbert, his wild eyebrows lowered. 'Purges too? Blood cleansing? A balancing of the humours and restoration of the male parts?'

Humbert was staring too. He looked like he wanted to tug his beard. 'Didn't I say a proper leeching? Clean the wax from your ears, Arthgallo.'

'My lord Humbert—'

'Clap tongue, man! We agreed to this!'

'Wait,' said Roric, looking from the leech to his foster-lord. *Male parts? He wants to purge my male parts?* 'You've been deciding for me in my absence? Humbert—'

'And you clap tongue too, boy!' Humbert said, close to snarling. 'You agreed, not an hour ago. Your health is Clemen's health and I'll do what I must to see both in proper mettle. So you'll swallow what pills and potions you're given, no mimbling and no questions – unless you'd see every curs't hope we've worked and bled for come to naught.'

A gentle touch to his arm. 'Your Grace,' Arthgallo said softly, 'all I want is for you to be well.'

'And Lindara? Can you promise me she'll be well?'

'Promise, Your Grace? Leechery is no place for promises. But I'm confident. Yes. I'll say that.'

Looking into the leech's gaunt face, Roric could see only earnest good intent. But he was coming to learn, painfully, that he was a man who could be fooled.

'The herbs my wife took, Arthgallo, that have made her so sick. Where did she get them?'

Arthgallo met his gaze without flinching. 'Not from me, Your Grace.'

'*Then where?*'

'I told you!' said Humbert. 'She trusted some travelling herbary woman. Heard a foolish maid babbling of wondrous cures. The woman's gone now. Forget her. Arthgallo—'

The leech turned. 'Yes, my lord. The body remains intact. Barely. Even with my best efforts it—'

'Body?' Roric frowned. 'What body?'

Arthgallo gestured towards the leechery's rear chamber. 'This way, Your Grace.'

There was, indeed, a body. Rotting and rank. Naked. Crammed into a wooden box packed with damp sawdust and blocks of softening ice. Not even Arthgallo's most pungent remedies, or the bunches of fresh herbs hung from the ceiling beams, or the sacks and barrels of dried herbs crowding the room, could disguise the stench.

Halted in front of the trestle bearing the stinking corpse, Roric pressed his forearm to his nose and mouth. 'By the spirits, Humbert. That's foul.'

'Everything about this is foul.' Humbert nodded at Arthgallo. 'Amuse yourself elsewhere. We'll call you when we're done.'

'Of course, my lord,' said Arthgallo. 'Take your time. I shall prepare a strengthening tincture for His Grace.'

As the door closed behind the leech, Humbert jerked his chin at the body. 'Look at his face, Roric. D'you know him?'

'What face? Humbert—'

'*Curse it, Roric. Look at him! Is he yours?*'

Breathing shallowly, he stared at the monstrosity that once had been a man. 'I need more light.'

Humbert snatched up a glowing horn lamp from a nearby crowded bench and held it over the corpse. 'Well?'

'Why would you think he's mine?' he said, looking more closely.

'He was wearing a falcon badge when he died.'

The dead man was of medium height. Medium build. Thin before the bloating, and stringy with muscle. Cropped brown hair, crusted with dried blood. A long, narrow face. A pointed chin. Perhaps the nose had been hooked, once. But so much of that face was dagger-slashed and boot-crushed, lips half-torn off, teeth broken. He doubted the dead man's mother would know him. But even so . . .

He stepped back. 'He's not mine.'

'You're certain?'

Abruptly, patience deserted him. 'Enough mystery, Humbert! What is this about?'

Instead of answering, Humbert thumped the lamp on the trestle beside the corpse and turned away. Fingers tugging at his beard, he muttered something under his breath. Then he swung round, his eyes glittering.

'Did you write to me from Cassinia?'

'*Write* to you?' he said, bewildered. 'No.'

'You sent no letter, ordering me to seek the death of Harcia's Marcher men. To abandon any hope of justice in a Crown Court, or friendship with Harcia's duke.'

Roric felt a chill of dread run through him. 'I wrote you no letter. And falcon badge or not, I don't know this man. And now you'll answer me, Humbert. *What the fuck is going on?*'

Beard tucked in, his gaze distant, Humbert was tapping calloused fingers to his chest. 'There was a letter. This butchered man, wearing a falcon badge, carried it. And I'd have sworn your hand held the pen that wrote it. Vidar agreed. But—'

'Show it to me.'

Humbert shook his head. 'I can't. I looked for it after that curs't skirmish, but the road was shambled to a slop of blood and mud. The letter's lost. As it was I nearly didn't retrieve the body.' He tugged at his beard. '*Fuck.*'

A spike of pain was pounding through his skull. 'What?'

'My life on it, Roric.' Humbert was near to spitting, his face reddened with rage. 'This is Balfre's doing. It was his man Waymon claimed he was attacked, by him—' He jerked a thumb at the corpse. '—unprovoked. And it was Waymon daggered the life out of him

428

and dropped him dead at our feet and afterwards tried to stop me claiming the corpse. If he'd not fainted from loss of blood . . .' His fists were clenched, his jaw working. 'They were trying to start trouble and couldn't afford him being questioned – or you seeing his murdered body.'

'So you think all of this was Balfre's doing? He forged a letter in my name, killed a man, to cause strife?'

'Yes.'

'But Humbert . . .' He raked his fingers through his hair. 'Murder, I'll grant you. I'd believe Balfre capable of that. But forgery? How could he? I never wrote to him.'

Humbert's eyes narrowed. 'You wrote to his brother.'

'You're saying Balfre and Grefin conspired together. With Aimery too, I suppose. My lord, this is—'

'Who else, Roric? If not Aimery and his cockshite sons, *who else*?'

No. No. What Humbert was suggesting? No. Because if his foster-lord was right then he really was no more than a blind fool, a gullible child, tricked by Harcia's duke into believing a lie.

'Whoever it was betrayed Clemen to Cassinia's regents.'

'*What?*' Humbert choked. 'You'd accuse one of us? Roric—'

'No, Humbert, listen!' he said, desperate to be heard. 'I was right. The regents' steward all but told me. Our miseries in Cassinia are the fault of—'

'Who?' Humbert spat, his disbelief like acid. 'Did this *steward* give you a name?'

'No. But—'

'But *nothing*!' Humbert banged a fist to the corpse's trestle. 'That treachery belonged to one of the widow's people. *This* treachery belongs to Aimery, Balfre and Grefin. A one-eyed mule could see it! But not you. *You* look for one of your own lords to blame. What the *fuck's* gone awry with you, boy?'

Red and black spots, dancing before his eyes. In his ears a distant roaring. The stinking chamber spun like a plate atop a jongler's stick.

'Enough, Humbert! You forget yourself. I might not be Harald, wanting every man to bow and scrape, but—'

The spinning room spun harder. His mouth dried. His lungs

429

emptied. All he could smell was death. He felt his eyes roll back and started to fall.

A strong arm caught him.

'There now, there now,' Humbert murmured, guiding him to the stone floor. 'Worn to rags, you are, just like Arthgallo said, and what a fool I am to ignore it. Head down. Breathe deep.' A moment, then a handful of dried meadowsweet was pressed against his face. 'This'll ease the stink. Breathe, boy. And lean on me.'

Shivering, humiliated, Roric let himself slump against Humbert's broad, robed chest. Felt Humbert cradle the back of his neck. He'd fallen like this when he was told Guimar was dead. Humbert had held him then, too. Been his bulwark to lean on, his shelter in the storm. He drew in a shuddering, scented breath, then pushed aside his foster-lord's herb-filled hand.

'I'm fine.'

'You're not,' Humbert retorted. 'Be still. And tell me what happened in Cassinia.'

The last thing he wanted to talk of was Cassinia. But like an arrow in flesh, the truth had to be plucked out.

'I failed, Humbert. The prince's regents won't bend. They wouldn't even see me. I went all that way for nothing.'

Silence. Then Humbert sighed. 'Not for nothing. The loss of false hope isn't nothing. And it was a false hope, Roric, to think Cassinia's regents would save us.'

'Like forging peace with Harcia was a false hope?'

'You know the saying. If it's peace you want, prepare for war.'

'Humbert . . .'

'Harcia covets Clemen, Roric. It always has. That won't change.'

'But I wanted it to,' he whispered. 'And I thought – Humbert, I honestly thought—'

'I know you did, boy. You were wrong.'

'About everything, it seems.' He rubbed the heel of his hand across his burning eyes. 'Berold's blood runs thin in me.'

Humbert cuffed him. 'Clap tongue on that.'

The time-smoothed granite flagstones beneath him were chilly. Despite his leather leggings, the cold was seeping into his bones. And he was Clemen's duke. He couldn't sit here like a child for the rest of the night. With a warning shrug, he pushed himself unsteadily to his feet. Humbert let him go.

'So, my lord,' he said, forcing himself to calm indifference. 'Is it to be open warfare between Clemen and Harcia?'

Some pained grunting, as Humbert stood. 'Perhaps. Much will depend on what you do next.'

'Here's what I won't do. I won't pour oil on the fire Aimery has lit. If he's so desperate for war let him be the one to start it, in the open, without any provocation from us.'

Humbert glanced up from dusting his hands free of dried meadow-sweet. 'And if he does?'

'Then I'll do what I must to protect Clemen. But *only* if Aimery – or his sons – strike first. We have troubles enough to contend with as it is.' He rubbed his eyes again. 'Who killed Harcia's Marcher lords? Do you know?'

'I don't.' Humbert's face tightened with bleak memory. 'It was a bloody rout, Roric. We were fighting for our lives. I saw Balfre's man Waymon slaughter Wido. Tried to reach him, but . . .'

'And Jacott?'

'I didn't see who gutted him. And he doesn't recall. But does it matter which Harcian hand held the dagger?'

'I suppose not.' Turning, Roric frowned at the corpse on the trestle. 'Still. I wish I knew—'

Humbert jabbed a pointed finger. 'We know enough.'

Yes. They did. And now here he stood amidst the ruins of his childish, faery-fed dreams, soaked in the stench of death.

'You did well, Humbert,' he said, trying to smile. 'However bad it was, if you'd not been there . . .' He shivered. 'I don't want to think of it. Only—'

'What?' Humbert prompted.

'Why name *Vidar* as Marcher lord?'

'Because we have no man better suited to the task,' said Humbert, beard bristling. 'Vidar knows the law. He knows the Marches. Crippled and half-blind, he held his own against Harcia. He saved my life. Our Marcher men have seen he's not to be trifled with. What's more, Harcia has seen it. And he wants to serve.'

'Even so. Surely Aistan, or Scarwid, or—'

'They'd go if you commanded it, but not willingly. They have their established lives and they serve a purpose on the council. Roric . . .' Humbert smoothed his beard. 'If you must know, Vidar's not happy in Eaglerock.'

Wilfully forgotten guilt stirred. 'Because of Lindara?'

'What?' Humbert blinked at him, startled. 'No. That was a trifling fancy, long dead. No. Roric, too many still see Vidar as Godebert's son. It may not be just, but the stain of his father's misdoings has never washed clean. He knows it. He feels it. In the Marches he'll be his own man. He'll be judged by what he does, not what his dead father did. He'll thrive there, you'll see. He's to wed Aistan's daughter. The one Harald—' He frowned. 'You know. It's a fresh start for him. He's earned it. And he'll keep Clemen safe. Remember how well he served you at Heartsong? Trust me, Vidar will keep that cockshite Balfre in line.'

Surprised by Humbert's praise, he frowned. 'All right. If you truly think he's the best man to serve me, I'll confirm Vidar's appointment. But I'd not leave him there alone.'

'He's not alone. Egann's with him.'

Egann. Humbert's canny, uncorruptible, iron-forged man. Though he was weary to the point of physical pain, Roric laughed. 'You're a crafty old fox, my lord.'

'That I am,' Humbert agreed, grinning. Then his amusement faded. 'Roric. There is one more thing.'

Of course. Swallowing a groan, he braced himself. 'Tell me.'

'The council knows you went to Cassinia. I'm sorry, boy. I had to tell them.'

Because of the Marches. He grimaced. 'They were always going to find out.'

'They won't like the outcome.'

'No. But like me, they must learn to live with disappointment. Humbert—' His legs wanted to fold again. 'Are we done? I want to sit with Lindara.'

A muscle leapt in Humbert's cheek. 'We're done. Go. Be with your wife. I'll stay. Arthgallo and I will see to disposing of the corpse.'

Reluctant, Roric looked at the almost-faceless dead man on the trestle. 'I wonder who he was. D'you think we'll ever know?'

'I don't,' said Humbert. 'But never fret, Roric. Clemen will avenge him all the same.'

Brooding over the corpse he'd brought home with him from the Pig Whistle, Humbert heard the small chamber's door open again, then close, as Arthgallo came in. He waited for the leech to say something. Waited. Waited.

'*What?*' he demanded. 'Out with it, man.'

'You know what, my lord,' Arthgallo said quietly. 'I am troubled, and you know why.'

'You've nothing to fear. This falls on my head. Not yours.'

'So you say. I doubt His Grace would agree.'

'His Grace will never know.'

'You hope.'

Humbert turned. '*He'll never know.*'

'My lord . . .' Arthgallo came closer, his spindly fingers clasped before him like an exarchite at prayer. His brown eyes, flecked green and gold, were wide with distress. 'We should tell him the truth. It's not too late. If we—'

'The truth would ruin him! You said it yourself, man, he's strained to breaking already. Should he learn of my daughter's betrayal, I fear—' Hearing his voice crack, Humbert paused. Breathed hard. 'Roric is like my own flesh and blood. I won't do that to him, Arthgallo. Say what you like, I won't.'

Arthgallo's distress turned to disapproval. 'I understand your feelings, my lord. But he is more than a son to you. He is your duke. He is *my* duke. In withholding the truth from him, I commit treason.'

'D'you tell me you've never prevaricated with a sick man? Never lulled him a little because telling the truth would do more harm than good?'

'No, my lord. I have done so. Not often, but—'

'Well, then.'

'But this is not—'

'*Yes, it is!*' Taking hold of the leech's bony shoulders, Humbert shook him. 'If you confess all to Roric, you'll set Clemen on fire. You'll open the floodgates to Harcia and the duchy will be destroyed. *That's* treason, Arthgallo. What you and I do? 'Tis an act of loyalty.

Of love. There is no treason in protecting our duke.' He stepped back. 'Now. When can you start to purge Roric of the witch's filth my daughter fed him?'

Arthgallo sighed. 'On the morrow, my lord. Provided he passes an easy night.'

'Good. That's good. Now—'. With a reassuring smile, hiding his own trepidation, Humbert gestured at the burdened trestle. 'Let's see about laying this poor bastard to rest.'

Come the morning, after a difficult night beside unwaking Lindara, Roric summoned his council. Because he knew precisely what he'd be facing, he chose to meet with his lords in the Falcon Throne audience chamber. Where he might sit, and they must stand, and he could remind them who ruled as Clemen's duke. Likewise he took immense care with his clothing. As a rule he was most comfortable in a serviceable leather doublet and huntsman's leggings. He rarely wore his coronet. He disdained ostentatious jewels. Peacocking was for Harald and lesser men like Ercole. A man should be judged by what he did, not what he wore. He'd always believed that, and proudly lived as he thought.

But he could no longer afford to be self-effacing and modest. The Roric who took Clemen from his cousin not because he wanted it, but because there was no one else. The Roric who could be tricked by Harcia and treated with contempt by Cassinia because they saw him as weak. Because he was weak. Because, in his heart, falling prey to self-loathing, he'd never forgiven himself for Liam's death.

That Roric had to die.

So instead of his favourite leathers, he dressed himself in rich black velvet. Placed his coronet on his head. Pinned diamonds to his doublet and pricked a ruby through his ear. Rubies on his fingers. Gold buckles on his shoes. Wearing the wealth of Clemen, he went forth to claim his throne.

'My lords,' he said, cordial, as the council warily entered his presence. 'Welcome. I won't keep you long.'

They exchanged cautious glances: Aistan, Humbert, Farland, Scarwid and Ercole. The chamber's doors were closed behind them. Still wary, they approached.

'Your Grace,' said Aistan, nodding. 'You're safely returned, I see.'

Keeping his hands loose on the arms of his throne, Roric smiled. 'I am.'

'A mercy,' said Scarwid. 'We were most concerned for your safety, Your Grace.'

'Not to mention surprised by your clandestine leaving,' Ercole added. 'Surely it would've been prudent for you to discuss it with us first, the wisdom of courting Cassinia's regents. We are your councillors, Roric. You owe us—'

'Clap tongue, pizzle!' Humbert snapped. 'This is your duke, not your manservant!'

'No, Humbert. Ercole is right,' said Aistan. 'It was a foolish, foolhardy action – and you were foolhardy to support it. You had no business lying to us. We should've been told from the start!' He turned. 'Your Grace, dare I ask the outcome of your ill-considered visit to Cassinia? Was the risk you took worth it? Or did you make matters worse?'

With a roar of outrage, Humbert buffeted Aistan's shoulder. And just like that, the council was brawling. Raised voices. Raised fists. Threats and imprecations.

For a little time Roric did nothing but watch. These men. These contentious, arrogant men. Yes, even Humbert. It was time they learned their place. Time he heeded Harald's warning. Time he reminded them he was their duke.

He stood. '*Be silent! Or be divested! My lords, the choice is yours!*'

Shocked, their tongues stilled mid-shouting, they stared at him. Certain of their attention, he sat.

'Was my visit worth it, Aistan?' he said coldly. 'I believe it was. Not because I managed to coax the regents into granting Clemen even one small trading concession. Unfortunately, in that I failed. But I didn't leave Cassinia empty-handed. Indeed, while there I learned several important lessons.'

'Roric.' Alarmed, Humbert stepped forward. 'Roric, don't be hasty. You can't prove—'

'Be quiet, Humbert.'

Humbert's gaping mouth shut with a snap. In his eyes, a flash of

435

temper. But he couldn't afford to care about that. He had this moment to finally claim his authority . . . and if he let it pass, unclaimed, he might as well give his throne to Ercole.

'I learned,' he said, looking at the lords of his council one by one, 'that not every friend can be trusted. I learned that personal ambitions, personal hatreds, can lead men into betraying the one thing they should hold most dear. My lords, I learned – to my bitter disappointment – that not every man standing before me holds Clemen's best interests at heart. And so I give you all fair warning: I am an excellent student. I'll consider these lessons . . . and surely put them to good use.'

No answer. His lords stared at him, blank-faced and mute.

'That's all,' he said. 'For now. You can go.'

CHAPTER TWENTY-SIX

The bells of Carillon were ringing, cascades of pealing notes falling onto the air. Imprisoned within her long-dead husband's carriage, talons of pain ripping her flesh with every breath, Berardine closed her eyes.

Will they ring for me when I, too, am dead?

She thought they would, but not for long. Leofric and his fellow regents were careful. They knew they daren't discard Ardenn's traditions entirely. It was why they'd always permitted her this weekly ride through Carillon's streets, why she still appeared on the palace's public balcony when a new proclamation was read out, and why every action throughout Baldwin's stolen duchy was taken in her name.

So the bells would toll for her, sonorous, sorrowful, in accordance with Ardennese tradition. And then, in less than a week, she'd be forgotten. Encased in the ducal tomb beside her beloved Baldwin.

Labelled Berardine, wife of the late duke. No more than a faint footprint in Ardenn's long history.

And what will become of my poor Catrain then?

Her other daughters had long been lost to her. Scattered across Cassinia. Married off at the first chance to noble sons of the regents' choosing, part of their husbands' grand families now. Was she made a grandmother yet? Of course. She must be. But she'd never know for sure. As soon as she realised that asking gave her keepers the pleasure of denying her even that much shallow comfort, she'd held her tongue. Put those lost daughters out of her mind.

But try as she might, she couldn't forget Catrain.

Eleven years since they'd seen each other. Had her daughter married Roric she'd be a wife, a mother. Instead, like her, Catrain was condemned to a living death. Locked away in the Prince's Isle with no hope of liberty . . . or love. Once a year Leofric permitted Catrain to write. For the longest time she'd feared her daughter's letters were a fraud. Found it hard to trust them. Hadn't she trusted the witch, Izusa? That had not ended well.

But tucked beneath her bodice, a tattered, fragile sheet of rush-paper. As often as was safe, she wore it against her failing heart. A travel-stained letter, smuggled to her by ways she'd never know. And for the past five years that letter had kept her alive.

I have seen her. She misses you. She is unharmed. And it was simply signed: *Roric.*

How he'd found Catrain, she couldn't imagine. What it had cost him to send the letter, she didn't care. She'd thought all hope was lost. His letter had pulled her back from the abyss. But now not even a handful of words could sustain her. She was forty-one and dying. And she was desperate to see Catrain before the end.

Carillon's bells were still ringing, joyous and free. But as her carriage swung to the right she heard their timbre change, heard the deeper, more portentous tolling of the bell called the Old Duke. Massive and beautifully sculptured, it hung in the belltower of the city's oldest exarch-house. Then the sound of the carriage-horses' hooves changed from crunch-crunch to clop-clop. Gravel to cobbles. They were driving along Baldwin Fairway, Carillon's most splendid thoroughfare. Her palace, her prison, lay directly ahead.

Seated opposite her in the carriage was the man who'd taken dear Howkin's place. Master Corbert. He kept her close and reported her every sneeze and wince and moan to the regents. Leaning forward, he pulled upon the carriage's window cord. The green velvet curtains drew back, letting in the light.

'Wave, Madam,' he said, in his dry, clipped voice. 'The people expect it.'

Madam. How laughable. When they called her *Madam*, did they think she thought they meant it? That she didn't understand she was being taunted, as though they sprayed perfume on a whore and called the drab *my lady*?

Perhaps. Or perhaps they didn't care. What she did know, full well, was that to the regents she was a whore. A vixen. Unrepentant and unnatural. A woman who thought to rule like a man. They despised her and she despised them in return. But still she waved at the waving Ardennese who'd gathered along the Fairway to watch her go by. She even smiled, because Corbert was not beyond withholding her syrup of poppy if he thought her insufficiently compliant. And without that small mercy, the pain would surely kill her before she saw Catrain one last time.

Returned to her apartments, she used the old, well-worn excuse of needing her water closet to hide Roric's letter. Then her gelded body servant, Ervin, helped her out of the rich ruby velvet gown that these days hung on her like an empty flour sack. One servant for Ardenn's duchess. One gelded man. Leofric refused her female companionship because he feared a woman's soft heart. How little he knew women.

Ervin almost carried her to the bed. 'Will that be all, Madam?'

Swathed in comfortable linen, she sank onto her pillows and patted Ervin's arm. He wasn't unkind, merely indifferent. She found herself grateful for it. Kindness would be impossible to bear.

'I'd see the physick, Ervin.'

A gelded man had no authority of his own. Ervin asked Corbert and Corbert agreed. The physick came and, as Corbert watched, an eager carrion bird, he handled her meatless bones and swollen belly as carefully as he could.

It was a torment to speak afterwards, but she was Baldwin's wife. 'How long, Joppa?'

The physick looked to Corbert, asking permission to answer. Oh, how that galled her. But she was powerless in her own palace. A broken doll, soon to be discarded.

Permission granted with a nod, Joppa clasped his hands before him. Such a neat little man. Never once had she seen a spot of blood on him that wasn't her own.

'We are close to the end, Madam.'

She raised her thinned grey eyebrows. '*We*, Joppa? What – are you dying too?'

'Madam.'

And that was Corbert, with a warning. They'd deny her everything, even the brief solace of sarcasm.

'How close, Joppa?' she asked. 'Will I see summer's end?'

'No, Madam. I'm sorry.'

Her raddled body had already told her, but she'd wanted it said aloud in Corbert's presence. She'd wanted a witness.

'Don't be, Joppa. The sooner I'm released from this misery, the better.' She rolled her head on the pillows. 'Master Corbert, you've heard the verdict. I'll not plague you for much longer. Please, I beg you. Let me see Catrain.'

Corbert's bulbous brown eyes glittered with his dislike. 'That's for the regents to decide, Madam.'

'Then ask them for me. Tell them I went down on my knees. It's not a lie, Master Corbert. My dying soul is on its knees to you, ser.'

Corbert looked at the physick. 'A sound dose of poppy, I think, Joppa. The duchess is upset, and in pain.'

She swallowed the sickly sweet syrup without protest, because she was in pain and because if she refused Corbert would find a small, mean way to punish her. The weight of the poppy dragged her eyes closed before her keeper and the physick left the room.

For nearly five weeks, Corbert never answered her request. She didn't ask again. That too would earn punishment. And she had so little now she couldn't bear to lose any more. Perhaps that made her a coward. She didn't care. What courage she still possessed she needed for the daily battle to get out of bed. To face her wasting self in the mirror. To take a breath, and then another breath, and not fall to the floor. Death had dawdled for so long . . . but now it was running. And she no longer had the strength to outrun it. What meagre strength she did have she was keeping for Catrain.

But Catrain didn't come. And with every passing day it seemed more and more likely her request would be denied. The pain of that was worse than everything else she endured. Not even Roric's letter could ease the suffering. No longer daring to keep the rush-paper within touch, for fear of Ervin discovering it, she felt as though her last hope had died. So she took refuge in sleep, and dreams of better days.

When she heard Corbert's voice she thought she was tricking herself. Groaned a weak protest, and turned her face away.

'*Madam*. Do you understand me? Your daughter is here.'

Trammelled in her bed with pillows and bolsters, fending off the afternoon's chill with goose-down quilts, Berardine slowly opened her eyes. There was Corbert, the carrion keeper, his beaked nose wrinkled at the sly, sour smell of impending death. At his side, a tall and slender young woman. She was weeping. Her tears fell from Baldwin's blue eyes. She had honey-gold hair bundled maiden-loose into a plain caul. Her dress was dark green linen, scarcely embroidered, and girded round her hips with a modest leather belt. On a choked sob, she clutched at Corbert's sleeve.

'Ser, might I have a little time alone with my mother? I know she has sinned greatly against Prince Gaël and his regents, and deserves every punishment that might be devised – but look at her. She is no more a threat to the prince than a starving sparrow in the weeds. If you could show her mercy . . .'

'Lady!' Corbert pulled his arm free. 'This is most unseemly. Did you not swear to the regents that—'

'Yes, I swore, Master Corbert!' The young woman flung herself at Corbert's feet and snatched up his hand. 'And I swear to you, on my life, I am no less the prince's obedient servant in this moment than I was the day I left his court. But my mother is near death. Please, have mercy. Set aside her wickedness and grant me leave to speak of womanly things with the woman who birthed me. I'll have no other chance.'

Hugely discomfited, Corbert prised her fingers loose. 'Get up.'

The young woman stood. She was limber, and graceful. 'Please, ser, forgive me,' she whispered, her gaze submissively downcast. 'That was shameful.'

Confused, Berardine stared at her. This was Catrain? It couldn't be. Catrain was Baldwin's irrepressible, hoydenish daughter, a wild spirit who stole out of borrowed houses without permission and dashed into burning stables to save someone else's horses. She wasn't meek. She wasn't mewlish. She didn't sob or beg.

Corbert's doublet was blue velvet, robustly stitched with gold thread. He smoothed the nap, then plucked at the extravagantly waxed point of his gingerish beard.

'Given the circumstances I will forgive your unwomanly boldness,' he said, so pompous. 'For all your unfortunate breeding, the regents report you as a well-behaved maid. Since you humbly acknowledge your fault – and your mother's manifest disobedience – I will grant your request. But be warned. Abuse my generosity and you'll be whipped to a bloody mess.'

Yet again, the young woman plunged to her knees at his feet. 'Thank you, Master Corbert! What a good man you are!'

Fighting the ever-present pain, Berardine watched Corbert withdraw from her apartment's heavily curtained, lamplit bedchamber. Watched the young woman wait until the door was closed, then raise her hand and make an obscene, soldier's gesture.

'Rampant old fart,' she muttered, rising to her feet. 'And a henwit to boot. What I wouldn't give to whip *him* bloody!'

Berardine felt her laboured breathing catch. She knew that scornful voice. She remembered that impetuous temper. Not meek at all. In no way mewlish. A terrible joy welled.

'Catrain!'

The young woman leapt to her. 'Yes, Mama, it's me.'

No amount of agony could have kept her from clutching Catrain to her breast. Weeping, she pressed her sunken cheek to her daughter's smooth face and cradled the back of her head as she'd done when her child was an infant. But then she let go, because there wasn't enough time.

'Catrain, my love. I can scarce believe it. I was sure the regents would keep you from me.'

Kneeling beside the bed, Catrain smeared the back of her hand across her wet cheeks, a childhood gesture so familiar, Berardine bit her lip.

'They were going to,' her daughter said, unsteady. 'They squabbled with each other for days.'

'And then they let you come. Why?'

'Because of politics. For appearances. They've decided I'm to be the duchess of Ardenn after you.'

And that was unexpected. '*What?*'

Catrain pulled a face. 'In name only, Mama. They won't let me rule. Or marry. I'm to have a privy council answerable to Leofric and the others. The council will make the decisions and I'll sign the writs, so everything is legal.'

'As they have done with me.' Aching, Berardine tried to smile. 'Still. At least they're sending you home. At least they—' But she couldn't say it. Even the thought made her quail.

'Haven't killed me?' Catrain snorted. 'I think they would have, years ago, only they didn't dare. They failed to keep my presence at court a secret and the dukes' men watch closely. If any ill befalls me, the dukes will take it as a personal threat.'

'Then won't they help you escape the regents' clutches? There must be a way to reach them, Catrain. Baldwin was their brother duke. Surely—'

'Perhaps if I were Baldwin's *son* the dukes would act,' Catrain said, temper snapping. 'As a woman, as your daughter, it seems I deserve my fate. Their concern for me is selfish. They want to be sure the regents get no taste for ducal blood.'

She bit her lip again, harder. Had to know, had to ask, though she dreaded the answer. 'You're well-treated? You're not abused?'

'I'm fed,' Catrain said, after a moment. 'I'm clothed. The regents are strict but I give them no cause for complaint.'

And that was the truth. But not the whole truth. 'Catrain . . .'

Her daughter shivered. 'Oh, Mama. The prince's court is a viper's nest. Its air reeks of treachery and greed. Everywhere you look, you'll see somebody scheming. Only one soul in the palace truly cares what happens to me.'

Berardine blinked away fresh tears. Eleven years in a viper's nest. *Forgive me, Baldwin.* 'Who, child?'

'Prince Gaël. We're friends, he and I.'

'*The prince?* Then—'

'But he's mad,' Catrain whispered, her brief smile fading. 'And there's no hope for him. Or me. Nor any hope for the Principality, I fear. What will happen when Gaël comes of age is anyone's guess. All I know for sure is that the dukes would see Cassinia's streets run with blood before yielding so much as a thumb's-worth of the independence they've gained since an infant inherited the crown.'

'You sound like your father,' she said softly. 'Baldwin had the keenest mind of any man I ever knew.'

'I think of him often. And I think of you, every day. Mama—' Catrain's voice broke. 'I'm so sorry. Your captivity, the way they treat you, it's my fault. If I'd not been naughty in Eaglerock, if I hadn't offended Roric, then—'

'*No*, child! We were undone by another man's malice and the regents' lust for power.'

'I saw him, you know,' Catrain murmured. 'Roric. Five years ago, in the palace garden. We spoke, and I—'

'I know. He sent me a letter.'

'He did?' A flush of colour tinted Catrain's cheeks. 'I begged him to get word to you that I was – but I never *dreamed* he could – the regents are still punishing Clemen because we – he *wrote*?'

'When I thought to drown in misery, that letter – his kindness – saved me,' she said, her voice unsteady. 'I think perhaps it could save you.'

Catrain stared. 'Save me? How? Roric is—'

She pressed a finger to Catrain's lips. Swallowed a moan as sickening pain surged through her. It was madness, surely, to even consider once more trusting in Izusa's vague prophecies of her daughter and Clemen's duke. The witch had abandoned her. The witch was made of lies.

Only . . . only . . .

Against every chance, Catrain and Roric had met again. She begged him for a favour and he risked everything to help her. Now I'm dying, and she's to be Ardenn's duchess . . . and Roric, in Clemen, is almost close enough to touch.

She'd long ago lost her faith in Izusa. But Baldwin never did

– and she still believed in Baldwin. Besides. She was desperate. If a leaky boat was the only boat, then that was the boat to row.

Ignoring the pain, Berardine clasped her daughter's face between her hands. 'Listen, child, carefully, for I doubt we've much more time. You've done well to cozen the regents into thinking you a meek, obedient maid.'

Catrain almost laughed. 'If I'd been myself at court I think they'd have risked the loss of me. So I put on a mask and became who they wanted. It's served me well. What cat fears a trembling mouse?'

Oh yes, she was Baldwin's daughter. 'You denounce me, loudly and often?'

'Yes.' Catrain blinked back tears. 'Though it breaks my heart.'

'No. You do the right thing.' She took hold of her daughter's cold hands. 'And when I'm dead you'll go on denouncing me. The regents must *never* have reason to suspect you. Continue to play the mouse in public – but in private, be a lion. As best you can, keep Ardenn loyal to you, and to Baldwin's memory. Most importantly, you must find a way to reach Roric. Clemen's duke is fated to help you. A witch foretold this. She abandoned me but – for your father's sake, I—'

'A *witch*?' Catrain shook her head. 'Mama, I can't. Why would you—'

'Please, child, you must trust that I—'

The chamber door swung open and Corbert strode in, not even the courtesy of a single knock. 'It grows late. Say good night, lady.'

'Ser,' Catrain said, hiding her hatred behind swiftly lowered lids.

Berardine gathered her close. 'Trust Roric,' she breathed. 'It was your father's dying wish.' Letting her arms fall, she collapsed against her pillows. 'Farewell, daughter. Be sure to heed my advice.'

'Advice?' said Corbert, swiftly suspicious. 'What advice?'

'Why, ser,' Catrain replied earnestly, turning, 'that I should remain obedient to the regents and be guided by them in all things.' She turned back. 'I'll do what you say, Mama. I give you my word.'

The strength she'd hoarded like a miser was now all but spent. With trembling fingers Berardine touched Catrain's cheek. Smiled with trembling lips, so her child would know she understood.

See, Baldwin? Here's our daughter. Our beautiful, brave Catrain.
Hope is not lost. Perhaps, with Roric's help, she can still save Ardenn.

Plague returned to Clemen like a whisper on a breeze. Softly. Stealthily. Hiding in plain sight. A slight cough. A runny nose. A trifling pain in the fingers. Nothing so alarming as swollen pustules and blood. No reason for Eaglerock's harbour leeches to raise the alarm. For weeks it spread, unheeded. Tainted sailors whoring in dockside taverns kissed it into bored, painted mouths. Merchants home from their travels, harassed and coin-pinched and infected, sweated it onto their wares. Smacked it onto their unruly children. Loaded it onto their mule trains and traipsed it around the duchy.

The very young. The very old. The already weak. They were its first victims. Their deaths were slow. They perished lazily, sauntering to their graves. Laboured breaths. Blue faces. Joints twisted out of shape. A little wasting of the body, but most could eat until the end. And only at the very end did they start to vomit blood.

Like scattered raindrops, harbingers of a coming storm, word began to spread of the new affliction. Rumours, to begin with. Gossip. *Have you heard?* For some weeks, those who answered could say no. Or say yes, they had heard, but they'd not seen it for themselves. They didn't want to see it. Hadn't Clemen suffered enough these past years? Poor harvests. The blistermouth. A crippling of trade. The duke taking more and more coin from their purses and still not giving them an heir in return. What was he doing, safe in Eaglerock castle? Didn't he care how the people of Clemen were in strife?

But then, as the stealthy pestilence spread, more and more folk could give witness of their own eyes. Rumour turned into reality. The scattered raindrops became a flood. And instead of whispering, the plague started to shout.

The exarchite Ignace was short and fat. What hair he had left to him was clipped close to his scalp. Like many who hailed from the Danetto Peninsula, he was swarthy, with dark eyes and a thin nose and not enough teeth. And, like most of his brethren – dark and fair – he breathed out sweetness with every hushed word. No matter which city state they hailed from, Danettans doted on dried and syruped fruit. They thought of honey as liquid gold and tended to eat as though each meal was their last. Not even Clemen's ongoing, never-ending trading difficulties, it seemed, could stem the flow of Danettan sweet-meats into the exarchite houses that had sprung up throughout the duchy over the past five years.

And because he needed the Exarch's grey-robed priests, Roric couldn't afford to levy taxes on their greed. It was just one more cause of friction between himself and his council. Before long there'd be enough causes to burst them all into flame.

'As you can see, Your Grace,' Ignace said softly, 'we are now sore-pressed to nurse any more of Eaglerock's afflicted. Not without we find and furbish another sickhouse.'

Which he'd be expected to pay for. Only with his ducal coffers perilously close to empty that was out of the question. Unwilling to say so, Roric nodded.

'I'll be sure to raise the matter with the council, Ignace.'

He and Ignace stood side by side at the entrance to the exarchite house's hospice. A high-roofed stone building sited close to the harbour, it had once been a warehouse for goods from Sassanine. But internal strife there, and the lack of Clemen coin for extravagant purchases, meant that Sassanine's ruler had ceased trading in the duchy and let the warehouse lease lapse. Yet another blow to Clemen's faltering finances. Not everyone on the council, or in the township, was pleased the exarchites had taken the lease, but the stark truth was unavoidable. Clemen needed the coin.

The sole reminder that the building had been a warehouse was the row of high, narrow windows under the sloping roof. Not even a lingering scent of exotic Sassanine spices remained. Instead the air was heavy with burning pastilles of sage and morning glory, thought by the exarchites to repel ill humours. Beneath it, the grim odour of failing flesh and rotten blood. End to end and wall to wall, the old warehouse was full of Eaglerock folk who'd succumbed to the latest plague. Men, women and children lay listless on straw pallets, moaning as Ignace's brother exarchites tended to their needs. No privacy here. No modesty, either. Only misery and weeping.

'It was good of you to come, Your Grace,' Ignace murmured, with a touch to his arm. 'Foolish, perhaps, but good.'

Roric drifted his gaze across the pinched, pale faces before him. 'These are my people suffering. How could I not come?'

'Easily,' Ignace said, shrugging. 'I am from Pruges, Your Grace. There is nothing a man can teach me about the indifference of dukes.'

At the far end of the old warehouse a child twisted on its pallet, crying out in pain. One of the exarchs moved swiftly to the child's side. Knelt close and bowed his head in prayer. The child twisted again, then began to cough bright blood.

Roric took a step forward. 'This is unbearable. There must be—'

'No, Your Grace,' Ignace said, catching his elbow. 'You can't help. That child is already dead.'

'But—'

Ignace pointed. 'See? It is done.'

The child shuddered hard, head to toe. Shuddered again, its thin limbs flailing. And then . . . nothing. Lips silently moving, the kneeling exarchite pulled the bloodstained sheet over its small face.

'You should go,' Ignace said softly. 'Your place is not here.'

The child's brief, brutal death had stirred no response from the exarchites' other patients. Either they were too sick to notice – or they'd grown used to such sights. Staring at them, his throat tight, Roric didn't know which was worse.

'Then where is my place, Ignace? Where would you and the Exarch and your god have me be?'

Ignace folded his hands across his full moon of a belly. 'Kneeling in penitent prayer before our chapel's shrine, Your Grace. Sin unrepented is always punished. If you would but give yourself into the Exarch's keeping, the people of Clemen would follow your—'

'No, Ignace, for the last time, abandon these attempts to convert me and my duchy. What a man believes in is his own business. Not mine. Or yours. Or the Exarch's.'

Ignace bowed his head. 'Your Grace.'

'I must go. You know my chief steward, Nathyn. Be sure to tell him if there's anything you need.'

Turning his back on Eaglerock's sick and suffering, and the infuriatingly persistent priest, Roric left the shadowed hospice. His personal men-at-arms were waiting outside, holding his horse for him, stoically patient.

Captain Pero raised an eyebrow. 'Your Grace?'

'I'm done.' He took his reins and mounted. 'I'd return to Eaglerock.'

'Your Grace! Your Grace, a word. If you please.'

Riding back to the castle, Roric had found himself – and not for the first time – running a gauntlet of fearful, disappointed stares from Eaglerock's townsfolk. His face still burning, more shaken than he wanted to admit, he flung Humbert a quelling glance. He was in no mood for one of his foster-lord's scolds.

'Not now.'

Heedless of the staff and courtiers in the castle's entrance hall, Humbert moved Pero out of the way with a glare and fell into step. 'Yes, Your Grace. *Now.*'

They were in public so he couldn't curse in Humbert's face. Such a pity. A full-throated bellowing match with Lindara's father would sear the memory of that dying child from his mind. Deafen him to its pitiful cries – and the jeers he'd heard from a few of those staring townsfolk. Pero and his men had silenced them, but not swiftly enough. Their anger echoed, flaying him like a whip.

There he is. Our duke, Berold's grandson. Or so they say. But I say he's not so much as a pimple on Berold's arse!

Surprisingly nimble, Humbert slipped in front of him, blocking his way. The oak entrance hall staircase rose majestically behind him.

'Your Grace—' Splendid in a deep-rose-coloured gown over a crimson velvet doublet and black hose, a flat black velvet cap gracing his head, Humbert narrowed his stare. 'I must insist.'

They were attracting the wrong kind of attention. With nerves in Eaglerock stretched taut, any hint of strife between Clemen's duke and its great lords would feed the rampant fires of gossip, adding to the general unease.

Roric forced a smile. Patted Humbert's vast shoulder. 'Of course. Come. We'll sit privily, and talk.'

'The small audience chamber,' Humbert muttered. 'It's empty.'

Dismissing Pero and his men with a nod, he led the way upstairs to the modest receiving room adjoining the grand Falcon Throne chamber. The moment he and Humbert were safely alone, his foster-lord turned on him.

'*The exarchite hospice*, Roric? What curs't madness is this?'

'Not madness,' he said, teeth gritted. 'Necessity.'

'*Necessity?*' Scarlet-faced behind his beard, Humbert strode about the room like a man in search of somewhere to thrust his sword. 'It was *necessary* for you to risk your life in that filthy place?'

'Yes, Humbert! It was! I had to be sure. I had to see for myself.'

'See what? Be sure of what? And keep your voice down. You've a gaggle of men next door, twiddling their thumbs waiting on you. Blane and Arthgallo and a few others.' Turning, Humbert stopped in mid-stride, barrel chest heaving, bearded jaw jutted with affront. 'And that's another thing. Why are they summoned? I had no word of it. Neither did Aistan know anything till I told him. But that cockshite Ercole's there. *He* knew.'

Because Master Blane must have told him. Cosily wed with the trader's grand-daughter, these days Ercole conducted himself more like a merchant than a councillor of Clemen. Curse him.

'Humbert . . .' Abruptly weary, a familiar pain leaping to life behind his eyes, Roric raised a placating hand. 'I'm sorry. I'd intended to speak with you and Aistan first thing this morning. But Lindara had a poor night and—'

'Lindara?' Humbert's breath caught, and his face tightened with fear. 'Is aught amiss? Has Arthgallo seen her? What—'

'*Humbert.*' He took hold of his foster-lord's arm. 'She slept fitfully, that's all. But it gave me a difficult start to the morning.'

United by their misgivings, they stared at each other. Two early miscarriages and an untimely stillbirth Lindara had suffered since his return from the disastrous journey to Cassinia. He and Lindara had grown brittle with each other, no words for such calamity. She was newly with child again . . . but he was afraid to hope. So was Humbert. They both startled at shadows and feared to hear her sigh, terrified that this babe would perish like the rest.

Humbert tugged at his beard. 'All right, then. But now you *will* tell me what this—' He pointed at the door that led into the Falcon Throne audience chamber. '—is about.'

'You recall we discussed in council that the harbour might have to be closed?'

'It was discussed, yes,' said Humbert, frowning. 'But no firm decision was—'

'*I've* decided. Until we can be sure this new pestilence has burned itself out, no ships will enter or leave Eaglerock harbour.'

'Roric—'

'I know I had my doubts,' he said quickly. 'That's why I went to the hospice. I needed to see the pestilence for myself.' He breathed out, hard. 'Humbert, it was terrible. And the people are blaming me. Something has to be done.'

He waited, then, half-expecting Humbert to contradict him, bluffly assert that the people blamed him for nothing. But Humbert stared at the floor. Tugged at his beard again, his lips pinched tight. Which meant he'd been told of the recent stares, and the jeering.

'Humbert—'

Humbert lifted his head. 'So you've decided to close the harbour. Good. If you recall, it's what I suggested from the start. But what has it to do with Blane, and the rest?' Another frown. 'Wait. Don't tell me you're thinking to ask their leave?'

'No. But I'm mindful that closing the harbour will—'

'Be mindful of this. You're Clemen's duke, boy, and a duke doesn't ask permission to do what must be done! What if the fucking merchant and those other pizzles say no?'

'Humbert . . .' Roric sighed. 'How can they? I'm their duke. I've asked them here because they'll be useful in keeping the harbour quiet when the news breaks.'

'You hope!' Humbert retorted. 'And hope is no remedy in these perilous times!'

As if he didn't know that. 'Withdraw to the throne room and advise Blane and the rest I'll be with them presently.'

'No, Roric,' Humbert said, shaking his head. 'I'd have you think on—'

Fury, sudden and ungovernable. 'Clap tongue, Humbert, and for once do as you're fucking told! Or say to my face here and now that you do but indulge me in a fantasy that I'm your duke!'

Humbert's jutting beard trembled once, then tucked close to his chest. He blinked, his face smooth as carved ice. 'Your Grace.'

Roric watched the adjoining door close. Heard wood thud against wood. Bile scorched his throat, and his hands were shaking. As though he'd been the one chastised, instead of—

I had the right. I've been Clemen's duke for eleven years. Nearly twelve. And still he questions every choice I make. He still calls me boy. No other lord would dare it. And while he dares, while I permit, I am neither man nor duke.

And yet he could weep for the look in Humbert's eyes. Did every son and father battle so? He supposed they must. But there was no one he could ask.

Harald always said that to be a duke was to be lonely. I never believed him. But I believe him now.

He took a little time, to smooth his hunter-green velvet doublet and buff the diamond pin on his breast. To wait for his sickness over Humbert to ease. The clamour that greeted him as he entered the throne room had him longing for a whip so he could thrash his visitors to silence.

Why the fuck must men be so contentious?

Crossing to his throne, Roric considered those he'd summoned to court. Blane and two of his fellow merchants, Lander and Gilmyn. Hoggard, the wealthiest of Eaglerock's warehouse owners. Shipmaster Garith, who owned six galleys. Arthgallo, for his leechery advice. Like Humbert, Aistan had come uninvited, his eyes hooded and unreadable. And there was Ercole, clearly torn between standing with his goodfather, Blane, or with Aistan and Humbert. He hovered between them, trying to look like he supported both. Still sulky-faced, was Ercole, but at Blane's well-fed table he'd grown a prosperous paunch.

Roric sat. '*Gentlemen*. What is this stir?'

Blane, who'd accumulated as much influence as coin these last few years, cleared his throat. 'We're told you intend to close the harbour, Your Grace.'

Staring at Ercole, Roric drummed the arm of his throne. A brief struggle, then Ercole dropped his gaze, defeated.

'I do, Blane.'

'Your Grace, you *cannot—*'

'I can. And I will. In case it's escaped your notice, Clemen is afflicted with plague.'

'If you close the harbour, Your Grace,' said Shipmaster Garith, booted feet spread as though he rode his galley's deck, 'we'll perish anyway. From lack of coin.'

'Garith's right,' said Hoggard. 'Eaglerock harbour is our lifeblood. Close it, Your Grace, and every ship will sail past us to find a port in Harcia.'

'It's well known Harcia's waters are treacherous, and the duchy has no decent harbour to speak of. The shipmasters who sail there before coming to us swiftly rue the decision.'

'Your Grace, they'll risk the dangers,' Garith said grimly, 'if you force their hand. And let but a handful succeed and we'll not get them back to Eaglerock harbour again.'

'Without the little trade that's left us,' Blane added, 'the waterfront will wither and die – and as we die so dies all Clemen!'

'Arthgallo,' Roric said sharply. 'Explain to these good men what they don't understand.'

Because he was Arthgallo, he'd not thought to change his stained smock or strip off his tatty canvas cap. His dusty hose were saggy and threadbare at the ankles and his right shoe was held together with string.

'Your Grace,' he said, with a vague attempt at a bow. ''Tis a foolish man who dismisses the plagues and distempers brought to us from foreign lands. Strange indeed are the humours bred in Agribia and Khafur and in the stewpits of Danetto's city states. Though this pestilence is somewhat mild, I fear—'

'To no good purpose,' said Ercole, with contempt. 'You leeches are all alike. A man sneezes and you cry plague and seek to empty his purse for remedies!'

Roric looked at Humbert, who stood a little distant. As a rule, that kind of arrogant outburst had his foster-lord growling threats and thumping fist. But this time Humbert said nothing. Might have been an old man, lost to deafness and scattered wits. Hiding dismay, he leaned forward.

'You think this pestilence a fraud, Ercole? Visit the exarchite hospice down at the harbour, as I have. Watch a child die in blood and agony, as I have. Then tell me again how Arthgallo and his brother leeches do perpetrate a fraud.'

Discomforted silence. Blane cleared his throat. 'You set foot in the hospice?'

'I did.'

'A child died there?'

'Before my eyes.'

Blane turned to Arthgallo. 'Could you not prevent it?'

'No,' said Arthgallo, staring. 'I wasn't present.'

'He means in general,' Ercole snapped. 'You're Eaglerock's most esteemed leech. Why haven't you done more to cure this outbreak of pestilence?'

Arthgallo's thin nostrils pinched. 'I do what I can, my lord. I am only one man. Why didn't you prevent it from spreading in the first place? You and Lord Aistan, here. Since the blistermouth, aren't you the lords charged with safeguarding the harbour?'

'We are,' Aistan said, before Ercole could fly at the leech. 'But despite our best efforts, this time we failed.'

Surprised, Roric looked at him. Aistan had argued against closing the harbour. Was he changing his mind? It was hard to tell. Since his return from Cassinia, theirs had been a distant, suspicious relationship. His fault. Humbert was right. He'd been unwise to make accusations of treachery without proof.

'Gentlemen,' he said, sitting back, 'people are dying. Not in their hundreds, I admit, and many who sicken don't die. Certainly Clemen has been afflicted with crueller plagues in the past. But that's no reason for us to be complacent. The duchy is weakened. Should the unthinkable happen and another more deadly plague strike our shores . . .' He watched them swallow fear. 'Every one of you remembers what it was like last time. None of us was untouched. We all buried people we loved. Do you want to live through that horror again?'

Blane exchanged glances with the other harbour men, then heaved a sigh. 'You're determined to do this, Your Grace? Close the harbour?'

'I am.'

'And how long will it remain closed?'

'No longer than needed.'

'Then we must bow to your good judgement. Your Grace.'

'Yes,' he said. 'You must. And you must also do your part to see the harbour reconciled to my decision. Yours are influential voices. Put them to good use.'

Another exchange of glances. Blane nodded. 'Yes, Your Grace.'

It was a victory, but their reluctant capitulation left a sour taste in his mouth. One by one he watched them offer their obeisance, and leave the chamber. Arthgallo excused himself to look in on Lindara.

'Aistan, Ercole,' Roric said, once he and his councillors were alone, 'I trust you to see the harbour speedily closed. Be intolerant of mischief. I want no trouble.'

'You might not want it,' Humbert said, staring after the departing Aistan and Ercole, 'but you're bound to get it. Best you put the castle guard on alert.'

He already intended to. But he'd snarled at his foster-lord enough for one day. 'A wise suggestion. Humbert—'

'No, Your Grace,' Humbert said, subdued. Reminded of his sons' deaths, his eyes were bloodshot. 'I'm an old man and I'm weary. I'd have a little peace if it's all the same to you.' Turning, he stamped his way to the throne room's doors. Then, as he reached them, he turned back. 'One last thing. I received word this morning. Berardine of Ardenn is dead. Catrain's been acclaimed duchess.' He straightened his velvet cap. 'I thought you'd want to know.'

As the castle guard sealed the chamber doors after Humbert, Roric closed his eyes. Berardine dead? Catrain made duchess? Did that mean the regents would let her go home to Ardenn? If they did, what would that mean for Cassinia's mad prince? According to Catrain, she was Gaël's sole friend. He had no doubt of that. Nor, remembering them together in the palace garden, did he doubt how much she loved the boy. Two hard losses. He could only imagine the grief she was suffering. If only he could help her. But with Blane so wary of him, these days, Ercole nastily whispering in his ear, he had no hope of smuggling a second letter into Ardenn.

All he could do was think of her . . . and hope for the best.

CHAPTER TWENTY-SEVEN

Dappled with early-morning sunlight, the autumn-turned woodland glowed gold and tawny and red. The first leaves were falling, oak and beech spreading a fiery carpet upon the damp earth and the damp moss, covering delicate, pale green ferns. Toadstools squatted in the shadows, their red caps dotted cream. The cool, rich air promised snow in winter. Believing it, squirrels scurried, collecting acorns, filling their secret larders for the cold days ahead. Glossy black crows croaked and cawed, congregated in the thinning tree tops. A fox, sly eyes gleaming in its narrow, black-masked face, its rusty pelt thickening, trotted boldly between the trees.

Settled belly-down along a crooked branch, watching it, Balfre regretted his lack of a bow. But this day, he wasn't the hunter. This day, he was prey.

Somewhere to the left, a startled squawk. A clatter of wings. The fox froze in its tracks, head lifted. A flick of its white-tipped brush and it was gone, darted into the tangled undergrowth.

Balfre grinned.

Moments later, two men came into sight. Both fair-haired, dressed in scarcely-worn huntsman's leathers, they moved with clumsy stealth. Their booted feet scuffed and slipped through the bright leaves. Cracked half-rotten, fallen branches. Left an easy trail to follow in their wake. Each man had drawn his sword and his dagger. The dappling sunlight glinted on the bared steel. Stubbled faces tight with trepidation, they kept themselves close and tried to look in every direction at once.

Balfre waited. Waited. Let them pass beneath his branch. And then, with a sinuous twist, ignoring the pull of the half-healed sword cut in his thigh, let himself drop the length of his arms, hands tight upon the weathered bark, and sent both men flying with a kick each between their shoulder blades. And as they sprawled ungainly, face-first on the damp ground, dropped lightly to his feet, plucked up their dropped daggers and pricked each man in the throat with his weapon's point.

'You're dead,' he told them. 'You fucking fools.'

'My lord.'

'My lord.'

They'd dropped their swords, too. Were this a skirmish against Vidar's men these green shites would be gutted now, like sheep. He pricked the dagger points a little deeper.

'Where are you from?'

'Oakford, my lord.'

'Wallington.'

'You're second sons? Third sons? Your fathers are in trade?'

'Yes, my lord. He's a blacksmith.'

'I be orphaned, my lord.'

He snorted. 'And you thought you could serve me as men-at-arms in the Marches.'

'Yes, my lord.'

'Yes, my lord.'

The men's voices had grown small. Unpricking them, Balfre sat back on his heels. Tossed the daggers so he held them blade-first, and rapped each man hard on his head with a hilt.

'Had I a month to spare I'd still lack the time to tell you every stupid fucking mistake you made.'

'Beg pardon, my lord.'

'D'you mean to send us home?'

He rapped their heads again, harder. 'No. And no.'

This time, wisely, the fucking fools said nothing.

Ten new men, Paithan had sent him from his family estate. Like Joben and Lowis, he never sent more than ten. That was the rule. It was important Vidar never noticed any great difference in the number of Harcian men-at-arms riding in the Marches. And that Aimery never realised what his heir was about. Next week, or the week after, some eight or ten seasoned men-at-arms would be sent home to Paithan.

He'd put them to good use, training more men-at-arms at home or serving Aimery at Tamwell castle, or himself, or some other impeccably loyal lord. A handful would go to the Green Isle, the ones who could be trusted to keep an eye on Grefin and report what they saw.

And every man he trained, every man he sent home, was a man he could count on once he was made duke. Since coming to the Marches, he'd trained nearly six hundred men. He planned to train many more. An army of fierce men-at-arms, loyal to Count Balfre and steeped to the gills in hatred for Clemen.

The two fools sprawled before him were the last of Paithan's most recent gift. He dealt with them as he'd dealt with the other eight. Lashed each man's wrists behind his back with thin strips of leather then pinned him between his sword and his dagger, plunged into the dirt at his head and his feet.

'Stay here,' he told them. 'And stay down. Move so much as a thumb's width and I'll use you for archery practice.'

'Yes, my lord.'

'Yes, my lord.'

His horse was hobbled in a clearing, not too far distant. Retrieving it, he released the hobbles, mounted, and returned to his manor. Waymon was in the library, at the reading table, working his way through an armory report. He looked up and burst out laughing.

'All ten trussed like chickens? Truly?'

Tossing his gloves onto a low table, Balfre shrugged. 'What the fuck do you think?'

'I think Paithan might be losing his touch.' Waymon shoved the report to one side and sat back. 'Are there no better men to be found in Harcia?'

Shrugging again, he crossed to the sideboard and poured himself a goblet of wine. 'They're young and strong. The rest we can thrash into them.' He nodded at the scattered pages. 'What damage there?'

'Enough,' Waymon said, scowling. 'More than can easily be accounted to the duke.'

Balfre swallowed wine. *Fuck*. It cost coin to train men-at-arms. Green men broke swords. They killed horses. They wore out their leathers, snapped arrows, snapped their bones, unravelled mail. Some of those expenses he could slip by Aimery and that sharp-eyed fuck

Curteis. And some he could pay for out of his own purse. But not all of them. So, faced with failure, he did what had to be done. Not often. Just often enough.

It was Waymon who'd suggested it, the first time he realised there were cobwebs in his coffers. When he was forced to accept the harsh truth that without sufficient coin at his disposal, his dreams and ambitions must wither on the vine. Because of that he'd agreed to thieving. And agreed too, there could be no witnesses left alive after. To be sure, murder was distasteful. But a duke – a king – must above all things be ruthless. Be prepared to shed blood in defence of his crown. And he'd killed at the Pig Whistle. Killed a Harcian lord and Harcian men-at-arms.

Of course, Bayard and Egbert and their men-at-arms had failed Harcia, and in failing had betrayed it. Death had been a fitting punishment. Whereas the traders who came through the Marches were, for the most part, innocent men. Innocent of harming Harcia, at least. It was harder to reconcile the killing of an innocent man. But what choice did he have? He'd needed the coin then. He needed more now. And so another innocent man must die so the reborn Kingdom of Harcia might live.

Such were the burdens of a crown.

'Don't fret yourself,' said Waymon, watching him. 'I'll take care of it. There'll be traders coming back from the autumn fair at Meckersly. I'll find one travelling on his own who won't be missed.'

He didn't doubt it. Like every other time, Waymon would neatly slit the trader's throat and take his purse or coffer and dispose of his body with no more conscience than a butcher. That was Waymon. If he'd learned anything since becoming Aimery's Marcher lord, it was how right he'd been to choose this man as his companion.

He drank the rest of his wine. 'Very well.'

Crossing back to the sideboard to refill his goblet, he glanced at the mantelpiece over the hearth. With Paithan's latest recruits had come letters from Harcia. He'd read all of them save one. Wished he could toss the last of them in the library fire unread, because it was from Jancis. But Aimery would know if he'd not answered her and be angry. He couldn't afford Aimery angry. His father, clinging stubbornly to life, must at all costs be kept sweet. So, fortified with more wine, he snatched up the letter from the mantel, where he'd left it, and cracked the wax seal. Dropped onto a stool and cast a swift, jaundiced eye over his unwanted wife's spidery scrawling.

Aimery was well. The leech Grefin had found for him continued to work wonders. Grefin was well, too, and Mazelina, and their children. She was well. She hoped he was well. Emeline had been poorly. But Aimery's leech had treated their daughter and the dear child was on the mend.

That was a pity.

Harcia was abuzz with tales of plague in Clemen. Aimery, being a good duke, had sent leeches to the towns and villages nearest the Marches border. So far there was no sign of sickness in their duchy. She was very frightened and begged him to take care.

Yes, yes, he knew all about Clemen's latest pestilence. Did his fucking fool of a wife think Aimery had failed to warn him? Did she imagine his men-at-arms didn't know what to do?

Finally, she said, she would be an obedient wife. Did he want her to join him in the Marches, all he had to do was ask.

Ask Jancis to join him? He'd hack his balls off with a rusty dagger first.

Irritated, because she never failed to aggravate, he drained his goblet a second time, tossed his wife's letter to the flames, then stood. 'I'm going out.'

Waymon smirked. 'Izusa?'

He turned away so Waymon couldn't see his face. Wouldn't see the way his blood burned beneath his skin. *Izusa.* Her name alone was enough to stir him. Sometimes he wondered if he wasn't half-bewitched. If she didn't fuck magic into him with every wild thrust of her hips. Maybe she did. What of it? Without her, his self-imposed exile to the Marches would kill him.

He picked up his gloves, pulled them on. 'Wait a full turn of the hour glass, then go and find those fucking turds I left in Bramly Woods. Run them back to the barracks.'

'Run them?' Waymon pulled a face. 'What if they trip over their own feet and break an ankle?'

'For their sakes I hope they don't.'

Waymon sighed. 'And then what?'

'The archery butts,' he said, after a moment's thought. 'Till sundown. And this time, Waymon, don't let them shoot each other. It's a waste of good arrows.'

Hand pressed to his heart, Waymon offered a sardonic, seated bow. 'Yes, my lord.'

'And you can tell them, from me, that any man who doesn't shoot at least three bullseyes before the sun sinks will forfeit his dinner.'

'Well, 'tis one way of saving coin.'

He grinned, even as anticipation began to burn. 'Fuck you, Waymon. And finish reading that report.'

There was a time, Molly remembered, when the roads that crossed just outside the Pig Whistle were thronged day and night with folk travelling in and out of the Marches. When anyone who stopped to listen would hear a dozen different shouted conversations in a dozen different, twisty tongues. When a soul could easily let slip an hour gazing at the foreign faces and the foreign clothes of the traders come to ply their wares wherever folk had coin to spare, and the dust kicked up by their horses and mules and donkeys threatened to choke the air. When folk from the towns and villages on either side of the Marches crossed their borders cheerfully, and nobody here minded too much that they were duchy-folk – so long as their purses were fat. And when them who lived in the Marches went about their work whistling and didn't fear the Marcher lords and their men-at-arms, or stay locked indoors at night.

There was a time . . . but it was five years past. Five years since the bloodshed over the Crown Court that never happened, and nothing had gone right for the Marches since.

Standing in the crossroads, Molly shaded her eyes and stared down the road that guided a traveller into and out of Clemen. Even a year ago she'd have been taking her life in her hands to stand there. Now the crossroads were empty. The road was empty. She couldn't recall the last time she'd had to turn someone away from the Pig Whistle because all her beds were taken. Or curse herself red-faced because she'd run out of pies. And if that wasn't misery enough, there was plague come into Clemen. Again. Thank the faeries Izusa had warned her, and told her what to look for in any soul with the taint, and given her secret, special charms for herself and Iddo and the boys, and the Pig Whistle, to keep them safe. She'd not stumbled across any sign of the new pestilence yet. But she'd heard tell of folk touched by it who were caught along the Clemen border of the Marches. Of course, that might be rumour. But if the stories were true . . .

A hint of movement, where the road to Clemen curved out of sight. Squinting, Molly tried to figure who it was. Not one of Vidar or Balfre's men-at-arms. They rode swiftly, careless, as though they owned the beaten earth beneath their horses' hooves. Who was it? And then she laughed out loud, because she saw it was a mule-train. *Traders*. There were traders on the road to the Pig Whistle.

'Spirits be praised,' she whispered, blinking away tears. 'Be praised.'

She'd long fallen out of the habit, but tonight she'd light a candle and burn a twist of honey-soaked wool beneath the flowering rowan beside the inn's henhouse. Perhaps if she'd shown more respect for the old ways, if she'd not spent more time cursing than praising, she wouldn't be able to count so many grey hairs these days, or lose so much sleep.

Not wanting to be caught sight of by her approaching customers, she hurried back to the inn. Her return to the public room raised a chorus of complaint from the handful of folk come to sup ale and eat bread and cheese. Every last man a local, though. They'd had no fresh news for over a week.

'Where be Iddo?' she demanded, as they waved their empty tankards at her. 'Oh, pipe down, ye cockerels. Ye b'aint in danger of dying parched.'

She took their empty tankards and sloshed them full of more ale. Collected their copper nibs, locked the coins in her kitchen coffer, then went in search of Iddo. She found him out back of the Pig Whistle, in the vegetable garden, brawling with Willem. The imp was muck from head to toe, and so was her precious Benedikt.

'—working, ye scabrous little shite, not 'ticing Benedkit to wickedness and throwing clods of dirt!'

Up went Willem's pointed chin, his scarred face tight with temper. 'We was working, Iddo!' Scornful, he kicked the woven rush-basket half-full of dug up carrots and leeks, sitting on the grass between him and Benedikt. 'See?'

'Curl yer lip at me, would ye, ye thankless snipe? When there b'aint a scrap of food goes into yer mouth ye don't owe to my sweat?' Iddo raised his hand. ''Tis no wonder Benedikt's turning to the bad. Ye—'

'No, I b'aint, Iddo,' said Benedikt. 'And Willem didn't 'tice me, neither. I wanted to throw the clod back at him and—'

'Shame on ye, then!' Iddo shouted. 'Ye should know better than to let this scunny—'

Molly sighed. She'd heard enough. 'Now then, now then,' she said briskly, clapping her hands. 'Boys, take them carrots and leeks to the kitchen and see 'em scrubbed clean. Then ye can scrub the pots in the scullery, and the kitchen table too. Go on. And when ye be done there, romp off and see what Iddo's rabbit snares have caught. There be traders on the road. I'll need to cook some pie.'

'Traders?' said Iddo, distracted, as the boys scuttled by him. It hurt her to see how he was afraid to be hopeful. 'How many?'

'Couldn't say,' she said. 'But there do be a mule-train. Best ye tell the stables. Then come in so ye can be useful, 'stead of bellowing at them boys.'

Iddo's face darkened. 'Ye go too soft on that Willem, Moll. He be doing Benedikt a mischief. Ever since that Alys died ye do naught but find excuses for his muckery!'

'I do not,' she protested, but she did, and because she knew it she couldn't look Iddo in the eye. There was a worm of guilt lived in her belly and it never stopped gnawing. Because of that Alys. Because of Willem's scarred face and crooked nose. No matter she'd hurt him to keep him safe. Every time she looked at the boy she remembered what she'd done. Imagined what he'd say if he ever learned the truth. The fear of it near stopped her heart, for she loved him near as much as she loved Benedikt.

Iddo was shaking his head. 'Moll . . .'

'Never mind that,' she said, poking him. 'Or being surly. Warn the stables. I've work indoors.'

There was a new face in the public room. Lord Vidar's man, Egann, travel-stained and weary. She didn't mind Egann. Stern but fair, he was. And not a lord, so no airs about him. She filled a tankard with her best ale and pushed it across the bar to him.

'We've not seen ye for some days, Master Egann.'

He drank deep, belched, then wiped his sleeve over his mouth. 'I did have business in Eaglerock.'

'Ah.' Hearing a stir in the forecourt, she looked through the open public room door. The traders had arrived. 'What tidings from Clemen?'

The question made him scowl. In his leathery face, a harsh sympathy she wasn't used to seeing. 'Nothing you'll want to hear, Mistress Molly. His Grace has closed the harbour.'

She felt her mouth dry. 'For how long?'

'Till the pestilence has run its course.'

'Oh.' Feeling sick, she fumbled for her cloth to blot some spilled ale. With the harbour closed there'd be no more traders coming to the Pig Whistle. Hard times had grown harder. How much more could they bear? 'Well, then. 'Tis good of ye to tell me, Master Egann. Now I—'

But she had no time to finish. The traders she'd seen on the road, four of them, were stamping into the public room. And she had to play the merry innkeep, ply them with ale and pie even though all she wanted to do was cover her face and weep.

Shuddering, Balfre emptied himself with a shout of pleasure then pulled free of Izusa's hot, wet clutch.

'By the Exarch's balls, woman,' he said, rolling off her. 'You're a fucking good fuck.'

She smiled. 'Thank you, my lord.'

He sat up, wincing as the half-healed sword cut in his thigh caught him. His own fault, a mistake in training his men. 'Fuck.'

'Show me,' she said, and pushed him down again. Rolled him a little so his leg caught the candle light. 'When did you last put my ointment on it?'

'A few days ago,' he muttered, as her clever fingers teased at the scabbing edge of the wound.

She slid off the rumpled bed. 'A Marcher lord should know to take better care of himself.'

Watching her cross to a cupboard against the cottage bedroom's far wall, admiring the copper-red curls against her pale shoulders, her naked, dimpled buttocks and the seductive sway of her hips, he felt lust stir again.

'Mind your tongue. I don't come to you for scolding.'

'I know what you come for, my lord.'

He laughed, then caught his breath as she turned back to him, jar of ointment in her hand. She had glorious tits. He could fuck her for her tits alone. Two bouts already, they'd had, yet the blood was rushing again to his cock.

'Curse my leg, you lusty bitch.' He snapped his fingers. 'Come here.'

'My lord—'

'*My lord! You're needed!*'

And that was Waymon, banging on the cottage door.

'Go,' Izusa said. 'I'll be here when you're done.'

'You'll be sorry if you're not,' he said, standing, and when she joined him bit her nipples to prove it. Her cry of pained pleasure made it doubly hard to scramble into his clothes and leave.

Remounted on his horse and waiting, Waymon pulled an apologetic face. 'Sorry, Balfre. But you said you wanted to know when next we caught Clemen scum trespassing.'

'How many this time?' he demanded, untying his horse's reins from the tree beside the cottage door.

'Five.'

He swung himself into the saddle, no longer caring that the wound in his thigh burned. Five more of Roric's people, crept into the Marches. Skulking in Harcia's Marcher lands like rats on a river barge. That made nineteen in nearly two months. It seemed Vidar hadn't made Harcia's position on the crime clear enough to his bastard duke.

'Where are they?'

Waymon's eyes were alight with anticipation. 'Dead Dog's Pond.'

Not so very far out of bounds, then . . . but far enough. 'Fine,' he said, and spurred his stallion. 'Then let us deal with them.'

They rode hard to the pond, where a half-dozen men-at-arms held the trespassers at sword-point.

Staring at the Clemen folk kneeling on the goat-nibbled rough grass by the pond's muddy edge, Balfre shook his head. A family, it looked like. Husband, wife and three children. Hollow-eyed and thin with hunger, their clothes little more than rags.

'Where are you from?'

'Dipford,' the man said, his voice shaking. 'My lord—'

'Dipford is in Clemen. These are the Harcian Marches.'

'We did never mean to trespass!' the woman cried, trying to shelter her snivelling brats. 'We thought this was—' A hacking cough swallowed the rest of her excuse. When she lowered her hand from her mouth, it was blotched with blood.

'*Balfre*,' Waymon muttered, as the men-at-arms stepped back.

He was hard put not to step back himself. *Plague*. Aimery had told him in detail what to look for. How to know if a man was sick with it. Had commanded him to act without mercy if he had to.

It was one of the few times he and his father had ever agreed.

Looking more closely, he saw that the oldest Clemen brat had blood crusted in its nostrils. Its father's knuckles were swollen, fingers twisted. His bloodshot eyes popped with fear.

'Please, my lord,' he said, his voice strangled. 'My wife's touched with an ague.'

Unlikely. More likely they'd been driven from Dipford to spread their pestilence somewhere, anywhere, else. Into the Harcian Marches and then Harcia itself. Rage kindled.

'Waymon.'

It was butchery, brief and brutal. When it was done, Balfre ordered the trespassers' heads struck off. Sent one of his men-at-arms to the goat-man's cottage on the far side of the pond, with orders to bring back two burlap sacks, rope, and lamp oil to burn what remained of the bodies. Waited in silence for the man to return and when he did, put the heads in the burlap sacks himself then secured them on either side of his stallion's saddle.

'What's in your mind?' Waymon murmured, as the headless corpses were doused in oil.

'A thought that it's time Vidar was taught a lesson,' he said. 'The fuck doesn't seem to understand we'll not be jostled like this.' He mounted his horse. 'Make sure the bodies are well burned. Then go

465

and inform Clemen's Marcher lord there's a gift waiting for him at the Pig Whistle. But make no mention of plague. Tell the men likewise, on pain of them losing their tongues. When Vidar comes to me, protesting, then I'll break the news.'

Waymon smiled, slowly. 'Yes, my lord.'

Mistress Molly of the Pig Whistle knew better than to keep Count Balfre waiting. Summoned, she hurried out of the public room and into her forecourt, wiping floury hands down the front of her apron.

'My lord,' she said, her brows pinching as she caught sight of the bloodstained sacks tied to his saddle. 'How can I help ye?'

He could hear a rabble of voices coming from inside. 'Call out your customers. And your barkeep.'

Wary, she obeyed him. A moment later the rabble stumbled out of the inn. Marcher folk, they looked like. Or folk from Harcia and Clemen, passing through. Only four foreigners. Traders. Their golden skin and bronze eyes marked them as Zeidican. The inn's customers stared at him, some still chewing bread like cows with their cud. A few clutched ale-filled tankards. He heard a muffled belch.

'For those of you unfamiliar,' he said coldly, sliding his dagger from its sheath, 'I am Balfre, heir to Aimery of Harcia. As a lord of these Marches, I am the law.' He flicked his wrist, left and right, and severed the ropes tying the burlap sacks to his saddle. His stallion tossed its head as they thudded to the ground. With a nudge, he sidled the animal out of the way. 'Barkeep. Empty them.'

The barkeep, Iddo, glanced at Molly. Insolent fuck. Then, his lips thin with distaste, he took a burlap sack in each hand and heaved until the severed heads tumbled out.

'Spirits save us!' Molly shrieked, as the rabble gabbled its dismay.

Dispassionate, Balfre looked at the rolling, gore-smeared heads. Then he lifted his gaze to the gibbering rabble.

'Like vermin, they crawled their way from Clemen into the Harcian Marches,' he said. 'They weren't the first to trespass. But they were the first to die. Spread the word, Mistress Molly. And you men there, no matter where you call home. Spread the word and be warned. From this day forth *every* man, woman and child found trespassing will meet the same fate. Likewise any man, woman or child found harbouring such vermin, or breaking *any* Marcher law, shall perish. I am not a cruel man. In the past I have been lenient. But it seems leniency breeds contempt here. And therefore leniency ends.'

Slack-jawed staring from Mistress Molly and her barkeep and the rabble. He heard someone start to retch.

'Vidar of Clemen will come to collect the heads,' he said, sliding his dagger into its sheath. 'Till then leave them where they lie, untouched.'

'Iss, my lord,' Molly whispered. 'We'll do as ye say.'

He shrugged. 'For your sake, I hope so. Your life will be forfeit if you fail.'

As she clutched at her barkeep, he spurred his stallion out of the forecourt and turned its head to the west. He was going back to Izusa, to fuck the bad taste out of his mouth.

Iddo was a bastard, but he knew how to set a rabbit snare.

With a grin at Benedikt, Liam bent to untangle the first of three dead coneys caught deep in the woods behind the Pig Whistle. Grinning back at him, Benedikt untangled the second. Then they wrestled each other to see who'd get the third. He won, because he was taller by a hand and he didn't mind wrestling dirty. Benedikt did. Laughing, panting, he rubbed a handful of fallen leaves in his brother's face, then leapt up to take the last coney out of Iddo's clever snare.

There was another snare set even deeper into the trees. But instead of doing what they were s'posed to, check it quickly and quickly get back to the Pig Whistle to help with the henhouse and the stables, they plopped the dead rabbits onto a tree stump and wrestled some more. After all that grubbing in the vegetable garden and the scrubbing in Molly's kitchen, there was nothing better than running wild in the woods.

Wriggled free like an eel, bounced to his bare feet, Benedikt snatched up a tumbled stick and waved it.

'Ha! Ha! Ye be a villain there, Lord Willem!'

They were Marcher brats, not duchy lords or sworn men-at-arms. They were strictly forbidden sword-play. But they were alone in the woods, not a soul to see them, and a stick wasn't a sword so they

467

weren't *really* breaking the law. Besides. Willem of the Pig Whistle was only pretend. Really he was Liam, the rightful duke of Clemen, and that meant he was born to hold a sword.

Hooting, Liam snatched up a branch of his own. 'Ha yerself, Lord Benedikt! I'll run ye through, I will!'

Shrieking with laughter, they thrashed at each other with their pretend swords, slipped and slithered on dead leaves, swung on low-hanging branches . . .

. . . until Iddo found them.

'What be ye doing, ye mad goblins?' he roared, and his face was so terrible they near pissed themselves with fright. Not letting them speak, he fastened bruising fingers round their arms and hauled them back to the Pig Whistle, and Molly.

The dead rabbits got left behind.

Molly listened, dreadfully silent, while Iddo told his tale. Then, deaf to any excuse or explanation, she dragged them out to the inn's forecourt and showed them five horrible, fly-smothered, cut off heads. Then she dragged them down to the ale cellar. Her right thumb and forefinger were pinched so tight on his ear Liam thought she was going to tear it clean off his head. He tried to see past her aproned bulk to Benedikt, but all he could glimpse of his brother was one flailing arm and two bare heels, kicking.

Iddo thudded the cellar's heavy wooden door closed, then hung his big lantern on its convenient hook. Shadows shifted across the windowless stone walls and splashed onto the inn's supply of barrels neatly stacked around the walls, beer and ale and wine in three proper rows. Iddo ruled here and liked things kept in their place.

The whipping barrel sat alone in the middle of the worn flagstone floor, fat with promise and fed on bad dreams.

'*Right*,' said Molly, unpinching her fingers. 'Who be first?'

Rubbing his burning ear, Liam slid a look at Benedikt. *I went first last time*. That was how they sorted themselves. It was never about whose idea had tossed them in trouble.

'Ma—' said Benedikt, his voice small. He was milky-pale beneath his freckles, one shoulder hunched a little as Iddo thwacked his leather-gaitered leg with the seasoned whipping switch. 'Ma, please—'

Molly shook her rough fist in his face. 'Hold yer tongue! I be so

468

thwarted with ye I could skin ye both and use yer hides for dishcloths! Now shuck yer hose, Benedikt, and take what ye've earned!'

Liam watched, mouth dry, as Benedikt puddled his mud-splashed woollen hose round his skinny ankles then shuffled to the whipping barrel. His teeth sank into his trembling bottom lip as he leaned over the splintered wood. In the friendly lamplight his skinny white arse looked like two hard-boiled plover's eggs, freshly peeled.

Still flinty, Molly nodded at Iddo. 'Welt him proper. But don't draw any blood.'

With a whistling crack the switch landed across Benedikt's twitching arse. He let out a choked squeal, his fingers cramping on the barrel. A livid line sprang to life where the switch had struck. Two more blows. Two more squeals. Benedikt's arse was criss-crossed scarlet, each hot line swelling hard and fast. He started dancing on his toes, hopping anguished and whimpering from side to side as his fists drummed a protest on the barrel.

'Hold still, ye little shite!' Molly snarled. 'If it were Count Balfre's men found ye, ye'd be run through on a proper sword for what ye did, and yer head cut off like them heads in the forecourt. That be what happens now for them as breaks Marcher law.'

Benedikt tried to stop dancing but the pain wouldn't let him. Iddo cracked him another one and on a howling shriek he burst into sobs.

'Please, Ma, I'm sorry, Ma, I won't do it agin, it hurts, Ma, please, Ma, *please please please* . . .'

Liam watched Molly blink back tears. But a flick of her finger told Iddo to crack Benedikt again. Again. Again. Again. Benedikt sobbed so hard he was gulping for air, tears and snot running unchecked into his open mouth.

'All right, Iddo,' Molly grunted. 'That'll do.'

Iddo lowered the switch to his side and took a step back. Benedikt held his breath a moment, waiting. When he realised his whipping was done with, he hobbled away from the barrel, spread-fingered hands hovering over his bright red welted arse. He was blubbing like a girl. Liam, looking away, felt sorry and angry and could've cracked Benedikt himself. It was what Iddo and Molly wanted, to see him shamed and broken.

'Right,' said Molly, pointing. 'Willem.'

Heart pounding, Liam took his place at the barrel then shoved his hose down.

I'm a duke. I'm a duke. Dukes are brave. Dukes are strong.

A few steps away, Benedikt's knees buckled and he folded to the cellar floor. Face hidden against his arms, welted rump stuck high, he rocked to and fro, weeping. One flattened hand slapped the flagstones, pounding out his pain.

'Willem,' said Molly. Her voice sounded ragged. 'I don't know which of ye thought to play swords and ye needn't bother telling me. I don't care. Iddo's right. The two of ye lead each other into mischief turn and turn about and I've been soft on it. But ye b'aint babbies no more. Ye know if ye be found playing swords it be yer life, and Benedikt's, and this inn taken off me and me thrown into a ditch to starve. Ye *know* that, and still ye 'ticed Benedikt to break the law, or ye let him 'tice ye, 'cause yer be heedless and ye never want to believe there be rules ye have to obey. Willem, I tell ye truly, today ye'll learn to believe.'

He heard Iddo's switch make a whistling sound before it cracked across his arse. The pain was so bad he nearly bit through his tongue. He watched his fingers spasm on the whipping barrel, felt rough splinters poke his skin. The first welt was rising like breakfast bread in the oven. The switch cracked his arse a second time. He howled.

No, no, I'm a duke, I'm a duke, I'm brave – I'm –

But he couldn't think through the whistling cracks that set his arse on fire. All he could do was press his belly across the barrel and stare at the stone floor as Iddo whipped him and whipped him 'cause he and Benedikt had played swords. Not even proper swords, just bashing about with sticks. Why was that agin the law? Why did that call for dying and Molly starving in a ditch?

He was blubbing now, like Benedikt. Iddo was whipping the tears out of him. He could feel himself dancing, just like Benedikt danced. But Molly wasn't his mother so he didn't beg her to make it stop. She wouldn't listen if he did. She hadn't listened to Benedikt and she wasn't his Ellyn.

Crack . . . crack . . . crack . . . crack . . . crack.

'That'll do,' said Molly, sighing. 'Let 'em smart on their lonesome. And let this be the last time ye tell me I go too soft.'

'For once ye were hard enough,' said Iddo. 'They'll smart a goodly while, I'll lay.'

Through his fiery pain, Liam heard an odd note in Iddo's voice. Snot-slicked and weeping, he looked behind him – and saw in the man's face a flash of gloating satisfaction.

Serves ye right, ye little shite, it said, loud as a shout. *I hope ye smart till Crackbean morning.*

Which was nigh three months away.

Hatred surged, even hotter than the roaring fire roasting his whipped arse.

You'll be sorry for that, Iddo. One day I'll make you sorry.

And so would Molly be sorry. One day, somehow, he'd make both of them pay.

Molly and Iddo closed the cellar door, leaving the lamp with its warm light and flickering shadows. Shuddering, Liam forced the tears back behind his eyes. Still holding onto the whipping barrel, 'cause he couldn't risk letting go. If he could stay on his feet he could believe he wasn't defeated.

Benedikt had stopped pounding the flagstones with his hand, but he was still blubbing. His welted arse still stuck in the air. And then, slow as an old tortoise, he curled onto his side with his muddied hose a tangle round his ankles.

'I'm sorry, Willem,' he whispered, all jerky with tears. 'This be my fault.'

'I didn't have to play,' he whispered back, sounding the same. 'It's my fault too.'

'My arse hurts, Willem. It hurts ever so bad.'

He saw again that flash of gloat in Iddo's heavy, stubbled face. 'Mine don't. And neither does yours.'

Benedikt whimpered. 'It does, but. And—'

'*No, Benedikt, it don't!*'

Silenced, Benedikt stared at him. Then he closed his eyes and blubbed some more. Sorry for shouting, Liam let go of the whipping barrel and curled on the flagstones beside his weeping brother, even though every move made him want to howl. Shame was a hot coal burning its way through his guts. Sick with anger, he did his best to stamp it out.

I'm a duke. I'm a duke. I'm brave. I'm strong. I'm a duke.

CHAPTER TWENTY-EIGHT

'Vidar? Vidar, where do you go?'

Seething with a barely controlled rage, Vidar glanced up as his fingers continued to belt on his sword. His timid wife, Aistan's ruined daughter, stood in the doorway that led from the manor hall to her dayroom, and twisted her fingers in the folds of her green linen skirts.

'To see Balfre on Marcher business,' he said, trying to gentle his voice. She flinched and startled so easily. Aistan had been woefully wrong when he said the exarchite women's house had healed her. 'I'll be back soon enough.'

'Balfre.' Hesitant, Kennise entered the hall. 'I wish you wouldn't go. The man is dangerous, and we'll be losing the light before long.'

The man had that morning murdered five desperate, defenceless Clemen innocents. Dangerous didn't begin to come near it. And Waymon, who'd so arrogantly told him to go play hide and seek at the Pig Whistle, he was no better. Mad dogs, the pair of them. For Clemen's sake they should be put down. If only Clemen's duke could be made to understand that.

He tied the end of his sword-belt out of the way. 'I must go, Kennise. Don't fret. There'll be moonlight enough to ride by.'

'Why must you go? Why can't it wait until morning?'

She didn't know about the murders. He had no intention of telling her. He'd brought the severed heads back with him in the burlap sacks Balfre had used, and given them to Humbert's watchdog Egann, for soaking in pitch. Egann, who'd brought his own dire news from Eaglerock.

Roric's closing the harbour? What was Aistan thinking, letting him get away with that?

But he couldn't give himself over to pondering Clemen's woes. He had woes enough of his own, trying to keep peace in the uneasy Marches. Keeping his men-at-arms from fright over the rumours of plague. Keeping himself from provoking outright confrontation with Balfre. From worrying and wondering over Lindara. She was with child again. Punished with silence, with distance, it was all he knew for sure. His poor Lindara. She'd suffered so much since they were forcibly parted. A day never passed when he didn't think of her with pain.

'Balfre . . .'

He turned on the woman he'd mistakenly made his wife. 'Kennise, *I must go*. You'll not be alone. Egann is here, and he'll stay with you till I return.'

She was fearful, and damaged, a lump of ice in his bed. That frozen wasteland had somehow delivered him two daughters. No son, as yet, though he still had hope. But despite her failings Kennise was also Aistan's daughter, which meant she was no fool.

'Something's happened,' she said, taking another step towards him. 'Tell me, Vidar. Stop treating me like a silly child.'

Irritated, he pulled on a fresh pair of gloves. The pair he'd worn to the Pig Whistle were ruined. 'I don't. I'm not.'

'Is it the pestilence? Has it breached the border with Clemen?'

'*No*,' he snapped. Fuck. Let that maggot fester and she'd wake screaming out of sleep every night for a week. Turning, he took hold of her frail shoulders. Wanted to shake her. Instead he pulled her close. 'No. Balfre's done something . . . unwise. It could stir violent feelings, which is the last thing we need. I must have it out with him at once, lest he take my delay as permission to go his way unchecked.'

She shivered against him. 'Then take Egann with you. There are servants here. I won't be alone.'

Take Humbert's watchdog, and give the man more gossip for his letters to Lindara's unforgiving father?

'Egann has his own duties in the barracks,' he said, releasing his wife. 'Have you so little faith in me, Kennise, that you think I can't scold Balfre without coming to blows?'

473

She flushed. 'No.'

'Well, then.'

'But if you won't take Egann, take a horde of men-at-arms instead. Please, Vidar. Do you want me sick with fretting?'

He did not. 'Very well.' He kissed her cheek. 'I'll be back in time for dinner. You might see a flagon of Evrish red opened. But refrain from emptying it yourself before I return.'

'Be careful,' she called after him. Then her breath caught. 'Vidar—'

Pausing, he looked back. 'What?'

'How much longer must we live in the Marches? I miss my family. I want to go home. Can't you tell Roric it's time he called you home?'

He almost laughed. Tell Roric? As if he could. That bastard Humbert stood between him and Roric in all things, and Roric so loved the old rump there was no shoving him aside. Just as there was no softening Humbert's animosity. Egann's continued presence was proof of that.

'The Marches are your home,' he said harshly. 'And as loyal subjects of Clemen's duke, you and I must live here for as long as it pleases him. As for family – what am I and your children, for you to say such a thing?'

She bowed her head, fingers clutched and trembling. 'I'm sorry. I didn't mean—'

'I don't care what you meant. Put Eaglerock out of your mind. I am Clemen's Marcher lord, Kennise. My duties are here.'

The ache in his hip as he rode to Balfre's manor house was a grinding reminder that he should send again for Izusa. Despite her foreign strangeness, it seemed she had the knack of healing. Certainly no other leech he'd ever met could ease his pains so well.

If only she had the remedy for a broken heart. I'd pay her whatever she asked if she could numb my life as she numbs my body.

Of course, hoping for such respite was a fool's errand. For the crime of loving the wrong woman he was sentenced to a living death here in the Marches. Only when Humbert died might he find a way to escape his prison. Rebuild his life into something closer to what he'd dreamed it would be, when he was a younger man.

Provided Roric's not been poisoned utterly against me these past five years. And that's a frail reed for a drowning man to clutch.

Balfre's hard-bitten serjeant, Grule, challenged him and his escort of four men-at-arms as soon as they appeared at the Harcian's manor house gates.

'Stand and be recognised – or meet the point of my sword!'

It was a formality, nothing more. Grule knew him well enough. Marcher law held that in the interests of keeping the peace, every Marcher lord had right of way to ride the length and breadth of the Marches. Past skirmishes between the old lords Wido, Jacott, Bayard and Egbert had oft had the abusing of that right as their cause. But Aimery's son put those former lords to shame. Every week he disported himself in Clemen's Marcher lands. When the mood took him he spilled blood the way other men pissed out beer. Since the confrontation at the Pig Whistle he'd spilled only deer's blood, and boar, and once hanged two Harcian Marcher men for breaking the law.

But now, with the butchery of this helpless family from Clemen . . .

Ignoring Grule's men, belligerently ranged behind their serjeant, Vidar rested his hand upon the hilt of his sword. 'Lord Vidar to see Count Balfre. Stand aside.'

Grule nodded, accepting that much. Then his gaze raked over Clemen's men-at-arms. 'You have leave to pass, Lord Vidar. Your men-at-arms do not.'

Marcher law again. A raised hand told his escort to hold fast. Then he kicked his horse forward, past the serjeant and his staring men, and cantered over cut grass to Balfre's front door.

As he dismounted in the manor house's forecourt, Balfre came out to meet him. 'Take Lord Vidar's horse,' he told the stable lad who'd come running. 'See it to water. But don't stable it. His lordship won't be here that long.'

Vidar threw his reins in the lad's face and limped to confront Harcia's next duke. 'Balfre! What the *fuck* is wrong with you? Execute thieves and rapists and murderers if you must, but *children*? Starving *peasants*? What manner of nobility did you learn at Aimery's knee that you'd slaughter—'

'A criminal is a criminal, Vidar,' Balfre retorted, strolling insolent towards him. 'Those peasants by their own admission trespassed on sovereign Harcian soil. And today's thief is tomorrow's murderer when coin's not surrendered swiftly enough to suit.'

'*Children*, you murderous fuck! No more dangerous to you than a mouse in the wainscot! When Roric learns of this—'

Balfre laughed, mocking. 'He'll doubtless wring his hands, weeping. From what I hear it's all he's good for. Vidar, your outrage is as twisted as your lame and crippled body.' Abruptly, his laughter died. 'Those peasants had the plague.'

He stared. 'I don't believe you.'

'Why would I lie?'

It was a fair question. He didn't know how to answer it.

'I did what I had to do, Vidar,' said Balfre, and shrugged. 'I'll not grovel apology for it. Only a fool kisses pestilence on the lips.'

'How are you so sure they were diseased?'

Balfre lifted an eyebrow. 'Has your duke left you ignorant of the plague's appearance?'

'Of course not. But even so, you had no right to—'

'I had every right. They were trespassing. Marcher law is on my side.'

'Fuck the law and fuck you,' he said, his vision blurring with rage. 'I'll take your word they were trespassing and I'll accept they were diseased – though you can offer no proof of either. But you didn't need to kill them. You could've given them to me. I'd have sent those peasants close-kept to Eaglerock and seen them first healed, if they could be healed, then punished for their crime. Why did you have to put them to the sword?'

'Because I don't *trust* you! Not with Harcian lives.' Balfre sneered. 'How noble. You'd have seen your precious peasants to a leech. But Vidar, you and I both know there is but one sure way to cure plague. Kill those infected and burn their putrid bodies after. Which is what I did. You're welcome.'

'You kill and burn infected *sheep*, Balfre! Those people weren't *sheep*!'

'Well, Vidar . . .' Balfre shrugged again. 'They were from Clemen. So there is an argument to be made.' Then he sighed, like a man fast running out of good will. 'My lord, don't be a fool. Sixteen other Clemen criminals have my men-at-arms found trespassing before today, and sixteen times I kept Harcia's sword in its scabbard and handed the trespassers to you. Much good that mercy did me. Do you think my patience has no limit? Even if those villagers hadn't been diseased, did you think I'd wait till a Clemen dagger slit a Harcian throat in the middle of the night before—'

'I should've slit *your* throat, Balfre, when I had the chance! That would've been blood well spilled!'

'Try again if you dare, Vidar,' Balfre taunted. 'I'm not so glutted on Clemen blood that spilling yours would cost me sleep!'

He wore a sword and a dagger, but he yearned to beat Aimery's arrogant son with his fists. Heedless of his painful hip, his halting stride, the edge of youth that favoured Balfre, blinding himself to the murderous bastard's strength and speed and violence-honed instincts, he shouted and leapt.

Balfre scythed his legs out from under him and smashed him to the ground with one fisted blow to his face. Breathless, he lay there. Then, body screaming with pain, humiliation setting him on fire, he struggled to rise.

'Stay down, Vidar, you fucking fool,' Balfre advised, and dropped to a knee beside him. 'It ill becomes me to beat a cripple.'

Though Balfre had struck him with a naked fist, no mail or gauntlet to lend power, still he could feel his eye and cheek swiftly swelling. A good thing the blow had landed on his blind side or he'd be wholly useless. Betrayed by his scarred and shuddering body, he stayed down.

'Plaguish or not, it ill became you to murder those peasants,' he said, choking. 'Your sense of honour is inconstant. You're owed a thrashing for those deaths, Balfre, and if I'm not the man to beat some shame into you, surely I will find the man who is.' He twisted his lips in a stinging smile. 'I'm sure Roric would be interested.'

'And here I thought I was the only hot-head in the Marches.' Amused, Balfre shook his head. 'I like you, Vidar. I shouldn't, since you're of Clemen and you did press a blade to my throat once, but . . . I like you. Roric's a fucking poor excuse for a duke but you're loyal. I can admire that.'

Breathing hard through his nose, Vidar glared at him. 'Should I feel flattered?'

'I don't give a fuck what you feel, Vidar.' Balfre stood. Tipped his head to one side, considering. 'I think we're done here. Only – one last thought. If I were you, I'd not trumpet how close the Marches came to plague. I said nothing of it at the Pig Whistle and my men know to keep their mouths shut. If you're wise, you'll follow my lead.'

If he was wise. So many things he'd have done differently, if he was wise. But Balfre was right. Let word escape that the plague had crossed from Clemen into the Marches, no matter how briefly, no matter it was contained . . .

'Agreed,' he muttered.

'And can we also agree that you should exercise increased vigilance along your Marcher border with Clemen? Those peasants came from Dipford. You might warn Roric of that. And Vidar?'

'What?'

'Here's fair warning from me. How you deal with those found sickened is your affair. My remedy you already know. I'll not hesitate to use it again.'

Vidar swallowed. Butchery and burning. The spirits have mercy on all of them once Balfre was made a duke.

He couldn't stand without help. Hating the man, hating himself, Vidar took Balfre's offered hand and without grace found his feet. Re-mounted his horse, his hip an agony, and rode away from the manor house feeling Balfre's following gaze like a dagger stuck in his back.

The Pig Whistle was quiet that night. Word of the severed heads had swiftly spread. The four Zeidican merchants ate supper early and hid themselves after in the dormer. A weeping pity that, no chance of wheedling gossip from them to sell. Some dozen or so regular customers had braved the chill, though. Molly served them pies and ale, cheerful as always, but her smile was forced and they knew it. Their smiles were forced too, and nobody called for music. What man made merry upon the graves of the dead?

As a rule, Clemen folk and Harcian folk mixed under her roof without a blink or a growl. They were all Marcher folk first, that was the way of it. She never thought she'd see anything different. But tonight men from the Harcian Marches sat apart from Clemen folk. And while they knew better than to start a ruckus, with Iddo and his cudgel at the ready behind the bar, still there were some nasty glares swapped back and forth. Angry mutterings. Nobody spoke aloud of those five slain Clemen folk, but every man in the place was thinking of nothing else.

A little after nine o'the clock it started to rain. She wasn't sorry. Though a bad night cost her coin, this night she was heartsick. She kept seeing those dead children's severed heads, their dull, staring eyes fringed thick with blood-crusted lashes. More than anything she wanted to lie beside Iddo in their bed, in the darkness, and feel his rough hands stroking her skin.

Taking an empty tray back to the kitchen, she paused at the bar. 'Keep things sweet out here, Iddo. I do want to cast m'eye over Benedikt and Willem.'

Iddo gave her a look. 'Moll, them boys got no more than what they deserved. They b'aint at death's door.'

He'd welted them on her say-so, because she was beside herself frightened after what Count Balfre had promised in her forecourt. The thought of Benedikt and Willem being killed for playing with sticks, it was enough to drop her howling where she stood. However hard it had been, listening to her boys' weeping as Iddo whipped them, better that than seeing them dangling from a tree branch or run through with a sword.

'I know,' she said, resting a hand on his arm. 'But it were a right proper welting. I'll be back agin directly.'

Without giving him time to argue, Molly left the tray in the kitchen then made her way upstairs to the attic room, which she'd given over to the boys. She didn't need it for a bar wench any more. First that Tossie, then Alys. Ellyn. Live-in help caused too much strife. She hired one of the girls from Birch farm when the inn was set to run her off her feet. Which of late was hardly never. Anyway, the boys were old enough now to serve in the public room and help her and Iddo keep the Pig Whistle neat and trim.

One lamp burned on the staircase to the attic, another inside the low-ceilinged room. Breathing softly, she eased the door open. The air stank of Izusa's best ointment. And there was her heart, her son, her Benedikt, curled on his side with the tip of his thumb in his mouth. His dark eyelashes trembled, and he whimpered softly as he slept. Guilt smote her again, like the crack of a birch stick.

479

But I had to do it. To save him. Any loving mother would.

She looked at Willem, on the other bed. Curled on his side like Benedikt. Both boys had ate their dinner standing, too sore for a stool. Willem's scarred face was lightly flushed, his reddish hair sweat-damp and trying to kink. He was her other son, and she loved him, but she feared him just as much. Even though she was sure he'd long since forgotten that cursed girl and her faery tales, even though his burned face and crooked nose meant he didn't look like anyone but himself. It didn't matter. She was afraid. He was an odd child, and always had been. So much friction t'wixt him and Iddo, if she could she'd send him away, get him 'prenticed on a farm. Only Benedikt would never forgive her. So, for her son's sake, she kept Willem at home.

Satisfied they were well enough, she drew the door closed again and went back downstairs, then whisked about playing the innkeeper until it was time to chivvy the stragglers home and set the inn to rights for the night.

At last, crawled into bed, tucked beneath quilt and blankets, she pillowed her head on Iddo's shoulder and smoothed the wiry hair on his broad chest.

'Iddo . . . about them boys . . .'

Hidden by darkness, he grunted. 'Woman, I do know what ye want to say so I'll say this afore ye. The brat deserved a harder welting than Benedikt. That sword mischief were his doing. The little shite leads our boy astray.'

She'd still never told Iddo the truth about Alys's dying, or what she'd heard the girl and Willem talking on that night. She'd go to her grave keeping her mouth shut on that. Some secrets were too dangerous to share, even with her man of oak. But she worried that Willem's oddness was grown out of the tales the girl had told him, that some part of him believed he was different, *better* – and that was why Iddo misliked him so. 'Twas a tricky path to walk between him and Willem. Tricky to love both of them when they didn't want her to.

'Sometimes he does,' she admitted. 'But Benedikt b'aint faery-blessed, Iddo. He be an imp too, ye can't deny that.'

Another grunt. 'That Willem, Moll. There be a hot defiance in him. He drives me proper wild, he does.'

'And ye weren't never defiant, Iddo, when ye were a boy?'

'Not like Willem. I tell ye, Moll, there be a look in his eyes . . .'

Oh, didn't she know that? Hadn't she seen for herself the look he meant, and didn't it fright her spitless?

'Ye'll not beat it out of him,' she said firmly. 'Beat a horse, beat a dog, beat a boy, Iddo, ye'll turn 'em vicious.'

'So ye'd have me tickle him the next time he picks up a stick?'

She was making him angry. 'No, Iddo,' she soothed. 'If it be a welting he's earned then it be a welting he'll get. Him and Benedikt. Ye think I don't know a boy's spoiled without welting? Only . . .' She trailed her fingertips lower, to dance along his quiet cock. 'It has got to be earned, Iddo. And no harder than what be fair.'

He rolled on his side, away from her. 'Fine, woman. Next time ye can welt them boys yerself.'

'Iddo . . .' She let her forehead fall against his broad, muscled back. 'Don't ye be cross with me. Ye did what was needful. I b'aint resenting ye for that. I only said—'

'I heard what ye said, Molly. No need to say it agin.'

She knew that tone. Iddo was done talking. But he'd be sweet enough, come morning. He wasn't one to hold a grudge. At least not with her. So she rolled to her own side of the bed, not crowding him, and soon enough, despite her guilt and the worry that never left her these dark days, fell into sleep.

'Willem! Willem, wake up. 'Tis morning. Cock's crowed. Ma, she'll be shouting. Willem?'

Twisting in his bed sheet, Liam heard Benedikt's voice faintly, as though his brother had hidden himself in the henhouse and was shouting from out there.

'Willem! Ye got to roust up. We got to start chores. If Iddo welts me agin I think I'll drop dead!'

He twisted some more, remembering. Iddo. The cellar. Benedikt rocking on the floor, bare arse in the air as he sobbed. His own welted arse, burning. His hatred for Iddo burning hotter than that. All his body, burning.

He dragged his heavy eyelids open. The window shutters were pulled back and the attic room was full of pale first light.

'Benedikt,' he muttered, 'I b'aint feeling right.'

'I b'aint neither,' said Benedikt, already dressed in woollen hose and a homespun shirt. 'My arse still hurts a mort. But—'

'Not just my arse. My head. And my bones.'

'What d'ye mean?'

Benedikt's anxious face was blurry. Squinting, Liam tried to see him properly. But he couldn't, his brother was dandelion-fuzzy, the way the world had gone fuzzy that time he snuck beer from the cellar and they'd drunk themselves silly. Iddo welted them that time, too. Iddo loved his switch and the sound of boys blubbing.

'Willem? Be ye sick?'

'Iss,' he said, talking Marcher. He did that sometimes, when it was easier than remembering how Ellyn had wanted him to speak. 'I b'aint right.'

Sucking in a sharp breath, Benedikt patted him on the shoulder. 'I'll fetch Ma.'

Hot and cold and shivering, Liam hugged himself beneath the blanket. His skin felt sore, like sunscorch, and he wanted to scratch his eyes.

A thudding of feet on the attic staircase and Molly came in, Benedikt at her heels.

'See Ma? T'aint playing. Willem b'aint right.'

Liam shrank against the wall. Molly's fury in the Pig Whistle's forecourt, then the cellar. How she told Iddo to welt them, the cold way she treated them in the kitchen last night. She'd turned into a stranger. When she touched his forehead, he flinched.

''Tis a fever,' she murmured, then stroked his hair. 'Run to Iddo, Benedikt. Tell him we need Izusa.'

Benedikt bolted.

'Don't ye fret,' Molly said, sitting on the edge of his bed. 'We'll have ye feeling rightsome soon enough.' She smoothed her apron over her knees. 'Willem, ye d'know I care for ye, just as I care for Benedikt?'

He used to. He wasn't sure now. But to be safe, he nodded. 'Iss, Molly.'

'And ye care for Benedikt, don't ye? Ye love him like a brother, just as ye were raised?'

'Iss, Molly.'

Molly frowned. 'Ye say iss, Willem, but do ye? D'ye love him enough that ye'll leave off being impish? Instead ye'll be the one who says *no* when he wants to be romping? D'ye love him that much?'

'Iss, Molly.' And it was true. In every way that counted Benedikt was his brother, as much a part of him as his hand or his crooked nose. 'I swear.'

Bending down, she caught his chin between her work-rough thumb and finger. 'D'ye know the world be turning dangerous, Willem? D'ye know it be them with the swords as make the rules? And us folk here in the Marches, pinched t'wixt Harcia and Clemen, we matter no more to them great lords than a flea to be cracked t'wixt their fingernails? D'ye know that?'

She was hurting him. He pulled free. 'Iss, Molly.'

'I hope ye do,' she said, still frowning. 'For here at the Pig Whistle we be ordinary folk. T'aint one thing great about us, Willem. We serve them fine lords when they want serving and we don't *never* go looking for strife.'

Squinting at her, shivering, he saw fear slither behind her eyes. And then, with a shock like lightning blasting a tree, he realised what she was afraid of.

Molly knows who I am.

Moaning aloud, as though his fever was getting worse, he pulled his knees to his chest and hid his face in his pillow. He wasn't only pretending. He really did feel sick.

She knows. How does she know? Did Ellyn tell her?

She must have. But why would Ellyn tell Molly? It was meant to be their secret. He'd kept it their secret. Never breathed a word to Benedikt though he wanted to, so bad. Every night before he fell asleep, every night since Ellyn died, he told himself his story. Promised to take back his stolen duchy. Kill the bastard Roric and avenge his murdered father. Most of all he promised that he'd never breathe a word. He felt his eyes sting.

Not fair, Ellyn. You said it were our secret.

Molly was stroking his hair again. Maybe she did care for him, even after the cellar. But he didn't show her his face. He might give himself away. Show her that he knew what she knew about him.

And then a thudding of feet on the stairs.

'Ma! Ma! Izusa be sent for!'

'Hush, Benedikt,' Molly chided. 'No shouting when Willem be poorly.'

'Sorry. Ma, can I stay till Izusa gets here?'

Face still hidden, Willem felt his saggy bed shift as Molly stood. 'No, Benedikt. There be chores. Come away and let Willem rest.'

Any other morning, Benedikt would try a wheedle on his mother. This time he didn't, and Liam knew why. He wasn't fevered so bad he couldn't still feel Iddo's whipping. Not even for him would Benedikt risk a swat on his welted arse.

'Iss, Ma,' his brother said, his voice small.

He didn't want Benedikt to think he was angry 'cause of not wheedling, so he uncurled himself a smidge and opened his eyes. Caught Benedikt's woeful gaze and managed a smile.

'Off ye go then,' said Molly, pointing to the open door. 'Ye can see Willem later.'

Cheered, Benedikt nodded. 'Iss, Ma!' he said, and did as he was told.

Time drifted feverishly after that. Liam drifted with it, hot and cold, his bones aching. Izusa came. He felt so poorly he didn't care that she stripped off his nightshirt and saw him naked back to front and head to toe. When she saw the welts on his arse she hissed like an angry cat. Her fingertips touching them made him moan. But then she shouted at Molly, and if his head hadn't hurt so bad he would've laughed out loud.

'Answer me, Molly!' Izusa said, her voice shaking. 'Did you do this?'

Molly made a funny sound. 'I had to, Izusa. Him and Benedikt, they—'

'You had to whip him into sickness? For that's what you've done!'

Listening to Izusa scold, and Molly make excuses, it was almost like he had Ellyn with him again. He turned his face into the crook of his elbow and smiled and smiled.

'This was very wrong of you,' said the healer, as though she was a lord. 'Willem is a sensitive boy. You and Iddo must treat him gently.

484

Didn't I tell you that, Molly, the time you burned him with the rabbit stew?'

Risking a glance, Liam peered with half-closed eyes. Molly was red-faced. She looked almost ashamed.

'Y'be certain 'tis the whipping that do fever him?' she said, fingers twisting in her apron. 'Willem b'aint touched with plague? Him and Benedikt, they—'

'If it was plague I'd say so, but it's not. The charms I gave you make sure of it. This is *your* doing.'

'Oh,' said Molly. She sounded small as Benedikt.

'You can go,' Izusa told her sharply. 'Wait for me in the kitchen, and put water to boil. There's a tea to be brewed that'll help with his fever and pain.'

Molly left without another word.

Izusa fed him poppy syrup. He remembered that muck from the time his face was burned and his nose broke. It still tasted dreadful. Then she put fresh ointment on his welted arse and helped him drink the tea she made. It tasted like pepper-grass. Within moments, he fell asleep.

When he woke again it was night. Benedikt sat on the floor beside the bed, cross-legged on a pillow, his candlelit face so miserable he looked near to sobbing out loud.

'Benedikt? What's amiss?'

'Willem!' Benedikt's chin trembled. 'Willem, I be sorry.'

Cautiously, he sat up. The ache in his bones was gone. His skin didn't feel sunscorched and he didn't want to scratch his eyes. Even his arse didn't hurt so much. He felt tender, but not terrible. Not like before.

He frowned at his brother. 'Sorry for what?'

'I heard Ma and Iddo in the kitchen. They were brawling on what Izusa said. Willem, it be my fault ye got yer arse welted. That makes it my fault ye—'

'Don't be a feggit.'

Benedikt sniffed. 'It does. I be the one who called ye Lord Willem. I picked up that feggit stick and—'

'And did ye twist my arm so I had to pick up one too? No, ye didn't. Benedikt—'

'Ma said Izusa said—'

'I don't give a feggit for what Molly said. Remember when Iddo welted us for drinking that ale? Did ye blame me then, when I were the one did the pinching of it?'

Shoulders hunched round his ears, Benedikt wiped at his runny nose. 'That weren't so bad a welting. I never got sick from it, I never—' Another gulp, a heaving gasp. 'Ma said Izusa said ye could've *died*.' Oh.

Benedikt was rocking again, hurting as bad as he'd hurt in the cellar. 'I be sorry,' he wailed. 'I never meant for any trouble.'

It was worse than Iddo's welting, seeing his brother hate himself and all 'cause of him. He couldn't bear it.

'Benedikt!' he said, hearing his voice catch, 'can I tell ye a secret?'

Slowly, Benedikt looked at him. 'Iss. Course ye can.'

'But if I tell it, ye can't never tell another soul. If ye tell another soul, Benedikt, even Molly or Iddo, I really could die.'

His brother's eyes popped wide as soup bowls.

Heart thumping, Liam swallowed. Ellyn had told Molly. That meant he could tell someone too. And if he couldn't trust his own brother . . .

'My name b'aint really Willem,' he whispered. 'It's Liam. My father was Duke Harald of Clemen. That makes me a duke.'

Benedikt hiccuped. 'Ye b'aint!'

He couldn't be cross with Benedikt for not believing him at first. 'I am,' he insisted, then leaned closer, confiding. 'Alys weren't Alys. She was Ellyn. She was my nurse when I were a baby. When Roric the bastard murdered my da and ma and burned Heartsong castle, Ellyn ran away with me. And she ended up here.'

From the look on his face, Benedikt didn't know whether to laugh or fart. 'Ye b'aint cribbing?'

'I swear,' he said solemnly, 'on Ellyn's grave.'

Benedikt knew what that meant. His eyes popped again. 'Ye be a *lord*? Like Balfre and Vidar?'

'No, a *duke*. Like Balfre's da in Harcia.'

'And Roric.'

'Roric's a thieving bastard,' he said, scowling. 'I'm going to kill him one day.'

Benedikt scrunched himself small. '*Willem.*'

'I have to. For Duke Harald. And so I can be Duke Liam properly instead of pretending to be Willem.'

'How?'

'I don't know,' he said, after a squirmy moment. 'But I have to. I promised Ellyn.'

'Willem . . .' Benedikt bit his lip. 'I believe ye, I do, but . . .'

'I can prove it. There were a Clemen duke named Berold. He was my great-granda, and I've got his ring.'

'Where?'

'It be hidden. I'll show ye, by and by.' He stared at his brother. 'Ye do believe me? Truly?'

Slowly, Benedikt nodded. 'I do. I promise. And I won't peep a word.'

There was a girl living in Clemen's Marcher lands who was ready to drop her husband's first son. Knowing Izusa as a fine healer, the woodsman had parted with coin he could ill afford, to be sure the birth was sweet. But his wife was badly built for breeding and he was a brute. His rutting had half-ruined the girl already and his child was set to do the rest. Having seen in the stones what must come to pass, and when, and needing a fresh baby's head, Izusa had taken the man's money and promised to do all she could.

Returned from healing Liam at the Pig Whistle, and knowing the girl's time had almost come, she set wards around her cottage that would turn away every seeker of her help – save Molly, because of Liam, and anyone sent by the pregnant girl's husband, and Balfre, of course. He must never be turned away. Then, protected, she sank herself into a trance . . . and waited.

A day later, the girl went into labour.

Summoned, Izusa saddled the fine horse Balfre had given her after the old nag died of colic, and rode hard to the woodsman's cottage. The girl's cause was hopeless, as she'd always known. Herbs eased her pain but nothing could save her. She died swiftly, in a gushing of blood. Holding the barely breathing baby, Izusa showed a sympathetic face to the stunned and silent husband.

'I grieve with you, Syme,' she said softly, capturing his will with her steady gaze. 'But you're young yet. You can sire another son. Now, I'll be taking the child. You don't want to see the poor mite. Bury your wife quickly, and say it's with her.'

She tucked the dying baby into her herbary bag and rode back to her cottage. Safe inside, with doors and windows once more warded, she unwrapped the failing child and settled with it in a chair. No larger than a rabbit, pale as fresh candle wax beneath the dried birthing blood, it lay limply in her arms and faded a little more with each weak breath. An eyelid flickered. A curled nostril flared. The tiny ribs, frail as leaf stems, struggled to rise and fall. She watched, feeling nothing. Anxious only for Salimbene.

At last, with a twisting shudder, the newborn baby died.

It was a brisk business, discarding the old head and making ready the new. A single stroke of her dagger cut through the infant's neck. There was very little blood, another reason for preferring a newborn. With the old head crumbled to ash at a word, she rubbed its smoky remains into the new head's pale, fresh skin. Placed it ready in its wooden box. Chanted the sorcery that would bring it to life. And then, while she waited, disposed of the baby's headless body and put dried pease to soak on the hob, after.

'*Izusa. Izusa.*'

She ran to the baby's head in its box. 'I'm here, Salimbene.'

'*A fresh conduit. Most pleasing.*'

'Newborn. It will last a goodly while.'

'*What news, Izusa?*'

He made no comment as she spoke of the simmering tensions between Harcia and Clemen, the whispers of plague, of Vidar's unhappiness, and the trespassing family Balfre had slaughtered. Only when she spoke of Liam did the dead baby's lips move.

'*The boy is unharmed?*'

His rage made the cottage's candles flare and smoke. 'I've broken his fever, and the welts will soon fade.'

'*The innkeep is a menace. She has endangered the boy twice.*'

'She was trying to save him.'

'*Kill her, Izusa. Before she kills him.*'

'Not yet. Salimbene, Liam still needs her.'

Silence. The candle flames shivered. Izusa held her breath.

'*Then let her live. For now. But if you are wrong, Izusa, you will pay a heavy price.*'

She bowed her head. 'I am yours, Salimbene, always, to do with as you will.'

'*I know.*' The baby's lips curved briefly, a cruel, mocking smile. Then its closed eyes tightened. '*And who is that?*'

A fist banging on her cottage door. A familiar voice calling her name.

'Balfre. He's here to fuck.'

A whispery chuckle. '*Fuck him well, Izusa. The Harcian is dear to my heart.*'

Another chuckle, and he was gone.

'*Izusa!*' Balfre bellowed. 'Are you there? Open this fucking door!'

She covered the box with its runed cloth that kept it hidden from unwanted gaze, then unwarded the cottage door and opened it.

'Balfre,' she said, smiling. 'Come in, my lord. I was just thinking of you.'

CHAPTER TWENTY-NINE

'Goat-hunting, Grefin? You'd take Jorin goat-hunting?' Mazelina stared, hands fisted on her hips. 'On Lamphill Moor?'

Grefin shrugged. 'It's where the goats are, my love.'

'I think it's a goat I'm looking at now!' she retorted. 'Lamphill Moor is treacherous. It's no better than a graveyard. This past year alone four lords' promising sons have perished there. No, Grefin. You go if you must, if you can't bring yourself to deny Terriel his routish pleasures. But I won't have you taking Jorin. What need has our son to risk himself so?'

They faced each other across a straggle of trailing pale yellow bas-blossom in the formal garden of their Green Isle castle, Steward's Keep. Overhead, the pale blue sky was scudded with grey-tinged cloud, promising stormy weather to echo their own personal storm. Carried to them from the tilt yard on the cool, fitful breeze, a clashing of swords and the shouting of men as they trained for battle. Jorin was one of them. Kerric, another. And were it possible, their daughter, Ullia, would be staggering about in mail and a leather jerkin with them. As it was she insisted on prancing to and fro behind the tilt yard's railing, brandishing a wooden sword.

'Mazelina . . .' He shook his head. 'Don't. I gave way to you and kept Jorin home instead of sending him to be fostered. Kerric, too. But you can't think I'll soften further than that. Would you have him mocked behind his back by the very men he now trains to lead?'

'I would have him safe, Grefin! Why does that desire make me a villain?'

'It doesn't,' he said, skirting the flower bed to reach her, and take her hands in his. 'Not the desire. Don't you think I share it? But if I let you persuade me to leave Jorin behind . . .'

He tugged her with him across the short, vividly green grass to stand atop the hillrise overlooking the tilt yard. Below them, the men-at-arms Balfre recently sent him from the Marches danced their deadly way through a drill with the Green Isle men who served in the Steward's Guard. Dolyn, his hard-bitten castle serjeant, had them paired off and facing each other with daggers. To be disarmed was to be defeated. A time-tested exercise, this one. Watching Jorin and Kerric warily circling, feinting, memory stirred. He almost smiled. How many times had he and Balfre faced each other in Tamwell castle's tilt yard, dancing the same dance under Ambrose's unforgiving eye? He'd lost count. Before that, when he was still too young to risk at sword play, he'd watched Balfre dagger-dance with Malcolm. The memory pricked. Odd, how he could go for months and months without thinking of his dead brother . . . and then suddenly feel the pain of his loss, as fresh as though they'd entombed him only the day before.

Sometimes Kerric reminded him of Malcolm. With a head tilt. A crooked smile. The way he'd frog-leap over his horse's rump and into the saddle. The little quirks of family. Blood ties echoing down through the years.

A laughing shout of triumph, as Jorin feinted past his brother's guard. Seized his wrist and neatly twisted his dagger from his grasp. Cursing, Kerric dropped to one knee then held up his other hand in recognition of defeat. Not content with one victory Jorin, grinning fiercely, spun round to challenge a Marcher man who'd just disarmed his Green Isle opponent.

Pleased, Grefin nodded. That was well done. If Kerric held echoes of Malcolm, then Jorin put him in mind of a young Aimery – and Balfre.

'I'm not a fool,' Mazelina said, her voice tight. 'I know our sons must train for bloodshed. And confirm the good opinion of the Green Isle's lords and their men with their prowess. But Grefin . . .' She slipped her hand from his to fold her arms across her chest. 'Despite all your misgivings, and Aimery's – yes, and mine – Balfre has kept the peace in the Marches. Whatever Roric's natural belligerence, he's safely contained. And yet you and Terriel and the other great barons do little more than prepare for war.'

Not shifting his gaze from his eldest son in the tiltyard, Grefin slid an arm around Mazelina's tense shoulders. 'We must. Since Harald's fall, little has gone right in Clemen. The duchy is full of unhappy people, ruled by an even unhappier duke. Let Roric for one moment think us weak and he might well decide to lift his spirits with plunder.'

'I know you and Aimery and Balfre think so,' she said, unconvinced. 'But be honest. Roric hasn't so much as *hinted* that's his plan. Never once since the Harcian kingdom was sundered has Clemen attempted to force its way through the Marches and lay waste to this duchy.'

'It only takes once,' he said grimly. 'My love, Clemen is near beaten to its knees. The little we have, compared to their riches, used to make us feel *poor*. And now . . .'

'I understand that. But it doesn't reconcile me to Lamphill Moor. If you and Terriel must hone your skills hunting game, can't you find somewhere else to—'

'No, my love, because—'

'Because Lamphill Moor is where the goats are,' she snapped. 'I know.'

'I'm sorry,' he said, after a moment. 'I don't like to distress you.'

'You may not like it, but you'll do it.'

'For Harcia?' He nodded. 'Yes, my love. I will. After so many years of marriage, please don't pretend you're surprised.'

Down in the tilt yard, Dolyn called a halt to dagger play and ordered his men-at-arms to the quintain, where a rough-hewn wooden trolley waited. So. Not horseback training this time. Instead the men would take turns standing on the trolley with a lance held hard to their ribs, being pushed towards their target. First they'd have the use of both hands, both legs, and unrestricted vision. Then, run by run, they'd face greater disadvantage. One arm tied behind their backs. One leg bound behind them. A slit-eyed helmet so they could scarcely see. Warfare was bloody, blinding and dangerous. Make training for it kindly and men were trained to do little more than die.

'Will you stay long with Terriel?' Mazelina asked, breaking the silence.

'A few days. He's been hinting at unrest among the Green Isle's eastern barons. While I'm at Tangallon I'll summon them. Nip their discontent in the bud. I won't have them disturbing Aimery.'

She turned to him, lingering resentment vanished in concern for his father. 'Why? Is there bad news come from the leech?'

'No,' he said swiftly. 'He promises me Aimery travels well, for a man of his age. But I'll not take that for granted.'

'So the goat-hunting is an excuse? A way of meeting with the eastern barons without stirring their resentments?'

'Not entirely. The castle must be provisioned. But what could be more natural than Terriel hosting a feast after? And once those cantankerous lords are stuffed with good food and wine I'll have an easier time of it, rapping their knuckles.' Grefin tucked a tendril of hair behind his wife's ear. 'I'd have Jorin beside me for that, so he can watch and learn.'

Mazelina bit her lip. 'You think there's a chance he'll be Steward after you.'

'I think it's plain, that Balfre will never get a son from Jancis. And even if he were made duke tomorrow, and married elsewhere the day after, and a year after that was dandling a boy-child on his knee—'

'Jorin would still be Steward. If something happened to you.'

'But it won't,' he added, reaching for her, because her eyes were full of distress. 'We're safe here, my love. I promise.'

'Even with Lamphill Moor?' she said, muffled against his chest.

He laughed. 'Yes, Mazelina. Even with Lamphill Moor.'

To no one's surprise, Jorin was jubilant at the thought of hunting wild goats on Lamphill Moor. Just as unsurprising, Kerric protested at being left behind. So did Ullia, who persisted in the fantasy that she was as much a boy as her brothers.

'Don't gloat,' Grefin advised his eldest son, under cover of Kerric and Ullia's heated bickering at dinner. ''Tis unbecoming. You're my first born by chance, Jorin, not design. It could as easily be Kerric chosen and you the one slighted.'

Jorin had his mother's quick wits and Aimery's sense of fair play. Balfre's fiery temper he'd been taught early to control. He glanced at his squabbling siblings, then nodded. 'Yes, my lord.'

'Good.' Grefin tousled his son's hair. Wondered, a little ruefully, what Jorin had inherited from him – apart from a love of music, which had little use save at a dance. 'We'll leave at dawn, be at Tangallon castle by sunset. Doubtless there'll be a feast to honour us. I'll warn you now – be sparing with the wine. You've a man's heart but a boy's stomach. Keep your hands off the serving wenches. And be courteous to Lord Terriel, no matter what he says.'

'Like you, my lord?' Jorin said, grinning.

He grinned back. For all that he and Terriel were fast friends these days, the road to amity had not been smooth, and even now they could roar at each other. But there was no harm in it. Terriel's loyalty was like rock.

'Yes, my son. Just like me.'

As the sun rose next morning behind Steward's Keep, Mazelina, Kerric and Ullia waved them goodbye. They trotted out briskly, a token escort of two men-at-arms and one pack-horse at their heels, confident of clear weather and an untroubled day's journey to Tangallon.

493

After reaching Terriel's castle a breath before dusk, they were indeed feasted to celebrate their arrival. Like a good son, Jorin was polite to blustery Terriel and only fondled the castle's serving wenches once or twice. They rose from their beds early the next morning, dressed in plain huntsman's leathers, washed down cold beef with tankards of ale, then assembled in Tangallon's bailey for the hunt on Lamphill Moor. Riding with them and Terriel was the lord's grown son, Alard, his three rambunctious nephews and four men-at-arms – Grefin's two, and two belonging to Tangallon. No need for hounds in this hunt, since the moor was open ground with nowhere for the dogs to bail up their game, but Terriel's kennel-man and his boys were set to follow behind the hunters with a horse and open cart so they could bring home the kill.

The moor's wild goats were wily and fleet. From the moment they spied the hunters' horses they scattered, bucking and leaping as they tried to escape.

'After them!' Terriel bellowed. 'Every man 'ware himself!'

Then there was nothing but the drumming of hooves on the flower-pocked moor, the singing of arrows, and the panicked bleating of goats as they were brought down.

Exhilarating madness. Sweat and blood and danger. A startled shout as one horse stumbled. Looking, Grefin saw a man pitch out of his saddle and crash to the turf. His heart stopped. Then he saw it was one of Terriel's nephews. Not Jorin. Cursing, Kierron staggered to his feet and snatched at his horse's reins. Cursed again as the animal lifted a foreleg, dead lame.

Nothing to be done for him. He'd have to limp home. The hunt hunted on and only came to a tattered end when the last goat was felled and the rest were scattered too far for slaughter.

Running sweat, heaving for breath, Grefin looked around for Jorin. There he was, not crushed beneath a falling horse or drowned in a moor bog like those other lords' sons, but laughing, clouting Terriel's heir Alard on the knee. Never mind the quiet man was a dozen years his senior.

'Jorin!' he called, his belly clutched with relief. 'With me. We've work to do yet.'

Not every arrow killed cleanly, and a good hunter left no beast to suffer if he could help it. Leaving their horses to stand, and the other men to wait, they ended the wounded goats' suffering with the mercy of a blade.

'That's it,' Grefin said, when the last goat within reach was dead. 'Terriel's kennel-man will get the rest.' He slapped Jorin's shoulder. 'You did well.'

His son's smile was almost shy. 'You taught me well, my lord.'

'Boast a little to your brother, if you like,' he added. 'But if I were you I'd say naught to your mother and sister. Women, you know, are apt to be squeamish.'

Jorin hooted. 'Not Ullia! She told me to bring home a goat's tail for good luck!'

'Ullia did? That girl is—'

'*Grefin!*'

Startled, he turned. Terriel was pointing. A horseman, riding fast towards them over the moor's greenish-brown tussocked turf. A small distance behind him, Terriel's kennel-master and his goat-laden cart.

'Mount up,' he told Jorin. 'This looks like strife.'

'My lord Steward!' the horseman gasped, reaching them. It was Tangallon's serjeant-at-arms, Revel. 'My lord Terriel. Word's reached the castle. Potterstown's besieged by raiders.'

Lean, weathered Terriel cursed, then began to retie the leather strip on the end of his braided, silver-streaked hair. Alard and Robion, the nephew who'd not been unhorsed, sat straighter in their saddles, the joy of the goat-hunt doused. The four men-at-arms turned to counting what arrows they had left. Grefin glanced at Jorin. His son's face had paled beneath its dirt and dried sweat.

'Raiders,' he said to Revel. 'Are you sure?'

Revel's eyes were white-rimmed. 'The boy who rode to warn us foundered his pony reaching the castle. My lord, I believe him.'

Raiders. Murdering bastards. Seeking coin and plate and jewellery, spoils easy to run with, they'd burst upon the Green Isle's north coast at the tail-end of summer. In and out so quickly, without warning, there'd been no time to react. Their swift, narrow boats pierced the coastal creeks like needles, stitching ruin and drawing blood, leaving widows and orphans and butchered men in their wake. Not a soul knew how they could navigate the Green Isle's dangerous waters, with their shifting sandbars and rips and treacherous tides. Not when every other ship that made the attempt drowned.

Grefin turned to Terriel. 'They must have come ashore at Dackle, then rampaged inland along Snakespine Creek.'

'Likely so.' Terriel's fingers worried at the hilt of his dagger. 'It seems we were wrong, Grefin.'

Never in Harcia's history – as kingdom or duchy – had their sovereign soil been plundered by outsiders. The first two raids had made them uneasy, but they'd told themselves the raiders were fly-by-night. No real threat. At the very worst, rogue pirates who'd been blown off-course.

But Potterstown was their third attack, and with every strike the raiders grew bolder. More than seven hundred Green Isle folk called the market town home.

'How many raiders, did this boy say?' Terriel demanded of his serjeant.

'That he wasn't sure of. A score, at least.'

Almost twice as many as before. And with Kierron's horse lamed, they were but ten men. Eleven, counting Revel. If he counted Jorin a man.

'My lord,' said the serjeant, 'I have eight Tangallon men-at-arms waiting at the edge of the moor.'

Grefin frowned. 'Only eight?'

'The rest are about the district on other business,' Terriel muttered. 'Since you came, Grefin, we've grown used to peace.'

That was true. And until this moment, he'd been proud of himself for it. But now there were raiders, with longswords and axes that could cleave a horse's head from its neck in a single blow. He didn't dare look at his son.

'That brings our strength to nineteen,' Alard said, uncertain. 'Is that enough?'

'Alard, we face them no matter how many they are,' said Grefin. 'It might be too late to save Potterstown – but we must try.'

'And if we can't save it,' said Terriel, his voice rough with rage, 'we'll chase those murdering bastards till we catch them and cut them down like goats.'

Goats. Grefin looked at the butchered animals on the ground. 'Quickly. We have to salvage as many arrows as we can.'

'No need, my lord Steward,' said Revel. 'My men-at-arms have brought plenty. We near emptied Tangallon's armory.'

He gave the man a swift, grim smile. 'Then let us fetch them, Revel, men and arrows, and make these murdering raiders weep blood.'

Potterstown, on the far western side of Lamphill Moor, was the largest market town in the Green Isle's centre. There, Harcia's best clay was lovingly crafted into plates and bowls and sturdy ale mugs. But the township was known for more than its pottery. Its folk were artisans and bakers, blacksmiths and herbalists, leatherworkers and poulterers and weavers and meat-smokers and orchàrders. Every week, almost year round, its market square was thronged.

Sick with apprehension, Grefin rode hard along rutted Potterstown road, Terriel at his left hand, Jorin at his right, the rest of their hunting party galloping behind. From early boyhood he'd trained with lance and sword and dagger. But all he'd ever done was joust in play and pretend to draw blood. He'd killed goats and stag and boar out hunting . . . but he'd never killed a man. Never skirmished in the Marches. Never risked his life. Now he was risking his life, and his son's life, and the lives of seventeen other men. He was leading them into a slaughter, asking them to fight brutal, axe-wielding raiders being armed only with swords and daggers and arrows. Inside his gloves, his hands were sweating.

He'd never been so afraid.

A league distant from the town they encountered a pitiful handful of women and children, fleeing. With a raised fist he ordered his hunting party to halt.

'Please, my lord, help us,' one of the women sobbed, a baby clutched to her breast. 'The raiders are camped in the market square, drinking and raping. And the men and boys they've not killed they've bound for taking away to be sold as slaves!'

A ripe curse from Terriel. 'Fucking slavery? That's new.'

Grefin looked at the women. 'We'll do what we can. You make your way to Tangallon castle. You'll be safe there.'

As the women and children moved on, Terriel cleared his throat. 'Grefin, I know you want to kill these bastards. So do I. But we should keep one alive. A heated sword to his cock will have him spilling secrets we can use against them.'

Mordant laughter from the men-at-arms. Ignoring it, Grefin nodded. 'Yes, with luck. If we can make sense of raider talk. But you'll leave that to me.' He nudged his stallion to readiness. 'Now, come. The people of Potterstown are waiting for us to save them.'

The township stank of fire and death. Grefin smelled the spilled blood and entrails before he saw the first body, butchered to pieces on the narrow bridge spanning Snakespine Creek. The man's severed hand clutched a bill-hook and his eyes stared with blind horror in his bloody, severed head. Stinking smoke from burning cottages wreathed the creek's banks, the sluggish water, the bloodstained timbers of the bridge.

Their horses' hooves boomed hollow as they crossed into the town.

'Hark,' said Terriel, scowling. 'The bastards are still at their sport.'

Drifting with the smoke and stench, faint screams for mercy. The suffering of men and women they'd come too late to save. Grefin kicked his horse ahead along the narrow street, then swung it round and halted. The others halted in front of him, tense and waiting.

He stared at his eldest son. 'Jorin—'

'My lord,' Jorin whispered, eyes wide in his set face.

Oh, the anguish of Jorin being here. He could scarcely breathe past the dread. His bones wanted to melt. *He's barely fourteen. I never should have brought him. I should have sent him to Tangallon with those women and let him hate me for it.*

'You've trained for this,' he said hoarsely. 'You all know what to do. Deliver justice to these raiders, and do your best to live.'

A small, special smile for Jorin. Then he looked at the others, the rough lords and men of the Green Isle. Showed them with a grim nod how much their courage meant. Met Terriel's fierce gaze and saw his own terror shining back at him. Not for himself but for Alard, his heir. And for his dead sister's boy, Robion. It didn't matter that men were used to breeding their sons for war. In that moment he and Terriel were brothers. Bonded soul to soul.

'Swords or bows, my friends. Pick your weapon and let's make these raiders rue the fucking day they were born!'

The scything, singing music of swords sliding free of their scabbards. Then with shouts of vengeful fury they spurred their horses into a gallop.

The market square was the town's heart, found at its centre. Leaping the bodies of Potterstown's dead and dying sprawled in the streets, following the fallen as a wolf-hunter tracked the spoor of his prey to its lair, Grefin remembered what Balfre had told him of killing in the Marches.

'They're not men,' he'd said, shrugging. *'Forget their faces. If it's on the wrong end of your sword, Grefin, it's a brute beast meant for slaying.'*

They burst into the market square to find a scene wrenched out of nightmare. Children hacked to pieces. Naked women, old and young, their breasts sliced off and their bellies opened, bodies ploughed and then discarded in scarlet pools. Old men butchered like bulls past their seeded prime, rheumy eyes gouged from their sockets and their aged pizzles cut off and stuffed in their toothless mouths. Three young men, bound for slavery, screamed like dying horses as raider cocks rammed up their arses. The rest of the murdering bastards were drinking and laughing and dancing around the square, bone necklaces and seal-hide jerkins and leggings outlandish, their copperbright hair hacked short and their brawny, tattooed bodies daubed in Harcian blood from head to toe.

Nearly blinded by horror, Grefin raised his sword and sank his spurs into his horse's flanks. With a bellow the maddened stallion plunged into the fray.

Shouting. Screaming. Howls to curdle a man's soul. Blood and shit and piss, turning the market square's grass to slop. The ringing clash of sword on sword, sword on battle-axe, the whining hum of loosed arrows, the wet cleaving of steel through flesh and the splintering crack of bone. As he fought for his life in a scarlet haze, Grefin dimly glimpsed his son and Terriel and Terriel's son and nephew and the men-at-arms and the murderous raiders slashing and flailing and falling around him, even as his own sword sliced through bellies and faces, spilling guts and scattering teeth, and his lethally trained stallion stove in skulls with its iron-shod hooves. No time to be afraid for Jorin. No time to be afraid.

And then the single sweep of a battle-axe took his horse's front legs off at the knees. The stallion went down, squealing. Falling with it, Grefin came near to drowning in the twinned gushing fountains of blood. In its death throes the horse rolled off him. Stunned, he staggered to his feet, shouting at the pain in his left leg and hip. Heard as an echo Balfre's mocking advice.

Whatever you do, Grefin, don't drop your fucking sword.

And there it was, still in his hand. He heard – felt – someone behind him. Spun round awkwardly, his bruised leg treacherous, and plunged his blade into a wide, screaming mouth. A shock up his forearm as tempered steel punched through the raider's skull. A second shock as he wrenched the blade free and a third as he cut off the dying man's head.

Even as the sundered raider's body toppled, and he lost his balance, toppling with it, a sword-thrust took him through his right shoulder from behind. He felt the blade scrape bone. Felt a sunburst of pain. Looking down he saw bloodied steel jutting from his flesh, saw his blood spurt as the sword pulled free. Watched his own sword fall from his nerveless fingers and tumble slowly to the ground. He couldn't remember how to pick it up. A dead man, he lurched round to look his murderer in the eye.

'*Grefin!*' shouted Terriel, and with a furiously swinging battle-axe hewed the raider almost in two.

Blinking, from far away Grefin watched the body fall. Watched Terriel turn, swinging again, to bury the axe in the chest of another blood-soaked raider.

An agonised cry to his left. Terriel's nephew, Robion, feet tangled in spilling entrails, slipping in spilled Potterstown blood. A raider heard his cry. Hefted his wicked, bloodstained axe, grinning.

Clumsy, Grefin bent and picked up his fallen sword with his left hand. There was pain in his right shoulder, but it felt oddly muffled. The blade felt awkward. Unpractised. He was a right-handed man. Balfre's voice sounded in memory, angrily contemptuous as only his brother could be.

500

Don't be a lazy fuck, Grefin. A man who can't fight with either hand is a fool.

He took the grinning raider with a sword-thrust through the throat. As the body crumpled he helped Robion to stand. Was he dreaming, or had the sounds of battle almost stopped? Blood and sweat dripped down his face, stung his eyes, blurred his sight. He used his right arm to blot his skin and hissed at the pain.

Robion took in a slow, shuddering breath. 'My lord Grefin. I think – I think it's done.'

Staring around the stinking market square, he saw Terriel's serjeant, Revel, bury a battle-axe in the skull of a weakly flailing raider. Saw a young girl, her face slashed open, pick up her own severed hand. Saw dead men-at-arms. Dead horses. The dead of Potterstown. Dead raiders. Saw Terriel's son, Alard, his injured left arm clutched close to his chest. Keening through the smokey air, the moans of the wounded and dying. Jorin. Where was Jorin? His knees threatened to buckle. His shoulder was on fire, his leg and hip burned. His son. His son. He couldn't see his son.

'*Grefin.*'

He turned. Slowly. Painfully. Terriel stood behind him, blood-soaked and weeping. He held a sword in one bloody hand, battle-axe in the other. His huntsman's leathers were ripped in countless places, slashed flesh showing here and there, his silver braid half-dyed red. His son, Alard, lived and so did Robion, his nephew – but tears were trailing down his bloody face.

Grefin shook his head. 'No.'

With a groan, Terriel dropped to one knee. Bowed his head amidst the carnage. 'My lord Steward, I am sorry. Your son Jorin is dead.'

Along with serjeant Revel, three other men-at-arms had survived the battle. All their horses were killed, though, so they took Potterstown nags in their stead. Two men-at-arms rode to Tangallon castle, to see the district alarm raised and help sent back to the town. Alard and Robion scoured smouldering Potterstown to be sure no raider had escaped them, and gather any hiding survivors at the bridge over the creek. Revel and the third man-at-arms worked with Terriel in the market square, laying their own dead and the village's slain in neat rows for later claiming and burial, or a return to Terriel's castle. The wounded were placed on makeshift stretchers and taken to join their fellow villagers at the bridge. Terriel's kennel-master would come with a cart by sunset, so the dead horses could be butchered for their meat. The slaughtered raiders they hauled into a pile for burning, setting aside the longswords and axes to be used in other battles. The air was foul with the stink of smoke and blood and lamp oil and shit.

As the aftermath unfolded around him, Grefin sat on the churned grass in the market square with Jorin's body, his wounded shoulder roughly bound and viciously throbbing. It was Terriel who'd ministered to him, and afterwards taken charge. He felt vaguely ashamed of himself, as though he'd failed his father, failed the Green Isle, because his legs wouldn't hold him upright and he'd forgotten how to speak.

Balfre never said what battle is like, after. He never said it makes you a moonwit, leaves you weak and gasping and trying to recall how to be a man.

Nor had his brother told him what it was like to lose a son. He thought he'd known, because of Malcolm. And Herewart, who'd lost Black Hughe. He'd seen his father's grief, and that old rump's tears, and so he'd thought he understood. But he understood nothing. When it came to grief, he was a child.

Jorin lay quietly on the ground beside him, his face mercifully unmarked. The dreadful wound that killed him was hidden beneath the partly burned, bloodstained sheet covering his body from neck to feet. Terriel said it was a mighty blow. Jorin would likely not have felt a thing. It was meant as a comfort. Perhaps one day it would be – but not yet.

'My lord Steward.' Crouching, Terriel laid a gentle hand on his unhurt shoulder. 'Alard and Robion have found carthorses and carts. We can take our dead and the living back to Tangallon. From there I'll see you and Jorin safely home to Steward's Keep.'

Home. *Mazelina.* He covered his face with his hand. Moistened his dry lips. 'Good.'

'Grefin.' The hand on his shoulder tightened. 'When first you came to the Green Isle, I was ready to hate your guts. I called you *Aimery's second fucking failure*, because I'd heard much ill of Balfre and I thought you'd be the same. I was wrong. You're a good man.

A son to make Aimery proud. A man I'm proud to serve, and call my friend. Your son died. Mine lived. My house is yours, my blood yours, until the day *I* die.'

Terriel's harsh sympathy broke him. As he pressed his face to the rough lord's chest, he heard a roaring sound, smelled burning oil and flesh and seal-skin. Someone had set fire to the heaped pile of dead raiders.

'Hold fast, my lord,' Terriel said softly. 'This is terrible, but you'll survive. You must, so you can help the Green Isle survive. So you can make these fucking raiders pay for this slaughter. Come now. On your feet. 'Tis time to go home.'

Restless, Mazelina prowled the narrow, wind-swept battlements of Steward's Keep, a warm shawl clutched around her and dread churning in her belly.

Something was wrong. Something had happened. She was no witch with the far sight. No soothsayer who could read omens. If there was special meaning in a streaking comet or the birth of a headless chicken, she could no more tell what it was than leap from these stone battlements and fly.

And yet she knew, she *knew*, she was right to be afraid.

Since before dawn, she'd been here. She'd watched the morning star set. Watched the sky turn pearly and the sun fright the moon away. Listened to the sweet piping of larks and thrushes, the scolding cry of plovers and the mournful complaint of the castle's peacocks as they sauntered about its lawns. Now, with the sun risen, the castle's horses whickered in the bailey stables, eager for hay and grain. Men-at-arms were at play in the tilt yard, sunlight catching the edge of each sword.

Watching them, she shivered. Felt so sad and oppressed. As though the lightening sky had turned thunderous, and threatened to kill the bright sun. One of the castle boys joined the mock fighting. And then she realised, no, that was Kerric. Even so high up, so distant, she knew him. Her younger son danced across dirt and grass and flag-stones like a jongler, light-footed, light-hearted, always laughing, never a tear. Though he'd come close to weeping when told he couldn't ride with Grefin and Jorin to hunt goat on Lamphill Moor.

And there was her fright again, stabbing like a knife.

'Mama? Mama, why are you up here?'

'Ullia,' she said, turning. 'Where's your shawl? It's cold.'

Ullia wrinkled her nose. 'I'm not cold. Mama, can we go hornberry picking? Siddly Copse is full of berries and if we don't pick them soon the rooks will get them.'

Instead of answering, she looked again over the battlements, down to the long, straight stretch of greensward that led from Steward's Keep to the countryside beyond its guarded stone gates. It was foolish to think she'd see Grefin and Jorin riding towards her. Tangallon castle was a day's brisk travel distant. The earliest she'd see them home was sunset.

'*Please*, Mama,' said Ullia, coaxing. 'Kerric says he'll be in the tilt yard till nightfall. If he can have the tilt yard, why can't I have Siddly Copse?'

Mazelina managed a smile. There were a dozen reasons, but she didn't have the heart to utter even one. Poor Ullia. Always wishing to be like her brothers. A sword was out of the question, but there seemed little harm in Siddly Copse. Besides. A few hours' berry-picking might prove a welcome distraction.

So they collected their rush-baskets and went to Siddly Copse, to pick hornberries and plan the Winterheight Feast the Green Isle's Steward held every year for his great barons. Ullia had heard from a travelling acrobat about a troupe of jongler dwarves in the Exarch's palace. The acrobat told her that sometimes the jongler dwarves travelled to other courts and palaces and great lords' castles, where they jongled on tables and danced with their clever dogs and wouldn't that be wonderful at the Winterheight Feast? Wouldn't that make Papa the best Steward the Green Isle ever had?

'Isn't he already?' said Mazelina, pretending to frown.

'Oh, yes,' said Ullia, so matter-of-fact. 'But Mama, I heard whisper that some of the eastern barons complain of him. I don't think they'd complain if there were jongling dwarves.'

Mazelina ate a hornberry so she wouldn't laugh out loud.

With their baskets full and the copse's rooks loudly cawing disapproval, they wandered hand-in-hand back to Steward's Keep.

'Look!' said Ullia, delighted, and pointed. 'Papa's home from Lamphill Moor.' A little gasp. 'Oh, Mama. He's hurt his arm!'

Grefin stood waiting in the Keep's forecourt, alone. A bandage showed bulky beneath his loose brown wool tunic, and his right arm had been tightly bound across his chest. Beneath an ugly rainbow of bruises, his stubbled face was pale. He saw them and half-raised his left hand in greeting. Then he let it fall again. His eyes were wide and dark.

'Ullia,' Mazelina said, hearing her voice oddly calm, 'give me your basket then go down to the tilt yard. Tell Kerric he's wanted.'

'Yes, Mama, but can't I first—'

'*Ullia. Go.*'

Not even brash Ullia challenged that tone of voice. 'Yes, Mama,' she whispered, and gave over her basket, and ran.

Like a woman in a waking dream, she slowly crossed the gravelled forecourt. Halted before her husband, put down the baskets, then folded her hands.

'Jorin?'

'It wasn't the moor,' he said unsteadily. 'It was raiders. They struck Potterstown. Mazelina, I had to defend the village. I'm Steward of the Green Isle.'

Yes. He was. And she was the Steward's lady. And Jorin was his heir.

Grefin's eyes filled with tears. He was so pale. He looked ill. Like a man soaked to drowning in death.

'He didn't suffer.'

'I hope not,' she said, and felt a shiver, harbinger of a greater storm. 'Take me to him.'

She followed her husband into the castle, into the austerely grand Great Hall where the Steward held his Winterheight Feast. Poor Ullia. There'd be no jongling dwarves this year. Jorin lay still and peaceful on a trestle covered in black velvet. His long, limber body, wrapped tight in shrouding bands, lay beneath more black velvet. His bloodless face was uncovered, his closed eyes sunken, his lips pale blue. Scented candles burned around him, sweetening the dead air.

Walking like an old man, Grefin shifted around the trestle until he was standing on its other side. He smoothed his shaking hand over Jorin's neat, dark hair. His knuckles were scraped and bruised and he hissed a little, as though even that much movement pained him.

For a long time Mazelina looked at her murdered child. She'd seen death before, many times. She didn't think he might be sleeping, wonder if any moment he'd open his sunken eyes, spring up sudden from the trestle, laughing. *Just a tease, Mama! Tell me I fooled you!* No. She'd seen death.

Her first-born son was dead.

'Do you remember,' Grefin whispered, 'when he was three – no, just turned four. He slipped into Tamwell's stables and somehow climbed onto my warhorse. By rights the beast should've killed him, but—'

'But instead, it fell asleep,' she whispered back. 'And you were so proud of his horseman's prowess you wouldn't let me whip him.'

'Papa! Mama! Why did Ullia make me—'

Mazelina turned to see her living son, Kerric, scuffed and sweaty from the tilt yard, halt sudden and stare open-mouthed at the burdened trestle. Ullia dodged around him. Saw the trestle. Let out a cry.

'Jorin? No – no – Papa – *no!*'

Her grief broke, a tempest. The storm swept her to Grefin, into his one-armed embrace. Swept her own arms around their trembling children. Swept them clinging to each other and left them wrecked and abandoned upon an unknown shore.

CHAPTER THIRTY

Summoned back to Tamwell castle with no explanation given, Balfre was deeply unamused to be told by Aimery's steward that His Grace was captured by another matter and would see his Marcher lord son in due course.

'Another matter?' Balfre glared, longing to slap the smirk off the insolent shite's face. 'What matter, Curteis?'

'My lord, forgive me,' said Curteis, seated at his cluttered desk in the castle steward's chamber. 'I'm not permitted to elaborate.'

'Then elaborate on why and for how long I was called back to court at all! I trust Waymon well enough but the Marches—'

'Count Balfre, you're to wait upon His Grace's pleasure. More than that, I cannot say.'

Balfre glowered. 'You mean will not.'

'Alas, my lord.' Curteis picked up his pen, hinting. 'When all's said and done, 'tis one and the same.'

This was about those fucking Clemen peasants. He didn't need Curteis to say it, he could see the condemnation in the steward's watchful eyes.

Judge me, you shite, would you? Wait till I'm your duke. I'll give you a lesson in judgement you won't soon fucking forget.

There was no point arguing further. Leaving his father's steward to hopefully trip over his own feet and stab himself through the eye with his fucking quill pen, Balfre went in search of Jancis. His wife was in the castle somewhere. She wasn't Izusa, but fucking her would pass the time. And then he'd go in search of his good friend Paithan and settle down to get drunk.

'Balfre!' Pale and prim, too skinny, her insipid beauty fast fading, Jancis stared as he entered her privy apartments. 'When did you – I didn't know you were—' She smiled, unconvincing. 'Welcome home, my lord.'

By the Exarch's balls, she was *nothing* compared with Izusa. Dismissing her trio of ladies with a look, he waited for the door to close then dropped into the nearest chair. 'Aimery calls me, I come.'

'Do you stay long?'

'No.'

If she was disappointed, she hid it well. 'Grefin's here. Have you seen him?'

Grefin? 'No.'

'He arrived late last night, but we've not spoken. Whispers have him wounded.'

'Wounded?' Baffled, he tried to make sense of it. 'How?'

'I don't know,' she said, flinching. 'I'm sorry.'

He leapt up. 'Yes, you fucking well are.'

So much for Jancis. Abandoning his useless wife, he went to find his brother and father. Let Curteis try and stop him. He'd break the steward's fucking neck.

Instinct and experience sent him first to Aimery's privy audience chamber. The man-at-arms posted outside the door showed him he was right.

'Count Balfre,' the man said, wisely nervous. 'My lord, I can't—'

'Say *can't* to me again and see your tongue ripped from your mouth. Stand aside.'

'Balfre!' his father snapped, as the man-at-arms wisely obeyed. 'Would you tally more reasons for my displeasure? Curteis has instructed you—'

'Forgive me, Your Grace,' he said, kicking the chamber door shut. 'Jancis told me Grefin was here, and wounded.' Looking past his father, he felt a stab of shock. Dressed head-to-toe in unrelieved black, face sickly, eyes smudged with shadows, his brother looked like a living corpse. '*Fuck*. Grefin?'

'And I see the Marches have done as little to curb your foul tongue as your temper!' Aimery added. 'By all the powers, Balfre, if you've hope of *any* sweetness from me then—'

'Please, Your Grace,' said Grefin, wearily. Instead of standing, as was usual, he sat on a stool against the wall, his left shoulder leaning on a faded tapestry. 'He's here now, and he needs to know what's happened.'

Choked with gall, Balfre watched his father's pallid, age-spotted face soften and his yellowish eyes fill with tears.

'Very well,' Aimery said, his voice choked, and had to clear his throat. 'Balfre. There is grievous news. Grefin's son – your nephew Jorin – is slaughtered by raiders. They nearly slaughtered your brother. But, thank the spirits, he survived.'

Silenced, Balfre stared at Grefin. So long since they'd seen each other. Out of sight, out of mind. With the Marches singing so sweetly for him, independence and authority and Izusa to fuck, he'd hardly thought of his brother. And when he did, could even think of him fondly. And now this. *This*. The brutal, naked pain in Grefin's face hurt him. It was Malcolm's loss all over again, yet somehow worse.

'Gref, I'm sorry,' he said, meaning it. 'Fuck. *Fuck*.'

Aimery sighed. ''Tis a tragic loss. When the news breaks widely, all of Harcia will weep.'

'He was killed by raiders, you say? I did hear whisper of something, weeks ago, but—' He shook his head. 'Raiders from where? Are they pirates?'

'We don't know,' Grefin said. 'I can't find anyone who's seen their like. They torched Potterstown. Murdered hundreds. Had others trussed to take for slavery. The things they did to those people . . .' With a shuddering breath, he banished the memory. 'I fear if they're not stopped at the Green Isle, they'll over-run Harcia entirely.'

Aimery punched a feeble fist to the arm of his gilded chair. 'Then, Grefin, we will stop them. I have, in the past few days, received assurances from every lord of the Green Isle. They swear to shed their blood to the last drop in defence of our sovereignty – and to avenge Jorin's death.'

Grefin frowned, his face grief-pinched. 'My son's death is but one among too many.'

'I know that,' Aimery snapped. 'But it's his death – your great loss – the barons feel most keenly. Terriel wrote unstinting of how you fought in Potterstown. He calls you fierce and fearless. A Steward without blemish.'

Balfre raised an eyebrow. 'High praise.'

'And well-deserved. Grefin—' Aimery leaned forward, urgent. 'The Green Isle's barons love you, and would die for you, which is what Harcia needs. 'Tis what *you* need, as their Steward. Men bound to you by more than lip-service obligation. Without that depth of loyalty we'll not defeat these raiding barbarians before they can sink their teeth into this duchy.' He sat back. 'Now. To the question of how we'll defeat them.'

As Grefin and Aimery began debating strategy, Balfre stared at the floor, his thoughts frantically awhirl. While tensions in the Marches had been simmering ever since his arrival, his ambitions meant he'd kept them from coming to the boil. And that meant his men-at-arms weren't yet properly blooded. When the time came at last for him to claim his kingdom of Harcia, he'd need blooded men to fight for him against Clemen. Letting his men-at-arms sharpen their swords on these raiders would answer that dilemma nicely. Of course he'd lose some in battle. But the rewards he'd reap were well worth any loss.

'—agree with that bullish shite Terriel's suggestion,' Aimery was saying. 'A string of garrisons around the Green Isle coast, each one within easy reach of where these raiders are likely to strike.'

'A sound notion, in theory,' Grefin said, dubious. 'But we'll need so many men. I doubt—'

'You'll have them. I'll see our castles here emptied, if I must.'

'And I won't refuse them.' Grefin shifted his gaze. 'Balfre? What do you think?'

'Me?' He frowned, showing nothing but pained concern. 'I think, as Aimery's heir, I should join you in defending our duchy.'

Grefin was too sombre for smiling but his eyes warmed, briefly. 'A generous offer. But word of these raiders will trickle into Clemen. You can't leave the Marches, Balfre. Roric might take your absence as an invitation to test our resolve – and our strength.'

'Then I'll send you men-at-arms.'

'Which, again, will leave the Marches vulnerable.'

'Roric won't test me. I have Vidar's measure – and Clemen's crippled lord has mine. They both know full well that—'

'Yes, Balfre,' said Aimery, darkly. 'And I know too. We'll shortly discuss *your measure*, and how far you'll go in testing Roric!'

'I'm sorry,' Grefin said. 'I don't understand.'

Aimery frowned. 'You will.'

Ah. So his summoning was about those fucking villagers. 'My point, Grefin,' he said, 'is that I have men I can spare to help you fight these raiders. As for our strength in the Marches, send me green men to train and I'll soon make that good.'

Grefin looked at Aimery. 'Your Grace?'

'Winter's close,' said Aimery, after some thought. ''Tis likely the northern storms will keep these raiders from the Green Isle till next spring. By then you'll have the garrisons established and men-at-arms enough for their stout defence. As for Balfre's offer . . .' He glanced sideways, grudging. 'Some of the men he's trained serve now in this castle. Ambrose gives me good report of them.'

'Oh, I don't question their competence,' Grefin said. 'There are Marcher men-at-arms at Steward's Keep. I'll gladly take all the men

Balfre can spare me, so long as it doesn't endanger us in the Marches.'

Aimery grunted. 'Very well. And when you leave you can take men from Tamwell with you. Talk with Ambrose on that.' He thumped the arm of his chair a second time. 'Now. Balfre. Let us discuss your recent conduct.'

With a hiss of pain, Grefin stood. 'I'll leave you. Perhaps later, Balfre, we can—'

'No, Grefin,' said Aimery. 'You'll stay. For what I have to say to your brother concerns you as well.'

Fuck. Balfre sighed. 'Your Grace, I—'

'Hold your tongue! I am speaking!'

He couldn't help himself. He flinched. 'Your Grace.'

'Roric's herald even now resides in the East Tower,' Aimery said coldly. 'My guest until I send him home with an answer for your actions that will satisfy his grossly offended duke.'

'Roric's herald is *here*? Well, I hope you had him leeched for plague before you let him up the stairs.'

Aimery's brows lowered. 'You think this a matter for puerile jest?'

'Your Grace, how am I the villain? Why do you—'

'*Because you murdered five of Roric's people! Three of them children! Or do you deny it?*'

'No, but—'

'Balfre? What is he talking about?'

He turned to his brother. 'They were dead already, Gref. Clemen's peasants were rotten with plague.'

'Even so . . .' Grefin swallowed. 'You killed them?'

'I put them out of their misery. And I broke no law doing it! Fuck, I *upheld* the law.'

Aimery snorted. 'Under Marcher law the penalty for trespass is not death.'

'They did more than trespass. They brought pestilence into the Harcian Marches!'

'So you say,' Aimery retorted. 'Clemen denies it. Clemen claims you killed its people without just cause. And you have no proof elsewise.'

'I have the proof of my own eyes. I have Waymon and six men-at-arms.'

Another disbelieving snort. 'And none of them would lie for you.'

'They don't have to lie. It's the truth.'

'You burned the bodies and spoiled the severed heads with pitch, to prevent—'

'To prevent the pestilence spreading! And if that cowardly shite Roric had done the same when he first had the chance, Clemen wouldn't now be in a muck sweat and we wouldn't be paying the price for his failures!'

Aimery pointed a shaking finger. 'Do not raise your voice to me!'

'Your Grace.' With an effort, Balfre gentled his tone. He could feel Grefin's wounded stare. It made him want to kick something. 'However distasteful, what I did was necessary. I am this duchy's Marcher lord. I'll not beg pardon for keeping Harcia safe.'

The corners of Aimery's mouth turned down. 'If your actions were so noble, why did I learn of them not from you, but from that bastard Roric's herald?'

'*What?*'

'I thought you'd changed, Balfre,' Aimery said, his face bleak. 'I thought you'd discovered wisdom and self-restraint. But I see I was mistaken. Your hatred of Clemen would not be held in check. Now peace between our duchies is once more precarious. Roric threatens reprisals! He threatens fines and sanctions and restrictions upon our merchants. Harcia cannot afford it! Especially now, with this new threat from these raiders. What were you thinking? Were you thinking at *all*?'

Bewildered, he pinched the bridge of his nose. '*Wait*. Your Grace – how can you think I'd not tell you what happened? I despatched a report to you the next day. I don't know why—'

'And I don't care to hear your excuses!' Aimery shouted. 'I received no report, Balfre. But even if I had, it would make no difference. *They were Roric's people and you should not have killed them!* Nothing you say will convince me elsewise. Nothing you say can undo the damage you've wrought. Get out of my sight – and take this warning with you. Misstep again and I will disown you. I'll strip you of all nobility and name Grefin as my heir.'

Balfre swallowed. A cold sweat soaked the soft linen shirt beneath his leather doublet. 'Your Grace.'

He blundered from the audience chamber. Stumbled along the corridor until he came to one of the spiral staircases that led up to Tamwell castle's roof. Climbed the timeworn, tightly winding stone steps until he reached fresh air, and the deserted battlements, and could show the sky his unmasked face.

'Balfre? Balfre!'

Grefin.

He turned. 'Stay the fuck away from me or I'll throw you off this fucking roof! Let Aimery bequeath his precious duchy to your corpse!'

Grefin took a limping half-step closer, then stopped. 'He didn't mean it. He's distraught over Jorin. I'll talk to him. I promise. I don't want to be duke.'

'*Fuck!*' He would have laughed if he weren't so close to weeping. 'You expect me to *believe* that?'

'Balfre – Aimery made me Steward over you and, right or wrong, I bowed to that. But I'll bow no further. You're his heir. I will never usurp you.'

'Never is a long time. And power is power.'

Stark honesty had crowded out the grief in Grefin's eyes. 'You know I don't care about power! You think if Aimery discards you. I'll break my word? Why? After my first year as Steward, I told him I was done. You heard me tell him. It was Aimery who wouldn't release me. *I kept my word, Balfre.* Why doubt me now?'

He nearly said, *Because I caught you plotting with Aimery and Roric behind my back.* Only it was better his brother didn't learn what he knew. Knowledge was power, too. That titbit might yet prove useful. Besides. By happy accident, Grefin had done him a favour. He'd likely not be Harcia's Marcher lord without that little conspiracy. Anyway . . . what Grefin said was true. His brother lacked ambition. Without Aimery's interference he'd never have become Steward. Grefin had never wanted anything beyond Mazelina and his brats.

'I mean this,' Grefin insisted, breaking the silence. 'Take out your dagger. Prick my finger. I'll give you an assurance written in my blood.'

His blind rage was fading. 'I don't want your fucking blood.'

Grefin shrugged, one-shouldered. 'Still. It's yours.'

'*Fuck.*'

'Balfre.' Grefin took another halting step towards him. 'I don't want us at odds. Not now. Not after . . .'

One of these days he'd learn how to stay angry with his brother. 'I'm sorry. For Jorin.'

Looking over the battlements at Cater's Tamwell's busy afternoon streets, Grefin smeared dampness from his cheek. 'You saved my life in Potterstown. The things you told me about fighting in the Marches? They saved my life.'

'Good.'

'But they didn't save my son.' He flinched. 'No. That's not fair. *I* didn't save him. It's my fault Jorin's dead.'

'Mazelina told you that, did she?'

Grefin's silence was an answer.

'You didn't kill your son, Gref, any more than you killed the people of Potterstown. Jorin was born with a sword in his hand. Like you were. Like I was. Bloody death is our birthright. How badly were you wounded?'

Grefin touched his right shoulder. 'More than a tickle. It's healing. And I bruised my hip. My leg. I'll live.'

'I know,' he said, gently. 'Come on. Let's find old Ambrose. Talk to him about the men-at-arms you'll need for the Green Isle.'

Silver striped in a sliver of moonlight, Aimery sat beside his sleeping son. Grief had driven Grefin to bed down in the Tamwell chamber he'd claimed as a boy. A few of his boyhood tunics were still in the chest at the foot of the bed and an old, splintery wooden sword was propped in a corner, collecting cobwebs. The chamber had no window, only an arrow loop. He used to play Constable of the Castle here with Balfre, when bad weather or a childish gripe kept him indoors. More than twenty-five years ago, that was. By the powers . . . twenty-five years. Time was an untamed horse, galloping heedless towards the abyss. Galloping him with it. He was grown an old man, infirm despite his costly leech. Not an hour raced by him these days without pain or worry in it. Every pain, every worry, sapping his remaining strength. But he wasn't dead yet. Nor would he die, till he was certain Harcia would be safe.

Such hope he'd had. Cautious at first but in the last few years steadily firming. Balfre in the Marches, keeping the peace, upholding the law, had proven himself a man worthy to be called a duke. Or so he'd thought. But now Balfre butchered children. What was he to do with that? With him?

Grefin shifted under his red fox coverlet, breath catching as he muttered. The words were garbled, but ripe with distress. Aimery fumbled for the horn lantern by his chair and lifted it, anxiously peering. Grefin shifted again, his eyes restless beneath their closed lids, and the coverlet slid aside to reveal his bare, bruised chest and the healing sword-thrust through the top of his shoulder. The wound was inflamed around its horse-hair stitches. So nearly a killing blow – and more killing blows to come, if his suspicions were right and the raiders returned to the Green Isle in the spring.

If he dies . . . if they kill him . . . then will I die too. If I lose Grefin not even Harcia will keep me.

Doubtless it was shameful to feel he'd not die if he lost Balfre. He loved Grefin without pause. But love was too simple a word for what tangled within him whenever he thought of his heir.

The lantern was heavy. But as he lowered it, forgoing its muted, muddy glow, Grefin uttered a sharp cry and opened his eyes, his sound arm lifting as though to ward off attack.

'Lie easy,' Aimery said. 'Or I'll summon the leech.' He set the lantern on the floor at his feet. 'You dream of Potterstown?'

A finger of moonlight traced Grefin's face in profile as he rolled his head on the pillow. 'Of Jorin.'

'Ah.'

'I lost sight of him,' Grefin murmured. 'In the fighting. My horse was killed underneath me and it was madness, after. I lost sight of him in the fighting. And then . . . I lost him.'

Malcolm. Aimery pressed a fist against his chest. 'I wish I could promise you the pain will ease.'

'But it won't.' Grefin tugged the coverlet higher. 'What are you doing here?'

'I couldn't sleep. I was afraid you might be fevered.'

A small, boyish smile. Then it faded. 'Father. About Balfre. What happened in—'

515

'No!' He raised a hand. 'Don't defend him. Would you break my heart, defending him?'

'And would you break mine, demanding I choose between you?'

Aimery sat back. 'What do you mean?'

'You know what I mean!' Grefin elbowed himself upright. 'For all our quarrels, I love Balfre. You had no right to threaten him with *me*.'

'I had every right! Old and frail I may be, yet I am still Harcia's duke. And as duke I'll do what I must to keep the duchy safe.'

'Even side with Clemen against your own son?' Grefin protested. 'When it's Clemen in the wrong? Trespass is a crime, and those people had the plague.'

'So Balfre says. But he can't prove it.'

'Which makes him a liar? A murderer? Is that what you believe?'

'What I believe doesn't matter! It's what Roric believes that counts.'

'It matters to Balfre,' Grefin said quietly. 'Father . . . he made a mistake.'

'Another mistake like that one and we will be at war!'

Wincing, Grefin rubbed the heel of his hand against a bruise. 'I doubt that. From what I hear, Clemen has no coin to pay for it.'

Were his son not griefstruck, Aimery would have slapped him. 'Did you wait for coin before you raised a sword against those raiders in Potterstown? And when you face them again, Grefin, will it take coin for you to avenge Jorin's cruel death? What starts in blood must *end* in blood. Maybe they did carry plague, those trespassing Clemen folk. But Roric won't remember that. Not a husband or a father in his duchy will remember it. All they'll remember is that Clemen folk died and Harcia killed them!'

'I understand your fear,' Grefin said, frowning. 'But it was Harcia killed a Clemen woman in the Marches, Your Grace. We didn't go to war over that.'

'That was different. The facts then were in dispute. But not this time. And Balfre—' He heard his voice crack. 'Balfre killed *children*.'

A difficult silence. Grefin lay down again. 'He's gone, you know. Back to the Marches. He left after you retired to your bedchamber.'

He grunted. 'Without seeking my leave. I know. Curteis told me.'

'I tried to dissuade him. It's dangerous, riding at night. He wouldn't listen.'

'Balfre?' He raised an eyebrow. 'How unlike him.'

Another brief smile. 'Did Curteis also tell you he left a letter for the herald to give Roric? I read it. He was surprisingly contrite.'

'He doesn't want me to disown him.'

'It wouldn't matter if you did. I won't take Harcia from Balfre. I've given him my word.'

A surge of anger. 'You had no right, Grefin. That promise isn't yours to give.'

'Even so. I gave it. And I'll not take it back.'

He stood. Stooped, and picked up the lantern. ''Tis very late. We'll talk more in the morning.'

'Yes, Your Grace. Good night again, Your Grace.'

'Pah,' he said, and left his defiant son to sleep.

In no mood for company or dallying, Balfre rode hard from Tamwell castle back to the Marches. Stopping only when he had to. Snatching meat and drink in haste. Pursued by inconvenient memories. His brother's grief. His father's fury. The hostile smirk on that fucking Clemen herald's face. It had nearly killed him, writing that letter. But it wasn't yet time to clash swords with Clemen. No matter what it cost him, he had to keep Roric sweet. So his pride was scorched. Better his pride than the Marches. Probably he should've left a letter for Aimery, too. Except there was only so much pride he was prepared to burn.

He knew Waymon would be waiting for him at the manor, with information and barracks reports and more coin – provided he'd managed to poach them a trader. And with his promise to Grefin of sending more men to the Green Isle, there were decisions to be made. But he was in no mood for Waymon or barracks talk. Through the long ride home, he could think of only one thing.

Eager, hungry, he crossed into the Clemen Marches and rode straight to the cottage that had become his second home.

'Izusa! Izusa! Open the fucking door!'

With a last fisted thump on the stubbornly closed carved timber, he stepped back. Shook his stinging hand and waited.

'*Izusa!*'

Nothing. His weary stallion lifted its head. Startled birds clattered skywards from the bare woodland around him. But the cottage door didn't open. She didn't come at his call.

'Bitch!'

Feeling outrageously thwarted, like a child denied its promised sweetmeat, Balfre retreated to sit on the storm-felled tree trunk Izusa used as chair and table when she wanted fresh air.

'Bitch,' he said again, but longingly, and dropped his head into his hands. No point trying to kick his way in. She had the cottage charm-protected, with foreign runes from across the sea.

'*I'm a woman alone, my lord,*' she'd protested at his protest. '*Your men-at-arms can't shadow me night and day. But don't worry. My little magics will never turn against you.*'

As a Marcher lord he should have her whipped for her spell-play. He should banish her from the Marches or thrust her at a passing exarchite. Those grey-robed miseries gave witches short shrift. But he couldn't. He wouldn't. Izusa was far too good a fuck. And whatever else she knew, but shouldn't, she had a knack for healing. All fucking aside, he'd keep her safe for that alone.

The cottage's grassy horse yard was empty of the palfrey he'd given her. With nothing better to do, not wanting to leave without seeing her, he stripped his tired stallion of its saddle and bridle and penned the animal safe with a pail of water from the well. Found himself a puddle of late-afternoon autumn sunshine and sat in it, eyes closed and face tipped to the branch-latticed sky. Breathing in, breathing out, his body hummed with fatigue. He felt as hard-handled as his stallion. A good thing, perhaps, that Izusa wasn't here. His cock was soft-soap, not iron. Good for pissing and nothing else.

He fell asleep. Dreamed and drifted until pleasure woke him, keen as a whetted blade.

His eyes opened on a strangled gasp, showed him Izusa in the sinking sunlight, her red hair wild, her eyes wilder, naked skin moon-pale, laughing as she took hold of his cock and thrust him home between her legs.

She rode him without mercy, shrieking like a falcon in flight. The slap of her thighs and arse against his leather breeches was a torment.

He wanted to feel her skin to skin. But he was helpless beneath her, a ruthless man being ruthlessly fucked. All he could do was rear up and bite her nipples and weep aloud his triumph as she broke him to pieces and sucked him dry.

'Fuck,' he moaned, shuddering. 'Fuck. I'll kill you for this.'

She leaned close, her sweet breath brushing his cheek. 'Kill me with fucking, Balfre. That's the best way to die.'

The cottage door stood wide open. Inside, all the candles were lit. They staggered over the threshold, laughing, and then she stripped him of his clothing. Poured a herbed honey posset into his parched mouth and pressed a slender finger to his sticky lips.

'*Wait, Balfre. Wait.*'

Moments later, his blood caught fire.

He did everything to her, and she let him. When he faltered she urged him on. Pain was pleasure, pleasure pain. There was no end and no beginning, only the pumping need to purge. Twice more she fed him her intoxicating potion. The sun exploded behind his eyes. His body unravelled itself, flying apart. As he sank one last time into darkness, he felt Izusa's gossamer touch.

'Sleep, my lord,' she whispered. 'You're safe here, in my arms.'

'Izusa . . .'

Freshly bathed, and dressed in a simple linen shift, she turned from the bedchamber's unshuttered window. 'My lord?'

'Izusa.' Sprawled naked on her bed, Balfre rubbed the back of his hand across his eyes. 'I'd have the truth. *Are* you a witch?'

She'd left three candles burning. In their mellow light the marks of her teeth and nails showed boldly on his scarred skin. Her own skin was unblemished now. An important distinction.

'My lord,' she said, tilting her head, 'what is a witch?'

'A foul, degenerate creature, full of deceit and lies and treachery. A misshapen monster spat from the reeking depths of the dark kingdom, spawned to wreak chaos and destroy men's souls.'

She rolled her eyes. 'Or so the exarchites say.'

'Yes. So they say.'

'But what do you say? Am I a misshapen monster? Have I destroyed your soul? Answer your own question, my lord. Am I a witch?'

A slow, remembering smile curved his lips. 'I can't answer for my soul, but I think you destroyed my cock.'

She laughed. 'Then is every woman born a witch.'

'Every woman but my wife.' His smile vanished. 'Why do you stand so far away? This bed is cold and empty without you.'

'As the Marches were cold and empty with you ridden to your father's court.'

His shadowed face clenched like a fist. 'Don't speak of my father.'

'Oh.' She crossed to the bed. Sat beside him. 'Your heart is hurting. If I have any power, I have the power to feel that. Your pain called to me while I did heal a goatman of bloody flux, out by Dead Dog Pond.'

'Dead Dog Pond?' he said, every muscle going still.

Watching a tumble of emotions play behind his eyes, she gently laced her fingers with his. 'If you think your swift justice troubles Harcia's people in the Marches, think again. Your people welcome it.'

'Then I wish my people had Aimery's ear,' he muttered. 'Aimery cares more for Roric's opinion than mine or any Harcian's. *Roric*. That fuck's such a piss-poor duke he can't even feed his people or keep them from disease. Plague-struck, they must creep into the Harcian Marches to steal our food.'

'Aimery didn't praise you for averting disaster?'

'*Praise* me? He threatened me!'

Just as Salimbene had foretold, in Balfre's absence. 'I'm sorry, my lord.'

Balfre sat up. 'It was odd. He claimed the first he knew of those Clemen I killed was what he heard from Roric's herald. But I sent a man-at-arms to Tamwell castle with a full report. He returned to the Marches safely and told me himself he'd spoken with Aimery.'

Because that was what she'd sorcelled Balfre's man-at-arms to say. Obeying Salimbene, she'd intercepted him before he left the Marches. Drugged him. Kept him. And when enough time had gone by, released him to ride home again as though nothing was amiss. The man was dead now, of the slow-acting poison meant to end his life while Balfre was at Tamwell castle. The death had looked natural. A flux of the bowels, not plague. She didn't know why she'd kept him, or killed him. Salimbene wanted it. That was enough.

'My lord. How did Aimery threaten you?' When Balfre didn't answer, she traced the silvery scar crossing his ribs. 'What you say to me is never repeated. What we do here isn't known.'

He grimaced. 'Waymon knows.'

'He knows we fuck. Not that we talk, after.'

'And what good is talk?'

'A burdened heart is an unhappy heart. I told you, my lord. I feel your pain.'

Balfre punched a fist to his knee. 'Aimery threatened to disown me. To make Grefin his heir in my place.'

'No!' she said, and reached for him. 'The wicked old man!'

He laughed, bitter, muffled against her breast. 'It's my own fault. Grefin found the old bastard a canny leech to keep him breathing and I held my peace. I had to. I couldn't afford Aimery dying too soon. Now it seems he won't die at all. The stubborn fuck clings to life like a tick.'

'Your brother. Lord Grefin,' she said, stroking his hair. 'Does he stand with you, or with your father?'

Balfre eased free, not a man to long give himself over to comfort. 'With me. He says. He swears. But . . .'

And there was his heart, uncovered. Never truly trusting. Always a useful seed of suspicion, ready to take root.

'But?' she prompted.

He scowled. 'I never heard him say the same to Aimery's face.'

She pressed her palm to his cheek. 'Are you hungry, my lord? I've braised rabbit keeping warm. Rest, while I fetch you a bowl.'

'None for yourself?' he said, as she returned with a generous serving of rabbit and a goblet brimming with red wine. 'You're no scullion, Izusa. You can eat in my presence.'

'I ate while you were sleeping. Come, Balfre. Fall to. You're a man in need of strength.'

He ate and drank, ravenous. When he was finished she took the emptied bowl and goblet out to the tub by the front door, for later washing. As she slipped back into the chamber, he looked up. In the candle-light his face was vulnerable, in a way she'd never seen.

'You're right, Izusa. It's not just the fucking I come for. There's a restfulness here I can't find anywhere else.'

'Good, my lord. Every great man deserves some peace.'

'I think . . .' He half-smiled. 'Did you call me *Balfre*, before?'

'An impertinence. Forgive me.'

'No. I like the sound of my name on your lips. I'd hear it again, Izusa. Whenever we're alone.'

She smiled. '*Balfre*.'

'Come,' he said, patting the blanket. 'You've fed my belly, woman, but my cock is hungry too.'

Though he tore the shift from her body, still in his own way he was gentle. She encouraged that, whispering pleasure and praise. So long as she must fuck him, she'd have a say in how it was done.

Sated and drowsy after, he let her hold him. 'I think you must be some kind of witch. I fuck you like a faery king. Enchantment lies between your thighs.'

She raked her fingernails lightly over his buttocks. So many men were flabby, but Balfre was pleasingly taut. 'I'm no witch as the exarchites would have it. But if you'd know the truth, Balfre . . . I'm not without power.' She slapped him when he snorted, lascivious. 'Not all power comes from fucking. I know much of the world beyond these narrow Marches. I've breathed the scorching air of Agribia. Watched the Great Eclipse atop the highest mountain in Zeidica. I know the twisting alleys of Lepetto and the wide, tree-lined streets of half-forgotten Pruges. I've seen men drown in the Sea of Sorrows and wept to the ringing of Carillon's bells. I can help you, if you'll let me.'

For a long time Balfre said nothing. She waited. There was no need to push him. At last he eased free, rose on his hands above her. His eyes were dangerous. Trapped beneath him, she met his stare calmly. To show fear would be a grave mistake. She knew him inside and out.

'*Who are you, Izusa?*'

She pressed her hand lightly against his chest, over his heart. 'I'm a storm-tossed leaf, Balfre. I'm a woman come to rest. The first time I saw you, at the Pig Whistle, after that bloody skirmish with Clemen? I knew then my purpose was to see you achieve your desire.'

Taking his full weight onto one arm, Balfre captured her left breast in his hand. Smiled to feel her thudding heart, even as she felt his. 'And what do I desire, Izusa?'

'A crown, my lord Balfre,' she said, covering his grasping hand with her own. 'A kingdom long since lost, that should be yours, and will be.'

His smile faded. 'How do you know that?'

'Does it matter? *I know*. And I see you crowned a king. All you need do is trust.'

His breathing was ragged, his body rampant. 'In you?'

'Yes, Balfre.' She wrapped her legs around his narrow hips. Lifted her own hips, shamelessly begging. 'In me.'

He was desperate to believe her, but his thorny nature pricked too hard. Eyes cold, he almost snarled. 'You know I'll kill you if you're lying.'

Capturing his gaze, she poured all her power into her stare. Melted his suspicion. Bound him, heart and soul. 'I'm not. Now fuck me before I die of desire.'

He plunged into her, groaning. The honey potion she'd fed him was potent. He'd want to fuck for hours yet. But she was sick of it, so she rode him hard to a swift spilling. And when she brought him more wine, laced with a strong soporific, urged him to drink deeply. He drained the goblet in a single swallow. Moments later, even as he tried to fondle her, his eyelids began to close.

'Sleep, my lord,' she murmured, 'and fret no more on your father, or Roric, or your loyal brother Grefin. When the time is right I'll help you rid the world of Aimery. I'll see you to your ducal crown, and after that a throne.'

He smiled at her, drowsy. 'Then you are a witch, Izusa.'

'Witch enough for your purpose, ser.' She kissed him, lightly. 'And that's all you need to know.'

CHAPTER THIRTY-ONE

J ust on sunrise, and Eaglerock was stirring to life. In Baker Street the apprentices coaxed ovens to greater heat or struggled to knead their risen dough well enough to please their masters. Bread already baking scented the air with mouth-watering promise. The town's other early birds, the piemakers and dairymen, the apple-girls and curd-sellers and tallowmen and tanners, they blinked in the cloudy morning light as they went about their tasks. Yawning lightermen extinguished their lanterns, shouldered their poles and wandered home to sleep the day through, scarcely listening to the bellow of cattle penned in the Shambles for slaughter. Hand-pushed scurrel carts creaked in and out of puddles, down narrow, hunchbacked alleys and along the town's wider streets as its scurrel-men collected the corpses of dogs and cats and vermin that had perished in the night. Human corpses they left untouched for the township's men-at-arms to carry away. Small boys ran with early, urgent messages, leather-clad feet slapping and splashing as they dashed. The dogs that hadn't died barked and howled to hear them and challenge the clopping horses who pulled the fish-wagons down to the harbour for the morning catch. On the waterfront the never-sleeping brothels, busy again, spat out sleepy sailors and docksmen who rubbed their eyes and hauled up their breeches to cover naked arses. And the whores who plied their trade in daylight hours opened chamber shutters and muslin chemises and flaunted their tits.

Swathed in a battered leather travelling cloak, and with a canvas cap worthy of Arthgallo hiding his head, Roric walked down to the waterfront with Humbert. Like himself, his foster-lord's familiar appearance was concealed by cloak and hood. Lacking the men-at-arms that usually surrounded Clemen's duke, they looked no more important than any other early-rising townsfolk. And those who did stir hardly glanced their way, too intent on their own troubles.

'So,' he said, keeping his voice low, and looked sideways at Humbert. 'What do you make of Vidar's latest report? Is he right? Does Balfre oversee the training of so many Harcian men-at-arms because of these raiders? Or does he have a more sinister purpose?'

Humbert shrugged. 'To my way of thinking, Balfre farts with sinister purpose.'

'Doubtless he does, Humbert, but you don't answer the question.'

'Because I've got no answer, Roric. Save to say we should hope Harcia does turn its Green Isle into a graveyard for those raiding cockshite butchers. Better their men-at-arms fight such a battle than ours.'

A good point. The thought of those ruthless northmen slaughtering their way through the Marches and laying waste to Clemen kept him awake at night. Waiting for a stinking manure cart to roll by them on its way to the shite-pits, Roric frowned across rutted Fleece Street and down to the slowly rousing warehouse district.

'It seems Balfre's brother proves himself a wily knight. If the rumours are true, he's foiled four raids already and we've only reached the last gasp of spring.'

Humbert pulled a face. 'The raiders killed his son. I can think of no better spur for vengeance.' A sideways glance. 'You think Grefin's cause for Clemen to worry?'

The manure-cart passed. As they picked their way around smelly puddles and between wheel-ruts, Roric felt a splatter of rain on his face and looked up. The sky was swiftly crowding with more clouds. They'd had a wet spring already. If the summer followed suit there'd be yet another poor harvest. The thought of Clemen's fields rotting black with ruined crops made him falter.

Not again, by all the powers. Please. Not again.

Too much rain in Clemen. Too little in Cassinia. And with pirates keeping Danetto's merchant galleys penned in their harbours, it seemed the world was swiftly running out of grain.

To distract himself from that dire thought, he looked again at

Humbert. 'I worry what might happen when Aimery breathes his last. Should his belligerent sons grasp the same sword and look southwards, how can Clemen hope to prevail?'

'They won't,' Humbert said, wiping rainwater out of his eyes. 'Balfre's a stone-hearted, murdering bastard but Grefin's not that style of man. He keeps his belligerence for the raiders and his sword sheathed elsewise.'

'Speaking of Balfre . . . for a stone-hearted, murdering bastard he's been uncommonly well-behaved of late,' he mused, as they turned into Griddle Lane. 'Since he killed that family from Dipford the Marches have been still.'

'Because after you threatened reprisals Aimery threatened to name Grefin heir in his place,' Humbert said, grimly amused. 'Balfre knows the old nob would make good on his promise, so he minces like a lady's palfrey and does naught to stir shite.'

'Who told you that? Vidar? He's never mentioned it to me.'

'Vidar?' Humbert's lips thinned. 'I don't gossip with Vidar. I know other men in the Marches. They hear things, and pass them along.'

'And you don't, it seems.'

'Now, Roric . . .' Humbert stopped. 'There's no need to wrong-foot me on this. The whisper only just reached me. I wasn't keeping tattle secret. Why would I?'

Halted, he met Humbert's hurt stare steadily. Over the past trying months they'd worked hard to heal their wounded friendship. Lindara's growing belly helped. The hope of an heir. The chance for a future with children in it. But Humbert still chafed against the notion that the boy he'd fostered was now a grown man, and his duke. So they continued to tiptoe on eggshells round each other and sometimes it seemed as though that might never change.

'You wouldn't. I know.' He started walking again, taking Humbert with him. 'But I'll tell you this. Just because Balfre's thought better of killing Clemen-folk in broad daylight doesn't mean he's not killing them in the dark. Vidar wasn't wrong, Humbert. People have gone missing from Clemen's border villages.'

'There was plague in those villages. You'll find those missing folk dead and tossed in a ditch.'

'Some, perhaps, I'll give you,' he said. 'But not all.'

They emerged from Griddle Lane onto sloping Ironmongery Street. Stamping his way downwards, Humbert blew a tremble of raindrops from his nose. 'You're frighting at shadows, Roric. You can't truly believe Balfre's murdering Clemen-folk under cover of night and burying the bodies before sunrise!'

Spoken aloud, his fear did sound ridiculous. But he couldn't shake loose his feeling of dread. 'Tell me again who was it called Aimery's heir a stone-hearted, murdering bastard?'

'And so he is,' Humbert growled. 'But I never once called him a fool.'

'Then what's your explanation?'

'I say that with all this rain the land's turned swampy along the border. Could be those folk have trickled south for better luck. Or they're skulking in the Clemen Marches, living rough.'

'Vidar says they're not. Do you call him a liar?'

Humbert hunched his cloaked shoulders round his ears. 'You know the Marches, Roric. Half of it's woodland. There are plenty of gnarly places where folk can hide. And rabbits and roots and berries so they'll not starve.'

Which was true. But it didn't explain the crawling sensation on the back of his neck or the queasy roil of his belly. Though it defied common sense, smacked uncomfortably of soothsaying and omens, he knew in his bones a storm was coming.

And I'm a man chained to a rock in its path, unable to escape.

'Roric?' Alarmed, Humbert seized his arm. 'Are you ill? You've gone pale as a fish's belly, boy.'

The burst of rain had eased, but still he had to blink and blink to clear his vision. 'No. I'm fine.'

'I'll send for Arthgallo when this business is done with,' said Humbert. 'He can—'

'I said there's nothing amiss!'

Humbert let go. 'Yes, Your Grace.'

They walked the rest of the way in stiff silence.

Despite the early hour, Eaglerock's waterfront tumbled like an ant hill. Not quite two months since the harbour was declared open again, and everyone who relied on it now rushed to make up their lost time and coin. A jaunty breeze blew in from the open water, its

527

salty freshness mixing with the stink of tar and fish and spilled spices and sweating men. No more taint from the plague ships, which had been anchored well out in the harbour.

An unpopular decision, that, to round up the sick and suffering of Clemen and house them on galleys. The exarchite Ignace had been furious in his opposition. And it was true, many souls had died on those ships. But the decision had kept the pestilence from spreading further through the duchy. Lives were lost, yes. But more had been saved.

Their purpose served, the disease defeated for now, the plague ships had been burned to the waterline and let sink into memory. Instead of fearful cries and moans of suffering, shouts and curses and laughter filled the air with working music. Filled Roric with the faintest hope that hope wasn't lost for Clemen.

'There,' Humbert said, pointing. 'There's Garith.'

The shipmaster stood on the dock beside his pride and joy, the impressive trading cog *Watersprite*, as his sailors and docksmen laboured up and down the gangplank with small chests and barrels. A winch swung canvas-stitched bales of wool or linen high overhead to be dropped into the galley's open belly. Large barrels sloshed full of Clemen ale and brandy were stacked beside the bales. Nimble dock-boys darted like minnows, following shouted instructions, cat-calling back and forth and mischievously tripping each other when Garith had his back turned.

Roric threaded his way through the mayhem, Humbert at his heels. 'Shipmaster Garith!'

Garith turned, his canvas smock a far cry from the figured brocade doublet he wore when visiting court. His weather-beaten glare shifted to a wary frown of welcome when he recognised his visitors.

'My Lord,' he said, with a polite nod. 'Let's jawbreak our business within.'

If the sailors and dock-men and darting boys realised who'd come to break jaws with their master, not a one of them showed it. Roric and Humbert followed Garith into the tarred wooden dockside hutch that served as his office, and waited as he closed its door then hurriedly pulled out two battered stools.

'Sit, sit, Your Grace, my lord. And I thank you for coming down to the harbour. It be a short tide and I can't afford to miss the turn.'

Perching on the nearest stool, Roric waved a hand. 'It's no great matter, Garith. I'd not interfere with Clemen's merchants unless I have to.'

The shipmaster's eyebrows quirked. 'Of course, Your Grace.'

'No need for pulling faces, man,' Humbert growled, seated with his fists braced on his knees. 'You well know Eaglerock would be a township of wraiths if His Grace hadn't put his foot down and closed the harbour when he did.'

'I do, my lord, I do,' said Garith, sighing. ''Twas a lucky escape we had.'

'Luck had nothing to do with it. His Grace's good judgement saved us. A pity the duke of Rebbai lacked Roric's good sense. Word is that duchy's half-charnel house these days.'

Garith sighed again. 'Indeed, my lord. 'Tis what I've heard too. But if you'll forgive me, Rebbai's troubles don't concern me as much as Clemen's. Your Grace—'

'Speak freely, Garith,' Roric said, glancing at Humbert. 'I'm no child to have his feelings spared.'

'Then I won't spare you,' said Garith. 'Your Grace, I sailed into harbour late yesterday after profitable trading in the Treble Kingdom's main port. And—'

'You take coin from those scabrous vermin?' Humbert demanded. 'Shame on you, Garith!'

'My lord, I do think there be more shame in starving,' Garith retorted. 'And letting the men who sail my ships, and their families, starve. I did warn you there'd be a cruel price to pay for closing the harbour and I pay my share of it by trading with any scabrous vermin as can part with genuine coin.'

'Enough, my lord,' Roric said, when Humbert took a breath to let loose his temper. 'We're not here to debate the merits of trade.' He looked at the shipmaster. 'What did you discover in Port Izzica that was so dire I must be summoned here at sunrise to learn of it?'

'Your Grace, you know they buy and sell slaves in the Treble Kingdom?'

A leaping of blood. 'I do, Garith, yes.'

'When I went ashore in the port there was a dockside auction. And Your Grace, I saw Clemen folk being sold. Harcians, too.'

'Slavery is a terrible thing, Garith. But we all know sailors risk much when—'

'They weren't sailors, Your Grace! They were ordinary men and women, as you'd find here in Eaglerock or any township beyond the Marches.'

'That can't be,' said Humbert, stunned. 'I won't speak for Aimery, but His Grace would *never*—'

'I don't say it was His Grace selling our people! Lord Humbert, I'll thank you not to put sour words in my mouth!'

'*Peace*,' Roric said sharply. 'I've no interest in you two brawling like tavern rats. Garith, did you make any attempt to buy these poor wretches yourself?'

'Of course I did, Your Grace. Well. Our folk, at least. But I was too late. I didn't realise they were our folk till coin had changed hands. I offered to empty my purse but the Osfahr bastard who bought them wouldn't sell them on to me. I watched them taken away in chains, weeping.'

'But how did they end up in a slave auction at all?' said Humbert. Bewildered now, and grief-struck.

'I asked the auction master that,' said Garith, his eyes haunted. 'He said he bought them from pirates and those curs't northern raiders.'

'You're saying we've got pirates and raiders loose in Clemen and nobody noticed?' Humbert stared. 'Garith, your wits have shaken loose.'

'I only tell you what I was told, my lord!'

Roric touched a warning hand to Humbert's arm. 'What else were you told, Garith?'

'The auction master said he'd sold others from Clemen,' said Garith, stepping back at the look on Humbert's face. 'But when I pushed to know more he had his bully-boys chase me off.' He stood a little straighter. 'Tweak my nose for running, Your Grace, if you must. But I'm a plain sailing man. Swords and suchlike and killing, that I leave to you and Lord Humbert.'

'As well you should. Your corpse feeding the fish of Port Izzica would do us no good.' He pinched the bridge of his nose hard, against the stabbing pain behind his eyes. 'And yet you can still fight for Clemen in your own way. Where do you sail next?'

'Cassinia, Your Grace,' said Garith, sounding wary. 'I stop in every duchy port, save Gevez and Carillon. Then it's home again.'

'And in every port there's a tavern, yes? A place you sailing men gather to drink and talk of matters close to your hearts?'

Garith rubbed a calloused hand over mouth and beard. 'You want me to listen with a wide ear for talk of pirates and slavery?'

'And encourage gossip with coin, if coin will help. Discreetly, though. Caution your crew against wild tattling and don't talk of this in Eaglerock. I must know how our people are being taken but I'd not see Clemen stirred to fresh panic. Not with our plague-fears so newly laid to rest.'

'I understand, Your Grace. Only . . .' Garith pursed his lips. 'Tavern talk don't come cheap.'

'I'll send a purse to you before you sail. Or if you must sail before it reaches you, keep close tally of your costs. I'll not leave you out of pocket.' With a strained smile, Roric stood and held out his hand. 'Do what you can, Garith, but guard your life. I don't want your death in my dish.'

Clasping him wrist to wrist, Garith bowed. 'Yes, Your Grace. I promise, I'll do my best.'

'I hope we can trust him and his crew not to tattle tongue,' Humbert fretted as they hurried back to the castle. 'Let word of this run riot and I fear the result.'

It was raining again, hard enough to keep most people off the streets. Though water plastered his canvas cap to his skull and defeated his leather cloak to trickle between his shoulders, Roric was grateful for it. The fewer people who saw his face, the better. He couldn't be sure it was perfectly schooled.

'Garith's a good man. He proved himself trustworthy when I closed the harbour and he kept his word that he'd not stir trouble after. He helped find us plague ships and never once complained at their burning, though the loss of his galley cost him coin, and some of the other shipmasters and merchants shunned him for that help and their losses.'

'This is different. But it's done now.' Puffing as they turned into Castle Way, the sharply up-sloping street leading directly to Eaglerock, Humbert dashed water from his face. 'I'll set Nathyn to summoning the council. We must—'

'Not yet. I want time to ponder this matter before I must start arguing with Aistan and Ercole and—'

'*Ponder?* You'd *ponder*? Roric—'

'Yes, Humbert, I'd ponder!' Frightened, furious, he glared. 'It seems our people are being stolen from their beds with me none the wiser. Do you think I should give the council another reason to doubt me? I will ponder and make my own enquiries and when *I* am ready to discuss the situation more broadly I'll—'

'Roric, what's to ponder?' Humbert demanded breathlessly. 'It's Harcia behind this wickedness. Make no mistake, boy, this is Aimery's doing. You threatened him, rubbed his nose in Balfre's murderous perfidy, and now he takes his revenge. Stealthily. Hoping no one will realise he's behind it.'

'And sells his own people why, precisely? Because he's short of coin?'

'Because he'd throw us off his scent. I tell you, Roric, I'm right. Harcia's filthy fingers are all over this.'

There was no point arguing. 'Perhaps. But till that's proven, Humbert, you'll clap tongue. Clemen is only just finding its feet again. The last thing we need is for tensions to rise again between our duchies, and the sleeping Marches to wake.'

And so they walked in stiff silence for the second time that day. But any thought he'd had of taking some time to sit quietly to try and make sense of Garith's news and decide who else he could send out nosing for answers was chased away by Nathyn. The agitated chief steward rushed to him as he and Humbert stamped through the persistent rain and spreading puddles across Eaglerock's deserted forecourt.

'Your Grace! Your Grace! 'Tis the duchess, Your Grace. Her ladies attend and the midwife is sent for.'

Angry impatience forgotten, Roric clutched at Humbert's arm. 'It's too soon. The babe's not due till late next month.'

'A pox on the midwife,' said Humbert. 'Send for Arthgallo. My daughter will have the best leech in Clemen.'

He took a deep breath, trying not to vomit. 'Arthgallo chose the midwife, remember? He said from the start he was no—'

'I don't care what he said!' Humbert bellowed. 'Do you love my daughter or not?'

Not, as it happened. Though he wanted to, and every day hated himself for wishing she was Catrain. A secret he'd keep from her father at all costs.

'Nathyn,' he said, trying to sound calm, 'fetch Arthgallo.'

Leaving Nathyn to obey, Roric let Humbert hustle him into the castle and up countless stairs to Lindara's apartments. They were met in the empty dayroom by her barnacle of a lady's maid, Eunise, limped out of retirement to serve her mistress again. Seeing them, she spread her blue linen skirts and offered a creaking curtsy.

'Eunise,' Humbert snapped, 'where are Her Grace's ladies? They should be in attendance. Do they dare—'

'Her Grace dismissed them, my lord,' the nursemaid said, her voice cracked and quavered with age. 'And she requests that you and His Grace do not come to her. She'll see you once the child is born and no sooner.'

Humbert growled. 'Stand aside, you decrepit besom. I'm her father and the duke is her husband. She'll see us when I say she'll—'

'Peace, Humbert,' Roric said, as Eunise lifted her whiskered chin and backed against the closed bedchamber door. 'Are you widowed so long you forget a woman's vanity? Whenever did you know Lindara wanting anyone to see her with a hair out of place?' He managed a smile. 'Except for after the toil of a good hunt, of course.'

'Exactly so, Your Grace,' Eunise said. 'Now, if you'll excuse me? I'd return to my lady.'

'Go. Be with my wife. And tell Lindara her husband and father sit vigil for her.'

'Miserable old bitch,' Humbert muttered, groping for the dayroom's padded settle. 'She was a sweeter piece thirty years ago.'

'Weren't we all, my lord,' he murmured, and chose a gilded chair.

Soon afterwards, the midwife and her assistant came. On their heels, Arthgallo. They uttered vague, encouraging platitudes then vanished within the mystery of Lindara's bedchamber. Eaglerock's most senior exarchite arrived, uninivited, trailing an acolyte and incense. In no mood for hearing a lecture on powers that might or might not exist, Roric sent them away – but politely. To be safe. The candle-clock above the fireplace melted through the hours. Servants brought them dry doublets and hose and robes, and he and Humbert changed out of their rain-soaked clothing to avoid an ague. Other servants brought messages of support from the council, and at noon carried in trays of food and wine. Roric and Humbert ate, needing something to do other than wait in frightened silence. And the braised beef helped calm bellies churned by the muffled cries from behind the stubbornly closed bedchamber door. At sunset servants brought roast capon and sweet cider. Again they ate. What else could they do? Arthgallo emerged once to utter more vague reassurances, then shut himself away with Lindara and the midwife again. Soon after that there were raised voices, then Eunise was sent out. The old woman left the chamber protesting her dismissal, but Arthgallo would not be moved. Eunise left Lindara's apartments and didn't return.

Midnight crept closer, and still no word of a child. Light-headed with fear, Roric pressed a shaking hand to his face. Stubble prickled, and his skin felt like ill-cured parchment.

'I can't bear this, Humbert. We've had so many false hopes and disappointments. What if—'

'Clap tongue,' said Humbert, rasping. 'I'll not listen to gloomy wallowings. You'll soon be a father, Roric. Tell yourself that.'

He let his hand fall. 'My lord, I'm trying.'

'Try harder.'

With no heart to scold Humbert's frightened rudeness, Roric closed his eyes and waited, as wood burned in the fireplace and the night crept towards another sunrise on leaden, hobbled feet.

Some two hours later, a woman's piercing cry leapt him out of his chair. Humbert leapt with him, and they stared at each other with fear and terrible hope. Moments later they heard the mewling, high-pitched wail of a newborn babe. Then the bedchamber door opened, and Arthgallo emerged.

One look at him, and Roric felt his legs threaten to give way. 'No. No.'

Beneath his stained, rumpled canvas cap, the leech's face was haggard with strain and grief. 'I am sorry, Your Grace. The child breathes . . . but not for long.'

Overwhelmed, unable to offer comfort to groaning Humbert, he followed Arthgallo into Lindara's candlelit chamber. His wife lay weakly panting and sweat-soaked on the birthing board, her linen shift rucked to her waist, her spread thighs smeared with blood. The bloodstained midwife, as sweaty and exhausted as her charge, murmured low encouragement while kneading Lindara's lax, emptied belly in rhythmic circles. Her young assistant, cheeks tear-runnelled, stood beside her and stared at the floor.

'Your Grace.'

Tearing his gaze from Lindara, Roric turned. 'Arthgallo?'

The leech cradled a small, linen-coddled bundle against his chest. 'Your Grace, here is your daughter.'

Daughter. Even as the word hammered iron through his heart, he was holding out his arms. And then, as Arthgallo surrendered the babe to him, he felt a terrible wave of relief.

If it must die, better it should die a girl. Not a son. Not my heir.

He looked down. Felt his breath catch. No relief now, only revulsion. Even after so many years, he remembered little Liam on the day of his birth. Pink and plump and gusty with life. But this – this – *creature*? So pale, almost grey. Wizened and wrinkled, limbs twisted. Face deformed and pinched with pain. Tiny mouth gasping for air. For life. It looked hardly human, looked more like a faery changeling, as though the old tales had come true.

This is what springs from my seed? This – this thing?

'Roric?'

He couldn't show Humbert. The old man might drop where he stood. He kept his back to the open door. 'Arthgallo's right, my lord. There's no hope. Leave us. I'd not have you distressed for no reason.'

'Fuck that, boy. I'll see my grandson.'

''Tis a girl, Humbert. Lindara birthed a girl.'

'Even so, I'll see it.'

Low, skin-crawling laughter from the bed. 'Do you hear that, Your Grace? *Even so, he'll see it.* What magnanimity. What generosity of spirit. Am I not blessed among women, to have a father like him?'

'*Clap tongue, Lindara!*'

'No, Humbert. I will not *clap tongue*. After all these years with my tongue clapped I've birthed a living child and now, my lord, *now*, it is my turn to speak!'

Shocked by her raw bitterness, Roric shifted to look at them. Humbert and Lindara stared at each other with such malice, such hatred, it threatened to freeze his blood. The midwife with her bloody hands and canvas apron backed away from the bed, beckoning her assistant to join her beside the fireplace, out of the way.

Arthgallo moved to Lindara's side, his stained hands raised to calm. 'My lady, please, contain your passions. 'Tis not wise for a woman newly delivered to so upset herself. You've not passed the childbed yet and you won't be out of harm's way till that's done.'

Lindara laughed again. This time she sounded wild. 'You stupid fuck of a leech, I won't be out of harm's way till I'm dead.'

'*Lindara*—'

'No, my lord!' Arthgallo said, stepping between Humbert and Lindara. 'Harness your temper. The lady's in my care and—'

'And much good it's done her!' Humbert roared. 'Clemen needed a son from this birthing, Arthgallo! One that would live, and thrive, and carry the future on his back!'

'Don't you blame him!' Lindara spat, struggling to sit up against her pillows. 'This is your doing, old man! That gross lump of flesh in Roric's arms, that is what your meddling has wrought!'

Bewildered, Roric looked down at the barely breathing thing he held, then up again. He felt like a man stumbled into the midst of a mummers' play, watching a story unfold that they knew and he didn't.

'Humbert, what is this? What does she mean?'

Humbert turned, and for the first time his gaze fell upon his daughter's child. He shuddered, one hand lifting as though he'd ward away evil. ''Tis a tragedy, Roric. One of nature's cruel tricks. But don't despair, boy. There's hope yet. You must try again and—'

'My lord, I don't advise it,' Arthgallo said, his voice low. 'I did warn you after Her Grace's last stillbirth. Your daughter—'

'My daughter has no say in this! She will do—'

'*Nothing!*' said Lindara, sweat pouring down her face. 'And *you* will do *nothing*. You have done *enough*, Humbert. And after this I'm *quit* of you! I'm quit of you, I'm quit of Roric, I am quit of all the lies!'

'What lies?' Roric demanded. 'Arthgallo, you say you warned Humbert? Warned him of what?'

Humbert stabbed a pointing finger. 'Clap tongue, Arthgallo! What we spoke of is privy. Roric—'

'You want to know what your dear foster-lord and his tame leech spoke of?' Lindara taunted. 'Then I shall tell you, husband. It's been a night for birthing, so let me at last deliver the truth. And when you hold it like you hold that repulsive monstrosity I hope you—'

'Not one more word, Lindara!' Humbert shouted. 'This is on your head, all of it. Woe to me that ever I sired such a traitorous bitch.'

'Enough, Humbert!' Roric said, dizzy with dread. 'That is my wife. Your daughter. If you can't deal with her gently then—'

'Of course he can't, Roric,' Lindara panted. 'You blind fucking fool. He hates me. I've ruined everything. And I don't fucking care. I'm glad his dreams are ruined. They were never my dreams. They were his and yours and I delight in their destruction. You fucking bastards ruined me. You ruined my poor Vidar. And now—'

'Vidar? What has Vidar to do with this?'

Humbert took a step towards the bed, his rage shot through with fear. 'Lindara, I forbid you. I *beg* you. Do not—'

'You beg me?' Lindara shrieked with laughter. 'But my lord, *I* begged *you*. On my knees and weeping I begged you not to force Roric upon me, not to destroy my hope of happiness, not to banish Vidar to the Marches, not to – not to—' Tears were coursing down her cheeks, washing away the sweat. 'Humbert, I *begged* you. So let me answer you now as you answered me then. *Fuck* what you want. I—'

Before Roric could stop him, Humbert snatched the mewling, misshapen child from his arms. Thrust it at Arthgallo and seized the leech by his arm. 'Get out.' Then he turned on the staring midwife and her assistant. Realised, too late, what the two women had seen and heard. 'You as well. Wait in the dayroom. And if I hear one *whisper* I'll see your corpses swinging on Gibbet Hill.'

As the shaken women scuttled from the chamber, Arthgallo stood tall. 'I will not abandon the lady Lindara. She is my patient and—'

'And she is my daughter! Take that monstrosity she spawned and leave us alone!'

Staring at Humbert, his gaunt face stiff with distaste, Arthgallo shook his head.

'Very well,' said Humbert, a wild-eyed stranger. 'The leech can stay, and we'll go. Come, Roric. There's nothing for us here.'

Though the room was warm, Roric felt cold to the bone. Frozen blood. Frozen marrow. A heart turned to ice. He looked at Arthgallo, so frightened he could hardly breathe.

'I think the truth is here. I'd stay to hear it. Arthgallo, what warning did you give Humbert? And do you know why the babe is so deformed?'

The leech's eyes were full of pity. Holding the child close, he sighed. 'After learning . . . certain things . . . I warned his lordship that a happy union between you and his daughter was unlikely. As for the rest . . .' He shrugged. 'Your Grace, ask your wife.'

'Arthgallo—' Breathe. Breathe. Ignore the crackling of frost. 'These *certain things*. They touch on me?'

'They do, Your Grace.'

'And yet you never told me.'

'No, Your Grace. To my shame. I was persuaded to keep silent.'

'Persuaded by my wife?'

'No, Your Grace. By her father.'

Humbert. 'Thank you, Arthgallo. Wait in the dayroom with the midwife and – take the child with you.'

As the chamber door closed behind the leech, Humbert lifted his whiskered chin. 'Now listen to me, Roric. This is no time to be hasty. Come away and we can—'

He closed the fingers of his raised hand slowly, until he held up a fist. '*Enough*.' Then he turned. 'Lindara?'

His wife had rolled onto her side, knees pulled to her chest, fingers twisting in the bloodstained hem of her shift. He didn't care. She could suffer. Until he knew the truth, she could suffer.

Lindara met his stare with familiar defiance. 'Your precious seed is tainted, Roric. For years, I tainted it. Humbert found out eventually but by then it was too late. Arthgallo's done his best. Did you never *wonder* at all the pills he gave you? He tried, but you'll never sire a normal son.' She smiled. 'Nor even a normal daughter, it seems, but I doubt you care for that. You or my father.'

Tainted. He was tainted. He could hear his own heart beating, a long way away. 'And this was your revenge? Because Humbert made you marry me?'

'No, Roric. I intended to bear Vidar's son and let you think the child was yours. *That* was to be my revenge.'

Another blow. He was almost too numb to feel it. 'You were fucking Vidar?'

She smiled again, a grimace of pain and contempt. 'From the day you and I were married, whenever and wherever and as many times as I could. Until Humbert sent him to the Marches, I was fucking Vidar. I love Vidar, Roric. I never loved you.'

'Yet you never bore him a son.'

A tear trailed down her cheek. 'Arthgallo suspects that in tainting you, I tainted myself. He fears I shall never give birth to a healthy child.'

Such stillness inside him. Such a vast, aching cold. 'And you don't care.'

'No. Not if it deprives you of an heir.'

He passed a shaking hand over his face. *Catrain*. He could have, should have, wed with Catrain.

'I don't understand. It's true we never shared a great passion, but Lindara . . . I did love you. As best I could. Why would you—'

Lurching upright, she hissed at him. 'As best you could, Roric? Your best was *shite*. You love your cock. You love Humbert. You love Clemen. Nothing else. I was only ever a womb to you, something to spill your seed in so you could have a son. Vidar loved me, Roric. Not you. *Vidar*. He *begged* you not to marry me and you didn't care. Remember?'

He couldn't look at her any more. Instead, he looked at Humbert. 'You knew?'

Humbert tugged at his beard, his face heavy with despair. 'Roric—'

'You knew.'

'Roric—'

'You knew and you didn't tell me.'

'Tell you what, boy?' cried Humbert, anguished. 'That my daughter is a fucking whore who cuckolded you for years right under my nose? That she consorted with a fucking witch to poison your seed with her potions? How could I tell you that? How could I—'

'*How could you not?*' Fighting the urge to empty his belly, Roric clutched at his pounding head. 'You said it yourself! My first, my

539

greatest duty, was to give Clemen its next duke, to confirm Berold's bloodline and close the door on the past. For years I've been trying and for years I have failed and in failing I've blamed *myself*! Believed I was being punished because at Heartsong I failed to save Liam's life. *You should have told me!'*

'Nothing would have changed! Don't you see, boy?' said Humbert, reaching for him. He was weeping. 'By the time I discovered my bitch of a daughter's treason it was too late. The damage to your seed was done. Arthgallo tried to tell me but I didn't want to believe him. I wanted to believe there was still a chance, still hope, and so—'

'And so you lied to me.' Roric stepped back. 'You bullied Arthgallo into lying. And you sent me back to Lindara's bed knowing she'd betrayed me, knowing that she *hated* me, knowing—' He turned away, afraid of what he might do. 'Humbert—'

'I stayed silent for you, Roric!' Humbert cried. 'I knew this would break your heart, I knew how you'd—'

'*Liar!*' he said, spinning round. 'You stayed silent for *yourself*! So you wouldn't be shamed, so you wouldn't be blamed, so you could make up for the loss of Lindara's brothers and claim yourself Berold's equal in the bloodline of Clemen's dukes!'

'No, Roric, no, I never—'

'I *trusted* you, Humbert. With my life. With this duchy. Since I was seven years old I have loved you like a father. Obeyed you as though I were your dutiful son and raised you to be the second-highest man in Clemen. And *this* is how you thank me? *This* is my reward?'

In the bed, Lindara laughed. 'Don't sound so surprised, Roric. He might love you like you're his flesh and blood but I *am* his flesh and blood and that never once stopped him from—'

'Lindara?' he said, as she doubled over on a dreadful cry of pain. 'Lindara! Humbert, fetch Arthgallo!'

As Humbert blundered to the door, Roric crossed to the bed. Took hold of his wife's ice-cold hand and dropped to one knee. 'Be brave, Lindara. Hold on. Help is coming.'

Moaning, she dragged open her sunken eyes. 'Tell Vidar I'm sorry. Tell him I know I wasn't always kind.'

The request stole his breath. Mute, he stared at her. Seeing his hurt, her face twisted.

'Fuck you, Roric,' she whispered. 'Fuck you. I hope it all ends in tears.'

And then came the gushing blood, like a raging scarlet river bursting its banks.

CHAPTER THIRTY-TWO

Another sunrise. Another day in his life. Looking over the parapet of Eaglerock castle's harbour-side balcony, watching the white-caps on the water and the first scurrying skiffs, the previous day's clouds and rain a memory, Roric breathed in the damp air and breathed it out, a hollow, whistling sound.

Widowed. I am widowed. My wife is dead. I'm alone.

The deformed baby was dead too. That grey-faced, mewling thing Lindara had pushed out of her body with so much screaming effort and pain. He couldn't think of it as his daughter. Could hardly think of it at all. After pronouncing Lindara dead, Arthgallo had taken it away and returned a short while later with a different dead babe to be entombed with Lindara. Another girl. One that looked nothing like a changeling faery. Where the leech had procured it, where its mother was, how it died? He didn't know. He never wanted to know. Every part of his body felt bruised and broken. Like a man unhorsed in a melee and trampled by countless hooves in the mud.

I am a widowed, childless cuckold. Oh, yes. And a bastard duke.

Duke of a struggling duchy. Duke of a dispirited people who were now being stolen and sold into slavery. A duke made incapable of siring an heir. Though Arthgallo, after doing what had to be done with Lindara's bloodsoaked body, had urged his duke not to lose hope. There might yet be herbs in the world, rare and obscure, capable of restoring some life to His Grace's seed. He would hunt for them. His Grace must not despair.

Poor Arthgallo. The leech was inconsolable over Lindara's death and the disaster of her pregnancy. Weeping, on his knees, he'd begged forgiveness for failing Clemen, for not telling his duke the truth. But the lies, the omissions, weren't the leech's fault. There Humbert was to blame, so Arthgallo had been forgiven. And because he'd already proven himself to be an honourable man, his sworn oath never to reveal what he knew was accepted.

Sadly, the midwife and her assistant were another matter. Even now they languished in Eaglerock's dungeons, where they could tell no one what they'd seen and heard. And whether they'd ever look upon the light of day again, well . . . that was a question without an answer, for now.

The only remaining loose end was Humbert.

Eaglerock's servants kept the hinges of every door in the castle well-oiled, but even so Roric heard the portal behind him swing open. Heard hesitant footsteps and a cautious clearing of throat.

'Your Grace?'

Nathyn. Cool of head and steady of nerve. Discreet, reliable, loyal Nathyn, who'd sobbed once when he was told of Lindara and after that said nothing but *Yes, Your Grace* or *No, Your Grace*, or *I will see it done, Your Grace*.

Roric kept his gaze upon the harbour. 'Well?'

'The proclamations are being given to the heralds now, Your Grace. They'll be riding out shortly. And soon the passing bells will toll in Eaglerock. Indeed, in every corner of Clemen.'

Indeed. 'But not in the Marches.'

'No, Your Grace. Though word will spread.'

Yes, but not swiftly enough to interfere with his plans. 'Her Grace's body? Her apartments?'

'The duchess and – and the child – lie at peace in the Great Hall, Your Grace. Three exarchites stand with them, saying prayers for their souls. And Her Grace's ladies even now oversee the setting to rights of her bedchamber.'

'When that's done, tell her ladies to sit vigil with the duchess. Then have the apartments sealed.'

'Yes, Your Grace.'

'Something else, Nathyn?' he said, when the steward didn't withdraw.

'Yes, Your Grace.'

'Humbert?'

'His lordship is here, Your Grace, and would speak with you.'

He'd sent Humbert home after Lindara died. Hadn't known if he could trust himself not to find a sword and strike. Told his foster-lord not to show his face at court until he was summoned, knowing, even as he said it that Humbert would ignore him.

'Very well. Give Lord Humbert permission to approach and then leave us.'

'Yes, Your Grace.'

Nathyn retreated. A low murmur of voices, then heavier footsteps crossing the balcony. They stopped.

'Roric.'

He waited, to see if the sound of Humbert's voice would reawaken the hot desire to find a sword and run it through his foster-lord to the hilt. But no. He felt strangely calm. As though the cold, lonely hours after Lindara's death had bled him dry of passion.

'*Roric*.'

Still staring at the harbour, he raised a hand. 'No, my lord. Not any more.'

A small sound of distress. 'Your Grace.'

'You wanted something?'

'Your Grace – curse it, *Roric* – we're family, boy. The only family either of us has left.' A harsh breath. Almost a sob. 'I know you're hurt. But will you not even *look* at me?'

He had no desire to lay eyes on Humbert ever again. But they had unfinished business, so he turned around.

'My lord, you presume upon familiar acquaintance. I am your duke. That is all I am to you, or will ever be.'

Humbert's eyes were red-rimmed, his hair and beard disordered. He still wore the rust-brown doublet and hose he'd changed into after the harbour. The sleeveless, marten-trimmed robe he wore over them had a tear in one seam. He was dishevelled, all the confident

543

belligerence beaten out of him by grief. For the first time in his vigorous life, he looked an old man.

'So that's it?' he whispered, stoop-shouldered. 'I've lost you too?'

'You didn't lose me, Humbert. You tossed me away.'

'I didn't. Roric, I never—'

'*Your Grace*.'

Humbert's bulky body flinched. 'Your Grace.'

Roric narrowed his gaze, considering. 'You do understand, my lord, that you're entirely dishonoured?'

Another flinch. In the strengthening daylight, a glitter of tears. 'Yes.'

'What would you do to earn your honour back?'

'Your Grace?'

'You heard me, Humbert. What would you do?'

'Anything,' Humbert said, his pale, drawn face stiff with hope. 'Boy, I'd do anything to have things as they were.'

He clasped his hands behind his back, so Humbert couldn't see them shaking. 'Things will never be as they were. If that's your dream, let go of it now.'

Humbert dropped his chin to chest. 'Your Grace.'

'But if you mean what you say, then—'

'I do!' Humbert said eagerly, his head jerking up. 'I mean it heartily. This night just past, I—'

'However you spent last night, my lord, believe me when I say you spent it more kindly than I did.'

'*Roric . . .*' Humbert's grieving eyes widened with shock. 'My daughter is *dead*.'

Perhaps he'd been mistaken. Perhaps some passion remained after all. 'Yes, my lord,' he said, his jaw tight. 'She is. A great many things died last night. Among them any care I ever felt for what you might suffer.'

Humbert rocked where he stood, like a jouster buffeted by a lance.

'We waste time,' he added, deliberately brisk. 'Would you learn how you can reclaim your squandered honour, or shall we simply agree that—'

'No, Your Grace,' Humbert said, hands lifting. 'What would you have me do?'

544

'Remove yourself to the Marches. You can best serve Clemen now by taking Vidar's place.'

Humbert blinked. 'And Vidar?'

'You'll see him escorted back to Eaglerock by a score of the castle's most seasoned men-at-arms. After that, you'll put him from your mind. Your daughter's treasonous lover is no longer your concern.'

'Your Grace—' With an effort, Humbert swallowed. 'I think he must be my concern. For your sake, he must be. Vidar might be a disloyal cockshite but—' He took a step forward, his lax hands fisted. 'Roric, you can't—'

'Stand where you are and clap tongue, my lord! Every right you ever had of me is now and for ever forfeit! Do you not *grasp* that? Don't you know what you've *done*?'

Breathing hard, Humbert stepped back. 'And what of Vidar's wife? She's Aistan's daughter, you can't—' Pinched lips. Another shuddering breath. 'You're in no position to provoke the council.'

'Aistan's daughter and her children are innocent in this. They'll also return to Eaglerock, under my protection.'

'And how will you explain her husband in chains?'

Roric raised an eyebrow. 'I am duke of Clemen. I don't need to explain it.'

'Ah.' Humbert's face tightened. 'That's what Harald used to say.'

'Harald might've been a bastard but he wasn't always wrong.'

Humbert opened his mouth to reply, then changed his mind. Stamped to the balcony's red stone parapet and grasped it hard with both hands as he stared down at the slowly waking township. 'When should I leave?'

'How fast can you pack?'

'Can't wait to see the back of me?'

'No, my lord. I can't.'

Humbert's head dropped. 'Doubtless I deserved that.'

That, and much more. But he was weary. He wanted this done with. 'Leave tomorrow, at first light. Ride as hard and as fast as you can. Vidar's manor house is staffed and provisioned. You can send for whatever else you need at your leisure.'

'Tomorrow?' Humbert's fingers whitened on the parapet. 'I'd prefer to leave after Lindara's funeral.'

'No.'

'As you wish, Your Grace.' Letting go of the parapet, Humbert straightened. 'What about Garith? The Clemen folk being sold abroad?'

'That's not your concern. Look to the Marches. There is your domain now.'

Humbert sighed. 'Vidar won't simply take my word for it, you know. He won't suffer himself to be brought back here on my say-so alone. Not under armed escort.'

'Don't fret. You'll receive an official letter to take with you.'

Humbert turned. Still grieving, but with anger stirred beneath the sorrow. 'And if he demands to know what's behind his sudden disgrace?'

'Did I tell you to mention anything about disgrace?'

'You mean to cozen him, then? Lull him with platitudes and pap? You're a fool if you think he'll believe it. Vidar's sly as a fox.'

'And I'm trusting you to outfox him. Or do I ask too much?'

Humbert hesitated, then dragged a hand down his face and over his beard. 'No, Your Grace. You don't.'

'Good,' he said, smiling thinly. 'Then be about your business. If you need help with anything, speak to Nathyn. He has my full confidence.'

Another hesitation. 'You're sure about this, are you?' Humbert said at last. 'You think the Marches will be safe in my hands?'

'I wouldn't send you if I wasn't. I know how much you love Clemen. I know you'd give your life to protect it.'

'And you, boy,' said Humbert, his voice breaking. 'I'd give my life to protect you.'

'I wonder,' he said slowly. 'Did you ever say that to Lindara?'

For a moment, he thought he might see his foster-lord drop dead at his feet. He'd seen men die in the Marches with that stricken look in their eyes.

'Farewell, Humbert. Go to the Marches. And there redeem yourself, if you can.'

* * *

The draggle of villagers huddled in the wooded clearing at sword-point were so ragged, filthy and hungry Vidar almost felt sorry for them. But only almost. Leaving his five men-at-arms to keep them docile, he jogged his horse back and forth across the overgrown woodland track and gave his temper free rein.

'*Doltards!* Don't you know we stand not a stone's throw from the Harcian Marches? Were your dirty fingers stuck in your ears the day Roric's heralds rode into your village and told you what happens when trespassing Clemen-folk cross paths with Balfre of Harcia?'

The oldest of the villagers, a man in his middle years, took a cringing step towards him. 'My lord, we were desperate. Root-rot took half our crops and a river flood took what was left, then washed away near every cottage.'

'And did it wash away your sense of direction too? Why not head up-river to Branstock? They lost people in the pestilence. You'd have found yourselves homes there.'

Uneasy, the man exchanged glances with his fellow villagers. 'You ain't heard, my lord?'

'Heard what?'

'There do be rumours of folk going missing round Branstock way.'

'*Missing?*' He stared at the man. 'Faeries took them, I suppose. No – hold your tongue, man. I've heard enough.'

Fuck. Strict treaty governed how many folk could live in the Marches. Every year there was a head count, with Clemen testing Harcia and Harcia testing Clemen. Not to mention gossip and the excitement provoked by unfamiliar faces. Even if he wanted to, he couldn't risk letting a dozen villagers remain.

'You can't stay in the Marches,' he said roughly. 'Go to – to Cobley. I'll send men-at-arms with you, to make sure—'

'No, my lord! Not Cobley!' a skinny woman protested, two skinny children hanging from the ragged hem of her dress. 'There be black-lung broke out in Cobley, my lord.'

'Black-lung?' Vidar jabbed at his horse's mouth, hauling it into retreat. 'You fools have brought *black-lung* into the Marches? *Fuck.* I should run a sword through you where you stand!'

'No, my lord!' The man threw up his arms, pleading. 'Soon as we heard there was black-lung, we bolted. Came here to be safe. We never walked anywhere close to Cobley. There be none of us sick. Not with black-lung. Not with anything. We be cold and hungry, no more than that.'

Now the village brats were crying, five of them wailing and snotting, making their mothers shriek. Tempted, so tempted, to act on his threat, Vidar backed his horse until its rump struck a low-hanging tree branch. Was the man lying? He and the others weren't coughing up clots of blood, and beneath the copious dirt they seemed unblemished.

Black-lung? Why hadn't Roric sent a warning and closed the Marches road?

'How long have you been skulking here?'

'Three days, my lord,' the woman said, clutching her snotty brats.

'And when did the black-lung start?'

'Some seven days ago, I think.'

Seven days. And with Cobley not important, likely that explained why the news of black-lung was yet to reach Eaglerock. Three days was enough time for the illness to take hold. So it seemed these fools – and the Marches – had escaped infection.

'Bodham.'

Lowering his sword, the serjeant approached. 'My lord?'

'We're near Hogget's farm. You and the men herd these churls there. Hold them on my authority and send a man to fetch Izusa. If she counts them clean, borrow a cart from Hogget and take them over the border to – to—'

'Craikstone?' Bodham suggested. 'It's not so far.'

'Fine. Craikstone. Tell its people to take these fools, by order of their duke. Have Hogget feed them, and provide bread, cheese and ale for the road. He can send a reckoning of his costs to the manor but warn him I'll know if he thinks to cheat me.'

Bodham's thin face twitched near to a smile. 'Yes, my lord. That's very – strict – of you, my lord.'

Bodham was an impertinent bastard.

He rode away from the gratefully babbling villagers without a single backwards glance. The day wasn't quite half over, but before he did anything else he needed to send word of the black-lung outbreak to Roric. So, once clear of the confining woodland, he spurred his horse into a canter and headed home.

There was a score of Eaglerock men-at-arms cluttering up his stables and rear courtyard.

'My lord,' their unfamiliar serjeant said, indifferently bowing. 'We're with Lord Humbert. He waits for you in the manor.'

He handed his horse's reins to a goggle-eyed stable lad. 'Does he, indeed?'

Still indifferent, the serjeant nodded. 'Yes, my lord.'

Given the upheaval of their generally quiet life, Vidar thought he'd be met indoors by Kennise, overflowing with tears and questions. But the manor's entrance hall was empty.

He found Humbert in the Great Hall.

'Vidar,' he said calmly. As though they'd laid eyes on each other only a day or so before.

Vidar halted just inside the doorway. 'Humbert. How unexpected. Have you been waiting long?'

Lindara's grizzled, travel-splashed father wore mail beneath his green wool surcoat. A sword and a dagger were belted by his side. 'Some little time. It doesn't matter. You're here now.'

'I was taken up with Marcher business. A dozen Clemen villagers found in Hogget wood this morning. My serjeant and some men will shortly take them back to Clemen. A close-run thing. They all but trod on Balfre's toes.'

'But you've dealt with them,' Humbert said, frowning.

Vidar smiled, like a good host. 'I have. Tell me, you've been served refreshment?'

'It was offered. Vidar—'

He wandered a little further into the hall. 'Egann will be sorry he missed you. He's in the western Marches, training a handful of new men-at-arms. He's a good man, Humbert. I'll confess, when first you foisted him on me I was far from pleased. I know you sent him here to spy. I know you thought – you hoped – he'd catch me in some grave misdoing. But it turns out we work well together. Have you come to take him home?'

Humbert's hands were tucked under his surcoat. His shoulders rose and fell as he breathed. 'No.'

'Good! By the way, I have news. There's black-lung not far over the border. In Cobley. Did you know? Does Roric?'

'I didn't,' Humbert said, his chin tucked to his chest. 'His Grace might. I've been riding hard for some days.'

'Yes. You do look weary.' Abruptly aware of his silent house, Vidar glanced around. 'You were offered refreshments, you said. By my wife? Where is she?'

'Upstairs. With your children.'

'I see. And tell me, if you've not come to take Egann home, just why *are* you downstairs, Humbert, standing in my hall?'

In answer, Humbert withdrew a sheet of folded, sealed parchment from beneath his surcoat. 'I am here on His Grace's behalf.'

Oh, but there was something gone horribly wrong. Looking closely, he could see Humbert was more than weary. He was butchered with grief. The pain in his bearded face was the same pain he'd failed to hide when years ago he lost his wife and then both his sons. But if Roric was yet living, then who . . .

Lindara.

Feeling sick, he moistened his dry lips. 'Humbert, what has happened?'

Lindara's father thrust the parchment at him. 'His Grace has written to—'

'And what's this *His Grace* shite? He's Roric to you.' He grimaced. 'Or boy.'

Humbert winced. 'Read the fucking letter, Vidar.'

'You read it,' he said, trusting in the clamour of instinct. 'Out loud. That way we'll both know what Roric says.'

'Very well.' His gloved fingers unsteady, Humbert broke the parchment's crimson wax seal. Unfolded the letter. Tipped it a little to one side so it caught the light streaming through the hall's window. '*My lord Vidar, after some years of serving me in the Marches I can only imagine how you long for home. Therefore you may relinquish your Marcher lordship into Lord Humbert's faithful hands and return to Eaglerock with your family so I might reward you as you deserve. Roric. Duke of Clemen.*'

Vidar swallowed, close to gagging. Not for a moment did he believe a word. Not with Humbert standing there, looking like death. His world, his world, it was tumbling down.

'So. Roric knows. After all these years. He knows.'

Carefully, Humbert folded the parchment. 'Yes.'

'Everything?'

A flicker in Humbert's eyes confirmed it. 'You're to leave at once, Vidar. You and your family. Eaglerock's men-at-arms will escort you to the castle.'

His skin was slicked with sweat. 'You mean Roric's men-at-arms. I'm under arrest?'

'There's no mention of arrest in the letter, Vidar.'

'Fuck the letter! *He knows*. Who told him, Humbert? You?'

'No.'

He almost laughed. 'Of course it was. It had to be. Lindara would never betray me. Fuck, why would you *do* it? When I've done everything you wanted, stayed away, buried myself here in these fucking Marches, never once tried to reach her.' He bent double, hands braced on his thighs, fighting to breathe, not to vomit. 'What the fuck possessed you, Humbert?'

Humbert said nothing.

Slowly unfolding, Vidar stared at the pale and shaken old man. 'You ask me to believe it *was* Lindara who told him? Why would she tell him? She wouldn't.'

Still, Humbert said nothing.

And now the fear was building, roaring in like a tempest. He was rarely a man for weeping and yet he wanted to weep.

'What's Roric done, Humbert? Fuck. Has he killed her? Don't tell me you're standing there doing that bastard's bidding and she's lying dead somewhere because he's *killed* her!'

Humbert shook his head.

Grinding a fist into his damaged hip, Vidar struggled to keep his balance. 'But she is dead. Isn't she.'

Humbert pressed a calloused hand to his face and wept.

Lindara. If Roric didn't kill her, then how could she be dead? And then he remembered. She was – she had been – pregnant.

'It was childbirth?' he said, choking. 'Are you saying childbirth killed her?'

'Yes,' said Humbert, muffled.

'And the baby?'

'Deformed by the witching poisons you and she fed to Roric.'
Humbert let his hand fall, and now his face was full of rage. 'And
so the truth gushed out, you cockshite, like the blood that gushed
between my daughter's legs.'

He had no words. Only pain and sickness and a tempest of grief.
If I weep for her now, I think Humbert will kill me.

'What does Kennise know? What have you told her?'

'Nothing,' Humbert said. 'You can tell your wife. Whatever you
like. I don't give a fuck. Only tell her now, Vidar, so I can get you
out of my sight.'

Lindara.

How could one man's body contain such a loss? Surely he should
be bleeding. Surely his bones should break.

He bowed, awkwardly. 'Then if you'll excuse me, my lord?'

'Never,' said Humbert, his eyes savage. 'But you can go.'

'Vidar!' Kennise leapt to her feet, shaking with nerves. 'Why is Lord
Humbert here, and all those men-at-arms? Is it Harcia? Does Balfre—'

He shoved the chamber door shut. 'No. This is nothing to do with
Balfre. Where are the children?'

'In their dayroom, with Inogen. I didn't want them to see me
afraid. Vidar—'

'*Fuck, woman! Be quiet! Can't you see I need to think?*'

Tearful, she stood and waited, fingers pressed against her lips. He
hated her for being so docile. Lindara would've slapped his face if
ever he spoke like that to her.

Lindara.

'Vidar!' Kennise cried, and rushed to him. 'Are you ill? Should
I send for that healer woman? Vidar?'

He had no choice but to let her help him to the settle where he
could sit, and try to breathe. She had his hand in hers, she was chafing
his cold fingers. Her touch sickened him. Fuck. *Fuck*. He couldn't
go back to Eaglerock. Roric was going to kill him. Or seal him in a
dungeon for the rest of his life. Death would be kinder. Roric wouldn't
be kind. After what he'd done, no man would be kind. Fuck. *Fuck*.
He couldn't stay here.

Sweating, he sat straight. Made himself look into his wife's eyes, with kindness. 'Kennise, my love, I need you to keep company with Humbert. He comes to us with dire news. Lindara is dead in child-birth. So – you should comfort him. His only daughter is dead and I can't – I'm not—' He laced his fingers with hers. 'He needs a woman's care.'

'Oh, Vidar,' she whispered, tears spilling. 'Poor Humbert. Poor *Roric*. Of course I'll comfort him. But—'

'Tell him I go to see his men-at-arms settled in the barracks. As soon as that's done I'll join you and together we'll do what we can to ease his grief.'

She pulled a kerchief from her narrow sleeve and began dabbing her cheeks dry. 'Yes. We must.'

He had to explain the men-at-arms. 'Kennise, Humbert's men are here to escort us home. We're returning to Clemen.'

'*Vidar!*' Disbelieving joy lit her, and then she faltered. 'Oh. Oh, I shouldn't be happy. How wicked of me to be happy when—'

'No. Not wicked.' He stood, drawing her with him. 'This is a painful tangle. Be happy with me . . . but grieve with Humbert. Now go. He needs you.'

'Do you come downstairs?'

'Not yet. Recall that I knew Lindara, and liked her well. I'd have a moment, Kennise, to – to—'

'Of course,' she murmured, and kissed him. 'She was your friend. I'm so sorry.'

The chamber door closed gently. Heart racing, sick with grief and fear, he crushed his hands to his face. He couldn't stay. He had to run. Now, while Kennise distracted Humbert and the men-at-arms were tired and hungry after their hard ride from Eaglerock. He had to run. He had to run.

If only he knew where.

Pleasantly exhausted after a good night's fucking with Izusa, Balfre ambled his horse into his manor's torchlit stable yard. It was late. Closer to dawn than midnight. No stable lads scurried at the sound of hoofbeats. Obedient to his lightest whim, they remained ignorant in their beds. It meant he must act as his own groom but that was a small price to pay to keep his business privy.

The other horses shuffled and whickered, roused by his arrival. He returned his horse to its stable, stripped it of saddle and bridle, covered the animal with a horse blanket against the night's chill, then carried the tack into the tack room and left it on the bench for cleaning.

In the lamplit feed room, scooping oats into a wooden pail, he heard a faint, hesitant shuffle in the glooming shadows. Caught the rank scent of stale human sweat. Easing his dagger clear of its sheath, he let the oat scoop fall.

'Step into the light and I might gut you,' he said. 'Skulk in the corner and I will certainly gut you. Either way, you fuck, you've picked the wrong place to trespass.'

'Have I?' rasped a familiar voice. 'Are you sure about that?'

Astonished, Balfre turned. A painful, dragging sound . . . and Vidar limped into the lamplight. Filthy. Unkempt. Doublet and hose stained and torn. His raised hands were red with bramble scratches. More scratches marred his already marred face. In his one good eye, the gleam of utter desperation.

'Balfre.'

'By the Exarch's balls,' he said, raising an eyebrow. 'What the fuck are you doing here?'

'What does it look like?'

Keeping hold of his dagger, he leaned a hip against the oat bin. 'It looks to me like you've been playing hide-and-seek in the Marches – and losing. It looks to me that you are a man on the run. Dare I ask why?'

Vidar scowled. 'In my experience, Balfre, there's nothing you wouldn't fucking dare.'

'True.' He laughed. 'So, Vidar. Let me guess. This has something to do with Humbert's noisy arrival in the Marches yesterday. Twenty men-at-arms, I'm told.' He shook his head. 'Tut, tut, my lord. What *did* you do?'

Vidar didn't answer. Turning aside, he groped at the bin of horsebread for support. He looked tormented.

'My lord, your choice is simple,' he said tartly. 'Tell me all and keep a free man, or keep your counsel and be delivered to Humbert.'

'Fuck,' Vidar muttered. 'You really are a cockshite, Balfre.'

'And yet here you stand. More or less. In need of my help.'

That earned him a one-eyed glare. He waited, indifferent. Considered the tumult of emotions playing over Vidar's face. Smiled as he witnessed the moment of collapse.

'Roric's wife is dead in childbirth.'

'Is she? Well, it does happen. But what has that to do with—'

'Her name was Lindara.' Vidar's voice cracked on the name. 'She was Humbert's daughter.'

'That's common knowledge, even in Harcia.'

'She was *mine*, Balfre. Roric stole her. With Humbert's connivance.'

Understanding dawned. 'You cuckolded your duke? And in her death throes the bitch confessed?'

'She was no bitch!'

'Now, Vidar. Keep your voice down. Unless you want my men-at-arms to come running.'

'She was no bitch,' Vidar said again, but quietly. 'She was beautiful and I loved her.'

The grief was genuine. Intrigued, Balfre tapped fingers to his dagger's hilt. 'Then why did you leave her for the Marches?'

Vidar's face turned sullen. 'Humbert discovered us.'

'But kept the truth from Roric. To save his daughter, yes?'

'And himself.'

'Of course. Family honour.' Balfre rolled his eyes. 'And he had you exiled here. But now the truth's come out. *Secrets*. They do have a nasty habit of finding the light. And that's the whole sordid story?'

Vidar closed his eye. 'Yes.'

No. That was a lie. 'Vidar . . .'

'What do the details matter?' Vidar demanded, his voice cracking again. 'You know the broad strokes and the outcome is the same. Roric seeks revenge, and I would keep my life.'

'Details matter because I say they matter,' he retorted. 'What madness makes you think you have any power here?'

'Fuck you, Balfre! My madness was in thinking I could ask you for help!'

'And it could be that I am mad enough to give it. But unless you tell me everything, this conversation will end on the point of my sword!'

In Vidar's scarred face, another struggle. And then, soon after, another collapse. 'My son was to be Clemen's next duke. Not Roric's. *Mine!*'

Silence. Nearby, in the stables, horses shifted in their straw.

'Fuck,' he said at last, admiring. 'No wonder Roric wants you dead.'

'Yes,' Vidar said raggedly. 'He must hate me almost as much as I hate him. So will you help me, Balfre? You'll not regret it.'

'Why come to me? Your mortal enemy?'

'Where else could I go?' With a contemptuous flick of his hand, Vidar indicated his face and hip. 'I'm hardly inconspicuous. Or fleet of foot.'

'You could've surrendered to Roric.'

Vidar laughed. 'Would you?'

'And what of your wife? Your daughters?'

'Aistan will protect them. Roric won't cross him.'

'And your duke? Surely he'll hunt you.'

'Not if he believes I'm dead.'

He grinned. 'So. You'd have me counterfeit your demise and thereby protect you from a vengeful Roric. And in return . . .'

'I told you,' said Vidar, his face stiff. 'You'll have no regrets.'

Balfre looked at him, eyes half-lidded. Then he pushed away from the oat bin and paced a little, deep in thought. Hide Vidar from Roric. It was an interesting idea. The man knew Clemen and its duke better than anyone else he had to hand. And knowledge was power. Vidar could be his secret weapon. A knife to be hidden until the perfect time to strike. But there was danger in keeping him. Vidar's was a familiar, unforgettable face. Unless . . .

Izusa. She was a witch, and had sworn to help him. She had to know some way of keeping Vidar unknown.

'Are you fit to ride, my lord?'

With an effort, Vidar straightened. 'Why?'

'Are you fit? Yes or no?'

'I can ride. Where are we going?'

'What do you care? Do you want my help or not?'

Vidar's breath caught. 'Yes.'

'And you'll have it. But in return, you'll do as you're told.

Whatever I ask, you'll answer. Whatever I want, you'll give. Agreed?'

Vidar's lamplit, ruined face told the story of his last and hardest struggle. So did his battered body and the way he gasped for air. Watching him, Balfre smiled. An easy treachery was no treachery he could trust. But a man in pain? That was useful. Men in pain were easily wooed . . . and won.

'Vidar?' he said kindly. 'Let me help you.'

With another unsteady inward breath, Vidar opened his one good eye. Then all the fight went out of him. His sigh was a shout of surrender.

'Thank you,' he whispered.

Balfre smiled. 'You're welcome.'

Roric rested his elbows on the arms of his chair and steepled his fingers. Rain washed the stained-glass window of his privy audience chamber. He tried not to notice it. Tried not to see fields full of rotting grain. Before him stood Aistan and the lord's youngest daughter, Kennise. Vidar's widow. She clutched her father's hand as though she were still a child, looking to him for every answer. He felt the old guilt prick him. What she was, Harald had made her. And because he'd been young and elsewhere, he'd done nothing to stop his cousin. Now she was suffering again, the innocent victim of another man's crime. Just when he thought he couldn't hate Vidar any more . . .

'I'm sorry, my lady,' he said gently. 'I'm afraid it's not good news.'

Aistan stiffened. 'Vidar is dead, Your Grace? You're sure of it?'

He was. Humbert's men-at-arms had discovered the body in a creek. After several days in the water it had been somewhat the worse for wear, but his clothing was recognised, and a well-known family ring, and enough had remained of him that Humbert could vouch some scars.

'Tis Vidar, he'd written. *He guessed the truth and ran rather than face you. I swear, Your Grace, I never thought him such a coward. I know you wanted him punished. So did I. But at least the cockshite's dead.*

Scant comfort. He'd wanted to look Vidar in the eye and tell him, without mercy, how Lindara had died.

'Your Grace?'

He looked up. 'Quite sure, Aistan. His remains are on the road back to Eaglerock even now.'

'I don't understand,' said Aistan, puzzled, as his daughter softly wept. 'Why did Vidar run when Humbert brought him such happy news?' Then he flushed. 'Your Grace, forgive me, I did not—'

'Peace, my lord. I know what you meant. And Humbert's news was surely welcome, in part.'

'In part it was, Your Grace,' Kennise whispered. 'For though my dear husband and I were pleased to serve you in the Marches, it was a sorrow to be kept so long from Eaglerock and my father.'

'And a greater sorrow yet that the cause for their return was your loss, Roric,' Aistan said, his face folding into grief. 'No wonder Humbert begged you to let him escape bitter memories in the Marches. It was generous of you to give him what he asked for. I know how much he means to you, and how he'll be missed.'

'As to that . . .' Roric looked at them steadily, showing them what they expected to see. 'I think Humbert wasn't the only one to be tormented by grief. Vidar and my wife cared for each other like brother and sister. Humbert suspects Vidar's wits were disordered by her loss.'

'A tragedy compounded,' Aistan murmured. 'So much misery.' Lifting his daughter's hand, he kissed it. 'Your Grace . . .' He settled his shoulders. 'It's no secret we've had our differences. But even so, I have never lost faith in you. Never once doubted that you are Berold's heir. And you should know that everything I do . . . anything I have ever done . . . was only done with this duchy's best interests at heart.'

Staring at him, Roric sat back in his chair. And what was that? A confession? Was Aistan admitting his part in Cassinia's vendetta against Clemen, and Berardine, and innocent Catrain? He thought the man was. After years of deceitful silence, and with so much harm done, he should be angry. But he was too weary, all his anger spent on Humbert. Besides. What good would raging at Aistan do him now? Not even a witch could change the past.

It was curious though, that Aistan chose now to confess, however circumspectly. Had grief for his duke, and his daughter, and for Humbert, driven him to it? Or had guilt finally taken its toll? Whatever the reason, it didn't matter. Aistan was useful, so he'd use him. With Humbert in the Marches he had need of someone to stand with him against the likes of Ercole – who could no longer be dismissed or derided, thanks to his ties with Master Blane.

'Aistan,' he said, gravely, 'I'll treasure those words. My lady—' He slipped from his chair and moved to embrace Kennise. 'There is no sharper grief than the grief we feel for a lost love.'

Her thin arms tightened around him. 'No, Your Grace. But at least I have my children. I wish – I'm so sorry—'

'So am I.' Releasing her, he stepped back. 'Don't fear the future, Kennise. Coldspring remains yours. And when the time comes, I'll help you find your daughters good husbands.'

'Your Grace.' She curtsied, a pale, plain woman who'd never stood a chance against Humbert's brilliant daughter. 'You are a good man.'

'Thank you, Roric,' Aistan murmured. 'I'd take her home now.'

'Of course. See to your daughter, my lord.'

Alone again, Roric returned to his chair. Dropped his head to his hands and closed his eyes, crushingly tired. Harald dead. Liam dead. Lindara dead, and their babe. Vidar dead. Humbert banished to a living death. And Catrain, imprisoned in Ardenn like Berardine before her, she might as well be in her coffin. So what did that leave him?

Clemen.

It would have to be enough.

CHAPTER THIRTY-THREE

Molly and Iddo were fighting again.

'Ye be a right fulsome feggit, Iddo! Feed them boys less, ye say? Willem and Benedikt be sixteen summers old, man! They b'aint babbies. D'ye want them dropping skin-and-bone dead on me, is that what ye want?'

The sound of a thump, as a fist struck wood. 'Ye b'aint never been a woman as wants to look the truth of them boys in the face,' Iddo shouted back at Molly. 'Be there work enough in the Whistle for me and Benedikt and that Willem? Coin enough for food to fill our bellies? Ye know there b'aint. Times be grim and growing grimmer. Ye got to 'prentice Willem out, Moll. 'Tis the only way we'll last.'

Sitting with Benedikt on the attic stairs, nursing a night candle and shamelessly listening to the muffled brawl in the kitchen, Liam felt his lip curl. There was Iddo, trying to get rid of him again. Ever since that whipping in the cellar, seared in his memory and never to be forgot, hardly a day passed that the Pig Whistle's barkeep failed to find reason to cuff him, complain about him, niggle Molly to shove him into some ditch. But even if she wanted to, on account of knowing he was the true duke of Clemen, and being afeared of that, which she was, she never would turn him out.

He wished she ignored Iddo for his sake, but it was Benedikt she kept him for. His brother was clutching his ankle, spluttering over Iddo's demand. He banged his knee against Benedikt's shoulder, to say *I know!* and *Clap tongue!*

Molly stopped clanging her cast-iron pots. 'Ye'll 'prentice Willem over my dead body, Iddo! The Marches will come good agin and till they do, we'll manage. Now why don't ye leave me to m'kitchen and see about chaining the dog out and putting the public room to rights and making sure all them doors and windows be locked and shuttered for the night.'

More iron banging, and the angry thud-thud of heavy booted feet on the floor. Liam nudged Benedikt, and with a rolling of eyes they walked tip-toe up the stairs and into the attic room they'd shared for years.

'That feggit Iddo,' said Benedikt, dropping onto his pallet bed. 'Ma should 'prentice *him* out.'

Liam latched the door, then used the night candle to light the tallow taper stuck in the wall beside Benedikt. 'Moll never would. He warms her bed too toasty.'

'Feggit!' Benedikt muttered, squirming. 'Don't ye make me think on that.'

Grinning, he lit his own taper. 'Bounce bounce bounce.'

'Clap tongue, ye bogshite!'

'Any road,' he said, relenting, then set the night candle in its iron holder, pinched it out, and collapsed with a grateful sigh onto his own bed. 'Feggit or not, Iddo's right to wrangle. Coin's scarce and so be easy pickings. It be weeks since we snared a rabbit in the home wood.'

'Or slingshotted a wild duck,' Benedikt muttered. 'I know.'

Truth was, they'd killed and eaten pretty much everything they were allowed to lay their hands on within a half league of the inn. That was the lawful limit of their hunting. Hardly a beast or bird was left. And though deer a-plenty crossed their path in the home wood the law said they weren't allowed to lift a finger agin them. Deer belonged to the Marcher lords. No mercy on a feggit fool caught with a haunch of venison. Even Lord Humbert, proven not a cruel man, though folk were well frighted by him at first, even he hanged a deer-thief. Regular Marcher folk were forbidden to take boar, as well . . . though that weren't so much a temptation. A man would need to be worse than a fool to face a boar without a lordly boar spear and a pack of snarling dogs.

Frowning, Liam scratched at the ugly burn scar on his cheek. The pain of it was a distant memory, but the bubbled skin still itched him now and then. His belly grumbled too. Supper's pease pottage hardly stuck to his ribs. How could it when Molly scarce waved a lump of bacon over it? He was hungry for rabbit stew or mowled duck or scrap'o'mutton or anything that weren't feggity boiled eggs or pease pottage with no bacon.

'Willem . . .'

He looked across the shadowy room at Benedikt. Saw the candle-lit gleam in his brother's eye and knew what he was thinking. He always knew what Benedikt was thinking.

'Bell Wood!' they said, together.

'After morning chores,' Benedikt added. 'We can say we be after rabbit in the home wood.'

'Iddo, he'll kick about it.'

'Let him. It be Ma as makes the rules.'

And wasn't that the truth. Molly was queen of the Pig Whistle, everyone in the Marches knew that. If she said him and Benedikt could go hunting then that's what they'd do. And she would say it, 'cause he wasn't the only one sick to death of boiled eggs.

Folding his arms behind his head, he thought about Bell Wood. They'd have to run hard as Count Balfre's greyhounds to reach it, more than a league to the east. But Bell Wood was their best hope of finding lawful game. Since the black-lung burned through it last winter, putting thirteen families in the ground, folk shied away from the woodland like farm horses side-stepping round a flyblown corpse.

'And it b'aint like proper trespass,' said Benedikt. 'With no folk living there these days.'

Which was Benedikt knowing what *he* was thinking. Half the time they didn't need feggity words at all.

Liam yawned. 'Still. We'll want to look lively. Bell Wood runs close to Harcian land and you can't turn a corner without falling over one of Balfre's men-at-arms.'

'Feggits,' said Benedikt, snuffing the candle closest to him. 'Blow out yer taper, Willem. It be burning low, and ye do know Iddo measures 'em with his feggit thumb.'

Another yawn, wide enough to split his scarred, broke-nosed face in two. Lurching upright he pinched out his candle. Wriggled and rolled until he was out of his hose and roughspun smock and under his blanket. Waited for the sounds of Benedikt's wriggling and rolling to stop, then curled onto his side.

'Story time,' he whispered, because the truth had to be whispered, and only in the dark. That's what he'd promised Ellyn. He couldn't see her face any more but he remembered how she hugged him tight and kissed his cheek all wet and blurty to make him laugh, and how every night she told him who he really was. Story time was how he loved her. 'Folk call me—'

'Willem. D'ye reckon I could tell it this time?'

Startled, he blinked. 'Why?'

'Well . . .' The sound of Benedikt wriggling under his blankets. 'I been thinking. I know 'tis yer story. But when ye told me who ye truly be, ye made it my story too.'

562

He'd never thought on it like that, but Benedikt was right. 'Tell it, then. But if ye tell it wrong I'll thump ye.'

Benedikt snuffled, laughing. 'Ye can try.' Another wriggling sound, then a little sigh. 'Folk call ye Willem,' he whispered, his voice solemn now. Serious. 'But it b'aint yer true name. Yer true name be Liam, and ye be the rightful duke of Clemen. *My* name be Benedikt. I be yer brother. 'Tis my oath to keep yer secret and see ye on the Falcon Throne.'

Oh. Tear-pricked, Liam stared at the low attic ceiling.

'Willem? Be that all right?' Benedikt whispered, sounding anxious.

'Iss,' he said, after a moment. 'It be fine.'

Another sigh, relieved. 'Yer da was Duke Harald. The bastard Roric killed him. One day, when the time be right, ye'll take yer revenge.'

'And ye'll help me, iss? Ye'll help me kill Roric?'

'Course I will.'

More prickling tears. 'Go on. Tell the rest of it.'

'Ye had a nursemaid. Her name were Ellyn. The night Roric the bastard came for ye, she saved yer life . . .'

His eyes drifted closed, lulled by Benedikt's soft voice. It was different when someone else told his story. When he all he had to do was listen, he could somehow see it happening in his mind. When someone else told his story, somehow . . . it was more true. Listening, smiling, he sank into sleep.

Molly and Iddo were still prickly with each other over breakfast next morning. Liam pulled a face at Benedikt and they kept their heads down eating their eggs. After that it was scrubbing the tables and benches in the public room, and hauling out the empty ale barrels, and changing shitty straw for fresh in the henhouse. When their chores were done they asked if they could go coney-hunting in the home wood. Iddo said no. Molly straight away said yes. Sullen, Iddo gave way.

Grinning at each other, they escaped outside. Snatched up their snares, their slingshots, their hooks-and-lines and their canvas bags and their small knives and pretended to saunter off to the home wood.

As soon as they were out of sight they started running, and didn't stop till they reached the mysterious and bountiful Bell Wood, where the game was fat and plentiful and waiting to be caught.

But it wasn't till they were splashing knee-deep across sun-dappled Wiggim's Creek, running higgledy-piggledy through Bell Wood's green, mossy heart, that Liam heard the fighting.

'Listen!' he hissed, snatching at Benedikt's arm.

Burdened with rabbit and duck, 'cause it was his turn to carry their spoils, his brother slithered to a tippy-tilt halt on the creek bed's slippery pebbles.

'What? I don't hear – *oh*.'

Still as mice in the stables, they strained their ears. Heard shouts and cursing. Clashing swords. Screams of pain.

'*Trouble*,' Benedikt whispered. 'Willem, let's go—'

'No. I want to see.'

The bank was steep on this side of the creek, and peppery with stinging nettles. Heedless of the danger he plunged out of the lazy water and scrambled up the damp bank, biting his lip against the nettle pain, bruising his knees and elbows in his haste. Benedikt, cursing, scrambled behind him. At the top of the bank they flung themselves down shoulder to shoulder on their bellies, panting. Swiped sweat out of their eyes and stared.

Some dozen or so men-at-arms fought each other among the spindly trees a long stone's throw from the creek, bloodied swords and daggers flashing in the fingery light. The men wore leather jacks over their tunics, arrow-full quivers on their backs and spurs on their booted heels. No sign of their horses, though. The battle must've started somewhere else.

Benedikt made a little sound in his throat. 'They do look in a killing mood. What d'ye s'pose—'

'Hush!' Liam said fiercely, jabbing an elbow into his brother's ribs. 'Y'feggit.'

Benedikt cursed again, then snapped his teeth shut.

His brother was right, though. Humbert and Balfre's men looked set to slaughter each other to the last breath. They were gasping hard, grunting and groaning as they set about each other with their swords. One man leapt backwards to avoid a swinging blade. His foot slipped on a patch of moss and he thudded to one knee. The man fighting him slashed his blade down, taking his fallen enemy's sword arm at the elbow. Blood spurted. The man shrieked. Another blow near severed his head. But then his killer was run through from behind and *he* died – and then *that* man died before he could wrench his sword free. Another man fell backwards on a scream, his belly opened left to right through his boiled leather jack as though he were a roast goose being carved. The fresh woodland air was rank with blood-stink now, bloody as a shambles, loud with shouts and bubbling moans, the wet, cracking sound of blades slicing flesh and bone, and the musical steel ringing of sword upon sword. Another arm was lopped off. A hand at the wrist. One man's face was cleaved in two, teeth and split tongue tumbling as he toppled like a tree.

Then there was silence, 'cause there was no one left to die.

Benedikt was shaking. Not crying, really, only tears and snot running down his face. '*Willem*.'

His face was wet too, and he wanted to heave up his eggs. Only he was Liam, duke of Clemen, and dukes were braver than that. So he lay on his churning belly beside Benedikt and bit his lip until the urge passed.

'All the *blood*,' Benedikt said at last, hiccuping. 'And that man's *teeth*, Willem. Did y'see his teeth fly, when – when—'

He pulled a face. 'I saw.'

'It be what we'll have to do, Willem,' Benedikt said, his face greenish. 'To get back yer Falcon Throne.' Another hiccup. 'I dunt know – I dunt know if I can—' Benedikt swallowed. 'Willem, d'ye think ye can?'

He stared at the dead men, the blood and the guts, breathing in air that stank like Hogget farm at slaughter time. 'I have to. I promised Ellyn.'

'Iss, but *how*? We dunt know one of end of a sword from t'other. We dunt *own* a sword. We *can't* own a sword.'

'I can't tell ye how!' he said, his fingers clenching. 'But I *will*. I'll make the Falcon Throne mine, I'll punish them lords who betrayed Duke Harald *and* I'll kill that thieving, murdering bastard Roric.' He jerked his chin at the slaughtered men-at-arms. 'I'll leave him chopped to pieces, just like them.'

Looking down, Benedikt poked a finger into the damp earth.

'Wish I knew which bastards it was killed my da. If I knew I'd go and find 'em. And I'd kill 'em stone dead.'

His brother hardly ever talked about his murdered father 'cause, he said, it made Molly sad to speak of him. And Iddo didn't like it. He elbowed Benedikt's ribs again, but kindly this time.

'When I'm duke we'll find them. And then ye can kill them any way ye please.'

'Iss?' Benedikt wiped his snotty face on his sleeve. 'Good, then.'

An eerie silence had settled over the blood-soaked woodland, broken only by the harsh croaks of ravens as they gathered in the trees. One flapped down to curl its talons in a dead man's bloody hair. Another landed on a still chest and poked its sharp, questing beak into an open wound.

'T'aint no more to see,' said Benedikt. 'And could be there'll be Humbert or Balfre or someone come looking for their men. We ought to—'

Struck by a thought, Liam took hold of his brother's shoulder. 'Not yet. You were right. We need our own swords.'

A moment, then Benedikt saw what he meant. His mouth dropped open. '*Willem*. Be ye cracked in the nod? Ye *can't*—'

He grinned. 'Iss, I can.'

'No – wait – *Willem*—'

Fumbling to his feet, he darted from the top of the creek bank into the spindly woodland where all those men lay dead. The ravens flapped away, croaking hoarsely, their beady red eyes resentful.

This close the stench of death was overpowering. Shite and piss and blood and opened guts spoiling the sweeter woodland scents. Gagging, he nearly tripped himself trying not to soak his shoes in scarlet pools. Dead mouths gaped. Dead eyes stared. Dead fingers loosely grasped the hilts of fallen swords. He made himself look at them. He'd have to do this to men himself one day.

'Willem, come on! Let's go!'

Benedikt was right again. They couldn't stay here any longer. He snatched up the two nearest swords and put a fallen dagger in each dead man's empty hand. Surely it would look as though they'd lost their long blades somewhere else in Bell Wood. Heart pounding, he turned back to his brother – and stopped on a startled gasp. Both swords slipped through his fingers.

One of the men wasn't dead.

Living eyes blinked slowly. Living nostrils flared. Living lips, blood-crusted, moved as he tried to speak. There was a wound in his throat. Blood on his shoulder. Blood on his leg. A sword-cut through his leather jack, showing broken ribs beneath. The blood there was frothy. Chances were the man would die. Only . . .

Liam looked down at him, sweat stinging. The man wore a Harcian badge. That was good. A duke shouldn't kill his own men. He felt his belly heave, thought he could taste blood. Felt like someone else, not himself, as he bent to pick up one of the stolen swords.

I have to. He's seen my face.

The blade pushed easily through the wound in the man's throat. He felt its point strike bone and pushed harder. Harder again. Felt bone break. A single moan. A spurt of blood. The man's flaring nostrils stilled.

'*Willem!*' Benedikt called from the top of the creek bank. 'Willem, we got to *go*!'

The heavy swords were hard to run with. Staggered back to his brother, he took one look at Benedikt and gave him a hard shove with his shoulder. 'You right with them rabbits and ducks?'

His brother nodded, still greenish. 'If we be found with them swords it won't be a whipping in the cellar, Willem.'

'Don't be a feggit. We'll hide 'em.'

'Willem—' Benedikt chewed at his lip. 'It looked like – with one of them swords – that man, did ye—'

'I did.'

Benedikt swiped his hand over his mouth. 'Did he see ye?'

'Iss.'

'Was it awful?'

'Iss.' But not as awful as he'd feared.

'D'ye feel sick?'

'No. I'm wholesome,' he said, filled with relief. He'd half thought Benedikt might turn from him – and what he'd do without his brother he surely didn't know. 'Now let's get on back to the Whistle, afore

Molly sends that feggit Iddo looking for us. We can find somewhere to hide the swords on the way.'

Hands on her hips, Molly looked at the game laid out before her on the kitchen table. Eight rabbits. Six duck. Four silver-scaled darts. Beyond the leather curtain a babble of voices in the public room, and Iddo laughing. A rare sound these days. It warmed her fretting heart to hear it. A good thing the Pig Whistle was near to half full. Better that Iddo be caught up out there serving ale and gathering gossip than in here tossing sharp questions at her boys.

Suspiciously docile, Benedikt and Willem stood shoulder to shoulder and said nothing.

She poked her finger into the rabbits and then the ducks. Pursed her lips. 'These be fine conies, boys. Goodly meat on their bones. And the ducks? Plump as pigeons. Fine eating, they'll make. The darts, too. Good fish for smoking.'

Willem's lips twitched. Benedikt beamed. 'Iss, Ma. That be what we thought.'

'Iss. Fine eating,' she mused, then slapped the flat of her hand to the table. Even Willem jumped. 'And now ye can tell me where 'twas ye took 'em! For ye never took 'em in the home wood, that much I know fer sure!'

'Molly—'

She shook her finger in Willem's scarred face. 'Not a word from ye, Willem. I be asking Benedikt on this.'

'Cause Benedikt, her sweet boy, had a face she could read. But Willem? Willem baffled her. His amber eyes hid too many thoughts. If only she could 'prentice him somewhere. She'd sleep better at night.

'Benedikt?' She gave him her best stare. 'Where'd ye take 'em?'

Her son glanced at Willem. The swift look knifed her. And when Willem twitched his lips again, saying *tell her*, loud as a shout? That twisted the knife till she wanted to cry out in pain.

Benedikt shuffled his feet. Dried mud flaked from his leather shoes to dirty her clean kitchen floor. 'Bell Wood, Ma. We took 'em in Bell Wood.'

Bell Wood? She thought of the danger, and shivered. To take such a risk! She could slap them. She should slap them. But then she thought of the home wood, bare as a starveling's pantry. Looked again at the silver fish and the fat rabbits and the plump ducks, and felt a dreadful relief.

'No one saw ye?'

'No, Ma!' said Benedikt. 'Not a soul, Ma!'

''Tain't no one in Bell Wood, Molly,' Willem added. 'But there be a mort of game.'

'And goats!' Benedikt was bouncing on his toes, gig-a-hoop. 'Ma, we saw goats, run wild in the wood 'cause of the black-lung. We could—'

'No, ye couldn't,' she snapped. 'Kill a goat with a slingshot? Not even Count Balfre could do that.'

'Then we could catch some. Herd 'em back for ye, Ma. Goat's milk and goat's meat and—'

'And explain 'em how, ye little feggit? No goats today, a herd of goats tomorrow? Ye d'know how folk be chancy just now. There'd be someone whispering of it a half-day later and *faugh*!' She clapped her hands. 'Men-at-arms on the doorstep demanding to see the note of sale. No goats, Benedikt. Put the thought from yer mind.'

Willem was watching her closely. 'No goats, Molly. But rabbit and fish and duck you'll nod at?'

Folding her arms, she brooded at the table. Rabbit and duck she could vouch for. Rabbit and duck and fish she could smoke, so the flesh'd keep in the cool cellar. She looked up.

'What do men-at-arms care for rabbit and duck?'

'And fish,' said Benedikt. 'There be a mort of fish in Wiggim Creek and Silver Pond.'

There were two creeks running through the home wood. Fish could be explained. She rapped her knuckles on the table.

'Rabbits and duck and fish, and that be all. No more than once a tenday, boys. And not a word to Iddo.'

Benedikt's eyes popped owlish. 'Ma?'

'Iddo frets himself overmuch. And he do have a face as a blind man could read. So ye'll not breathe a word to him.'

'What if he asks?' said Willem. 'Iddo b'aint a man you can tell *none of your nevermind*.'

569

There'd been other whippings since that bad day in the cellar, but only a stripe or three at a time. She'd made sure of that. Even so, she watched Willem walk wide around Iddo. Not frightened. But wary. The boy had no trust. Just as Iddo didn't trust him. Some days she thought it was like living in a tinder box. And 'cause that was her fault she worked hard to keep the peace. It had changed things 'tween her and Iddo, but there weren't a thing she could do about it.

'Iddo's mine to deal with,' she said firmly. 'If he asks, ye come to me. Now, ye can take them ducks and rabbits and fish and do what needs to be done with 'em.'

The boys grinned at each other, then snatched up the game they'd killed and rough-and-tumbled their way outside to skin and pluck and gut.

'Molly!' Iddo called, elbowing the kitchen's leather curtain aside. 'Three bowls of stew here!'

With mutton still hard to come by, and pot hens twice the price they used to be, most days she made barley, dried pea and carrot stew. It broke her heart, but times were as they were.

'Front table,' said Iddo, jerking his chin towards the far end of the public room. 'Bascot be in from Clemen.'

Bascot? 'Twas a while since she'd seen him. She took the tray of steaming bowls down to the table by the door, where Bascot, his brother Tapster and his scrawny nephew Philbert huddled over their tankards of ale.

'Sers,' she greeted them, with her best innkeeper smile. 'A fine thing t'see ye under m'roof agin. How d'the cloth trade be treating ye? And what be the news from Clemen?'

Bascot, whose sober brown wool tunic belied the richness of the fabrics he traded, exchanged gloomy glances with his brother and nephew.

'Sad news, Mistress Molly,' he said, accepting his bowl of stew with a nod. 'For there be a fresh round of ducal courts travelling throughout the duchy, levying taxes and fines on folk already light in their purses from the last time His Grace foisted up the fees.'

'Not that Clemen's lords do be feeling the pinch,' Tapster added, and wiped at the ale foam plumping his lip. 'The duke's council and the rest, high on the hog they're living. Aye, and their men-at-arms too. Only the second decent harvest we've had in six years, Mistress Molly, and the poor folk of Clemen with their rib-bones like the spars of a wrecked ship. Does His Grace take pity and think of the hungry before his coffers?' He thumped a fist to the bench. 'He does not. The harvest be taxed thrice over. You'll find folk the length and breadth of the duchy, weeping for a crust. But not Roric. Bastard or not, he's that bastard Harald's true blood and no mistake. Berold's blood, it's turned to water. His blood's been pissed away.'

'Easy, Father, easy,' young Philbert murmured, glancing around the chatter-filled public room. 'Who's to say what ears are flapping?'

Molly bent lower. 'Don't ye fret, now. I can name every man in here and not a one of 'em belongs to Lord Humbert or his man Egann.' She straightened. 'And I be right sorry to hear of yer troubles. Babbies starving for a crust of bread? T'aint right. Do I misremember, or don't the dukes of Clemen buy in grain from Cassinia?'

Bascot splashed his emptied spoon into his stew. 'If them goblins had grain to sell, aye, we'd be buying. But ain't word reached the Marches, Mistress Moll? Drought's got Cassinia by the parched throat again, it has.'

'And the grain ships from Danetto?' Tapster snorted. 'Pirates got them.'

Yes, she'd heard that a few weeks ago, from a passing Pruges merchant. 'There do be grain grown in Sassanine, b'aint that right?'

'Aye,' said Tapster. 'Only Aimery of Harcia wooed them Sassanine goblins with fine horseflesh. They do have a treaty or some such now, horses for grain. No grain to any folk else. Leastwise not in Clemen.'

'Thanks to Duke Roric,' Bascot added. 'He taxed the Harcian horse-merchants so hard last summer they threw up their hands and now they stay home.'

So that explained why she'd not lately seen hide nor hair of her regular Harcian horse-coping guests. Was Roric of Clemen a doltard, to be kicking such holes in his suffering duchy's coffers?

'There's them as saw it coming,' Tapster muttered. 'Not two month ago, I heard a soothsayer give warning in Gramply Ford. Blood on the moon for a week, he said. A foretell of calamity. And not a hand of days after—'

Bascot was shaking his head. 'You don't want to pay any mind to that. Omens and foretells and suchlike. Blood on the moon. Blood in his eye from sour ale, *that* be—'

'*Not a hand of days after*,' Tapster said, slapping the bench, 'we got word of the ducal courts starting agin. And what have we seen since but innocent folk bleeding coin from their purses?' He looked up. 'You do know there be signs and portents in the world, for them with eyes open to see, don't you, Mistress Moll?'

The first rule of innkeeping was never argue with a customer. Besides, didn't she burn her little offerings to the spirits and keep about the place the charms Izusa made for her, just in case?

'Well,' she said, being careful, 'I can't say as I've ever laid eyes on a foretell, or been shown an omen, or fallen foul of a soothsayer. But—' She smiled at Tapster. 'I can show ye plenty of folk in these parts who have. The old ways b'aint so popular as they were, what with them exarchites traipsing all over, but folk don't altogether forget what they was raised to believe. They just . . . nudge it aside.'

Especially when it didn't seem to be helping 'em no more.

Tapster poked his brother with a sharp finger. 'There, Bascot, y'see?'

'Feh,' Bascot grumbled. 'I still say that old soothsayer were ale-blind. But I can't deny we're seeing some right tricksome times.'

Molly rested a sympathetic hand on his shoulder. 'And if ye are, 'tis no wonder ye be gloomy.'

'Gloomy? Mistress Molly, we be grim. The ducal courts, they don't just levy taxes and fines. Roric's men-at-arms be marching off folk heard raising their voices against the duke and his council.'

'You can stare, but it's true,' said young Philbert, woeful. 'Ten silver ducats our trading warrant cost us. Last time we sold into Harcia, Mistress Molly, our papers cost us four. With Clemen's roads unchancy, we thought this venture to join with another clothier and his man. But Master Fenwick protested at paying twice double for his papers. He and his man were marched off, and that was the end of them.'

Molly nearly dropped her wooden tray. 'D'ye tell me they be *dead*?'

'Who can say?' said Bascot, shrugging. 'We left Fenwick wailing. Didn't dare speak up for him, I'm sorry to say.'

'And I be sorry to hear it,' she said. 'I knew Clemen had its troubles, but not so bad as this.'

'Tell her about the slavers,' said Philbert. 'D'you know about them, Mistress Molly?'

'I be sorry to say I do. Folk plucked from their beds, I hear, up and down the length of the duchy. Been going on a goodly while. D'ye say Duke Roric b'aint nipped it?'

Philbert glowered. 'He tries, but he can't. All he can do is foist taxes. What use is a duke as can't keep his people safe?'

'My, my. And here's me only ever hearing good things about Clemen's duke.'

'Times change,' Tapster said sourly. 'And men do change with them. Remember that, Mistress Moll.'

'Indeed I will, Master Tapster,' she said. ''Tis good advice. Now I'll leave ye to—'

The public room's door banged open and Lord Waymon strode in. At his heels, a pack of Harcian men-at-arms, no better than snarling dogs. She didn't recognise a one of them. So many new Harcian men-at-arms in the Marches, it seemed every other week she saw a face she'd never met before. Prickled by the sudden silence, Molly turned back to the bar, where Iddo stood staring. But the boys weren't with him, thank the faeries. They must still be outside plucking and gutting what they'd killed. And praise the faeries, let 'em stay out. She never wanted Lord Waymon to once notice her boys.

'Mistress Molly!'

She looked round. Bobbed a curtsy, tray and all. 'My lord.'

'I come on Count Balfre's business,' Waymon said, his cold stare sweeping round the room. His hunter-green velvet doublet was sewn with topaz. Gold dangled from his ear. 'And what I say is for every man under this roof to hear. Earlier this morning Clemen did, without lawful leave or provocation, attempt to extort coin from some innocent Harcian merchants. When these merchants rightly refused to pay, Clemen did meet them with violence. I have six slain men-at-arms even now being carried out of Bell Wood.' His head whipped round. 'Mistress Molly? What d'you know of this?'

Fear was a cockroach, scrabbling in her throat. 'Nothing, my lord.'

His cruel eyes slitted. 'No? You seem somewhat struck.'

'I am, my lord,' she said, forcing her gaze to hold his. 'I be right shammeried, my lord, to hear such a dreadful thing.'

'Really? With the Pig Whistle so used to bloodshed?'

'Not for some years, my lord,' she said, fighting to keep her voice no more than politely reproachful. 'We be peaceful here, as ye d'know.'

After a terrible long time, he shifted his stare. 'You men. I don't know you.'

Master Bascot frowned at his brother and his nephew, then stood. 'I am Bascot, my lord. A cloth-trader of Clemen.'

Waymon's thin lip curled. 'Thinking to trade your rags in the Harcian Marches? And in Harcia?'

'Thinking to trade, my lord, with all proper papers.'

'Not today. Harcia has had its fill of Clemen today. You may present yourselves to Count Balfre five days hence. He will decide then if you can trade in Harcia, or not.'

Bascot looked with some alarm at his brother. 'Five days, my lord? You'd have us tarry here idle five days? But—'

Waymon's hand found his sword-hilt. 'Man, you and your friends can tarry or you can fuck each other for all I care. What you won't do is set foot on Harcian soil before Count Balfre allows it. Not without offering forfeit of your lives.'

Face flushed, Bascot sat. 'My lord.'

'Mistress Molly,' said Waymon, pinning her again with his dreadful stare, 'best you make it known to your customers. Harcia has no stomach for Clemen treachery. Any man, woman or child found aiding Clemen in violence against us, or dishonesty, or trickery, or any knavish jest, that fool will perish upon the point of a sword. You hear me?'

'Iss, my lord,' she said faintly. 'I do hear ye right well.'

'And so do these men-at-arms hear me,' said Waymon. 'Every man of Harcia knows his duty and will do it. Never doubt that, Mistress Molly.'

She curtsied again. 'No, my lord.'

'What walking filth is *he*?' Bascot spluttered over the raucous chatter, after Lord Waymon and his men-at-arms had gone. 'I declare, Mistress Molly—'

'I know, Master Bascot,' she sighed. 'That be Lord Waymon of Harcia. Count Balfre's trusted man.'

'Ha! Trusted *cur*,' Tapster retorted, shaking with anger like his brother. 'Trusted *pizzle*. Trusted *shite*—'

'Have a care, Master Tapster. That bench there be crowded full of Harcian farmers.'

Philbert glowered at them. 'And you'd soil your fingers with their coin, would you?'

'Philbert!' Tapster struck his son a blow on the arm. 'What's the first rule of trading? Coin is coin. It has no friend or foe. Forgive him, Mistress Molly. He's a hot-blooded lad.'

Though her nerves were still jangling, she gave the three men her best smile. 'I do, Master Tapster. Now be peaceful. I'll send Iddo to ye with ale on the house, for the disturbance.'

'Moll,' said Iddo, as she hurried to take the tray back to the kitchen. 'Moll—'

When it counted, she could count on him. She'd always known that. She pressed her hand to his cheek. Felt the tight muscle over his jaw. 'Don't ye fret, Iddo. That shite Waymon don't scare me. See ale to Master Bascot, iss? Our coin, not his.'

Leaving him to grumble, she pushed into the kitchen, dropped the tray on the table, stirred the stew in its pot, turned her curd pies in the oven, then went to find them ructious boys.

They were out the back, cross-legged on the dusty grass, carefully picking through a pile of rabbit and duck guts for the bits they knew she'd want to use.

'Benedikt! Willem!'

Surprised, they lifted their heads. One look at her face and they bounced to their feet.

'Ma?' said Benedikt. 'What be amiss?'

She could weep, she was so frightened. 'There were bloody trouble in Bell Wood this morning, Benedikt. What did ye and Willem see?'

Benedikt's gaze slid by her. 'See, Ma? Nothing. Just coneys and fish and birds and goats.'

She knew her son better than any soul living. Better than herself, better than Iddo. She knew when he was lying. Trouble was, she weren't sure she wanted the truth.

'Who said there were trouble, Ma?'

'Lord Waymon. Boys, he was murdering angry.'

'He's always murdering angry,' said Willem, careless. 'Waymon's a man as'd kill you by way of saying hello.'

Her hand lashed out and slapped him before she could stop it. 'D'ye think I be jesting, Willem? Be this a smile on m'face?'

'*Ma!*' Benedikt protested.

Willem said nothing, only stared at her with his strangely grown-up amber eyes. The skin around the scar she'd given him was blotchy red from her blow.

'Ye'll mind yer step the next few days,' she said, glaring. 'Stay close to the Whistle. I won't have ye roaming far.'

'Yes, Ma,' said Benedikt, crestfallen.

Willem never said a word.

With a last hot look at them, she picked up the skinned and gutted game carcases and went back inside.

CHAPTER THIRTY-FOUR

Settled discreetly behind a tapestry screen in Balfre's manor house library, Vidar nursed a goblet of wine and listened to his beloved Lindara's father bellow.

'Extortion?' A heavy thump, as Humbert struck something made of wood. 'You pizzling cockshite, this was no fucking extortion! Your merchants had no proof of road-tolls properly paid. And when they were challenged they did provoke the confrontation. This blood's on your hands, Balfre. When Roric hears of the Clemen men your wild dogs killed in Bell Wood he'll—'

'Do nothing,' said Balfre. 'Humbert, I admire your loyalty but why do you persist in making threats we both know your duke will never honour?'

'You're a fine one to be talking of *honour*, Balfre.'

'You should know, my lord,' Balfre said, his voice cutting, 'that my father was of a mind to send Clemen grain from Sassanine. A gesture of friendship, full knowing how the people of Clemen do hunger for bread. Alas, when he hears of your men-at-arms' wanton belligerence against our traders . . .'

Humbert was breathing like a set of aged bellows. 'Wanton belligerence? You'd speak to me of wanton belligerence, when there are still innocent Clemen folk sold into slavery abroad?'

Balfre's laugh was ripe with contempt. '*This* again? How many times must I say it? Harcia has nothing to do with pirate raids upon Clemen's villages. I could as easily accuse Clemen of being behind the northmen who pillage the Green Isle.'

'Pillage yourself, Balfre!' Humbert retorted. 'And heed this warning. Roric stays his hand not out of cowardice, but care for innocent blood. Push him any harder and you'll force him to stop caring.'

A heavy thudding of boots as Humbert stormed from the room and slammed its heavy oak door in his wake.

'Old fool,' Waymon muttered. 'Roric must be in dire straits if he's Clemen's best choice for Marcher lord.'

'Humbert's a wily old fox,' said Balfre, not for the first time. 'You dismiss him at your peril. Isn't that so, Boice?'

And there was his invitation. Vidar drank the rest of his wine, set down the goblet, then twisted off his stool and walked, not quite steadily, out from behind the screen.

'Fuck,' Waymon said, disgusted, eyeing the empty goblet. He stood close to Balfre's chair, like the guard dog he was. 'He's drunk again. What worth is this shite's counsel?'

'It's been nearly four years, Waymon,' Balfre said mildly. 'When did I last keep a man beside me four *days* if I found no worth in him? Enough pettiness, my friend. Instead give some thought to those matters we discussed earlier. I'll join you in the tilt yard shortly. We can talk them over after we've trained.'

'My lord,' said Waymon, resentful, and withdrew.

'Well, Vidar?' Slouching against his chair's high, cushioned back, Balfre raised an eyebrow. 'Are you drunk?'

He shrugged. 'A little. I have no choice, unless you want Waymon to wonder why Boice is sporting a sudden limp.'

'Ah. Your hip?'

'Is troubling me, yes. Izusa's concoction isn't holding.'

'Unlike her face.'

Yes, the face. It kept him safely unrecognised, kept him alive, the face Izusa had made for him. But every time he caught sight of it – in a mirror or a darkened window or in a splash of water – he was shockingly reminded of all he'd lost. Reminded that the woman who'd made it for him was no harmless healer, but a witch. *A witch*. And instead of denouncing her, he was concealing her. Day and night he wore the charm she made him that gave him his new face. Kept it secret beneath his shirt, against his skin, where it burned him and chafed him and never let him fully rest.

Or perhaps that was his conscience.

'Sit, Vidar,' Balfre said, waving his hand. 'I don't like to see you in pain.'

Gritting his teeth against the grinding ache from his old wound, Vidar crossed the intricately woven Khafuri carpet and lowered himself stiffly into the padded oak cross-frame chair beside the fireplace. It was an old piece, beautifully carved. Godebert had owned one something like it. The chair made him feel closer to the home he'd abandoned and would never see again.

'Brandy?' Balfre offered, standing. 'My brother's sent me a keg. The best the Green Isle has to offer. It seems he and his doughty barons have beaten back yet another horde of raiders.'

'That's good news.' But Balfre was frowning. 'Isn't it?'

'Grefin was wounded.'

'Badly?'

'Badly enough. But he says he'll live.'

And whether that was good news, or bad, who could say? What Balfre felt for his brother remained something of a mystery. In no mood for solving riddles, Vidar let his gaze drift around the library. Like the rest of the manor, it was remarkably gracious. A fire crackled cheerfully in the slate-lined hearth, and the flame-warmed air was lit to a golden glow by scores of beeswax candles burning in wrought-iron candle-wheels. Books he'd now read several times over crowded a wall of shelves. Time-faded tapestries of frolicking nymphs and faeries decorated the other walls, while heavy damask drapes hid the lead-lined glass window. It was a room that had become painfully familiar since the night he'd thrown himself upon Balfre's mercy . . . and to his surprise been caught.

'Vidar!' said Balfre, impatient, standing at the sideboard holding an unstoppered jug. 'Brandy. Yes or no?'

No matter what Waymon thought, he rarely let himself get drunk. It was too dangerous. But Green Isle brandy was potent, and the pain in his hip was sharp. 'Yes.'

Balfre splashed a pewter goblet a quarter full then gave it to him. 'Here. And don't be mopish. I'll get something from Izusa later tonight, to ease your woes.'

It was galling how well Balfre had learned to read him. He emptied the goblet in one smooth swallow. Fermented apple burned a mellow path from his gullet to his gut.

'Fuck, Vidar!' Balfre protested. 'Only a hog guzzles good brandy!'

Savouring the aftertaste, he half-smiled. 'You say *fuck* a lot.'

'Fuck, yes, I do,' said Balfre, grinning, and dropped back into his chair. 'And every time I say it I stick a finger in Aimery's eye. The duke pretends himself above crudity, but in truth he can swear a man-at-arms thrice blind.'

'You really don't like your father, do you?'

With extravagant ease, Balfre flung his right leg over the arm of his chair. 'Not a whit. But then, name me one man – besides my faery-kissed brother – who'll admit to liking the fuck who sired him.'

'I liked mine well enough. Though I'll admit, affection cooled at the end.'

His own goblet paused at his lips, Balfre smiled an odd, secret little smile. 'I think it's the fate of an heir to resent his father. Always, always, the old man stands in the way. Second and third sons have it easier. All play and no work for them.'

'You call fighting hordes of northern raiders a game?'

Balfre shrugged. 'But war is a game, Vidar. You know that.'

If it was then he'd lost badly, the very first time he played. 'You don't like your brother, either?'

'Did I say so?' Balfre sipped from his goblet and gave a small, pleased grunt. 'Grefin and I would often sit by a good fire and drink and talk. In the Croft. In Tamwell castle. Wherever Aimery decided we should lay our heads next. Perhaps that's why I squander fine brandy on you, Vidar. Perhaps I pine for my little brother and you're the next best thing.'

He dropped his emptied goblet onto the carpet. '*Fuck!*'

'Ha!' Balfre was grinning again. 'Now tell me. What d'you make of Humbert's interfering with our merchants? He's a sly fox, but he's not wolfish.'

'You think Roric put him up to provoking the bloodshed?' He retrieved the goblet. 'I doubt it. Roric's first instinct is for peace, not slaughter.'

Balfre rolled his eyes. 'The way you talk, you make him sound like a woman. Or an exarchite.'

'If you'd seen him slay Harald you'd not call him either.'

'Roric slew Harald a long time ago. People change.'

Perhaps. Perhaps not. Roric would never have brought Harald undone if not for Humbert, whispering in his ear.

'*If* Roric told Humbert to chivvy your traders,' he said slowly, 'I'd wager that cockshite Ercole and his merchant goodfather Blane are behind it. The more coin that's gouged from foreign merchants, the less Clemen's merchants must pour into Eaglerock's coffers.'

Balfre grimaced. 'What kind of duke allows himself to be bullied by a merchant?'

'The kind who owes that merchant more coin than he can repay. Roric's been in debt to Blane for years.'

'Has he?' Balfre said softly. 'I don't recall you mentioning that before.'

'Because I haven't.'

'Why not?'

He met Aimery's son stare for stare. 'My knowledge of Roric and Clemen is like a dagger sheathed at my hip. But if that sheath is empty . . .'

'Meaning what?'

'Meaning I don't trust Waymon.'

'You have nothing to fear from Waymon.'

'*You* have nothing to fear from Waymon, Balfre. I have . . . nothing but fear.'

Balfre drained his goblet of brandy then got up and refilled it. 'You're safe here, Vidar. I've sworn it. Don't insult me again.'

If he'd learned nothing else since coming to live under Balfre's roof, it was that his host had a dangerously changeable disposition. He sat a little straighter. 'No insult was meant.'

Balfre's cold stare thawed. 'More brandy?'

He retrieved his goblet and held it out. 'Balfre, you know that Humbert will go back to Roric claiming you're behind the trouble in Bell Wood. He'll say you tasked your merchants to deny Clemen its lawful coin in the hope of provoking a confrontation.'

'And is that what *you* think?' Balfre said, returning the brandy to the sideboard. 'That I defied Aimery to stir violence when he, like your Roric, prefers peace to war.'

He thought it entirely possible but wasn't fool enough to say so. 'No. And don't call him my Roric. He is not fucking mine.'

'So it would seem,' said Balfre, amused. 'But is he Humbert's? Is he the council's? Or does he belong to Master Blane? Tell me, Vidar. Who truly rules in Clemen?'

He swallowed more brandy, savouring the heady swirl of fermented apple fumes. The leaping flames in the fireplace blurred across his vision, smearing the library orange and gold. Time smeared with it, and he was staring at the past.

'From the moment it was decided that Harald must go,' he murmured, 'Roric leaned upon Humbert like a lame man on his staff. Even now I'm not sure he's learned how to stand alone. The news from Clemen these past months gives me pause. Leaving aside the poor harvests, the inclement weather, pirates raiding the duchy's coastal villages – if indeed it's pirates – there is misery caused by the travelling courts, the punitive fines and imprisonments, the increased taxes and imposts, the discouragement of Harcian traders . . .'

'All of it meaning what, d'you think?'

He looked at Balfre. 'That instead of leaning on Humbert, he's now leaning on men like Ercole. And Blane. Men who have him at a disadvantage, who care more for themselves than Clemen. Roric's greatest fear, always, was of becoming another Harald. That fear has made him ever reluctant to wield power.'

Balfre pushed out of his chair and took a slow turn around the library, sipping brandy as he paced. 'So men with less power now seek to wield him – and because he lets them, his greatest fear is coming true.'

It struck Vidar cold, hearing the words spoken aloud so starkly. 'Of course, I could be wrong.'

Balfre nodded. 'Of course.'

'The loss of Lindara—' He flinched, that pain always close to the surface. 'Roric never loved her as I did, but neither was he – indifferent.'

'And grief, like time, changes people.'

It certainly did.

Balfre considered him, quizzical. 'You sound almost sorry for the bastard.'

'I'm sorry for Clemen. Roric has ruined everything he's touched.'

'Truer words were never spoken,' said Balfre. 'And for your duchy's sake, Vidar, I hope the tide will turn soon, so that Clemen might enjoy peace and prosperity again. In the meantime, I'd ask you to join me and Waymon in the tilt yard. Dusk should be falling and I want our new men-at-arms to get a taste of training in the dark.'

Two days earlier some thirty green youths had descended upon them, to be changed from clumsy gawkers into lean, fighting men. Vidar shook his head. 'I find it hard to fathom you've anyone left in Harcia who still doesn't know how to hold a sword.'

Balfre shrugged. 'You'd be surprised.'

'Why do you need more sword-ready men? Didn't you say your brother had defeated the northern raiders? And word from Cassinia has pirates beating them back, too. Surely the danger has passed.'

'Not quite,' Balfre said, idly. 'Baldassare and his vermin care only to protect their own killing ground. They won't lift a finger to protect the Green Isle. And these raiders are persistent fucks. For all I know, Grefin will be fighting them every spring and summer for the next twenty fucking years.'

What a thought. But he couldn't regret it. Balfre's brother, the Green Isle's barons and the men-at-arms he was helping Balfre train were keeping the persistent fucks off Clemen soil.

But even so . . .

'You know, Balfre, Waymon holds no high opinion of my ability to train green men.'

'I don't care what Waymon thinks. Your Marcher experience remains invaluable.'

'My experience remains a spur pricked to his flank!'

Balfre's eyes lit with amusement. 'Exactly. When you and he cross swords, the men learn swiftly what it means to fight with passion.'

'And one of these days I might be teaching them how to die in a welter of blood!' he retorted. 'Izusa's potions, for the most past, kill my body's pain. But they don't unmake the damage. One false step, one stumble, and—'

'Fuck that, Vidar. Lame or not, you're a brilliant swordsman.'

'I'm flattered. But—'

'But what?' Amusement fading, Balfre stared. 'You grow tired of your refuge here? You long for a return to Clemen skies? Or perhaps my generosity has become a burden. I'd understand if that's the case. I have been very generous.'

Fuck. Awkwardly, Vidar stood. 'Balfre—'

'But I forget,' Balfre said, sweetly vicious. 'You can't go back to Clemen, can you? Thanks to me, Clemen thinks you dead. Which you will be, should Roric learn the truth. How does Sassanine appeal? I'm sure I could smuggle you there in a dung cart with the next shipment of Harcian horses!'

Mouth dry, skin prickling, Vidar raised a hand. 'I'd rather you didn't.'

'Does that mean you'll come with me to the tilt yard?'

'Of course. I'm sorry.'

With an irritable flick of his wrist, Balfre tossed the last drops of brandy out of his goblet and into the fire. The flames roared, blue-tinged.

'Don't fucking apologise, Vidar! Just – do as I ask.'

Mutely, he nodded. Hating himself. Hating Balfre. Hating Roric most of all, for making him into this helpless, servile thing.

For over an hour he trained green men-at-arms by the light of a flaming torch. By then he could have wept for the pain in his hip. Noticing, at last, Balfre called a halt to the sparring.

'See what happens when you make me lose my temper?' he said, too softly for nearby Waymon to overhear. 'Now, you're done for the night. Waymon and I have further business. I'll see you again at breakfast.'

Upstairs, alone in his lavishly appointed bedchamber, Vidar sat on the edge of his wool-stuffed mattress and dropped his aching head into his hands. He could still taste Balfre's brandy in the back of his throat. It held the tang of betrayal. If Lindara could see him, she'd be so ashamed.

Except I do this for her. For the memory of her. I do this for Clemen, though no one will understand.

In those first, dark days of hiding, he'd been a wounded beast gone to ground. Grief and rage had consumed him. He'd thought the agony of Lindara's death would kill him. Thought he deserved no less. Instead of fighting for her, he'd deserted her. Abandoned her to Roric's loveless bed. He was contemptible. A coward. A eunuch, not a man. Imagining her final hours, the blood, the pain, the fear, he'd reduced himself to a torment of skin and bone.

Balfre's ruthless pity saved him. And for a time, as he recovered his lost strength, he'd fed his soul on dreams of revenge. Harcia wanted him? Harcia could have him. Roric had thrown him away. For the price of a safe roof over his head he'd sold Balfre Clemen's secrets. It was the only way he could punish Roric, who'd married the one woman he'd ever love.

But then, slowly, surely, as he spent more time in Balfre's company . . . listened to him and Waymon talking . . . lay in bed at night making sense of the hints and whispers all around . . . he came to understand the breadth and depth of his mistake. Because behind the smiling human mask, Aimery's son was a rabid wolf with an appetite for conquest. He'd be Clemen's blood-soaked future if he wasn't stopped.

Worse, it became painfully clear that Clemen couldn't rely on Berold's bastard grandson to stop him. Disgraced Godebert's disgraced son would have to stop him. There was no one else.

A terrible realisation . . . and easier said than done.

He had to wait for the right moment. If he spoke now, no one would listen. If he spoke now, he'd die. Roric would kill him, because of Lindara, or Balfre would, for his betrayal. But if he stayed his hand and kept compliant, if he did whatever Balfre asked, he could help Aimery's wolfish son defeat Roric. And then, with Roric thrown down, he could return to Clemen and heal what Harald's bastard cousin had hurt.

It was how he consoled himself, found a way to live with the fact that it was possible to enjoy his life in the Harcian Marches – and even Balfre's company. Sometimes.

Standing, he stripped off his fine clothes and crawled into bed. As the relief of sleep closed over him, he breathed out his nightly plea.

I love you, Lindara. Forgive me. Help me. We must keep Clemen safe.

'The thing is,' said Balfre, calloused fingers idly roaming, 'I almost feel sorry for the old rump.'

Lying with him in her cottage bed, tucked into the curve of his arm, Izusa pushed a strand of sweat-damp hair out of her face. 'Why? Humbert's your enemy.'

Balfre chuckled. 'I know. But there's a ruthless streak runs through him that I could use, were he Harcian. Instead, most likely he'll die.'

'But not yet.'

'No. Just like Vidar, he'll be useful till I'm made Harcia's duke. Which will be *when*, Izusa?' With one of his abrupt mood shifts, Balfre pinched her inner thigh. 'You said the tainted ink I use to write my letters to Aimery would kill him. You swore it. And still my father is breathing. How much longer must I wait?'

A dilemma. Nothing Balfre wanted would come to him before Harald's son was ready. And Harald's son was not ready yet. So the ink she'd been making was sorcelled to weaken, not kill. To keep Aimery feeble, Balfre eager, and give Liam time to grow.

And not a word of that truth could she share with Aimery's son.

Propping herself onto one elbow, she traced the strong arch of his eyebrow with a gentle fingertip then lowered her forehead to rest on his.

'I'm sorry,' she murmured. 'It's not given me to tell you what you want to know. All I can say is what I've said from the start. You will be duke of Harcia . . . and after that, a mighty king.'

With a roar of frustration he shoved her out of the bed, then pounded the wall behind him with his fist. Though she was freshly rune-charmed, she felt fear. Magic could fail – and Balfre had a raw power all his own.

'Don't, my lord,' she said, touching his arm. 'You'll hurt yourself.'

He pulled her back in beside him. '*Fuck.*'

Waiting for his temper to cool, she idled her fingertips on his chest. 'You're unsettled. Has something happened?'

'Grefin's wounded, fighting northmen,' he said, after a brooding pause. 'If he dies before Aimery I could be named Steward. I don't want to be named Steward. I need to bide my time, in the Marches.'

'And you will.' She caressed his lips. 'Grefin. You're frightened for him.'

'Did I say that?'

'No. But you are.'

'He's my brother,' Balfre muttered. 'Whatever our disputes . . . he's my brother.'

He was no use to her melancholy. 'Vidar needs stronger potions for his pain. I have some ready for you to take. And more ink.'

That had him staring. 'How do you know what Vidar needs? I never—'

'I'm a witch,' she said, taunting. 'There's very little I don't know.'

Balfre never cared for being challenged. 'Witch or not, Izusa, you're still a fucking woman! Don't presume to—'

In one lithe move she straddled him, and rubbed herself against his cock. 'I *am* a fucking woman. Did you want to fuck?'

Distracted, he seized her breasts. Pinched her nipples. Laughed at her gasp. 'Does a dog piss on three legs?'

She rubbed him harder. 'Let me think . . .'

His turn to gasp as his face flushed with desire. 'Before the thought escapes me,' he panted. 'The slaving raids into Clemen will have to stop. Humbert's making accusations. Until Aimery's safely dead I'd not pour oil on his flame.'

'I'll stop them. You pour oil on *my* flame.'

'Fucking witch,' he groaned, shuddering as she took him in. '*Izusa.*'

She finished him quickly, and he left her cottage soon after. The moment her front door closed behind him she hurried back to her small bedchamber and unwarded the baby's head, where it sat hidden in plain sight on a shelf near the bed.

'Salimbene?'

In the open ash box, the sunken eyes shifted beneath their greyish, papery lids. The little rosebud mouth pursed and relaxed. Then its lips parted.

'*Izusa.*'

'You were watching, Salimbene?'

'*I was. You handled him well.*'

A thrill of delight, more potent than a hundred thrusting cocks. 'You heard what he said about Humbert?'

'*Baldassare will be told.*' The dead lips curved in a brief, sardonic smile. '*The loss of ready coin will keep him restive. A good thing for a pirate. I'd not have him made sleek with easy pickings.*'

'Balfre grows so impatient,' she confided. 'I fear—'

'*Fear is weakness, Izusa. Be strong. Balfre will wait.*'

Foolish, to show misgivings. She bowed her head. 'Yes, Salimbene.'

'*The future ripens in our favour, Izusa. Harald's son has killed his first man.*'

She looked up. 'At last!'

'*Tonight I will send you a dream, Izusa. At dawn you will find the place you dream of and rune it from all eyes save his. You will rune the swords you find there. They belong to Liam and the innkeeper's son.*'

She trusted Salimbene without question. But *swords*? If Balfre or Humbert should stumble across the secret . . .

The baby's grey lips stretched in another brief smile. '*Your runes will keep them safe, Izusa. Sleep now, and wait for me.*'

'Salimbene.'

Alone again, she closed up the box and wreathed it in muffling charms. Then she fetched a stained piece of linen from the chest at the foot of her bed. The blood on it belonged to Harald's son. It was years old, but no less powerful for the passing of time. Taking her dagger, she slashed free a narrow strip of the rusty-red stained linen. She pissed on it, to start the magic brewing, then lay down to sleep . . . and dream.

*   *   *

The morning after the slaughter in Bell Wood there were chores. No great surprise, that. The Pig Whistle was full of chores. More chores than customers these days. For once, Liam and Benedikt didn't feel like moaning about them. Last night's story telling had been sombre, restful sleep hard to find – and full of blood.

Since they both hated pot-scouring, they tossed a copper nib to see who'd lose.

'Rough!' Benedikt called, but the coin landed smooth-side up on the kitchen floor. 'Feggit. Be ye fiddling it, Willem? That be four tosses in a row I've lost.'

Liam thumped his brother just hard enough to ache. 'Fiddle yourself, pizzle.'

Molly looked up from scraping carrots. 'I'll fiddle ye both 'less ye get to rolling up yer sleeves. And mind yer tongue, Willem. I'll have no rough talk from my boys.' Then she wrinkled her nose. 'Leastways not where I can hear it.'

'Iss, Ma,' said Benedikt, to avoid a cuff on the ear. 'Ma, since it be a splashy day, can we fish Chibbum Pond once chores be done? Fish do rise something easy in the rain. And ye always do say there b'aint no such thing as too much smoked fish.'

Lips pursed, Molly started on a fresh carrot. 'Be ye wheedling me, Benedikt?'

'Not wheedling, Ma. Just asking.'

'Chibbum Pond? No place else?'

Liam looked at his brother, and his brother looked back. Lying to Molly made Benedikt feel sick, after. She was hinting about Bell Wood. And while the swords weren't hidden there, they weren't at Chibbum Pond, neither.

'No place else, Moll,' he said easily, because he could lie to her all day. 'Promise.'

Scrape, scrape, scrape went Molly's paring knife. Little curls of carrot skin fell to the kitchen table, soft as snow. Molly's fingers were stained orange. She never cut herself.

'When yer chores be done,' she said, not looking up. 'But don't stay gone all day. Be best all round if Iddo finds ye here when he gets back, come dusk.'

Liam grinned at Benedikt. Sousing Iddo was near as much fun

as fishing. And with the day to themselves they'd have plenty of time to take a few fish and talk about sword-work. His fingers itched like fire to wrap themselves round a hilt.

'*Chores!*' said Molly, glaring. 'Willem, scrub the public-room benches with hot water and soft soap. But if a customer comes, mind, ye'll put yer bucket and brush aside and serve him.'

But it wasn't a local farmer or travelling merchant who cast his shadow over the Pig Whistle's threshhold. It was Harcia's Lord Waymon, mud-splashed and reeking of pride.

'Boy, I'd have words with Mistress Molly. Fetch her.'

Dropping the scrubbing brush into the pail of cooling soapy water, Liam stared at the Harcian lord. Arrogant shite, he'd never dare that tone of voice if he knew it was Clemen's rightful duke he spoke to.

'What words, my lord? Only Molly, she be—'

Waymon struck him. '*Fetch her!* Or fetch your head as it rolls across the floor.'

Scarred cheek burning, Liam dropped his gaze so Waymon wouldn't see the molten fury leaping inside him. 'Iss, my lord. Sorry, my lord. Never meant no harm, my lord.'

He fetched Molly, then retreated to the shadows between the bar and the kitchen so he could listen to what Waymon had to say.

'My lord,' Molly greeted him, bobbing in and out of a curtsy. 'How might I help ye?'

Beneath his leather riding cloak, Waymon's doublet was midnight blue and stitched with pearls. Its sleeves were slashed, showing silk beneath them. He wore a fat drop-pearl in his ear and gold rings on his gloved fingers. His muddy riding boots reached past his knees and his silver spurs glinted hints of gold in the public room's lamplight. Scowling, Liam fingered his own scratchy, roughspun wool sleeve.

When I'm a duke I'll dress like that. When I'm a duke I'll wear gold and pearls.

Waymon stared down his narrow nose. 'Count Balfre is deep displeased with Clemen. At every turn its duke and lords and men-at-arms seek to do us harm. I think you know this, Mistress Molly.'

Molly put up her chin. 'Lord Waymon, I b'aint any part of what dukes and counts and lords might do. The Pig Whistle be an honest inn, and we keeps to Marcher law.'

'Mistress Molly . . .' Waymon smiled, unfriendly, 'these are turbulent times. I'd think you would welcome a friend like Count Balfre.' He looked around the public room. 'The Pig Whistle is popular, but folk can be fickle. The Marches boast other inns. A few hints from Harcia's men-at-arms and you might find yourself wanting for custom. And of course life is unchancy. Accidents happen. People die.'

Liam saw the flinch run through Molly's stout body. 'D'ye be threatening me, Lord Waymon?'

'You'd take friendly advice as a threat?'

'Lord Humbert of Clemen, he be a man as offers friendly advice.'

'No doubt. But I do doubt he'll lift a finger when your son's taken for theft.'

'*Theft?*' Molly stepped back. 'My Benedikt's no thief!'

'A mother's love,' said Waymon, shrugging. 'And who will trust it when Count Balfre's Serjeant Grule swears he saw your son at trespass on his lord's manor estate, looking to take deer?'

'But it b'aint true!' Molly cried.

Waymon sneered. 'It's true if I say it is. And then your son hangs.'

Sick with rage, with fear, Liam watched Molly tremble. She knew he wasn't Willem. She knew he was Harald's son. What if she gave him to Waymon for a promise Benedikt would be safe? Would she do that? Should *he* do that? Benedikt was his brother. Could he let his brother hang?

And then Molly slumped, surrendering. 'What must I do?'

'Whatever I ask,' said Waymon. 'Share gossip from Clemen and further afield. The names and privy business of travellers seeking shelter under your roof. And from time to time you'll mention certain things in passing to men who'll take your words with them back to Clemen, and into the wider world.'

'I will,' said Molly, stifled.

'Remember,' Waymon said, his eyes narrowed. 'Your son's life depends on your obedience and good sense. For should I learn you've run bleating to Humbert of this . . .'

Benedikt would hang. Shaken, Liam watched Waymon leave. The moment the bastard was gone, he stumbled out from behind the bar.

'Molly! Waymon can't do that, can he? Ruin the Pig Whistle? Hang Benedikt on a lie?'

She turned to stare. '*Willem!*'

These days he never could be sure she loved him. Not when she feared him on account of who he was. But – she could've given him to Waymon and didn't. So she must love him a bit. And they both did love Benedikt.

'Ye can't let Waymon do this! Ye can't—'

'This b'aint yer concern, Willem!' she snarled. 'Run along. Catch me some fish. And if ye breathe a word to Iddo or Benedikt I'll whip the skin right off yer arse.'

No point arguing. He ran.

'That feggit Waymon!' Benedikt said, kicking the wet grass as they reached the home wood's far western edge, which ran up against Froggy Bogmarsh, where folk didn't go. Where they'd carefully hid the swords. 'I wish faeries were real, Willem. Then I could catch one and make it put a chant on him to shrivel his cock black and make it fall off!'

Liam slung his arm around Benedikt's shoulders. 'I know.'

'She can't do it, Willem. She can't tell lies for Harcia.'

'I think she has to. She b'aint got a choice.'

'But what if Humbert finds out?'

Then there'd be a mort of trouble. Only he didn't want to think on that now. 'He won't. Who'd tell him?'

'Maybe I should tell Iddo,' Benedikt muttered.

'*No!*' Stopping, he gave his brother a hard shake. 'Not a peep, Benedikt. Moll can look after herself.' Wishing he'd kept his mouth shut, he let go. 'And when I'm properly duke, I'll make feggit Waymon pay. The pizzle be a dead man walking. Promise.'

Benedikt sniffed. 'All right.'

'Any road,' he added, trying to be cheerful. 'We be here.'

'No.' Benedikt shook his head. 'This b'aint the right place.'

'Y'going blind, Benedikt?' He pointed. 'Look. There's the oak tree with the lightning scar halfway up its trunk. And there, just aside it, there's the hollow log where we hid the swords.'

Benedikt squinted. 'Where?'

'Feggit!' He grabbed his brother's arm. '*There!*'

'Oh,' said Benedikt, and laughed. 'Now I see it.'

He puffed out a breath. 'Maybe I should think twice afore crossing swords with you. If ye can't even see a feggit oak tree three times taller than—'

'I can see it! I can see it!' Benedikt elbowed him in the ribs. 'Come on. Don't forget we have to catch Ma her fish and get back to the Whistle afore dusk.'

They raced each other to the hollow log. Took out the precious swords, left their fishing lines and hooks for safety and plunged back into the sheltering trees a stone's throw from the stinky bogmarsh, where they could kill phantom men-at-arms with not a soul to see them.

'Wait!' Liam said, as Benedikt rushed to slaughter a seeded sapling. 'Benedikt, wait.'

Disappointed, his brother stopped. 'What?'

'This b'aint a game,' he said slowly, feeling the weight of the sword in his wrists, his forearms, all the way to his shoulders. The weight of what it meant, and who he was, and what one day he'd have to do. 'I'm duke of Clemen, Benedikt. And you be my trusted lord. We have to do this solemn. We have to do this *right*.'

'Right how?' said Benedikt, uncertain. 'Willem, we b'aint knights. We scarce know one end of a sword from t'other.'

'We saw them men-at-arms in Bell Wood. They knew what to do. Just . . . let's think on them. Y'know. How they held their swords and – and—'

'Screamed when they got their hands cut off?'

He glared at his brother. 'Y'know what I mean!'

'Iss, iss,' said Benedikt, rolling his eyes. 'All right then. We'll do like ye say.'

'Good.' He took a deep breath and lifted his blade. Felt the weight of the sword. The weight of his future. Felt the rightness of forged steel and felt himself smile. 'I reckon we start like this . . .'

Standing at his closet window, Humbert scowled through the gently persistent rain falling on a dozen men-at-arms at their sword-training in the tilt yard.

'Furthermore,' he growled, 'His Grace can tell that jackanapes Ercole to spit on himself for a nock-doddled pizzlewit. His Grace knows full well Balfre's a cockshite looking for tendered reason to shove a pike up our arseholes and only a brainless mankworm would oblige him! Yes?'

Brentton, his trusted personal herald, stoically nodded as he scribbled ink across a sheet of paper. 'My lord.'

'So His Grace should know this,' he continued. 'His appointed Marcher lord won't bow to pizzlewit pronouncements. If it's war in the Marches he's after, he'll need to find himself a new Humbert. This Humbert intends to leave law-abiding Harcian traders well alone from now on, and if Ercole and his coin-grasping goodfather don't like it let them be the ones to wade knee-high in blood.' He glanced at the herald. 'Yes?'

'– high . . . in . . . blood,' Brentton muttered, then nodded. 'My lord.'

Humbert grunted. Brentton had lightning fingers, and put together a cypher no soul but himself could read. Next to Egann, the herald was his most important servant. 'His Grace should also know said cockshite Balfre prances yet more green men-at-arms into the Marches. Since that bloody mess in Bell Wood I've laid eyes on a half-score new Harcian faces. My serjeant tells me others are rode away, just as before, so we'll still not pinch the shite for treaty-breaking. But I don't like it. Yes?'

Brentton dipped his quill in the inkpot. 'My lord.'

Fingers tugging at his beard, Humbert turned away from the window and wrestled with the need for self-preservation, set against love. Self-preservation lost.

'Roric,' he said, 'I'd have you think carefully on whose counsel you lean the hardest. Our men-at-arms perished in Bell Wood for no good reason. A worthy duke preserves his people. He doesn't toss them to rabid wolves on a whim. When he taxes, he taxes fairly. And when he imprisons, he turns the key with just cause. Don't squander your duchy's love for you. In hard times love is oft hard to find. It's harder to keep – and woeful easy to lose.'

'My lord?' said Brentton, when the silence had stretched for a good while. 'Is that all?'

Humbert roused himself from brooding. 'Yes. Ride hard for Eaglerock. Read what I've said to His Grace in privy audience. And if for any reason you're stopped unlawfully between here and the castle—'

'Destroy the letter.' Brentton bowed. 'Yes, my lord.'

'And tell Laffet to ready my palfrey. Rain or not, I'd ride the Marches a while. With luck a steady face and a friendly smile will go a little distance in calming fluttered hearts.'

But he'd not hold his breath for it. Pizzlewit Ercole and cockshite Balfre had between them stirred the Marches to a fever pitch of mistrust and resentment and naked, bloody fear. How could Roric not see that? How could he go on putting his trust in men like Ercole and Blane and the like, when their selfish advice served only to harm him – and Clemen?

Feeling a shudder of ill-omen, he rubbed the tips of his fingers against his closed eyes.

Roric . . . Roric . . . I wish you'd let me come home. I know you think you don't need me. But you're wrong, boy. You do.

CHAPTER THIRTY-FIVE

The mood in the crowded guildhall was ugly.

With Aistan seated by his right hand on the makeshift dais, Roric stared at the resentful faces of Broadthorpe's pinch-pursing, miscreant men of means. Swept his gaze around the sullen townsfolk seated behind that crowded front row. A sleepy, southwestern artisan township, Broadthorpe, one long day's ride from Eaglerock. Prosperous before the duchy's hard times, and still not broken. Full of silversmiths, weavers, blacksmiths and fine leatherwork. Foolishly its leaders had chosen to defy the lawful demands of their duke.

'Good people,' he said, keeping mellow, hoping that reason would yet carry the day, 'your disobedience serves you ill. This is Clemen not Zeidica or Borokand where despotic tyrants hold sway, caring nothing for the people they rule. What I ask of you, I ask out of concern for your welfare and love for this duchy.'

'Ha!' Broadthorpe's bullish mayor jutted his chin. 'Love for our coin boxes, more like.'

'Curb your insolence, Jarvas,' Aistan snapped. 'Or do you look for accommodation beneath Eaglerock castle?'

Broadthorpe's mayor stood, ponderous with the weight of his forty-nine years and bloated self-regard.

'Your Grace,' he said, glancing angrily at Aistan, 'since the arrival of your herald last week, we in Broadthorpe have talked most mightily on your demands for greater tithes, and taxes, and tollage of our bridges and roads. We do wonder now that you failed to ask a tollage for the air we breathe and the deposits in our nightjars. Mayhap you'd care to tax our eyelids for opening, our nails for growing and our arseholes for farting! In short, Your Grace, you ask too much!'

The townsfolk of Broadthorpe loudly applauded their mayor. Some shouted their support of him, others drummed their heels on the wooden floor to create an ominous thunder.

Aistan leaned close. 'Now will you stop placating them, Roric?' he said, pitching his voice below the uproar. 'These people are in need of a mailed fist holding a sword, not an empty hand stretched out in friendship.'

'You'd have my men-at-arms spill Clemen blood? See the people tremble at the mention of my name?' He shook his head. 'If that's what you're after, Aistan, you should've left Harald where he was.'

'I understand your reluctance,' Aistan said sharply. 'At one time I shared it. But Clemen can't support such rank defiance. Would you have Broadthorpe's pernicious rot spread throughout the duchy till we're mired in open revolt?'

He touched Aistan's arm. 'It won't come to that.'

'No?'

'No.' Sitting back, he waited for the townsfolk's clamour to die down. When the hall was almost quiet again, he steepled his fingers. 'Mayor Jarvas, have you come to hear reasoned argument or simply for raucous, closed-minded dispute?'

'We've come to tell you there's no more coin for Eaglerock!'

Jarvas retorted. 'We're citizens of a chartered township, Your Grace. Not cows to be milked whenever you fancy you've a thirst!'

'Thirst?' He laughed, derisive. 'You're a fool, Jarvas. It's starvation we face.'

Jarvas thrust out his chest, pigeon-wise, be-ringed fingers clutching the front of his black velvet robe. His gold and peacock-blue enamel chain of office winked in the torch and lamplight as he rocked on his heels.

'You look plump enough to me, Your Grace. You and Lord Aistan. Aye, and the rest of Clemen's council and its barons and your men-at-arms. D'you think the people of Broadthorpe don't know how things are done in Eaglerock?'

A fresh swell of muttering in the guildhall. Roric felt himself tense. He'd spurned Aistan's suggestion that he appear at this meeting wearing mail beneath martial leather and he'd left his serjeant, Homb, and his other men-at-arms outside rather than range them around him in an unspoken threat. Had he made a mistake? Were Broadthorpe's hackle-raised townsfolk about to start snarling and snapping?

Perhaps. But only if they scented fear.

Ignoring Aistan's choked-off protest, he stood and stepped down from the dais to confront Jarvas face to face. Waited for the townsfolk's muttering to cease, for their mayor to deflate his puffed chest. When he was sure of their attention, he looked Jarvas in the eye.

'You speak of whispers, man. Gossip. Let me tell you what I know. I know our harvests are yet meagre. I know intemperate weather is not our friend. I know plague and black-lung and slough and chalk-bone still stalk through Clemen, despite the precautions taken in Eaglerock harbour and no matter what our leeches do. I know desperate men take desperate measures to feed their hungry families, and though we've beaten back the pirates who came ashore to steal innocent Clemen-folk and sell them into vile bondage, they are still plundering those few merchants brave enough to dare the open waters. And most of all, Jarvas, most all, *I know this*. It takes coin to repair our ravaged duchy and *every man*, however great, however humble, must bear the burden of supplying it.'

Jarvas blinked. 'Your Grace—'

'You people of Broadthorpe!' Swinging aside, Roric began to pace between the dais and the township's prominent citizens seated in the front row. Swept his cold gaze across their wary faces. His sword, belted close, thumped against his leg with each stride. 'You hear scurrilous whispers and shout from your rooftops that they're true! *They are not true.* I demand coin and *more* than coin from my barons. I command them and their sons to raise their swords in Clemen's service. I tell them their men-at-arms must serve me first, leaving their homes and families at the mercy of any danger. And those men-at-arms I hold ready to protect any town or village in Clemen, should it be threatened by a foe. To *die* for you, uncomplaining. And you begrudge me coin? You ask Clemen's barons to pay for *everything*? You should hang your heads in shame.'

In the hush, as Broadthorpe's people exchanged uneasy glances, their mayor's nervous cough sounded loud. 'Your Grace—'

Still pacing, Roric raised a hand. '*Be silent.*'

The townsfolk stared, frozen, as Jarvas closed his mouth. No more raucous clamour. No drumming heels now.

'You boast of Broadthorpe's charter,' Roric said, giving his contempt free rein. 'Where do you think it came from? Who granted it? A *faery*? It was granted you by Harald. And what one duke can give you, another can take away. So here is fair warning, Jarvas. You know, and I know, it's within your means to pay Broadthorpe's reckoning. So within a tenday you'll see that exact amount surrendered to an official from Eaglerock's treasury – or you'll learn, to your great sorrow, what it means to wake my wrath. Broadthorpe's charter will be revoked, its independence shattered. You'll once again be chattel to be disposed of as I see fit.'

Jarvas swallowed. 'Your Grace.'

Halting, he seared the mute townsfolk with a measuring glare. 'I am not Harald. I do not punish imagined slights or shed blood capriciously. *But do not mistake my mercy for weakness.* Heed this warning, Broadthorpe. You defy me at your peril.'

The frozen silence continued, unbroken, as he and Aistan swept out of the guildhall and into Broadthorpe's market place. Serjeant Homb and his men-at-arms, seeing them, came to straighter attention.

Roric glanced sidelong at the man who'd taken Humbert's place. 'Well, Aistan? Satisfied?'

Aistan smiled briefly. 'I am.'

'I thought you might be.' He nodded at his serjeant. 'Let's go.'

They journeyed back to Eaglerock sweating. The weather was sultry for so late in the year, charcoal-grey clouds gathering, a threat of thunder and lightning and more crop-rotting rain. Water lay in stagnant pools along both edges of the sunken clay road that meandered some three leagues from the township to the edge of Cudrotham Wood, and the open fields on either side of them were so green their brilliance hurt the eye. Brindled milch cows, hides scabby with rain-scald, stood in grass so high it brushed their pendulous udders. Their swishing tails were soaked in liquid manure, the waterlogged grass so plentiful they seemed content to do nothing but drowse.

With the road too slippery and potholed for riding faster than a slow jog, Roric was able to peruse Aistan at his leisure. They were riding side by side, leaving their men-at-arms escort to discreetly bring up the rear.

'You're pensive, Aistan,' he remarked, after they'd ridden in silence for some time.

Aistan grunted. 'I'm weary. The years have crept up on me.' He patted a disordered lock of his horse's mane into place. 'And, if you'd know, I worry about Kennise.'

He rarely mentioned his youngest daughter. 'How does she go on? I hope time has eased her grief.'

'Kennise was ever fragile,' Aistan said, eventually. 'Harald left his mark on her. And it seems her life with Vidar was not as content as she let me believe.' He released an unsteady breath. 'But I think she improves, now the Marches are behind her.'

Roric blotted trickling sweat from his temple. Poor Kennise. One way and another, his family hadn't done well by this man's youngest daughter. 'I'm sorry she's had to endure so much pain.'

'I know.' Aistan frowned. 'And you, Your Grace? How do you go on, without Lindara? At least Kennise has her daughters. But you—' A heavy sigh. 'Forgive me. I don't mean to pry.'

He watched his gloved fingers tighten on his reins. 'I'd know who asks the question, Aistan. Clemen's councillor . . . or my friend.'

'Are we friends, Roric?'

'You tell me, my lord.'

'I'll tell you this,' said Aistan, sombre. 'After Humbert's sons perished, leaving you fostered alone beneath his roof, I watched Harald deliberately set you apart from Clemen's other young lords who would gladly have drawn you into their company. He made sure to deny you natural companionship so he might keep you tied to his whims and selfish generosity. Played up your bastardy even as he pretended to ignore it.'

Roric stared sidelong, jogging his horse stride for stride with Aistan. 'You think I don't know that?'

'I think . . .' Aistan smoothed his silvered beard. 'Roric, I've long suspected there is some darker truth behind Humbert's shift to the Marches. A reason beyond Clemen's safety that keeps him penned there. What it is, I don't need to know. Nor would I call him home. Humbert serves us well as a Marcher lord. But without him, without Lindara – and thanks to Harald's machinations – you are bereft of family. I think it unhealthy. Both for you and for Clemen.'

Pasture had given way to hedgerows on either side of the sunken clay road. Roric listened to the rustling and chep-chep of hedge-birds in the dark green foliage. Listened to the soggy, rhythmic thud of hooves striking damp clay. Their horses' bits jingled. One of the men-at-arms behind them coughed. The cloud-bruised sky seemed to sink lower towards the ground.

'I take it you've a remedy in mind.'

'I have a sad, lonely daughter, Roric. And you need a son.'

Laugh or weep. They were his choices. 'You'd give me your family, Aistan? Since I lack one of my own?'

Aistan turned to look at him, his eyes deep and shadowed. 'I'd give you a way to put the past behind you. A chance to make a happier future for yourself, and Kennise, and Clemen.'

By wedding and bedding the woman Harald had ruined. The woman Vidar had married because he couldn't have Lindara, who'd birthed him two daughters and now lived like a mouse in her father's manor. Coldspring sat empty, a waste of good land.

'I don't know what to say.'

'You can say yes,' Aistan replied. 'Roric, surely you know your childless state has long concerned the council. Given how Lindara died we've said nothing, to spare your feelings, hoping you'd come to admit the urgency of this for yourself. But you can't, or won't, and we can keep silent no longer. Indeed, to keep silent is to be derelict in our duty.'

His skin was crawling. 'I see.'

'You're displeased. I understand that. And were you an ordinary man the choice to wed or not would be yours, no one else's. But—'

'But I'm a duke. Which means my cock and seed belong to Clemen.'

'Crude. But true.'

'Except were I a stallion, Aistan, instead of a man, an astute horsekeeper would've have gelded me long since. Or has it slipped your mind that before I was widowed I sired no living child?'

'Why so quick to blame yourself? The fault might have been Lindara's. Roric—' Shifting in his saddle, Aistan fixed him with a steady stare. 'You stand today in the same place you stood the morning after Heartsong. Now, as you were then, you are a duke in want of an heir.'

And if that wasn't a cruel faery-trick, he didn't know what was. So many things Aistan and the council couldn't be told. Truths he had to keep secret lest Clemen be torn apart. But the alternative was impossible. Marry Kennise, another reluctant daughter? And who would *she* fuck, to numb her hurting heart?

He shook his head. 'You honour me, Aistan, but—'

'If you think I'd force Kennise to wed any man, even you, after all she's suffered,' Aistan said quickly, 'you're mistaken. Beneath my daughter's sorrow there is sweetness. I'd see it bloom. Kennise has always admired you. She often speaks of your kindness to her at Vidar's funeral, and since.'

Kindness. He needed no more lessons on how little difference kindness made in a marriage. Make Kennise his duchess? What had that woman ever done to deserve such a fate? Arthgallo was still treating him with noxious tinctures and pungent herbs, but the leech couldn't say for certain that his duke's seed was restored to health. How could he in good conscience bed Kennise not knowing if because of him she'd give birth to something foul as Lindara did?

'Aistan—'

'Roric, you must give Clemen an heir! If not by Kennise then by some other suitable woman. Without one, seeing us vulnerable, what do you think Balfre will do when Aimery dies and he's made duke?'

'You don't need me to answer that.'

'I think I do,' Aistan retorted. 'I need to be sure you understand the stakes!'

Fuck. As if anyone could understand the stakes better than he. Did Aistan and the council think he never *once* considered what would likely happen should he trip over his own feet and break his neck falling down a flight of stairs? *Fuck.* For months now he'd been thinking of little else. Knowing he should wed again, even though it would be a lie. Knowing he couldn't tell the truth, that Lindara had likely ruined him. Knowing that whatever he did it would be the wrong thing.

Somewhere, beyond the great divide between the quick and the dead, Harald was laughing.

He looked at Aistan. Time, at last, to know the truth for certain. 'Tell me. Was it you who told Cassinia's regents that Berardine of Ardenn had offered her daughter Catrain to me?'

Aistan's eyes widened. Then he nodded. 'Yes, Your Grace. It was.'

Surprised to silence, Roric blotted more sweat from his face. Looked ahead to Cudrotham Wood, perhaps a quarter league distant. The sunken road's footing was getting boggier. He slowed his horse to a walk. Aistan slowed with him, as did their men-at-arms.

'Odd,' he murmured. 'I suspected, but never thought to know for sure.'

'I believed I was doing the right thing. If you'll recall, Roric, I told you once that never did I do anything with a heart bent on harming Clemen.'

'And yet Clemen was harmed. Some might call that treason.'

'And you'd not wed a traitor's daughter?'

'I'd not wed any man's daughter, Aistan. Save that it seems I must. And since I must, why confess the truth now? After so many years, when you'd have me for Kennise?'

'Because I'd have you for Kennise,' Aistan said, shrugging. 'If you'd never asked the question, Roric, I'd have taken that truth to my grave. But you did ask and if I'd lied you'd have known it, I think. Then whatever trust there is between us would've died an ugly death.'

Trust. Too small a word, surely, for the gaping wounds left behind at its loss. He'd trusted Lindara, and Humbert, and both betrayed him. But what of Aistan? Had he truly betrayed Clemen? Or was it that in trying to protect the duchy he'd simply made a mistake.

'When you wrote to Cassinia's regents,' he said quietly, 'was it because you didn't trust me? Because I met with Berardine in secret? Did I give you cause for doubt?'

Aistan frowned at his horse's neck. 'You were young. Green. Seeking to establish your authority apart from Humbert. As for me, I was angry. My great dignity offended. By the time I understood your thinking, it was too late.'

In other words, yes. He was partly to blame. 'It was wrong of you to tell the regents of Berardine's offer. But it was wrong of me to meet with her before first consulting with you. Especially after all you'd risked, standing with me against Harald.'

Another silence, then Aistan glanced sideways. 'Does this mean I'm forgiven?'

The road ended, and Cudrotham Wood began. Passing from cloudy light into dappled shadow, Roric nudged his horse to a brisk trot as they struck the leaf-littered path. A moment, then Aistan caught up with him. Creaking leather, jangling bits, as the men-at-arms followed suit.

Roric looked again at Aistan, trotting beside him. 'Humbert swore Lindara loved me. He lied. Our marriage was a misery. Lindara never loved me a single minute of one day, and when she was dying she cursed me.'

Not even the woodland shadow could mask Aistan's shock. '*Roric*.'

'I know I have to marry again. I know I have to sire a son.' *Somehow*. 'But for pity's sake, at least for the moment, let's talk of something else. Broadthorpe. What are your thoughts?'

'If they deliver the coin they owe in timely fashion you won't hear me complain,' Aistan replied. 'But Broadthorpe is one township. You did well to shame them but will you wear out your tongue shaming every tardy town and village in Clemen? Or will you do as your council advises and let your lawful sword speak for you?'

'Berold never thought to raise his sword against his own people!'

'Berold never faced such perilous times – or the disobedience of those who'd seek to thwart the will of their duke.'

Mindful of the men-at-arms riding behind them, Roric lowered his voice. 'You agreed to depose Harald because you could no longer defend his actions. By that reckoning, Aistan, should I drown my sword in Clemen blood you'd be forced to depose *me*!'

'I don't advocate wholesale slaughter,' Aistan retorted. 'But you cannot shrink from making an example of the next reprobate who'd shake his fist at you, like that turd of a mayor Jarvas. His conduct sets a dangerous example. It teases others to test your bounds. Did you learn nothing from turning a deaf ear to the jeers of the malcontents in Eaglerock?'

He didn't relish the reminder. His willingness to tolerate a little rowdy discontent had led to a riot in the Shambles. A harsh lesson he wasn't keen to repeat.

'I take your point, my lord. I'll stomach no more men like Jarvas. And that's enough talk of Broadthorpe. Tell me of this new falcon you've procured.'

'Ah!' said Aistan, brightening. 'Now there's a pretty thing!'

Relieved, Roric let Kennise's father wax eloquent about his latest acquisition from Khafur. Trotting and cantering in turn, they made their way deeper into Cudrotham Wood.

The first arrow took Roric's palfrey through its throat.

As the horse dropped like a stone, taking him with it, he heard the high-pitched thrum of more arrows singing out of the weeded gloom. Lying winded on the damp ground, ankle trapped beneath his palfrey's carcase, he saw another arrow find the rump of Serjeant Homb's horse. It squealed and bolted, taking Homb with it. More arrows quivered in tree trunks, struck branches, impaled his dead horse.

'Stay down, Roric!' Aistan shouted, battling to keep his horse steady, positioning himself as best he could to draw fire. An arrow jutted from his thigh. 'Don't make yourself a target!'

The other men-at-arms had scattered in pursuit of their assailants. He could hear shouts and thudding hoof-beats off to the left, heading deeper into the woodland. No more arrows were flying.

'Roric, are you sore hurt?' said Aistan, his voice tight with pain.

His breathing almost returned, he shook his head. 'Bruised only.' He hoped. 'Who—'

The sound of uneven hoofbeats turned his head, had Aistan wrenching his horse about. But no danger. It was Serjeant Homb, his thin, sunweathered face slick with blood from an open welt across his left cheek. His grey horse's rump was daubed scarlet.

'Your Grace! Are you fettled? I swear I didn't run. My horse—'

'Bolted, I saw,' Roric said. 'And who could blame it, with an arrow in its arse?'

'My men ride down the shites behind this. Your Grace—'

'Don't fret, man. I'm breathing. But help me out from under this brute. Lord Aistan is wounded.'

Alarmed, Homb turned to Aistan then slithered from his saddle. Wincing, Roric did his best to help the serjeant lever the dead horse's hindquarters off his ankle. Groaned as he was half-pulled, and half-dragged himself, free. Propped on one elbow, he tried to argue with Aistan as the lord insisted that Homb first render aid to Clemen's duke.

'Leave me, Serjeant!' he snapped, giving up on Kennise's father. 'My leg's bruised, no more. Lord Aistan caught an arrow. See to him *now*.'

Dismounted and seated on a half-rotted log, his lined face pale, Aistan gritted his teeth as Homb inspected the wound.

'Could be worse, my lord,' Homb said. 'You've dribbled a bit, but there's no gushing pumper. The arrow's not in too deep to cut out, but I hesitate to inflict battle butchery on you.'

'Cut the shaft close to his leg, Homb,' Roric told him, on his feet, warily letting his bruised ankle take some weight. 'Leave the arrow-head embedded, and tie it off with a strip of linen. That should last well enough, Aistan, till we can get you to Arthgallo.'

Stoic, experienced, Aistan bore the serjeant's rough leeching with scarcely a sound. When it was done, his bloodied thigh bound tight with strips torn from Homb's shirt, he blinked his eyes free of sweat and looked around them.

'No experienced archers did this. One horse dead, by luck more than skill? Not a man killed but a dozen slaughtered trees. A shoddy business.'

He snorted. 'Then let me say I am all in favour of shoddy. Given I think we both know it should be me dead on the ground and not my horse.'

'Your Grace,' Homb said, his gaze seeking untoward movement in the shadows. 'I'd take Lord Aistan's horse and see how my men fare.'

Roric nodded. 'Go, Homb. And be wary.'

As the serjeant vaulted into the saddle then hustled the horse in pursuit of his men-at-arms, Aistan tried to stand.

'Don't be a fool,' Roric said. 'Nurse your strength. You think I don't remember what it's like to catch an arrow?'

''Tis good, I'll prosper,' Aistan muttered.

'I know you will, my lord.' He limped to the fallen log and lowered himself, stiffly. 'Especially by sitting quietly till we've no choice but to ride on.' He checked the strip of linen binding Aistan's thigh. Bloody, but not sodden, no major vessels breached. A piece of good luck. He rested a hand lightly on Aistan's shoulder. 'And I'll not forget how you put yourself between me and danger. It was—'

'My duty, Roric,' Aistan said, faintly smiling. 'And my privilege. I'd not—'

Then they both turned, at the sound of approaching horses. Roric stood, slowly, then limped to the middle of the path. Unsheathed his sword and waited. The hot stir of battle was fading. He felt chilled, and deadly. A few moments later Homb trotted into sight, his men behind him. Halting, he tossed onto the path three bows and three quivers emptied of arrows.

'Your Grace,' he said, nodding. 'We have them.'

He raised a hand and three of his men rode forward. Each had a body slung face-down across his horse in front of his saddle, bound at wrist and ankles with leather ties. Two of the captives wriggled. The third hung limp and dead. A snap of his fingers and the three assailants were shoved off the horses and onto the damp, leaf-littered ground. They fell awkwardly. Rolled face-down.

Roric smiled at the pained cries from the living. 'Well done, serjeant.' With an effort, masking the sharp pain, he closed on his assailants without revealing his lameness. Looked down at them, outwardly indifferent, then sliced the ties binding their ankles. Pricked them between their shoulderblades with the point of his sword. 'On your feet, cockshites.'

They were young men, no older than fifteen or sixteen. Brown haired, loose-limbed. One had brown eyes, the other green. They looked no more remarkable than any youths to be found on the streets of Eaglerock township. Beneath the mud and leaves plastering them, they seemed well fed. Respectable. Their doublets and hose were hardly extravagant but weren't pauper wear either. Brimful of frightened defiance, the youths stared at him. Roric stared back, no longer smiling.

'Do you know who I am?'

The taller youth sneered. 'Roric.'

He raised an eyebrow.

'Duke Roric,' the other youth muttered, sullen.

'And why did you attempt my life?'

Though his wrists were bound, the taller youth clenched his hands to fists. 'You be a tyrant! And a greedy bastard. You thieve the coin from honest Clemen folk so you might live high and mighty in Eaglerock castle. You've no care for our suffering so long as your belly's full!'

Pain stabbed through his chest but he kept his face stern. 'You come from Broadthorpe? All three of you?'

The youths looked down at their dead companion. The back of his brown doublet was ripped and blotted with drying blood. Lips trembled. Eyes widened. Then they exchanged glances and clamped their unsteady lips tight.

Roric shook his head. 'You come from Broadthorpe.'

The woodland hush had deepened further. Its gloom as well. No birdsong or clatter of wings in oak branches, or ash. No furtive scuttling of lizard or any warm-blooded creature through the undergrowth. The dappled sunlight was fading. Were those storm clouds closing in? Roric thought they must be. He could feel Aistan's eyes on him, and Serjeant Homb's. The eyes of every man-at-arms, angry and expectant. He kept his own gaze fixed on the two defiant, frightened young men before him.

'You are wrong about me. I am no tyrant. If you'd come to me in Broadthorpe with honest complaint, I'd have listened. Over the protests of my loyal councillor, Lord Aistan, whose life you also attempted, I'd have sat down with you. Broken bread with you. Listened to your grievances and helped you where I could. Instead you have cast yourselves into the midden. All that remains now is the choice you must make.'

The shorter youth, with green eyes, licked his dry lips. 'Choice?' he croaked. 'What choice?'

He held their wide-eyed stares steadily, showing them nothing but cold rage. 'Your lives are forfeit. You are lost. But if you answer my questions honestly I will spare you torture in Eaglerock's dungeons. Instead I'll give you a swift and merciful death. I will not mount your heads above the entrance to the castle and I will spare your families a similar fate.' He waited for his words to sink through their shock. 'But if you refuse to answer me, or you insult me with lies, believing that with you safely dead I'll never learn the truth of who you are, I will hurt your loved ones in ways you cannot imagine. Because I will learn the truth of you. You have nowhere to hide.'

Their defiance lasted mere heartbeats. Then the young men's knees buckled and they fell against each other, eyes white-rimmed with horror. And then, stammering, weeping, they answered his curt questions.

No, they'd not told their families they intended to do this terrible thing. They'd told no one in Broadthorpe. They were friends who listened to their fathers and the men in the township complaining and threatening but doing nothing about anything, 'cause they were bags of hot wind who blew and blew and blew nothing down.

They'd not been allowed in the guildhall for the meeting but they'd been outside. They'd heard enough to realise the mayor wasn't going to stand tall for Broadthorpe. That Jarvas was going to surrender with hardly a shout, barely a raised fist. It made them so angry they knew they could never let it pass. Someone had to speak for Clemen's ordinary folk. Strike a blow against the tyrant duke, the tyrant Harald's cousin, Roric. So they'd run, they'd fetched their horses and their weapons, and they'd galloped ahead to wait in Cudrotham Wood.

'And this is the truth?' Roric demanded, when they finished amongst a flurry of sobs. 'You swear it on your families' lives? On every scream of agony they'll utter if I learn you've lied?'

They swore it, incoherent. Believing them, Roric slid his sword back in its scabbard and instead withdrew his dagger from its sheath on his hip. Then he held out his left hand to Aistan, who withdrew his own dagger and tossed it into his grasp.

'Can you die like men?' he asked, looking at the ashen-faced youths. 'Or must my serjeant hold you down like sheep in a shambles?'

They nodded, shaking so hard their teeth chattered.

'Good, then.' Roric closed on them and cut the leather ties binding their wrists. 'Open your doublets.'

With trembling fingers, faces running tears and snot, they bared their hairless chests to the cool, damp air. His own fingers steady, his eyes dry, not letting himself think of what this meant, only how best to do it, he lightly rested the tip of each dagger against the flesh between their third and fourth left-hand ribs. The daggers heaved in time with his would-be murderers' desperate breathing, blades catching what little of the day's light still filtered through cloud and trees.

The taller youth stared. 'You – you never asked our names,' he said, bewildered. 'You don't know who we are.'

'I don't care who you are. You tried to kill me.'

The daggers punctured their hearts cleanly. Roric released his hold on each hilt as the bodies fell, so there'd be no dying gush of blood to spoil his clothing. Feeling cold, and strangely distant, he stared at the dead men. *What begins in secret must end in secret*. One of Harald's favourite sayings. One of the few Humbert ever agreed with. Secrets. Lies. Duplicity. All shades of the same uncomfortable colour. Once, for the greater good, he'd set discomfort and scruples aside.

And now it seemed he had no choice but to set them aside again.

'Homb,' he said, looking up at his serjeant. 'Lord Aistan and I will ride on to Eaglerock with two men. You and the rest stay behind to deal with this.'

Homb nodded. 'Yes, Your Grace.'

'Take these fools as deep into the woodland as can be reached. Strip them first so Cudrotham's scavengers aren't hindered. Keep their clothes and weapons to burn somewhere else.'

'Yes, Your Grace. And what of your horse?'

'The same, as far as you're able. Strip its tack, drag it as far off the path as you can and leave it for the wolves. Take the saddle and bridle with you to Eaglerock.' He frowned. 'We're down two horses. I'll have yours. You find the horses these cockshites rode here. That'll leave one spare. You can lead it. And one of your men will have to walk your wounded horse home.'

Homb's broad, leathery face creased in a wry smile. 'We'll manage, Your Grace.'

'There's to be no talk of this. You understand?'

Homb shifted in his saddle to look at the other men-at-arms. Shifted back. 'No talk of what, Your Grace?'

Feeling grim, Roric bent to pull the daggers from his would-be murderers' unmoving chests. As Homb and his men busied themselves with their orders, he wiped the blades clean on the dead men's hose, sheathed his own at his hip, then limped back to Aistan, still seated on the fallen, half-rotten log. Aistan took back his proffered dagger, eyes hooded with pain. The wound in his thigh was sluggishly seeping. He needed another bandage, something to staunch the blood.

Aistan read the thought. 'It can wait, Roric. I'm not dying.'

Ignoring Aistan's impatience, he took one of the dead men's stripped off linen shirts and slashed it to bandages and re-bound Aistan's wounded thigh, pulling an apologetic face as the man sucked in a sharp breath.

'Sorry.' Satisfied, at least for the moment, that Aistan wouldn't drop dead out of his saddle between here and Eaglerock, he took a deep breath, let it out very slowly, and made himself meet Aistan's considering gaze.

'So, my lord. Are you sure you still want me to wed with your daughter?'

'Roric, if you'd not put those curs down, *then* I'd be having second thoughts.'

'Ah.'

'This was not murder.'

No, it wasn't, any more than the Harcians he'd killed skirmishing in the Marches were murdered, or Harald slowly sliding off the length of his sword. He was Clemen's duke. The young men had attempted treason, the punishment for which was death. Everyone knew that.

And yet . . . and yet . . .

Aistan cursed. 'You did not fail them, Roric. Those young fools failed you. You were their duke and they *betrayed* you. They betrayed Clemen.'

It seemed Aistan knew him better than ever he realised. 'Then why does it feel as though I betrayed them?'

With another curse, Aistan pushed to his feet. 'If you feel that, it's because you're a good man, Roric. Would I have stood with you against Harald, would I be offering you my daughter, if you were *not*?'

'Aistan, you thought Vidar was a good man.'

'And he was, in his way. But never did I think him as good a man as you.'

There was nothing he could say to that, not without destroying lives for no good purpose. Instead he looked at his hands, his killing hands, that had pushed those daggers home without a heartbeat's hesitation.

'I find it peculiar,' he said slowly, 'when I think back to the night we decided to abandon Harald. All of us declaring our fealty null because he was so poor a duke, a man no man of conscience could support. And yet, under Harald, the duchy prospered. No blistermouth. No pestilence. No rotting crops in the fields. Our traders were free to roam Cassinia as they liked. The treasury was full and Clemen had its heir. If Liam had lived, if I'd not failed him, or if I'd left well enough alone? He'd be a young man now. And perhaps Clemen—'

Heedless of his wounded leg, Aistan pushed him. 'Enough, Roric. Harald was brutal. He had to be stopped. There was nothing but cruelty in him and he'd have raised his son the same. For Clemen's sake, we did the right thing. You *cannot* regret it now.'

Oh, but he could. 'You call Harald cruel, Aistan. And he was. But so am I. Even now my men-at-arms are disposing of those young men's bodies with no more care than if they were dogs. Their families will endure agony, never knowing their sons' fates.

''Tis better they suffer than their sons' attempted murder of you, made public knowledge, light a fire in Clemen to burn this duchy to ash.'

'And is that how I'll sleep at night? Is that how we'll sleep?'

'Roric,' Aistan tried to smile, 'I'll sleep because you're living. I'll sleep because they failed.'

Was that the answer? He thought not – but it would have to do for now. 'We should go, my lord,' he said, clapping Aistan lightly on the shoulder. 'Daylight trickles through our fingers, and you have an appointment with Arthgallo.'

CHAPTER THIRTY-SIX

'*You look plump enough to me, Your Grace. You and Lord Aistan. Aye, and the rest of Clemen's council and its barons and your men-at-arms and the rich folk you choose as your friends. D'you think the people of Broadthorpe don't know how things are done in Eaglerock?*'

A heated, disdainful accusation. Such resentment on the mayor of Broadthorpe's face. Dining with Master Blane and Ercole in the merchant's lavishly elegant Eaglerock townhouse, Roric couldn't help but wonder, yet again, if he'd not wandered far astray. The dining room's walls were hung with finest Pruges tapestries. Exquisite hand-woven Osfhar rugs graced the polished oak floor. Carved alabaster and carnelian horses pranced along one sideboard. So much wealth in one small chamber. Was Jarvas right?

'Your Grace? Is something not to your liking?'

He blinked away the vivid, discomforting memories of Broadthorpe. Forced himself to smile at his host, as though his life were sweet as roses. As though he'd not scant days ago, daggered to death two misguided and desperate young men.

'No, Blane. 'Tis all most pleasing.'

'Good, good.' Blane gestured at a servant. 'I'd have you taste this tarragon chicken, Your Grace. The recipe is new, in from Lepetto.'

611

The chicken was served. He tasted it. Said something vaguely complimentary, though in truth he could be eating charcoal and not know the difference. He'd hardly slept since returning from Broadthorpe. Cudrotham Wood haunted him. Just as Liam's death still haunted him, and the death of that unknown child in the exarchite hospice. Vidar's death. Lindara's. The death of their monstrous babe. His nights were crowded with wailing ghosts. Was it any wonder he feared to sleep?

'Your Grace.' Blane set down his dainty knife on the table. Sent the servants from the dining chamber with another curt gesture. 'While 'tis always a pleasure and a privilege to host you beneath my roof, I must confess I asked you here tonight with a wider purpose.'

He sat back. 'Indeed?'

'Indeed.' Blane picked up a napkin, dabbed creamy sauce from his flaxen beard. 'But I'll let my goodson unfold the mystery. Ercole?'

Ercole swallowed his mouthful of wine, hastily. 'Some time ago, Master Blane confided in me concern over whispers he'd been hearing from various sources in and around Eaglerock harbour – and abroad.'

'Whispers?' Roric sipped from his own wine-filled goblet. 'Touching upon what subject?'

'Many subjects, Your Grace,' said Blane. 'But alas, all with one theme. How venturing to do business with Clemen might prove hazardous to health.'

A sharp pain came to life behind his eyes. 'In what way hazardous?'

Ercole fiddled with an emerald ring, so that its smoothly planed facets caught the candle light. 'Unjust imposts. Lawless roads. Corrupt men-at-arms. Judicial thieving. And other suchlike tales.'

'That is untrue. All of it.'

'Most of it,' Blane said gently. 'But the little that is true has been grossly distorted.'

'By whom?'

'That is a tricky question to answer.'

'But I believe the reason is simple to see,' Ercole added. 'Someone wishes to hurt Clemen, and you with it. And, from what my goodfather tells me, there has been some success.'

The pain was pulsing in time with his fast-beating heart. 'Does this someone have a name?'

Blane shrugged. 'We suspect Aimery of course. Balfre. I'm sure that comes as no surprise. But the matter proves less straightforward than that.'

Of course it did. 'How so?'

'Well . . .' Blane smoothed his beard. 'At first I dismissed these whispers as the sour complaints you'll hear in any dockside tavern, or where merchants of different stripes gather to share news. But when the whispers persisted, I took it upon myself to make enquiries. I am uniquely placed to do so, I'm sure you'll agree. Your Grace, there is more than one common theme at play here.'

'Your Grace . . .' Ercole leaned a little across the table. 'We've discovered that these damaging, ill-founded rumours sprang to life in the Marches. Out of the Pig Whistle Inn.'

The Marches. *Humbert*. Roric drank more wine. 'How long have you and Master Blane been pursuing this, Ercole?'

Ercole and Blane glanced at each other. 'Some four months, Your Grace,' the merchant murmured. 'I'd beg you not to look harshly upon my goodson for keeping silent. 'Twas at my insistence. As you well know, I'm a cautious man. It has taken years for my trading ventures to recover from the storms that have buffeted Clemen. I was in no rush to upheaval them.'

Ercole was shaking his head. 'Master Blane seeks to protect me for his grand-daughter's sake. He loves my wife dearly and would not see her suffer for my misjudgement. The truth is that I share responsibility for not speaking of this sooner. You bear so many burdens already, Roric. I was reluctant to mention anything without more than vague whispers to show you.'

Because he was tempted to empty his goblet in one swallow, Roric nudged it out of comfortable reach. 'I see.'

'There is something else.' Ercole folded his plump hands on the table. 'I'm sorry, but I think you must know. When my goodfather told me of the Pig Whistle's involvement, I wrote straight to Lord Humbert and asked him to make enquiries of his own. Being Clemen's Marcher lord he is best placed to uncover the truth of this mischief.'

'Humbert has said nothing of it to me, Ercole.'

'Nor has he answered my requests. Which is why I do mention the matter to you here and now, privily. There is much history between you and Humbert. I'd not stir trouble in open council.'

And here was another of the great reversals in his life – that he could be taking earnest counsel from Argante's indolent half-brother, while the man who'd helped raise him, had loved him like a son, now languished in exile, swirled about with dark doubts.

'Ercole . . .' Roric looked up. 'Do you suggest Lord Humbert conspires with Harcia against us?'

'I suggest nothing. But, as I said – I thought you should know.'

He didn't want to hear this. How could he even *suspect* Humbert of such treachery, let alone believe it? And yet had anyone told him that Humbert would one day lie and cheat and torment his own daughter to make her a duchess, inveigle a good man like Arthgallo to lie and cheat for him, place his own desires and ambitions above Clemen's interests . . .

'Go to the Marches, Ercole,' he said curtly. 'Speak with Humbert. Whatever the truth is here, I'd know it.'

''Ware, my lord! Behind you!'

The warning came half a heartbeat too late. Humbert shouted in pain and anger as the sell-sword's blow thudded across his back. He heard his leather doublet split, felt the iron rings of his mail bite through wool and linen into flesh.

'Cockshite!' he bellowed, and on a pivot drove the hilt of his sword into the Sassanine's tattooed face. Sell-sword blood spurted and the turd crashed to the muddy ground. Another pivot and his sword was plunging through the turd's throat. He pulled it free, sweat and blood slicking his face, stinging his eyes. A blink, a headshake, and he could see again. More trouble. Stepping over the sell-sword's twitching body, he turned a little and drove his shoulder into the back of another Sassanine about to dagger one of his men. It hurt like fuck but the sell-sword went down. Before he could catch his breath, his man-at-arms had finished the task.

'Lord Humbert! That's all of them!'

Four sell-swords. Four corpses. An anxious check of Clemen's men-at-arms – and he could smile. Every one of them still on his feet. Some blood, some bruises, but no limbs lost, no bellies slit, no throats cut from ear to ear. Groaning, he braced a fist on his thigh and bent over, let the red haze of battle drain out of him like blood.

'My lord! Are you sore hurt?'

And that was Egann, sliding a hand under his elbow, helping him to stand straight. His spine cracked. His head spun. The back of his shoulder was on fire.

'Don't fuss, man. Do I look dead to you?'

Egann grinned, his teeth ghastly in a mask of red. He had a dagger-slash across the bridge of his nose and into his right cheek. 'My lord, you look doughty. But take a breath. We've time.'

Did they? He wasn't so sure of that. Huddled on the side of the muddy road, three Harcian spice merchants clutched at each other and stared in horror at the spilled blood and the dead sell-swords and the sharp blades of the two Clemen men-at-arms holding them under guard.

Stupid *cockshites*. What were they thinking?

Humbert fished beneath his doublet and mail for the tail-end of his linen shirt, pulled it free, and wiped the worst of the blood from his blade. Then he shoved the sword back in its scabbard and stamped through shallow puddles to the merchants.

'You.' He jerked his beard at the gabblemonger who'd spoken for all the merchants when they were first challenged. 'Care to reconsider showing me your trading papers?'

'I can't,' the spice merchant said, quavering. 'Your slaughtering men-at-arms frighted our mules! They've likely bolted themselves to broken legs and the ruin of our wares. This is a disgrace. I protest—'

Humbert bared his teeth. 'You protest? *Cockshite!* It's Clemen protesting here, you scabrous, pissing pizzle. You brought *sell-swords* into the Clemen Marches. And that means you dragged them with you all the way here from Eaglerock harbour!'

'We had to!' the merchant shouted. 'Everyone knows Clemen's unsafe these days. Lawless men riding the highways, lurking about inns and hostelries, cutting throats with no fear of capture or justice. If Baldassare's pirates weren't plundering every merchant galley and Sassanine grain ship they could sink we'd not have set foot in your pestilent duchy. We were protecting ourselves. We've done nothing wrong!'

'*Nothing wrong?*' He could've struck the shite. 'You broke Marcher law. No swords here but those worn by a lawful man-at-arms. And don't tell me it wasn't deliberate! Look where we are.' Despite the pain in his shoulder, he swept a pointing finger around them, at the encroaching straggle of trees and the rough, rutted road. 'Half a league from the main trader road through the Marches. You thought to creep your way past my men-at-arms like rats in a pantry.' He jutted his beard. 'Your mistake. When *I'm* through protesting you'll never trade through Clemen again. *Egann!*'

Egann joined him. 'My lord?'

'Send a man to find these pizzles' mules. I doubt they've gone far, roped together.'

'Yes, my lord.'

He looked again to the merchant, whose face was turned the colour of spoiled milk. 'The sell-swords. I know they were Sassanine. Where did you hire them?'

'A tavern,' the merchant muttered. 'In Eaglerock harbour.'

Oh, Roric. 'Well, I'll not be fouling Clemen soil with rotting sell-sword flesh.' A glance at Egann. 'Tie the bodies to the mules after you find them. These pizzles brought them here. They can take them away.'

Gasping, the merchants exchanged horrified stares. 'You can't do that!' cried the gabblemonger. 'The blood – it might ruin our spices!'

'Do I look like a man as gives a witch's tit for your spices? Find yourselves an exarchite house in Harcia and leave the corpses there. Those grey miseries like to be charitable.'

The gabblemonger merchant shut his mouth. A little wisdom, far too late.

'Egann.' Humbert turned his back on the anguished Harcians. 'After what happened in Bell Wood there'll be a stink on this like a bathful of old fish guts. I want their trading papers. Once you have the mules, the papers, and the bodies tied to the mules, escort these cockshites safe into the Harcian Marches. Balfre can worry about them after that. Then you can leave the men to their business and bring the papers to me at the manor.'

Egann nodded. 'Yes, my lord.'

'Unless—' Belatedly, he took a second look at the wound in Egann's face. 'D'you need leeching first?'

'No, my lord. I'm doughty.'

He clapped Egann on the arm. 'You are that. Go on, then. Why are you still standing about?'

When it came to skirmishing, Clemen's Marcher horses were trained from first handling to shift out of reach of swords and daggers once their rider was dismounted then wait to be caught. Humbert retrieved his stallion from the nearby woodland, hauled himself wincing into his saddle, and made his bad-tempered way back to the manor.

'Lord Humbert!' Ffolliot, the manor steward, gaped in horror as he came in from the stables. 'What – are you – should I—'

'Peace, man,' he growled, stripping off his bloodstained gloves. 'Most of the red's not mine. Send down for the barracks leech.' He tossed the gloves onto the comfortably shabby hall's sideboard. 'And to the kitchen for something hot. Killing sell-swords stirs the appetite.'

'My lord,' Ffolliot said faintly. Fastidious, he retrieved the gloves and held them like a housemaid dangling a dead mouse. 'Should I not send a boy to seek Izusa?'

She was certainly sweeter to the eye than Greyne. But he wasn't near to dying and besides, the barracks leech was at hand. 'Greyne will do. He'll find me in the dayroom. Bring me some food there and a fresh shirt, doublet and hose, then don't disturb me after.'

Leaving Ffolliot to mutter unhappily under his breath, Humbert retreated, aching, to the equally shabby dayroom. Ffolliot was known to mutter about that, too, but he had no patience for frippery. The manor was his barracks. He'd not spend Roric's scant treasury coin on nonsense.

He was partway through a bowl of hot mutton pottage when Greyne arrived. The barracks leech was no Arthgallo but he did well enough. They were all much the same, leeches and healers and bone-breakers. Never content lest they were causing a man grief.

He yelped as Greyne helped him out of his battered leathers and mail. Yelped again as the leech poked strong fingers into his shoulderblade. 'Shite, man! Are you trying to finish what that cockshite sell-sword started?'

Ignoring him, Greyne turned aside to his leeching bag. 'The flesh is a little pulped, my lord, but not badly pierced. The bruising goes down to the bone, however. As for your nicks and cuts, none of them need stitching. This time. You'll be sore some goodly days.' A scolding frown. 'You should take better care.'

'By that you mean send my men-at-arms where I fear to go myself?' He snorted in disgust. 'Pizzle. Stick to your leeching.'

'Courage oft survives beyond a man's strength to support it,' Greyne said, undaunted. 'It's no shame to admit you're not a young bear any more.'

'I know my years and what's to be done with them, Greyne. I am my duke's Marcher lord. When the law's broken, and wicked men draw swords, I must fight.'

'Yes, my lord,' Greyne murmured, and busied himself with slopping together a stinking poultice.

Waiting for him, stripped to his hose, Humbert spooned down the rest of his pottage then brooded into the dayroom's warming fire. Five months, just gone, since that deadly skirmish in Bell Wood and hardly a day without some kind of strife in it to give him a megrim. When he wasn't confronting that arrogant shite Waymon for chivvying Clemen merchants, or trading barbs afterwards with Balfre – who'd never kick that shite in the balls when he should – he was breaking up taunt-fests between his men and Harcia's and settling pizzling disputes among Clemen's Marcher-folk, all of them on needle-point and looking daggers at each other. He'd not had to hang anyone yet but he feared that was only a matter of time. Not a soul in the Marches, it seemed, who wasn't eggshell-close to cracking.

And now he had *sell-swords* to deal with. *Fuck*. Because where there were four there'd be more. He'd wager his best doublet on that.

'Lord Humbert?'

Blinking, he looked at Greyne. 'What?'

The leech held up his slop-filled mortar. 'The poultice is ready.'

He cursed when the stinking slop woke his wounded shoulderblade to fresh burning. As it dried, Greyne dabbed ointment on his small wounds and bruises then trussed him in a linen bandage to hold the poultice in place.

'And if I thought you'd heed me, my lord,' he said, when he was done, 'I'd say rest that arm and shoulder in a sling.' He held up a stoppered glass bottle. 'Here are comfrey and poppy pills. You know how to take them. Leave the poultice a full day. I'll look at you again on the morrow.'

'My thanks, Greyne. Be warned, the men who fought with me will be back at the barracks by-and-by. Pay special heed to Egann. He took a dagger to the face.'

Greyne raised an eyebrow. 'And yet I do not see him here, seeking my help. But then – did I tell you I was shocked, my lord, I'd be telling you a lie.'

'Ha,' he said sourly. 'Think yourself a jongler, do you? Help me into my clothes.'

Dressed again, and Greyne departed, Humbert poured himself a goblet of strong porter. The ruby-red wine bit his throat and seared his gullet. Beyond the dayroom's window the sky was bright, but he could feel a melancholy descending, damp and dismal as a cloud. He could have lost his life skirmishing with those cockshite sell-swords. To fall in Clemen's service, that was a noble death. But to fall so far from Eaglerock, unreconciled with Roric, with his beloved duchy floundering . . . that, he couldn't bear.

The dayroom door opened. 'Ffolliot, are you ramshackle? Did you not hear me—'

'I told your steward to stand aside, Humbert.'

Stunned, Humbert turned. 'Ercole?'

Closing the dayroom door, Argante's wilted pizzle of a half-brother offered him a perfunctory smile. 'My lord.'

Ercole. Well, well. Since last they'd met, the little shite had gained flesh and an air of unctuous superiority. What he lacked of his dead half-sister's extravagant good looks he more than made up for with the richness of his clothing. Pink Khafuri diamonds winked on his fingers, in his ears, and his gold-stitched violet doublet was brocaded silk.

Humbert put down his goblet, then pretended it wasn't there. Be curs't if he offered a grubby mankworm like Ercole a single drop of his wine.

'I don't know why you're here,' he said, 'but as it happens—'

Wandering the dayroom as though he owned it, the arrogant pizzle,

Ercole fluttered fingers crusted with jewelled rings. 'I've come at Roric's request, Humbert. There are disturbing matters he'd have explained.'

Roric. How greasily the name slipped from Ercole's meddling tongue. 'Disturbing?' He scowled, feeling his temper leap like an oil-fed flame. 'I'll tell you what's disturbing, Ercole. Being set upon by sell-swords from Sassanine, *that's* disturbing!'

Taken aback, Ercole halted. '*Sell-swords?* Why were—'

'Clap tongue and I'll tell you. Harcian spice-merchants did hire four of the murderous cockshites in Eaglerock harbour, then doddled with them all the length of Clemen and into the Marches. I was riding out with Egann and some of our men-at-arms. We crossed paths with the merchants and their escort, my hackles went up, and when I challenged them—' He spread his hands wide, then clapped them sharply. 'The cockshite sell-swords attacked.'

'But how did they—'

'*How?* 'Twas a simple matter, Ercole. Because not a man of yours in the harbour, not a man-at-arms *anywhere* in the duchy, did notice three cockshite Harcian merchants with *Sassanine sell-swords* trailing behind them like farts.'

'Humbert, you—'

He crashed a fist to the sideboard. The flagon of porter leapt and wobbled, splashing wine like blood. 'What are Roric and the council playing at down in Eaglerock? How did you let this slip under your noses? *Sell-swords* roaming free on Clemen soil. Do you know what Balfre will do with this? Do you know the trouble he'll cause here now? Because it was Harcian merchants who hired those sell-swords, and Harcian merchants we pointed our swords at, and Harcian merchants who'll run to Aimery's son shrieking that Humbert of Clemen did threaten their lives!'

'That is not His Grace's fault, or mine!' Ercole protested. 'You are the Marcher lord here, Humbert. 'Tis your task to keep the peace. Which you have not done as well as you ought, and if you think Roric hasn't noticed that, you're sadly out of touch. Now moderate your tone, my lord, for I'll not be spoken to in such fashion!'

'I'll talk to you any pizzling way I please! By a wonder none of my men was killed putting down those Sassanine fucks. But Egann near had his face sliced right off his skull!'

Ercole blanched. Mincing little pizzle. Never on his best day did he do himself credit with a sword. The sight of blood was known to send him swooning, like a maid.

Breathing heavily, feeling every cut and bruise and the pulped flesh beneath his poultice, Humbert tugged at his beard. 'You'd best tell Roric of this the moment you get back to Eaglerock. Tell him to keep a closer eye on merchants coming through the harbour. And any merchants already prancing their merry way about the duchy. There'll be sell-swords with a mort of them, I'll stake my good name on it.'

'Certainly I shall inform His Grace of this unfortunate confrontation,' Ercole said stiffly. 'But first you will listen to what I have come to say. Roric is—'

Humbert held up his hand. 'Wait.'

Something was tugging at him, something important. A niggling itch at the back of his mind. Sell-swords. Spice-merchants. *Everyone knows Clemen's unsafe these days*. And something about the pirate Baldassare . . . and grain ships . . .

Ercole drew in a sharp breath. '*Humbert!* I will not—'

'You will if you care what happens to Clemen,' he retorted. 'Harcia's been bartering grain from Sassanine. You recall?'

'Grain?' Ercole stared. 'Humbert, I've not ridden all the way from Eaglerock to be shouted at and—'

'*Clap tongue*, you pizzle! Roric needs to hear this! Or is it that you remember me as a man who flaps his tongue to no good purpose?'

Pinch-lipped, Ercole grasped the back of a nearby chair. 'My lord, you are unwise to speak to me as to a servant. I stand most high in His Grace's esteem.'

And if that was true, then shame and woe upon Roric. For should a man like Ercole be so highly placed in his confidence then surely the boy had lost his way.

'Perhaps,' he said softly, a terrible ache in his chest. 'But I advise you to listen nonetheless. I have this from one of those cockshite Harcian merchants. Baldassare's taken to plundering the grain ships running from Sassanine to Harcia. Let Harcia's people grow hungry and where do you think Aimery will look to find bread for their empty bellies?'

Ercole let go of the chair. 'Oh.'

'It might not come to anything,' he added. 'The cockshite merchant might've been lying. Or wrong. But Roric must be told. Aimery's duchy is more precarious than it was. What if in the end Grefin fails to hold the Green Isle against those northern raiders? You've seen horses panicked by wolves, Ercole. They'll run and they'll run and they don't care what they trample.' He tugged his beard. 'Now. What was it you came to say?'

Waspish, Ercole smoothed the front of his doublet. 'So I'm to be permitted to speak at last, am I?'

Abruptly weary, he sank onto a padded settle. 'By all means, Ercole. For the sooner you've flapped your tongue, the sooner you can leave.'

A nasty light glittered in Ercole's pouched eyes. He reached within his doublet, retrieved a small folded, wax-sealed letter, and held it out.

'Read this first.'

He had no choice. He was forced to rise and take the letter. It made of him a supplicant. Resentment curdled his blood. He cracked the wax seal and unfolded the paper.

Ercole speaks with my authority. Answer his questions. Roric.

He tossed the letter on the settle. 'What's this about, Ercole?'

'Roric wants to know why you've failed to quash the ugly rumours flooding out of these Marches like stale piss from a brothel.'

'What rumours? I know nothing of—'

Everyone knows Clemen's unsafe these days.

Ercole smirked. 'You know nothing? The look on your face says otherwise, my lord.'

'Wind,' he said, glowering. 'Ercole, what shite are you stirring now?'

'I doubt Roric would care to hear you dismiss his grave concerns as *shite*. I can tell you, Humbert, he is already most distressed. These lies spreading from the Pig Whistle are being whispered so far afield as Maletti.'

'The Pig Whistle? What's the Pig Whistle to do with this?'

'The Pig Whistle lies at the heart of Roric's dismay. As do you, Humbert. His Grace can't understand why you've not pursued this invidious matter as I asked.'

Humbert stared at the little cockshite, dumbfounded. He'd not hit his head fighting those sell-swords, had he? Or perhaps he was tiddly, his one goblet of porter rushed straight to his noddle.

'You've asked me for nothing, Ercole. As for these so-called rumours, this is the first I've heard of them. One of those Harcian spice-merchants said something, but aside from that? You're full of piss.'

'Humbert.' Ercole sighed. 'I did indeed instruct you to investigate the rumours, and the Pig Whistle. Why you chose to ignore that, I can hardly say. It's not me you'll answer to for your dereliction, but Roric.'

The mankworm was lying. There might well be rumours spreading, harmful to Clemen, but this fucking little pizzle had never written of them to him. Worse, the malicious glint in Ercole's eyes said the shite knew there was no way to prove his claim false. Here was base treachery. An attempt to topple him into disgrace in revenge for past slights. His heart thudded with a sick swiftness that stole his breath. *Roric*. The name was like a bruise. All the old pain rewoken, the old resentment made new. Everything he'd ever done had been for love of Clemen, and that boy. Always, *always*, he'd acted out of love. And in return . . .

'You little turd,' he said, and couldn't keep the tremor from his voice. 'I was shedding blood for Clemen when you were shitting in your nappy. If Roric wants an accounting from me then Roric can fucking well come here and ask for it himself! And you can scuttle back to Eaglerock and tell him I said so!'

'I am here for an accounting on Roric's behalf!' Ercole retorted. 'Or did your ageing eyes misread the letter he sent? Your duke wants the truth of this matter, my lord. Should I scuttle back to Eaglerock and tell him Humbert pisses on truth? How long before you exchange this manor for a dungeon, d'you think, did I tell Roric *that*?'

'Isn't a dungeon where you want me?'

'Humbert, I want you dead!' Ercole spat. 'My sister was slaughtered because of you, her child burned alive in the castle that should've

623

kept him safe. Every day since Heartsong I have dreamed of your destruction. But I won't destroy Clemen to have it. I don't need to. I have wealth and family and Roric's trusting ear. You're old and alone and cooped up in these Marches. That's vengeance enough.'

Turning aside, Humbert battled his own fury, that urged him to plunge a dagger between the cockshite's ribs. If only he could disbelieve Ercole's concern for Clemen. But if his hatred was honest, so was the rest.

'You've no doubt these rumours against Clemen spring from the Pig Whistle?'

'None. My goodfather and I have spent months seeking the truth of this.'

Fuck. He was tired. He was aching. He had a stinking poultice bound to his back. But if Molly of the Pig Whistle had thrown her lot in with Balfre – and it had to be Balfre behind this, there could be no one else – he must find out for himself. And if it was true then he must make her rue the day she sold herself to Aimery's son. Yes. Times were hard. But they could always get harder. Something Molly should have thought on before betraying Clemen to Harcia.

He looked at Ercole. 'Wait here. I'll return shortly.'

'You go to the Pig Whistle?' Ercole lifted his chin. 'Then you'll not go alone. *I* speak for Roric in this matter. Not you.'

'Ercole . . .' He tugged his beard again, hard. 'Molly might be a sly, conniving bitch but they don't call her queen of the Pig Whistle for naught. You'll never browbeat her. She could break you in half with one hand.' He looked the shite up and down. 'Especially now, when a blind goat could see you're better pastured than a hog fattened for the high board.'

Ercole flushed. 'Salve your pride by insulting me, if you must. I won't stay behind, Humbert. And you'd be wise not to test me.'

He'd be wise to snap the cockshite's neck, bury his body and pretend to the world they'd parted friends. A pity he was a fool.

'Fine,' he said. 'But if you're wise, Ercole, you'll remember this is the Marches, not Eaglerock, and which of us here is the Marcher lord.'

After five months of careful practice, Liam liked to think he knew which end of a sword was which. And why wouldn't he? Ever since

Bell Wood, twice a week and sometimes thrice, he and Benedikt had managed to sneak free of Molly and Iddo and find somewhere safe to wield a blade. This afternoon they were meant to be wood-fetching. And they were. Or they'd get round to it. Once they'd danced a while with their swords.

In the early days they'd not dared face each other. How could they explain a sword-cut to Molly? Instead they'd sliced the air to ribbons. Stabbed nettle-stacks. Killed thistles. Then, once their muscles hardened and their wrists toughened and the swords began to feel like their own flesh, not steel sticks, they'd gingerly begun pretend-fighting. That was when they made sure to wrap their blades in strips of burlap sacking pilfered from Gwatkin's stables. It muffled the sound and kept them safe.

But ever since he'd opened his eyes that morning, Liam had felt oddly restless. Felt he and Benedikt were somehow cheating with the burlap. He wanted to hear the true steel ringing of blade against blade, feel the shock of each blow unmuffled as it thrummed through his bones. Training with a wrapped blade? That was no better than playing with sticks.

He told Benedikt his plan on the way to fetch Farmer Spurfield's horse and cart from nearby Tiddy Pond farm. The Pig Whistle's carting mare was lame in a hindleg. Spurfield was helping out in return for a share of the wood they gathered.

'I dunt know, Willem,' his brother said, pulling a doubting face. 'Swords make a mort of clash. I know the far side of Froggy Bogmarsh hushy, but still. What if someone hears?'

'We got axes,' he said, hefting his. 'For wood-chopping. Who's going to think it be swords? Benedikt, we got to clash blades proper sooner or later.'

Benedikt rolled his eyes. 'Fine. Only if I cut yer hand off, Willem, don't ye dare throw a tantrum.'

And that was that. He'd won. He nearly always won.

They trundled the horse-and-cart from Tiddy Pond farm out to their swords. Tied the nag's reins to a stout sapling, then ventured into the nearby woodland with their unwrapped swords and the axes and the familiar, heady excitement of sword-play bubbling in their blood.

Facing his brother, Liam raised his naked blade and grinned. 'Ready?'

'Iss,' said Benedikt. 'No. Willem, be ye sure?'

'Don't fret yerself. Ye won't hurt me.'

They danced and danced, laughing, like real men-at-arms. But in the end he wasn't the one who bled.

'*Willem!*' Shocked, Benedikt lifted his spoiled, roughspun smock and bared his sword-slit skin to the air. 'Ye gormless pizzle!'

Liam stared at the red trickle down Benedikt's ribs. Swallowed. ''T'aint so bad.'

'How would ye know?' Benedikt poked at the wound with the tip of his grubby finger. 'It hurts!'

'Ye b'aint *dead*, Benedikt,' he said, feeling his knees turn wobbly.

'Feggit,' Benedikt muttered, and let fall his smock. 'I be done with this, Willem. No more crossing blades when they b'aint wrapped. It be too risky.'

He hated to give up. He wouldn't give up. But he'd have to wait a while. Benedikt could be mule-stubborn when he liked.

'Anyway,' his brother added. 'There b'aint no more time for swords. We got to fetch and chop wood, then cart it back to the Whistle, empty the cart, take it back to Farmer Spurfield and leg it home agin afore dark! 'Cause if we dunt, ye d'know Iddo will make our lives a feggit misery.'

He sighed. That was true. They might've grown too big for whippings in the cellar, but Iddo was still a mean bastard.

'Iss,' he said. 'I know.' Reaching out, he tousled his fretsome brother's hair. 'Sorry I stuck ye, Benedikt. Come on. Let's chop wood.'

Rushing back and forth between kitchen and public room, Molly started to regret sending them boys out to fetch more wood for the Pig Whistle. With coin so tight she'd long since had to give up hiring a pair of hands to help her and that surely did make for aches and pains when her inn got busy, like it was just now on account of Lord Humbert's clash with those Harcian spice-merchants and folk wanting to chinwag on it. Sell-swords in the Marches! The faeries protect them, what next? Soon enough Marcher folk wouldn't be safe in their beds. But though the news was surely alarming, there was a part of her couldn't be sorry, as such. Sell-swords in the Marches meant her public room was nigh on half-full. She couldn't remember the last time she'd sold so many tankards of ale.

Coming back into the kitchen with a tray of emptied pottage bowls, she caught a whiff of burning. Cursed, abandoned the tray, and dragged a stew pot off the hob. The bottom had caught. Now she'd have folk complaining of spoiled rabbit.

She fetched a clean pot and a ladle and began scooping untainted meat, gravy and vegetables into it. The swollen knuckles on her right hand protested, shooting pain up to her elbow. *Joint-ill*, Izusa called it. An affliction of advancing age. She didn't like to think of that but facts were facts and couldn't be outrun. Her son was almost a man now. Handsome like his father, with the same heart-melting smile. Soon she could step back and let him shoulder the heavy burden of the inn. Him and Willem. Them boys were still joined at the hip.

Iddo wouldn't like it but she'd talk him round. He deserved a rest as much as she did. He'd hurt his back a month before and it still pained him. Izusa's pills helped with the worst discomfort – hers and his – but there it was. Even in lean times the Pig Whistle was a mort of hard work and between them they'd been working it day and night for nigh on twenty years.

'Molly! Molly!'

Iddo, sounding fretsome. She set down the pot and ladle, crossed to the unshuttered kitchen window and leaned out. 'Iss?'

'How long did ye tell them boys to stay out after wood?' he called, standing at the top of the cellar stairs. 'Only I need 'em for hauling up ale kegs. Can't slake a man's thirst on promises and air!'

'And I can't bake pies and cook stew with a cold hob. Nor heat bath-water for them as takes a bed, neither. Bung open a keg where 'tis and ye can fill jugs till them boys come home.'

'Fill jugs?' Iddo pulled off his canvas cap and dashed it the ground. 'Run from bar to cellar and back again with jugs? From now till when them boys see fit to show their faces? Molly—'

She slapped the wooden sill. 'D'ye stop yer hollering, Iddo! Ye'll be pleased enough in yer hot bath tonight with a tenday's worth of dry firewood in the shed.'

He swiped up his cap and stamped lopsided down into the cellar. As she turned again to her burnt stew, a hand-bell clanged out in the public room. That meant a customer wanted her. Whenever Iddo had to leave the bar, and she couldn't leave the kitchen, there was the bell. Something else she didn't care to dwell on. That kind of shoddy she'd always left for the Marches' other inns. Her Pig Whistle was better than that. But while coin was tight what choice did she have?

Forcing a cheerful smile, she swept aside the leather curtain. 'Iss, iss, how can I serve ye?'

'Mistress Molly,' Lord Humbert greeted her, standing at the oak bar. His face was hard, his eyes unfriendly. He wore mail beneath his leather jack and his cheek was marred by a livid bruise from his skirmish with the sell-swords. Another lord stood with him. Soft and pampered, he was. She'd never seen him before but his eyes were just as cold. 'We'll step outside to the forecourt. I'd have words with you.'

CHAPTER THIRTY-SEVEN

Molly smoothed the front of her stew-splashed apron. Behind Humbert and the other lord she could see her customers, some Clemen folk, some Harcian, and a handful of traders, all of them agoggle, staring and whispering and letting their pottage and stew go cold in the spoons stopped halfway 'twixt bowl and belly.

'Lord Humbert,' she said, hearing her voice faint and frightened. She never could see him now without feeling her heart frog-dance in her chest. 'I did hear of yer skirmish this morning with them sell-swords. Shameful doings.'

'Shameful, indeed,' he agreed. 'But it seems shameful doings are in no short supply these days. The forecourt, Mistress Molly.'

Humbert knew. She could see it in his face, in his eyes. *He knew*. She wanted to flee. She wanted to weep. She wanted to throw herself on the public room floor at his feet and beg forgiveness. Tell him *I never wanted to do it, but what choice did I have*? Only – after her wickedness, however could she trust Humbert to protect Benedikt from Waymon?

Ever since the dreadful day Balfre's man threatened to trump thievery against her Benedikt, and see him hanged, she'd done as she was bid and told lie after lie about Lord Humbert and his duke and all the terrible things they did to poor folk in the Marches and in Clemen. Lied to every passing trader and merchant who'd listen about the hardships they caused foreigners and how Clemen weren't safe, knowing they'd believe her because she was Mistress Molly of the Pig Whistle inn.

Even after Humbert and his men-at-arms protected the Pig Whistle from rough Clemen men come into the Marches bent on mischief, she lied. After some of Balfre's men-at-arms had caused a drunken row and Humbert's man Egann risked himself alone to confront them, she lied. And when Iddo hurt his back, and it was give Izusa coin or pay the poulterer, and Lord Humbert stepped in with a silver ducat and a kind smile, the next day, the *next day*, she told a silk merchant from Pruges that she'd heard Clemen was looking to impose a special tax on every bolt of trader silk. So many, many lies she'd told. 'Cause if she didn't, Waymon of Harcia would hang her innocent son for a thief.

But Humbert wouldn't care why she'd lied. Not now. She'd long since lost her chance to ask him for help or mercy.

The soft, pampered lord she didn't know snapped his fingers in front of her face. 'Why do you stand there gawping, woman? Are you loose in your wits?'

'This is Lord Ercole,' said Humbert. 'Come from Duke Roric in Eaglerock.' He scowled. 'The forecourt, Mistress Molly.'

Tears pricking, she bobbed a curtsy. 'Iss, my lord.'

The Pig Whistle's forecourt was crowded full of Clemen men-at-arms on horseback, led by Humbert's wiry, unamused serjeant, Derron. Not once since he was made serjeant after Bodham died had she ever seen the man smile. More mounted men-at-arms sat watchful in the road, two of them holding their lords' fine horses. Eyeing them warily, looking at all the hands resting suggestive on sword-hilts and daggers, Molly halted with her back to the Pig Whistle's front wall. Her mouth was dry as old straw.

'My lord, I d'wish ye'd tell me what—'

'Mistress Molly,' Humbert said, booted feet wide, fists on his hips. 'There are rumours swirling abroad, touching on Clemen and its duke. False rumours, filthy lies, that plunge a dagger in my duchy's honest heart.' He leaned close. 'Rumours I'm told were started here.'

Her joint-swollen fingers twisted in her apron, the pain a welcome distraction. Overhead, the sun was sliding. Them boys would be looking to trundle home soon, surely. She felt her heart sieze.

Stay away, imps. Striggle-straggle. Hunt rabbits. Don't ye let this be the first day ye did ever rush to heed Iddo.

She made herself meet Humbert's glare. After so many dreadful lies, what was one more? 'My lord, I dunt know what ye mean. If there be nasty rumours swirling they b'aint naught to do with the Pig Whistle.'

Lord Ercole, soft and pampered, slapped her so hard she stumbled sideways. 'She's lying, the treacherous bitch. Don't tell me you can't see it, Humbert.'

'Molly.' There was pain beneath Humbert's cold rage. 'You'd take Harcian coin to hurt Clemen? To hurt me? I've done you no harm. I thought we were friends.'

She pressed a palm to her throbbing, burning cheek. 'I never took no Harcian coin, my lord. I never—'

'I've heard enough,' said Lord Ercole, turning. 'You there! Serjeant!'

Derron nudged his horse forward a few steps. 'My lord?'

'Ercole,' Humbert said, warning. 'Recall what I told you.'

Pampered Lord Ercole jabbed a ringed finger at Humbert's chest. 'Then cease your lamenting and deal with this, Humbert!'

'Derron,' Humbert said, his loathing stare not shifting from Lord Ercole's face. 'Take half the men, search the Pig Whistle and its outbuildings roof to floorboards. No cupboard's too small, no mattress unlikely. I want every coin and scrap of paper. The rest of the men can stand ready. Any man or servant tries to flee, take them.'

Derron nodded. 'Yes, my lord.'

'No!' Molly protested. 'Lord Humbert, I've guests here b'aint lifted a finger agin ye. What'll happen to the Pig Whistle d'they talk of being hounded and frighted and jostled by men-at-arms?'

Humbert's look was like another slap. 'Then they talk, Mistress Molly. And you'll learn how words can wound.'

There was nothing she could do to stop him. Fighting tears, she stood where she was, on pain of custody, and watched as Humbert's serjeant and his men-at-arms rousted her customers into the forecourt. Rousted Gwatkin and his two lads out of the stables to stand with her. When Iddo didn't join them she started to tremble. Then Gwatkin, grown old in his years at the Pig Whistle, brushed gnarled fingers agin her elbow and touched his prunish lips to her ear.

'Iddo's gone to fetch Lord Waymon. Word is he and some of his men-at-arms be down the road a-ways. 'Tisn't right, what Humbert be doing. We'll let Harcia set him straight.'

She pressed her fingers to her lips, to keep back a laughing sob. And when Humbert demanded to be told Iddo's whereabouts she handed him a brazen lie, not sorry at all. Iddo was off with her boys, fetching firewood. And not a soul who heard her, and knew elsewise, breathed a word to Clemen's bullying Marcher lord.

Heartsick, she huddled with Gwatkin and listened to Humbert and Lord Ercole and Clemen's men-at-arms rampage through the inn, breaking pottery, splintering timber, wrecking the life she'd sweated to build. Trembled as her customers' belongings were dragged downstairs from the dormer and into the forecourt to be rummaged through and strewn about. The traders from Khafur and Cassinia thickened the cooling air with loud, foreign protests. And when Clemen's lords and men ignored them they shouted their outrage at her instead. All she could do was shake her head and spread her hands and say how she was sorry.

Then Lord Waymon came, with a score of his men.

Humbert left the crowded forecourt and stamped into the road to meet him. 'You can turn back, Waymon. This is naught to do with you.'

'I'll turn back when it suits me,' Waymon retorted, halting his horse. His men-at-arms halted behind him, their faces surly. 'Clemen doesn't yet rule in the Marches.' He stared at the Pig Whistle. 'What's this uproar?'

'None of your business.'

'But it must be my business, Humbert.' Waymon pointed. 'I see Harcian Marcher-folk there.'

'There are Harcians everywhere,' said Humbert. 'More's the fucking pity.'

Waymon laughed. 'And my duke does wonder why the Marches are so contentious.'

'If the Marches are contentious, Waymon, that's your doing.'

'I don't recall rousting innocent Harcian spice-merchants and killing their escort. Are you sure that was me?'

'They weren't innocent!' Humbert shouted. 'They broke the law hiring sell-swords!'

'Our merchants would have no need of sell-swords did Roric keep a proper peace!'

'Humbert! This is no time for gossiping!'

Molly watched, almost entertained, as pampered Lord Ercole elbowed his way across the forecourt then strutted to stand with Clemen's Marcher lord. She hated Waymon enough to vomit but she'd cheer him if he struck the man who'd slapped her face.

Waymon was staring at him, astonished. 'Fuck, Humbert. Who's this prissy turd?'

'Lord Ercole,' said Humbert, over the snide laughter of Waymon's men. 'One of His Grace's councillors.'

'By the Exarch's balls. Your duke is in sore need of better men.'

'And *your* duke should take care,' Lord Ercole retorted, red-faced. 'Roric knows full well he is behind the mischief made against our duchy. The lies and calumnies being told of Clemen both at home and abroad. I promise you – Waymon, is it? Harcia's slander will not go unrewarded.'

'So truth is slander now?' Waymon demanded. 'Should I next look for dogs to shit gold? My lord turd, Clemen is a cesspit. 'Tis true Harcia has known that longer than most, but how is Harcia to blame if more people do discover it?'

Lord Ercole snapped his fingers at the nearest Clemen man-at-arms. 'You there. Bring me the innkeep.'

The man-at-arms dismounted his horse and started towards the Pig Whistle's forecourt. Molly felt her knees buckle as Waymon turned his head. In his cold stare she saw the promise of Benedikt hanging should she confess the truth of what she'd been doing – and why. She squeezed her eyes tight shut, shivering. Where was Iddo? She needed Iddo. She couldn't face this without her man. Around her, frightened, prisoned customers were milling and shifting like sheep penned for slaughter.

'Here now! Here now!' Gwatkin protested, his old voice cracking. 'Leave her be! This b'aint right!'

Hard hands took hold of her, bruising. She cried out. Gwatkin protested again, and she heard a fist strike flesh, heard the old stableman grunt in pain. Opening her eyes she saw him on the ground and writhing, and then Clemen's man-at-arms was dragging her across the forecourt towards the road and Waymon, who'd kill her precious Benedikt if she dared open her mouth.

'Leave her be, ye bastard! Get yer filthy hands off my Moll!'

Iddo, shoving his way through the press of men-at-arms in the forecourt. He was panting, sweating, first with running and now with rage. She nearly fainted with terror for him. Her Iddo never could think straight when he was in a rage.

'No – no – Iddo – no—'

But Iddo wasn't listening. Anger had stopped his ears.

Pulling free of the man-at-arms she lunged towards her bullish man, her man of oak, and tripped over the scattered belongings of a Hentish trader. Crying out, she fell hard against another man-at-arms. Startled, he drew his dagger. She felt the blade punch through her belly and screamed. Heard Iddo scream, a shattering howl of fury and fear.

'Molly!'

Dazed, blood pumping between her fingers, she sank to the ground. Iddo tried to reach her but Humbert's men-at-arms knocked him down.

'Murder!' Waymon shouted. 'Butchery! Harcia, have at these fucking Clemen dogs!'

A rabble of answering shouts as Harcia's men-at-arms threw themselves at Humbert and Lord Ercole and Clemen's men. Gasping for air, Molly snatched a glimpse of Humbert as he caught Waymon's arm and hauled him out of the saddle. Saw pampered Lord Ercole with a dagger. He was waving it in a Harcian man-at-arm's face. Then the furious fighting spilled into the forecourt and she lost sight of the brawling Marcher lords.

Crying out with every kick and buffet, she dragged herself across her own forecourt to slump beside the Pig Whistle's front door. Her customers had run away, Marcher-folk and traders all. After this she'd likely never see them again. And then booted feet trod on her as Waymon's men-at-arms pounded into the public room in pursuit of their Clemen foe. The clash of sword against sword. A scream. A triumphant shout. Then angry shouts fading as the men-at-arms battled their way upstairs.

Iddo. Where was Iddo? There was Gwatkin on the dirt, unmoving, poor old man, but she couldn't see her Iddo.

Someone close by was moaning in terrible pain. Then she realised. *Oh. It be me*. The hand clutching her belly was drenched scarlet. So was her apron. She looked again for Iddo but couldn't see him. Her eyelids were heavy, wanting to close. Biting her lip, she bullied them open.

Benedikt. Benedikt. Wherever ye be, chick, stay there. Whatever ye do, my precious lamb, don't come home.

By the time they'd filled the back of the cart with firewood it was nigh dark. There'd be no time to unload the wood into the Pig Whistle's shed, never mind taking the borrowed horse and cart back to Tiddy Pond farm. They'd have to do that come sunrise.

As Spurfield's nag picked its way along the rutted cart track leading to the back of the inn, Liam gloomed on what Iddo would have to say about that. Likely he'd spit nails. Then the cart's front left wheel hit a rock. The lurch shook Benedikt out of his slumping drowse.

'Be we home yet?'

'Nearly.'

Benedikt sat up, yawning. 'Good.' Then he leaned forward, peering. 'Willem? We should be able to see the Pig Whistle by now.'

He'd been so busy glooming on Iddo he never noticed. But

Benedikt was right. No lamps glowing in the stables. No light spilling from the kitchen's back window. No familiar glow in the upstairs dormer.

They leapt down from Spurfield's wood-cart, tethered the old nag to a handy tree branch, and ran.

There was dim light in the public room. Two horn lanterns. No candles. No fire. Molly was there. And Iddo. Not a soul else. Every table, bench and stool knocked over and splintered, plates and bowls and tankards and spoons and knives scattered. The air stank of spilled stew and ale. Blood was splashed across the floor, up one wall, over the wrecked furniture.

'*Ma!*' said Benedikt, stumbling to her.

Someone had settled Molly on a folded blanket by the cold hearth. Grey-faced, her apron dagger-ripped and drying in stiff, dark red folds, she heaved in a shuddering breath and opened her eyes.

'Benedikt,' she murmured. 'M'little chick.'

'Ma, what—'

'Benedikt.' Liam touched his brother's shoulder. 'Sit with her. I'll look to see we're safe.'

Molly coughed. 'Iddo.'

Iddo lay on a blanket in the corner by the bar, badly beaten, sluggishly bleeding. A gleam of lamplight caught his eyes, half-opened in his bruised, swollen face.

Staring down at him, Liam shrugged. 'He'll keep.'

'Willem—' Benedikt twisted to look at him. 'Ma needs Izusa. Can ye run, can ye—'

It seemed to him Molly was beyond healing, but he couldn't tell his brother that. 'Iss. I'll go.'

But first things first. He snatched a lantern off the bar and picked his way to the attic stairs. Climbed them. Felt his heart give a sickening thump as he saw the bedroom door kicked open. Inside, everything was upended. His bed and Benedikt's had been daggered so their straw-and-wool stuffing spewed out like guts. The pillows were gutted too. Spare shirts and smocks and hose slashed to ribbons. Even their good leather shoes were butchered useless. Heart thumping even harder, Liam fell to his knees under the open window and prised up the second floorboard from the wall, so hasty and careless he made his fingertips bleed.

And there it was. Berold's ring, his future, wrapped in its scrap of sacking. Lamplight brought its mellow gold and precious tiger eye to life. He strung it on a bootlace and hung it round his neck, under his linen smock, where no one would see it.

Every other room in the Pig Whistle was ransacked the same. Finding no one in hiding, only mess and ruined belongings, he went out to the stables. One horse. It looked like a man-at-arms's mount. But no traders' mules or regular horses, not even lame Brown Betty. No Gwatkin or his lads. No one lurking in the ale cellar, neither, or crouching in the henhouse. When he and Benedikt had left that morning, the inn was home to six traders. Now they were all gone. Faery-taken, like in the old tales.

But then he found a man-at-arms slumped in the Whistle's forecourt. Dead, with not a drop of blood on him. He wore a falcon badge stitched to his leather jack.

Liam felt a cold sweat spring. Felt disbelief and rage rise. The man's sword was in its scabbard, his dagger still on his hip. He'd not been fighting. He'd been standing guard. *Waiting*. For him and Benedikt? To take them away, like the others?

A falcon badge. That meant treacherous Humbert had done this. Ransacked the inn, hurt Molly. Humbert, following orders from his bastard duke Roric. And sooner or later the traitor would be back.

Feggit. We can't stay here.

'*Willem!*' Benedikt glared. 'Where the fuck have ye been? Where be Izusa? I thought—'

'Benedikt,' Molly chided, feeble, 'mind yer tongue.'

Benedikt chafed Molly's limp hand. 'Hush, Ma. Save yer strength. Willem—'

'No, chick. Sit with Iddo. I don't want him lonesome and I need a word with Willem.'

Anguished, Benedikt shook his head. 'No, Ma, ye—'

'Do as yer told. Or I'll slap m'wooden spoon across yer arse.'

On a choked sob, Benedikt obeyed her.

'Willem.' Her crooked finger barely moving, Molly beckoned him close. 'I'd have ye heed me.'

Wary, he set the lamp on the floor beside her and dropped to one knee. Seeing the fresh blood on her apron, wet and shining, he bit his lip. She wasn't Ellyn. She'd never been Ellyn. But she wasn't Iddo neither. And when she could've betrayed him to Waymon to keep Benedikt safe, she didn't.

'Willem.' Molly coughed, a skin-crawling rattle. 'This be Humbert's doing. He found out I were telling lies for Lord Waymon.'

Of course. What else would put Humbert in such a fury? 'How'd he—'

'I dunt know. It don't matter. Willem—' Her eyes were clouding, but still something fierce burned. 'I know yer secret.'

'Oh!' He dropped his mouth open, so she'd not know it weren't a surprise. 'Did Alys tell ye?'

'Iss.' Her fading gaze shifted. 'I learned it of Alys. But I never told a soul . . . Liam. And now I never will.'

He thought she was waiting for him to thank her. But why should he? Nothing had been the same since the night Ellyn died. Molly had looked at him different after. And even though Iddo never knew the truth, he knew Molly. So Iddo got harder and she never stopped him. Not giving him to Waymon didn't make up for that.

'I did right by ye, Willem,' she said, as though he'd complained out loud. 'I took ye in when I had no need. Kept ye on after Alys died. Loved ye, in m'own way. Ye do owe me for that.' Her blood-stained fingers clutched at him. 'Whatever ye think about who ye be and where ye belong, whatever giddy thoughts be whirling, *ye'll leave my Benedikt out of it*. If ye don't, ye'll get him killed.'

Liam pulled his arm free. 'Benedikt does as he pleases.'

'Willem—' Tears mingled with her sweat. 'I *beg* ye. Don't put my chick in harm's way, don't—' Another cough, harsh and hacking. Then blood gushed from her belly.

'Benedikt!'

Tangled, Liam retreated as Benedikt hurtled to Molly. Stood for a moment, watching his brother's frantic sorrow, remembering the attic stairs and Ellyn dying. He never knew sleeping pain could wake so fierce. He wanted to say something, for Benedikt, but he didn't know what. So he went back to Iddo.

The lamp on the floor beside him washed the miserable bastard in weak light. Blood glinted. Split flesh gaped. One arm hugged his ribs, as though they were cracked. He looked to be suffering.

Good.

A nudge to Iddo's knee with the toe of his boot. The barkeep stirred. Blood-crusted eyelashes fluttered as he looked up. 'Willem.'

Liam crouched. 'One of Humbert's men lies dead in the forecourt. Did ye kill him?'

'No.'

'Then who?'

Iddo closed his eyes. 'I dunt know.'

'Molly says Humbert did this.'

Painfully, Iddo squinted. 'Him and Waymon.'

'*Waymon?* Why?'

'Ha.' Iddo tried to smile. 'I asked him for help.'

He bit at his lip, thinking. So . . . Waymon fought Humbert over the Pig Whistle because Humbert found out Molly was telling lies for Harcia and Waymon didn't want the secret to spill wider. Only now the Pig Whistle was ruined, Molly was dying, and Humbert had left a man behind to take the innkeeper's sons.

Fuck.

'Where be Gwatkin and the stable lads? Tam, and little Coop?'

'Humbert took 'em,' Iddo mumbled. 'And the traders. Said he had questions. Wicked doings here, he said. There was a Clemen lord as died. Izusa couldn't save him.'

That was all right. One less for him to kill when it came time to take the Falcon Throne. 'Izusa was here?'

'After. Humbert wouldn't let her help me and Moll. So she went off with Waymon.' Iddo tried to laugh. 'The bastard were daggered good and proper.'

And with luck he'd die too. 'Twas a pity treacherous Humbert still breathed. Every lord and man who knew anything about this muckery, who might want to stir shite about the Pig Whistle and Clemen? He wished they were dead. Molly's lies touched too close to him, made him unsafe.

Feeling Iddo's stare, he looked down. The barkeep's face was twisted with more than pain.

'Ye did bring this on us, didn't ye, Willem? I dunt know how, but this be yer fault. Ye been naught but a troublesome shite yer whole life. When ye did turn up on our curs't doorstep with that slut Alys, Molly should've drowned ye in a bucket. Like a rat.'

Liam smiled. Remembered, like it were yesterday, that afternoon in the ale cellar when Iddo had done his best to whip him half to death and how he'd gloated on the pain he'd caused. He remembered every cuff, every snarl, every glare the barkeep gave him. Remembered how this wasn't the first time Iddo had wished him dead.

He leaned close. 'Molly's dying.'

'What?' Iddo seemed to shrink. 'No.'

'Iss.'

Blood and tears ran down Iddo's pulped face. 'Ye be a lying shite, Willem. Molly. I want Moll—'

Iddo died quickly, like the man-at-arms in Bell Wood. One hand to smother his nose and mouth, the other to crush his windpipe. As life fled from the bastard's eyes, Benedikt let out a harsh cry.

'*Ma!*'

Curse it. Liam wiped Iddo's blood from his hands onto the man's ripped hose, and stood. They didn't have time for any more grieving. If they didn't move quickly they'd have no time at all. He hauled weeping Benedikt to his feet and shook him.

'Benedikt, we got to go.'

Benedikt hiccuped. 'Go where? And what about Iddo?'

'Iddo's dead.'

'*Dead?*' Benedikt's face crumpled again. Iddo had always treated him like a proper son. 'But—'

'It happens,' he said roughly. 'Most like he was hurt inside. Nothing to be done. Benedikt—'

Dazed, his brother stared around the wrecked public room. 'Willem, we can't go. There be the Pig Whistle, and—'

'*Fuck* the Pig Whistle! Humbert thinks we've broke Marcher law. He do already have Gwatkin and the lads and he left a man-at-arms behind to take us. Only he be dead, so—'

'Ye *killed* him? Willem—'

'I b'aint that big a fool! He's just dead. I dunt know how. Come *on*, Benedikt. We have to run.'

Stepping back, his brother dragged a sleeve across his grief-stained face. 'And Ma? Iddo? Willem, I got to bury 'em. I can't leave 'em to rot!'

Shite. There wasn't *time*. 'What about a funeral pyre? Y'know, how they do it in Sassanine, like that trader told us one time.'

'Y'mean . . . burn the Pig Whistle?' Benedikt said, uncertain. 'With Ma and Iddo inside it?'

'They won't feel anything.'

'*Willem!*'

It was hard not to slap him, or shake him till his teeth fell out. 'What does it matter if the Pig Whistle burns? Ye weren't never going to be an innkeep, Benedikt! When I'm the proper duke of Clemen ye'll be my greatest lord. Ye'll be a count, like Balfre. Ye'll be a second-best duke. We'll be living in Eaglerock, not in the Marches.'

'I know,' Benedikt muttered. 'Only the Pig Whistle be my home.'

'It be four walls and a roof,' he said, roughly wheedling. 'And even say we don't burn it, if ye think Humbert'll let ye come back here then ye b'aint got the noddle of a lackywit hen.'

The truth of that struck his brother almost as hard as Molly's death. 'All right.' His breathing hitched. 'We'll burn it.'

'*I'll* burn it,' he said, scalded with relief. 'You see what food be in the pantry we can take, then go and unharness Spurfield's nag. It'll find its way home agin. Make sure the hens got food and water too, in case they get forgot a day or so. And there's a horse in the stables. Belongs to Humbert's man, I think. Tether it somewhere safe in case the stables catch. When I'm done, I'll meet ye outside.'

'We should fetch down our spare clothes.'

'Can't. Humbert's men cut 'em to pieces. Iddo's, too.'

Benedikt scowled. 'Bastards.'

'Don't fret on it. I'll see they pay, when I'm duke.'

He stood well back and stared at the floor, so Benedikt could kiss dead Molly goodbye without feeling squirmy. Touch Iddo's shoulder in farewell. Then his brother moped out of the public room and he got busy with the lamp oil. Doused Molly with it, and Iddo, and everything wooden that would burn. Struck by a thought, he dragged the dead man-at-arms into the public room and doused him with lamp oil too. Took out the man's sword and dropped it beside him, since he couldn't bend the stiffening fingers round the hilt. Next he dragged

Iddo closer, to make it look as though there'd been a fight. Fetched the barkeep's cudgel from behind the bar and put it in his hand. Then he ran upstairs, splashed lamp oil in every room, and one by one set fire to them with a lit candle. The flames took hold greedily. He scrambled back downstairs to the stink and sound of burning.

Last of all he set fire to Molly, Iddo, the man-at-arms and the Pig Whistle's public room. For a moment he stood in the doorway, watching. Then Benedikt came back and he had to hustle his brother, into the forecourt. Hold him hard while Benedikt hid his face and wept.

The Pig Whistle burned like a winter bonfire. Side by side they watched the embers fly, their childhood going up in smoke.

'So what d'we do now, Willem?' Benedikt whispered. 'Even with Berold's ring on yer finger, t'aint like ye can just march into Clemen and tell Roric to hand back the Falcon Throne.'

He'd asked himself the same question while he was splashing lamp oil around. And as far as he could see, there was only one answer.

'We go to Balfre.'

'*Balfre?*'

'Iss. And ask him to take us as men-at-arms.'

'He never will! We b'aint Harcian.'

The flames were roaring, leaping through holes in the Pig Whistle's thatched roof. Too hot and too dangerous for them to stand so close. Tugging his brother into the road, Liam gave him a little shake.

'Balfre won't care for that. He'll care we hate Clemen. And he'll train us proper to use a sword. We'll fight Clemen here in the Marches. We'll serve Harcia and bide our time. And one day . . .' His fingers found the hard, round shape of Berold's ring, safely hidden beneath his smock. 'I'll get my chance to kill Roric. And then the Falcon Throne will be mine.'

Benedikt tore his gaze from the burning inn and stared at him, wondering. 'Y'do never doubt that, Willem, do ye?'

He smiled, grimly. 'No, Benedikt. I never do.'

Vidar was walking along the corridor from his manor bedchamber to the stairs, on his way to the tilt yard, when he was startled by a shout as he passed Waymon's room.

'You stupid *fuck*, Waymon! What were you thinking?'

Balfre. Visiting his surly friend for the first time since the Pig Whistle skirmish, and clearly unamused.

'I was thinking you'd not want Humbert getting proof we've been stirring shite!'

Waymon, attempting to defend himself. For three days he'd been kept in bed, full of stitches and syrup of poppy. What was the wager he wished now that he'd died?

A muffled thump, as though a fist had struck the wall. 'You should've come to me first, Waymon. I'd have sweetened Humbert, fuddled him with a story to suffocate suspicion!'

'I don't think so. The innkeeper—'

'Would've kept her mouth shut to save her son! Now she's dead, her man's dead, the Pig Whistle's a pile of charcoal, somebody killed that fuck Ercole and Humbert's out for blood!'

'But Balfre—'

Grinning, Vidar moved on. No regrets that Waymon was in disgrace. No regrets that Ercole was dead. Clemen would be better served with that cockshite in the ground. Roric had ever been a fool to keep him. As for Humbert, perhaps now he'd realise just how dangerous Harcia was.

Down at the tilt yard, Grule was bullying a handful of sweating new recruits through a series of sword drills. Leaning on the yard's railing, Vidar considered the would-be men-at-arms . . . then frowned, and gestured at the serjeant to join him.

'Lord Boice,' Grule said, with a friendly, respectful nod.

'Grule.' He pointed. 'Those two. They show some promise.'

'Ah.' Grule nodded again, pleased. 'They be Willem and Benedikt. Molly's boys, as weren't killed at the Pig Whistle.'

And that was why they looked familiar. He'd seen them before, at the inn. 'Which one's which?'

'Benedikt's got the dark hair. Willem's the one with the scarred face.'

Vidar watched the innkeep's brats methodically count their way through the drill. 'Yes, indeed. They show promise.'

'Taken to swordplay like ducks to water, they have. Ye'll see, my lord. I'll soon have 'em teaching Humbert's shiting men a lesson.'

He smiled, slowly. 'They're out for revenge?'

'Iss, my lord. And who can blame them?'

'Not I, serjeant,' he said, watching their swinging swords catch the sunlight. 'For some of us, revenge is what keeps us breathing, even more than meat and drink.'

'I hear ye, my lord,' Grule said, approving. 'D'ye care to come train a while with me? I could use yer canny eye.'

'Thank you, Grule. I do care.' Vidar gestured. 'After you.'

Izusa. Izusa. Come to me.

Salimbene's whisper tugged in her mind as she was plucking feathers from the chicken she'd killed for supper. Leaving the half-naked bird on the butchery tree stump, she dabbled her fingertips in the fresh blood then hurried indoors. The baby's head in its box sat uncovered near the cottage hearth. Kneeling before it, she drew in a deep, calming breath.

'I'm here, Salimbene.'

The head's tiny, shrivelled nostrils flared. Its dead lips moved, like a whisperer in the wind. Flakes of grey skin sloughed from its withered cheeks.

I smell blood.

She dabbled her scarlet fingertips on the head's bald skull, and its lips. Its shrivelled tongue darted in and out, tasting, swift as a striking snake.

This head ages, Izusa. Soon it will fail.

'I seek a new head, Salimbene. But there are fewer babies born.'

The head chuckled. More skin sloughed free, to drift and float like featherdown in the breeze wafting through the open door.

Give it blood, Izusa. It will last long enough.

Her pulse leapt. 'Is it time?'

It is time. When next Balfre comes to fuck you, Izusa, give him the fatal ink. Aimery will perish and Balfre will be duke.

'And then?'

Then your exile in the Marches will end.

Her pulse leapt again, tumultuous. 'And I can go home to Lepetto? I can return to you?'

You will return to Ardenn, Izusa, and serve its captive duchess Catrain.

643

He was sending her back to Carillon? Disappointment, dark as death. Acid tears scalding her eyes.

You will do this for me, Izusa.

She flinched. Sighed. 'Yes. I will.'

You know how to leave the Marches. You know what must be done.

Another sigh. Her heart was aching. 'I do. I'm ready.'

Remember the blood, Izusa.

And Salimbene was gone.

Disconsolate, she finished plucking the chicken. Ripped out its innards for burying in the herb bed then put it in a pot on the hob to simmer for pottage. Cleaned her butchering axe and knife. Fed and watered the horse. Tossed grain at the hens. Reworked the charms around her cottage. Dusk fell slowly, dragging starlit night by its heels. Tasks completed, she lit the torch by the front door and went inside to prepare, as far as she could, her last ink for Balfre. Exhausted afterwards, her nerves on fire, her belly raw, she curled up on her bed and plunged into sleep.

Balfre's impatient knocking woke her. It was late. Hours past midnight. Feeling muzzy, raw still from her dark runings, she opened her door to him.

'My lord Balfre. Come in.' He pushed past her roughly and she closed the door. 'I'd abandoned hope of seeing you. I take it Lord Waymon heals neatly, since you've not called me back to the manor.'

Balfre didn't answer. Didn't kiss her. Instead he tossed his leather riding cloak to the floor and paced the cottage's cramped living room like a man on the eve of battle.

'Balfre?' she said, puzzled. 'What's amiss?'

His face was pale, his eyes haunted. He'd been careless in his dressing, wore only a plain linen shirt and dark blue hose. No rings. No pendants. He looked like a peasant.

'Nothing's amiss. I'm weary.'

'How weary?' Slipping in front of him, she slid his hand inside her shift, to her breast. 'Shall we fuck?'

He snatched his hand free as though she'd burned him.

'*Balfre*. What's happened? You're not yourself.'

Turning, he stared at the flames lazily flickering in the hearth. 'Perhaps my cock is tired of you.'

'I don't believe that.'

A long silence. Then he shook his head. 'I dreamed tonight. Of Aimery. And when I woke, I was weeping.'

Ah. Stepping close to him, she pressed her cheek against his back. 'Don't fret, my lord. 'Tis only the powers, calling your name.'

She felt the shock run through him. Stepped back, so he could turn again to face her. Hot colour in his cheeks, now. Desire in his eyes. 'I don't understand.'

'I dreamed tonight too, Balfre. I was given the answer we seek.'

'It's time? Izusa—'

She smiled, gently. Held out her hand. 'Come. I need you.'

Compliant, like a small boy, he sat at her table where the unfinished ink awaited in its unstoppered glass vial. Watched unprotesting as she sliced his finger with her silver knife and dripped his eager blood over the letter from Aimery he'd given her weeks before, that she'd held safe for this moment. She could feel the incant building, insidious and deadly, as his blood soaked his father's quavering signature until it was sopping red. When she scraped the mix of blood and ink from the parchment into the vial of tainted ink, the surge of power was almost blinding. A murmured chant. A binding rune. And then it was done.

Fascinated, Balfre lifted the stoppered vial before his eyes. 'You're certain this will kill him?'

'Yes. And with no more sign of violence on him than there was on the man-at-arms I killed for you at the Pig Whistle.'

'You were certain of the other inks, too,' Balfre said, his glance doubting. 'But Aimery prevailed against them.'

Because he was meant to. Her secret, and Salimbene's. 'I told you, Balfre. I dreamed. Would you question my powers?'

He hesitated, then shook his head. 'No.' A frown. 'How soon will he die?'

'Once he touches the letter you write with this ink, Aimery of Harcia will be dead within a month.'

'So long?' he said, disappointed, and thumped the vial onto the table.

She needed a month, to be sure of her leaving. But he couldn't know that either. 'It might be sooner. I err on the side of the caution.'

She tapped the table. 'And so must you, my lord. This ink is lethal and blood-bound to you as well as the duke.'

'What?' he said, staring. 'You'd put me at risk?'

'Not willingly. Balfre, this is killing magic. Darker than any we've yet touched. Of course there is a risk. There was no other way to ensure Aimery's death.'

'You could've warned me.'

'My lord, I am warning you now.' Leaning forward, she captured his gaze with her own. 'Be sure to wear gloves when you write with this ink. When the letter's done, seal it quickly. Then straight away burn gloves, quill, and what remains of the ink. Do you understand?'

'I understand I want to fuck you.' He laughed, his eyes warm again. All his ghosts chased away. 'Izusa . . . Izusa . . . you must be a witch.'

CHAPTER THIRTY-EIGHT

Seal Rock castle stood at the edge of the world.

Or so it felt, sometimes, to a man standing on the clifftop beyond its imposing stone curtain wall. A sheer drop to the waves pounding far below, to the rocks humped out of the restless water, where seals gathered to hunt fish and laze in the sun. The rocks were empty this morning, the seals frolicking somewhere else.

Shading his eyes, Grefin stared out to the horizon, to the cold and empty north. The sky overhead was a pale, thin blue. Cloudless. Beneath his feet the salty turf was sheep-cropped and damp. The chill salt wind scouring his face and tousling his hair had sculptured the stunted gorse bushes into tortured, fantastic shapes. It bit through his martial leathers and the wool shirt he wore beneath them.

Seven weeks and four days since he'd killed a northern raider. Any morning now the first ice-laden gale of winter would sweep in across the shifting waters of the Silver Expanse. It meant the Green Isle would be safe for another season. And when spring returned, then they'd wait and see if the raiders had finally abandoned their hopes of Harcia. He was beginning to think it could happen. This past year had seen fewer raids, and they'd been foiled in their attempts to breach Cassinia and the Danetto Peninsula.

But he didn't dare speak his hope aloud for fear of tempting a malicious faery.

He heard a faint, skirling cry in the wind and looked up. Wheeling high above him, an arrow-tailed kite. As he watched, it raised its bronze pinions and hovered, beautifully deadly. Waiting, waiting, for the right moment to strike. Some might call it an omen. A soothsayer's warning. He called it nature, caring to look no deeper than that. Aimery always scoffed at omens, and had taught his sons the same.

'My lord Steward! My lord!'

Grefin turned, smiling. Watched his handsome son – his only son – stride over the turf towards him, a young, wiry-haired deerhound bounding by his side. The arrow-tailed kite shrieked and wheeled away.

'My lord,' Kerric said, reaching him, 'you slipped out early. Are you hiding from our guests?'

Of course he was. 'No.' Grefin fondled the deerhound's ears. 'What a thing to say. Why? Are you?'

When Kerric laughed he looked so much like Jorin that it hurt. Stung, Grefin shifted his gaze back over the sun-sparkled water so Kerric wouldn't notice. He'd promised himself he'd never let his youngest child feel less for not being his dead brother. Because of Malcolm, and watching Balfre, he knew how that felt. Knew how a father's undying grief could poison a living son's heart.

Flicking him a concerned glance, Kerric moved to stand with him and stare northwards. 'Are you worried, my lord? Do you think the raiders wait to spring one last surprise before winter?'

He rested a hand on Kerric's shoulder. So tall, his son had grown. And strong. Battle-hardened, blooded, and scarred. As good as a man, though many would still call him a boy. Mazelina still hadn't forgiven him for giving Kerric a sword and throwing him at the raiders. Not after Jorin. She loved him, loved both of them, but she couldn't understand. Kerric, a warrior born, lived to avenge his slain brother and protect Harcia. As a father, as the Steward, he'd not have it otherwise.

'I don't,' he said, tightening his fingers, to reassure. 'But I can't help wondering if somewhere, out there—' He pointed towards the distant, watery horizon. '– a northern father stands with his son, looking towards us and saying *Come spring, my boy, we'll take them.*'

Kerric laughed again. 'Saying is one thing. Doing is another. Let those shites throw themselves at the Green Isle till the sun plunges into the sea. The northmen won't defeat us. Not while you're our Steward.'

Warmed, despite the cold wind, Grefin started to reply, but then the deerhound started barking. He and Kerric turned, to see the young dog losing its manners over a straggle of black-faced sheep.

'Shite,' Kerric muttered, and whistled for the dog to heel. 'Don't tell Darby. The hound means no real harm. And I am training him, truly.'

''Tis our secret,' he promised. 'But it's likely best we remove him from temptation.'

'You know that means braving the barons' gauntlet?'

Grefin rolled his eyes. 'Better the barons than Darby. That man sets uncommon store by his sheep.'

Companionable, and escorted by the chastened deerhound, they returned to Seal Rock castle. It was full to overflowing with the Green Isle's barons and lesser lords, some twelve men in all, and their chosen serjeants, gathered to celebrate the end of what had come to be called *raiding season*. But there was more point to this coming together than the relief of feasting and wine and a respite from killing. The living were honoured, the fallen mourned, and a detailed review was undertaken of the season's failure and success.

'Ha! There he is, our mettlesome Steward! Come, Grefin, break your fast with us! Your wife presides over a hearty board!'

Terriel, the mightiest lord, bellowing, as they entered the Great Hall.

With Kerric a half-pace behind him, Grefin made his way between the hall's crowded trestles up to the high table where Terriel and his son Alard, who'd lost his right arm to the raiders earlier that year, sat with Mazelina and Ullia. Joben was there, and Paithan, travelled to Seal Rock from Aimery's court. Servants scurried, carrying pitchers and platters and baskets of bread. Hounds slunk under the trestles, barked and snapped and snarled over bones in the corners, begged for morsels with mournful eyes. Some two score of voices clashed and mingled and bounced around the walls.

He made slow progress because they all wanted to speak with him, the Green Isle's nobles. Ask a question, offer advice, shake his hand, share a loss. Though they could be fractious, disputatious, quick to offence and slow to forgive, still . . . in his years as their Steward he'd come to love these men. Even the ones he didn't like very much. The serjeants, too, were eager to greet him. Tough men who oft made the difference when it came to defending the Green Isle's raided villages.

At last, reaching the high table, he took a seat between his wife and his yet-unwed daughter. Kissed Ullia's pretty cheek and Mazelina's prim mouth. She wasn't fond of Seal Rock castle, his wife. Cold, brute and masculine, she called it. Made for swords and bloodshed, not familial warmth. He couldn't argue. He, too, preferred Steward's Keep. But it was Seal Rock that guarded the Isle's north coast, so in Seal Rock he must stay, and think of her, missing her, in the barren months they lived apart.

She touched his knee. 'Grefin . . .'

Turning from Terriel, who'd started to ramble, he looked at his beloved wife. Since Potterstown, and losing Jorin, Mazelina had become his mirror. In her face he saw every scar on his battered body, every bleak memory behind his eyes. How much he'd changed and was still changing. What he'd sacrificed for the Green Isle and what he yet might have to give.

'My love?'

She nodded at the end of the hall. 'I think – something's happened.'

Nicholas, Seal Rock's steward, stood in the hall's doorway. His face was grave. Realising himself noticed, he half-raised his hand then took a step back. A warning. A plea.

'My lord?' said Kerric, breaking off conversation with Alard. 'What is it?'

'Doubtless nothing,' he said, standing. 'Tarry here. I'll not be long.'

He could feel the curious stares follow him, hear how the babbling voices changed. Every man thinking it, not a one speaking the thought. *Are the raiders come back? Do we celebrate too soon?*

'My lord,' Nicholas said, drawing him into the corridor beyond the Great Hall. A good man, quietly efficient. 'This is just come from Tamwell castle.'

Grefin looked at the rolled parchment, waxed fast with Curteis's device. He felt his throat close, his belly roil. His recently scarred fingers shook as he splintered the crimson seal. He read the note quickly, then nodded at Nicholas as he handed it back.

'Thank you. The herald should return at once. Tell him to find the swiftest cog in Naseby port and hold it till I arrive. Then send to the stables. My family and I will need our fleetest horses made ready to depart within the hour.'

Nicholas bowed. 'Yes, my lord.'

As he walked back into the Great Hall, for once not hiding behind his Steward's mask, the Green Isle's lords and their serjeants fell awkwardly silent. So did the servants, halted in their tracks. Even the squabbling dogs hushed. His people stared and waited until he was standing before the high board.

'My lords,' he said, wishing above anything that he could hold his wife's hand. 'My friends. I must return to Cater's Tamwell, with my family. Duke Aimery is fallen gravely ill and—' His voice broke. He had to clear his throat. '—and the leech fears for his life.' He turned to look along the table. 'Terriel. I'd not abandon our purpose here. Can I ask you to play my part and see all good services performed?'

Terriel nodded, his eyes brilliant. 'Of course, my lord Steward. Take the Green Isle's love and good hopes with you to His Grace.'

'I will, Terriel.' His gaze shifted. 'Joben. Paithan. As members of the duke's council, I assume you'll travel back with us?'

His cousin and old Herewart's son looked at each other. They'd come to Seal Rock at Balfre's request. Close to him still, after so many years. 'We will,' Joben said, sombre. 'I'm sorry to hear this, Grefin.'

Was he? Was Paithan? With Aimery dead and Balfre made duke they'd be showered with largess. That made it a trifle difficult to believe in their grief. But it wouldn't be wise of him to show any doubt.

'I know. I'll have the stables ready your horses.'

'Come, Ullia,' Mazelina said, an arm around their weeping daughter. 'Kerric?'

'Yes, Mama,' Kerric murmured. He took his sister's hand and together they started from the hall.

Grefin turned again as someone grasped his elbow. Terriel. 'Don't fret yourself on us, Grefin,' he said roughly. 'And if your father dies, send word. The lords of the Green Isle will come to Tamwell and stand with you.'

He'd break if he tried to speak again. So he nodded, then followed his family through the silence and out of the hall.

For the first time since his life as the Green Isle's Steward began, Grefin returned to Tamwell castle under cover of night. This wasn't a moment for fanfare or celebration. It was raining, a dull, mournful drizzle of damp in keeping with his mood. After the brutal ride across the Isle, north coast to south, and then the rough water crossing to the mainland, he was exhausted. Pain-wracked. So were Mazelina and their children. Joben and Paithan showed the strain too. Only the men-at-arms who'd journeyed with them seemed indifferent to their hardships.

Curteis was waiting for him in Tamwell's bailey, his face drawn in the sputtered torchlight.

'My lord Grefin,' he said, bowing. 'You've made excellent time. I did fear—'

As the steward's voice failed, Grefin took hold of his arm. 'His Grace lives?'

'He does, my lord. But . . .' Curteis rallied. 'He is determined to see you.'

Grief like a raider's axe, cleaving him in two. 'Where's my brother? I'd speak with Balfre before—'

Glancing past him to Joben and Paithan, Curteis turned a little aside. 'My lord, His Grace has not sent for Count Balfre. He would speak only with you.'

Ah. 'Then I won't keep him. Look to my family, Curteis, and these good men-at-arms.'

'Of course, my lord. You'll find your father in his chamber.'

He kissed Mazelina and Ullia swiftly, patted Kerric's stubbled cheek. 'Go with Curteis. He'll coddle you warm and dry and make sure of a meal.'

'Give your father our love,' Mazelina whispered. 'Grefin—'

He couldn't break. Mustn't break. 'I know. I'll see you soon.'

The journey from bailey to Aimery's chamber was the longest of his life.

The first sight of his father choked him to silence. The bold, vigorous man of his childhood was entirely vanished. Even the older man he'd become lately – diminished, yes, but still vital – that man was gone too. Aimery had become a frail, pathetic creature, propped up in bed with pillows and tucked beneath bearskin. A half-dozen burning candles lent dishonest warmth to his face. Wrinkled skin draped over jutting bone. Once-keen eyes peered, yellow and rheumy. Thick hair thinned to gossamer strands was plastered to his crusted scalp.

'Grefin!' Aimery said, his voice a raven's croak. 'You've come.' His clawed fingers jabbed at the chamber's attendants. 'Get out. Get out. I'd be alone with my son.'

'My lord.' Somehow he managed to cross from the doorway to the bedside without falling to the floor. Paid no attention to the servants sent scuttling from the room. ''Tis good to see you.'

Aimery held him close. He smelled of disease and creeping death. Then his wasted arms fell away. 'Let me look at you, while I can.'

There was a chair, but Grefin sat on the bed beside his father. Fought against tears as Aimery's clouded gaze roamed his face.

'You've grown thin, fighting northmen. How many more of their ships have you taken?'

'Two score, or thereabouts,' he said, forcing a smile. Knowing the tally would give Aimery pleasure. 'Stored safely inland with the rest, against the day Harcia dares to sail again. Your Grace—'

'Good, good.' Then Aimery frowned. 'And you? What wounds have you, since last we met?'

'None worth mentioning. Your Grace, why—'

'Liar.' Aimery poked him. 'Did you think your wife forgot how to wield a quill?'

Ah, Mazelina. 'No, your Grace. Why have you not sent for Balfre?'

Aimery gestured at the silver pitcher set on a table against the wall. 'Wine. And don't stint.'

He was a husband, a father, and Steward of the Green Isle but he obeyed Aimery as neatly as though he were still a child. The pitcher held Lombardi sunwine, its spicy scent rich and familiar. He half-filled a silver goblet and returned to the bed. Eased his father's cold, twisted fingers around its stem. But even so simple a task as raising it to his lips was now beyond Harcia's duke. Eyes burning, Grefin helped him drain it, to prevent the crueller shame of spilled wine. And then he pretended he'd not done that, just as long ago Aimery had pretended not to see that his small son, taking his first jousting pass in the tilt yard, had wept for being knocked out of his saddle and onto his arse. Setting the emptied goblet aside, he held his father's hand and waited for him to speak. The chamber was hushed, its only sound the crackle of flames in the hearth. Iron braziers, filled with smouldering peat, added to the warmth.

And yet . . . and yet . . . the hand in his was icy cold.

Stirring, Aimery cleared his throat. 'We've had strife in Kirby Bedwin. Poxy mudder knights, looking for mischief. Men Balfre trained in the Marches then sent home again so he could train more.' He grimaced. 'Insolent young cockerels. They bare their arses to my ban on havey-cavey jousting and rough melee.'

'You don't punish them?'

'I tell your cousin Joben to punish them. He swears to me he will, he has, and then last week in Kirby Bedwin two bands of mudder knights clashed in the street. Wine and strumpets. Four dead. A score bloodied. Honest guildmen with their shops set afire.'

Aimery was gasping, trembling. Gently, Grefin pushed him back to his pillows. 'Please, Your Grace. Don't distress yourself.'

'I've told your brother to curb his appetite for men-at-arms,' said Aimery, fretful fingers plucking at the bearskin. 'Use the ones he's got till they die of old age – or the colic. He bares his arse at me on that, no better than a mudder knight. Sends Joben or Paithan to chew my ear on the matter. They visit him often then come back from the

Marches to tell me how Balfre's in the right, Clemen's a menace, I must give him more farmers to make into men-at-arms.'

'Send your troublesome mudder knights to me, my lord. Let them bare their arses at those northern raiders.'

He'd meant for Aimery to be amused, but his father only frowned. Rubbed a thumb across his signet ring. Picked at a scab on his bony wrist.

'Your Grace . . .' He straightened a fold in the bearskin, smoothed its ruffled dark brown pelt. 'You should send for Balfre. It isn't right he's not here.'

Aimery's blueish lips pinched. 'Roric of Clemen,' he muttered. 'The bastard's foaming at the mouth. I'll let you guess why.'

Over the killing of that Clemen lord in the Marches. He'd received Aimery's letter on it a few days before his summons home. 'Surely he foams without cause. You said Balfre places the blame for Ercole's death on Humbert. That Humbert and Ercole and Clemen's men-at-arms ransacked some Marcher inn, unprovoked, and Waymon did all he could to prevent the slaughter.'

Aimery rubbed his sunken eyes. 'I know what I said.'

'You don't believe him?'

'*Roric* claims Balfre was using the innkeep to stir trouble in Clemen, and Waymon provoked the slaughter to keep the truth from coming to light.'

'Then Roric's lying.'

'What if he's not?' Aimery whispered. 'What if your brother had Ercole killed on purpose? What if he seeks to force Roric's sword from its scabbard?'

Grefin stared at his father. Aimery stared back.

'No,' he said, and slipped off the bed. 'My lord, how can you take Roric's word over Balfre? He serves you well in the Marches. I've heard you say it many times.'

'And how many times did you hear Balfre say that every duke of Clemen sat his arse on a stolen throne?'

This again? Grefin wanted to weep. 'Your Grace, those doubts and fears are long since put to bed. 'Tis your illness that wakes them. I *beg* you, don't—'

Aimery's clawed fist thudded against his bony chest. 'I was

654

warned, Grefin. Years ago. In Piper's Wade, I was warned. *Beware the long-tailed comet, Aimery. Chaos is coming. A long-tailed comet cannot lie.* I see that comet, Grefin. I feel the coming chaos. I—'

'My lord, this is nonsense! You don't believe in omens!'

'I don't believe in *Balfre*! I thought I did. I let you convince me he'd changed. But this business in the Marches – the murder of Clemen's lord – I tell you, Grefin, your brother can't be trusted. As soon as I'm dead he'll provoke a war with Clemen. I want *you* to be my heir!'

'I can't, Your Grace. I won't. I'm your Steward. Nothing more.'

'You're my son!' Aimery cried, spraying bloodied spittle. 'And I am your father! You owe me your *life*!'

He had to blink to see properly, his tired eyes blurred to blindness with tears. 'But not my honour. I swore Balfre an oath. I won't take from my brother what isn't yours to give.'

'Then get out,' Aimery said, choking. 'I don't want you, I want Curteis. Fetch me Curteis!'

Grefin dragged a hand down his face. He couldn't leave. How could he leave? How could he—

'*Didn't you hear me? I said get out!*'

He reached for Aimery's hand. 'Your Grace – Father – if you'd only send for Balfre we could—'

On a gasping rattle, his father's yellowed, bloodshot eyes rolled back in his head. Then he started to shake like a man dying of plague. Grefin bolted for the chamber door. Flung it wide.

'Fetch the leech,' he told the nearest attendant. 'Fetch Curteis. *Run.*'

The attendant gasped, then fled. Grefin slammed the door shut. Stumbled back to the bed where Aimery shuddered, moaned, and with a stifled groan took hold of his father.

Please, my lord. Don't die.

The woman had been a peddler, crossed into the Marches from Clemen to sell her paltry wares. Whittled spoons. Carved acorns. Flimsy buttons made of clay. Sunk deep in a rune-trace, Izusa felt her approach and knew the peddler was what she needed. Just as a rune-trance had shown her that farmer's pregnant young wife when she needed another baby's head for Salimbene.

It was no hard thing to find the woman struggling through the rain on the Marches road, offer her a warm, dry bed for the night and a chance to sell some spoons. She'd killed her swiftly. Silently. And now the peddler's body lay hidden, runed against rotting, as she waited for word from Salimbene that Aimery was dead.

A month and four days after giving Balfre the fatal ink . . . five days after she'd found and killed the peddler woman . . . the shrivelled baby's head in its ash box called her out of sleep.

Izusa. Izusa. Harcia has a new duke.

And so, with a sigh, with a sloughing of grey, dead skin, her life in the Marches was brought to an end.

Balfre came the next day to tell her what she already knew. Giddy and laughing like a little girl. Nothing like a man who'd murdered his father.

'I leave for Cater's Tamwell tomorrow,' he crowed. 'The day after Aimery's entombed I'll be acclaimed duke. And soon after that *king*.'

She sat on a stool. 'And your brother?'

'Grefin?' A careless shrug. 'If he's loyal he can steward the Green Isle till a northern raider kills him.'

'And if he's not?'

Balfre frowned. 'Have you runed those letters I gave you?'

Letters he'd forged incriminating Grefin in treason against Harcia, that he'd use if his brother couldn't be turned to his purpose. She'd steeped them in fuddling chants so that anyone who read them would never question their lying truths. Difficult runings that had cost her dear in blood and pain. But she'd not begrudge the suffering because it was for Salimbene.

She pointed. 'On the table.'

Grinning, he reached for her. One hand cupped the back of her neck, the other plundered beneath her loose shift, fingers pinching her nipple. She gave herself to him without restraint. Took genuine pleasure in his fucking, which she'd not done for some time. A sweet farewell, though he didn't know it. When he was done, shuddered empty, he pulled up his hose.

'I'd fuck you the rest of the day, if I could. Alas, I must return to the manor. But don't weep. I'll make up for it when you join me in Cater's Tamwell.'

She pretended surprise. 'My lord?'

'Did you think I'd leave you to rot here alone, Izusa? Fuck, no. When things are settled you'll join me in Harcia.'

'But Balfre – you have a wife.'

His face turned ugly with scornful contempt. 'Jancis isn't the kind of woman any man would make a queen. Besides, we both know I can't do this without you.' He bit her bottom lip. '*Witch*.'

He wanted her to be pleased, so she showed him pleasure. 'My lord, I'm honoured.'

A mischievous smirk. 'You should be.'

'But first things first. What of Vidar?'

'He suspects nothing. Do you have the poison?'

She fetched a glass vial from her bedchamber, filled to the stopper with a pale green liquid. Enough to kill a dozen men, though he had in mind but one. At least for now.

'A few drops in his wine. He'll not taste it.'

Balfre smiled. 'Quick or slow?'

'Quick enough. He'll be dead before sunrise.'

He slipped the vial inside his doublet. 'And then he'll be a cat among the pigeons. Poor, crippled Vidar. Useful to the end. I've already forged his confession. You'll find it with his body. As for what comes after, you're sure of your part?'

'I am, my lord. Never fear.'

'Fear, Izusa?' He kissed her again, savage. 'What's that?'

She put the runed letters in a satchel for him, then stood outside her cottage and watched him ride out of her life, towards a future that only Salimbene could see. When he was gone from her sight she went back inside. Very soon now it would be time to leave for Carillon.

'Benedikt!'

Terrified, heedless, Liam threw himself at the Clemen man-at-arms in front of him. His mail-clad shoulder struck a boiled-leather belly and they both went down. He heard something break. Waited for a burst of pain through his body. But it was the Clemen bastard who screamed, the Clemen bastard whose sword dropped to the ground, who rolled grunting as he clutched his snapped forearm.

There wasn't time to kill him. Liam scrambled to his feet, kicked the bastard in the balls, then barged through the melee to his fallen brother.

Benedikt, ye pizzling shite. Don't ye dare be dead.

A swinging Clemen sword caught him high across the back. He staggered, lost his balance, crashed to one knee, flailed upright again. Sweat stung his eyes. He could hardly breathe or see. The screams and shouts and clash of battle raged around him. A flash of blade to his right. He turned, his own sword raised, and felt the shock as steel met steel. Teeth bared, snarling, he threw his weight against Clemen's man. Tilted his enemy's balance just far enough to hook a booted foot round the bastard's ankle. The man went down hard. Liam hurdled him and kept going.

Gloved fist into this face. Jabbing sword-hilt into that throat. Grule called him a green-shite, a know-not, a boil on battle's arse, but he knew that was farting wind. He was a duke, and born to fight.

'*Benedikt!*'

His brother sprawled face down in the Clemen dirt, unmoving. Abandoned, as brawling men-at-arms brawled somewhere else. Sobbing for air, sobbing, Liam grabbed Benedikt's shoulder and hauled him over. His brother's eyes were closed, his face a filthy, bloody mask, his scalp split scarlet along his mud-clotted hairline. He'd lost his boiled leather skull cap. But his chest moved. He was breathing. Liam thumped his brother's limp arm.

'*Benedikt!*'

A cough. A strangled groan. Benedikt opened his eyes.

'Willem? What—' A gasp. 'Willem!'

But he'd heard the thud of running feet, was already turning. He blocked the Clemen bastard's down-swinging sword slash, slid blade along blade, smiled to hear the steel sing. Blocked three more swift strokes, gasping as the blows slammed through every bone in his body. There was blood in his mouth. He'd bitten his tongue. He spat red, tried another ankle-hook, failed, slipped in the mud, rolled clear of a sword-swing, staggered up, muscles screaming, defended himself, defended again, again, fuck, this Clemen shite knew what he was doing, attacked, slipped *again*, saw a chance as his enemy slipped, stamped his booted foot on the man's outflung wrist, grinding hand and blade into the mud. Their eyes met. They stared, desperate.

Then startled as a hollow, metallic booming sounded over their heads.

Liam turned. It was Humbert, that murdering, treacherous bear of a man, standing on the farmhouse steps with a gong and hammer in his hands. Behind him huddled the farmer and his wife and the thieving pizzle who'd started this. Clemen's Marcher lord struck the gong again, harder. The last few fighting men-at-arms fell back, confused and panting.

Humbert threw down the gong and hammer and stamped down the steps. 'What is this shite? Who provoked the skirmish?'

Stepping a prudent distance from the Clemen man-at-arms he'd put on the ground, Liam watched as his serjeant, bloody and limping, faced Humbert.

''Tis Marcher law, and well-known, that we might pursue a poacher to any lair, Harcian or Clemen.' Grule pointed to the huddled family. 'While riding on our lawful business we came upon this Clemen farmer's son taking Harcian game in Harcian woodland. He must answer to Count Balfre.'

'Lord Humbert, he's lying!' Clemen's serjeant shouted, shouldering forward. 'They do—'

'Clap tongue,' Humbert ordered. 'You're cockshites to a man. Spill blood over venison? You'd see Clemen and Harcia tearing throats for a deer?' He scorched them all with his fearsome glare. 'You make me fucking tired.'

Clemen's serjeant gaped. 'My lord? It be a clear case of Harcian trespass! And I do have men—'

'*Clap tongue, I said! Are you deaf?*'

Mute, Clemen's serjeant shook his head.

'Good,' said Humbert, glowering. Then he reached within his lace-fronted brown doublet and pulled out a small purse. Shifted his glare to Grule, tossed the purse at the serjeant's feet. 'For the deer. If Balfre wants more, tell him to come fetch it himself. Now you and your men ride home to the Harcian Marches, serjeant, before I lose my temper.'

And that was that.

As Clemen and Harcia drew apart to take stock and fetch their scattered horses, Liam helped unsteady Benedikt to stand. 'Ye be in one piece? B'aint no holes poked in you?'

'My head aches,' Benedikt said, gingerly swiping clotted mud from his cheeks. 'But I b'aint skewered.'

The fighting over, he was suddenly aware of his own bruises, a split in his scarred cheek, a shattering exhaustion. This was their fourth skirmish with Clemen's men-at-arms since Ercole was killed at the Pig Whistle. Harcia's men-at-arms were under strict orders from Aimery not to spill blood, but with Clemen's men-at-arms ready to take offence at a fart, excuse every kind of Clemen lawbreaking on account of dead Ercole, any fool could see blood was going to be spilled. But not much of his this time, or Benedikt's. Their luck was holding.

He grinned. 'Nor me.'

'Willem—'

He looked up from shoving his sword back in its scabbard. 'What?'

Benedikt was staring across the trampled grass to where Humbert spoke some last stern words to the farmer's son. 'He ought to be on his knees t'ye. Humbert. Bowing and scraping. Begging forgiveness. Calling ye "*Your Grace*." D'ye never wish ye could just march on up to the pizzle and—'

All the time. He had dreams of seeing Humbert humbled, and worse, for betraying Harald. But he took care not to talk on them. Not while he lived in Balfre's barracks.

'Clap tongue, Benedikt!' he muttered. 'D'ye want someone to hear?'

They rode back to Balfre's manor with Grule and the other men. From the look on his face the serjeant was wondering what Aimery's heir would have to say about clashing swords with Clemen. Nothing pleasant, most like. Balfre weren't a pleasant man. But when they reached the barracks, they found riotous uproar. Grule slid from his saddle and snatched a running man by his jack.

'Towser! What's happened?'

'Word's come from Harcia!' Towser panted. 'Duke Aimery's dead!'

Liam looked down. Aimery dead? Then Balfre was duke. He hid

a smile. One step closer to Roric . . . and the Falcon Throne. He could feel Benedikt beside him, trying not to grin. Still looking down he waggled a rude finger at his brother. *Mind yerself, pizzle. We got to watch our step.* Then Grule barked at them to keep moving. No rest for the weary, or a Harcian man-at-arms.

In the hours left till sunset, first they suffered at the hands of the barracks leech, counting their cuts and bruises and stinging them with foul muck, then worked their way through every task Grule gave them and a few more besides. The barracks was worse than an ant hill, heaving and clamouring with the men who'd been chosen to escort Harcia's new duke to his castle in Cater's Tamwell. Lord Waymon barged in and out, cursing and cuffing and threatening to dagger any fuck who did dare to make Balfre late or slow or seem anything less than a duke. They'd be leaving at dawn. By then every horse must be groomed spotless. Every saddle and bridle and leather jack and doublet cleaned and oiled and gleaming. Swords sharp. Daggers deadly. Everything fucking perfect or there'd be a pike up someone's arse.

Liam and Benedikt rolled their eyes at each other and kept out of the feggit lord's way as best they could.

Come supper, crowded in the noisy barracks mess with fifty hungry men-at-arms, Benedikt near fell face-first in his rabbit stew. 'I got to get some shuteye, Willem,' he said, yawning wide enough to swallow a horse. 'Be ye coming?'

Liam played with a crust of bread. He should. His bruises and bones were aching and his burn-scarred cheek stung where it was cut. Even so, he was too jittery for sleep.

'Soon,' he said. 'I got things to think on first.'

Benedikt yawned again. 'Suit yerself.'

A few tilt yard torches were still burning, throwing light and shadow onto the scuffed, patchy grass. Ducking under the rail with his sword, he wandered into the middle of the empty training ground and started working through the drills Grule had shown him. He'd spent enough time these past months watching Balfre with a blade to know that Roric, raised the same way, would be a lethal man in a fight. Bastard or not, he'd killed Duke Harald. So Harald's son had to train every chance he got, no matter he was tired and aching, if he wanted a hope of killing the man who'd stolen his throne.

'You're dropping your right shoulder, Willem. It puts you off-balance. I've told you that before.'

Startled, he turned. Lord Boice, Balfre's strange guest, was watching him from the tilt yard railing. He nodded. 'Iss, my lord.'

'Go again,' Boice said, encouraging. 'And keep that shoulder high. Else you'll be asking for a Clemen blade between your ribs.'

He did as he was told. But after a few moments Boice cursed and ducked himself under the railing. 'No. Here.' He held out his hand, approaching. 'The sword.'

'My lord,' he said again, and handed it over.

'You're doing *this*,' Boice said, hunching a shoulder to his ear. 'When you should be doing *this*.' His shoulder dropped. 'You see the difference?'

'Iss,' he said, scowling. Not because he resented the correction, but because he hated to be wrong. 'Only I—'

'Boice! What the fuck are you doing?'

And that was Balfre, sauntering down the torchlit path from the manor to the tilt yard, Lord Waymon by his side. They were carrying heavy silver wine goblets. Balfre had two.

'Saving your man-at-arms's life, I hope, my lord,' Boice said, handing back the sword. 'Or should that be Your Grace?'

'Not quite yet. But the sentiment is appreciated.' Balfre held up one of the wine goblets. 'Waymon and I were were sharing a drop of sunwine. Toasting Aimery's memory. Care to join us?' His gaze shifted. 'You, there. You can go.'

As Boice crossed the tilt yard, Liam pretended to obey . . . then drifted unseen into a deep pool of shadow. Any chance he got to watch Balfre, he took. When serving a man, 'twas good to know him. Especially when that man must later be thrown down. Balfre, the arrogant shite, never looked twice at the man-at-arms he'd dismissed. Thought an order given was an order followed. Fucking fool. Surely he'd prove no obstacle when the time came to push him aside.

Boice ducked back under the tilt yard railing, then took the goblet Balfre offered him. Lifted it, in wry salute. 'To His Grace, Duke Aimery of Harcia. And to his noble son.'

'Hear, hear,' said Balfre and Waymon, sipping. But Lord Boice drank deep. The look on Balfre's face, watching him empty his goblet, made Liam think of a cat with its paw on a mouse. It was the same gloating look he'd seen on Iddo's face, that day in the cellar. His breath caught.

Shite. What was going on here?

Smiling, Balfre laid his hand on Boice's shoulder. Shook him a little, as though they were friends. 'Ah, Vidar. I am going to miss you.'

Liam felt his blood leap, even as Lord Boice lost his balance where he stood. *Vidar?* He remembered that Clemen pizzle from the Pig Whistle. Had sworn vengeance on him too, for betraying Duke Harald. But – Vidar was dead. And half-blind and crippled when he was living. Boice weren't neither.

Boice was staring at Balfre, his unscarred face stiff with shock. Then he looked at the goblet. Cursed. Threw the heavy silver cup on the ground. 'Balfre?' he said hoarsely. 'What have you done?'

So . . . he *was* Vidar?

Astonished, Liam watched as Balfre snatched at Boice's neck. Pulled something free from under his shirt and doublet and snapped it loose. Waymon was staring too, just as amazed.

'Fuck, Balfre. I believed you when you said you'd given Vidar a different face, but – *fuck*. It *is* him.'

'Not for much longer,' said Balfre, grinning at the man everyone in the manor had called Lord Boice. 'What have I done, Vidar? I've killed you.'

Boice turned from him, the movement spilling light from a tilt yard torch onto his true face, Vidar's face, with its one eye and its ragged scars. He looked stricken.

'Balfre . . . *why?*'

'Why do you think? Am *I* half-blind? Or too doltish to notice you'd had a change of heart? You only played the traitor. However bruised by Roric, your loyalty always belonged to Clemen. Take him, Waymon. Lock him in his chamber. He'll be dead by sunrise.'

Waymon's smile was wolfish. 'And buried in the midden an hour after that, yes?'

'The midden?' Balfre laughed. 'What a waste that would be. No, Waymon. I've a far more useful resting place in mind.'

Silent, stumbling, like a man half-dead already, Vidar let Waymon hustle him away.

Balfre stayed behind, his fingers caressing whatever it was he'd snatched from around slowly dying Vidar's neck. Watching him from the shadows, Liam saw him smile. Then Harcia's new duke picked up Vidar's discarded goblet. Tossed it in the air, caught it and turned for the manor.

Too frightened to move, Liam waited till Balfre was safely out of sight. Then he bent himself double, whooshed the burning air from his lungs in one long, astonished rush. Growing up in the Pig Whistle he'd heard Marcher folk whisper of *faeries* and *goblins* and *omens* and *witchery*. He'd seen their fingers flick as they warded off bad luck. Iddo always scoffed at them, but Molly never did. She used to call on the faeries and leave charms around the inn. True, the faeries and the charms never saved her but did that mean she and the Marcher folk were wrong? 'Cause how could Balfre have given that treacherous bastard Vidar a different face if he weren't a man as dabbled in dark muck? He couldn't. Which meant he was that man. And that meant Liam, Duke of Clemen, had best watch his step.

'Shite,' he muttered, shivering . . . then returned to his solitary sword drills.

CHAPTER THIRTY-NINE

'Mama, we're worried about Papa.'

Sickeningly weary, scoured raw with grief, Mazelina looked up from the dull distraction of needlepoint. Cool sunlight from the dayroom window played across her children's pale, unhappy faces. And they were still her children, though Kerric was pushed too soon into manhood and Ullia, her brash Ullia, had grown to love fine dresses as well as swords and was sought after by several young

Green Isle lords. She still danced ahead of them – but soon she'd let herself be caught.

'My loves.' She stabbed her needle safe in the half-finished cushion cover and put the embroidery to one side. 'Your father mourns his father. You must expect him to be a little distant. 'Tis not even a week since Aimery died. I think he's only now beginning to realise his loss. And you remember . . .' She hesitated. 'We all remember how it was, when we lost Jorin.'

Kerric shook his head. 'This is different.'

'Everyone in Tamwell knows Papa has sent for Uncle Balfre,' Ullia said. 'I don't think Aunt Jancis has stopped crying since. And Emeline – Mama, Emeline looks as though she'd leap from the west tower. She never says a word but I know she's terrified of her father.'

'Mama—' Kerric sat beside her on the settle. 'Is Papa afraid of what Balfre will do now he's duke?'

'Kerric! What a thing to ask!'

'That's not an answer.'

Agitated, trying to hide it, she stood and crossed to the unshuttered window. The day outside was blustery, the sky scudded with high cloud. Keeping her back to her son and her daughter, she clasped her hands tight to stop their trembling.

'Kerric, Ullia, your father would be most hurt were I to tell him what you've said. So I won't. And if you love him, you'll not repeat it.'

'But Mama—'

'*Enough*, Ullia. Comfort Emeline. She's your cousin, and needs a friend.' She glanced over her shoulder. 'As for you, Kerric, make yourself useful to poor Curteis. He and Aimery were very close. And there's a great deal to be done in Tamwell before Balfre returns.'

'Mama,' her children murmured, chastened.

As soon as they were gone, she fetched a shawl and went to find Grefin.

He was in Tamwell bailey's smithy, alone, hammering out his pain on old, worn horse-shoes. It was a trick he'd learned on the Green Isle. A way of conquering his feelings without alarming his family or the lords who'd come to love and trust him.

Stripped to his hose and heedless of struck sparks and molten metal, he lifted his head as she entered. Caught his hammer on its downward stroke. The scars and knots on his bare torso, gifts from the northern raiders, were slicked with running sweat.

'Don't look at me like that, Mazelina,' he said curtly, before she even tried to speak. 'I don't know what I'm going to do.'

The shawl she'd needed to cross the bailey was stifling in the smithy's heat. She let it slip to her elbows. Made sure her voice was gentle because his grief had made him brittle. Like badly tempered steel.

'And you won't know, my love, till you decide who you believe. Aimery . . . or Balfre.'

He threw down the hammer, filling the smithy with ringing echoes. 'How can I decide, Mazelina? How can I choose between my father and my brother? All my life I've been torn between them, like a piece of meat between two wolves. I'm *exhausted*. And I can't – I can't—'

Weeping, she went to him. Held him hard. Waited for his storm to pass so he could hear what she had to say. When at last she felt all his muscles soften she leaned away from him, just a little, and pressed her palm to his hollowed cheek.

'Then don't decide, my love. Don't choose. Let Balfre choose for you. Let him show you who he is. And when he shows you, because he will, then you'll know what to do.'

Grefin rested his cheek on her hair. 'Do you know how much I love you?'

'As much as I love you.'

'Mazelina . . .' He breathed out, slowly. 'I'm tired of hammering horse-shoes. Take me inside.'

Closeted in his study, Humbert cursed as he read the the latest spidery-scrawled letter sent him by an increasingly desperate Lord Scarwid. The news from Eaglerock wasn't encouraging. Though the worst disruptions to trade in Cassinia had settled, the dukes there dabbling in peace for a change, Clemen's fortunes continued miserable. His Grace was cold and unforthcoming, growing grimmer each passing day. Master Blane blamed him for Ercole's death, with a chorus of his brother traders echoing the man's grief – and rattling their coffers.

No longer generously inclined, they wanted their loans repaid. Roric was despondent and would scarce listen to any advice in council, save it came from Lord Aistan. To appease the merchants there was to be another increase in taxes. Eaglerock's tradesfolk were crying foul. And the township's exarchites also stirred trouble, attracting malcontents, muttering strife. Wasn't there any way Humbert could come to Eaglerock and guide His Grace in person? For it seemed any written advice he offered Roric was being ignored.

Sighing, Humbert pinched the bridge of his nose. Scarwid's plea for intervention wasn't the first he'd received of late. Several lords had written to him in the past few weeks, nobles who'd supported the move against Harald and were then in full agreement that Roric was their only hope. Now they begged him to be their spokesman a second time, encourage the duke they'd chosen to soften his stance. Listen to wider counsel. Ease his throttling grip upon the duchy.

He had no idea what to tell them.

A sharp knock, and then his study door pushed open. Egann, with a most peculiar look on his face.

'My lord, you should come. There's strange trouble at the Pig Whistle. Folk are claiming Lord Vidar is there. Dead.'

Humbert stared. 'Man, are you *drunk*?'

'I wish I were,' Egann said grimly. 'But I've a sober man-at-arms outside who'll swear he's seen the body.'

'*Vidar's* body?'

'Yes, my lord.'

'That you hauled out of Crooked Creek and I sent to Eaglerock to be buried. *That* body.'

'The very same.'

'Egann, has the shiting world gone *mad*?'

'It would seem so, my lord.'

'*Shite*.' He stood, shoving his chair back. 'You'd best show me.'

They rode hard to the Pig Whistle inn – or what remained of it. By Marcher Law its blackened ruins should have been cleared and a new inn planned to take its place, the freehold leased to any soul with the coin to pay. But some Marcher folk claimed the burned-down Pig Whistle was haunted and didn't keep secret what they thought they heard and saw. With the susperstitious Marches already uneasy, and bad blood splashed far and wide over Molly's death and the inn's burning, better to let things rest a while – or so Humbert thought. Balfre didn't seem to care either way. And after Ercole, and Harcia's treachery, he wasn't in the mood to sit down and chat. So nothing had been done.

Only other folk, valuing coin over fear and sentiment, had taken matters into their own hands. They knew there were merchants and traders coming into the Marches who were ripe for something to eat and drink by the time they reached the Crossroads. Eager for somewhere to ease their weary bones and horses and mules. So while there was no longer an *inn* to offer hospitality, that didn't mean they must be disappointed. Not wanting any more ructions, sensitive to the Marches' mood, Humbert had decided to turn a blind eye. For a while.

'Fuck,' he muttered, as he and Egann and the man-at-arms who'd brought the unwelcome news came in sight of the Pig Whistle's charred, rainsoaked skeleton. 'You'd think it was market day in Eaglerock.'

They eased their horses from fast canter to slow trot and approached with caution. Enterprising Marcher folk had set up carts and trestles and barrows in the burned inn's forecourt. Canvas tents flapped their awnings to one side, straw pallets inviting the weary to rest. On the other side, rows of horselines with water and hay and oats for sale. The damp air smelled of pies and pasties and hot pease pottage and ale and horseshit and burning peat and wet charcoal. Dogs barked. Men shouted. Women shrieked and flapped their skirts. Some in the gathered crowd were Marcher folk, some were foreigners, and some – *shite* – looked to be travellers in from Clemen. A handful of men-at-arms tried to keep order. Halting, Humbert slid from his saddle, threw his reins to Egann and stamped his way through the excitement until he reached its cause.

Vidar. Dead on the ground in the middle of the muddy, trampled forecourt. Dagger slashes in his doublet, fresh blood spilled from the wounds. Kneeling beside him, the healer woman Izusa. She seemed nigh witless in her distress. Seeing him, she scrambled to standing.

'Lord Humbert! My lord!'

A ragged silence fell, slowly. Humbert scowled at the woman, then the body at her feet. *Shite*. Behind him he could hear whispers and muttering. *It is him. I told ye. That be Lord Vidar.* No hope now of keeping this secret. What a cockshite fool he'd been to wink at the Marcher folk come to ply their trade in this curs't place.

'Izusa,' he said heavily. 'This is—'

'My lord, forgive me!' Izusa held out bloodied hands in appeal. 'I found him not far from my cottage, stabbed and crawling on all fours. I tried to help him but he commanded I take him on my horse to your manor. He had desperate news for you, Lord Humbert. I didn't dare disobey him – but I fear I cost him his life.'

She was close to babbling, her eyes wide, tears streaming. Horribly aware of the folk crowding close, he did his best to soothe.

'Izusa, I've no doubt you're not to blame. Whatever misfortune did befall Vidar, then—'

'Here—' She pulled a folded paper from within her blouse, thrust it at him. 'Vidar said it would explain all. He said Clemen is in great danger. Aimery of Harcia is dead and—'

Shocked gasps. Humbert flinched. 'Aimery's dead? You're sure?'

'Vidar swore it. Even now Balfre rides to claim his birthright. My lord, your duke and Aimery's son, with Vidar's help, they long ago made a pact. Once Balfre was duke, Roric would freely give him Clemen and its Marches in return for a fortune in gold and jewels so he could live out his life in exile.'

'*Never!*' Humbert protested, as the crowd in the forecourt started to jostle and shout. '*Vidar* said that, Izusa?'

'His dying words. On my life. And he wrote it down.'

Stunned, he looked at the the confession she'd thrust at him. Dimly heard the crowd shouting. Felt himself elbowed and pushed and kicked. Looked up to meet Egann's horrified stare. Then somebody took hold of his arm and turned him. Norbert of the Clemen Marches, who ran pigs in Fallow Copse.

'Is it true, my lord? Are we sold to Harcia?'

The young man's frightened demand was like the first gust of wind heralding a storm. Within heartbeats a gale of questions raged around him. Hands clutched. Fingers pinched. Some of them belonged to Clemen men-at-arms, their duty and training wiped away by panic.

'No, 'tis *not* true!' he said, loudly. ''Tis a misunderstanding! Nothing more!'

But they didn't want to listen. Most all of them knew Izusa and trusted her word. And they'd seen Vidar, not a memory of mouldering bones but a man newly dead. Egann stepped in to help him, and the few men-at-arms who hadn't lost their wits, but it took time and threats of violence before the crowd dispersed.

Not till then did Humbert realise Izusa had fled.

'Find her,' he told a man-at-arms. 'And bring her to me. But gently, mind. The woman's overturned. Egann—'

'My lord,' Egann murmured. Dishevelled and sweating but still the rock he'd always been.

'I'm taking Vidar's body back to the manor,' he said, his voice low. 'You ride for Eaglerock. Find Roric. Tell him Aimery's dead and I have news bearing on it he must hear from me alone. Tell him he's to ride back with you without delay, and press on him he can tell no one where he's going, or why, nor in any way reveal himself as Clemen's duke. Yes?'

Egann nodded. 'Yes, my lord.'

'Then go. Ride as hard and as fast as you can. For once I don't care how many horses you kill.'

Cater's Tamwell was a township in mourning.

Riding through its grieving streets on a black destrier, dressed in black huntsman's leathers, unadorned save for his signet ring and a blood-ruby in his ear, Balfre acknowledged the townsfolk's half-hearted cries of welcome with a sober nod of his head, the restrained wave of one hand. His escort of men-at-arms, led by Waymon, trotted behind him, hooves drumming the high street's hard-beaten earth. Clouds gathered overhead like a spreading bruise. There'd be rain before nightfall. A weeping sky for Harcia's dead duke.

Tamwell castle brooded melancholy over the slow-flowing river.

In Harcian tradition a black flag flew above the battlements. Black sacking was draped between the arrow loops in the curtain wall. Exultation hidden, Balfre cantered across the stone causeway and into Tamwell's bailey. The castle guard's men-at-arms, many of them familiar to him from the Marches, had gathered to greet him. Joben was there. Paithan, and Lowis. Not privy to his intentions like trusted, complicit Waymon, but trustworthy enough. Unlike his nephew,

Kerric, warlike for all his youth, tall and a wicked scar puckering his chin. Behind them a score of barons and lesser nobles come to see Aimery locked at last in his tomb. He knew every lord in the bailey save two – a whipcord-lean man somewhat younger than Harcia's dead duke and another man, younger still, missing half his right arm. He'd not met them before. And of course that doddering old fuck Curteis was there, bloodless with grief.

'Curteis!' He slid from his saddle. 'Where's Grefin?'

The steward bowed. 'My lord, he—'

'*Your Grace.*'

Slowly, Curteis straightened. His face was a blank mask but his eyes were lively with derision. 'Your Grace. Lord Grefin sits with your father. The lady Jancis and your daughter, and the lady Mazelina and her daughter, await you inside.'

Ah. Family.

'See my escort housed and fed,' he said. 'Then tell the ladies I beg their indulgence. I'd speak with my Steward first. Where does Aimery lie?'

The faintest colour touched Curteis's sunken, sallow cheeks. 'In the game larder, Your Grace.'

He nearly burst out laughing. Aimery hung with his butchered venison? Fuck. How *apt*. 'Make sure Grefin and I are not disturbed.' He gestured. 'Waymon?'

Waymon, who'd caught up with him and his escort after seeing to the final business with Vidar, dismounted his horse. 'Your Grace?'

'You know what I want. Explain it to Curteis.'

Waymon smiled. 'Your Grace.'

'Curteis? Assume anything Waymon asks of you is a command from me.'

Curteis bowed again. 'Your Grace.'

Servants curtsied and bowed as he made his way down to the game larder below Tamwell's kitchens. Gesturing at the man-at-arms at the door to remove himself a short distance, he slipped inside.

The chill, slate-lined chamber had been emptied of game and made colder still with blocks of lake ice cut the previous winter. Dozens of beeswax candles burned, gilding the frosty air. In its centre, beneath rows of empty meat hooks, Aimery's corpse was laid upon a broad trestle draped with crimson velvet. He looked like a wax doll floating on a lake of blood.

Grefin slumped on a backless stool beside their dead father. Dressed for mourning, in black velvet, no crude martial leathers, no sword or dagger, he was shivering. Pale as Curteis. He didn't look up.

'He wants to be buried at the Croft. Not here at Tamwell.'

Balfre closed the larder door behind him. 'He told you that?'

'He told Curteis.'

'But . . . you were here with him. At the end.'

It was a guess. A sudden suspicion. But the smallest tremor in his brother's clasped hands confirmed it.

'I was sent for.'

'And I wasn't.' There was no second stool for him to sit on, so he wandered to the crimson-covered trestle and perched on one corner. 'Why? Was Aimery so far gone he couldn't remember where to find me?'

Wincing, Grefin lifted his head. Then he frowned. 'Get off that.'

He waited, just long enough, then slid free of the makeshift bier. Took a moment to savour Aimery, so still in his cloth-of-gold tunic, gnarled fingers neatly curled around the hilt of *Benevolence*, his favourite sword. The naked blade lay unmoving along his sunken chest and belly, steadily reflecting the beeswax candles' thin, honey-scented flames. No hint in that dead face of final suffering. Did he die swiftly, poisoned by Izusa's deadly ink? Easily? A quiet slipping out of life? Or was his end violent and agonised, a raging of despair?

He wanted to know. But if he asked, would grieving Grefin tell him?

'I spied two unfamiliar lords in the bailey when I rode in,' he said, smoothing a small wrinkle in Aimery's golden sleeve. 'With but three arms between them. A trifle careless, don't you think?'

The faintest of sighs. 'Terriel and his son. Alard lost that arm to a raider in Mosswich, last spring.'

So. The greatest baron of the Green Isle and his heir had reached Tamwell before he did. 'Do I have this right, Grefin? You sent for them before sending to me that Aimery was dead?'

Grefin was staring at the floor again. 'The Green Isle deserves a voice here. It deserves its own witness.'

'And what do I deserve? I'm your brother. I'm your *duke*. If you look to be my Steward you'd best show better loyalty than that.'

'Loyalty?' Slowly, Grefin lifted his bleak gaze. 'An odd word coming from you, Balfre. Was it *loyalty* that prompted you to stir shite in the Marches until blood was spilled and a lord died? To spread lies about Clemen so that in his final, painful days our father was plagued with Roric's threats and fury?'

He smiled, even as his muscles tensed and his fingers itched to unsheath the dagger on his hip. 'And there I was thinking Aimery's last thoughts would be of love and family and forgiveness. But it seems he couldn't help himself. A vengeful, dishonest man to the end.'

The stool crashed onto its side as Grefin leapt up. 'You're saying Aimery lied? And Roric, and Lord Humbert? Everyone lies except you. Is that your claim?'

'I claim Harcia. As for the rest . . .' He shrugged. 'What does it matter? Men die every day. Even lords. Even dukes.'

Grefin stared, as though they'd never met before this moment. 'Have you wept for him, Balfre? Have you squeezed out even *one* tear?'

'Do I need to? From the look of you, Grefin, you've wept enough for both of us.'

'Be careful.' Grefin's eyes were glittering. 'Or you'll have me thinking you're glad he's dead.'

He pressed a palm to his heart. 'I'm glad his suffering is ended. Does that make me as poor a son as he was a father?'

'He was a *great* father! And an even greater duke! He ruled this duchy with justice and mercy and he forgave *you*, Balfre, when—'

'When *what*? When I lived and Malcolm died? Are you fucking blind, Grefin? Aimery *never* forgave me for that!'

Turning away, Grefin raked shaking fingers through his untidy hair. 'Not Malcolm again. Malcolm died years ago. His death has nothing to do with this.'

'And by *this* you mean my legitimate grievances against Aimery? Fine. We'll leave Malcolm out of it. Let's talk instead of the plan you and Aimery hatched behind my back, to broker a puling peace with the bastard Roric of Clemen. So that when I became duke I'd be no more than our dead father's puppet!'

Grefin turned round. His eyes were stunned. 'What?'

'*What?*' he mimicked, vicious, then laughed. 'Fuck, Grefin. If you could see your face.'

'I don't know what you're talking about.'

'Now who's telling lies?'

Silence, but for the sound of two men breathing. Then Grefin bit his lip. 'How long have you known?'

'From the beginning.'

'How did you find out?'

'What does it matter?' he countered. 'Your little scheme fell apart soon enough. As I'd have told you it would, if you'd bothered to ask. You can only trust Clemen to be treacherous, Grefin. In a changing world, that's the one thing that stays the same.'

Grefin was staring, guilt and grief and uncertainty in his eyes. 'I never wanted to go behind your back. I fought Aimery on that, as hard as I could.'

'Really?' He raised an eyebrow. 'As hard as you fought against being made the Green Isle's Steward? That hard?'

Grefin's lips tightened. 'So this is how we mourn our father? We rake over the past, looking for ways to sour the future?'

'Forget the future, Grefin! The present's so sour it would fell a charging boar. You've been *sour* to me since I set foot in this fucking tomb.'

'I'm not sour!' Grefin protested. 'I'm heartbroken. Not only because Aimery's dead, but because you don't seem to care! *Fuck*, Balfre. Please, tell me you *care*.'

He threw his arms wide. 'Fine. I care. Now what?'

Another silence. Grefin pressed his hands to his face. Let them fall. 'Before. You said: *I claim Harcia*. Is that all you claim?'

'Meaning what?'

'*Meaning is that all you claim?*'

'Ah.' And another suspicion was confirmed. 'So now we know why Aimery sent for you and not me when he realised he was dying. Tell me, Grefin. What did he want to say that he didn't want me to hear? Something about disinheriting his lawful heir, perhaps?'

Grefin looked at their dead father. Seemed almost ready to weep some more. 'He was afraid. And now I'm afraid.'

'Any man loyal to me has no need to fear.'

'Oh, *Balfre* . . .'

He watched his brother turn away, again. Watched him reach a hand out blindly to the game larder's cold wall and lean against it, as though he lacked the will or strength to stand alone. As though he stood on the brink of a precipice and didn't know whether to jump . . . or fall.

And so he'd come to it. The question he had to ask, dreaded to ask, because – stripped of all disappointment, resentment and complicated memory – this man was his brother. There was love, as well as rage.

'Are you loyal to me, Grefin?'

No answer. Balfre took a step closer. Almost reached out to lay a hand on his brother's resolutely turned back. All their lives, even while Malcolm lived, Aimery had stood between them. Now the miserable old fuck was dead and *still* he stood between them.

'Grefin,' he said, hearing himself close to pleading. Hating it, hating his weakness, but desperate to deny their father a final triumph, the complete severing of their frayed brotherly bond. 'When Aimery asked you to be his Steward, though by rights the Green Isle was mine, you say you argued. But in the end you surrendered. When he asked you to conspire with him and Roric against me – against our duchy – again, you say you argued. But in the end, you surrendered. The last—'

'Balfre, you can't—'

'*I haven't finished*. The last time we saw each other you'd just lost Jorin defending the Green Isle from raiders and I'd saved the Harcian Marches, and Harcia itself, from a Clemen plague. Aimery chose to see you as a hero and me as the villain. It was ever thus. He threatened to disavow me and make you his heir instead.'

'I remember,' Grefin muttered. 'But—'

'You *swore* to me you refused him,' he continued, implacable. 'Do you remember *that*? Do you remember promising you'd never usurp me, no matter what Aimery said?'

'Yes.'

'But when you saw him on his deathbed, Grefin . . . did you surrender?'

On a growl of frustration, Grefin swung round. Crossed the cold floor towards him, his grief-thinned face darkening with sudden rage.

'*No!*' he shouted, with a hard shove. '*Fuck.* You're so eager to condemn me you forget I never swore not to be the Steward. And I never swore not to seek a lasting peace with Clemen. But I *did* swear I wouldn't usurp you and I fucking well kept my word!'

Balfre blocked his brother's angry attempt to shove him again. 'So Aimery did try to disinherit me!'

'He was raving, Balfre! He was dying! And *you'd* incited riot and murder in the Marches against his express desire. Or will you stand there and deny it?'

His turn to shove, hard enough to knock Grefin back a step. 'I don't have to justify myself to you. Besides, what I did or didn't do in the Marches doesn't matter. What Aimery wanted doesn't matter. He's dead. I'm Harcia's duke. And as duke it is my duty to see our duchy restored.'

'To what? A *kingdom*? So Aimery wasn't raving? Despite all your protestations you never did abandon that mad, childish dream of wearing a king's crown.'

The incredulous contempt in his brother's voice burned like acid. 'Not mad. Not childish. And not a fucking dream.'

'You intend to invade and conquer Clemen.'

'*Reclaim,*' he retorted. 'Clemen land is rightfully ours. It was stolen from us—'

'It wasn't stolen. It was lost in a family squabble, nearly two hundred years ago. Balfre, you can't—'

'Two hundred or two thousand, theft is still theft. And it *was* theft. Freyne stole Clemen from his brother, the rightful king.'

'And if he did?' Grefin threw up his hands. 'After so long, how can it *possibly* matter? And anyway, it's too late. You can't rewrite the past!'

'True enough, but I *can* write the future. *Fuck,* Grefin. How can you be my brother and not know me? When was I *ever* another

Aimery? Did you truly believe I'd leave this duchy diminished? Harcia was a *kingdom* and it will be again.'

'Mazelina was right,' Grefin murmured, shaking his head. 'She said you'd show me who you really are, and you have.'

'*Mazelina*.' Resentment stabbed. 'I might've known your fucking wife would try to poison you against me. She's no better than Aimery. You made a bad mistake, Grefin, marrying that bitch.'

Grefin stepped close, fingers clenching. 'Watch your tongue.' Then he blew out a hard breath. 'Balfre, you can't believe Roric will surrender his duchy. Or that Clemen's people will welcome you with open arms. They won't. They'll resist with every dagger and pitchfork and cooking pot they can find!'

'Let them. Roric and his people can learn the hard way what it means to defy Harcia.'

'And then what, after you've defeated them? You'll be king of a shambles, Balfre. Is that what you want? To sit a throne of bloody bones?'

'I'll sit a throne, Grefin. Whether it's bloody or not will be Roric's choice.'

'Balfre . . .' Grefin dragged a hand down his face. 'You can't think Harcia's barons will risk their lives and their sons' lives in unprovoked war for no better reason than you want to put a crown on your head!'

'They'll risk what I tell them to risk because I am their duke!' Then he grinned. 'And because I'll reward them with Clemen plunder and land.'

'So you'd be a pirate king? A king of murder and rape and theft?'

'It's not theft when you're taking back what was stolen from you!'

'Fuck,' Grefin whispered. 'You really have gone mad.' He blinked, his eyes suddenly brilliant in the candlelight. 'I'm sorry, Balfre. Truly. But this must end.'

Balfre felt his own eyes sting. 'Don't do it, Gref. Don't choose Aimery again.'

'I'm not! I'm choosing *you*! I'm trying to save you from yourself!'

As his brother pushed past him, heading for the game larder's door, Balfre seized his arm. '*I don't need saving*.'

For a handful of thudding heartbeats they stared at each other. Then the look in Grefin's eyes shifted from sorrow to savagery. A sharp twist and he was free, a dagger glinting in his grasp. Balfre slapped at the emptied sheath on his hip. Fuck. His brother had disarmed him. Aimery's velvet-covered trestle was two, perhaps three, wide steps to his left. Not shifting his gaze from Grefin's tense face he bridged the distance in one sideways leap, struck the trestle, lost his balance, snatched *Benevolence* from his dead father's grasp and recovered his footing even as he swung the sword's point towards his brother. Grefin lunged at him, the stolen dagger slicing low. Hot pain as his own dagger sliced across his thigh. A strangled yelp from Grefin as *Benevolence* slid along his ribs. Then he was twisting again, out of reach. Balfre swallowed a curse and followed. Sword against dagger? Grefin should be dead. But his brother had survived seasons of raiding, butchering northmen. Now it was clear why.

Panting, cursing, they fought as only brothers could. Every slash of blade, every drop of blood, every sting of pain a tit-for-tat. *You broke my sword. You stole my friend. You chose Aimery instead of me.* The game larder was cold but they were sweating. Their harsh breathing misted the air as they laboured across the granite flagstones, candle-flames flickering in their wake. Grefin lunged again, feinting right, then slashed the dagger sharply left. Balfre saw blood spurt from his opened forearm, with his next breath felt searing pain. His brother lunged again, seeking to cripple. He flung himself backwards, vision blurring. Bruised his hip on the corner of the trestle. Clutched at crimson velvet to stop himself from falling, caught sight of Grefin closing in, spun – and sliced *Benevolence* through Aimery's face.

Grefin howled. His fingers loosened on the dagger. Balfre spun again, snatched it from Grefin with his other hand and sank the short blade up to the hilt in his brother's belly. Without thinking, shifted and twisted it. Made it a killing blow.

A choked cry. A startled gasp. Grefin sagged, then folded to the granite floor. Balfre went down with him, not letting go of dagger or sword. Kneeling, he looked at his brother, and Grefin looked back. Puzzled. Regretful. A bleeding away of pain. Two men breathing. Two men breathing. Two men breathing.

One.

Balfre stood, awkwardly, and limped to the door. Cracked it open, called for the guard, and sent him to fetch Lord Waymon. Then he waited, holding his slashed forearm, wondering if he was going to weep.

'Fuck,' Waymon said, when he saw Grefin's body. 'Should I be sorry?'

He didn't know. 'Gather our men-at-arms, Waymon. I want Curteis, Kerric, the leech who treated Aimery, that bitch Mazelina, her son and her daughter and my useless wife and her daughter taken into custody – *discreetly* – and locked in a cell. Then assemble the barons in the Great Hall. Come back when it's done and bring the leather scroll-case from my saddlebag with you.'

'Yes, Your Grace.'

'And make sure that fuck of a guard outside stays well away.'

'I will.' Then a frown. 'You're bleeding, Balfre. How badly are you hurt?'

'Badly enough to be useful. I'll survive. Now go.'

While he waited for Waymon's return he used *Benevolence* to saw ragged strips of crimson velvet from the trestle-cover, so he could roughly bind his wounds. Then he picked up the kicked-over stool and with a stifled hiss of pain sat down. Glanced sideways. The sword-cut through Aimery's face gaped bloodless, revealing a pustuled tongue, rotted teeth, and the ulcered inside of one withered cheek. Which answered his earlier question. The old bastard had suffered before he died.

He was careful, while he waited, not to look at Grefin. Thought instead of Izusa and how, when she joined him, they'd fuck in Aimery's bed.

Eventually Waymon returned, carrying the scroll-case. Smiling fiercely. 'It's done, Balfre. And the barons attend at your pleasure.'

'Good,' he said, standing. 'Then let's not keep them trembling on sword-point any longer.'

When he limped into Tamwell castle's Great Hall, his bloody, daggered forearm held close his chest, the gathered lords of Harcia gasped almost to a man. Joben, Paithan and Lowis, standing a little apart, startled to see him and would have rushed to his side. Waymon, like a watchdog, forestalled them with a frown and a shake of his head.

The hall's ceiling was hammer-beamed and lofty, the pennants of every noble Harcian house hanging proud and brightly coloured. Small wooden shields painted with noble house devices – dogs and spotted cats and boars and swords and stallions and oak trees and eagles and lions rampant and suchlike – decorated the walls between mighty spreading antlers of stags killed years before. Iron wheels crowded with burning candles dispelled shadow. It was a hall filled with history, intended to impress. At its far end a painted, gilded dais, upon which stood Aimery's ducal seat with its bear-claw decorations. But the bear was dead. The wolf had taken his place.

Balfre made his limping way foward, Waymon a half-pace to his side, carrying the scroll-case. At his back, the barons' mumurs rose louder. He reached the dais. Ascended it. Stood before the throne. Waited for silence and then, when it didn't fall, raised the arm Grefin hadn't slashed wide with his dagger.

'*My lords! I'd have your attention!*'

The babbling faded until the only sound in the hall was the scrape of boots on the flagstoned floor, the creak of leather doublets and the faint chinking of mail as his Marcher men-at-arms quietly entered.

'My lords,' he said, sweeping their bewildered faces with a sorrowful gaze. Paying special attention to Terriel and his one-armed son, from the Green Isle. He had to capture them first or see them lead the rest into doubt and disputation. 'There is no kind way to break this news, so I shall simply tell you. My brother Grefin, Steward of the Green Isle, has been found in most foul treachery against our father, the late duke, and our beloved duchy of Harcia. These wounds I bear, which you can plainly see, were even now caused by him when I did confront him with the proof of his transgressions. Alas, my lords, Grefin – in an extremity of guilt, and fearing his deserved harsh punishment – made attempt upon my life and in defending myself I did slay him.'

A stunned silence. And then uproar. Loudest shouting of all from Terriel, who bullied his way to the foot of the dais, his one-armed son at his heels, and brandished a clenched fist in defiance.

'Grefin a traitor? *Never!* I've fought with him and bled with him and comforted the dying with him since the raid on Potterstown! Nothing you say, Balfre, will convince me his heart is black!'

'Then, my lord, let Grefin himself convince you,' he replied. 'For I have here the proof I showed him. Letters in his own hand between himself and a man I – to my great shame – trusted as a friend.'

'Who?' Terriel demanded. His shout was echoed by the lords at his back, in mourning for Aimery and shocked to unseemly outcry. 'Who is it you'd trust more than your own brother, my lord?'

Balfre stared at Terriel until the man surrendered, shifting his gaze. '*Your Grace.*'

'Your Grace,' Terriel muttered, as his son leaned close and touched his elbow. Then he rallied. Brought up his chin, looked around at his fellow lords. 'We've a right to know who it is you claim Grefin's conspired with.'

It was said that in Agribia there lived men who tamed wild beasts and paraded them for entertainment. It was how he felt now, faced with Harcia's volatile barons.

'Claim?' he said, frowning. 'Terriel. Do you think I'd speak if I weren't certain? Or that you could be more dismayed and hurt than *I*? This matter touches my family to its *heart*. Were I not who I am I'd be weeping like a woman. My life is in *ashes*, everything I believed in proved a lie. You want to know who suborned my brother to treachery? It was Vidar of Clemen.'

'Roric's Marcher lord?'

'The same. He came to me – he said – seeking shelter from Roric's vengeance. Touched by his plight, and seeing in it some advantage for Harcia, I agreed.'

'Did Aimery know?'

And that was Joben. A hint of suspicion in his voice. Balfre smiled at his cousin, who was only now beginning to understand how many secrets had been kept from him. But let him be offended. Once he was gifted with, say, Coldspring manor, his hurt feelings would swiftly heal.

'He did, cousin. And like me, he felt the rewards were worth the risk. Alas. My father and I were mistaken.'

Another look around the hall, then Terriel snorted. 'Vidar hoodwinked you?'

The important thing was to seem contrite. 'You'd chide me, my lord? Well. Doubtless I've earned it since, far from being disgraced, Vidar was deep in the bastard Roric's confidence, conspiring with him – and then Grefin – to plunder our duchy, fatten ruined Clemen at our expense, and at the end of the day place Roric upon our ducal throne. To my great sorrow I didn't suspect his duplicity till the damage was done. But then I took steps to uncover his plotting and had the truth from him – and Grefin's letters – shortly before receiving word of Aimery's death.'

'And Vidar?' said Joben. 'What of him?'

'Dead by his own hand.'

More consternation from Harcia's nobles. Terriel turned to glare at his fellow lords, then waved a hand to silence them. As the noise died down again, he turned back.

'I've no doubt Roric schemes to plunder Harcia. But why would *Grefin* betray us like this?'

'Thwarted ambition,' he said, sorrowful. 'Being Steward of the Green Isle wasn't enough for my brother. He wanted to be duke after Aimery. And when our father refused to disavow me he turned elsewhere for the riches and power he craved.'

Still, Terriel fought him. 'Forgive me, Your Grace, but there must be some mistake. I tell you I *know* Grefin. Vidar of Clemen was lying. Balfre, you killed an innocent man.'

For all he'd lived all his life on the Green Isle, Terriel's courage was legendary throughout Harcia. His opinion bore weight. And Aimery's heir had a motley past. The duchy's other barons, uneasy, muttered and exchanged doubting glances.

Balfre eased his pain-throbbed daggered arm. 'Waymon.' Waymon withdrew the forged letters from the scroll-case and handed them over. 'Terriel, I take it you know my brother's style with a quill? Then read the proof in his own hand and tell me again he was innocent.'

As Terriel read the runed forgeries, Balfre took his place on the throne. Watched the pugnacious baron's face change as the plausible lies and Izusa's sorcery took hold.

'Pass the letters on,' he said. 'I want everyone to read them. I'd have no doubt among my barons that what I've said is the truth.'

Hand to hand, the letters travelled around the Great Hall. Man by man, Harcia's barons fell to Izusa's power. The silence after was like the world's hush at midnight.

The letters returned, Balfre let them fall at his feet. Showed Harcia's lords the grief and devastation they wanted – needed – to see.

'This is a dark day for Harcia,' he said, his voice breaking. 'And darker days are coming, for Clemen means to swallow us whole. But *I* say we don't wait for the bastard Roric to strike us. *I* say Balfre of Harcia and his nobles strike first!'

The roar of his barons' approval was balm on an open wound.

Grefin's dead. I killed him. My little brother's dead.

CHAPTER FORTY

The bells of Carillon were ringing, sweet silver and bronze echoes sounding over the township and the harbour and rebounding off the steep, encircling hills. Catrain smiled to hear them. Carillon's bells made her think of her mother. Sometimes, when she heard them, she thought she could hear Berardine singing. Feel the brisk stroke of a loving hand over her hair. Oh, how she hoped her mother knew that she'd never meant to fail. But she had failed. She was no more Ardenn's true duchess than a candle could be called the sun. Baldwin's palace was his daughter's gilded cage . . . and, just like poor Gaël, she remained the regents' prisoner. Their puppet, meekly dancing whenever they pulled a string.

In the streets beyond the palace, Carillon's exarchs would be gathering for their nightly sunset ritual – the walking of Baldwin Way, with their golden orbs full of incense perfuming the twilight air with cinnamon, cedarwood and amber. Their long grey robes would swish the cobbles, their leather sandals slap-slapping, as they chanted in counterpoint with the ringing, singing bells. She remembered, vividly, being taken to watch their stately, mysterious procession with her sisters. But now her sisters were gone, as though they'd never been born, and the breathlessly beautiful procession was denied her. All she had left were memories.

And memories, no matter how sweet, must fade.

Hands braced on the balcony parapet, Catrain closed her eyes and leaned into the fading light, into the rising breeze, into ageless silver music that helped her survive each lonely day. Helped her forget, for a few moments, the promises she'd made . . . and couldn't keep.

'*Catrain.*'

An unfamiliar voice. She turned, thinking the regents, or the privy council they forced on her, had found yet another sour guardian to clip their prisoner's wings a little closer to the bone. But the woman standing before her was no dragonish old hag. Dressed in a dark green wool gown, she was young and oddly beautiful. Creamy pale skin, depthless green eyes and wildly curling red hair.

'Who are you?' She looked past the woman into her dayroom. Couldn't see the keepers who counted her every breath. 'How did you—'

The woman smiled, a lazy curve of sculptured lips. 'I am Izusa. I knew Baldwin, and Berardine.'

Catrain felt the stone parapet hard against her back. Recalled Berardine's frantic whispers at the end. Knew, without knowing how, who and what this woman was.

'You're the witch.'

Izusa's smile widened. 'You don't need to be afraid.'

'I'm not afraid,' she said, lying. 'Only curious. You say you knew my father. But Baldwin has been dead for years. Did you meet him when you were in your cradle?'

'Catrain . . .' Izusa chuckled, a disarming sound. 'I *am* a witch. And what woman doesn't desire to smooth away time's unkind touch?'

She was in no mood for mockery. 'What do you want?'

'What do *you* want? Madam?'

Madam. And there was a cruel taunting. 'You must already know if you're truly a witch.'

'I have always known.' Izusa's smile faded, leaving her beautifully austere. 'But I need to know if you know. So I will ask again. What do you want?'

She could feel a bead of sweat, trickling down her spine. Hear the echo of her mother's voice, desolation mingled with the dregs of hope. Remembered the look on Master Corbett's face when he told her Berardine was dead. Her chest tightened, and her fists.

'Where have you been, Izusa? My mother *needed* you!'

Izusa spread her slender hands, graceful. 'Someone else needed me more.'

Just like that. Without remorse or even a hinting of sympathy. No wonder witches were thought of unkindly. 'Why do you come now?'

'Because now you need me,' Izusa said, eyebrows raised. 'Catrain, *what do you want?*'

The simple complexity of the question almost made her laugh. What did she want? What didn't she want? But the things she wanted most not even a witch could give her. So she'd have to settle for the things that might be within her grasp. Things that might, were she granted them, help her put right everything that was gone wrong and rotten in Cassinia.

'Freedom. Power.' She swallowed, remembering more. *A burning stable. A scented garden. A man with sad, tender, eyes.* 'Roric of Clemen.'

'And you shall have him,' Izusa said, her voice shimmering with amusement. 'And freedom. And power. But only if you trust me.'

Carillon's bells were singing. They sounded like Berardine. 'My father trusted you, Izusa. And my mother. They're both dead.'

Izusa shrugged, indifferent. 'Everyone dies. I never promised Baldwin or Berardine endless life.'

And now the witch sounded like Regent Leofric. Cool, detached, embracing the impersonal like a lover. Her head was tipped a little to one side, her green gaze measured. Touched with arrogance. Gifted – or cursed – with unnatural powers. Staring at her, Catrain felt a wave of sickening disbelief. Her parents *trusted* this woman? Confided their hopes, their dreams, their secrets, to this witch? What had possessed them? Why would they do it?

'Then what did you promise them, Izusa? Duke Baldwin and his duchess were unswerving in their obedience to the Exarch, who abhors all things supernatural and unclean. I can't believe they would endanger their souls, not for—'

'Catrain . . .' Izusa laughed. 'You say you want power. But what use will it be if you fear to wield it? Fear to wield it and how can you call yourself Baldwin's daughter? Hope to follow in his footsteps? Your father knew the truth of ruling. Do you?'

The witch's mockery set her teeth on edge. 'Pretend I don't.'

'It's simple,' Izusa said, her green eyes sharp. 'There is nothing a duke abhors, should the having or using of it be necessary to protect his duchy and his people.'

A sinking in her belly. Izusa was right. A duke – a duchess – unwilling to risk all in defence of Ardenn was no better than a murderer. To leave Baldwin's people in bondage to the regents would be an act of gross cowardice. And for what? Her *soul*? What was her soul, compared to all the souls Baldwin and Berardine had placed in their daughter's keeping? Every man, woman and child in the duchy waited for their duchess to free them from the regents' dominion. Poor Gaël waited too, trapped in his palace. In his gilded cage of the mind. She was his only friend, his sole hope of justice. What would Roric think of her, did she turn her back on Cassinia's true prince? How could she save horses from a burning stable but abandon Ardenn's people? *Her* people? And how could she claim a birthright she refused to fight for with every weapon she could lay her hand upon . . . even if one of those weapons was a witch?

'Catrain.' Izusa's smile was gentle again, all mockery muffled. 'I can help you. I will help you. But you must trust me first.'

Trust a witch.

Despite knowing all the reasons why she should, every instinct rebelled against agreement. Instinct had served her well so far. Was it wise to abandon the inner voice that guided her? Most likely not. But this was what Berardine wanted. What her father had done before her. And in the end what choice did she have? She was a pale, power-less shadow drifting about a palace that once she'd called home. A daughter who made promises to her dying mother . . . and so far had failed to keep even one.

Freedom. Power. Roric.

Heart drubbing her ribs, Catrain lifted her chin. 'When do we start?'

Izusa laughed. 'We already have.'

'And what must I do?'

'Nothing to alarm the regents or their council,' Izusa said, so calm, so confident. 'Be what they think you are, Catrain. A meek, compliant mouse. As for the rest? Leave that to me. We are part of a living tapestry . . . and the colours are about to change.' She pointed to the darkening sky. 'See how Abdiel shines? 'Tis an omen of good fortune. All will be well.'

Catrain turned. Stared at the brilliant white star pulsing high above the bell tower of Carillon's grand exarchite chapel. An omen? Truly? But that was superstitious nonsense . . . wasn't it? She turned back to ask.

But Izusa was gone.

And then her haggish attendants were bustling into the dayroom, crying out that she must dress for dinner, or offend her privy councillors by keeping them waiting.

She bit her lip. Schooled her face. *I am Catrain, Ardenn's duchess, a meek, compliant mouse*. And as Carillon's bells faded to silence she did as she was told. For the first time not minding, because singing in her mind like those silver bells, Izusa's promise.

Freedom. Power. Roric.

She would have them all.

'Balfre?'

Standing on Tamwell's battlements, overlooking the river where it curved around the night-dark township, Balfre pulled his leather cloak a little tighter to keep out the blustering breeze. It was late, past midnight, and below him, in the castle, the barons slept after a subdued, sober feast. Overhead, the black mourning flags snapped, loud in the chilly silence. With the earlier threat of rain passed, the sky was cloud-clear and starry. A threequarter moon washed silver light over the flowing water and sloping roofs and open fields of Cater's Tamwell. Torches burned in cast-iron holders, touching a golden glow to the silvery air.

'Balfre,' Waymon said again, more insistent. 'What did the leech say? The barracks leech, I mean. Not Aimery's leech.'

'I know which leech you mean, Waymon.'

'And? What did he say?'

'*Keep still, Your Grace. This might pinch somewhat.*'

A faint scraping of boot on gritty stone as Waymon approached. 'But you're stitched without trouble? You'll not be impaired?'

'It seems unlikely.' He frowned. 'No thanks to my brother, who did his best to cripple me and bleed me like a winterfeast hog.'

Waymon stopped. Cleared his throat, sounding awkward. 'About Grefin. His body yet lies in the game larder, with the duke. What shall I do with it? I know by rights a traitor's corpse is quartered around the duchy and the head mounted over Tamwell's main gate, but . . .'

But Grefin was never a traitor. At least not the kind of traitor that Harcian tradition would recognise. Balfre pulled a face. Try as he might, though he'd tainted his brother before Harcia's barons, he couldn't quite bring himself to inflict the final humiliation. What that said about him he didn't know. Didn't care to learn, just now.

'Leave him,' he said, wearily. 'It's cold in the game larder. He'll keep a day or two. But you might want to add some more ice.'

'Ice,' Waymon said, after a moment. 'Yes. I'll . . . arrange for more ice.'

And so much for Grefin. 'Has word gone out to the men-at-arms we sent home from the Marches?'

'It has, my lord. And come morning, the barons are set to ride home to their own castles and bring back their people.' A satisfied chuckle. 'Roric is in for a nasty surprise.'

Not before time. 'And Izusa? You've sent for her?'

'I – not yet. I wasn't sure. Of course I will, Balfre, if you're sure. But – I wasn't.'

Izusa. He hungered for her like a man starving in the wilderness. 'I want her safely out of the Marches before we strike at Clemen. Humbert's old but he won't show his belly like a grey-muzzled hound. He'll fight till he's hamstrung and a sword takes his head and his men-at-arms will follow him. What makes you think I'll risk Izusa in such a slaughter?'

'Of course you wouldn't,' Waymon said, hasty. 'But we have time. And – well—'

He wasn't widowed yet. Speaking of which . . . 'That other matter. You've seen to it?'

'I have,' Waymon said, after another, longer pause. 'All's ready. Again – if you're sure.'

Balfre looked over his shoulder. In the torchlight Waymon seemed out of character uncertain. 'Fuck. After everything you've done, don't tell me you're *squeamish*.'

'Cautious,' Waymon said, warily. 'As you should be.'

He stared again at the moon-splashed river. 'Do you tell me they'll be missed? Any of them?'

'No.'

'Do you think I should keep them caged somewhere, like moulting parrots with lice? Because it's sad to kill them and who can say? They might not spread disease, so let's risk it?'

'No, Balfre. You don't have a choice. I understand that.'

'But?'

'But nothing. As I said. All's ready, and the men-at-arms you requested are waiting downstairs.'

He turned. 'Then let's be done with this, shall we? I'm tired. I'm hurting. And I want my fucking bed.'

Of course it was that bitch Mazelina who leapt to her feet when the solid wood-and-iron door to Tamwell's most solitary prison cell was unbarred and opened.

'*Balfre!* What's the meaning of this? Where's Grefin? Let us out!'

On principle he didn't answer. Never again would he bow to someone else's demands. Especially not hers. It was Mazelina's fault, more than anyone's, that Grefin was dead.

Kerric grasped the bitch's arm, urging her to silence. 'Your Grace, can't you tell us why we were taken into custody?'

Because Grefin's wife was unpredictable and his surviving son was dangerous, despite his youth, he'd told Waymon he wanted five men-at-arms to accompany them into the castle's torchlit and cobwebby rabbit-warren dungeon. Two men between them carried a cauldron of mutton stew, a pitcher of ale, and a pail full of dry bread, bowls, cups and spoons. As they delivered the stew and the pail, setting them down just over the cell's threshold, and Waymon and the other three men-at-arms stood wary with their swords drawn and pointing, Balfre looked at his meagrely lamplit prisoners.

They all stared back at him, fear and confusion in their eyes. His goodsister. His niece. His nephew. His wife. His daughter. Tamwell's steward and Aimery's foreign leech. Seven people who'd be dead by sunrise because he'd poisoned their mutton stew. He held his breath a moment, waiting to feel something. *Anything*. But he felt nothing. Not even for Jancis, who'd once shared his bed, or for the plain, tear-stained girl she'd borne him, who was his own flesh and blood.

But then Grefin had been his flesh and blood. And if he couldn't weep for Grefin . . .

Mazelina wasn't tear-stained. Even fearful, she kept her wits. Shook off her son's hand and took a half-step towards him, heedless of the men-at-arms' raised swords.

'This is *outrageous*, Balfre. I want to see my husband!'

'And I want to know by what right you hold us here,' Kerric added, emboldened by Mazelina's defiance. 'We've done nothing wrong, Balfre.' He'd taken hold of his pretty sister's hand. A pity Ullia had to perish. But there it was.

He nodded. 'I know.'

'Then why are you doing this, my lord?' Jancis whispered, clutching her useless daughter. 'Have we displeased you somehow? Tell us what we've done and we'll make amends.'

That earned her an irritated glare from Mazelina. Anger had blinded the bitch. She seemed oblivious to her danger. Curteis, though, the aged fuck, knew what was coming. The knowledge of impending death was in his dull eyes. But he looked half-dead from grief already. Likely for him this was a mercy. As for the silent leech, well, that was unfortunate. A good leech was ever useful and this one had worked wonders keeping Aimery alive for so long in the face of Izusa's sorcery. But not even Curteis was as intimately acquainted with Aimery's health. It would be madness to risk belated questions or doubts now, with victory close enough to taste, like fresh blood.

'I'm sorry to frighten you,' he said gently, caressing them all with his mildest stare. 'And I'm sorry you're kept here, in such discomfort. Certain matters are come to light that must be untangled as a matter of grave urgency. But I assure you they will be. You'll not be kept prisoned long, and you'll see Grefin soon.'

'What matters?' Kerric said, suspicious. 'Are we accused of something, Balfre?'

'If we are, it's a mistake,' his pretty sister added. 'Please, uncle, if you'd tell us what you think we've done so we can explain ourselves, then—'

He raised a hand. '*Please*. You must know there are protocols I am forced to follow. As Harcia's duke I can't be seen to favour family above the law. Aimery would never forgive me.' Smiling again, he showed them the reasonable ruler. The loving uncle. 'Be patient, Ullia. All of you, be patient. Let me see to this mystery. In the meantime, eat and drink and try to rest.'

His brother's bitch of a wife was still protesting as the cell door closed in her face.

'Stay,' he told Waymon, as his men-at-arms barred the door. 'And no matter what you hear, do nothing. Understood?'

If Waymon was distressed, no man would ever know it. 'Yes, Your Grace.'

'Then I'll see you again at sunrise.'

Accompanied by his men-at-arms he limped away from the barred cell . . . and didn't look back.

The night before Egann arrived in Eaglerock castle uninvited and unannounced, Roric lost hours of peaceful sleep to ravaging, blood-soaked dreams. Startled awake a half-dozen times, sweating and gasping, his heart pounding so hard he thought he must choke. In the end he abandoned any hope of sleep.

Lying in the darkness, in the vast and empty bed that had witnessed the desolation of his marriage to Lindara, the futility of his tears, the arid wasteland of his rage over her death, his child's death, at Humbert, he tried to ignore the crushing sense of dread that threatened to grind his bones like chalk. Tried to tell himself, he was no better than a churl frighted by falling stars. But the self-scolding didn't help.

When the sun rose, he rose with it. Suffered himself to be dressed by his body servant and ate a lonely breakfast. Then Egann came, dread made flesh, and sleeping nightmare was turned to waking dismay – which only deepened when Humbert's loyal whipcord of a man refused to say why it was so important for Clemen's duke to spirit himself out of the castle with a smothered identity and ride with all urgency to the Marches.

'Forgive me, Your Grace,' was Egann's only reply. 'Beyond news that Aimery's dead, all I can tell you is Lord Humbert doesn't waste your time.'

For Humbert's sake, he hoped not.

The ride from Eaglerock castle to Humbert's manor was brutal. They foundered three good horses between them, came close to foundering themselves. Arrived at last at the manor's stableyard, Roric all but fell from his saddle. As stable lads scurried to take the exhausted horses, Humbert stamped out of the manor and hustled him to what looked like an abandoned dairy. Inside its cool cellar, an open coffin on a trestle. In the coffin, a corpse packed in sawdust and ice. It was greenish and bloating, stinking the chilly air with death.

Roric stared. '*Another* one? Why is it you insist on showing me rotting bodies? Humbert, if this is why I've near killed myself riding from—'

'Clap tongue and look at him!' Humbert said, with a push. 'I know he's a bit ripe, but can't you see it's Vidar?'

'Vidar,' he said blankly. 'Humbert, are you—'

Another hard push. '*Look!*'

He looked. Looked again. Then he started to laugh.

'You think this is *funny*?' Humbert demanded.

'No. Yes. No. It's just . . .' Roric rubbed his eyes. Wondered if he'd fallen into some kind of mad dream. 'I was thinking of marrying Kennise.'

As though he'd not heard that, Humbert banged a fist to the side of the coffin. Looked as though he'd rather bang it against his duke instead. 'It's *Vidar*, Roric.'

He made himself look again at the body in the coffin. Though its face was grossly disfigured, he knew it. 'I can see that.'

'And?'

'And this is the second time you've told me Vidar's dead. How sure are you there won't be a third? Or a fourth? Perhaps even a—'

'*Roric!*' Beside himself, Humbert stamped around the cellar.

'What's the *matter* with you? Don't you want to know where he's *been*? Aren't you—' And then he stopped stamping. 'What the fuck d'you mean, you're thinking of marrying Kennise?'

Helpless, they stared at each other, a rush of terrible memories flooding to fill the silence. So long since they'd stood face to face. So much rage and pain between them and no way to go back.

'Fuck, boy,' Humbert muttered. 'You look like shite.'

'You look old. And you've grown a coarse tongue.'

'That's the Marches. They do coarsen a man.'

It seemed they did more than that. Humbert's years of skirmish and exile had carved deeper lines in his face. Thinned his hair and whitened what remained. He'd lost weight, his bones and muscles showing closer to the surface. In his eyes shadowed memories, unshared. He was a different man. But then, so was his duke different. With all that had happened since last they'd met, it was a wonder they even recognised each other.

'So. Vidar.' He looked again at the one-eyed corpse in the coffin. 'You say you know where he's been?'

'I know where I was told he's been. In the Harcian Marches. Living as Balfre's guest.'

A punch of dread beneath his breastbone. '*Balfre?*'

'I've no doubt he sold Aimery's son every Clemen secret he could think of.'

Of course. 'His revenge for Lindara.'

Their eyes met, briefly, then they both looked away.

'How did he die?' Roric said, after a difficult moment. 'Do you know? Has it anything to do with Aimery's death?'

'Perhaps. I can't say for sure.'

'Then what can you say for sure?'

Humbert's tired eyes narrowed. 'I was also told,' he said, his voice rough, 'that with Vidar's help you and Balfre recently came to an arrangement. When Aimery died you'd give him Clemen and its Marches in return for a fortune in gold and jewels so you can live out your life in exile.'

He felt the cellar tilt around him, felt a rush of bile into his throat. A sick rage that left him dizzy. '*Who told you that?*'

'A Marcher woman. And Vidar, in a written confession.'

'What confession? Show it to me!'

'It's in the house,' Humbert said, his beard jutting. 'I'll show it to you presently. But you should know I think it's written in his hand.'

'I don't care what Vidar's confessed.' He was sweating, icy drops against hot skin. 'None of it's true. Tell me you believe me, Humbert. Tell me you don't believe Vidar.'

Humbert looked at him in disgust. 'Believe that cockshite? Don't be a fucking pizzle.' Then he sighed. 'But the claim was made in public, Roric. You can trust it'll soon be whispered in taverns the length and breadth of Clemen. That won't do folks' tempers much good.'

Another sickening rush of bile, drowning relief. 'This woman, Humbert. I'd speak with her. I'd know why—'

'You can't. She's dead. So's the man-at-arms I sent to fetch her.'

'Dead how?'

'Ah.' Humbert tugged at his silvered beard, such a familiar gesture. Painful. Stirring more memories of kinder days, long gone. 'That's what you'd call a mystery, Roric. Her cottage burned to the ground with her in it. My man too. Could be she thought she'd somehow be blamed for Vidar. She was a Marches healer, and couldn't save him. It's hard to see now but he was stabbed to death. Could be she saw my man, lost her wits and . . .'

'Or,' he said grimly, 'she was part of this muckrakery and Balfre had her silenced. Had Vidar silenced too, so he could spread his lies unchallenged. Is he still in the Marches?'

'No. He's ridden home to Cater's Tamwell to be acclaimed Harcia's duke.'

'Is he behind this, Humbert? Is it all Balfre's doing?'

Flickered with candle shadows, Humbert's face was bleak. 'I'd say so. Just as those lies about you and Clemen were his doing, and Ercole's murder, and the Pig Whistle's burning. All of it done to stir shite for Clemen. I tell you, Balfre's the biggest fucking cockshite of a liar as ever drew breath.'

'And you think he has his eye on our duchy.'

Humbert snorted. 'I've been saying as much ever since you made me your lord of the Marches. Or did you never read a single pissing letter I wrote you?'

694

There was an upturned barrel in the cellar. Perching on it, wincing, Roric stared at the dirty stone floor. 'I read every one of them.'

'And yet Aistan's voice is the only one you hear. Or so I'm told.'

He looked up, sharply. 'I beg your pardon?'

Humbert tugged his beard again, a crease between his grey, bushy eyebrows. 'You looked and sounded just like Harald then.'

'*Don't*. I'm too tired. And we don't have time.'

'Was it Aistan's idea that you wed with his daughter?'

'What does it matter?' he said, as his muscles throbbed and his bones ached. 'I can't marry her now. Vidar's treachery taints her. It taints Aistan. *Fuck*.' He pressed his palms to his face. Hid in the dark, like a coward. 'If only you'd let me wed with Catrain.'

'Ha.' Humbert snorted again. 'Let you and me start with the *if onlys*, boy, and we'll still be flapping our lips when Balfre kicks down the door.'

He dropped his hands to his lap. *For this I killed Harald. I failed to save his son, for this.* He made himself meet Humbert's steady stare.

'Tell me, my lord, since you're so keen to advise. If you're right and Balfre does mean to ride against Clemen . . . have we any hope of stopping him? Or should I throw down my sword now and let the duchy pass to him without bloodshed?'

'*Surrender?*' Humbert's face darkened. 'You'd see us slaves in our own land, Roric? Or sold outright into Zeidica and Osfahr and the Treble Kingdom and Hent? Are you maggot-brained? Do you think baring our throats to Harcia will tempt Balfre into mercy? That cockshite wouldn't know mercy if it rammed a pike up his arse. *No*, Roric. *We don't surrender.*'

Roric pushed off the edge of the barrel. 'Then what should we do? Your own words would seem to condemn us to bloody slaughter! How often have you written to me of Balfre's skilled men-at-arms, his lethal training of them, Harcia's schooling in battle against those raiders? How can Clemen prevail? We have no coin for war, for the hiring of mercenaries!'

'It's not coin we need. It's heart and stomach and the will to defeat Harcia. And that comes from *you*, Roric! Courage flows from a duchy's duke!'

What courage? 'Humbert . . .'

Humbert took hold of his shoulders and shook him, as he'd done countless times since he was seven years old. 'It's not fear that defines a man, Roric. Every man feels fear. It's what he does *despite* the fear that shows his true mettle.'

Mouth dry, eyes burning, Roric stared at the man who'd made him, and destroyed him, and now sought to help him out of the mire. He remembered those two boys in the woodland beyond Broadthorpe, and all the desperate tyrannies that had followed in the wake of their deaths.

'Humbert,' he whispered. 'I fear you were right. I think I am become Harald.'

'No, boy. You aren't your cousin. Harald never doubted himself a fucking day in his life. You're the great Berold's grandson. And his greatness is in you.'

He'd never thought to see Lindara's father again, not till the old man's funeral. Never thought he could still care what the bastard's opinion of him was. Now it seemed he'd been mistaken. How galling. He took a deep, steadying breath, then felt his belly recoil at the sour stink of rotten flesh. Of dead Vidar, whose dreams of vengeance were now become Clemen's waking nightmare.

That recalled him to the dire present.

'If you're right and Balfre means to attempt Clemen,' he said, pushing aside complicated feelings, 'if we're to have any hope of saving the duchy, I think we must hold Harcia at bay here in the Marches. If we can bloody Balfre badly enough, we might well give him pause.'

'I was thinking the same,' Humbert said, frowning. 'And if you'll heed me, Your Grace, here's how we'll proceed. By your written and sealed command, we'll empty Clemen of swords and men to wield them, and muster them here to break that cockshite Balfre's black heart. While we wait for them to arrive, I'll send my stealthiest men-at-arms to spy out what they can of Harcia's intentions. You'll tarry here, and your presence we'll keep quiet till we ride into battle so Balfre's not tempted to take you prisoner – or worse. Aside from me and Egann, not a soul in the Clemen Marches can marry your name to your face. You'll be plain Master Berry. Agreed?'

His heart was thudding, a dull drumming against his ribs. 'Agreed.'

Humbert clapped him on the shoulder. 'Then let's not dilly-dally. There's ink, paper and sealing wax in the house.'

Ink, paper and sealing wax. Was that all he needed to shatter peace? Declare war? Make himself a duke of widows and orphans? His flourished name and his signet ring impressed in hot wax. Wax the crimson of fresh blood, to be spilled by the men of Clemen he'd sworn on his life to protect.

'*Roric*.' Humbert was scowling, his beard jutted more fiercely than ever. 'This is Balfre's doing, boy. Whatever mistakes you've made elsewhere, the blame here isn't yours.'

He wanted – needed – to believe that. But events had conspired to erode his certainties with doubt. Now he was a man stranded on rotted ice, knowing he must take a step, knowing that any step he did take would likely plunge him into darkness. Plunge his duchy into bloody death. He wanted to stand still – and knew he couldn't.

'I know, my lord,' he said, pretending a confidence Humbert must surely know he didn't feel. 'So let us make a start. I'm eager to school Balfre with a lesson he won't forget.'

Though Count Balfre – no, *Duke* Balfre – and Lord Waymon were gone to Cater's Tamwell, Harcia's Marcher barracks serjeants were so snarly the two great lords might as well not have left. Rumour and gossip thickened the barracks' air almost past breathing. Clemen had plotted war against Harcia with Balfre's brother and now a furious Balfre was preparing to punish the duchy and its duke. Battle would begin right here, in the Marches – and that meant every man-at-arms, no matter how young or green he might be, was to make ready to spill his blood in Balfre's cause. Horses clean, saddlery clean, swords and daggers sharp, leathers oiled and mail without so much as a speck of rust.

Cleaning mail was a sweaty, tiresome task. Liam and Benedikt cleaned theirs together, since it was easier for two men to toss the heavy iron links in a sand-and-bran-filled leather bag on the open ground out back of the barracks, between the dormer and the tilt yard. Besides, that gave them a chance to talk without being overheard.

After they'd turned the bag end-over-end fifty times, Liam bent to unlace it, wanting to see if the mail inside was scoured clean and oiled enough to satisfy snickety Serjeant Grule. As he fingered the shiny iron links, Benedikt straightened and pressed his fists to the small of his back. Kept on flicking him frowning glances, same as he'd been doing for a few days now.

Huffing out a breath, Liam looked up. 'What?'

'I wish ye'd tell me what be niggling ye, Willem, I know there be something. Ever since the skirmish with Clemen over that farmer's thieving son, ye b'aint been yerself.'

There was hurt as well as temper in Benedikt's voice. Looking down again, Liam re-laced the leather bag. He'd not told his brother about the tilt yard and how he'd seen Balfre murder Vidar. That night still made him sweat. If Balfre had seen him . . . if Harcia's new duke ever found out he'd been witnessed . . .

So it was safer all round if Benedikt never knew. Better bruised feelings than a wine cup full of poison.

But he couldn't say nothing. His brother was worse than a dog with a bone. 'I been thinking, is all,' he said, with a glance round to make sure they were still alone. 'About what to do when Balfre and Waymon get here with Harcia's army, and the proper fighting starts.'

'I know what to do,' Benedikt said. 'We scarper!'

He huffed out another breath. 'No. We don't.'

'But Willem, it be madness, us fighting for Harcia! Balfre don't need our swords to help him win. Clemen b'aint got a feggit chance, everyone knows that. So why risk it?'

'Ye want me to turn tail, Benedikt? How can I, when I—'

'Listen.' With a nervous look at the barracks, Benedikt came closer. 'I know ye got yer heart set on killing Roric, but *think*. He b'aint here. He might not come at all. And even if he does, or we end up fighting him someplace else – ye don't know what he looks like! He could stroll across the tilt yard right now and ye wouldn't have a feggit notion it was him. So how do ye think to—'

'I know!' he said, angry because he'd not thought of it himself till the middle of last night. 'Think I be a wigget, Benedikt?'

'No,' his brother said, sounding a touch doubtful. 'Only – d'ye say now ye b'aint looking to kill him?'

'Oh, I'll kill him,' he said, his blood hot. 'One day, Benedikt, I'll kill him.'

'Unless Balfre kills him first. Ye got to know Balfre wants Roric dead too.'

He did. And almost, *almost*, he could make his peace with that. If Roric came to the Marches and Balfre killed him in a skirmish, or took the bastard prisoner here or somewhere in Clemen and killed him after, it had to be the next best thing to killing Roric himself.

'Iss. I know.'

'So what d'ye plan to do?'

'I say we don't think on Roric,' he said, close to a whisper. ''Cause for all we know he'll not reach the Marches in time to cross swords with Balfre. We think on Humbert instead. Balfre hates him near as much as he hates Roric, and we know what that old shite looks like. So come the fighting we find Humbert, we take him prisoner, and give him to Balfre.'

'Ye reckon? Humbert be a canny swordsman.'

'Iss, but he's old. He'll not stand agin the two of us. And I do owe him vengeance.'

'So we take Humbert,' his brother said, frowning. 'Then what? Ye reckon that'll see ye shining in Balfre's eyes?'

'Course it will. And after Clemen's defeated, and Balfre's named himself their duke, he won't stay in Eaglerock. Not always. But we will. We can ask to be Eaglerock castle men-at-arms. And 'cause we gave him Humbert, Balfre'll say we can.'

Benedikt rubbed his nose. 'And then what?'

'Then we'll bide our time. Clemen's folk won't want a Harcian on the Falcon Throne. Sooner or later they'll want Balfre gone, and there I'll be. They'll fight for me. Harald's son. Their proper duke. And I'll take Clemen back from Balfre.'

'I dunt know, Willem. I mean, it do seem a good plan. Only an awful lot's got to go right first.'

'An awful lot's gone right already,' he pointed out. 'I should've died in Heartsong, when I were a baby. Ellyn and me, we should've perished on the road afore we ever found the Pig Whistle. When Molly and Iddo died? I was meant to die then too. And since you and me started fighting in the Marches, I b'aint hardly earned m'self a scratch.'

'Skirmishes,' Benedikt said, uneasy. 'When Balfre and Waymon come back it won't be skirmishing, Willem. It'll be proper war, like none of us have ever seen.'

They looked at each other, trying to pretend the thought didn't fright them.

'I heard Serjeant Huley talking to Serjeant Eadin in the shite-house,' Benedikt added. 'He caught another Clemen spy sneaking at the border. Huley said they pricked him some, to see what he knew of Clemen's plans. But he knew feggit so Huley hanged him. Cut off his cock and balls, stuffed 'em in his mouth and left him there as a warning.'

Which was what happened when a man was fool enough to get caught. 'They say anything else?'

'Eadin did. He said Balfre would surely be here soon, and it were a pity we don't have no camp whores on account of him wishing he could have a last fuck, just in case.'

'He should find himself a sheep. Not even a whore would fuck Eadin.'

'No, but Willem—' Benedikt tugged at his ear. 'That means—'

'It won't be long now afore we're swimming in blood.'

Another shared look. Deep breaths. Cautious smiles. And then the barracks bell sounded, and they had to haul their mail in its leather sack back to the armoury, where the endless grinding whir of the whetstone sharpening swords and daggers filled the air with a promise of war.

CHAPTER FORTY-ONE

Balfre rode out of Tamwell castle at the head of his army, flanked either side by Waymon, his cousin Joben and Lord Terriel of the Green Isle. Behind them rode four hundred fiercely trained men-at-arms. Between the castle and the Marches he would be joined by Harcia's other barons, their sons, and more men-at-arms. By the time he struck his first blow at Clemen, Harcia's army would be some eleven hundred swords strong. Humbert and his Marcher men had no hope of victory and little of survival. He'd sweep through their Marcher lands and into Clemen unopposed.

And if Roric was in the Marches then the Marches was where he'd die. Wherever he was run to ground, Roric was going to die.

The people of Cater's Tamwell township lined the high street to cheer their new duke as he pranced his great black warhorse past them under a blue sky. His gold-etched armour, hammered sleek by Aimery's renowned armourer, Master Perryn, shone blinding bright in the unclouded sunshine. Men shouted for spilled Clemen blood, women sighed over their handsome duke and his lords, children squealed and clapped and threw fresh horse dung at each other once the last men-at-arms had ridden by.

Trotting knee-to-knee with his duke, by his coveted right hand, Waymon laughed out loud. 'Harcia is with you, Your Grace. I'd wager a barge full of gold coin that Roric won't have three cur-dogs barking support for him.'

Balfre grunted. At his back loomed Tamwell castle, held safe by a barracks of experienced men-at-arms. Aimery slept in its grand family tomb, laid hasty to rest with a scant nod at Harcia's tradition of solemn, pervasive mourning. *The pressing needs of war* was the excuse given out, and not even blustery Terriel had questioned it. As for those other bodies, Grefin and the rest, they were coffined and quicklimed and stored deep beneath the castle, their deaths still a closely kept secret. Once Clemen was subdued, with Roric dead and himself proclaimed the rightful King of Harcia, word would go out of Grefin's ruinous treachery and how in raging despair he'd killed not only himself but his wife and his children, his royal brother's innocent family and two others as well. The barons who knew differently would be sworn to secrecy, on pain of death and the destruction of their families. Even Joben. And so the lie wouldn't be doubted. People loved a good tragedy.

Then would Izusa be named King Balfre's queen.

'Your Grace?' said Waymon, attentive. 'Is something amiss?'

With a shake of his head, graced with a beaten gold ducal coronet, he glanced past Waymon to Joben, who only that morning had complained of feeling slighted. He'd not yet drawn his prickly cousin completely into his confidence. Let Aimery's nephew prove himself against Clemen in the Marches, just as Waymon had proved himself these past years. That would decide how far he might be trusted, and with how much truth.

'Cousin,' he said, raising his voice above the drumming of hooves and the jangling of mail as they led his small army out of the township and onto the wide, stone-edged road that meandered towards the Marches. 'Between now and when first we draw our swords against Clemen, I'd have you heed all the advice that good Terriel, here, can impart. Not a man who's seen you lift a lance in the tilt yard could doubt your courage, but only since Aimery named me his lord of the Marches have I truly understood the difference between jousting and war.'

Joben frowned, wanting to take offence. But he knew better than to reveal his pricked pride a second time. 'All of Harcia knows Lord Terriel's martial reputation. I'd be honoured to have him school me.'

'The honour's mine,' said Terriel. 'Never fear, Your Grace. I'll keep Lord Joben safe.'

'I don't doubt it,' Balfre said, smiling. Pleased not by their acquiescence, which was his due, but for the binding strength of Izusa's wardings. Days and days since Terriel and the other barons had read those runed, incanted letters and not so much as a hint of weakened influence had he seen. They believed in Grefin's guilt as strongly now as they had in Tamwell castle. They were bound to him, their new duke, body and soul . . . and thanks to Izusa would remain bound until death.

They rode sure and steady towards the Marches until, with dusk falling, they reached the village of Dogger Hill, a good third of the way through their journey. There they were met by four more barons and their two hundred and thirty men-at-arms. The village, forewarned, had food and tents and horselines ready for them, and its one small inn emptied of guests for the convenience of His Grace the duke and his lords.

Balfre was halfway through his solitary, rustic supper of stewed rabbit when Waymon entered his privy chamber without invitation. He looked sick.

'Balfre . . .'

And without another word spoken, blinded by sudden premonition, he knew. He felt a dreadful stab of pain in his chest, felt the pewter spoon slip from his numb fingers. He wanted to vomit up every mouthful of meat he'd swallowed.

'Don't,' he said, hearing his voice turned strange, hoarse and pleading. 'Waymon, don't—'

'I'm sorry.' Waymon groped to close the chamber's crooked door. 'You hardly spoke of her, but even so I knew that you — that Izusa was—' A rasping, indrawn breath. 'So I asked Grule to keep an eye on her. Balfre, he's sent word. Izusa is dead.'

Because he'd needed Waymon with him in Tamwell he'd left his most senior serjeant behind with his lord's authority to safeguard the Harcian Marches. A good man, Grule. He didn't make mistakes.

Balfre cleared his burning throat. 'How?'

'No one knows for certain,' Waymon said, his eyes fearful. 'There was a fire. Her cottage burned. But there are rumours, Balfre. It's thought Humbert played a part. Because of Vidar.'

Vidar? And what did that mean? It had been Izusa's idea, that after he left for Cater's Tamwell she should be found with Vidar's body, with the false confession, so Roric and Humbert would be stirred to confusion, further weakening Clemen with internal strife before his attack. Seeing the advantages, he'd readily agreed — and trusted implicitly that she'd do as she promised. But he'd never dreamed she'd meet trouble, that she might—

Fuck. Fuck. Did I get her killed?

'Balfre,' Waymon said again, helpless. 'What can I do? What do you need?'

'I need Humbert's head on a pike,' he said, scarcely recognising his own voice. 'I need every creek in the Marches to run red with Clemen blood. I need to go deaf from the sound of Clemen men-at-arms, screaming. And right now, Waymon, I need you to get out.'

Waymon's stricken face tightened. 'Balfre, I—'

'*Get the fuck out!*'

The moment the chamber door banged shut he heaved up rabbit

stew and buttered bread and the two full goblets of wine he'd drunk with them. Heaved till his belly was empty and all he could spit onto the floor was yellow bile. And after that he wept, a salty rush of grief that left him snot-nosed and shaking.

Izusa. Izusa. You will be avenged.

In the end, Roric decided, it was the waiting that taxed him hardest. Having agreed to Humbert's plan that he remain unremarkable and unannounced, he kept himself to the manor house and its grounds while word went out for a mustering of Clemen's lords with their men-at-arms. But that meant he found himself with too much time alone, too many chances to question every choice, every decision, every twist and turn of his life that had led him to this sword-point moment. It was exhausting.

Throughout the slowly greening Marches, where spring was blooming late out of a cold winter, tensions had wound intolerably tight. Clemen and Harcia's men-at-arms warily circled each other like growling, raised-hackle dogs in a farmyard, each waiting for the other to bite first. But Humbert had given orders for their men to avoid trouble with Harcia on pain of death, and so far the tenuous peace was holding.

In an attempt to escape the pressure of that tension, and the merciless flogging of his own bleak thoughts, Roric spent hours in Humbert's manor barracks tilt yard, readying himself for the bloodshed to come. He didn't spar with Humbert, who – after finding an obscure resting place in the manor grounds for Vidar's disagreeable corpse and seeing it buried – spent his time riding the Marches, seeking to instil confidence in the superstitious, rumour-plagued folk who called this cousined pocket of Clemen home.

Once Roric would have regretted it, not sparring with his foster-lord. But now the lack of time they spent together was a relief. For all they shared a common goal and a roof, he and Humbert remained largely estranged. Every silence between them continued to echo the past; Lindara standing behind them wherever they were. That was exhausting too.

Instead he crossed swords with Egann, the only other man who knew him for who he was, or with any man-at-arms he could pull to his purpose. He also spent time in the armoury, piecing together mail and boiled leather to suit him. His own martial equipment had been sent for but there was no surety it would reach the Marches before Balfre's return.

The thought of that had him sweating. If only he knew when Aimery's son would arrive, how many men-at-arms he commanded, he'd have some idea of their chances. But every attempt to discover Balfre's plans had failed, leaving good men dead and grossly mutilated.

'It's a race,' Humbert said, as they shared their ninth supper in the manor house's candelit dining room. 'And like it or not, boy, that bastard Balfre has a leap start on us.'

'Even so . . .' Roric stabbed the point of his knife into a slice of roasted carrot. 'We have more swords coming, Humbert. Clemen's lords have answered the call.'

'I won't count it answered till I can count how many swords I have to stick into Aimery's cockshite son. And neither should you, Roric. It takes time to ready men for battle and travel them so they don't arrive half-dead with exhaustion.'

'I'm not counting unhatched chickens. I'm just trying to—' He put down the speared carrot, uneaten. 'You're the one who warns against dour brooding.'

'And against gilding the truth.'

The ungilded truth was killing his appetite. 'Humbert . . .' Frowning, he tapped fingertips to the stem of his goblet. 'D'you think there's any chance we're reading Balfre awry?'

'*Awry?*' Humbert choked on a mouthful of partridge pie. 'Roric—'

'Because right now, all we have are suspicions. Balfre's made no outright declaration of war.'

Humbert dropped his spoon to his plate and sat back in his chair, glaring. 'Does a wolf warn the sheep before it starts the slaughter?'

His own pie, though tasty, had turned to cold suet in his belly. The wine he'd drunk rose to burn the back of his throat. 'No.'

'No.' Humbert banged a fist to the table. 'So let's hear no more of *that* shite, boy.'

Boy. He'd never thought to miss hearing that. 'I'd have you know

'I did read your letters, Humbert. And I raised your concerns with the council. But Aistan – and Ercole, while he lived – made good arguments against spending borrowed coin to prepare for a war that might never happen.'

Humbert scowled. 'That they *hoped* would never happen. And you listened because it was your hope too. There always was a part of you that dreamed of a peace with Harcia. Just as you dreamed you could make Cassinia's regents bend to your will, and that marriage with Baldwin's daughter would see Clemen made rich. A maggoty notion if ever there was one. Look how a pizzling *hint* of the marriage had the regents breaking Clemen's back across their bent knees! It was the start of the duchy's rot and we've never recovered since!'

'You think our cause is hopeless?'

'Did I say that?' Humbert slapped the table. 'Clemen isn't run aground yet. Let us break Balfre's back over *our* knees, and then we'll see to steering the duchy into safe waters.'

He tried to smile. 'You make it sound so simple.'

'It's not. But it's not beyond us, either.' Pushing his plate aside, Humbert stood. 'It's late. Get some sleep. Tomorrow you'll start riding the Marches with me. If there's to be fighting in our future you need to know the ground you're skirmishing over and it's been a lot of years since last you were here.'

That was true. Sighing, Roric shoved back from the table. 'As ever, my lord, I am guided by your wisdom. I'll see you at sunrise.'

Two days he spent, from dawn to dark, riding the Marches with Humbert. Remembering his younger days, and how he'd skirmished here with Vidar and Humbert's heir, Ailred, who'd died so long ago it was hard to recall his face. Odd, how Humbert never talked of him, or his dead brother Collyn. But then Humbert never was a man given to sentiment. Perhaps he thought that seeing his sons buried was the same as them never being born at all. Or else easier. And if that was so, who could blame him?

Egann rode with them some of the time, impressive with his knowledge of terrain and tactics. Aistan had protested the lack of another lord in Clemen's Marches, but Humbert had fought hard for his man and clearly was right about him. When it came to drawn swords against Harcia, Egann was a fighter to have close at hand.

As he rode Clemen's Marcher lands, threading through copse and wood, splashing across creeks and around the boggy edges of marshland, feeling a faint ache in the thigh-wound Harcia had given him years before, Roric noticed how few Marcher folk they encountered hour to hour. Like canny wild creatures sensing the approach of foul weather, they kept to their cottages and holdings and hid themselves in woodland shadows. It only increased his sense of impending doom.

'The greatest pity is losing the Pig Whistle,' Humbert said, as they ambled their way back to the manor house at twilight on the second day. 'Did it not burn down, with all the comings and goings through its front door we'd know more of what goes on in Harcia.' He hawked and spat past his horse's shoulder. 'That cockshite Balfre knew what he was doing.'

'Can't prove he burned it, though, Your Grace,' Egann added, just as sour. 'A master of the sly whisper and hidden dagger, is Balfre.'

And this was the man they expected him to defeat with a handful of men-at-arms and a dispirited duchy. Roric felt his fingers clench. If he'd not felt dour before . . .

But there was better news waiting for them in the manor house study. Scarwid's heir, Rufier, had arrived, along with two other northern lords.

'Your Grace,' Rufier said, bowing. 'My father tenders regrets for his absence. His recent infirmity keeps him from the saddle. But I have answered your call in his stead, and hold some one hundred men quartered just over the Marches border.'

Roric felt a little of his twisting tension ease. 'That's heartening to hear. Your family has ever served Clemen with honour.'

'Lord Aistan is on his way with near twice that strength of sword.'

'To arrive when?'

Rufier shook his head. 'I'm sorry, Your Grace. I can't say for sure. Two or three days, perhaps?'

'Serril and I between us hold near ninety more men-at-arms, Your Grace,' Welden of Stony Bridge said, standing with his neighbour. 'Add our swords to Rufier's, and to those wielded by Lord Humbert's Marcher men-at-arms, and we'll pose a threat not to be discounted.'

He forced a smile. 'True.'

'I'm grieved the number's not greater,' Welden said, frowning. 'But alas—' He spread his calloused hands wide. 'Here in the north we lost many good men to plague and black-lung, and some to slavery too. Finding men to train in their places has been tricky.'

'And as you know, Your Grace,' Serril said, his round, bearded face pleated anxious, 'we keep your peace in northern Clemen, and have done for years. There's been no need for barracks tumbled full of men.' A sharp glance at Humbert. 'Or there hasn't been. So we thought.'

'Cast no dark looks at Humbert,' Roric said, as his foster-lord jutted his beard. 'No duke was better served by his Marcher lord than I am by Humbert. Balfre's made sure to keep his daggered intentions well secret.'

The three northern lords murmured apologetic understanding. But watching them closely, he caught an undercurrent of doubt. So, was Humbert proven right yet again? Had Balfre's lies about a treacherous bargain struck with Clemen's duke spread beyond the Marches?

'My lords,' he said, resting his hand on the hilt of his dagger, sheathed at his hip. 'With Eaglerock so far away, and your daily business keeping you for the most part in the north, we do not know each other well. To you and others like you, I'm a signet ring pressed into wax. A crudely etched face stamped into a coin. So let me share this much of myself. Whatever rumours you might have heard of clandestine dealings with Harcia, know them to be rank falsehood. I stand before you prepared to die in Clemen's defence.'

Rufier, who looked older than his twenty years, flushed beneath his reddish, barbered beard. 'Your Grace, I pay no heed to rumour. I grew to manhood hearing my father speak of you with naught but love. You have his undying loyalty, and mine.'

'And ours,' Welden said swiftly, his hand touching Serril's shoulder. They were both older than Rufier by roughly ten years, seasoned men who, like most lords in Clemen, had only ever played at war. 'Your Grace, I'd ask you not to mistake our natural dread in your presence for a lack of respect – or any misgivings.'

'His Grace is glad to hear it,' Humbert growled, unimpressed. 'My lords, you're welcome to a bed for the night. But come the morning you'll need to ride back over the border and fetch your men here.' He turned. 'Egann – play the host, man. See these good lords settled.'

Roric kept his temper in check until he and his foster-lord stood alone in the study. '*Humbert!* What—'

'Pardon, Your Grace, pardon,' Humbert said, lifting both hands. 'But whatever wrangling we must do I'd rather those chumbles weren't witness to it.'

'And what makes you think we must—'

Humbert's beard was jutting again, his eyebrows raised high. 'Well, you were about to send them back to their men and order them to hold fast across the border till Balfre drew first blood, yes?'

'And if I was?'

'You'd be mistaken.'

'The mistake, my lord, would be in provoking Harcia with a flood of Clemen swords. Fright the Harcian Marches with these lords' men and we give Balfre an excuse to blame the ensuing bloodshed on us!'

'*Roric!* When will you grasp it? Aimery's cockshite son *has* his excuse! He's made it up out of whole cloth and stitched it into a doublet he wears even now. And you know as well as I do that without those lords and their men there is *no* hope we can break Balfre here in the Marches.' He tugged at his beard. 'I can only cross fingers that Aistan and his swords arrive in time.'

Because if they didn't, Clemen would be lost with scarcely a blow being struck. The thought of that burned.

'It can't end like this, Humbert. Not after all we've fought for. All we've lost.'

'It'll end as it ends, boy. All we can do is defend Clemen with what we have.'

A terrible sorrow welled. 'Our poor duchy. What it's suffered. I should have been a better duke.'

'Cockshite and codswallop!' Humbert growled. 'Take pizzling thoughts like that into battle with you, Roric, and you'll be dead before your sword's out of its scabbard. Go and soak your head a while. Drown that maggoty doubt. We've supper to eat, and strategies to talk over with Scarwid's boy and the other two, and the last thing they need is a duke lost to moping.'

Roric rubbed his tired eyes. And there was Humbert in a nutshell. A handful of days only, they'd been back in each other's company. And yet he was ordering his duke about, foster-lord to squire, as though nothing had changed. As though there'd been no Lindara. No Vidar. No dead, deformed babe. As though Harald yet lived, and Liam, and Argante, and all *he* was, or could ever hope to be, was the bastard cousin of Clemen's hated duke.

A powerful man, Humbert. Not always admirable. A man who'd used his power to help and to hurt. Loving him was hard. And it was harder still to forgive him – or to know if forgiveness had been earned, or was even deserved.

But then . . . couldn't he say the same of himself? Humbert wasn't the only one to make mistakes.

'Roric,' Humbert said, his voice gentled, 'stop fretting. You've done all you can.'

'You know I haven't. I could've disregarded Aistan and Ercole's advice. The months I've spent with the travelling courts, in disputations, inventing new laws, new taxes, strangling unrest, seeking remedies for our empty coffers – if I'd spent that time preparing Clemen for war—'

'You'd have convinced Aimery that Clemen was a danger to Harcia. Had him thinking we meant to declare war against him – with Balfre urging him on.'

'So you're saying there was *never* any hope for peace?'

Humbert smoothed his disordered beard. 'If I've learned nothing else in these Marches, it's that Balfre's a belligerent fuck eager to wage war on Clemen. And there's not one shiting thing you or I or any man alive or dead could've done to prevent him from getting his way. Which means yes, Roric. Peace was always a pipe dream.'

'You truly believe that.'

'I do. *And* I believe that's enough philosophy for one night.' Humbert crossed to the study door. Opened it, and stood back. 'Now, boy, you might not be hungry but I'm ready to chew the hind end off a donkey. So. After you, Your Grace.'

Surprising himself, Roric laughed. And then he did as he was told, and led the way out of the study.

*   *   *

710

Creeping barefoot out of the snoring barracks, leaving Benedikt a huddled lump beneath the blankets, Liam made his stealthy way past the stables and the armoury to the fringe of old elm trees hemming the tilt yard's far edge. The air was cool, the moonlight meagre. Owls hooted softly from the depths of the nearby woodland. A horse whickered. A fox barked. Familiar night sounds. No need for alarm.

Berold's ring was hidden in a knothole between two branches halfway up the fourth elm tree from the left. After a childhood of tree-climbing in the Pig Whistle's home wood, Liam scaled the elm's trunk without needing to think. Found finger and toeholds by instinct, feeling the rasp of dry bark against his bare soles and palms like a friend's touch. His reaching fingers found the ring, strung on its strip of leather and wrapped in muslin and burlap, thrust deep into the slowly rotting knothole. Relief had him closing his eyes, just for a moment. It had been a risk, hiding the proof of his birthright in a tree but he'd had no choice. Wearing it in the barracks was impossible and he'd needed to keep it close so that when the time came, he could easily retrieve it.

And that time was upon him. An advance rider had come in from Harcia just before lights out. In a few hours Balfre would be returned to the Marches, with Waymon and more Harcian lords and hundreds of blood-hungry men-at-arms. Humbert and his few men, they'd be swept away like twigs in a flooded creek. And after that it would be Roric's turn. There was nowhere in Clemen the murdering bastard could hide where he'd not be found and killed. By himself. By Balfre. By some unwitting man-at-arms. In the end it was all the same. One way or another, Duke Harald would be avenged.

Grinning in the darkness, Liam unwrapped his ring, shoved its cloth wrappings back into the knothole, then slipped it over his head on its old bootlace. Tucked under his shirt, it rested against his chest – a promise of the greatness he was destined to achieve.

He climbed down the tree, neat as a cat. Turned to shadow-slip his way back to the barracks before he was missed – and was struck by a thought that nailed his bare feet to the chilly, damp grass.

Balfre might be duke of Harcia. He might command a thousand men-at-arms, or more. Have the power of life and death over every baron in his duchy, every baker, every whore. And though he believed that in riding to ruin Roric and claim Clemen he served no man but himself – he was wrong.

Everything Balfre does will help put me on the Falcon Throne. So even though he thinks he commands me, it's really me who commands him. His army is my army. His war is my war. And victory, when it comes, it won't be his. It'll be mine.

He slapped his hand over his mouth, to stop himself from laughing. And then he crept back to the barracks, unseen. Slid beneath the blankets on his cot, unnoticed. And fell into a light slumber imagining the look on Benedikt's face when he told his brother the joke.

Four hours after Balfre's tumultuous dawn return to the Harcian Marches, so many lords and men-at-arms to batter Humbert and his men that the barracks grounds spilled over and horse-lines were set up in the woods, word came from the serjeants riding the Marches' open roads that several score of men-at-arms had crossed the Clemen border.

A final, frantic whetstone honing of sword and dagger. Horses saddled and bridled, their shoes hammered tight. Men-at-arms rallied, formed into patrols and assigned to a lord or shouting serjeant. Each man given a bold red linen sash to tie across his body, because the Harcian Marches now overflowed with unfamiliar faces.

Encased in mail and boiled leather, lethally sharpened sword and dagger strapped to his side, and surrounded by countless other dangerous men, Liam sat his horse beside Benedikt, out in front of Balfre's manor house, and watched Balfre and Waymon confer with a half-dozen other Harcian lords and his Marcher serjeants. Shining in gold-chased silver armour over black mail, Harcia's new duke looked confident, his gestures emphatic and unhesitating as he gave his orders. Nothing about him suggested he expected anything less than victory or hinted at grief for his dead father.

Under cover of the muttering men around them, Benedikt leaned close. 'Ye be all right, Willem?'

They'd been ordered to follow Serjeant Eadin in their skirmishing against Clemen. A stroke of luck, that. Eadin was a feggity man, easy to give the slip. And no matter what Balfre planned, that was *their* plan: to slip out of the Harcian Marches first chance and go ahunting of Lord Humbert in his own back yard. That would be easy too. Growing up in the Pig Whistle, they'd run loose on both sides of the Marches more than any other man-at-arms in Balfre's service. Not even Serjeant Grule knew the Clemen Marches' nooks and crannies as well as they did. Likely they'd have to risk themselves fighting for a while, but that was fine. He weren't fretted. Him and Benedikt, they knew which end of a sword was which, these days. Hadn't Grule often praised them on their swordplay since they'd joined Balfre's barracks? Hadn't they already survived skirmishing with Clemen more than once?

He grinned at his brother. 'I be rosy, Benedikt. You?'

'Rosy enough,' Benedikt said, running a finger round the throttling neck of the mail beneath his leather jack. 'But I'll be glad to get started.'

And so would he.

Their wish was granted soon enough. At Balfre's command the huddle of lords and serjeants broke apart. As they went about mounting their horses, Balfre's destrier was brought to him by a liveried squire. A magnificent beast, black as pitch, with a bloody flame of rage in its eyes. Balfre swung himself into its saddle with enviable ease and pranced the animal closer to his gathered men-at-arms so he might be more easily heard. Harcia's duke lifted a gauntleted hand, and all the muttering conversation in the ranks ceased.

'Faithful servants of Harcia,' he said, his raised voice carrying clearly beneath the lightly clouded spring sky. 'I have but two words for you before we ride out to crush treacherous, warmongering Clemen, whose lies and deceit hastened the great Aimery's death. *No mercy!*'

His eager men-at-arms took up the cry. '*No mercy! No mercy! Avenge Aimery! No mercy!*'

'*No mercy!*' Liam shouted, thinking of Roric and of Humbert, who'd helped put the murdering bastard on his throne. He glanced sideways at his brother, lustily shouting with the rest. Caught Benedikt's eye and laughed, feeling his horse quiver with stirred excitement, and his own hot blood rise. '*No mercy!*'

Balfre's warhorse reared once, hooves raking the air. Then the serjeants joined their assigned men-at-arms, and Waymon and the

713

other Harcian lords, their armour far short of Balfre's splendour, fell in behind their duke as he spurred his destrier into a knee-snapping prance and led them, and his men-at-arms, towards the manor house gates.

Harcia was going to war.

They crashed through the Clemen Marches like a river in full flood. Ordered by Balfre to seek out Humbert's men-at-arms in Bell Wood, and from there chase their Clemen prey as they saw fit, with a steady push through Humbert's territory towards the border with Roric's duchy, Serjeant Eadin led his close-riding score of men-at-arms into the woodland at a brisk trot.

With a glance and a nod at Benedikt, Liam eased his horse stride by stride so the other men-at-arms could go by him. Benedikt did the same until they were bringing up the rear.

After that, it was just a matter of waiting.

Though they searched from side to side they found none of Humbert's men-at-arms skulking in Bell Wood. Furious, Eadin cantered them out of the newly budding woodland, over empty Bluebell Meadow and into straggling Tadpecker Copse. Not even ten strides deep into the trees they heard the steel ringing of blade against blade and the shrill shouting of men who were fighting for their lives. Another four strides and their horses were startled by a half-dozen riderless mounts come bolting out of the copse's heart.

'For Harcia!' Eadin bellowed. 'No mercy!'

They spurred their horses, plunging into dappled shadows and the madness of bloodshed. A good thirty men were skirmishing among the spindly trees, swords rising and falling, nearly a third of them unhorsed and Harcia's red-sashed men-at-arms outnumbered. Howling, Eadin barrelled his horse into the nearest of Clemen's mounted men. More shouts, some alarmed, some relieved, as the rest of Eadin's men joined the fight. Trusting Benedikt to look after himself, Liam charged an unmounted Clemen man pulling his bloodied sword from a burst Harcian eye. Rode his horse right over him, heard the cracking of broken bone beneath iron-shod hooves and the muffled shriek of agony as the injured fuck went down beside the man he'd killed. There was too much blood to see who it was. Then a blow to his back had him hauling his horse onto its haunches, wrenching around so he could slash his sword across his mounted attacker's throat. Blood spurting, the Clemen bastard toppled from his horse. Catching his breath, he saw Benedikt lean sideways to stroke his sword's whetted edge through an unmounted Clemen man's face. More spurting blood. Another corpse. The air stank of fresh blood and horse shit, shivered with the screams of the wounded and dying who littered the grassy, crimson-splashed ground.

He looked around. No sign of that treacherous bastard Humbert.

Then three Clemen men-at-arms spurred their horses clear of the frantic violence, trying to escape before they were cut down too.

'Benedikt!' Liam shouted, pointing. 'After 'em!'

Heedless of Serjeant Eadin's bellowed protest, they spurred their own horses in pursuit. Changed direction as soon as they were out of his sight, letting Clemen's men go their own way while they trotted cautious to the eastern edge of the copse.

'So,' Benedikt said, panting, once they'd looked hard at each other to make sure any blood splashed on them wasn't theirs. 'Now we find Humbert, iss?'

Liam tucked the hilt of his sword under his thigh, then dragged his forearm over his face to wipe away the sweat. 'Iss,' he said, taking his sword back. 'And we'd best get a move on, afore someone else finds him first.'

After that it was cat-and-mouse, cat-and-mouse, playing hide-and-seek with every man-at-arms in the Clemen Marches. Five more times they were tangled in a bloody skirmish as they criss-crossed Clemen land to find Roric's Marcher lord. The second time, not far from the burned remains of the Pig Whistle, Benedikt caught the trailing edge of a Clemen dagger down his right cheek. The wound wasn't killing deep but he bled like a stuck hog till it clotted. Battling their way through Clemen survivors at corpse-choked Crooked Creek, Liam had his left thigh sliced by a wildly swung sword. The blade opened his horse's side down to a rib, but neither wound was mortal.

Pretending he wasn't half-scared out of his wits, Liam bound the wound with a strip cut from his red sash, then put the pain out of his mind. He and Benedikt made a ragged escape, spurring their tired

715

horses without mercy, and kept on hunting. Hoped with every freshly slaughtered Clemen man they stumbled over that they'd not found Humbert. That the old rump yet lived, could be found and taken prisoner, and they weren't risking their lives for naught. Once, on the edge of sour-salty Badger Pond, they caught sight of Balfre on his destrier, close enough to see that none of the men-at-arms he harried was Clemen's Marcher lord. They saw Serjeant Grule, too, in Farmer Spurfield's rye-patch, battling Clemen men-at-arms alongside the grizzled old lord that someone in the barracks had said was famous Lord Terriel of the Green Isle. They saw the old man cut down, his hamstrung horse falling on top of him. But Humbert wasn't there either so they rode on quickly before someone looked up from the slaughter and saw them watching, not fighting.

'Fuck, Willem,' Benedikt muttered, his voice slurry because of his slashed cheek, as they jogged their tired horses away from Spurfield farm. 'D'ye think we'll find Humbert afore dusk? Or afore there b'aint no more Clemen shites to be killed and Balfre calls victory? Harcia's lost men but Clemen's lost a sight more. The skirmishing's got to end soon.'

Feeling an unwelcome clutch of nerves, Liam glanced at the late-afternoon sky. Benedikt was right. The day was dying and his chance to gift Balfre with Clemen's Marcher lord was dying with it. The thought of failure nearly had him snivelling like a babe.

'Willem?' Benedikt prompted. 'What d'ye want to do?'

Gritting his teeth against the throbbing pain in his thigh, the ache in his shoulders and back, crushed by the weight of his mail and leather jack, feeling his leather skull cap like a lead bowl, he pressed his spurs once again to his horse's scored flanks.

'Ride on to Spindly Copse. We haven't looked there yet.'

'And if we don't find him, Willem?'

Hating his brother for the difficult questions, for being right, Liam glared. 'I don't fucking know, Benedikt! Let's just ride to Spindly Copse!'

'Fine,' said Benedikt, sulky. 'If that be what ye want.'

What he fucking wanted was to find that fuck Humbert. He spurred his horse again, urging it into a reluctant jog, leaving Benedikt to catch up as he pleased.

CHAPTER FORTY-TWO

Just like Bell Wood, they heard the fighting in Spindly Copse before they saw it. The clashing of swords. The muted metal thumping of blade against iron mail and boiled leather. Harsh breathing. Grunts of pain. The deep, raw bellow of a wounded horse. Fingers of fading light reached down through the undergrown trees and their branches, gilding the spreading tangles of bramble bushes just coming into bud.

Another wounded horse bellowed, higher-pitched this time. A horrible, skin-crawling cry. Liam felt his own horse shudder and prop, ears flattening, haunches dropping beneath him as it baulked at what lay ahead. Benedikt's horse baulked with it, resentfully swishing its tail.

'Leave 'em,' Benedikt whispered, sliding his feet out of his stirrups. 'The poor shites have had enough.'

Nodding, Liam looked around to be sure they were alone. Then he dismounted, hissing as his wounded thigh threatened to give way when his boot touched the ground. Ignoring Benedikt's anxious glance, he secured his reins to a sturdy sapling, then made certain of his sword and his dagger as his brother did the same.

'Ready?' he said, when Benedikt was done.

His brother shrugged. 'I s'pose.'

With all the stealth that was left to them, they crept towards the ugly sounds of increasingly desperate battle. A few moments later came upon nine men in a clearing. Five were Harcian. Four were Clemen. And one of them was Humbert. No sign of the wounded horses, but scattered around them, eight bodies. Five of the dead were wearing a crimson Harcian sash. Liam felt a wave of blinding relief crash over him, and his hand went to the hilt of his sword. *At last.*

Here was his prize. But then Benedikt took hold of his arm and pulled him down behind a wild tangle of brambles that edged the clearing.

'Wait,' his brother hissed. 'We can't fight nine men. Let Humbert kill a few more first. Ye've seen him fight, ye know he will. Then we'll have him.'

It wasn't a risk he'd have taken by himself. But Benedikt had made the choice for him. They'd have words on that later. He pulled off his skull cap, desperate to ease the pounding pain in his head.

Humbert and the other eight men-at-arms were bruised and bloody, dirt and leaves and sweat plastered to their stained faces, their stained armour and boiled leather jacks and mail. No elegance to their sword and dagger-work, only a grim determination to kill first before being killed. Their footwork was clumsy, more a stagger than a dance. It was clear they were exhausted, worn to near-collapse by the day's relentless fighting. The cool, moist air heaved in and out of their lungs in shuddering gasps.

One of the Clemen men turned, awkward, and tripped over a dead man's leg. A Harcian man-at-arms – like the others his face was unfamiliar, they must have ridden in with Balfre – saw him off-balance and moved in for the easy slaughter.

Alerted, Humbert lurched round. Saw the Harcian's raised sword and raised his own. '*Roric! Roric! 'Ware behind you!*'

Liam forgot his resentment, hardly felt Benedikt's digging elbow. Heart thumping, fingers clenching, he stared in disbelief at the man who'd murdered his father. His mother. Who'd tried to murder him and had stolen his duchy. Tall and strongly built, closer to plain than handsome, with close-cropped greying chestnut hair and blood splattering his cheeks. He was dressed like a common man-at-arms. Looked nothing like a *duke*.

The bastard Roric's lunging blade took the Harcian through his throat, even as Humbert's sword slashed the back of the man's thighs. Then Humbert was turning again to block a new Harcian blade, and Roric was close-grappling with another of Balfre's men. The fight was evenly matched now, four against four. Liam watched, breathless, willing Humbert and Roric to prevail, for the other two Clemen men-at-arms to fall. Then he and Benedikt could take the last two Harcians, gulling Roric and Humbert into thinking they were saved. And then – and then –

A crashing through the trees on the far side of the clearing. Raised voices. Drumming hooves. Three sweat-soaked mounted horses burst out of the gloom. Not a rider among them wore a red sash. Hard on their heels, five more horses. The rider in front was Waymon, his darkly bronzed armour painted lavishly with blood.

Madness. One of the Harcians brought down the first Clemen horse, then severed its fallen rider's head with a single swing of his sword. Blood gushed like a wellspring as the wounded horse thrashed itself to death on the ground. Its wild throes frenzied the other horses, sent them rearing and spinning and trampling in panic.

Graceful as a jongler despite his armour, Waymon vaulted out of his saddle. He had eyes for no one but Humbert, who'd been knocked off his feet and was struggling to rise again. Struggling for breath. As Roric and his men-at-arms battled Harcia's swords, oblivious, Waymon hurdled the dead horse's twitching carcase, closed on Humbert in three swift strides and slit his throat with a dagger.

'*Your Grace! Your Grace! Lord Humbert, Your Grace!*'

So cried a Clemen man-at-arms. His horrified shout froze every blade mid-swing. Roric whipped round. Saw Humbert dead in a pool of blood, saw Waymon grinning, and beneath his mask of blood and sweat turned white as fresh chalk.

'*Roric!*' Waymon echoed. 'At last. A face to put with the name.'

Roric leapt for him, his eyes savage, tears washing through the scarlet on his face.

'*Shite!*' yelped Benedikt.

Hidden behind the brambles, they watched Waymon and Roric fight like men possessed by goblin-spirits, heedless of the bodies they trod on and tripped over and ground to mincemeat with their boots, of the bloodsoaked grass and dirt they were churning into stinking mud, and the blows they landed on each other's straining bodies. Watched the men-at-arms of Harcia and Clemen try to hack each other to bloody bits. Screams and curses and shit and death. A nightmare vision worse than any skirmish they'd ever seen or fought in.

Liam felt a chill rattle his bones. Fuck. *Fuck.* Never mind the men-at-arms. Waymon was winning. Any moment he'd have Roric on the ground, he'd have Clemen's bastard duke spitted and dying on his sword. And if Roric died now there'd be no Falcon Throne for murdered Harald's son.

'Willem, *no*!' Benedikt grabbed him. 'Willem don't, ye can't – don't—'

Sword unsheathed, wrenching his arm free of his frantic brother, Liam flung himself over the brambles and into the fight. He had one chance to take Waymon by surprise. To kill Balfre's trusted friend before the bastard killed Roric and with him any hope he had of reclaiming Clemen.

Roric saw him running, sword drawn. Let his own sword drop, startled. Distracted, Waymon hesitated. Glanced behind him, recoiled, then turned.

Liam struck him with all the speed and strength he could muster. The blow knocked the wind out of him. Knocked Waymon off his feet. Ignoring the shocking pain, bracing himself for more, he dropped to his knees on Waymon's armoured chest, raised his sword to his arms' length and plunged it into the bastard's gaping mouth, through the back of his skull and into the bloodied ground beneath his head.

Stillness. Muffling silence. A peculiar kind of calm.

Looking up, Liam met Roric's shocked stare. The bastard's eyes were the colour of warm amber. Seeing them, he remembered that this man was a kind of cousin. That they shared more than a bloody history. He remembered they shared blood.

'But – you're Harcian,' Roric said, dazed. 'Why would you—'

And then his face changed. His sword came up. Liam heard the thud of approaching footsteps, tried to pull his sword free of Waymon. Grunted as Roric roughly shoved him down and aside. As he tumbled off Waymon's body he saw a silver flash of swords, heard the clash of blade on blade, heard an agonised grunt then felt a spray of something warm and wet across his face and hair. He smelled the iron tang of fresh blood.

Fuck. Don't let it be Roric's.

The muffling silence vanished, and he was once more battered by the clamour of battle. Shouts and screams and ringing steel. Men were fighting almost on top of him. Sword lost, he pulled out his dagger. Smeared the blood from his eyes and looked for Roric. His father's murderer was struggling with another Harcian. The man-at-arms's sword-hilt struck Roric hard in the face. The bastard went down like an axed sheep. Following him, the Harcian struck again, then again. Another blow and surely he'd crack Roric's skull. Cursing, Liam scrambled to reach him. Then a shout went up and for a moment he thought he could hear thunder. But no, it was only more horses, Clemen and Harcian, thrusting and stamping and crowding into the body-strewn clearing. Cries of 'Clemen! Clemen!' and 'For Aimery! No mercy!' drowned out the other sounds of bloodshed and mayhem.

Buffeted by horses, he lost sight of Roric. Lost his dagger as it was knocked out of his hand. His grand plan was in a shambles. He'd be trampled to death any moment.

And then something struck him a violent blow from behind. The last thing he heard, as darkness claimed him, was a voice saying Sorry . . . and the thundering of hooves.

When he came back to himself it was night, and he thought he must have been sorely injured because the ground beneath him was gently rocking, and all he could smell was wet salt. His body was an argument of many different pains. Hurting worst of all his head, pain like the blade of a sword driving through it from side to side. He moaned.

That'll teach me to take off my skull cap.

'Hush, Willem,' Benedikt said softly. 'Sound carries over water and we're not so far from land.'

He had a fearsome thirst. Swallowing, he tried to sit up. His battling pains defeated him.

'Stay still,' said Benedikt. 'That were a mighty crack to yer noggin. Ye didn't ought to have pulled off yer cap.'

If he'd not felt so mizzled he'd have kicked his brother for that.

Having no choice, he did as he was told. Stared up into the star-pricked, lightly moon-silvered sky and listened to the gentle slap of little waves against wood. Beneath him he could feel timber boards, and smell tar.

'We're in a boat.'

'Iss. A wherry.'

'And we're off the Marches coast?'

'A ways along the Clemen coast by now,' said Benedikt. 'I been rowing for a while.'

'Rowing.' He sat up, grunting at the pain. 'Benedikt, how did we—' And then he stopped, because he realised that the leg he'd just kicked didn't belong to his brother. Benedikt was behind him, folded into the wherry's stern. 'What the—'

'*Hush!*' Benedikt urged him. 'Don't fuss, Willem. It's Roric.'

Dumbfounded, he peered at the shadowy slump in the wherry's bow. '*Roric?* Shite! What's he doing here?'

'Yes, Benedikt,' said Roric, his voice rough with weariness and pain. 'What am I doing here? I confess, I'd like to know. Why didn't you bind me and hand me over to Balfre? I'm sure the duke of Harcia would've been monstrous grateful. He'd have made you rich, most likely. Showered you with coin and praise. But here I am, unbound, in a thieved wherry, still alive.'

As Benedikt gaped, Liam groped around himself. 'Where's a sword? I want a fucking sword.' His scrabbling fingers closed around a cold, damp hilt. Not a sword, a dagger. But it would do. He pointed it at Roric. 'Never mind flapping yer tongue, *Yer Grace*. Sit there and keep silent, else I'll make yer wish ye did.'

The faint moonlight showed him Roric's teeth as he smiled, brief and mocking. 'You know who I am.'

Clemen's bastard, pretender, murdering duke. 'Iss. I know. Only seeing as how ye've just lost yer duchy, I don't reckon to call ye anything but Roric.'

'So.' Roric nodded at the dagger. 'You'd kill Waymon to save me, only to kill me yourself? You're a strange young man, Willem.'

Benedikt snorted. 'Ha. Ye b'aint wrong there.'

'Clap tongue,' Liam muttered, and elbowed him. 'Benedikt, what happened?'

'D'ye want me to clap tongue or tell ye? I can't do both, ye feggit.'

There was a lump the size of a goose egg on the back of his head. Gingerly exploring it with his fingertips, wincing, Liam flicked Benedikt a scowling glance. '*What happened?*'

'Well . . .' Benedikt cleared his throat, the way he did when he knew he was in trouble. 'Not to spin a long yarn, Willem. When

Roric went down it looked like he was done for. So while Harcia's men and Clemen's men were busy trying to slaughter each other, I rapped ye with a sword-hilt so it looked like ye were killed too. Then as soon as the fighting spilled out of Spindly Copse and they all rode away leaving the dead on the ground, and I saw Roric *weren't* killed, I tied ye both to a horse and got us out of the Marches and over the border to Lemmet Cove, as was left deserted on account of the black-lung and the pirates. Then I stole a wherry that not a soul wanted and rowed us out of Balfre's reach.'

Shifting until his back was against the wherry's side, Liam stared at his brother. '*You* put this fucking goose egg on my head?'

Benedikt's face was a pale blur in the miserly light. 'I had to! Them Harcian men-at-arms *saw* you kill Waymon! Ye'd be dead for it right now if the duke – if Roric hadn't saved ye!'

Roric folded his arms across his chest. 'You were watching?'

'Iss,' Benedikt muttered. 'We both were, till Willem saw Waymon had the best of ye.'

'You weren't fighting for Balfre? You were both wearing a scarlet sash.'

'Never ye mind whose side we're on,' Liam snapped, waggling the dagger at him. 'Me and Benedikt b'aint none of yer business.'

'But you and Benedikt saved my life,' said Roric. 'So I think that makes you both somewhat my business.'

Nosy bastard. Fine. When cornered, attack. Something he'd learned from Serjeant Grule. 'That lord what Waymon killed. Humbert. Who was he to ye?'

'My friend,' Roric said softly, not trying to hide his grief. 'My second father. I won't speak of him. Willem, why did you and Benedikt risk your lives to save me? Aren't your homes in the Marches? Don't you have family there?'

'We be brothers, Roric. Our family's dead. Murdered. It be just us now.'

'I'm sorry,' Roric said. 'Truly. As it happens, I'm in the same boat. No pun intended.'

So now he was trying to make them feel sorry for him? *Bastard*. 'Right.'

'Did you save me because you thought I might reward you with riches? If so, you're doomed to disappointment. As you say, Willem. Clemen is lost. Balfre has won. There's nothing but blood and death there now. At least for me. But you and Benedikt could still make a life for yourselves.'

'Weren't ye listening? Balfre's men know I killed Waymon. By now I reckon he wants both of us dead.'

And if that weren't a faery-curse, he didn't know what was.

'You could trade me for your life,' said Roric. 'You're two against one. And I've seen you with a sword.'

Benedikt leaned close. 'We can't risk it, Willem. Ye know Balfre loved Waymon like a brother. He'd say ye had a bargain then go back on his word and kill ye.'

And that was likely true. In his own way, Balfre was as big a bastard as Roric. What to do . . . what to do . . .

He glowered at the man who'd murdered his father. 'Where can ye go, Roric? Is there any place that'll have ye? Or do we toss ye into the water right now and wave goodbye as ye drown?'

'Yes, indeed,' Roric murmured. 'A very strange young man.' Then he sighed. 'Willem, in the past day I've lost nearly every man I ever thought of as a friend. And my people, who trusted me, are now at Balfre's mercy. And he is not a merciful man.'

Benedikt was frowning. 'Yer Grace—'

'*Don't call me that!*' Roric said with violent revulsion. 'There is not one speck of grace about me. There's more grace in both of you, two ignorant boys from the Marches.'

'Roric, then,' Benedikt said awkwardly. 'Be ye sure there b'ain't someone ye can turn to?'

A dragging silence. Water sloshed against the wherry's hull. At last, Roric stirred.

'There is someone,' he said, hesitant. 'Perhaps. But she's a long way from here. If we could get to Eaglerock harbour, find passage to Cassinia before Balfre's fist closes tight around Clemen's throat and from there make our way to Ardenn, then maybe—' He shook his head. 'But it's a fucking frail hope.'

'Frail be better than nothing,' said Benedikt. 'Willem?'

He blinked. 'Ye want us to row to Eaglerock? Benedikt, d'ye know how far that is?'

'Too far,' his brother said gloomily. Then he brightened. 'We could row part of the way. Couldn't we? Then leave the wherry beached somewhere and keep going on foot?'

'I s'pose,' he said, reluctant. 'But—'

His brother was glaring again. 'Willem, y'started this. Now y'can finish it. Or why the fuck did ye start it at all?'

He didn't know. Fuck. He didn't know anything. He was the rightful duke of Clemen and he didn't know a fucking thing.

'Fine,' he muttered. 'We'll make for Eaglerock.'

Staring at the man whose life he'd just saved, who'd murdered his father and stolen his duchy, Liam picked up the wherry's oars and started to row.

EPILOGUE

Dawn in Lepetto. Nightwings serenaded the blushing sky, greeting the new day even as they fled over countless red clay roofs to the somnolent safety of the city's famous, fragrant lemon groves. Standing naked on the high balcony of his deceptively humble home, lips curving as a salt-scented breeze caressed his supple, olive-brown skin, Salimbene watched the familiar early flight with half-closed eyes. Obsidian feathers shone irridescent, hinting dragon-green and the azure of Lepetto's lapping harbour, and lilting birdsong sang counterpoint with the first tollings of the great bronze bell atop the Exarch's distant palace. A peaceful, perfect sunrise. One of thousands he'd greeted since making this city state his home. After fleeing Zeidica, and his father. Bleached bones now, a mournful skull, the man who had sired him then sought his death. His royal seed long-since blighted. His kingdom a rubble of rock and regrets. Remembering, Salimbene smiled wide. Revenge was like nectar, like honey on the tongue.

Overhead, carved jet against the blue-bowl sky, the last nightwings thrashed through the gilded air, racing to catch up with the rest of their flock. Stragglers. Weaklings. Too young or too old or merely imperfect. Wide smile became thinned lips. Thumb and forefinger pinched. One nightwing dropped stoneish to the catseye cobbles far below. Startled to silence, the remaining birds darted out of sight.

The Exarch's bronze bell tolled on, lonely, waking marvellous, secretive Lepetto to life.

'*Salimbene . . . Salimbene . . .*'

Summoned, he stepped from his sunlit balcony into shadow and mystery, into the beating heart of sorcery. The balcony doors slammed shut behind him. Candlewicks ignited in the windowless room that kept his secrets. Dust stirred. Eyelids fluttered. Scabbed lips murmured his sleeping name. Here he conjured the past and the future, breathed the memory of his mother, touched with ancient fingertips the moist skin of long-dead flesh.

'*Salimbene . . . Salimbene . . .*'

It was the severed head connecting him to Izusa that called. The infant heads on either side of it, sitting on their little plinths, whimpered in sympathy. He snapped his fingers and the head's sunken blue eyes sprang open.

'What news, Izusa? Do you have Liam safe?'

'*Not yet. I must still cajole Catrain. She is wary of the regents, not yet entirely trusting. She—*'

Fury shook him, the tempest never far from his fist. 'I must have him! Liam is my wellspring. If you fail me, Izusa, I will—'

The severed head shuddered, brackish blood seeping with her fear. '*I'm sorry! Forgive me!*'

Her good fortune that she was far away, in storm-gathered Cassinia. He could punish her from here, but he needed his strength.

'Without him, Izusa, your life is forfeit.'

'*Salimbene,*' the head whispered, weeping, '*I will fetch him. I won't fail.*'

So she said. But he would pinch her out like a nightwing if she lied.

Still raging, though Izusa was banished from his presence, it was some time before he was calm enough to bend his wit towards the task that started and ended each day: his search for the Oracle of Nicosia.

Find it, my love, no matter the cost his mother had begged him. *Find it and destroy it. Only then will you be untouchable.*

And for nearly two hundred years, he'd tried. But the Oracle, his dangerous enemy, was ever elusive. Doubtless it knew he hunted it, sought to make himself the destroyer and not the destroyed. Sometimes he despaired of keeping that promise to his mother. Sometimes he even wondered if, in her dying delirium, she had been mistaken and he stood in no danger from the Oracle, or anything at all.

But then he remembered what he'd learned long after her death.

That she had been no ordinary witch, but the last great witch queen of Osfahr. And that even though he was Salimbene, he ignored her warning at his peril. So every night and every morning, he searched for the one thing in all the world that could harm him.

The bowl of blood on its carved ivory stand woke at his approach. Churned like a millpond, sensing his disquiet. He trailed his fingers across its crimson, coagulated surface, feeling the rush of power heat his bones.

'*Show me*,' he commanded. '*Reveal the Oracle of Nicosia to my eyes!*'

But again, yet again, the bowl of blood showed him nothing. He threw it stinking and scarlet across the windowless room. Cursed the Oracle. Cursed Izusa. Set the air on fire with his rage. But he was being foolish, and he knew it, so soon enough he turned the flames to ice. What matter that the Oracle continued elusive? Two hundred years. Two thousand. It was only time. And in time he would find the Oracle of Nicosia and destroy it. Then, as his mother had promised, he would be untouchable. As magnificent as the sun.

'I am Salimbene,' he whispered. 'From the shadows, I rule.'

ACKNOWLEDGEMENTS

My agent, Ethan Ellenberg, for his stalwart support and sage advice.

The international Orbit team, who never fail. Special thanks to Tim Holman, always, for everything. To Joanna Kramer, who didn't know what she was getting herself into. To Abigail Nathan, for not letting me look like an idiot. And Anna Jackson, who kept me sane and believed when I doubted.

My patient and meticulous beta readers: Kate Elliott, Glenda Larke, Elaine and Peter Shipp, Mark Timmony, Craig Slater and Mary GT Webber. And Larry Murphy, for the chain-mail.

Look out for

BOOK TWO IN THE
TARNISHED CROWN SERIES!

Trouble is brewing in the kingdoms
of the Tarnished Crown.

The fearsome Balfre's army sweeps into Clemen, subduing all
opposition. Meanwhile Liam, the boy who has vowed to reclaim
his father's stolen throne in Clemen, is adrift at sea with his foster
brother, Benedikt, and Roric – the man who killed his father.
Angry and confused, and in an unlikely allegiance with this bitter
enemy, he must plan his next move.

In the Principality of Cassinia, the duke's daughter Catrain will
do what she can to help Roric and Liam. But kept prisoner by
the council of regents, and being guided by the dark witch Isuza,
Catrain is unsure who to trust, and how long she must wait to
claim her royal birthright.

Meanwhile, the young prince Gäel has reached his legal majority,
ready to be formally crowned Prince of Cassinia. But many fear he
is unstable, unfit to rule – and not without reason. As his regents,
headed by his cousin, delay over his coronation, unrest is growing
strong among Cassinia's dukes, who distrust each other as much as
the council of regents itself.

As Cassinia's duchies balance on the edge of a blade, even one false
step is sure to draw blood . . .

www.orbitbooks.net

extras

orbit

www.orbitbooks.net

about the author

Karen Miller was born in Vancouver, Canada, and came to Australia with her family when she was two. Apart from a two-year stint in the UK she's lived around Sydney ever since. She has held a variety of interesting jobs and fell in love with speculative fiction at primary school.

Find out more about Karen Miller and other Orbit authors by registering for the free monthly newsletter at www.orbitbooks.net.

if you enjoyed
THE FALCON THRONE

look out for

THIEF'S MAGIC
book one of Millennium's Rule

by

Trudi Canavan

CHAPTER 1

The corpse's shrivelled, unbending fingers surrendered the bundle reluctantly. Wrestling the object out of the dead man's grip seemed disrespectful so Tyen worked slowly, gently lifting a hand when a blackened fingernail snagged on the covering. He'd touched the ancient dead so often they didn't sicken or frighten him now. Their desiccated flesh had long ago stopped being a source of transferable sickness, and he did not believe in ghosts.

When the mysterious bundle came free Tyen straightened and smiled in triumph. He wasn't as ruthless at collecting ancient artefacts as his fellow students and his teacher, but bringing home nothing from these research trips would see him fail to graduate as a sorcerer-archaeologist. He willed his tiny magic-fuelled flame closer.

The object's covering, like the tomb's occupant, was dry and stiff having, by his estimate, lain undisturbed for six hundred years. Thick leather darkened with age, it had no markings – no adornment, no precious stones or metals. As he tried to open it the wrapping snapped apart and something inside began to slide out. His pulse quickened as he caught the object . . .

. . . and his heart sank a little. No treasure lay in his hands. Just a book. Not even a jewel-encrusted, gold-embellished book.

Not that a book didn't have potential historical value, but compared to the glittering treasures Professor Kilraker's other two students had unearthed for the Academy it was a disappointing find. After all the months of travel, research, digging and watching he had little to show for his own work. He had finally unearthed a tomb that hadn't already been ransacked by grave robbers and what did it contain? A plain stone coffin, an unadorned corpse and an old book.

Still, the old fossils at the Academy wouldn't regret sponsoring his journey if the book turned out to be significant. He examined it closely. Unlike the wrapping, the leather cover felt supple. The binding was in good condition. If he hadn't just broken apart the covering to get it out, he'd have guessed the book's age at no more than a hundred or so years. It had no title or text on the spine. Perhaps it had worn off. He opened it. No word marked the first page, so he turned it. The next was also blank and as he fanned through the rest of the pages he saw that they were as well.

He stared at it in disbelief. Why would anyone bury a blank book in a tomb, carefully wrapped and placed in the hands of the occupant? He looked at the corpse, but it offered no answer. Then something drew his eye back to the book, still open to one of the last pages. He looked closer.

A mark had appeared.

Next to it a dark patch formed, then dozens more. They spread and joined up.

Hello, they said. *My name is Vella.*

Tyen uttered a word his mother would have been shocked to hear if she had still been alive. Relief and wonder replaced disappointment. The book was magical. Though most sorcerous books used magic in minor and frivolous ways, they were so rare that the Academy would always take them for its collection. His trip hadn't been a waste.

So what did this book do? Why did text only appear when it was opened? Why did it have a name? More words formed on the page.

I've always had a name. I used to be a person. A living, breathing woman.

Tyen stared at the words. A chill ran down his spine, yet at the same time he felt a familiar thrill. Magic could sometimes be disturbing. It was often inexplicable. He liked that not everything about it was understood. It left room for new discoveries. Which was why he had chosen to study sorcery alongside history. In both fields there was an opportunity to make a name for himself.

He'd never heard of a person turning into a book before. *How is that possible?* he wondered.

I was made by a powerful sorcerer, replied the text. *He took my knowledge and flesh and transformed me.*

His skin tingled. The book had responded to the question he'd shaped in his mind. *Do you mean these pages are made of your flesh?* he asked.

Yes. My cover and pages are my skin. My binding is my hair, twisted together and sewn with needles fashioned from my bones and glue from tendons.

He shuddered. *And you're conscious?*

Yes.

You can hear my thoughts?

Yes, but only when you touch me. When not in contact with a living human, I am blind and deaf, trapped in the darkness with no sense of time passing. Not even sleeping. Not quite dead. The years of my life slipping past — wasted.

Tyen stared down at the book. The words remained, nearly filling a page now, dark against the creamy vellum. Which was her skin . . .

It was grotesque and yet . . . all vellum was made of skin. While these pages were human skin, they felt no different to that made of animals. They were soft and pleasant to touch. The book was not repulsive in the way an ancient, desiccated corpse was.

And it was so much more interesting. Conversing with it was akin to talking with the dead. If the book was as old as the tomb it knew about the time before it was laid there. Tyen smiled. He may not have found gold and jewels to help pay his way on this expedition, but the book could make up for that with historical information.

More text formed.

Contrary to appearances, I am not an "it".

Perhaps it was the effect of the light on the page, but the new words seemed a little larger and darker than the previous text. Tyen felt his face warm a little.

I'm sorry, Vella. It was bad mannered of me. I assure you, I meant no offence. It is not every day that a man addresses a talking book, and I am not entirely sure of the protocol.

She was a woman, he reminded himself. He ought to follow the etiquette he'd been raised to follow. Though talking to women could be fiendishly tricky, even when following all the rules about manners. It would be rude to begin their association by interrogating her about the past. Rules of conversation decreed he should ask after her wellbeing.

So . . . is it nice being a book?

When I am being held and read by someone nice, it is, she replied.

And when you are not, it is not? I can see that might be a disadvantage in your state, though one you must have anticipated before you became a book.

I would have, if I'd had foreknowledge of my fate.

So you did not choose to become a book. Why did your maker do that to you? Was it a punishment?

No, though perhaps it was natural justice for being too ambitious and vain. I sought his attention, and received more of it than I intended.

Why did you seek his attention?

He was famous. I wanted to impress him. I thought my friends would be envious.

And for that he turned you into a book. What manner of man could be so cruel?

He was the most powerful sorcerer of his time, Roporien the Clever.

Tyen caught his breath and a chill ran down his back. *Roporien! But he died over a thousand years ago!*

Indeed.

Then you are . . .

At least as old as that. Though in my time it wasn't polite to comment on a woman's age.

He smiled. *It still isn't — and I don't think it ever will be. I apologise again.*

You are a polite young man. I will enjoy being owned by you.

You want me to own *you?* Tyen suddenly felt uncomfortable. He realised he now thought of the book as a person, and owning a person was slavery — an immoral and uncivilised practice that had been illegal for over a hundred years.

Better that than spend my existence in oblivion. Books don't last for ever, not even magical ones. Keep me. Make use of me. I can give you a wealth of knowledge. All I ask is that you hold me as often as possible so that I can spend my lifespan awake and aware.

I don't know . . . The man who created you did many terrible things — as you experienced yourself. I don't want to follow in his shadow. Then something occurred to him that made his skin creep. *Forgive me for being blunt about it, but his book, or any of his tools, could be designed for evil purposes. Are you one such tool?*

I was not designed so, but that does not mean I could not be used so. A tool is only as evil as the hand that uses it.

The familiarity of the saying was startling and unexpectedly reassuring. It was one that Professor Weldan liked. The old historian had always been suspicious of magical things.

How do I know you're not lying about not being evil?

I cannot lie.

Really? But what if you're lying about not being able to lie?

You'll have to work that one out for yourself.

Tyen frowned as he considered how he might devise a test for her, then realised something was buzzing right beside his ear. He shied away from the sensation, then breathed a sigh of relief as he saw it was Beetle, his little mechanical creation. More than a toy, yet not quite what he'd describe as a pet, it had proven to be a useful companion on the expedition.

The palm-sized insectoid swooped down to land on his shoulder, folded its iridescent blue wings, then whistled three times. Which was a warning that . . .

"Tyen!"

. . . Miko, his friend and fellow archaeology student was approaching.

The voice echoed in the short passage leading from the outside world to the tomb. Tyen muttered a curse. He glanced down at the page. *Sorry, Vella. Have to go.* Footsteps neared the door of the tomb. With no time to slip her into his bag, he stuffed her down his shirt, where she settled against the waistband of his trousers. She was warm — which was a bit disturbing now that he knew she was a conscious thing created from human flesh — but he didn't have time to dwell on it. He turned to the door in time to see Miko stumble into view.

"Didn't think to bring a lamp?" he asked.

"No time," the other student gasped. "Kilraker sent me to get you. The others have gone back to the camp to pack up. We're leaving Mailand."

"Now?"

"Yes. *Now*," Miko replied.

Tyen looked back at the small tomb. Though Professor Kilraker liked to refer to these foreign trips as treasure hunts, his peers expected the students to bring back evidence that the journeys were also educational. Copying the faint decorations on the tomb walls would have given them something to mark. He thought wistfully of the new instant etchers that some of the richer professors and self-funded adventurers used to record their work. They were far beyond his meagre allowance. Even if they weren't, Kilraker wouldn't take them on expeditions because they were heavy and fragile.

Picking up his satchel, Tyen opened the flap. "Beetle. Inside." The insectoid scuttled down his arm into the bag. Tyen slung the strap over his head and shoulder and sent his flame into the passage.

"We have to hurry," Miko said, leading the way. "The locals heard about where you're digging. Must've been one of the boys Kilraker hired to deliver food who told them. A bunch are coming up the valley and they're sounding those battle horns they carry."

"They didn't want us digging here? Nobody told me that!"

"Kilraker said not to. He said you were bound to find something impressive, after all the research you did."

He reached the hole where Tyen had broken through into the passage and squeezed out. Tyen followed, letting the flame die as he climbed out into the bright afternoon sunlight. Dry heat enveloped him. Miko scrambled up the sides of the ditch. Following, Tyen looked back and surveyed his work. Nothing remained in the tomb that robbers would want, but he couldn't stand to leave it exposed to vermin and he felt guilty about unearthing a tomb the locals didn't wanted disturbed. Reaching out with his mind, he pulled magic to himself then moved the rocks and earth on either side back into the ditch.

"What are you *doing*?" Miko sounded exasperated.

"Filling it in."

"We don't have time!" Miko grabbed his arm and yanked him around so that they both looked down into the valley. He pointed. "See?"

The valley sides were near-vertical cliffs, and where the faces had crumbled over time piles of rubble had built up against the sides to form steep slopes. Tyen and Miko were standing atop of one of these.

At the bottom of the valley a long line of people was moving, faces tilted to search the scree above. One arm rose, pointing at Tyen and Miko. The rest stopped, then fists were raised.

A shiver went through Tyen, part fear, part guilt. Though the people inhabiting the remote valleys of Mailand were unrelated to the ancient race that had buried its dead in the tombs, they felt that such places of death should not be disturbed lest ghosts be awakened. They'd made this clear when Kilraker had arrived, and to previous archaeologists, but their protests had never been more than verbal and they'd indicated that some areas were less important than others. They must really be upset, if Kilraker had cut the expedition short.

Tyen opened his mouth to ask, when the ground beside him exploded. They both threw up their arms to shield their faces from the dust and stones.

"Can you protect us?" Miko asked.

"Yes. Give me a moment . . ." Tyen gathered more magic. This time he stilled the air around them. Most of what a sorcerer did was either moving or stilling. Heating and cooling was another form of moving or stilling, only more intense and focused. As the dust settled beyond his shield he saw the locals had gathered together behind a brightly dressed woman who served as priestess and sorcerer to the locals. He took a step towards them.

"Are you mad?" Miko asked.

"What else can we do? We're trapped up here. We should just go talk to them. Explain that I didn't—"

The ground exploded again, this time much closer.

"They don't seem in the mood for talking."

"They won't hurt two sons of the Leratian Empire," Tyen

reasoned. "Mailand gains a lot of profit from being one of the safer colonies."

Miko snorted. "Do you think the villagers care? They don't get any of the profit."

"Well . . . the Governors will punish them."

"They don't look too worried about that right now." Miko turned to stare up at the face of the cliff behind them. "I'm not waiting to see if they're bluffing." He set off along the edge of the slope where it met the cliff.

Tyen followed, keeping as close as possible to Miko so that he didn't have to stretch his shield far to cover them both. Stealing glances at the people below, he saw that they were hurrying up the slope, but the loose scree was slowing them down. The sorceress walked along the bottom, following them. He hoped this meant that, after using magic, she needed to move from the area she had depleted to access more. That would mean her reach wasn't as good as his.

She stopped and the air rippled before her, a pulse that rushed towards him. Realising that Miko had drawn ahead, Tyen drew more magic and spread the shield out to protect him.

The scree exploded a short distance below their feet. Tyen ignored the stones and dust bounding off his shield and hurried to catch up with Miko. His friend reached a crack in the cliff face. Setting his feet in the rough sides of the narrow opening and grasping the edges, he began to climb. Tyen tilted his head back. Though the crack continued a long way up the cliff face it didn't reach the top. Instead, at a point about three times his height, it widened to form a narrow cave.

"This looks like a bad idea," he muttered. Even if they didn't slip and break a limb, or worse, once in the cave they'd be trapped.

"It's our only option. They'll catch us if we head downhill," Miko said in a tight voice, without taking his attention from climbing. "Don't look up. Don't look down either. Just climb."

Though the crack was almost vertical, the edges were pitted and uneven, providing plenty of hand- and footholds. Swallowing hard, Tyen swung his satchel around to his back so he wouldn't crush Beetle between himself and the wall. He set his fingers and toes in the rough surface and hoisted himself upward.

At first it was easier than he'd expected, but soon his fingers, arms and legs were tiring and hurting from the strain. *I should have exercised more before coming here. I should have joined a sports club.* Then he shook his head. *No, there's no exercise I could have done that would have boosted* these *muscles except climbing cliff walls, and I've not heard of any clubs that consider* that *a recreational activity.*

The shield behind him shuddered at a sudden impact. He fed more magic to it, trying not to picture himself squashed like a bug on the cliff wall. Was Miko right about the locals? Would they dare to kill him? Or was the priestess simply gambling that he was a good enough sorcerer to ward off her attacks?

"Nearly there," Miko called.

Ignoring the fire in his fingers and calves, Tyen glanced up and saw Miko disappear into the cave. *Not far now*, he told himself. He forced his aching limbs to push and pull, carrying him upward towards the dark shadow of safety. Glancing up again and again, he saw he was a body's length away, then close enough that an outstretched arm would reach it. A vibration went through the stone beneath his hand and chips flew off the wall nearby. He found another foothold, pushed up, grabbed a handhold, pulled, felt the cool shadow of the cave on his face . . .

. . . then hands grabbed his armpits and hauled him up.

Miko didn't stop pulling until Tyen's legs were inside the cave. It was so narrow that Tyen's shoulders scraped along the walls. Looking downward, he saw that there was no floor to the fissure. The walls on either side simply drew closer together to form a crack that continued beneath him. Miko was bracing his boots on the walls on either side.

That "floor" was not level either. It sloped downward as the cave deepened, so Tyen's head was now lower than his legs. He felt the book slide up the inside of his shirt and tried to grab it, but Miko's arms got in the way. The book dropped down into the crack. He cursed and quickly created a flame. The book had come to rest far beyond his reach even if his arms had been skinny enough to fit into the gap.

Miko let go and gingerly turned around to examine the cave. Ignoring him, Tyen pushed himself up into a crouch. He drew his bag around to the front and opened it. "Beetle," he hissed. The little machine stirred, then scurried out and up onto his arm. Tyen pointed at the crack. "Fetch book."

Beetle's wings buzzed an affirmative, then its body whirred as it scurried down Tyen's arm and into the crack. It had to spread its legs wide to fit in the narrow space where the book had lodged. Tyen breathed a sigh of relief as its tiny pincers seized the spine. As it emerged Tyen grabbed Vella and Beetle together and slipped them both inside his satchel.

"Hurry up! The professor's here!"

Tyen stood up. Miko looked upwards and pressed a finger to his lips. A faint, rhythmic sound echoed in the space.

"In the aircart?" Tyen shook his head. "I hope he knows the priestess is throwing rocks at us or it's going to be a very long journey home."

"I'm sure he's prepared for a fight." Miko turned away and continued along the crack. "I think we can climb up here. Come over and bring your light."

Standing up, Tyen made his way over. Past Miko the crack narrowed again, but rubble had filled the space, providing an uneven, steep, natural staircase. Above them was a slash of blue sky. Miko started to climb, but the rubble began to dislodge under his weight.

"So close," he said, looking up. "Can you lift me up there?"

"Maybe . . ." Tyen concentrated on the magical atmosphere. Nobody had used magic in the cave for a long time. It was as smoothly dispersed and still as a pool of water on a windless day. And it was plentiful. He'd still not grown used to how much stronger and *available* magic was outside towns and cities. Unlike in the metropolis, where magic was constantly surging towards a more important use, here power pooled and lapped around him like a gentle fog. He'd only encountered Soot, the residue of magic that lingered everywhere in the city, in small, quickly dissipating smudges. "Looks possible," Tyen said. "Ready?"

Miko nodded.

Tyen drew a deep breath. He gathered magic and used it to still the air before Miko in a small, flat square.

"Step forward," he instructed.

Miko obeyed. Strengthening the square to hold the young man's weight, Tyen moved it slowly upwards. Throwing his arms out to keep his balance, Miko laughed nervously.

"Let me check there's nobody waiting up there before you lift me out," he called down to Tyen. After peering out of the opening, he grinned. "All clear."

As Miko stepped off the square a shout came from the cave entrance. Tyen twisted around to see one of the locals climbing inside. He drew magic to push the man out again, then hesitated. The drop outside could kill him. Instead he created another shield inside the entrance.

Looking around, he sensed the scarring of the magical atmosphere where it had been depleted, but more magic was already beginning to flow in to replace it. He took a little more to form another square then, hoping the locals would do nothing to spoil his concentration, stepped onto it and moved it upwards.

He'd never liked lifting himself, or anyone else, like this. If he lost focus or ran out of magic he'd never have time to recreate the square. Though it was possible to move a person rather than still the air below them, a lack of concentration or moving parts of them at different rates could cause injury or even death.

Reaching the top of the crack, Tyen emerged into sunlight. Past the edge of the cliff a large, lozenge-shaped hot-air-filled capsule hovered – the aircart. He stepped off the square onto the ground and hurried over to join Miko at the cliff edge.

The aircart was descending into the valley, the bulk of the capsule blocking the chassis hanging below it and its occupants from Tyen's view. Villagers were gathered at the base of the crack, some clinging to the cliff wall. The priestess was part way up the scree slope but her attention was now on the aircart.

"Professor!" he shouted, though he knew he was unlikely to be heard over the noise of the propellers. "Over here!"

The craft floated further from the cliff. Below, the priestess made a dramatic gesture, entirely for show since magic didn't require fancy physical movements. Tyen held his breath as a ripple of air rushed upward, then let it go as the force abruptly dispelled below the aircart with a dull thud that echoed through the valley.

The aircart began to rise. Soon Tyen could see below the capsule. The long, narrow chassis came into view, shaped rather like a canoe, with propeller arms extending to either side and a fan-like rudder at the rear. Professor Kilraker was in the driver's seat up front; his middle-aged servant, Drem, and the other student, Neel, stood clutching the rope railing and the struts that attached chassis to capsule. The trio would see him and Miko, if only they would turn around and look his way. He shouted and waved his arms, but they continued peering downward.

"Make a light or something," Miko said.

"They won't see it," Tyen said, but he took yet more magic and formed a new flame anyway, making it larger and brighter than the earlier ones in the hope it would be more visible in the bright sunlight. To his surprise, the professor looked over and saw them.

"Yes! Over here!" Miko shouted.

Kilraker turned the aircart to face the cliff edge, its propellers swivelling and buzzing. Bags and boxes had been strapped to either end of the chassis, suggesting there had not been time to pack their luggage in the hollow inside. At last the cart moved over the cliff top in a gust of familiar smells. Tyen breathed in the scent of resin-coated cloth, polished wood and pipe smoke and smiled. Miko grabbed the rope railing strung around the chassis, ducked under it and stepped on board.

"Sorry, boys," Kilraker said. "Expedition's over. No point sticking around when the locals get like this. Brace yourselves for some ear popping. We're going up."

As Tyen swung his satchel around to his back, ready to climb aboard, he thought of what lay inside. He didn't have any treasure to show off, but at least he had found something interesting. Ducking under the railing rope, he settled onto the narrow deck, legs dangling over the side. Miko sat down beside him. The aircart began to ascend rapidly, its nose slowly turning towards home.